D0621262

Douglas L. Bland

UPRISING

A NOVEL

Blue Butterfly Books

THINK FREE, BE FREE

Blue Butterfly Book Publishing Inc.
2583 Lakeshore Boulevard West, Toronto, Ontario, Canada M8V 1G3
Tel 416-255-3930   Fax 416-252-8291   www.bluebutterflybooks.ca

Complete ordering information for Blue Butterfly titles is available at:
www.bluebutterflybooks.ca

First edition, hard cover: 2009

Library and Archives Canada Cataloguing in Publication

Bland, Douglas L
    Uprising : a novel / Douglas L. Bland.

ISBN 978-1-926577-00-5

    1. Title.

PS8603.L379U67 2009   C813'.6   C2009-903821-8

Design, typesetting, and maps by Gary Long / Fox Meadow Creations
Title page photo © Jeffclow/Dreamstime.com
Text set in Minion, titling in Helvetica Neue, maps in Myriad
Printed and bound in Canada by Transcontinental-Métrolitho

The text paper in this book, Rolland Enviro 100 from Cascades, is EcoLogo™ and Forest Stewardship Council certified. It contains 100 per cent post-consumer recycled fibre, was processed chlorine free, and was manufactured using energy from biogas recovered from a municipal landfill site and piped to the mill.

Blue Butterfly Books thanks book buyers for their support in the marketplace.

Dedication

This work is dedicated to the Cree Nation and especially to the Plains Cree who, in the spring of 1885, fought the North West Mounted Police and the Canadian Militia in a forlorn effort to take back their land. In the aftermath, they lost not only their land but also, it seemed for generations, the essence of their ancient culture—"the echo from the past." The People's greatest loss that spring was their belief that they would live a traditional way of life freely and forever in harmony with the Great Spirit on the generous, open prairies bounded by the Rocky Mountains, the Red River, and the endlessly flowing North and South Saskatchewan rivers. Among the Cree some now ask: is the ancient culture truly lost forever? Or is it alive, carried forward by the echo of the past that the Elders guard as the People await another day and the return of a great chief to lead the faithful?

Tecumseh's Vision

"MY HEART IS A STONE. HEAVY WITH SADNESS FOR MY PEOPLE; cold with the knowledge that NO TREATY will keep the whites out of our land; hard with determination to resist as long as I live and breathe. Now we are weak and many of our people are afraid. But Hear Me: a single twig breaks, but the bundle of twigs is strong. Someday I will embrace our brother tribes and draw them into a bundle and together we will win our country back from the whites."

— TECUMSEH, Shawnee chief, circa 1795

Quotation on Assembly of First Nations website—capitalized emphasis added by the AFN (http://www.afn.ca/article.asp?id=58)

"We have a right to be frustrated, concerned, angry—anger that's building and building."

— PHIL FONTAINE, Grand Chief of the Assembly of First Nations; CTV News, May 15, 2007

"It's time to quit being loyal Canadians … We don't need the white man's money. We need a share of our own wealth."

"There are only two ways of dealing with the white man. Either you pick up a gun or you stand between him and his money."

— TERRANCE NELSON, Chief, Roseau River First Nation, Manitoba; CTV News, May 15, 2007

SENATOR ROMÉO DALLAIRE: *"We have heard about the Aboriginal Day of Action. Is the internal security risk rising as the youth see themselves more and more disenfranchised? In fact, if they ever coalesced, could they not bring this country to a standstill?"*

THE RIGHT HONOURABLE PAUL MARTIN: *"My answer, and the only one we all have, is we would hope not."*

— Senate Committee on Aboriginal Peoples
Ottawa, Tuesday, April 8, 2008

"The little discomfort that I feel after this incredible journey pales in comparison to what our people suffer every single day."

— SHAWN ATLEO, newly elected Grand Chief of the Assembly of First Nations, after an exhausting all-night marathon of balloting; Calgary press conference, July 24, 2009

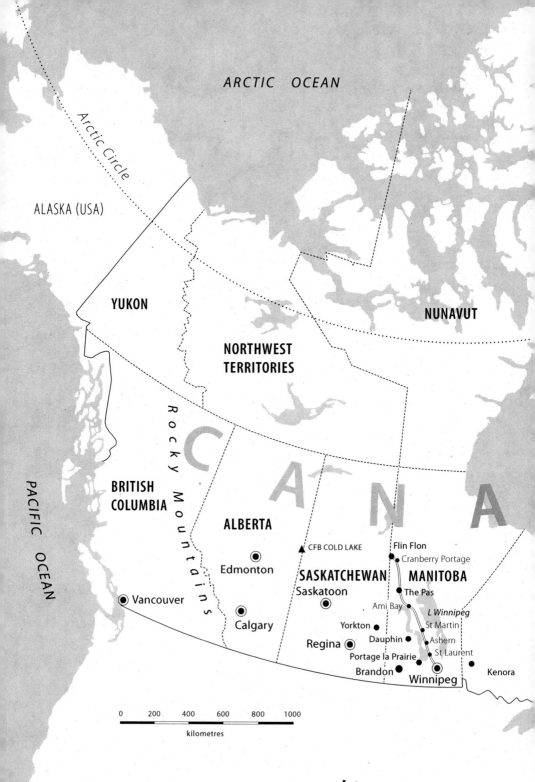

GREENLAND

Arctic Circle

NEWFOUNDLAND AND LABRADOR

D A

Hudson Bay

LABRADOR

NEWFOUNDLAND

Robert-Bourassa
hydro plant

hydroelectric plants

Radisson

Chisasibi

Sept Îles

La Grande Rivière

*James
Bay*

QUEBEC

Waskagonish

CFB
BAGOTVILLE

PEI

HWY 109

NEW
BRUNSWICK

NOVA SCOTIA

ONTARIO

Matagami

CFB VALCARTIER

L Superior

Val d'Or

Quebec

Montreal

Oka

Kahnawake

CFB GAGETOWN

Halifax

Sault Ste Marie

CFB PETAWAWA

OTTAWA

Akwasasne

Toronto

CFB TRENTON

Boston

New York

*ATLANTIC
OCEAN*

Philadelphia

STATES

WASHINGTON

DAY ONE

Sunday, August 29

Sunday, August 29, 2345 hours
On the Ottawa River, west of Petawawa

Alex cut the outboard motor and let his small boat drift into the dark, shallow bay of the island in the middle of the Ottawa River. One by one, the other five aluminum fishing boats of his makeshift raiding party pulled in near him. The boats were painted mud brown, their motors muffled by burlap covers. His party's weapons, as yet unloaded, were also covered, to avoid clattering against the metal hulls.

The current, always strong in the upper reaches of the Ottawa, tugged at the boats, threatening to pull them back into midstream. Luckily the crews had learned enough from their numerous rehearsals to jockey the boats into the planned order and keep them there for the next dangerous leg across the broad river and onto the beach at Canadian Forces Base Petawawa. Well, that's already something, Alex thought.

Twice he flicked his red-shaded flashlight, signalling the helmsmen to shut down their outboard motors in unison—the better to camouflage their number from curious ears. Another instruction remembered and carried out properly, even with the adrenaline pumping. That was good, because things were about to get a lot more complicated.

The boats had all been loaded according to his careful instructions. Backpacks, carrying-boards for heavy loads, first-aid kits, and an assortment of straps, ropes, wires, and cutting tools—"a place for everything and everything in its place," as his old Airborne platoon sergeant had never tired of reminding him. But the crews tonight—seven per boat, a helmsman and six carriers—though they styled themselves "warriors," did not have the experience of his old sergeant. Their description of themselves was in fact a wild exaggeration, for his troop was in reality a motley, inexperienced, mostly young, gang of natives.

They certainly weren't soldiers. Alex had shaped their enthusiasm as best he could over the past six weeks, and he figured if all went well they could at least keep some discipline on the march from the beach to the target and back again. Now he watched through the darkness as they unbundled their assorted rifles, shotguns, and the one automatic weapon picked up from "the merchant" at Akwesasne. The helmsmen checked the readiness of their boats and each then flashed two red signals back to Alex.

"So it begins," he muttered to himself. He knew that other raids were under way across the country, although he knew none of the details of any of them. For Alex and his team, what they were about to do in Petawawa was the only mission that counted.

Across the river, on Canadian Forces Base Petawawa, Military Police Corporal Joan Newman tried not to spill a lukewarm cup of instant coffee on her way to her patrol car. Join the Armed Forces, she thought bitterly. See the world. Yeah, well, they didn't mention the part about marrying a warrant officer who'd come back from Africa with a drinking problem. Or aiming for the paratroops and winding up a military policeman instead.

Now divorced, Joan was looking at spending the remaining four exciting years of her current enrolment patrolling half-empty bases on dark, lonely nights. And drinking too much while wondering what…Damn! She *had* spilled her coffee. No time to change her green military sweater either. Her boss was a real stickler for keeping to the regular patrol schedule, even though she, and no doubt other MPs, had pointed out it just made things more predictable for anybody up to anything worse than the occasional drunken fist fight. Not that anybody ever was. As she got into the car, Joan told herself for the hundredth time that this was not the life she'd planned for herself.

Alexander Gabriel, full-blood Algonquin (so his grandfather insisted), was born on the Golden Lake Reserve near Eganville, Ontario. Other kids on the reserve had made fun of him because he did well in school. When he turned eighteen, he enlisted in the army as an infantry officer cadet, partly for the adventure, partly to get away from the life the other reserve kids were heading for, and partly because he was in awe of his Uncle Simon's heroic and much-honoured service in Korea. Alex was sent to Royal Military College at Kingston to serve Canada; however, he promised his grandfather he would remain true to his people's traditions.

Unfortunately, he had quickly come to realize that there was little room for his native traditions in the army or anywhere else outside the reserve. When his classmates at "the zoo," as cadets refer to RMC, called him "chief" or "moccasin," they said they meant nothing by it. Yeah, right. They didn't single out other guys with racially based kinds of nicknames.

Even so, Alex liked military life and found he was good at it. After graduation, he advanced quickly from lieutenant to captain. Captain Alex Gabriel was marked by his superiors and peers as "a bright star" and a "streamer," a fast-rising infantry officer. His outstanding record won him a position in the new Special Service Regiment when it was established as part of the elite Canadian Special Operations Force Command.

Others had noted his rise also, and Alex could still remember the meeting when he had begun to see that the promising career the army seemed to be offering him might not be what he really wanted. It had happened a year or so after he had joined his unit. Alex arrived home on leave to find his grandfather waiting for him in his small cottage. To his surprise, three middle-aged men, all natives, were sitting quietly around the wooden table in his kitchen. Alex recognized one of them, a local chief from a nation across the Ottawa River.

"These elders would like to speak with you, Alex," said his grandfather. "I'm going fishing, so you can talk and I'll see you for supper. You're a good boy, Alex. You do what you think is best for the people." He turned and walked out the door before Alex could answer.

Without introduction, the chief beckoned Alex to a chair at the table. "Alex," he began, "I'll be brief. We represent a nation-wide first nations organization which I am sure you've never heard of before today. We're not from those guys who sit around Ottawa talking and not acting. Alex, we believe that the aboriginal people in Canada are a nation, not many nations, but one nation. We're not Canadians and we don't want to be Canadians. We don't want to be partners with people who stole our land and broke every treaty our ancestors made with them.

"If we want to be a nation, Alex, we have to start acting like a nation. That means we have to build the parts, the structure, of a real, modern nation. Otherwise, we'll remain a simple gathering, an ineffective assembly of nations. One of the most important parts of this new nation is its army.

"I won't go into detail this afternoon, Alex, but we wanted to let you know that we have been reaching out to our brothers and sisters in the Canadian army, and will continue to do so, to let them know that there is another way, a way to serve the people." He pushed a small envelope across the table to Alex. "Inside the envelope you'll find a contact number, and the address for a website. If you want to talk, just follow the signs.

"We don't expect any commitment from you now or even soon, but we may be in touch someday in the future. You're a proven leader, Alex, and a trained officer. The people are going to need you some day. Things can't continue as they are—a disorganized leadership without any long-term aims and our young folk falling under the influence of gangs and criminals. Only independence, real independence, not BS rhetoric from the Ottawa Indians, will get the people their land and rightful inheritance. You think about it, Alex. Think hard about who you are and who you should be. Then, when the day comes, Alex, you'll know what to do, and your choice will be clear and obvious."

Without another word, the men stood up, walked out the door to their truck, and drove away. Alex did think about it. And though he tried to dismiss the chief and the meeting, he knew from that day on, from deep inside his spirit, that one day he would have to a make a choice between his attachment to his people and the army life he loved.

That day rushed at Alex after what the government called "an unfortunate incident," a sloppily violent police reaction to the June Days of Protest across the country.

An incident involving pushing and shoving along some train tracks in southern Manitoba turned nasty, and caused a riot between enraged natives and an outnumbered, frightened, and poorly trained RCMP detachment. Constables Thomas Scott and Susan Lachapelle had panicked, and in a flash four native "warriors" and two teenagers they were using as shields were dead. When on-site CBC reports, inaccurately as it turned out, suggested government complicity in the police shooting, riots and violent incidents erupted elsewhere. In several locations in the East and West, informal native leaders, who elected officials of the aboriginal community described as "hot-headed radicals," used the events as an excuse to attack transportation and infrastructure facilities across the country. Thus began the spontaneous, and now infamous, August Week of Protests, the worst civil unrest in Canadian history.

The escalating native protests that followed were brutally attacked by local police and army militia units. But when the Special Service Regiment was called up in mid-July, "in aid of the civil powers," to maintain good order on the railway system between Toronto and Montreal, it was clear to Alex from his commanding officer's orders that the army was "headed for a final showdown with native protesters and whether they were armed or unarmed didn't matter." Alex knew then that he had no choices left. Reluctantly, he searched through his letters and papers and dug out the envelope the chiefs had left him at the end of the meeting in his grandfather's cabin. One day soon afterwards, he simply drove out the front gate at Base Petawawa and went home, taking his kit and weapons with him.

Now he was here. Returning to the base on a very different mission than the army had trained him for.

Sunday, August 29, 2345 hours
Canadian Forces Base Halifax

Inside the little guard's hut at the Canadian Forces Base Halifax ammunition compound, Fred McTavish leafed eagerly through his sports fisherman's catalogue. Page after page of sleek, shiny, aluminum boats, and on page twenty-two, the one he wanted: padded bow seats, whisper-quiet, four-stroke, fifteen-horsepower outboard motor, trailer, and everything. Oh sure, it would cost a bundle. But a man's entitled. Hadn't he worked hard all his life, done his tour of duty, worked in the shipyards, found other work when the yards shut down, paid his taxes, brought his paycheque home, and raised two honest kids?

"You bet I'm entitled," he told himself. "Three more months, just three more months, and I'll be hitting the lake in that shiny beauty."

His boys had moved away two years ago to go to university in Toronto and Calgary, but when Dennis was home last winter during reading week, he had told him, "Dad, you buy that boat. I'll be back in the summer and we'll go fishing every day for a week." That'll be nice, Fred thought.

The sudden roar of fast motors from two pickup trucks startled Fred. "What the hell are those jerks doing speeding up to the depot gate on a Sunday at this time of night? Must be lost." He reached for his flashlight and stepped out the door. Peering into the darkness, he watched the two pickup trucks coming down the road towards the gate. They were driving way too fast. "Stupid bastards!" Fred told himself. He flicked on his flashlight to wave them down. The lead truck slowed, then veered toward him and suddenly accelerated again. The collision crushed Fred's rib-cage and sent him flying backward into the doorway, rocking the table inside the guardhouse. The boat catalogue fluttered to the floor. Fred died, slumped sideways, half-sitting against the wall outside the little hut.

Sunday, August 29, 2359 hours
On the Ottawa River, west of Petawawa

Annie Connor, the helmsman and commander of the boats once the teams landed on the beach, nudged Alex Gabriel's arm. "We're ready," she whispered. She wasn't the chatty type and Alex liked that. She was twenty-three, quick-witted, and assertive; a natural leader. If the warriors hadn't elected her third-in-command, he would have put her into that position himself.

Alex fumbled briefly, reached over the side, cupped his hands, and splashed cold water onto his face. He checked his watch, then turned towards the invisible faces he knew were waiting for his order to go.

One red flash, a pause, then another flash. The motors raced briefly then dropped together to idling speed. Alex nosed his boat into the current, setting a course that would carry his little fleet north and clear of the rocky island upriver from Indian Point on the west shore. He swung west into the open river, calm on this windless night, and, guided by the intermittent flash of the base airfield's revolving beacon, headed towards "the officers' beach."

Petawawa, lit up against the dark southwestern sky, wasn't hard to find. It was as quiet as one would expect in the very first hours of a Monday morning in late August. Alex and the Central Committee that had planned and authorized the raid knew that most of the base was in "stand-down" mode for a special weekend leave at the end of the militia training season. Duty units were on half strength. Best of all, the front-line 1st Battalion of the Royal Canadian Regiment, the top-notch regular infantry unit there, was far away, chasing terrorists in Zimbabwe as part of a Commonwealth "stabilization force" deployed in the wake of the chaos that had followed the January assassination of Robert Mugabe. As a result, the only combat troops in the region were the 390 paratroopers in the three "commandos" of the Special Service Regiment at CFB Trenton, four hours drive away.

Natives still in the army and stationed at Petawawa had assured the Central Committee, through the special network that had been set up, that no unit would be in the training area that weekend—a fact confirmed by others who were members of various militia regiments. At best, there would be half a dozen military police on routine patrol, rattling doors and breaking up fights outside the canteens. The base defence force, a gaggle of office and supply clerks—donkey-wallopers and jam-stealers, as the infantry called them—was a standing joke and would take hours to organize itself. By then, Alex was determined to be long gone, back across the river. Nevertheless, he prayed that surprise would work, for he knew that if even a half platoon of airborne infantry were waiting for them, his band of warriors would be mowed down before they could even cock their rifles.

Following the procedure Alex's flotilla had practised night after night over the last few weeks, the crew chiefs manoeuvred their boats quickly into an "echeloned" line to his right rear, each boat keeping station just outside the wake of the one in front. They raced forward to cover the few kilometres from the island to the beach quickly. Alex hoped the noise, if anyone even heard it and wondered, would be taken for keen fishermen heading up the river seeking sturgeon and pickerel near the narrows at Point Mackey.

He watched nervously as the boats tossed over the bow waves of those in advance and fell in and out of line. Cold water splashed his warriors' faces as they gripped the sides and seats or grabbed for equipment they hadn't secured well enough. The crews watched the dark shore approach, more excited than anxious, too young and inexperienced to be afraid—unlike their chief.

Alex checked his watch again, timing the run he had made on several reconnaissance visits in the weeks before. He and Sergeant Steve Christmas, a native from the Oka band near Montreal, and another airborne deserter, had landed alone at night two weeks earlier and recced the ground to the target. As regular soldiers stationed at Petawawa, both had marched and run through the area countless times. But things change and, besides, both had learned well the maxim, "time spent in recce is seldom wasted." Both also knew that plans never work as well on the ground as they do on paper. For one thing, distances are difficult to judge in the dark, and sooner than he expected, Alex's boat bumped over the first sandbar just off the gently sloped, sandy beach.

Alex flashed a quick red light in warning to the others—too late: the boats criss-crossed each other's wakes, their motors whining in high revs as they bounced over the shallow approach to the beach before being shut down indiscriminately while oars and paddles clattered against the boats as the crews pushed and paddled to the shore. So much for the rehearsals, he thought, but at least they weren't shouting and hitting out at each other as they had on their first training run in another location upriver six weeks ago.

The crews lurched noisily up the sloping shoreline. Steve Christmas, the disciplinarian, directed a few well-aimed curses at particular stumblers then settled into his quiet, assured manner, restoring silence and order.

As they had rehearsed time and again, whispered words from Alex sent his two scouts sprinting a hundred metres ahead of the patrol into the edge of the tall grass fringing the beach. The carriers unloaded the boats, everyone, Alex hoped, remembering the particular items for which they were responsible. The boats were then quickly pushed out into deeper water where, under Annie's command, they would head back out into the river and hold about a kilometre offshore waiting for the recovery call from Alex.

As the scouts moved quietly and quickly forward, Alex waved the lead section of ten warriors off in single-file formation towards the road. He followed a couple of dozen metres behind with his radioman. The remaining fifteen warriors, divided into two sections, each forming a well-spaced though ragged, single-file line on opposite sides of the road, followed Alex. Steve Christmas brought up the rear. The patrol moved off the beach onto the bush-covered grassy field, crossed Passchendaele Road, then passed the empty tent grounds, angling west towards Brindle Road, always keeping careful watch for any lights on the horizon that might betray a vehicle approaching from the base.

Alex had drilled into his team the necessity of maintaining a high degree of alertness while on the march, with the prime directive to avoid detection and contacts on the way in and back out. He was pleased to see Helen Pendergast and the other two young section commanders, all selected by their peers, enforcing the order for quiet, vigilance, and proper spacing. After ten minutes, the patrol reached the end of the open fields and moved up onto Brindle Road, still heading southwest. As they hit the road, the sections closed up their open formation but held to their alternating pattern—one section on one side, the next on the opposite side. The scouts hurried forward to the top of the low escarpment to guard the Crest Road intersection two kilometres ahead. There they watched for oncoming vehicles or other signs of trouble as the patrol made its way up the hill. Once the lead section arrived, the scouts waited for Alex's signal to move forward.

The scrubby, pine-filled bush along the roads was deep and silent. The only noise was the crunch, crunch of boots on gravel and the soft grunt of people adjusting their loads and weapons as they began the climb up and out of the Petawawa plain. Alex checked his watch: on time so far. Up the Brindle Road hill to Crest Road: three kilometres to the target. All easier than the pace in their training exercises. Training ought to be harder than the real thing, and over the past few weeks Alex and Steve had made sure that it was.

When the patrol reached the junction of Brindle and Crest roads, Helen Pendergast raised her arm, silently signalling a halt. As the signal was passed down the line, Alex came up beside her and checked his map and watch again. The sections were resting in formation, some resting on a knee, others taking a drink of water or a nervous pee. A light northerly wind kicked up, rustling the spirits of the forest. Encouragement, he thought... or perhaps a warning.

Canadian Forces Base Petawawa is, of course, native land. At least it was until the white settlers occupied the region without any thought of compensation for the inhabitants. Some people say its name is from an Algonquin word, *petwewe*, meaning "Where one hears noise like this," referring to the fast water flowing over the rocks of the Petawawa River. But as a child, Alex preferred his grandfather's explanation that the area was named after his distant ancestor, an Algonquin woman who lived alone on the banks until the age of 115 years. She would have lived forever because she was married to the spirit of the river. But she died the moment she reached out to steady the first canoe of the first French explorers who touched the river bank at her feet.

Many years later, German immigrants built a settlement on native land near the same spot and tried hard to farm the harsh, rocky ground. Alex's people protested to the government, but in vain. "Why," he had once asked his grandfather, "did we not fight the settlers for the land long ago?"

The old man answered the young Alex sadly. "We were mostly peaceful people, and we thought we were simply lending a little piece of our vast lands to these poor devils so they wouldn't starve. In return, they gave us diseases that killed our bodies, and laws that confused our elders. Then they kept the land and tried to grow corn in rocks. They never understood that the land decides who lives and who dies. My forefathers," he added, "should have listened to the old woman by the river."

In 1904, the Department of Militia and Defence purchased 22,430 acres from the settlers, saving *them* from starvation but as usual ignoring the Algonquin people's claims. The army has occupied the land ever since.

Alex smiled wryly. Here he was on his own ancestral lands with a mere handful of young natives attacking a modern military base that was home to 4,400 professional soldiers.

Joan Newman peered wearily into the darkness. Nothing but a two-lane gravel road, and at the sides, nothing but the bush: rocks, trees, road, rocks, trees, road. As she scanned the way ahead, the same irritating little rhythm beat in her brain as it did so often on such nights. Stay alert. Don't hit a deer, please don't hit a moose—rocks, trees, road. Oh God, she thought, if I did hit a moose, would anyone care? Yeah, actually. My boss would care. The car would be totalled. All that paperwork to get rid of my corpse. He'd be really mad. Rocks, trees, road. Rocks, trees, road.

A wave of his arm sent Alex's scouts along Crest Road towards the target, this time with Sergeant Christmas in the lead. The patrol followed a few minutes later, the individual warriors in the surrounding darkness simply marching into the footsteps before them. They were confident in their leaders, especially Gabriel and Christmas, and they each knew what they were to do. Or rather, they'd been told what to do. "Follow the rehearsed plan; do your assigned part; don't worry about anything else. If there is a surprise, follow the drills." These rules had been hammered into their heads in training night after night for weeks. Weeks, Alex thought, not months. Five minutes of panic is all it would take to create total chaos. He took a deep breath. Too late to worry about that now. He had to focus on his own tasks.

The protective lights surrounding the Petawawa ammunition and weapons storage area, which was located on Menin Road on the outskirts of the base's built-up areas, shone brightly through the vegetation, allowing them to see it well before Steve Christmas and his scouts reached the compound. As they approached the outer perimeter, Christmas quickly surveyed the roadways, the first storage bunkers, and the wire—everything was as he remembered it, including being unguarded, as usual. He listened for a few minutes then sent young Patty Roy back to bring up the patrol. He sent his other scout, Denny Villeneuve, 200 metres down the road towards the base to warn of approaching vehicles. Then he sat back for a more thorough look at the compound.

Alex slid into the ditch beside his second-in-command. "Ready, Steve?"

"Yeah, guard's out. All quiet. Typical weekend night in Petawawa."

"Okay, let's go." Alex waved the first section into action.

The warriors, crouching, sprinted to the front gate, a high wire barrier topped with razor wire, no obstacle really—except to honest people. Alex was pleased to see Pierre Léger, following the drill, step forward, quickly cut the padlock, and push open the gate. He was less pleased to hear it swing open with a loud squeal, perhaps protesting the unexpected disturbance. Léger's section jogged through past the first bunker, down the lane to their assigned bunker. Up came his bolt cutters, *snip snip*, and the metal door was open. As the others wrestled off their backboards and packs, Léger scanned the interior with his flashlight, looking for the supplies on his list.

The other two sections moved into the compound, breaking into smaller squads as they too headed to their assigned bunkers. This raid was no random scavenger hunt. Each section and squad had received detailed orders to collect specific weapons and munitions. Though they had never been in the compound before, or even seen it up close, they recognized their targets from the maps and photos Alex had shown them over and over again, and from the scale model he and Christmas had built in the training camp.

The raiding party had a complete description of what was stored in each bunker, thanks to supply officers, military clerks, and civilian employees loyal to the Movement and the cause who were stationed in Petawawa and in the National Defence Headquarters in Ottawa. But they also had a carefully considered shopping list. The priority items were linked to the "grand strategy": anti-aircraft and anti-tank weapons; explosives (C4, plastic explosives, detonating cord, and primers and fuses); fragmentation and smoke grenades; small-calibre automatic weapons and ammunition; and, if the team had carrying space, a few anti-tank mines.

The ammo compound at Base Petawawa held supplies for most of Eastern Canada and for overseas deployments—everything the army needed: rifles, grenades, explosives, every calibre of ammunition, M72 and Carl Gustav anti-tank rocket launchers and ammo; and of special interest, Blowpipe anti-aircraft missiles. Many of the Canadian Forces' best weapons were outdated by the fast-moving standards of modern warfare, but they would certainly provide the Movement with a vast edge over any police opponents.

A hiss from Christmas's radio broke the silence. "Headlights approaching," whispered Villeneuve.

"How many...what speed?"

"Looks like a single, a car, I think. Not very fast—slow actually. Hey, it just pulled in front of the old building down the road, shining a light around."

Steve turned to Alex. "Company coming, single car. An MP, I think... checking buildings. Not too alert by the looks of it...just the routine meathead patrol."

"Right! Close the gate. Put the lock and chain back on. Pass the word— lights out. They know the drill." At least I hope they do, he thought.

Alex watched the nearest patrol anxiously as it stopped collecting its load and scattered into the shadows of the bunkers. Christmas, crouching, dashed outside the gate and dropped into the shallow ditch beside his leader. "Set."

Alex watched the approaching car. "Okay. We can't take a chance that the MPs might see something and then, after we let the car go, raise an alarm. We'll take them down. Okay, as we rehearsed the other night—once the car halts at the gate, I'll take the driver's side … you take the partner."

"Got it." Christmas crossed the lane and dropped into the ditch. Just like the ambush outside the camp in eastern Afghanistan, he thought as he struggled to flatten his large frame into the low grass. But this time, no inquiry.

Villeneuve warned, "Passing me now." He dropped into his backup position, hoping that the car would not try to reverse towards him if something went wrong.

The car pulled into the entrance lane as expected. Joan Newman shone a spotlight across the gate then casually over the compound as she had done on too many night shifts. "Boring, boring, boring," she told herself, "the usual Sunday night bullshit. I've got to get myself a life—maybe even that jerk, Jack."

The door flew open. Joan felt someone grab her collar and lift her sideways and backwards out of the car. She fell hard on the road, the impact taking her breath away. A dark shape loomed over her, pistol in hand, and stepped hard on her right arm. "Be quiet, don't do anything stupid, and you'll be okay."

The other front door was already open. She heard someone switch off the engine. Feet ran towards her. Joan caught her breath and growled, "If you guys are frigg'n' militia on an exercise, you're in big trouble. Let me up." She moved to sit up but was knocked roughly back down.

"Shut up, stay down. This is no exercise," Alex barked. He turned to the warriors. "You two, stay with me. The rest get back to the job. Sergeant, any commotion on the radio?"

"No." He glanced at the body on the ground. "Nice job, sir."

He meant it. One reason people followed Alex, in the army and now on this raid, was that he always led from the front. A simple concept, and not exactly stamped Top Secret, but a lot of officers never seemed to get it: leading means being in front. How else can you know what's going on? Call it "operational problem solving" or "dealing with the unexpected 101," just like bloody "Foxhole U," army staff college. You will have problems, like this one. Stay on top of them.

Alex hadn't wanted to get stuck with any prisoners, but of course he'd considered that it might happen. So what to do? Taking her along was out of the question. But he had a more immediate worry. The dispatcher would get suspicious and raise an alarm if she didn't report in soon. Buy some time and get things moving, he ordered himself.

And sure enough, the car radio crackled. "Three-two, this is three, what's your location?" the dispatcher droned over the MP radio net. "Three two, come on, Newman. If you stopped for a leak, wipe it and call in. Out."

Alex grabbed Newman. "Listen," he said, jamming his face into hers, "you get on that radio and tell them you're on your way, nothing to report, and if it's okay, you're stopping for coffee at the base coffee shop. I'll make a deal: you play the game and you go free—screw up and you're coming with us... at least part way. It won't make any difference to the base commander if you're a hero, prisoner, or corpse. You decide."

Newman looked into his eyes briefly, then reached into the car for the radio. "Three, this is three-two. Addy, I ought to report you to the CO, but he's worse than you are. I'm done for now and going for a coffee. Over."

"Three, yeah. You scare the crap out of me, Newman. Call in after your doughnut. Out."

"Good choice," said Alex. "Sounds like a swell unit."

He turned to Christmas. "Take the car into the back of the compound and hide it. Put her in it, tie her up, gently, and leave off the mouth tape."

He took a quick glance at his captive's name tag. "Have a good night, Corporal Newman, and just relax. They'll find you by morning." He nodded to Sergeant Christmas, who pushed the MP onto the floor in the back of the car. Alex left to check the section leaders. Best to move things along.

The sections returned to work, a bit more subdued. This minor incident drove home that this was no game. Leroy mumbled to no one in particular as he struggled to hoist a backboard loaded with M72s onto his shoulders. "That bitch had a gun and if she'd panicked or seen something, well... shit, it's a long way to the beach."

Alex was considering the return trip as well. Was there a code in that MP's message? Not likely. Security at Petawawa was generally as lax as it seemed. But still... And besides, how long would they wait for her to have a coffee and call in? Fifteen, twenty minutes? Likely a bit more. Unless some other incident came up, or another meathead decided he needed a doughnut too or they wanted some at the desk. Too many scenarios. Hope for luck but don't count on it. It's about thirty-five to forty minutes to the beach carrying all this stuff, fifteen minutes to load and get off the shore—at least an hour to comfortably break contact from here. No time for pissing around.

The section commanders reported loaded and ready. Christmas checked in. "The guest's resting well, although it looks like she may have wet her pants in the excitement. She seems tough and cocky enough, but Christ, sir, I still can't get used to women in the army..."

Alex laughed. "Give it time, sarge."

"Yeah, sure. Who's got that much time?"

"Okay, call in Villeneuve at the double." Alex watched the sections fall into formation, then waved the first one out the gate. He grabbed the two scouts and sent them on a jog back the way they had come, down Crest Road to the first intersection. Leaning close, he whispered into Jock Tremblay's ear to impart urgency, not panic: "Double your section down the road for four telephone poles, then walk them fast another four and double again. No bunching up and keep them quiet. You know the drill: if a vehicle approaches, slip into the bush and stay still; if we get separated, go to the beach and get across the river. Move out."

He passed the same instructions to each leader in turn. Only Helen Pendergast hesitated. "These loads are heavy and running with them..."

Alex grabbed her lapel and got very close to her. "Do as you're told! You move them along. I'm counting on you. Now's the time to lead." She swallowed hard and nodded. He let go of her jacket and his frown relaxed. "Go!" he said.

Turning to watch her section clear out, he glimpsed Steve Christmas, cool as usual, gathering up Villeneuve and fading into the darkness fifty metres behind the last section. Rearguard and follow-up. Then, out loud: "Everybody gets to the beach."

The plan had been to take a different route back to the beach, through a trail Alex and Steve had discovered in the bush. It was the classic patrol tactic—one way in, another way out. But good commanders change plans when they need changing. So far his warriors had done just fine, but time was short and he sensed them getting jittery. The first priority now was to get away from the compound, off the high road, and down onto the plain as quickly as possible, keeping the patrol together and under control, with no stragglers and no panic. The road was the fastest way.

If the MPs came looking for Newman, he assumed they would come from the main base, headlights on, worried about an accident, not an incident. If, for whatever reason, an MP happened to come from the other direction, from lower down, they'd be lit up and scanning the edges of the road for the missing car, and be most unlikely to see his patrol before his scouts saw the approaching lights. Yes, speed mattered more than stealth at this point. Alex jogged up the line of huffing warriors to his position behind the first patrol.

Run, walk. Run, walk. Measured steps. Get them into a rhythm. Encourage the leaders. "Good show. Keep it up, not too fast. Steady pace now. You all did well. Everybody remember to breathe." The comment brought snickers down the puffing line.

One hundred metres from the compound. Now two hundred. No lights, no sirens. Nothing but dogs barking in the distant married quarters and, close by, heavy footsteps, bouncing loads, and laboured breathing.

Clang! Bang! A couple of loads came undone and crashed to the ground. Some warriors kept moving, others stopped to help comrades rebuild their treasures. Soon the patrol looked like a Santa Claus parade—scattered individuals jammed up here, small groups bobbing up and down there. Only three hundred metres down the road. The wind picked up, rattling the trees, or were they guards moved by the spirits? Those who hadn't stopped picked up their pace.

Things were unravelling.

Alex fumed. I've got to stop this! He hustled forward to the first section leader. "When you reach the intersection and the scouts, move on down the road twenty metres, then stop and get your section together. You check personally that you have all your people—touch each one. Then let me know you're ready, wait till I give the word, then move out at a steady walk. Got it?"

"Got it. Are we okay?"

"Yes, right on schedule, just as we planned it," he fibbed. "I'm going to call the boats in to shore as soon as we close up, sort ourselves out, and get moving again. You just worry about your people. Remember: make sure you have *everyone* and that they've all got their loads." Alex repeated the word to each section leader, while encouraging individuals as they passed him in the road.

Sergeant Christmas came out of the darkness. "Fine night, sir. A guy should be getting home to the old lady, don't you think?"

Alex smiled. Who's encouraging who now? "Yeah, piece of cake."

"Reorg?"

"Yeah, Steve, I told the section leaders to pull their people together just past the intersection and then we'll force march them down the hill and across the plain. I'll call Annie in a few minutes and get the boats moving. I think we can trust Villeneuve and Patty to bring up the rear after we pass the intersection. You get ahead and mark the beach. Give us a quick light if necessary and guide us to the boats. Let's make it a smooth move into the boats and off the beach."

"Got it. See you on the beach, sir."

After stopping and sorting themselves out, the patrol was looser. Alex was relieved to find that they hadn't lost anyone or apparently any gear. But this was no time to relax. He'd seen this a hundred times, even with trained soldiers: once you got past the critical point, a little rest, a bit of adrenaline come-down, and the giggles and joking start. It's a dangerous mood. Alex had to use their confidence to cover the next few kilometres quickly, without letting it cause carelessness. He knew Christmas had picked up on the mood too and could hear the sergeant encouraging and admonishing the troops in the same sentence as he moved down the line to get forward.

"Morrison," Christmas stage-whispered for everyone to hear, "if I see you drop Her Majesty's ammunition again, I'll call your mom to come and carry it for you. You're an idle crow, Morrison."

"Actually, I'm Cree, sergeant."

"You're a no good smart ass! Get your gear sorted out!"

The others snickered at the exchange, partly glad not to be the butt of the sergeant's feigned wrath, but partly disappointed too. Thank God, Alex thought to himself, I have Steve Christmas as my second-in-command.

Alex saw the mood improve as if high morale were wafting through the air from one warrior to the next. Without any direction from him, they picked up the pace, improved their spacing, and started encouraging one another. Comments like, "Okay, let do it"; "Let's go, guys"; and "Beat you to the boats" replaced the furtive "Let's get away" of only minutes before.

And there was still no response from the base. Alex got a familiar sweet feeling of a mission coming to a successful close as he joined the dog-trotting warriors moving in good order down the hill towards the river. Pulling out his cellphone, he called Annie and gave her the code phrase to bring in the boats. "Hi, sweetheart, we will be home in about fifteen minutes. Can you open the doors to the barn?"

"Sure thing, I was getting worried, it's late. So you drive carefully. Bye."

As the patrol crossed Passchendaele Road, Alex saw Steve Christmas's light flashes marking the place on the beach, about a hundred metres to the west of the original landing point, where the boats were waiting for them. Christmas waited, counting his charges through to the beach. The rear guard came in a bit off course, but in good order.

Alex joined his sergeant, just as young Villeneuve came up. "Everyone clear from the road, Villeneuve? Anything left behind?"

"No, sergeant. Nobody we could see, but somebody dropped this ammo belt on the road."

"Okay. Good job both of you—get to the boats."

Alex watched as the warriors loaded the little craft. Quiet more from fatigue and ebbing excitement than self-discipline. It didn't matter. It was not a perfect patrol; he was sure that small bits of kit were back on the road and would eventually lead investigators to piece the plan together. But as he walked to the last boat, he wasn't worried; he felt sure he would never come this way again. His kids had done well and would have stories to tell. He walked proudly with Christmas to the water's edge.

Annie was all business and ordered Alex into the boat. Everyone else had done their job and could relax; she'd been waiting and biting her nails the whole time, and now it was her turn to get it done. She rallied the other helmsmen into line, the engines revved in unison, and they headed at full throttle towards the far shore and safety.

Alex glanced across the river to Quebec and the red dawn rising up from behind the eastern hills. "Red sky in the morning," he thought to himself. "Now there's a menacing sign."

"Everything okay, Alex?" Annie asked.

His face lit up. "Sure, Annie. Almost perfect."

Annie smiled broadly and couldn't resist a sudden impulse to reach out and squeeze his hand. She felt so proud to be with him, and proud also to be one of the warriors who'd really struck a blow for their long-suffering people.

DAY TWO

Monday, August 30

Monday, August 30, 0530 hours
Ottawa: National Defence Headquarters (NDHQ)

The night shift was coming to an end. Colonel Ian Dobson, the National Defence Operations Centre's director, was at his desk earlier than usual, filling in the last sections of his report, which would form the basis for the daily ops briefing at 0730 hours. He expected the day's "Morning Prayers," as these sessions were known at NDHQ, to be routine: a few words from the intelligence staff, brief reports on the status of deployed units and ships, summaries of the last day's activities from deployed units overseas, comments on major exercises, and the status of the one active search-and-rescue operation, SAR Harper, which was looking for a missing person presumed lost in Newfoundland's wilderness. Ten, twenty minutes tops, then off to the cottage to join the kids for one last precious week before they went back to school. Next year, Carolyn would be heading off to college and might not be around for the summer; Julie was going to junior high this year and was getting squirmy about family. They're growing up so fast, he thought. The last thing he wanted was something surprising that would cut into this one last blissful family week.

Refocusing, Ian turned his gaze to the room around him—a world far removed from his idyllic cottage. For all its importance and worldwide scope, Ian thought, the National Defence Operations Centre was not, in fact, very impressive. Only about the size of a corner store, cramped, and rimmed with electronic screens showing most of the general and current information concerning the whys and wherefores of the Canadian Forces, the NDOC was a windowless, rather drab facility.

Despite its unspectacular appearance, however, Ian knew how crucially important the centre was to Canada's military operations: it was its nerve centre. And access to this secure facility was tightly guarded. Entrance into NDOC, located on the twelfth floor of NDHQ, required passing through security checks at the main entrance, and further, increasingly stringent checks, which involved the supplying of highly secret codes, to get through the many doorways and elevators leading to the upper levels of the building. Ian, like everyone else in the room, wore a special security tag on a neck-chain, so that guards could easily identify individuals and their security clearances. On the twelfth floor, as on the other upper-level, high-security floors, guards randomly verified the identity of those walking the hallways and their purpose for being there. The inside joke, however, was that security was unintentionally assured by the confusion caused by the continual rebuilding and rearranging of offices, meeting rooms, and hallways that made the top floors into an impenetrable rabbit warren. If a bad guy were ever to get in here, Ian thought, he would never be able to find his target or his way out without a guide.

Inside the operations centre, the senior duty officer and several middle-ranking officers worked at individual consoles, keeping abreast of ongoing operations and developments by watching and responding to operational reports and situations in various regions and commands at home and abroad. The atmosphere was "24/7 busy normal." Computers hummed, telephones chimed softly, clerks carefully ordered the endless flow of paper, and officers, each responsible for a particular part of the world or some special function, spoke matter-of-factly to distant stations and other officers crammed into the NDHQ labyrinth.

Behind the main room, communications clerks, or comms clerks, as they were universally called, constantly monitored and operated the global Canadian Forces communications network, receiving and sending scores of messages mostly in secure and coded formats. Both sections of NDOC were hooked into the adjacent National Defence Intelligence Centre, a facility where even greater security prevailed, and "need to know" rules were even more closely defined.

Once Dobson finished his morning briefing, complete with the inevitable PowerPoint slides, at 6:45, he would walk down the hall and up the back stairs to the office of the deputy chief of the defence staff. The DCDS, Lieutenant General Carl Gervais, was (nominally, some said) the senior operations officer in the Canadian Forces. Together they would go over the details and discuss likely questions and answers on operational matters that he and Gervais would address at the 0730 meeting in Conference Room B on the thirteenth floor of NDHQ.

Over the past two years, Dobson had learned that Gervais liked to look as though he were in control and handle every question brought up by his boss, the chief of the defence staff, or any of the dozen or so officers and civilian assistant deputy ministers gathered around the large conference table. But Dobson knew also that Gervais expected him to jump in quickly if Gervais's sometimes shaky grasp of relevant details threatened to become apparent. As had become glaringly obvious over the years, when Gervais dumped a problem into Dobson's lap, he left it there.

Far better to prep the old man so he could blather his way past any uncertainty and then clean up problems later. Which wasn't easy, given Gervais's impatience with details during briefings and indeed with briefings altogether. So, after his quick meeting with the DCDS, Ian would return to his desk, make any final amendments to the script to steer around especially obvious holes in Gervais's knowledge, then rehearse the briefing with his assistant, who controlled the slides. At the appointed hour, he would walk over to the meeting room for his quick dog-and-pony show in front of the brass and the senior civvies.

It was just coming on 0615 hours when a call from across the room drew Dobson away from his report. Lieutenant Commander Dan Noble, halfway through a message one of the comms clerks had just handed him, called over his shoulder, "Hey, sir, I just got a flash message, a Significant Incident Report from Petawawa. You had better look at this."

"Bugger," Dobson said to no one in particular. Half an hour before he was to see the DCDS and what does he get? A SIR from, of course, Petawawa—that place was cursed. "What now? Did someone cut off another head at Chez Charlie's last night or have they just found more horses on the payroll?"

"Seems a bit more bizarre, even for Petawawa, sir. A female MP has gone missing with her car and all."

Dobson reached for the paper and read the formatted message. He paused a moment and turned to Noble. "Call the base duty officer and find out if we're talking about a deserter or what. Have comms get the deputy base commander, Colonel Neal, on the phone, and alert the DCDS's assistant. I might need to see the general earlier than usual."

"Aye, sir." Noble reached for his phone and hit the speed dial with one hand while beckoning a clerk over with the other.

Almost immediately, Dobson's desk phone buzzed. He flipped off his desk speaker and lifted the receiver. A voice announced, "Colonel Neal on the line for you, sir."

"Bob, Ian, glad to see someone else is up. What the hell is it this time?"

"We're not sure yet, Ian. The MP commander was called into his office about 0330 after his people couldn't raise this MP, Corporal Joan Newman. The desk sergeant already spent about two hours pissing around trying to find the car—figured it was broken down somewhere, had another car retrace the route she was on, the usual. They found nothing. Checked the guard house; she never left the base. And she's not shacked up for a quickie with her boyfriend—checked that too. Then the sergeant called his CO, who went over the same searches again with more people. Still nothing. So he called me. We're still looking. That's all we have."

"What do you know about the MP?"

"Good record, smart and reliable—this is way out of character."

"So what are we dealing with? Has she gone over the hill or had an accident, or is this some criminal act? What?"

Neal bit his tongue. He'd just said they didn't know what was happening. "Don't know, Ian. But shit, who'd take off with a police officer?"

"Has the media caught wind of this?"

"Not so far," Neal responded, refraining from pointing out that as it was 6:15 a.m., the only journalists out of bed were radio drive-in-show people too busy catching up on the morning papers to notice if the building they were in was on fire. "But the search has started the rumour mill and they probably will in short order."

"Yeah, okay. Keep me posted. I have to give this to the boss ASAP and then to morning prayers. The base commander can expect a call from the DCDS in thirty minutes. You guys are top of the hit parade again. Good luck, Bob."

Dobson put down the phone and called to Noble, "Keep on top of this; make copies of the SIR for the usual list of people but don't send it out until I speak with the general. Call the provost marshal and ask her to be at prayers—give her the bare facts. We need a complete description of the MP detachment up there and this Newman person's file. Now!"

Turning to the Canada Command desk officer, Ian warned her, "Cindy, get ready for an overlap in shifts for a few hours until this thing is cleared up and put away." As he turned back to his report, he thought, not for the first time, that if the military wanted you to have a family life they would probably have issued you one … an all-purpose, completely flexible one.

Monday, August 30, 0625 hours
On the Ottawa River, five kilometres south of Fort William, PQ

Alex Gabriel's flotilla touched down on the Quebec shore across from Petawawa. An assortment of trucks and pickups rolled down along a trail through the bush off Chemin Fort William to take on the precious cargo. A tall, sour-looking man walked towards Alex, and, pulling him aside, glanced over the packs, boxes, and weapons crates.

"What did you get?" he asked sharply.

"Much as we planned. We found the stores as described, carried away what we could and got out. We had a run-in with an MP, but she did no harm."

"Did you shoot her?"

"Of course not! What's the matter with you? We don't go around shoot-ing people out of hand." Alex's instant dislike for the guy grew legs. He turned to walk away. "I'll count the stuff off the beach once I've seen to my people."

"Nope. You leave that to me. My guys will take the loads from here on and we've got plans for the team."

"I thought we were going to use this stuff locally. Why the changes? And what plans for my team?"

"Best you remember not to ask such questions. I'll have your second-in-command get your people into those two trucks there, and you get in the van here. Someone wants to see you elsewhere."

"What's happening to the team?"

"I told you not to ask about things that aren't your business. Anyway, they'll be taken to a camp somewhere to eat and sleep, then we're going to prepare them for something else. We can't just let them go wandering around town. They'll get drunk or start fighting or bragging to who knows who about the whole exercise. The Mounties will be out in force soon enough without us spreading the word."

The late summer sun broke over the eastern hills, sending long shad-ows across the beach as strangers jumped from the trucks and grabbed the cargo, roughly pushing Alex's warriors to the side. He took one step to intervene, but the tall man grabbed his shoulder and pulled him towards a van parked near the road. Reflexively, Alex seized his arm and started a palm-strike but checked himself. For a moment they stood frozen, glaring at one another, then from the corner of his eye Alex saw Christmas step between the strangers and the team and start coaxing the warriors into the trucks. Christmas turned, flashed Alex a thumbs up, then jumped in the lead truck and slammed the door. Alex released the tall man's arm and started toward the van. The last he saw of his little team's effort was their boats being loaded into trucks and driven off the beach eastward towards the village of Sheenboro.

Monday, August 30, 0730 hours
Ottawa: NDHQ, Thirteenth Floor, Conference Room B

The room was arranged as usual for morning prayers. Name cards ranked in a never-changing order sat with parade-ground precision down each side of the long, dark, rectangular table. This odd habit always amused Ian—these people know each other, he thought. But the staff was simply doing what the staff had always done. A pad of paper and two sharpened pencils sat ready for each principal, although these pads were never used. No one took notes so access-to-information prowlers couldn't demand them.

Ian tapped his few pages of notes into order on the lectern at the front of the room as he looked down the table towards the chairs at the opposite end set aside for the chief of the defence staff—the CDS—and beside him, the deputy minister, the public service head of the Department of National Defence. Senior officers and officials moved into the room, dropping their own note pads at their usual places along the sides of the wide table. The room felt crowded, though it was actually less full than usual. It had been cleared of the hangers-on, the aides and staff officers who normally sat on the side walls, stationed and ready to provide their bosses with the details of any issue. In private, they called themselves ventriloquists. Ian was not the only one who wondered why they were not at the table with the generals and civilian officials.

Today, tension filled the room. People gathered in small factions, immersed in separate, tense conversations, and the absence of the customary banal chatter made the space feel cramped and airless. Ian shuffled his papers again, checked the slides and his boss's short briefing notes, which sat on the simple podium. As he glanced up, the DCDS was gesturing earnestly to Vice Admiral Marie Roy, the vice chief of the defence staff.

The CDS was late. That, Ian reflected, was rare, and meant bad news.

A few minutes later, General Andrew "Andy" Bishop marched through the door with Deputy Defence Minister Stephen Pope and, unexpectedly, the minister of defence himself, James Riley, Member of Parliament for

Winnipeg South. General Bishop motioned the minister into his own chair while a staff officer hurriedly brought another to the head of the table for the CDS as the attendees quickly took their places.

The CDS sat down, looked at the DCDS, and commanded immediately, "Let's hear it." His sharp tone brought all eyes to Carl Gervais as he stepped up to the podium.

"Minister, General Bishop, I'll begin with a television clip which we recorded an hour ago. Then I'll provide a brief situation report on last night's incidents. Colonel Dobson will provide greater detail on the intelligence background, and then the CDS will give us his thoughts on future operations." He looked down at his script while the staff in the next room clicked on the television monitor.

"This clip," Gervais continued, "was recorded at 0700 hours from the First Nations' Television Network. We do not know whether FNT was complicit in this broadcast or whether they were taken over electronically for the period by the so-called Native People's Army, but we suspect the latter."

Riley turned to the CDS. "Is it likely that the native groups have such technology?"

Bishop responded carefully. "Yes, minister. It's a relatively simple cyberspace technical procedure with the right equipment and the right people. In modern cybernetic warfare, even a secure network can be quite vulnerable. We have to assume that the natives have sophisticated systems and the people to run them."

The chief looked to Gervais. "Let's see the tape, Carl."

The DCDS nodded at an apparently blank wall and the staff monitoring proceedings from the projection room hit "Play."

The scene that appeared had an *al-Qaeda* ambiance, despite the mixture of modern camouflage gear and traditional native costumes and the giant Warriors' Brotherhood flag backdrop. A woman, simply masked, flanked by two men dressed in traditional native costume but carrying M16 rifles, sat at a desk. She glanced down occasionally at a handful of papers as she spoke quickly and forcefully.

The native people of North America were violated more than 400 years ago by European slave traders and invaders. Since that time, we have been assaulted by racists bearing weapons of mass destruction, germ warfare, and firearms. They poisoned our people with their drugs and alcohol and religions. Genocide from coast to coast has been visited on our nations across the Western hemisphere. Our forefathers tried to negotiate peace and understanding with the whites, but they simply played into the hands of the invaders. We remained "les sauvages," and nowhere were we so humiliated and cheated than in what you call Quebec—it is our native land, not theirs.

The lap-dog leaders of the First Nations, "white Indians" all of them, are totally discredited. They fill their pockets with bribes and tokens. They negotiate without our authority to give the whites our lands and future. We, the People of the Land, the true First Nations, will not negotiate. We already have what we need, sovereignty and liberty, and now we will use them. We will take what belongs to us from the ruling cliques in Quebec and, supported by the brave warriors of the Native People's Army, we will restore to our people their rightful heritage. Remember the genocide of the villain Champlain and the heroic defence of our land by the Iroquois Confederacy. Remember all our heroes and early resisters and today the brothers and sisters killed and wounded in the same fight for our land. A new day has arisen and the native people in the occupied lands you call Quebec will rise with it.

The tape ended abruptly and static filled the screen. The monitor went blank. While Gervais returned to his notes, the principals sat still and silent, except for the minister who shifted about in his chair, reached for a pencil, then changed his mind and tossed it irritably onto the table.

The DCDS resumed his presentation. "Last night, a series of obviously coordinated raids were launched against several military installations in Eastern Canada, apparently in support of this attack on Quebec. In each case, the targets were ammunition storage facilities and weapons lock-ups. The raiders were well organized and apparently had prior knowledge of just where various types of munitions were stored within the compounds and armouries." On cue a black-and-white map with red X's appeared on the monitor. "As this slide illustrates, raids were made at Halifax, CFB Valcartier, CFB St. Jean, two armouries in Montreal, and, the largest one, at

CFB Petawawa. There were no incidents at any other installations across the country.

"The raiders seemed intent on taking major and special weapons, including anti-aircraft missiles, anti-tank missiles, some anti-tank mines from Petawawa, mortar bombs, plastic explosives, small arms ammunition, radios, and other lesser equipment. The staff is still calculating the losses.

"The raiders were almost certainly members of various native people's organizations. Although we have no clear intelligence to confirm this assumption, the tape leaves little doubt that's what's going on."

Gervais flipped through his slides. "The raids were conducted from various approaches. For instance, the Halifax attack was mounted on heavy-duty pickup trucks which rammed through the gates in the early hours this morning, then made off into the local area. That raid, unfortunately, resulted in the death of a civilian guard, who it seems was run over trying to stop the raiders at the gate. In Petawawa, the attack seems to have come from across the Ottawa River, a rather daring idea that, ah, unfortunately, may be something our summer exercises in 2008 suggested to the native soldiers who were part of the scenario. In that scenario, Petawawa was raided from across the river by a 'rebel force' of, ah, factious aboriginal militants."

Carl Gervais, who had argued loudly against the exercise, couldn't resist a pointed extemporaneous observation. "You may remember that exercise, minister. I recall you praised the, ah, 'display of multiculturalism in action' involved in treating aboriginal grievances seriously."

Gratified to see the minister look away and reach for his glass of water, the DCDS returned to Dobson's notes. "We're still trying to reconstruct each of these incidents. In Petawawa, the raiders were interrupted by a female military police officer. She was captured by the raiders, but not harmed. A search party found her an hour ago, tied up in her patrol car hidden in the back of the compound. She is still being debriefed, but she told her commanding officer that one individual, whom she thought was the leader, was referred to by the others as 'sir,' and that while giving the others distinctly military-style orders, he called one of the others 'sergeant.' Her account of their language and discipline alike indicates not merely a high level of organization but the probable presence of several trained soldiers.

"Unfortunately, other raids caused a number of casualties. As I said a moment ago, in Halifax, a civilian guard, a commissionaire, was killed. As well, a brief firefight erupted when a military police patrol responded to a silent alarm in Valcartier, but they were overwhelmed by the raiders' weapons. Thankfully, the military police escaped without fatalities, but the two MPs were injured—not badly—and their vehicle was destroyed.

"Minister, CDS," Gervais continued, "we have put Canadian Forces bases on alert, launched searches, and mounted guard units around ammunition compounds and vital points at bases and militia locations. These precautions have been as unobtrusive as possible, so as not to alarm the local populations—we are advertising these raids as the actions of criminals looking for weapons to sell on the black market, and downplaying both the precision and success."

"Chief," the minister said, turning to Andy Bishop, "that message can't hold given the tape. I think the cabinet will have to—the prime minister—will have to make a public statement confirming briefly what we know and what we're doing about it. And he is going to have to do it today."

"I agree, minister. And so does the clerk of the Privy Council; she's scheduled a meeting in one hour with me, the commissioner of the RCMP, the chief of the Security Communications Establishment, the deputy minister of the public safety department, the prime minister's principal secretary, and others to thrash out a response along precisely those lines."

Jim Riley pushed back his chair and stood up. "Thank you, General Bishop, and the rest of you as well. I've things to do too. General Bishop, after your PCO meeting, I'll meet you in the prime minister's office. I'll let you know the exact time."

Monday, August 30, 0915 hours
Chisasibi, on James Bay

Will Boucanier looked out the small window as the Air Creebec Dash 8 made its long, slow approach into Chisasibi, an unattractive Cree village of some 3,000 souls on the La Grande Rivière, six kilometres from James Bay and about 100 kilometres from Radisson and the main James Bay hydro-electric generating plant. But it was home to Will—a soldier home from the wars and on his way to a new one.

Long ago, at age eighteen, Will had left the village and the band, travelled to Montreal, walked the streets, homesick yet incredibly happy to be away. The big city had been totally unfamiliar to him, weird, baffling, and threatening, but Will had never felt so safe. In Chisasibi, he had spent every night of his young life afraid, terrified, that Dad would come rolling in the door drunk, and, as Mom would say, "in a mood."

Fear and noise all night. Not in his room, but menacingly close, out there, down the dark hallway. He would lie in bed, whimpering, "Go away!" His thoughts made no difference.

"Get out. Leave me alone."

"Bitch!" A cry of pain, then scuffling, and in the morning, bruises, scrapes, and sullen silence.

Demons in his house and in his dreams. His younger brother, Jimmy, crying himself to sleep at night.

Morning. Dad sleeping it off, and Will and his brother slouching about the house, exhausted, hating going to school, but afraid to stay home. Will feeling guilty leaving Mom alone with her abuser, but he was just a kid. What could he do?

Mom, worn out, tangled hair, face swollen from tears, fists, and lack of sleep, wandering the kitchen in a floppy pink track suit. "Now, boys, don't wake your dad. Get yourselves ready for school. Will, make some porridge for your brother. Hurry now!"

Every day hoping to come home and find Dad had run off. Relieved when his "ways," as Mom called them, got him another thirty days in jail, and guilty for feeling it. The shame of the "drunken Indian" followed Will all his days on the outside. "Are we natives," he asked himself repeatedly and without answer, "doomed to be our fathers' sons?" Will had never had a drink of alcohol in his life. He'd never dared to.

"Sunday, we'll go to church," Mom said as if it would help. But the only good the priest ever did for him, Will recalled, was to keep him in school and send him running from the village.

Three weeks after leaving Chisasibi, Will had wandered off the street into the army recruiting office on Sherbrooke Street in Montreal and signed up. That decision he had never regretted, and he served for fifteen years with distinction. Right from the start he was recognized as a first-class recruit. Coming from his background, fieldcraft was as natural as walking, and weapons were second nature. His peers, mostly city boys, admired their "crafty redskin" comrade. Leather-tough, he was impervious to weather, long marches, heavy loads, and the purposeful harassment of his instructors; once he'd left home, no insult from outside could touch him on the inside. But what really set him apart—a natural gift for leadership, for being in front, for commanding—wasn't truly evident until he was promoted to infantry corporal, then, in just five years, to sergeant, and warrant officer in five more.

Warrant Officer Will Boucanier: stone cold, emotionless, dedicated to the army no matter the mission. He could look at the battlefield with a dry eye, as great captains must. He just focused on the job and got it done, and expected the same of those under him. In command, he took no back talk, no malingering, accepted no excuses and gave none. His "people"—though the word carried a profound ambiguity to his native ear—he treated with the utmost care. Everyone equal, everyone his prized responsibility. But he followed the rule: mission first, men second, myself last. He was never nasty, but never soft. That was his code, and the pride it engendered kept him going.

Will Boucanier, as everyone of experience in the army knew, "walked the talk." He won the Medal of Valour during the Battle of Medak Pocket— the night-long battle in the former Yugoslavia in which, on September 15, 1993, the 2nd Battalion Princess Patricia's Light Infantry—the Patricias—stood and fought a much larger Croatian force that was threatening four Serb villages with "ethnic cleansing." It was the first major battle for the unit in the post-Cold War era, and one the Liberal government hid from Canadians for years. There were no news stories, no ceremonies, no homecoming welcome or remembrance for the casualties, just officially imposed silence, lest Canadians discover the consequences of the "decade of darkness" which had starved the Canadian Forces.

But soldiers across the army knew what had happened in the Medak Pocket and then-Sergeant Boucanier's part in it. That night, he had led a six-man Joint Task Force 2 (JTF2) detachment attached to the Patricia battalion tasked to protect the four Serb villages isolated in the midst of the hostile Croatian population. In the darkness and chaos of that September night battle, Will watched through his powerful night-vision scope as Croatian infantry, supported by two T54 tanks and intent on slaughtering their neighbours, worked their way around the Canadians' right flank.

Will had reported the situation to the Patricia battalion commander, but he knew no one in the unit, already under heavy fire, could slow the assaulting force in time to save the villagers. However, he figured that his little force, off on the flank of the Patricia companies, might be able to surprise and distract the Croatian infantry. Will had stood up, gathered his soldiers, and led them in an attack on the enemy company in the valley below his position. The citation to his decoration read:

Sergeant William Boucanier MMV
Chisasibi, Quebec
Medal of Military Valour

On September 15, 1993, Sergeant Boucanier, commanding a JTF2 *Detachment allocated to peacekeeping duties in the area of the Medak Valley in Krajina, came under heavy Croatian mortar and small arms fire. During the ensuing engagement, he observed these same forces preparing to attack an undefended village inhabited by women, children and old people. Without regard for his own safety and under heavy fire, he led his small detachment into the village and there successfully defended the villagers from further assault. During the night, he was wounded twice, once seriously by mortar fire, but maintained command of his soldiers, encouraging them and adjusting their deployment to defeat the Croatian assault. Sergeant Boucanier's cour-*

*ageous and skilful actions helped prevent a massacre of the villagers
and secured the battalion's exposed flank until reinforcements arrived
at daybreak the next morning.*

All of that seemed a long time ago, though. Now, he was slipping and
sliding slowly into his hometown as the pilot dodged the rain clouds and
fought the high winds bouncing the small aircraft around above the bare,
grey, granite hills of the James Bay basin. It was the end of a long hip-
hop flight from Montreal through Val-d'Or and Waskaganish to Chisasibi. Some homecoming—a flight from modernity to cultural calamity and
personal trauma. But Will had steeled himself. The mission brought him
here, not family or home. Indeed, his family had disappeared: his brother
to Montreal, drink, and jail; his father long ago lost on the land; and his
mother in despair to the grave. He was home today because he was Cree,
because he knew the land, the language, Chisasibi and Radisson, and who
he could count on. The right man for the job. Still a soldier, he told himself.
Not a mercenary. A soldier and a man of honour.

Only last month, Will had abruptly taken his release from the army,
despite persistent, heart-felt urging from his superiors to stay, and unan-
swered pleas from the sergeants' mess for reasons. He was sick at heart to
leave the only home he'd ever known, a home made safe by order, merit,
and predictability; a home where things made sense. After a childhood
of chaos, of feeling worthless, he'd found a real home among soldiers, a
special group set aside by society for a special purpose. But just as he had
fifteen years earlier, he felt relieved as well as homesick. Across the country,
he knew, were villages like his, full of homes like his, and getting himself
out of there, no matter how successfully, had always felt a bit like running
away. Like going to school and leaving Mom alone with that man. Well,
not any more. He had fought the white man's wars, "for peace and freedom," they had told him. Now he was coming home to fight for the same
things, to fight the only way he knew against the despair he'd escaped so
long ago.

Boucanier, too, had been identified by the Movement. Its leaders had
reached out to him several times early in his career and as he advanced

in it, only to be rejected. But Will's gut-wrenching, mind-bending experiences in Yugoslavia, Somalia, and Afghanistan changed him profoundly. His sympathy for the people he helped in those places, people forced by history's whims to surrender their culture to the tyranny of the majority, affected deeply his sense of himself and his people and his homeland on James Bay. The political jumble that was Yugoslavia, which the UN and the Western allies had turned into the even bigger Balkan region mess, convinced Will that nationalism, not federalism, saves lives and cultures.

He learned also from watching certain Serbian patriots and Afghani communal leaders that strong leaders can achieve a great deal if they have the strength and determination to unite people around their own traditions. The key lesson Will took away from his experience, however, was that the people's success and security depend on one thing: cultural unity, protected by one unchallenged leader, and set free from distracting entanglements in other people's causes.

Will convinced himself as he watched the clandestine Movement grow, that it might just prove to be the organization that could create the winning, disruptive conditions that would allow him to set his family and his people and his culture free from its woeful history. He believed, he truly believed, what Molly Grace had told him at their first secret meeting after he contacted those chiefs who had approached him over the years: they really could "take back the land" and reshape it with the power of pride. What he did not reveal to anyone, however, was his longing, his ambition, to become the one to lead his people in their ancestral lands.

Wars change soldiers and the ones that he had seen had changed Will's faith in his army. The Canada he deserted had deserted honour first when it walked away from its pledge to the Afghanis he had fought to protect. For Canadian politicians, Will thought, honour is a pliable thing. He and a few others soldiers were the real army, the.army of soul, duty, singleness of mind and purpose.

He knew and accepted that race meant nothing in the army. There, only truth, duty, and valour command all. The creed needs no explanation, abides no excuses, and has no nationality. But his people, *his* people, were the Cree; he would not desert them. Instead he was now part of a different army, as honourable as *his* Canadian Forces, and it would fight as well and maybe even win. He promised himself long before he returned home that no matter the success or failures of the Movement, he would lead his people to his kind of peace and freedom.

Out the window, below, Will could see his old home, the James Bay territory: a mass of granite, part of the Canadian Shield, one of the oldest geological formations on the planet; endless mountaintops, smooth and peakless, ancient yet enduring, shaped by the grinding of advancing glaciers and the constant assault of wind, snow, and rain; and everywhere the sparse landscape commanded by black spruce, just "the forest" in his youth, but, as he had learned later, actually the largest single-species forest in the world. To the north, where the trees reluctantly gave way, the lichen—reindeer moss, as it was commonly called—covered the rocks and thin topsoil like a soft, pale green mat. *Cladonia rangiferina*. To the white man, strange green stuff on rocks, but to the people, vital food for the caribou they hunted and, sometimes, for the hunters as well.

His people, the Cree, and the Inuit with whom they shared the land in northern Quebec, had hunted the caribou, along with other animals, for millennia before the whites came. They had learned how to survive in this harsh place; and, Will thought, despite all the terrible changes the arrival of the whites had brought, they still managed to survive. For Will, the approximately 12,500 Cree and the few hundred scattered Inuit families who continued to eke out a living on the northern perimeter of the territory personified the tenacity of the human mind in the face of nature's indifferent outrages.

The outrages inflicted by the whites were more difficult to deal with. Not only had most of the animals on which the natives depended for their livelihood been killed, not only had the whites brought disease and the alcohol that had destroyed so many lives, but most of their land had been taken too. Today, they shared the territory with about 15,000 non-natives, many of whom were transients.

Will knew everyone in the territory was once a transient. The first inhabitants were migrating natives who settled on the land because they found just enough substance and a climate just tolerable enough to provide a precarious existence. Boucanier's distant ancestors had settled the area as fishers, hunters, and gatherers long before history came to these places.

They lived off the land—what else could they do? Like native people across northern Canada, they could not conceive of any other world, and only moved on to a new sameness that offered better hunting grounds once they had depleted the area where they had been living. Or they moved to escape savage, bloody competition with other bands and the "meat-eaters, the Eskimo." But nature was the real enemy, always unforgiving and deceitful, ready to snare anyone who ventured too far onto the land, or worse, the water. Will had no illusions about it. For centuries, sameness, violence, and hard nature had framed the Cree's existence. But they had found joy as well as hardship, and they had loved the land as well as they feared it.

Much later, Europeans moved through and into the territory, to trap, prospect for minerals, and to hunt and fish. Some settled in small communities to service the transients and the mines. Their coming meant trouble: not only disease and booze, but an alien religion based on fear of God rather than his people's religion founded on harmony between the people, the land, and the spirits. But at first, the Europeans who had stayed in the North shared the Cree's respect for the land and saw in the bleak wilderness an overwhelming beauty. Later, things had changed; more white men had come to alter the land—to master it, not live with it—and brought disaster to Will's people on a much greater scale.

The Cree might still be living a so-called traditional life, like the more northerly Inuit, had it not been for the white man's gluttonous appetite for electricity. But the hydroelectric dams came, and history decided that the Cree would now exist in the unsettled world between the shaman's animist vision and the complexity of modernity. Lured by jobs and the promise of broader horizons, many native people departed the traditional world to help export to the modern world the energy that drove its machines and its cities, that made European Canada thrive and grow, and in so doing helped the modern world bring disaster to traditional communities.

Negotiators from the communities had, of course, signed papers which all sides expected would at once bridge the gap between and protect the two worlds. These "treaties" supposedly allowed all the economic benefits, the good of the modern world, to be blended into the traditional native world. Unfortunately, the communities found that these papers were no barriers against all that was bad in the modern world. The white man's economy took away the reasons, the rhythms of the old ways, turning tradition into inertia, ignorance, and stale custom. But it didn't bring Will's people into its rhythms either; it left them wandering like vagrants between a world that no longer existed and one they couldn't enter.

No more. Will knew he was himself in part a product of the white man's world. He was a modern soldier as well as a traditional warrior, at home amid technology and organization as well as at home on the land. After today, he would dedicate all his skills to the service of the people—a promise, he sometimes pondered, that might one day make him king.

The airplane brought him back to his childhood world and his people, scattered in tiny communities with familiar names like Wemindji, Eastmain, and Waskaganish along the coast of James Bay, and in others such as Nemaska, Sakami, Waswanipi, and Oujé-Bougoumou farther inland. But it was Chisasibi on the south bank of the La Grande Rivière that held his special attention. His home village, yes. Near the James Bay coast. But also near Radisson, the administrative centre of the La Grande power project, and six kilometres from it, the Robert-Bourassa hydroelectric power plant.

Will tightened his seat belt as the Dash 8, banging and complaining, lowered its landing gear in the final approach to the runway. The pilot fought the strong wind, and the little plane, drifting sideways as it descended to the tarmac, bounced twice, and then, its engines roaring in protest, slowed to a halt just before running out of runway. As the Dash taxied toward the terminal, the young native attendant made the usual empty plea for the passengers to remain seated and said "Welcome to Chisasibi" unconvincingly in three languages.

Will reached for the bag under his seat and checked his watch. If his luggage had come through without damage, and his contact from the local cell was on time—and sober—he would get straight to work training whatever "warriors" the local band chief had assembled for him. He had low expectations for his new troops, but that was okay. He didn't need JTF2 for his mission. The kids only needed to do as they were told and show some steadiness in the initial attack. He would do the rest.

Monday, August 30, 1220 hours
Akwesasne: Native People's Council Planning Headquarters

Alex woke abruptly as the van slid roughly and halted at the entrance to somewhere. He pushed himself up on an elbow from his cramped back-seat bed and slid half-awake onto the floor with bright sunlight shining in his face. How long had he been out? More importantly, where was he?

Although Alex was a key combat leader in the NPA, he knew that his status didn't mean he was a trusted agent in the inner circle. Alex had learned this lesson some time before. When he had first agreed to join up, he had tried asking questions about the structure and plans of the Movement. However, he had been told that, for the sake of the Movement, such things must remain secret. Revolutionary organizations, Alex had been told, are secretive with good reason—they operate outside the law and threaten established governments and leaders. Governments use their considerable authority and means to infiltrate revolutionary organizations, even comic and inept groups, to gather information, plant disinformation, disrupt plans and the supply of resources, especially money, and to collect evidence of criminal activities for future use in courts. A revolution's best defence against these types of intrusions is internal secrecy and compartmentalization of information, people, and plans. Any clandestine movement that works on trust is soon destroyed, often from within. Molly, the Movement's leader, understood this rule very well. She trusted no one.

Alex until now had been kept in his own small box. He understood his operational task, was vaguely aware that other operations were underway at the same time he launched his, and that the Movement had some type of control centre on a reserve in Quebec near the U.S. border.

After he joined the NPA, he was moved irregularly from reserve to reserve across northeastern Ontario. Six weeks before he raided Petawawa, he was taken to a reserve on the Quebec side of the Ottawa River, and there he was given his orders and supplies and met his warriors. His "briefer," who Alex concluded had a military background, though not a Canadian one, was obviously experienced and professionally trained—likely some kind of mercenary. From his accent, Alex guessed the man hailed from the southwestern U.S.

As the van rolled through the village, Alex could see a few small houses, a fence in front of them, older vans and pickup trucks in the driveways, a mix of Ontario, Quebec, and U.S. licence plates. A wide river spread in the distance. The HQ, he guessed—on the St. Lawrence? Seems, he thought, I'm about to move into a wider world—or maybe this is actually the end of the line for me, now that my job is done. What the trip to the centre meant in fact he had no sure idea.

Armed men at the window scanned the interior of the van, questioned the driver, and, after an irritated response, waved them on into the village. They drove past more small houses, kids, and dogs, not very far, but Alex paid little attention, focusing instead on making himself physically and mentally alert. After what seemed a couple of kilometres, the van stopped near a small building covered in dull-grey plastic siding; the driver killed the engine and more armed people crowded up to the doors.

The tall, sour man threw the driver's door open, pushing them away. He stepped out of the van and spoke to a couple of older men in cheap camouflage clothes of the sort you could buy at any Canadian Tire store. They carried M16s which, Alex immediately noticed, needed a bit of maintenance. But the weapons, magazines in place, looked loaded, and so did at least one of the "Mohawk warriors," as he soon learned they liked to be called. A quick survey revealed other armed people near the building, and they weren't loafers. Their clothes and weapons were clean and they carried themselves in a soldierly manner. So there is a hard core to this outfit, Alex thought. And they're the guys to watch.

One of the serious ones came forward, slid the side door open, ordered Alex out in a decidedly unfriendly manner, then pushed him aside and searched the vehicle's interior, looking, Alex supposed, for a troop of Mounties. To the left of the grey plastic building, he noted a large Quonset hut, its curved walls supported by sandbag revetments about one and a half metres high and one metre deep. The entrance was guarded by more serious-looking people and draped with canvas to hide any light that might escape from inside at night.

The tall, sour man got back into the van and drove off, and most of the ragtag hangers-on drifted away and disappeared into the surrounding buildings. The new man in charge motioned Alex towards a small hut. A guard, no more than eighteen, in mismatched camo and an uncomfortable-looking army surplus store hat, stood in the doorway fidgeting with the trigger guard on his old army-issue FN rifle. That scared Alex a lot more than his admittedly ominous surroundings.

The serious man motioned Alex into the building and told the kid to watch him. Then, in one swift move, he grabbed the rifle from the boy's hands and cuffed him on the head, sending his hat flying into the dirt.

"I told you already not to load this thing! Do it again without orders and I'll kick the crap out of you. Understand?"

The kid nodded dumbly, bent slowly to pick up his hat but jumped back as his chief swiftly and expertly pulled the magazine off the rifle, snapped the breech open, emptied the chamber, and shoved the weapon back into his fumbling grasp.

As he walked away, he spoke over his shoulder to Alex. "Hard to get good help, captain. There's a washroom in the hut. You've got time to clean up. Sonny here will get you something to eat. Grab a nap. No telling how long before they call for you—maybe tomorrow morning."

Captain? Alex thought. He'd pegged the man without hesitation—or doubt—as a professional, a sergeant or warrant officer. But how did he know me? Do I know him? Uh, uh. He must have been briefed. Somebody here knows what they're doing.

The kid opened the door and motioned with his empty rifle towards a bench in the corner. Alex sat down and dropped his small pack on the floor. The raid had been tiring and the nap in the van uncomfortable and insufficient. Alex suspected, however, that he wouldn't get much rest in the next few days. Might as well shake off the stress hangover—hot water always worked—then grab what sleep he could.

Alex looked at the kid, slouching against the inside door, clearly unsure of what to do or what attitude to take to the person his boss had called captain. "Say, young fellow," Alex said. "Did anyone ever tell you that cleanliness is next to godliness?"

The kid shook his head, more confused than ever. Alex stood up and made a move for his small pack. "I need a shit, shave, shower, and shampoo," he said, and pointed towards the toilet room in the corner.

The kid waved his rifle vaguely. "There's no shower."

"That's okay, son," Alex said, slinging his pack over his shoulder as he crossed the room. "I'll use the sink." Please, God, he thought, don't let him reload that rifle. If I'm gonna get shot, I want it to be on purpose and not by some amateur's mistake.

Entering the bathroom, under the kid's uncertain gaze, he unwrapped his shaving kit, stripped off, set clean socks, underwear, and a T-shirt on the back of the toilet, and sat down to do his business. He let the water run hot in the sink, shaved cleanly and closely, watching himself in the mirror.

His thoughts swarmed randomly. Who are these people? They seem … what? Tense, aggressive, suspicious? What next? Where am I? What am I expected to do? He stopped shaving and looked firmly at himself. Get a grip, he silently told his reflection. Stay quiet, assess the situation, find out what they want, then decide whether to go along. Refilling the sink with hot water, he took a facecloth and improvised a sponge bath, put his old clothes and his kit into the pack with instinctive neatness borne of long military habit, and went back into the room, startling the kid who lurched nearly upright. "I think I'll get some sleep on that cot over there, if it's all right with you."

"Ah, sure, I guess so. No one ever tells me anything. They just yell at me."

"Welcome to the army, boy. And remember: keep your finger off the trigger!"

Alex dropped on the cot and, suppressing questions he couldn't yet answer, fell asleep immediately. The boy slouched into the corner chair baffled and seemed to ask his empty rifle, "Like who's the guard and who's the prisoner in this revolution anyway?"

Monday, August 30, 1300 hours
Chisasibi on James Bay

Joe Neetha was the senior Native Peoples Army "commander" in the Chisasibi area, and the only one outside the Committee besides Will Boucanier who knew the names and locations of the James Bay NPA "warrior cells." Neetha's family lived in the area of Mistissini where he grew up in the local custom. But Joe had been around; he'd travelled to Radisson, worked in a small store, then as a labourer for Hydro-Québec in town. There he'd fallen in with the native political community and worked for a time in the band office. It was there he was recruited into the Movement. Five years ago, he'd been ordered back to Mistissini to develop his own cell and join the local Canadian Forces Ranger patrol, one of nineteen such units in Quebec.

Although he knew all about the Rangers from living in the North, Joe had made a point of reading up on the group when he signed up. According to the official line, the Canadian Rangers, part-time reservists, provided military units to patrol isolated and coastal communities in Canada. They helped protect Canada's sovereignty by reporting unusual activities or sightings to the Canadian Forces, especially in the northern region. Defence ministers liked to say that the Rangers played an important role in advancing the self-reliance of Canada's First Nations and Inuit groups.

Joe remembered laughing when he'd read that—he didn't believe the average Canadian had any idea how much natives contributed to the defence of the country, but he had to admit that the small Ranger patrols, typically fewer than twenty people, were a highly efficient means of protecting Canadian sovereignty in the sparsely populated North. Ironically, given this purpose, they also provided an organized authority within communities, which made them a prime target for subversion by the Movement. A significant number of Rangers held leadership positions as mayors, chiefs, or band leaders, and had a powerful influence on their peers, especially the youth in the community, who were naturally attracted to the Rangers' martial image. So strong was the pull of the Rangers that the Canadian Forces in 1996 organized the Junior Canadian Rangers. The program unintentionally provided a perfect cover (as the Movement quickly realized) for indoctrinating new members and leaders into the NPA from the growing cohort of disaffected twelve- to eighteen-year-olds who were living boring, frustrating lives in remote and isolated areas of Canada.

Canadian Forces officers close to the program around the James and Hudson Bay regions watched the development of what they reported as "dangerous trends." They sent their misgivings to their superiors in Ottawa and explained that the Inuit weren't a problem, yet, but no one there took much notice. Some officers were even reprimanded for their "alarmist and insensitive" reports. Officers with long experience in the North who persisted in raising alarms or tried to redirect the program in the field were soon posted, often at the insistence of native leaders in the patrols, to desk jobs by officers who rarely left Ottawa.

When he enrolled, Neetha participated in a ten-day Basic Ranger Qualification Course in Mistissini. Like the other Rangers, he was given a uniform—flash-red Ranger sweatshirt, T-shirt, ball cap, brassard, vest, and toque—and also a Lee Enfield rifle and ammunition. He was taught basic drill, rifle training, general military knowledge, navigation with map, compass and GPS, first-aid techniques, search-and-rescue procedures, and formal radio communications techniques. Like many of the Rangers, his unit was also provided with snowmobiles and boats.

All of that material and training was given to him by the Canadian Forces. However, since his patrol operated in a "politically sensitive area," it also had some very modern military equipment, obtained for it not by the Canadian Forces but by the NPA. This equipment was stored well out of sight of the Canadian Forces officers who weren't part of the Movement.

The Canadian Forces sent Joe on "patrol sustainment training," which involved additional weapons and live-firing exercises, operational planning, and search-and-rescue drills. Outside these government-provided courses, Joe had joined other recruits in non-CF exercises designed to teach setting and reacting to ambushes, offensive patrolling, advanced map reading, and the care and use of grenades and explosives—all given by long-standing members of the patrols and by outsiders flown into the area by the NPA.

Joe had taken to the life easily. It was, after all, just another form of hunting. But he was noticed by his peers and Canadian Forces commanders as a leader, and that distinction marked him for advanced training beyond the regular Ranger schedule. Members of the NPA noticed as well. Joe soon found himself on new, exciting training at Canadian Forces bases in the south, at Gagetown, for instance, where his operational planning, patrolling, and leadership skills increased considerably. But the NPA had plans for him too.

Joe, under the cover of visiting distant relatives in the United States, began to train at American native reserves. There he learned how to han-

dle sophisticated weapons and how to plan and conduct sabotage operations involving several units. He also received large doses of propaganda,
which reinforced the grievances he had come to accept as the true history
of the Cree, and in fact of all the native people in North America: the
story of the natives as victims of the "genocidal invasion" of their land by
marauding Europeans.

As a Ranger, under close direction of regular forces officers, Joe practised the routine duties of "providing a military presence in support of
Canadian sovereignty" by collecting local data of significance needed
for military operations, and conducting surveillance/sovereignty patrols.
His Ranger patrol, like the others, assisted Canadian Forces activities by
providing local expertise, guidance, and advice; conducting Northern
Warning System patrols; helping local search-and-rescue activities; and
reporting unidentified vessels sailing along the coast. Joe had five years of
Ranger work behind him, and each year he became a more proficient and
dedicated soldier standing on guard. Just not for Canada.

Joe met Will outside the airport terminal, loaded his kit into an old Ford
pickup, and together they drove the dusty hundred kilometres into Radisson. They picked up a police tail somewhere just outside of town, Will
noted without surprise. At least the police communications system was
functional, he thought. At the Chisasibi airport he'd seen the local cop eye-
ing him carefully as he picked up his luggage. Naturally enough, the local
band police were always suspicious of natives they didn't recognize and
who seemed out of place. If you weren't a familiar face or a Hydro worker
returning for another three-week shift, you were "a person of interest,"
perhaps a drug-runner or an unemployed drifter home from the city. And
after fifteen years on the outside, Will Boucanier expected to be noticed.
Fine; he had a cover story ready.

Radisson was a typical resource industry company town—boring,
small, low-slung, a place for surviving until you could leave. About 2,000
people—workers and natives—existed in this town of one school, one hospital, and many bars. Will reminisced idly as the truck bounced over the
once-familiar terrain and finally stopped in front of L'Auberge Radisson, a
forty-room hotel of less than Holiday Inn standard.

Will and Joe walked together into the hotel and up to the front counter. "Boucanier," Will announced. "Will Boucanier."

"Yes, sir, Mr. Boucanier. Hope you had a good flight, a bit gusty and maybe bouncy, I bet." The short, slim, white clerk beamed and prattled on without waiting for an answer. "And I think you're staying for four days, is that right, sir?"

"I may be longer, a week in fact; it depends on the business." Will looked around the small lobby, just in time to see the local cop, a respectable-looking Cree, wander in and pretend to scan yesterday's newspapers, which were piled in disorder on the table near the door. "I might be opening a hunting and fishing outfit, bring in some tourists, you know. Got me a development grant."

"Fine, sir, you can let us know. A credit card for an imprint, please." Hotel clerks are the same everywhere, thought Will. Please and thank you, without looking into your eyes.

"There you go, sir. Just fill in the card and sign at the X. You're in room 312. Do you need someone to carry your bags?"

"No, thanks, I've got this savage here to do that."

The clerk started.

Joe only grunted, then leaned his large frame over the counter and growled, "Who is the savage in the room, do you think, sonny?"

"Sonny" had no answer. But the remark wasn't aimed at him. It was for the cop loitering near the door, who glanced coldly at Joe, then back at the newspapers. Joe picked up one of Will's bags and headed for the stairs.

After they were out of sight, the policeman sauntered over to the desk. "Let's see the card." The clerk handed it over with a worried glance toward the staircase. "Trouble, Bob?"

Bob Ignace ignored the question. "Did you ask him why he was here like I told you to?"

"Yeah. He said 'business.' Setting up a hunting and fishing camp with his new partner. Says he's got a government grant."

"Sure. We've all got government grants. But that's Will Boucanier from Chisasibi. He was a hero in the army. The only thing he's been hunting in fifteen years is people. So what's he doing here, with that big-mouth troublemaker, Neetha?"

The clerk flushed. "Well, he left a business card, so he must be serious."

"Boy, you're a regular Sam Spade," Ignace replied. "Let me see it." He read it without interest, then said, "Make me a copy. If they leave, call the station. Otherwise, keep your mouth shut. And don't go telling stories to impress that fat-ass squaw you're trying to screw, understand?"

The little clerk blushed crimson and pushed the card into the photocopier. "Sure, got it."

"Thanks," said Ignace. As he left, he tossed over his shoulder, "No way she's going to sleep with you anyway."

Up in room 312, Will dropped his bags and computer on the bed and glanced out the window in time to see the police car drive off. He locked his computer, locked it inside his bag, and then motioned Joe towards the door. "We can't talk here. Let's go for a walk."

He didn't speak again until they were in the parking lot. "I looked over your Ranger record," he told Joe. "You've been busy. Tell me about your people."

Joe pointed toward the centre of town, suggesting a turn along the noisy main street. "I have twenty members in my patrol. Two are ex-army—infantry, not too bad—but I have to kick their asses if they get near the booze. The rest are kids from around the village and nearby. Most have three years in and two had advanced courses outside. They're steady enough, but they've never done anything except throw a few grenades at our homemade range."

"Have they got the legs for the work?"

"Yeah, we're okay there. I work them pretty hard, lots of packing cross-country. And living on the land comes naturally, of course. But working at night is still a bit awkward—they see spooks and ghosts and stuff. I don't know exactly what you have in mind, but they can hump it and they do as I say."

"Okay. What about the other cells in the area?"

"I don't know. I mean, I know most of the leaders from Ranger courses and some from the States. But some I just met after I got the message from Montreal. As for their people, who knows?"

"Montreal? Who did you talk to and what did they tell you?"

Joe stopped walking and hesitated. "I don't think I'm supposed to talk about it," he said. "Except to say Maurice told me to follow your orders."

Will nodded. "Okay. I have a fair idea of the makeup of the cells and patrols, and their leaders' strengths and weaknesses, but I need a feel for their guts—are they disciplined, confident, more than just boys playing a game? What's your feeling?"

Joe thought for a minute. "They seem ready to do something more than training," he said. "They've got the bravado of all inexperienced soldiers who've been training. You know how people change when you hand out the live ammo. But their leaders are okay, and they understand the challenges. I think they can hold their people together with a pat on the back and a kick in the ass when needed."

They waited for a car to pass and then crossed the street. "Well," said Will, "they're going to get their chance, sooner than they might think. Okay. Here's what I want: a rental truck, civvy maps of the local area, and some safe place to store supplies heading our way. I'll call a meeting with the cell leaders, together if possible, some time later. But in any case, these guys had better be committed because they know too much already. If you have any doubts about any of them, come clean now."

"All the guys I know are all right, I'm sure of them," Joe said, looking into Will's eyes. "The ones I just met, I didn't get a bad feeling about any of them."

"Fine. I'm counting on you to lead your patrol and to back me up as second-in-command. Can you do that?"

"Yeah. If we need to, I'll have my number two back me up so I can back you up."

"Good. Here's what we'll do for now. I'll rent a pickup later this afternoon. Tomorrow I have business out of town that doesn't concern you. I'll meet you back here at the hotel, day after tomorrow, thirteen hundred. Don't be late. Lateness is one thing that really pisses me off. It gets people hurt."

Will reached into his jacket. "Here's two cellphones. Use one to call the leaders to meet you tomorrow at the RV north of Chisasibi you were told to select last week. The leaders are not to say a word to their members; they just have to drop everything, say they're going hunting, and make for the camp. They're to wait there for orders I will pass to you later in the week. Once you've reached them all, smash the phone and throw it in the river. Use the other as a backup or to find anyone you can't reach tonight, then get rid of it too. My cell number is on this pad; it's legitimate, so only use it if you have some real emergency. And then speak as if the Mounties were listening because they probably are. Got it?"

"So we're going somewhere, some real action?" asked Joe excitedly.

Will's easy manner changed abruptly. He turned to face Joe directly and stepped toe-to-toe into the young leader's space. "Don't ask questions unless you don't understand what I just told you to do." Will raised his voice just enough to convey the intended reprimand. "Do you understand what you're to do?"

Joe, startled, pulled his hand from his pocket and dropped his arms to his sides, awkwardly trying to stand to attention without attracting attention. He blushed. "Yes, sir!"

"Good. Then do it!"

Will walked away. Joe, a couple of steps behind, followed along in silence—the boundary between superior and subordinate clearly established. After a few steps, Will, without looking back, waved Joe alongside. "Come along, Joe. Let's get something to eat and an iced tea—do they make iced tea in this metropolis?"

Monday, August 30, 1530 hours
Robert-Bourassa Generating Facility

It was late afternoon when Will joined a small group of tourists on a trip to the great generating facility, to view, in the inviting words of the Hydro-Québec commercial, "the splendid northern vistas and colossal hydro-electric structures" that, together with the mechanics of the generating system, are the heart of the La Grande hydro project which supplies more than half of all the electricity generated in Quebec, and as such is a crucial component of a vast network of interconnected power grids serving eastern North America.

The project is in fact a giant stairway of dams and hydroelectric plants, all founded on the vast watershed of the east shore of James Bay and the steep, eternal cascade of the La Grande Rivière as it races towards the bay. The centrepiece of the project is a massive fifty-three-storey-high storage dam near Radisson and the immense reservoir behind it. Here the river is diverted through plunging tunnels into two underground powerhouses which together comprise the fifth-largest hydroelectric development in the world. By far the larger of the two powerhouses is the Robert-Bourassa plant, the pride of Hydro-Québec, the largest in Canada, and the world's biggest underground powerhouse. It was here that Will and the other visitors were taken.

The tourists were promised a view of "nature as you have never seen it"—a promise difficult to keep because the site is in every respect unnatural. Will marvelled at the awe on the faces of the visitors as his small group wandered, whispering, through the "true cathedral-like structure carved into the bedrock at a depth of 140 metres." They walked reverently amid the roaring generators and complex machines, staring at the high granite ceiling and pointing to the wonders not of nature but of man's invention.

The well-rehearsed guides, clutching electric torches, seemed to Will like minor officials in some great mediaeval European church, reciting sacred phrases to worshippers rather than offering technical guidance to the curious in a workshop. At each station, the guides' ever-respectful manner and the soft cadence of their words combined with the sheer scale of the site to transform the tourists into pilgrims of technology, much as a visit to Rome and the Sistine Chapel is said to convert every tourist into a Catholic pilgrim, if only for a moment.

But Will Boucanier was no idle visitor and he wasn't there to see the wonders of nature, the docility of tourists, or the marvels of technology. He was there to recce the complex and get a first-hand look at the control room, generating units, and the other underground works that produced the energy without which southern cities would die. Of course he already had a complete description of the system, and maps and sketches of all the facilities, collected and confirmed by native workers on the site. The NPA planning team at Akwesasne had used the very open Hydro-Québec website to locate critical features in the system, the mechanisms and structures whose destruction would bring the whole complex to a standstill.

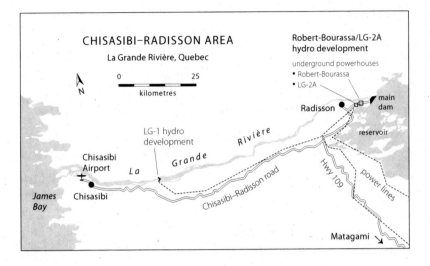

But websites can be wrong—sometimes deliberately so—or outdated, and sometimes even accurate diagrams fail to bring out important features of a target that are immediately obvious once you're actually looking at it. Soldiers will launch attacks based on maps if they must, but if the enemy leaves all the doors open, then they'd rather take a look for themselves. So Will had come to see his target at the invitation of Hydro-Québec and walked right on in.

The La Grande complex was, in military parlance, a soft target. It wasn't hard for the planners to figure out how to cripple these critical sites, or even how to gain control of them, because the project had been built and maintained since its inception without much regard for even low-level security. The plentiful information Hydro-Québec made available to the world on its website didn't conceal careful layers of security; the whole thing was as wide-open as it looked. The main problem for NPA planners was to conduct the reconnaissance, develop the operation, train the assault team, and assemble the resources and people for the raid without alerting the government.

With inexperienced leaders and followers, operational security is a major problem, even with a straightforward battle plan. In fact, the whole thing had almost unravelled twice in the spring of 2008. First, a patrol leader training his people to use explosives decided to try out some of

their stolen dynamite on a Hydro pylon south of Radisson. They succeeded in damaging the transmission tower and line, but as a predictable
result caused a wide-scale alarm that brought the Sûreté du Québec—the
SQ, as the provincial police were commonly known—and the RCMP into
action. Fortunately, the investigators couldn't find any links to anyone and
the government was happy to dismiss the attack as "some pranksters playing with stolen explosives." The RCMP suspected more and continued their
undercover investigation, but the politicians didn't want to hear about it
and there were no harmful consequences for the Movement, although the
patrol leader in question suffered a tragically fatal boating accident three
weeks later.

The second incident involved a group of CBC journalists who simply
strolled into the Radisson installation without being stopped by guards,
and then highlighted the problem for several nights on TV news. Premier Commeau asked both Hydro-Québec and the provincial police to
investigate the matter only after the CBC's French language network aired
its investigative report. That prime-time news event showed journalists
entering several power installations—including walking right up to the
command centre at the site, and driving unchallenged in an unmarked
van into another part of the site that provides power to millions of people
in Quebec and the United States.

"We have asked Hydro-Québec to give us reports on the state of security and asked the Sûreté du Québec to do an independent evaluation, so
we have a solid picture of what the security situation is," the premier said
in a news conference.

The utility company's chief executive officer said guards in fact had the
news crew under video surveillance at all times, but admitted to serious
security shortcomings. He admitted also that Hydro-Québec had promised to increase security at its sites after the terrorist attacks in the United
States in September 2001 but had not in fact done anything.

"In this case, it was just journalists," he said. "It is not acceptable … If it
was a terrorist, obviously, it would not be acceptable. And therefore, what
we have to make sure here is that intrusions like these can never happen
again."

As managers of power grids in Ontario and several U.S. states expressed
their concern, the federal public safety minister faced criticism in Parlia-

ment over the security breaches. She told Parliament that it was a matter for the company and the province to resolve.

Later, Premier Commeau responded saying, "The federal public safety minister is mistaken. The federal government has to provide more security funding for Quebec … something that they have failed to do since 9/11."

Fortunately for the Movement, the federal and Quebec governments continued to squabble over responsibilities and money, and did nothing after this intrusion. Hydro-Québec closed all tours of its facilities across the province for two weeks while it "reviewed" its security arrangements at James Bay. The review resulted only in an insignificant increase in unarmed guards near the control room and the installation of a few security cameras and alarms to provide a better view, but no better way to respond to a more serious incident. The changes were typically enough to keep honest people out of the facilities but no real inconvenience to Will and his comrades.

The tour proved to Will that the facility and its security arrangements were almost exactly what the NPA had believed, and that it was safe to proceed with the plan. Later that day, he walked around town to place in his mind the vital points that in the coming days would be the lead subject of every news broadcast across Canada. The walk didn't take long: down the street from the hotel past the three radio stations to the post office, then across to the police station, taking particular notice of the location and layout of the police car park, around to the town offices, and then back to the hotel.

He rented a pickup for tomorrow's recce outside town and the meetings with patrol leaders along the road south from Radisson. So far, everything checked out. Everything on the ground matched everything on the maps and the website, and there weren't any unpleasant surprises after Will had seen things for real. He was almost ready.

DAY THREE

Tuesday, August 31

Tuesday, August 31, 0530 hours
Radisson, on the La Grande Rivière

Will woke early, as always. He checked his e-mail messages, sent to him through a clandestine address—an "electronic letter drop" that allowed for contact between Will and the NPA. It was used to pass low-grade security information, but even so, the computer was never out of his sight. "Hot messages" went by cellphone, which were sometimes used only once. The plan required that Will be noticed by the police and the Canadian Security Intelligence Service and the electronic Communications Security Establishment. But if the decoy was to succeed, the authorities would have to work for their information, and Will's e-mail connections, multiple cellphones, and odd movements around Radisson were part of that lure.

He headed downstairs for his usual spartan breakfast of porridge, brown bread, and black coffee. Afterwards, Will loaded his pickup and drove out of town at 0624, exactly at sunrise, for another look at the approaches to the generating facilities. Part way there, he turned off the main road for a thorough check of an unassuming little cross-country dirt trail that in a few days, by his estimation of the Council's plans, would be central to his assault plan, and his secret reaction plan if things went off the rails during the La Grande operation. Satisfied that his recce had given him a complete feel for the ground, Will swung the truck around and headed out of town south on Highway 109 towards Matagami.

It was time to check the Movement's Radisson-Montreal operation, organizationally independent of the Robert-Bourassa scheme but an integral part of the James Bay campaign as a whole. Will drove south in the low early morning sunlight to meet the leaders who would put the highway part of the grand plan into action.

The basic idea was to lure "reaction forces" towards the James Bay complex, then trap them on the highway so they could not be used for other purposes. Several patrols or cells would independently stake out sections of the northern 600 kilometres of the 1,400-kilometre Radisson-Montreal highway, demolish structures, and harass police and military convoys on that road to cause confusion and delay any rescue of Radisson. Ideally, police and military commanders would send an initial force towards Radisson. Will's units would then trap it on the way to the La Grande by means of demolitions placed on or near the roadway before and behind it, and subject it to harassing fire, causing the police and military to send another force to rescue the first one. Small native units would then simply repeat the tactic, trapping the rescue unit itself on another, more southerly section of the road. Eventually the army's rescue of Radisson would become a mission to rescue the rescuers: a series of traps sure to draw in ever larger numbers of the troops and helicopters that neither the police nor the Canadian Forces had in abundance.

It was a tactic that had been used with great effect in the Vietnam wars, and Will had studied it carefully. The Viet Minh had used it against the French, and the Viet Cong used it a decade later against the Americans. Will would create for the Canadian Forces their own "street without joy" in the forests of Quebec. Operations of this type required only a few conditions: an isolated target valued by political or military leaders, a single overland route through difficult terrain between the target and the rescue force, and skilled teams of hit-and-run ambush and harassing squads to attack the rescuers from the shadows. The James Bay power complex and single access highway offered the ideal geographic situation, and now the social and military situations were right as well.

As Will drove south through the rough, rocky terrain, he automatically noted useful tactical positions and solved tactical problems, a field soldier's habit. The land provided many good ambush locations but overall it was far from ideal. Too much of the terrain was bare rock, devoid of useful cover. And while clever camouflage might overcome this disadvantage in static positions, once a unit moved, or was forced to move, it would be almost fully exposed, especially to air attack. Even at night, the army, with its Light Armoured Vehicle III—the LAV III of Afghan fame, capable of all-weather, day and night surveillance—and its helicopters and infantry patrols with night-viewing scopes, would make short work of anyone caught in the open. Yet the surrounding terrain left police and army units little choice but to fight their way along the road. Properly placed demolition of key stretches would hold them up. But harassing fire was also essential, and for that, careful selection of attack sites in this barren country was critical to success.

At around 0920, Will stopped his truck on a small bridge on Highway 109. Stepping out, he walked to the railing, looked over, and checked the structure. An ideal spot for demolition, much harder to repair than a mere hole in the road. But a hard target, he thought, one that would take a lot of explosive or very careful ... A smart "thwack" on an adjacent pond startled Will and drew his attention to his unknowing allies, a pair of beavers swimming directly away from the dam they had constructed just upstream from the target bridge. The pond stored hundreds of tons of water. An expertly released, extremely sudden flash flood would sweep this bridge away in moments—the beavers' revenge on man's slaughter of their ancestors for hats, and the people's revenge, using the white man's dull national symbol.

And Will had his human experts at his disposal too. Experts to handle this dam—and others like it—in the cells he would visit that day, former soldiers and construction workers who were thoroughly familiar with explosives. All along the road to Radisson, bridges meant streams and streams usually meant beavers. In some places they'd have to use less efficient means, but in literally dozens of places, Will's demo-teams could blow dams before and behind military convoys, washing away bridges and roads, trapping them in both directions. All this havoc with just a few dozen kilos of plastic explosives.

Simply flooding the roadway, without an accompanying firefight or even a smashed bridge, would pose a significant tactical problem for any convoy hurrying along a single road to James Bay. As soon as a couple of vehicles tried to cross a flooded road and fell into craters previously blown then hidden by the water from a destroyed dam, or were blown up on mines hidden in the water, the whole expedition would slow to a crawl. Commanders would begin to call forward engineers to check each flooded section. "Mine fright," a psychological phenomenon, would cause soldiers to creep slowly forward, fearful that their next step would be their last: expecting to have your balls blown up your ass does that to people, even to the female soldiers of the modern Canadian Forces. Will gazed at the stream as his mind wandered south along the road and forward in time watching his plan unfold.

The sudden approach of a fast truck heading north brought Will sharply back to the present. As it sped across the bridge and down the road, Will noticed the whip antennas that marked it as a police or game warden patrol, probably sent to spy on his journey. Or not. Perhaps he was overly cautious. But this was no time to get careless. He hurried back to his rented truck, stowed his binoculars under the seat, checked his map, and started down the road to his first rendezvous as the dust from the other truck receded in his rear-view mirror.

Will made four stops that day, as far south as the road off the highway to Waskaganish. Each time, he visited cell leaders who were unaware of the others' instructions or even, supposedly, their identities. In a community like this, though, it wasn't hard to guess who else was likely to be a committed militant. But it didn't matter now, so there was no point worrying about it. In any case, his instructions at each stop were the same: "Get your people ready. Watch for a courier who'll come by with cases of explosives, C4, fuses, detonators, detonating-cord, and small arms and weapons. He'll know who you are but be ready to be approached. When the courier arrives," he told each leader, "so will a small team, four or five guys. You take them wherever they want to go. Ask no questions, make no arguments."

Then he gave each road patrol leader a set of cellphones, codes, and maps. Finally, he gave them all a pep talk and, in case it didn't take, a veiled threat about what happens to traitors. "Last year a cell leader went over to the other side; they promised protection and money. He didn't get the protection and his widow didn't get the money. You know, boys, you can't trust whitey or the frogs."

Tuesday, August 31, 0600 hours
Akwesasne First Nations Reserve

Alex too was up early, relieved that his nap had turned out to be a full night's sleep. They hadn't summoned him at midnight or some such stunt to keep him off balance. But now someone was banging on the door. "Come on, captain, you're wanted in the Complex."

"The Complex" sat within a sprawl of trailers, vans, and makeshift huts, surrounded by a high wire fence—all set aside from the usual band residents and partially hidden on the far eastern section of the St. Regis, the American portion of the Akwesasne Reserve close to the Canada-United States border. The compound provided a secure headquarters and logistical base for the Movement and its leaders.

Akwesasne was a logical base for the Movement, Alex thought, and had obviously been chosen with care. Alex remembered details from an intelligence briefing he had attended during an internal security training exercise. Some 13,000 Mohawks lived in Akwesasne, a huge tract of land on the banks of the St. Lawrence River near Cornwall, Ontario, and about 150 kilometres west of Montreal. The reserve had gained notoriety with both the civil and military authorities because of the numerous illegal activities supposedly given cover by the fact it was, in the report author's words, a "jurisdictional nightmare." Straddling the international boundary between Canada and the United States, and governed under laws, agreements, and customs of these nations as well as the provinces of Ontario and Quebec, and the state of New York, the reserve was felt by many police and military leaders to be almost lawless. That this territorial maze was all subordinated to the Mohawk Council of Akwesasne, an elected council of twelve district chiefs and a grand chief, was considered by the report's author to be a further black mark against it, and another reason why the reserve was deemed the very antithesis of the Canadian ideal of "peace, order, and good government."

To be fair, Alex had to admit that the governing structure of the reserve was complex. Every aspect of life on the reserve was subject to negotiation and deliberation by all these governmental and bureaucratic bodies. The complexity of Akwesasne administration was illustrated by the fact that the security and policing of this small community could involve five legally separate police services: the reserve's own Mohawk Police Services, the RCMP, the Ontario Provincial Police, the Sûreté du Québec, and the New York State Police, not to mention other American federal police and security agencies.

As a result of this "jurisdictional nightmare," the reserve did attract criminals and criminal gangs, native and non-native, who saw it as an ungoverned space where overlapping judicial and police responsibilities provided room to manoeuvre. While most of the permanent residents of Akwesasne were peaceful, law-abiding citizens interested only in making an honest living and providing for their families and children within a society based in Mohawk traditions, over the years, Akwesasne had hosted drug, gun, and human smugglers. The illicit tobacco trade, Alex knew, was big business on the reserve too.

Although the conditions at Akwesasne provided the Movement with a safe haven and an environment where the organization could work and grow in relative safety from Canadian and American authorities, Molly Grace was determined to eventually sweep from every reserve in Canada all forms of corruption and gangsterism. For the moment, however, the security she needed required a few uneasy alliances with unsavoury characters. It was simply a burden the Movement would have to carry for now. Nevertheless, at Akwesasne, Molly and her enforcers were tolerated by the residents because she kept these "allies" outside the reserve, provided money and protection to the community and its many legitimate businesses, and backed up the Mohawk Police Services in their running battles with criminal gangs.

But Akwesasne's home on both sides of the international boundary offered an added bonus over any other Canadian reserve—almost unhindered movement across the border, and uncomplicated access to American aboriginal leaders and their rich and secure communities across the United States.

Alex opened the door a crack. "Right out. Just have to wash the soap off and dress."

The stunned kid had disappeared at some point during the night. Now, the dim light of the half-dawn showed only the outline of the big guy who had escorted him to the hut the night before, the one Alex had tentatively pegged as a warrant officer.

"Okay," said the voice. "But hurry up."

Alex quickly splashed water from the sink and improvised a sponge bath, dabbing his joints with soap and wiping off most of the water with paper towels and his dirty T-shirt. He dressed and grabbed his small pack. He felt alert and refreshed, though hardly clean.

As he walked out the door the "warrant officer" snatched the pack and threw it back into the hut.

"Hey," Alex protested, "never separate a soldier from his kit." Then he added, as casually as he could, "That's the rule, right, warrant officer?"

His escort smirked. "Nice try, captain, but this is a need-to-know place."

They walked across the compound, into the Quonset hut, and down a long hall towards—Alex had no idea what. By the time he passed through a second short hall into a second inner hut, his eyes had adjusted to the dull light. The various sections of the building were, he correctly assumed, separated by narrow spaces between their walls to guard against penetration by electronic-seeking satellites and direction finders.

The long, narrow inside hut was divided into small working areas, separated by standard movable partitions of different colours for different functions. But the deceptively simple layout hid a sophisticated computerized command and control capability. Every computer connected to the Internet or to the specially constructed secret First Nations network, which was protected by a sophisticated high-security firewall. The cables leading to external access points in the village were buried in deep, shielded concrete conduits. Alert armed guards kept the separate staffs from wandering into

the most vital areas, especially the code room in the communications centre far down the corridor in the heart of the compound.

This inner area—nicknamed the Complex, after the NORAD command
post in Colorado—was at the heart of First Nations Movement. And this
morning the staff was fully alert and very active. Alex was taken down
another tight side corridor, past a cramped meeting room. Before the door
could be hastily slammed in his face, he recognized a few senior chiefs of
the First Nations Assembly. His escort opened another door farther down
the corridor and directed him inside.

Alex stopped uncertainly inside the doorway. Instead of hushed darkness and a dozen people hunched over flickering screens, the space was
bright, nearly empty, and very ordinary-looking, like an unimportant
conference room. A thirty-something man in practical outdoor clothes
stood at the front of the room behind a two-metre-long folding table, with
papers and a map spread out before him. He put his steaming coffee mug
on the makeshift desk and waved Alex to a chair in front.

"Morning, Alex. I'm Bill Whitefish, chief of staff to the First Nations
Movement." He extended his hand, and then sat down. "Take a seat. Hope
you got some rest. Coffee?"

"No, thanks," Alex replied, before turning to move his chair. He stopped
in surprise. Behind him, in the far corner of the room, a woman sat silently
in an armchair, legs crossed, her lap filled with files, looking him over
with unsettling intensity. She wasn't much older than Alex. Dressed in
cords and a rose-patterned shirt, she was slim, conventionally attractive,
and, judging by her brown complexion, high cheekbones, and long, silky,
braided hair hanging over her left shoulder, obviously native—probably
Cree, Alex thought. She said nothing and pointed to the chair. Alex sat
down, uncomfortably aware of those large, black eyes burning through
the back of his head straight into his mind.

Bill Whitefish didn't introduce her. Instead, without preamble, he said,
"That was good work at Petawawa, just as we expected when you were
assigned to the mission."

Alex mumbled, "Thanks . . . my young people did well . . . I hope they're
being treated properly . . ." He resisted the urge to turn to the woman in
the corner. Disquieting as her stare was from behind, it wouldn't improve
things to look her in the eye, at least not now.

"Don't worry about them. They'll be fine, and thanks to your training, useful in the future as well. Amazing what a bit of pride and purpose can do to these supposedly wild kids, don't you think?"

Whitefish turned, uncovered a whiteboard behind his table, and pointed to a sparse organization chart. "Later today we'll talk to you about another mission we have for you. But first, it's time you got to know the details of the organization that's directing this campaign. What I'm going to tell you is for your ears only. Many others know some of the details, only a few know the full extent of our operation, and fewer still know who knows. Even the fact that you have been briefed is a secret. I know that you understand from your special ops background that there are government security clearances above top secret that are themselves a secret. So, assume the same thing here. What you learn this morning is not for gossip and not to be discussed with anyone. Got it?"

"Yes, of course."

"Good. Let me begin with the bare-bones details of the Native People's Movement, the NPM, and how we've built it up, especially after the government-inspired violence on and after the June Days of Protest some time ago. You remember that disaster?"

"Yes, sir." Alex couldn't help reverting to army subordinate-superior language in these situations. "I remember it, of course. That's why I'm here."

"Alex, just call me Bill. Anyway, we began to organize the NPM in detail once we understood that a serious conflict with the government was inevitable, since the government had repudiated the land settlement and national sovereignty deals we thought were cast in stone. We understood that a nationalist movement needed to be created. The NPM and its tactics are modelled on other successful 'people's revolts,' such as those in Algeria, Vietnam, and the ANC in South Africa, for instance. I think you're more than familiar with these histories?"

"I am, certainly—a major topic in my degree program and a long-time interest in any case. I assume T.E. Lawrence and his revolt in the desert is a major source of ideas too?"

"He is *the* central source," said a voice from the back of the room. "Go on, Bill."

"The NPM is composed of the Native People's Council, the NPC, and the Native People's Army, the NPA. We also have a Central Committee..."

Bill's eyes raised to the back of the room; he hesitated, then continued. "We will talk, perhaps, about the Committee later ... The NPC is composed of a select group of chiefs and some elders who represent regions across the country. They provide advice and counsel for the Movement as a whole.

"Early on, we adopted organizational structures taken from modern militant organizations and created as well a sophisticated, secret, business-like organization. We are very careful, and successful so far as we know, in cloaking our operations behind groups and governing agencies legitimately associated with the aboriginal community."

"On the reserves and so on?"

"Indeed, a member of a legitimate organization or a reserve might be at the same time a leader of a local revolutionary cell, and a band chief might be a member of the NPC, and one or both might be part of some federal negotiations task force, especially if we can convince, by whatever means, federal politicians to let us join or run such task forces and inquiries.

"These crossovers make it difficult for the government and law enforcement agencies to take any sort of action against us without risking trouble. It's a situation we exploit with some skill ... and ruthlessness, if I might say so.

"The Council is supported by three main offices. The Information and Intelligence Authority, or IIA, provides clandestine control over the First Nations' Radio and Television Network, the First Nations' Internet Service, and the Aboriginal Media Relations Association. Its job is to bolster native self-awareness and the community's sense of grievance and to deflect any criticisms of any native initiative or organization by playing on 'white guilt' and so on.

"We also send delegates to academic meetings and public events to beat the guilt drum and castigate anyone, especially politicians or academics, who dares criticize or raise doubts about native claims, rights, or activities."

"Bill, I assume this unit is related to some type of intelligence operations," Alex said. "Without it you'd be flying in the dark and very vulnerable."

"Of course. The Movement's intelligence unit, our second major unit, collects, analyses, collates, and disseminates intelligence within our organization. It employs a score of analysts—mostly former soldiers and police officers loyal to the cause—housed in a couple of innocuous-looking offices in Ottawa and Winnipeg, hidden within legitimate establishments operated by the native community. Its counter-intelligence wing works to prevent federal investigations of native governments and funding programs or any intrusive inquiries of any kind. It also develops 'sources' within the federal and provincial governments and within all the federal political parties."

"Within the political parties? Isn't that risky?"

"Well, it can be except when individuals and parties need money, if you see what I mean."

Alex nodded in disbelief.

"Our third main unit, Alex, is the Reconciliation Authority—the RA. Its public aim is to prompt reconciliation between native and non-native Canadians. Its real duty is to maintain and track the maze of legal battles and challenges to land and other claims made by the native community against Canada. It also clandestinely collects information, including records of ownership of farmland across the country, especially on the Prairies. We're building up a record of all the rulings involving native people, and who made them, in municipal, provincial, and federal courts and tribunals. We're in effect building a reconciliation invoice of the price to be extracted from Canadians in the future for their decisions and actions in the past."

"All very costly, obviously. How can you raise such money without the RCMP seeing it?"

"Well, we do it mostly in the open. Our Financial Unit manages three distinct streams of revenue. The first is public money. Government grants of all sorts, available in surprisingly large quantities, flow into the native community every year under incredibly lax controls. Most of the money is spent as intended, but we 'tax' a portion of it."

"Don't chiefs and others complain when your taxman shows up?"

"Some do from time to time, but they all eventually listen to reason after a visit or two.

"The second, and indirect, source of funding comes from smuggling. Drug and cigarette smugglers, native and otherwise, might not be sympathetic to the Movement. But they are willing and able to pay for our sophisticated intelligence information; if that doesn't interest them, our threats to betray them to the authorities always help us to reach a settlement with them. They would rather do business than fight us. The payout, though dirty, is highly lucrative.

"The third major source of funding may surprise you. We obtain substantial contributions from online operations. Sort of like political parties, seal lovers, and religious groups, we generate money from well-intentioned Canadians and from hundreds of people in other countries who are eager to support 'oppressed Canadian aboriginal people'. And since the beginning of the wars in Iraq and Afghanistan, we have also received large donations from 'sources' in those regions."

"Why would they send you money, Bill? I doubt, from my experiences in the region, that anyone, even the educated elites, cares a rat's ass about our problems."

"Perhaps not, Alex. But I think some people in the region who oppose your 'educated elites' would rather have our soldiers occupied in Canada and not wandering around opposing them in theirs.

"That's the tip of the iceberg, Alex. The Movement is large, active, and ambitious, and its funding base is considerable as well. We can turn on the tap, so to speak, whenever we need to by making 'requests' from politicians, large and small, and from officials, judges, police, customs agents and criminals on both sides of the Canada/U.S. border. Once touched by occasional payoffs and bribes or girl or boyfriends, we own them. They provide influence and information on demand as well. They're what we call 'the insurance.'"

The picture Bill Whitefish gave Alex left the soldier impressed, but at the same time uneasy. Even he had his prejudices. These guys obviously understood the theory, but could their followers manage an operation of this scale, sophistication, and seriousness. They were after all, just reserve Indians.

"Any questions?" Bill asked.

"Well, yeah," Alex stammered. "Lots, mostly details: how many people; where are we strong and weak; can I count on the young leaders; how does what we did last night fit the grand strategy, if, with respect, there is one. Things like that." He took a deep breath, then took the plunge. "Where is it all going? What's our endgame?"

The woman at the back of the room spoke up. "We can cover those matters later, much later in some cases. Today, we're situating you for the next operation and for a leadership role in it. Go on, Bill."

Alex turned from Whitefish to the woman, then back to Whitefish. Whatever they were up to, it was happening fast and he was in too deep to back out now.

"Okay, Alex," Bill went on, "let me put the Native People's Army—the NPA, the armed wing of the Movement—on the board. It's not so much an army as an idea. And the idea is simple—get lots of armed people concentrated in important areas, overcome the defences of Canada, especially where the Canadian Forces are weak, then stay there. The NPA is based on several related objectives: maintenance of an irregular armed force with reasonable levels of internal unity and discipline; the development of full-time combat commanders and leaders; the establishment of high skills in low-level tactics and technical capabilities; subversion of the police and the Canadian Forces; and the destruction of the Canadian army's public image as 'peacekeepers.'

"The crucial effort over the past three years has been to create in the minds of our people the belief that their army is just that, *their* army— an organization they can identify with and a source of communal pride. 'People's army, people's war,' that's the traditional revolutionary battle cry ..."

"Vo Nguyên Giap, the Vietnamese general," Alex interrupted.

Again Bill glanced at the back of the room. "Right you are, so I'm told. In any case, for some time the 'warrior society' has worked hard to gain credibility within the community, and I think we've had some success in becoming the legitimate protector of native people and their rights and traditional claims in the eyes of the people. When the *intifada* erupts, our people won't hesitate to identify our cause with theirs.

"Once things start, of course, it's crucial that the NPA doesn't melt away in the face of trouble. You know, Alex, how overstretched the Canadian army is, but you know it's a professional force. When and where its soldiers manage to get into action, they will perform effectively, and our guys have to be ready for that. That's why we knew we had to find sufficient competent, experienced combat leaders to train the kids and hold them together when the shooting starts—"

Alex looked at him sharply and Whitefish quickly corrected himself. "I mean, *if* shooting starts. Again, we looked to the federal government for unsuspecting assistance. First, we quietly encouraged young people who were beginning to see how things really were to keep their mouths shut and enlist, especially in officer training programs. Their job, as deep moles, wasn't just to learn the ways of warfare but to build their own connections to natives otherwise enrolled in the armed forces. As a bonus, as they progressed in rank and responsibility, they gained knowledge and access to government secrets and establishments, very useful during the raids this week.

"This strategy worked splendidly. The Canadian Forces, including the reserves, the militia, provided a steady stream of leaders to meet the Committee's needs. The government was eager to enrol native people in the armed forces, not just because they had long been a source of good soldiers, but to satisfy the demand for racial integration, multiculturalism, and diversity. We took full advantage of that. The leadership problem in the NPA has slowly sorted itself out as patriots arrived from the regular Canadian Forces and as native enrolment in the militia increased.

"Our training programs for those who haven't been in the Canadian Forces are not particularly sophisticated, but they don't need to be. We've got a small cadre, mostly former regular soldiers like yourself, trained to use explosives, lay mines, and build and destroy field obstacles, and perform basic field staff duties. Ordinary members only need to learn how to operate in small tactical units, employ basic small arms such as rifles and hand grenades, use radio communications systems, read maps, do as they're told, and not panic in the face of trouble. Instilling discipline was a major issue and, again, it's the regular members of the Canadian Forces who provided the way forward. They understand training, and the kids respect them. You know that; you were one of them and the team you trained did just fine. I'll leave it there."

"Thanks, Bill, the briefing was helpful. In fact, the simple force you described also describes the Taliban that I—we—fought and the Canadian Forces continues to fight in Afghanistan. And we all know how much trouble they were and still are."

Bill looked to the back of the room. "Molly?"

Molly Grace had watched Alex carefully during the briefing. She had a peculiar talent for seeing right inside people, and although she knew a great deal about him from the files, in the flesh he impressed her even more. She sensed the sureness with which he absorbed information and admired his poise in alien circumstances. Molly's aptitude for evaluating others was accompanied, perhaps even caused, by a failure of empathy; she rarely liked those she met, even those she admired, but she had an unerring ability to know when she had found someone useful to the cause, and she had a keen sense of how best to enlist their sympathy and support.

She stood up, walked to the front of the room, and balanced herself on the table's front edge directly before Alex. "I wouldn't normally say much more than Bill has just said, but I want you to fully understand how things work here and the reality of the Movement.

"Bill told you that the Native People's Movement is directed by the Council. That's not necessarily untrue, but it's not the whole story. I'm going to take you into my confidence, mainly because we are going to give you a great deal of authority and you may find yourself in a situation where some local chief, some member of the People's Council, might try to override what I have told you to do. I'm telling you this, Alex, because I can see what sort of man you are and because I think you appreciate the importance of discretion.

"The Council in fact provides me with a community consensus-building device, no more. It serves to involve some chiefs in decisions and that involvement commits them to supporting those decisions. Most of the chiefs know the outline of the strategic plan, but sometimes their knowledge isn't always... shall we say, complete.

"All revolutionary organizations depend for success on a few dedicated leaders. The Movement's plans, actions, and vital information are in the hands of the very small, secret vanguard, the Central Committee, those very few leaders who founded the First Nations' Movement.

"The Central Committee needs the first nations chiefs for one reason and one reason only—our people know them and trust them. They think the chiefs are in charge of everything and so they go along. We may be leading a popular movement, but we can't leave the revolution in the hands of the chiefs: it would fail if we trusted them to act."

Molly shifted around and began to pace the room, speaking as much to the walls as to Alex. "The Central Committee never intended to trust the revolution to those co-opted, high-living sell-outs in Ottawa, the First

Nations Federation leaders. That's why the Committee is in touch with some of the best, the firmest, young men and women in the organized youth groups, community governing councils, and healing circles across the land. These special young people are our eyes and ears, and sometimes our hands, in the communities, the essential link between our strategy and our ability to act.

"They communicate with the Central Committee, with me, indirectly by a specially devised system of procedures and rules of contact. For the most part, they wait for instructions and carry on 'legitimate' programs, but they keep their eyes open for real or potential opposition, traitors, weaklings, the dissolute, provide information to their Committee contact, and keep the people focused on the real causes of their problems: the white man's oppression and the government's hypocrisy.

"Discipline within the cells is strict. And when they have to, cell leaders take decisive action in their communities. Mostly they use persuasion, but sometimes, I'll be honest, they also use punishment, such as withholding band benefits and privileges or even expelling individuals from the reserve. Our access to resources, including taxing traditional trade outside the white man's control, is also useful with some of our less resolute brothers and sisters. The point to remember is that the Central Committee is, as they say, 'the vanguard of this revolution.'

"If we had time, which we don't, I would take you in to see the People's Council in action down the hall. They're definitely in touch with the problems of the people, and in their hearts they know the solutions. It's just a matter of keeping them from getting panicky about media reports of a 'native uprising.'

"Okay, Alex, that's enough for now. Bill will show you around and give you more immediate instructions for the next phase. You're going to Winnipeg. We'll talk later. Thanks for last night's work." Molly scooped up her papers and turned to leave.

Captain Gabriel, officer and gentleman, stepped forward to open the door and put out his hand. "Molly Grace, I assume? A pleasure to meet you. I wasn't sure you were real, but you certainly are that."

Molly recoiled, slightly wary of the unexpected courtesy and the obvious test. His actions were gracious, but her exit was softly blocked. She looked into Alex's eyes, and as she held out a hand, her voice lost its commanding edge. "You'll go far in this effort, Alex. I'm depending on you to work for the people. Lead and they'll follow you."

Tuesday, August 31, 1838 hours
Radisson

After a long day on the road, Will circled back to Radisson and his hotel late that night. As he pulled in, he saw Bob Ignace leaning against the side of his patrol truck in the parking lot.

"How's the fishing, Boucanier?" Ignace called out as he walked towards the vehicle. "Never knew you were much of a fisherman. Take some lessons in the army? Doesn't look like your rods even got out of the cases."

"Never had to take any lessons, Bob. Don't you know, we traditional natives have a natural sense about these things. Why, we can catch fish without a line and a hook, just call them out of the water and they jump into the boat. Isn't that what we tell the government inquiries?"

Will collected his kit and walked towards the hotel.

"Real smartass, Will. Tell me, since when have you been so interested in beaver ponds?"

Will paused, then without reply or turning around, walked on. Mission accomplished so far. He was getting out there and being seen. That was his prime directive, as they say in TV-land.

Tuesday, August 31, 1915 hours
Akwesasne: The Complex

It had been a long day for Alex too. He left the command centre with his head buzzing from a day of information and rhetoric. Molly Grace had grabbed his heart and his imagination, as she did with most people.

Alex's immediate instructions from Bill Whitefish were clear and simple, yet extremely puzzling. "Go to the stores building, get dressed and outfitted. A driver will take you by car to Trudeau Airport in Montreal. Stay at the Best Western Hotel there, and stay in your room, order room service. On Wednesday morning, use the ticket you'll be given and fly to Winnipeg, and there take a taxi to the Occidental Hotel on Main Street."

"Winnipeg? I thought I was here to fight."

"Someone will meet you there and take you to Sam Stevenson. I believe you know him."

"Colonel Sam Stevenson! I certainly know him. Everyone in the army knows Sam Steele—that's what the soldiers call him."

"He'll give you your next orders. Have a good trip."

Bill Whitefish shook his hand and walked away without another word.

Looking back at the day, Alex admitted to himself that he was a bit confused and more than a little suspicious of the various people he had met in the group. The most obvious question was: could these civvies actually plan and conduct the operation they had just outlined for him? But his bigger concern was: could Molly and her sidekick, Bill Whitefish, be trusted?

Tuesday August 31, 1900 hours
Ottawa: NDHQ, Thirteenth Floor, Conference Room C

General Bishop had deliberately chosen Conference Room C, a room just big enough that he could frankly brief Minister of National Defence Jim Riley without the inconvenience of too many of the minister's political staff or his own staff officers around to inhibit the discussion. It was precisely 1900 hours as the CDS held the door for the minister to enter the room first.

The Intelligence Centre director, Colonel Ed Conway, stood at the lectern ready to deliver the first part of the briefing. He waited while the principals found seats and for General Bishop to introduce the topic—it was the CDS's show all the way.

Andy Bishop was a tall, thin man with dark hair cropped close over a narrow face and long nose. It was difficult to imagine how he'd ever squeezed his frame into the cockpit of a fighter plane. But he had, and was by reputation a superb pilot as well as a proven creative tactical commander. In January 2010 he commanded the Commonwealth Humanitarian Intervention Force, CHIF, deployed to Zimbabwe under a UN "responsibility to protect" mandate issued by the Commonwealth leaders. He personally conceived and directed the strategy that destroyed Zimbabwe's air force in two days, eliminated its army's combat capability in seven, and put a Commonwealth "Save the People" directorship in place immediately afterwards. His reward was the thanks of Parliament, promotion to full general, and appointment as CDS.

General Bishop was also the first CDS in the history of the Canadian Forces to earn a Ph.D., having studied law and international relations at Queen's University, Kingston, and at Oxford. But he wasn't a people person. He was considered a cold fish by almost everyone, except intensely intellectual officers like himself. While he was not well known by the rank and file, he was greatly admired by the young, "new model" fighting officer corps he led. No matter his aloofness, nobody disputed his ethical principles or his orders once he had made a decision. The new Canadian Forces Headquarters he had established was, as another Canadian general officer in another era had demanded, "a small, thinking headquarters devoid of administrative detail."

The CDS would listen carefully to briefings and discussions but cut in quickly if they wandered from the point or glossed over crucial issues, and he was notoriously impatient if his incisive queries elicited vagueness. He trusted only a few staff officers—"Bishop's brats" as outsiders referred to them, though only out of earshot—chosen because they were well-educated and experienced in the field and at sea. They knew they could speak bluntly with Bishop; "frank unto the Kaiser" was the norm. They knew also that whenever the chief fell quiet or seemed unresponsive it was a good idea to keep quiet as well. Inexperienced officers, even senior ones, had been stiffly rebuked for interrupting the man while he was thinking over a question or situation. Thus Colonel Ed Conway, a senior "brat" who had followed the general through several positions, stood silently waiting for the CDS to speak.

Finally, after Jim Riley had settled into his chair, General Bishop poured himself a glass of water, finished adjusting his glasses, and got ready to speak.

"Minister, this evening we are going to put in a larger context our assessment of the raids we experienced on Sunday night. I want you to think in terms of vulnerabilities, not threats. The native people, if they're well organized—and we'll speak to this point during this briefing—are situated in bands and on reserves that sit astride the east-west lines of communications and transportation on which Canada's national economy depends. They sit next door to most of the major sources for our resource industries and on the north-south lines that take them to the industrial bases in Ontario, Quebec, and B.C. They also sit astride the oil, natural gas, and hydro lines that fuel southern Canada and a good deal of the United States.

"Northern Quebec and the James Bay power generation facilities are particularly vulnerable. The transmission lines from the facilities run south for nearly 1,000 kilometres. They are not only undefended but probably indefensible. On the Prairies, the natural gas and oil pipelines are the great vulnerability. The above-ground lines and transfer stations that keep things flowing are all unprotected. A few kilos of explosives, a mere fraction of what was stolen in the raids this week, would put them all out of action. The natives don't have to control the entire territory to cripple Canada. They just have to make raids on the isolated lines from the safety of reserves.

"Minister, the threat we face from the native population may be small in the sense that they can't seize and hold major cities or even towns. But our vulnerability to the threat they could pose is extremely high. In risk management terms, our economy, freedom to travel, and relations with the United States are in the hands of actors we can't control.

"Moreover, we have few ways to redress the threats or to substitute other things to diminish our vulnerability. We have thousands of what we call vital points to protect and very few people and resources to protect them. If, for instance, we were to stand still, guarding pipelines, the natives could attack other targets. If we were to try to chase them around, they could blend into the reserves and the peaceful population, and strike when we go somewhere else.

"In most of the scenarios we have constructed from the intelligence we have about what radical native leaders might be contemplating, we are in very big trouble. And as you will hear in these briefings, the opportunities we have left open for someone to attempt something dramatic are frighteningly large. This evening, over the next couple of hours, we're going to paint these vulnerabilities in bright colours."

Bishop left his assessments hanging before the minister's eyes, then he continued.

"Minister, I will make a few more comments, and then two of my senior officers will review the data for you. These remarks and briefings are intended to add some flesh to the image of the barebones vulnerability I just presented to you. We must assume after Sunday's raids that the facts and figures to follow—once the framework for the hypothetical threat—are now the framework for the probable future for Canada over the next several months."

General Bishop stepped towards the centre of the room, clasped his hands criss-cross at his waist, and again turned and faced Riley.

"Minister, an examination of the statistics for the native population in Canada reveals two general trends. First, there is an unprecedented growth in population on reserves. Second, despite this fact, and contrary to some media reports and public opinion, social conditions and health and welfare on some reserves are stable and even improving. Which is good news, of course. However, many investigators are worried that in the middle distance, rapid population growth and worsening social services are on a collision course. As you may know, minister, scholars warn us that revolutions often occur when conditions are improving and people's expectations of a better future are suddenly dashed."

Conway smiled to himself. He very much doubted that Riley knew any such thing, even though it was a concept particularly germane to Canada's present situation. But then, Canadian ministers of national defence tend not to know much about warfare, international relations, or history. But it didn't help to embarrass them—thus Bishop's tactful attempt to guide the minister through the fundamentals of revolutionary warfare.

"In the near future," Bishop continued, "the open question is whether the improvements in current standards of living can continue fast enough to avert a security challenge to the government of Canada, especially from the rapidly growing and increasingly frustrated young male population on reserves. Analysts who have applied the Canadian circumstances to models of, as they say, 'perceptions of disaffection' in so-called failed states, in the Horn of Africa for instance, conclude that the young members of the native community in Canada are a dangerously fertile ground for recruitment by radical leaders within that community. The concern here is not militant protest, minister. The possibility of a large-scale revolt by native people against Canada is, according to these models, very possible."

Riley broke in irritably. "Models, African failed states, surely this is just academic mumbling. We've got programs, comprehensive negotiations, we know they—"

"I'm afraid not, minister," the CDS interrupted quietly but firmly. "It's true that we're paid to take such notions seriously and be prepared for the worst while others hope for the best. But Sunday's raids and Molly Grace's television tape strongly suggest that the analysts' scenario is in fact very serious, plausible, and immediate, not some theoretical case concocted by defence academics."

"Well, I don't sympathize with these attitudes. Our government provides billions in cash and support to the First Nations and their chiefs every year."

"Indeed you do, minister. And that brings me to something else very serious, plausible, and immediate. Over the years, Canadian governments have deliberately created something approaching a parallel government within Canada run by native leaders. True, it is a reasonable way to work with the more responsible and moderate elements to improve conditions without provoking accusations of paternalism and trampling of the right to self-government.

"The problem is that, if these leaders fail to deliver or are found wanting, as seems the case in some regions, then this organization, this parallel government, is ripe for a coup staged by any well-organized native leader. Put simply, the official native leaders, the ones who get invited to Rideau Hall and to federal-provincial meetings, are extremely vulnerable, and the radicals wouldn't have to create a governing structure from scratch under difficult conditions, just take over the one we've built for them."

"Sure, yes, you're right," Riley acknowledged. "But the dilemma for the federal government is that it has to support someone, even ineffective leaders, even ones compromised in the eyes of residents on reserves, or risk the collapse of years of policy built with these leaders. We can't just throw out the whole framework for national policy."

"I understand the situation, minister, but the entire hollow structure that governments have created is highly vulnerable to an internal radical takeover." Bishop raised a hand to fend off an interruption from Riley. "If such a thing were to occur, it would likely come from someone within the middle ranks of the community, from some generally unknown radical chief, for instance.

"The chiefs and grand chiefs aren't likely to be the leaders—they've got too much going for them to take such risks. As you may know, minister, rebellions and revolutions are rarely directed from the comfortable bunch at the top of the hierarchy." In a flicker of the wit familiar only to his close associates, Bishop added, gesturing around the room, "That's why I always have to watch the colonels."

Riley smiled. "You should see it in my profession."

"Indeed, minister. Actually, I have." He paused. "I'll ask Colonel Conway to flesh out these thoughts with some detail of the facts we face today. This briefing is complex and longer than most, minister, but it can't be avoided if you're to get a good sense of the seriousness of the situation. As I said earlier in your office, we've been building this file with the RCMP and CSIS for years, but your colleagues on both sides of the House would have none of it. It's time you got the whole picture."

Ed Conway looked up from his notes, waited for the CDS to sit down, and then focused on Jim Riley. "Minister, the Native People's Army, the NPA, is a formidable force, deeply embedded in the native community, especially in the reserves. It is secretive, secure, and very difficult to penetrate by ordinary intelligence means. The force is lightly armed, although after last night's raids it has added significant capabilities to its arsenal. The NPA, in any case, has for a long time had access to, and possession of, heavy weapons on the reserves in Quebec and eastern Ontario, but the RCMP hasn't been allowed to confiscate them."

Conway paused just long enough to let Riley absorb that message then continued. "We believe that many leaders have had professional training in the Canadian Forces regular and reserves, and in U.S. Army units, including airborne battalions and special forces units. In fact, the American forces have been more successful in recruiting Canadian natives than we have over the years. We have tried to track the natives recruited by the Americans, but it is difficult to do, and in any case, the effort, though we thought it was clandestine, was challenged last year before the Privacy Commissioner by the Council of Native Leaders and the government lost the case.

"Our problem, minister, isn't just that a significant paramilitary force has been assembled on the reserves. The problem is more profound. So now I'd like to run briefly through the main issues relating to the native population." He glanced towards one of the two screens just behind his lectern as if to direct the minster to his slides.

"The aboriginal population of Canada—North American Indian, Inuit, and Métis—numbers nearly 1.2 million people—four per cent of the Canadian population. And it's growing very rapidly. Between 1996 and 2006 the aboriginal community grew by forty-seven per cent, six times faster than the non-aboriginal Canadian population.

"According to the 2006 census, approximately 700,000 people identify themselves as North American Indians and most identify themselves with one of 615 First Nations. This Indian community is expected to increase to 730,000 individuals by 2021, but the statistics are a bit dated and some scholars and policy analysts think the population is already larger than measured and will increase more dramatically by 2012.

"Approximately forty per cent of the population live on one of the 2,720 reserves of vastly different sizes that are scattered across Canada. The strongest concentrations, more than forty-eight per cent of the total Indian population, live on reserves in Manitoba and Saskatchewan.

"In 2006, the median age in the national Indian population was twenty-five. In other words, exactly half the population is older and half is younger than twenty-five. The norm in the general Canadian population is forty. The on-reserve population is very young—thirty-four per cent are children under fourteen years of age.

"Although there are exceptions, as you know, the majority of the natives on reserves live in miserable conditions, are poorly educated, and have few employment opportunities on and near the reserves. The 55,000 young people between fifteen and twenty-four years of age—that's a full twenty per cent of the on-reserve population—present a looming problem for education and health and employment planners everywhere, but it's greatest in the Prairie provinces. They present also a significant potential threat to national security and public safety.

"Now let me turn to the other segment, the off-reserve Indians, who represent some sixty per cent of the total Indian population. Off-reserve aboriginals include individuals residing on non-reserve rural land and individuals residing in Canadian cities. Of these two groups, the populations in cities make up the largest concentrations of native people anywhere in Canada, on or off reserves.

"Winnipeg, for example, contains more than 26,000 First Nations people and Vancouver and Edmonton each have more than 20,000 within their boundaries. In the smaller cities on the Prairies, the concentrations are even greater. In Thompson, Manitoba, and in Prince Albert and North Battleford, Saskatchewan, for example, fifteen to thirty per cent of the total population is Indian. These figures, of course, are dynamic, but the trend is toward increasing concentrations of these large urban, generally young populations in identifiable sections of the cities. Again, minister, the figures are not always trustworthy, especially in this case as many of the young people don't exactly take to filling in census forms and so on. So we're guessing about how many kids are in the urban populations.

"The problem of disaffected youth, both with natives and non-natives, is related to poverty and lack of education; however, these issues are of particular concern in the native population. As you well understand, there is a strong correlation between success in school and future employment. School enrolment for all natives between the ages of six and sixteen has remained stable at around eighty-six per cent since 1990. However, high school graduation rates on reserves remain low.

"For instance, on Manitoba reserves, only thirty per cent of aboriginals between twenty and twenty-four have completed high school. Among Canadians generally—including off-reserve natives—eighty-four per cent of the same cohort have completed high school. The general failure of young people on reserves to finish high school has an inevitable negative impact on their individual lives, of course. But it also has a cumulative wasting effect on the reserve community. Failure in school leads to failure in the work place, which leads to frustration and grievances, which leads to security vulnerabilities for the individual, the community, and the nation. It's no exaggeration in the context of on-reserve natives to speak of a 'lost generation' or more realistically about an unrecoverable, lost society."

Ed Conway took a breath. "Gentlemen," he said, "there is some cautionary good news in the data. Post-secondary enrolment rates remain low as well, but show marked improvement from historic figures. Today, the number possessing post-secondary degrees has increased dramatically."

"At least," Riley put in, "they offer role models for youth."

"Unfortunately, minister, while the data does show that these people are better off in many ways, it shows also that better-educated natives don't just leave the reserves but they tend to live outside urban aboriginal communities once they have completed their studies. That out-migration, in turn, leaves the worse-off, the uneducated young people, perhaps the most aggrieved, on the reserves and in the inner-city slums. It creates unbalanced communities, at least by Canadian standards.

"Sir, the employment figures support these general observations. Unemployment for on-reserve Indians remains far higher than the rest of the population, at 27.6 per cent. The unemployment rate of off-reserve Indians is markedly lower but, at 16.5 per cent, still over twice the general figure. The unemployment rate for fifteen- to twenty-four-year-olds, the most vulnerable group for radical propaganda and recruitment and therefore the main security concern for the Canadian Forces and the police, is 40.1 per cent on-reserve, against 9.2 per cent national average. This is indeed a worrying fact as native leaders have repeatedly pointed out over the years.

"Minister, General Bishop, that concludes my portion of the briefing."

As Riley began to lift his hand the CDS cut in quickly. "If you agree, minister, I suggest we go right into the next briefing. I've asked Colonel Ian Dobson, the Director of the National Defence Operations Centre, to cover the criminal native gangs aspects of this situation for you. Then we can move to your office to handle any questions and consider our planning options."

Riley reached for his water glass. "Sure, fine, whatever you suggest. It's a lot of information at once. And it's not good news, you know, especially the way you guys think of things—what's the old saw? For soldiers, nothing is ever safe enough."

Riley took a drink and turned towards the next briefing officer. Bishop's lean jaw clenched perceptibly.

Ian Dobson adjusted his reading glasses and took his classified notes from a folder. "Minister, there is another series of details you need to know. They're related, as General Bishop suggested, to the sometimes con-flicted relationship between NPA and native gangs, or what officials term Aboriginal-Based Organized Crime, ABOC."

Riley nodded, relieved by the change of topic, even to this unpleasant subject.

"The Canadian Criminal Intelligence Service reported recently that native gangs are a serious, growing threat to Canadian society. They are young, armed, and ruthless. They differ in structure from region to region: more like conventional organized crime in the East, especially along the Ontario/Quebec/U.S. borders, where the main business is smuggling.

"In the West," Dobson continued as a new PowerPoint presentation appeared on the screen, "they're typical violent street gangs of young men attracted by excitement and a sense of belonging, likely to work for organ-ized crime groups in a kind of adjunct and subordinate relationship. In Alberta the main gangs—the Red Alert, the Indian Posse, and the Alberta Warriors—are based mainly in Edmonton and Calgary. In Saskatchewan, the Native Syndicate has control of the action in Regina while the Indian Posse works out of Saskatoon. And in Manitoba, the main gangs are the Manitoba Warriors, the Indian Posse, and the Native Syndicate. They are—"

Riley interrupted. "Are these gangs with the same names part of a big-ger organization, like say the Hells Angels? When I was in the Manitoba government, the gangs were a bother, but not the national security threat you seem to be suggesting here."

"The gangs, minister, are loosely related, but very much locally con-trolled. They work together to transport drugs and weapons for instance, but they are territorial."

"Thank you, please go on."

"The gangs are recruited from local populations, thus tending to be band- or clan-oriented, which increases their appeal to young people and their internal cohesion and loyalty. Recruiters target young people drifting into the cities, and others in community centres and correctional institutions—police refer to the jails as gangland community colleges. Of course, the recruiters are active on the reserves.

"In every province except Newfoundland, gangs are expanding into smaller towns and recruiting more aggressively, creating successor generations of members. Expansion, competition for 'trade' and new members, and a general sense that they are untouchable due to the, uh, political optics of aboriginal issues, is increasing the number of incidents and the level of violent behaviour, and it is spilling over into peaceful, settled communities. Police, courts, and jails are struggling to address the problem. In most provinces, but especially in the West, many prisons are dominated by native gangs and cults. They are very dangerous places.

"The gangs have typically been motivated by the usual factors: money, status, and inter-gang power struggles. They are fed by drug- and gun-running profits, prostitution of white and native boys and girls, petty crimes, 'debt collections,' and intimidation—'tax collection' it's called on the street. Until recently there has been little sign of any political motives or orientation in the West, but some officials suggest that this fact may be changing.

"In the East, the gangs are more entrepreneurial and actually run large networks of drug, booze, tobacco, and firearms smuggling; they also launder money on a significant scale. And, like the reserves in the West, they provide tax-fraud havens for these and other illegal activities.

"Nevertheless, minister, the NPA and our own security forces may be running behind the actual development of some of these gangs. They may be reaching a stage of evolution, so to speak, where they will challenge both organizations." Dobson flipped to a new set of charts and maps.

"There are strong indications that some of the gangs are evolving into political organizations. That's to say, they're beginning to take an interest in political power as a way to advance their interests."

"You mean," Riley interjected, "they're bribing politicians and so on?"

"Yes, they do that, of course, but what is happening is that gang leaders are using their so-called street smarts to build alliances with other gangs, and in the case of the native gangs, to organize gang territories under a type of congress of leaders from various gangs. These, what some investigators call 'third-generation gangs,' work together to divide market shares and to dominate larger and larger territories. In cities such as Winnipeg, these third-generation gangs may already be in existence."

Jim Riley, unfailingly sensitive to matters connected with his riding, pointed to the slide. "Are there concrete examples where this is occurring? You have Winnipeg on your map. I know we have gang problems in Winnipeg. Are you suggesting we have, what did you call them, third-generation gangs there?"

"Yes, sir. These gangs now have virtually total control in several areas of the country—or at least ungoverned or contested spaces in many areas. In Ontario, the bands along Lake Ontario east to the Quebec border have a strong grip on the reserves in the area and are expanding into the rural community. The same is true in Quebec, especially along the St. Lawrence and near Montreal. The reserves in the north of most provinces are fast coming under gang political control and we can see this in the voting patterns for some chiefs—many are gang-related or supported, and voting is rigged more or less.

"Minister, many gang leaders have become popular figures. They dole out just enough cash and benefits to satisfy the poor native community— kind of bread and circuses—and 'tax' the legitimate native businesses in the zone, but not so much as to cause them to shut down. Every day they dig themselves into stronger positions."

Riley took a sip of water, set his glass down carefully, took a deep breath. "Well, that's a lot of info for one meeting. Look, we've created a sprawling bureaucracy to chase these Islamist terrorists, wild Indian kids, and the motorcycle gangs—I mean, Christ, we have the Department of Public Safety, how many people work in that maze? We have threat centres, cyber centres, operations centres, critical infrastructure protection centres, federal-provincial municipal conferences of ministers, Canada-wide policy networks. We just got rid of the gun registry, we have people in hazmat suits all over the place ... yet you guys are still painting a picture of wide-scale insecurity ..."

The CDS started to speak, but Riley waved him off.

"General, I know something about business and organization—might seem boring to you guys, but if I have a competitor who is fast and agile like this NPM and these gangs, I sure as hell wouldn't build a big blundering organization to beat him. That's what we have in Ottawa, battalions of committees—bureaucracy, public bureaucracy. People chasing budgets when they should be chasing bandits. How on earth is a big whole-of-government organization going to outpace an adroit, decentralized bunch like we are up against?

"As I said, that's an impressive load of data; all that about the native demographics and such. But how can you be sure of the outcome? What makes you sure we are facing a threat of any scale? I mean, the raids were certainly serious, ominous even, but . . . a threat to the nation?"

The room fell silent. Everyone knew that only General Bishop could respond.

"Minister," he began, "I have a great deal of sympathy for your point of view. My worry is that very few national leaders, or opinion makers, or members of the courts, seem willing to accept the central notion that as a first principle a liberal democracy has the right to defend itself against anti-democratic elements in its midst. So, minister, we do what we can within the limits our culture and democratic ways spell out for us. But I believe the evidence and this week's events more than suggest that we are indeed facing a national security threat that for whatever reasons is being encouraged and directed by elements in our aboriginal community. I know also that if the native community actively joined such a movement, we do not have the military or police forces to address a nation-wide insurrection."

Riley chose not to pursue the argument. "Well, I hope you're wrong, General Bishop."

Andy Bishop paused and looked Jim Riley in the eye. "Let me be absolutely clear, minister. You and the government will know exactly what we know, starting with this briefing. I expect directions from the government that are clear and appropriate. I want you to carry that message to the prime minister or I will take it to him myself. I apologize for my bluntness, James, but this is a damn mess and it's going to get a lot worse."

Jim Riley swallowed hard, twice, then stepped up and extended his hand to Bishop, "Thanks, Andy. I appreciate your bluntness. I promise you that I'll speak directly and frankly to the prime minister and impress on him the seriousness of the situation. I am sure he'll want to hear from you directly in short order; I'll make sure he does."

The minister of national defence looked around the room. "One thing

I want you and your officers to understand, general. I'm a Canadian too, and more to the point, one of the places you're talking about—Manitoba's Inter-Lakes region—that's my home and has been my family's home for generations. No one's going to drive us off our land anytime soon. I'll get back to you as soon as I can speak with the PMO."

DAY FOUR

Wednesday, September 1

Wednesday, September 1, 0900 hours
Air Canada Flight 8565, Montreal to Winnipeg

The flight out of Montreal was routine enough—a cursory once-over at the gate by bored inspectors more interested in their communal gossip than their dull jobs, a bad seat, and no in-flight meal. Alex always asked for a window seat on the right side of the aircraft when he travelled west. It was a three-hour trip over some of the most beautiful land in the world, especially as the aircraft sailed out high over Lake Superior's wondrous blue waters framed in grey granite dressed in autumn's red and yellow forests.

Alex dozed uneasily for the last thirty minutes of the flight. The thump of the landing gear locking into position brought him back abruptly to the world of metal and machines and bitter politics. He tightened his seat belt and watched the farms and fields slip under the wing as the aircraft pulled into a tight southerly turn, dropped over the Perimeter Highway and landed slickly on the windy runway. He followed the other passengers off the plane, through Gate T, and down the stairs into the lobby. Alex retrieved his suitcase, headed outside, and joined the taxi queue.

When his cab came, he got the door himself, settled into the backseat, and told the scarlet-turbaned Sikh driver, "The Occidental Hotel, Main Street, please."

The cabbie hesitated. "The Occidental? Are you sure, sir? Have you been here before? It's not in a very fancy place—kind of a beat-up area for a hotel, really."

"Yeah, well, business is tough in Ottawa these days," Alex replied, deliberately lying about where he was coming from, as he'd been instructed to, in order to cover his tracks. "We're saving money this month."

The cabbie shrugged, pulled away from the airport, and cut out on to Wellington Street. "Most of our visitors from Ottawa go to the best places." He paused for the traffic and grinned at Alex in his rear-view mirror. "Can you still tip?"

Alex smiled back. "Oh, sure—special rates, though."

The taxi turned down Flight Road to Sargent Avenue directly to the inner city. The driver cut across Cumberland, manoeuvred though heavy traffic out on to Main Street, and pulled up on Logan, stopping in front of a run-down, three-storey building, the famously infamous Occidental Hotel.

"Here you go, sir. Are you sure I can't take you somewhere else?"

"No, this is fine." Alex looked at the meter and passed the driver thirty dollars. "Keep the change, but I'll need a receipt." As Alex stepped out onto the noisy, dusty sidewalk, the driver said, "Thanks. Have a nice day. And watch your wallet in this part of town."

The cabbie hesitated at the curb, curious to see whether his wealthy-looking passenger was really going into the Occidental or, Alex thought grimly when he noticed the driver watching him, whether he'd make it inside without being hassled outside on the street. As Alex reached for the hotel door he saw the cabbie through the taxi's grimy side window shaking his head as the car eased away from the curb. The old Sikh would have a story for the guys tonight.

Wednesday, September 1, 1140 hours
Winnipeg: North Main Street

Alex was familiar with Main Street, and even the barroom of the Occidental, from his first posting several years ago to the 2nd Patricias, then stationed at Kapyong Barracks on Kenaston Boulevard. But his experiences then only added to his sense of apprehension this morning. If anything, the intervening years hadn't been kind to north Main Street or the old hotel-saloon. The Occidental was known by reputation to every Winnipegger, although few decent citizens have ever stepped into the place, except cops and the odd bunch of college kids on a dare. The three-storey building sat on a concrete island, isolated by the flow of traffic along Main and Logan streets and the busy Disraeli Freeway. Its uninviting front door faced the even less-inviting Bon Accord block across Logan, while its shabby rear, strewn with broken crates, boxes, and rubble, overlooked three dilapidated grey houses.

Still, the Occidental, perhaps in tribute to its sheer tenacity, was held in a kind of respect, a landmark residents would hate to see vanish almost as much as they'd hate to see its insides. The old girl displayed her aspirations in bold colours on a fancy sign hung on the Main Street wall: *Furnished Rooms, Suites, Private Baths. Special Discounts for Artists, Musicians and Students*. And, thought Alex, nightly brawls outside, no charge, join or watch, take your choice.

In the days of beer parlours and ladies-and-escorts segregated drinking establishments, the hotel had been the favourite of ordinary working white guys looking for ten-cent draft beer. They enjoyed the rough and the reassuring company of people like themselves. In those days, keen members of the Salvation Army would drop by to save souls from drink and damnation. The new locals, though less prosperous, drank beer there too, but they looked to other saviours and another religion. Alex grimaced at the sign over the entrance, *White Buffalo Spiritual Society*, then stepped inside.

The smell of old carpets and stale beer buffeted him on his way in the door. He blinked in the dim light and walked to the desk, where a middle-aged, unshaven clerk put down his paper and scowled at this unusual customer. "What will it be, chief? Nice suit. On welfare or are you one of those guys they hired in the government to make things look fair?"

"You have a room for me," Alex replied stonily. "The name's Grieves. Or do you have to ask your boss first?" He flashed a twenty and they settled for a draw. The clerk glanced at the register and said, "Yeah, sure, okay. Staying three days it says here. Prepaid." His eyes flicked up in genuine surprise, and a note of sarcasm crept in as he continued, "Top floor, 372, the presidential suite." He handed Alex a key and an envelope, taped shut and initialled. "Elevator's broke. Stairs are over there."

Alex crossed the small lobby and walked up the stairs, not too fast. He was conspicuous enough in his suit without taking the stairs two at a time; nobody that healthy had stayed in this hotel since 1953. He walked down the dark third-floor corridor to room 372, fumbled with the key, and pushed open the door. The room was small, just a creaky steel bed, a chest of drawers, and a well-used "private bath."

He threw his bag on the bed and tore open the envelope that had been waiting for him at the desk. It contained nothing but a card with a phone number written on it. He flipped open his cellphone and dialled the number. Two rings, then a grunted "Yeah?"

Alex replied to the voice according to the set of code-words and counter-challenges he had been given at Akwasasne.

"You left me a card."

The voice hesitated, then asked, "Birthday?"

"April."

"Party?"

"Tea."

"Okay, you're cleared. Clothes are in a sealed box in the closet. Put them on. Pack everything else except your shaving kit, take the back fire-escape, and drop the suitcase beside the dumpster. Toss the cellphone in the dumpster there, then go to Disraeli, cross Main, and walk up Alexander. Wander a bit. Check for tails. We'll be watching for 'em too. Take your time, then head to the Presbyterian Church on Laura at Alexander and sit in the pews. We'll make contact if you're clean." Beep. Click. Dial tone.

Alex tore up the card and flushed it down the toilet. He opened the box and found worn jeans, white socks, old Nikes, green plaid shirt, a thin red jacket, and a beat-up Blue Bomber tractor hat. At least they were clean. He changed quickly, packed, threw the keys on the bed, opened the door, and checked the hallway. Clear. He made his way down the fire-escape and out into the alley. As he passed the hotel dumpster, Alex chucked his cellphone into it and dropped his suitcase on the ground. That, he said to himself, will be gone within the hour.

Alex followed his instructions, moving along Disraeli, dodging across Main Street's several lanes, and up Alexander. Despite the clothes, he felt conspicuous, too upright in these beaten-down surroundings. He forced himself to discard his habitual upright, parade-ground posture, pace, and presence. Loser, he told himself. Think loser. Act loser. Look loser. Shuffle. Head down. Drift. He checked himself in the store windows as he walked along, trying to look as if he was stopping to ponder a smash-and-grab.

As he ambled along, he stopped at a bench in the churchyard park at Fountain Street. Maybe I should have brought a bottle, he thought. Nah, don't want cop trouble. Just look thirsty. He hung his head but quickly checked the street behind him, looking, he supposed, for a shady character even scruffier than himself, or maybe someone in a trench coat, who would suddenly stop walking, turn away, pull up his jacket collar, and light a cigarette. I watch too many detective movies, he told himself.

After another half hour of wandering up and down the streets of this depressing neighbourhood, Alex found it was unpleasantly easy to shuffle along looking discouraged. Time to get going, he thought. He headed for the rendezvous point. The church on Laura was just one of the many churches and fine buildings in this once-prosperous part of Winnipeg. The grand red-brick Canadian Pacific railway station on Higgins Avenue, built in 1904, had once been the centre of a lively local economy that supported numerous small manufacturers, warehouse businesses, banks, and one-product shops; a number of rival churches and synagogues had been built for the mostly east-European immigrants who had come to build a better life in the early twentieth century. But that was ancient history.

In the sixties, businesses had started faltering or had moved to newer parts of town. The closing of the CP station was a big blow. And then the demographics began to change. As the middle class moved out and welfare clients moved in, trade fell off, and other stores, banks, and services moved out. Residents moved to the suburbs and businesses left Main Street for the new malls on west Portage Avenue and Pembina Highway to the south. Then the native population swelled, displacing the white working poor, if not the derelicts.

Ill-prepared young natives moved from the reserves to the city in search of the life they'd watched on TV. They didn't find it. Instead, kids living on welfare, drugs, booze, and prostitution wandered the streets. Gangs began to multiply. More businesses left. More banks closed. Seedy hotels, pay-day "banks," and little else remained. Winnipeggers grew resigned to the native slum around north Main, Selkirk, Slater, and MacGregor: what can you do? Just don't go there, especially at night. Every election, the white politicians talked about doing something, and between elections they did nothing.

We will make something better for our people, Alex thought. We've got to. He reached the church on Laura and noticed the paint peeling off the door.

He went in and stood at the back, letting his eyes adjust to the darkness. He walked partway down the aisle and sat in a pew, not too far back, but not in front either. The place was empty except for a couple of old women several rows away, drinking from a bottle hidden carelessly in a paper bag. He watched them for several minutes and then an attractive little native woman came swiftly down the aisle, dropped onto the pew beside him, and immediately knelt as if to say a prayer.

Good grief, he thought. They don't watch enough detective movies. You are way out of place, lady. After a few moments of inaudible prayer she raised her voice and whispered, "Come with me and keep quiet." She rose as quickly and quietly as she had arrived and continued forward towards the altar. Alex got up immediately, wondering whether it was more obvious if he went with her or followed six feet behind her, and decided he couldn't afford to lose her.

Alex hurried after her, through a doorway beside the altar, along a hallway, down a flight of stairs to the basement, across an empty, cement room with faded yellow paint, out a creaking metal door, up four concrete steps, across a rubble-scattered backyard, through a break in a collapsing wooden fence, across another small yard, and down another set of steps into the basement of an old house on Ellen Street.

"Very complicated. Does the priest know about this setup?" Alex teased.

"The priests here are liberation priests, just like those fighting for justice in other oppressed countries," the woman replied tersely. "Now, no more questions. When we go outside, hold my hand like we like each other and walk with me."

"If I'm going to hold your hand, shouldn't I at least know your name—just in case we get stopped, of course?" Alex smiled as he took her hand, but the flush that crept into her cheeks was angry, not embarrassed. "I'm Deanna. But we won't get stopped. Let's go and stop talking." Alex stopped smiling.

They walked up a set of uneven wooden steps to a dismal kitchen, went out the back door, and followed the narrow stone walkway along the side of the house to Ellen Street. Deanna, if that was her name, led Alex to Henry Avenue, then east to King Street and turned towards the great Logan CPR train yard. They worked their way east along the tracks and climbed up to the Main Street overpass, crossed the bridge, and finally slid down into a muddle of ragged bushes to a basement doorway at the back of the rundown "Aboriginal Centre of Winnipeg Inc." on Higgins Avenue—the once-majestic CPR station, a gilded lady turned to new pursuits.

Deanna took Alex's arm, directing him to a small basement doorway, half hidden by scrawny vines. Inside, she pointed down the hallway to another door. "Go there!" With that she turned and walked away, cold, hard, tense, and bitter. Alex shuddered. God only knew what her life had been like before she had joined the Movement and what it would be like after Molly Grace was done with it.

Alex examined the door. It had a coded lock, and a surveillance camera covered it from a corner. To knock or not to knock? As he raised his hand to knock, the door swung open and a native half a head shorter than Alex, but about a foot wider, motioned him in then frisked him roughly.

"Come with me," he said, speaking and moving at the same time.

The burly man walked down the hallway to another closed door, grunted at the kid guarding it, and knocked once. A lock turned and the door opened. Alex stepped in. A small group, five young natives and an older man standing around a large table, stopped talking and looked up, interrupted in mid-conversation. The leader stepped back from the table, folding a large map over on itself as he did so.

Wednesday, September 1, 1235 hours
Winnipeg: Colonel Stevenson's Headquarters

Even a stranger would have seen that the older man was in charge. But Alex wasn't exactly a stranger. Though a few years had passed since he was under his command, Alex recognized Colonel Sam Stevenson at once.

"Okay, everyone, take a break for ten minutes while I speak with the hero from the Petawawa raid," the colonel said. Suspicion turned to admiration on five young faces as they filed out, leaving Alex and Sam alone. The colonel closed the door.

Habit made Alex straighten up, almost to attention, but a tiny motion of Stevenson's left hand said, "Stand at ease." His right hand gave Alex a firm, welcoming handshake.

"Glad you're here to join us, Alex. Good trip? You'll meet the others a little later. Have a seat." He motioned Alex to a chair in front of a smaller desk to the right of the main table. "Coffee, tea?" Alex declined both and sat down.

"Colonel Steele," as his regular force soldiers called him, was hardly a Hollywood Rambo-style soldier. His hair, slightly greying, was trimmed short and neat. He was Docker-dressed, as the saying went: matching shirt and trousers, both pressed and creased. But the colonel was short for an action hero, at most five-seven, slight, physically unassuming, his posture concealing rather than emphasizing his exceptional fitness for a man in his mid-fifties. He wore thin-framed reading glasses hung around his neck, librarian-style.

"Do you know why you're here, Alex?" Stevenson asked, dispensing as usual with small talk.

"Not exactly, sir. I was only told to come here to help you command the operation in this sector. Beyond which, Molly Grace told me you would fill me in. I must say, sir, that I am honoured to be with you, and I hope I can be helpful." Alex blushed. Damn, he said to himself, that sounded trite—like I'm some ass-kiss, first day on the job in NDHQ.

"Never mind. I'm sure you'll do fine, and like I said, I'm glad to have you.

In fact, you're here because I specifically requested you, before the raid on Petawawa. You have a fine record, brains, guts, and experience. That's what I need, and frankly I don't have enough of it here. They're keen, Alex, and they'll die for the cause, but they're not all soldiers and there isn't time to make them into soldiers. You're going to hold them together, Alex. I'm giving you a big job: I'm giving you command of the Winnipeg battle group, the garrison in effect.

"Here's the outline. Soon, when the operation begins, your mission will be to create a major disturbance, draw police and army units into the centre of the city, and then hold them there, pin them down, while we move the larger units from the north into the cities and vital points across the province. It's a diversion within a diversion, Alex."

Alex held out a hand. "Hold on please, colonel. With respect, you're suggesting that we're going to launch a full-scale attack on a major Canadian city, a city of some 700,000 people, with small groups of untested, so-called warriors, and intentionally invite the army and the police to counterattack us! Do you expect, one, that we'll be able to hold on until the other untested warriors come to our rescue, and, two, do you expect any of us to survive the experience?"

"Well, Alex, yes, I do expect you will be able to hold until relieved, mainly because we have been preparing the teams you will lead for many months. They're not all untested, as you say; the key sub-unit commanders are mostly trained soldiers with experience in the Canadian army and the U.S. Special Forces. And two, I'm not sending anyone on a suicide mission. You'll have plenty of backup, and once we draw the army and the police into the centre of the city—get them committed there—you're going to pull out.

"Remember, Alex, we have surprise on our side, and the army here is just the local militia, no better trained than our young people. As for the police, they're simply not prepared for the kind of action we're going to put them in.

"Let me give you the bigger picture, put things in context. After that, and once you've completed your recce of the area, if you have doubts or see a need to change the outline plan, well, we'll discuss the details and make whatever changes fit the bigger strategy. Fair?"

"Fair enough, sir. It just seems rather too bold. I mean, I can't think of many civilians who would believe the scenario even if we told them about it in advance."

"That's our major advantage, Alex, here and in the whole country. The Ottawa politicians just assume that the outrageous things they do can go on without any organized response from us, and they think, too, that we're too lazy or drunk to figure how to organize a nationwide resistance movement. Complacency and prejudice is a deadly combination in politics and war.

"So, let me explain why Molly Grace sent you west when the action seems to be in the East."

Alex nodded. "That would be helpful. I thought about it all the way here."

"Well, what's happening back there in the East is a bigger diversion, to draw forces into Ontario and Quebec so we can act here. Then we're doing it again, or rather, you're going to do it again. It won't be easy for us to get south in sufficient numbers if the army and the police are able to block the roads south and concentrate their troops north of Winnipeg. So your job is to make them think the problem is in the city, a kind of native *intifada*. We need them to commit to the city before they see us moving south, and then we need to hold them and prevent their move north. It's a kind of tar-baby strategy—a nice, little trap. But timing is everything. Here, look at the map."

Stevenson unfolded the map he'd hidden so obviously when Alex entered. It covered much of the table and illustrated the city and its environs in considerable detail, with aerial photos of specific targets. It also showed military symbols, a familiar second language to Alex, denoting vital points such as electrical and water works, military establishments and units, police headquarters and substations. Two smaller, more detailed maps at one side of the table showed the inner city and the airport plus its infrastructure in greater detail.

"You can see," Stevenson explained, "that we have two areas of concentration—the inner city with all its high-value targets, and the airport, because it's the most likely place where the army would try to concentrate a large number of troops for a counterattack on the downtown. If they try to come by road from outside the province, well, too bad for them. We'll trap them in skirmishes and by blowing up bridges and culverts all along the way."

The tactical picture rapidly took shape in Alex's mind and a stream of questions flowed from his quick intellect. "A rude question, colonel: hold till when? Until the cavalry arrives?"

"That's two questions, but good ones. I could say, 'Hold until relieved,' like the British did at Arnhem—or so the movie has it. But we're the Indians, remember? If the cavalry shows up, it's not on our side.

"No, your job is to hold the city centre until the enemy is thoroughly committed to the fight in Winnipeg. When he realizes that Winnipeg isn't the real target, he'll be too late to cover our move south. Once I'm sure the white guys are stuck into it here and it's too late for them to stop our bigger plan, I will pass the word to you that your job's done, and then you're to withdraw, taking your people north out of the city. It's a big, bold plan, Alex. It's been in the making for more than two years, and your operation is a critical part of the Central Committee's grand strategy—which, I guess you know, means Molly Grace's grand strategy. Come, sit down again and we'll do the staff college thing, at least in outline for now."

Despite the very different circumstances they were in now, Alex felt comfortable—like he was once again in uniform. And Alex and Sam were both soldiers, no matter that they'd taken off the Canadian Forces uniform. Colonel and captain, revered senior officer and trusted subordinate, played their parts automatically and effortlessly.

Stevenson opened his well-worn map folder and flipped through several pages. "Okay, Alex, here's the staff college estimate of the situation, and so on. You read the concept of ops then we can talk about the details." He dropped the thick document onto the table.

Alex sat up in his chair, reached for the brown canvas case, and stared at the document: *Operation Middleton*. The irony of the code name, the name of the British officer who had accepted Louis Riel's surrender in 1885, registered immediately.

Alex ran his fingers through the table of contents: "Concept of Operations"; "Allocation to Tasks"; "Logistics"; "Command and Signals"; "Annexes." There were also lists of code words and nicknames; descriptions of the ORBAT—the order of battle; target lists; and maps. Complete enough, at least on the surface. He started with the "Concept of Operations," the heart of the document.

OPERATION MIDDLETON

Aim: To capture southern Manitoba and install a provisional First People's government by no later than 30 September.

Phase I: Battle Group Riel, seven combat teams, three Special Forces sections, four combat engineer sections, and a headquarters and communications section capture Winnipeg's inner city and establish control over the downtown core bordering on Portage Avenue, Memorial Boulevard, the River Assiniboine at the Osborne Bridge to the Forks, north to Alexander Avenue and the Disraeli Freeway south to Ellis Avenue and Balmoral. Battle Group Riel will hold the area until relieved by Battle Group Winnipegosis advancing from northern Manitoba. Most important target is the legislative buildings, to be fortified in two lines: outer perimeter on the grounds to the River Assiniboine, and inner strong point within the building.

In Phase II, Battle Group Métis assembles combat teams in outlying areas north and west of the city and moves on the airport to capture Canadian Forces Base Winnipeg, destroy Canadian Forces aircraft, damage runways, and secure terminals. Security patrols would control the airport and deploy Blow Pipe anti-aircraft teams to defend against any air attacks or airborne attempts to reinforce the Canadian Forces in the area.

The whole "Western Territory" operation in Manitoba, Saskatchewan, and Alberta is under the command of Colonel Stevenson, first from HQ at the old CPR station in Winnipeg, then after the assault from a hangar on the military base at the airport.

Rules of Engagement: All troops, police, or other armed force not identified as NPA units to be engaged with deadly force within assigned areas. Civilians held as captives to be treated according to the Laws of Armed Conflict on pain of severe penalty to commanders. Other civilians to be escorted to the perimeter and released unharmed.

Alex looked up from the paper. "Every combat unit in Western Canada will come down on us like a ton of bricks. Have any of your people any idea how complicated this mission is? Have they any basic training at all? Being a soldier requires more than being able to mouth the words." He stopped, caught between his anxiety and his respect for Stevenson.

Stevenson wasn't at all upset. "Yeah, that's possible. Actually, with a bit of luck most of the army won't be in Western Canada. But if the army wants to tie up units fighting for buildings in the city or the airport, well, so much the better for the grand strategy. Your guys don't have to conduct open-field military operations, Alex, just irregular urban warfare.

"Of course it's a challenge, holding this mostly amateur native army crowd together," he continued, "and they're not much else. But that's your job. We always had it easy in the regular army, you know that. We commanded volunteers who wanted to be the best, who often set the standards for officers to live up to. If you couldn't get an 'outstanding' rating leading those guys, you were a real screw-up.

"Most armies aren't like that. They're like this ragtag outfit. If their officers don't lead from in front, and check everything, nobody steps up to do it. What's worse, your subordinates are keen but they'll get you killed if you don't watch out. And if they do, your operation will fall apart. Think of it as defensive leading. It's not easy, Alex. You have to be out in front but keep your bloody head down. And I don't just mean when bullets are flying. For this operation, with these guys, you have to change your expectations, but not your style. These guys will follow you as best they can, but who knows really how they're going to react once we turn the heat on. But that's why I asked for you to command them, Alex."

Alex nodded and returned to the document to skim through the plan again. Then he stood for a long while over the map. He'd always had a gift for being able to embed maps in his mind, to see the patterns on paper in 3D and as if moving through them in real time. "We come down here, there's that tall building and we ..."

Stevenson interrupted his concentration. "Okay, Alex, come meet my staff. After that, I want you to begin your recce of the area and the targets. Tonight you meet your sector commanders and we'll begin the detailed review and rehearsal of the operations. That battle drill sequence—recce, planning, orders, and deployments—will increase in intensity and extend down the chain of command until we get a warning order from higher. I'm not sure on the timing, it's pretty tight, but we're at three days notice to move so we have a bit of time to shake things out." The colonel opened the door and called in the staff.

Alex was partly relieved by the briefings, which were mostly clear and concise. Obviously this small staff had been trained somewhere and by professionals. When they were done, Stevenson offered Alex a couple of guides to show him around the city, but he refused them.

"I can manage, thanks. A group of Indians in old clothes walking about with maps taking notes might attract attention. I'll just take a cut out of the centre of the map for reference and see you back here early this evening. Can I meet with my own people, say around eighteen hundred?"

A few people at the table looked at Stevenson in surprise, but the colonel understood and appreciated Alex's independent style. "Sure. Matt here will be your chief of staff and you can begin your own battle procedure right now. Okay, folks, that's it for now. Planning meeting as usual at seventeen hundred. Alex, you can see your people after that."

Wednesday, September 1, 1400 hours
Winnipeg: Main Street

Alex picked up his map and a notepad and made his way out the rear entrance of the Aboriginal Centre. He scouted around the east side to Maple Street; it was immediately obvious that the entire site was easy to defend. Early settlers had seen its potential and built Fort Douglas nearby in 1812 as the headquarters of the Red River Settlement. Both the North West Company and the Hudson's Bay Company built defended locations near Point Douglas, taking advantage of the natural protection provided on three sides by sharp turns in the Red River. The grounds now housed various native facilities and exhibitions, but Alex looked first at the high buildings and the railway embankment around which he'd formulate his defensive plan for the north flank of the downtown position.

He began to construct his plan, asking himself, then answering, a series of related, complex questions he had been taught in staff college and in real operations. Where is the key terrain, the ground that must be held if the mission is to succeed? Where are the approaches to the key terrain that must therefore be defended? Where are the killing zones into which attackers could be funnelled? Where is the "dead ground," the possible avenues of attack we won't be able to see—behind buildings, for instance—from the natural defensive firing positions? Where are the best sites for which weapons and how many people will be needed in each location? What's the logical allocation of scarce weapons and people to tasks? How can the scattered sites best support each other?

Alex looked first at the east-west railway line where it crossed Main Street. That, he told himself, would be the northern boundary of his defensive position. With a few snipers and anti-tank weapons, it would be easy to barricade and defend the north Main Street approach where it passed under the tracks. Walking along Higgins, he decided he would have to barricade the Slaw Rebchuk Bridge at Salter, and the Disraeli Freeway as well, probably where they passed over Sutherland Avenue.

I can use buses and trucks, there and there, Alex thought, and support the roadblocks with a few well-placed gunners in the high windows of the Centre, in the tower of the abandoned fire hall at Maple and Higgins, and in the north-facing buildings on Higgins and Henry avenues. I'll also need to secure my western flank with snipers and build hasty barricades around Isabel and Logan.

He looked again at the core of his position, the Aboriginal Centre. It was a perfect strongpoint to close north Main Street and provide some security for his headquarters in city hall a few blocks away. The city hall, he reasoned, wasn't crucial to the overall plan, but from a military standpoint it was a useful outpost for protecting his main position, and moreover, the optics of a native flag of revolt flying from it on the TV news would help ensure a rapid rush by the Canadian authorities into the downtown. So he walked the back streets along King and Notre Dame to recce the city hall area, continuing to mark on his map the high buildings and narrow streets near the site, the ready-made firing points and spots for roadblocks.

After reconnoitring the approaches to city hall, he made a detour over to Dagmar and Notre Dame to check out the large fire and medical service centre there. His plan involved getting as many "first responders" as possible, along with their pieces of large equipment, deployed and stuck in separate street locations, not trapped in the station house. That would probably force the second wave of "rescuers" to find and extract the first responders who would be stuck all over the downtown area, further disorganizing the response. Besides, crippled fire trucks would become both convenient obstacles to military operations trying to retake the downtown, and potent symbols of chaos. He made another note on his map and headed to the next major target, Lombard Square, and the famous junction of Portage Avenue and Main Street.

Portage and Main, besides being Canada's windiest corner, is the heart of Winnipeg's financial district. In Stevenson's scheme to hold the downtown core and attract a counterattack, Lombard Square was the hard nut in the centre of the chocolate. Alex circled back from the fire hall to Main Street at McDermot Avenue, pocketed his map and notebook as a police car drove by, then strolled into the concrete garden at the foot of the Richardson Building. He grabbed a coffee from a street vendor and sat quietly on a bench sketching the site in his mind.

Winnipeg Square is the key terrain to controlling the downtown area, he thought to himself. Whoever controls these high buildings controls the Square, whoever controls the Square controls the city centre, and whoever controls the city centre more or less controls Winnipeg. Which was all fine and good, but the Square presented a tricky tactical problem. He gazed around, trying to pull the complex of buildings, streets, and avenues into a pattern.

Six main buildings offered themselves as strong points, he decided. Control of only one or two, even the most central, would mean nothing if the police or the army controlled the others and got snipers high up, dominating my positions. But controlling and defending all six would take a lot of people. Too many. More than I have. I could cause enough trouble to keep a fight going for a while, but not nearly long enough. I'd have to put too many of my people in the Square, then the army would wipe me out here and roll up the other positions.

Alex got up and strolled about the Square, trying not to be conspicuous. He paused at the southwest corner, where a plaque declared that the Bank of Montreal had been established in 1871. A tough-looking bronze army officer stood guard in honour of the warriors of the 1914–18 war. Alex

stopped to admire the statue and the idea it represented: liberty though strength and sacrifice. That's our creed too, he thought. I'm still a soldier, he found himself silently assuring the bronze officer.

After a minute, he glanced across the Square to the TD Bank building. It wasn't much of a fortress, despite its imposing height, especially because of the car garage behind it, overlooking Main Street. He drew a quick sketch of the area, awkwardly holding his notepad as he thought a street artist might, and marked imaginary interlocking arcs of fire from building to building.

He shook his head—the sketch confirmed his fears. If the police got into that garage, and they would, his guys wouldn't be able to move anywhere along the street or down lower Main Street. The Manitoba Telephone and the Scotia Bank buildings provided firing positions northwards if they fell to the police, and they would. If he couldn't hold or neutralize the TD building, life in the open Square would be miserable and short. A difficult situation, he thought. Too many options demanding resources and skills and people I don't have.

Alex followed the civilians and tourists making their way from one segment of the Square to another via several flights of stairs leading down into the underground hub connecting all the streets together. After a few confused attempts, he surfaced at the Main Street exit at the Richardson Building and strolled past it, trying to visualize a plausible capture and defence of that site. Damn. There just didn't seem to be a way.

At Lombard Street, his attention was drawn to the tall, elegant Union Tower building. A greenish plaque on its wall proclaimed it to be the site of the first Masonic Lodge in the Red River Settlement, established in 1864; the Northern Lights Lodge, led by Messrs. Shultz, Bannatyne, and Inkster. More land thieves, he thought sourly. He gazed up at the old structure's high windows, noted absently the "For Lease" sign in the ground floor window, and turned back to the perplexing Square. And suddenly he saw the way. He had his plan. So simple it was brilliant, or, if you prefer, brilliant because it was simple.

Why fight it out above ground? he asked himself gleefully. Why control all the buildings? He spun quickly in a tight circle, taking in the Square all at once. The aim was to tie down the police and the army. So start by grabbing a few city buses to barricade the streets, pick a couple of well-

protected sites to cover those barricades, and control everything not from above, from the buildings, but from below, from the underground concourse.

On his notepad he drew a circle linking all the surface exits from the underground mall. If I can seize the Union Tower, he thought, I can control the intersection and that troublesome car garage easily. Just a few snipers in the high windows of the Bank of Montreal give me the crossfire I need. But the key is the underground—with that in my hands, my people can move rapidly under cover from various parts of the square. I'll need a few commanders in high buildings to control the action and direct traffic.

But if the police want to fight it out at close quarters underground, so be it. Let's see who has the stomach for knife fighting in the dark. And anyway, win or lose, it would take hours for them to clear the area, and that would serve my aim just fine. I'm sure I can "hold until relieved," even in a messy cat-and-mouse fight in the underground mall and in the cellars of the buildings. Especially if I can keep my people off the street and tempt the army and the police into the killing grounds.

Much relieved, Alex set off westwards in the underground passageway along Portage Avenue towards his next major objective, the Hudson's Bay store at Portage and Memorial Boulevard. Obviously they would need to block the western approach to Lombard Square and the crossing routes north and south from the Bay. But that would be comparatively easy. Block the streets with buses again, and the Bay would provide a ready-made fort—a Hollywood Western cliché, Alex smiled, but this time the Indians would be on the inside. Plus, the Winnipeg Art Gallery across Memorial Boulevard would provide an excellent high shooting post, as would the open balcony of the Canada Centre on the north side of Portage.

It was all falling into place now. Alex spied a bonus feature, and his notebook acquired a new entry: the glassed-in walkways that pass over Portage Avenue at Vaughan Street. They would provide a handy gallery, letting his riflemen control long stretches of both streets and giving them a free run building to building under cover. Once the warriors were in place, the police would have a miserable time gaining control of the area. Trying to manoeuvre around the outside of the occupied buildings and clear them from exposed positions while the native forces moved easily under

cover inside would create lots of vacancies for promotion in the city force in a hurry. The classic advantage, Alex noted instinctively, of interior over exterior lines.

As he turned towards the government offices a few blocks down the Memorial Boulevard, he saw in the distance the "Golden Boy" shining in the sunlight atop the big prize, the Legislative Building.

The Legislative Building and its surrounding grounds insulted the native community every day that they remained. It hurt Alex even to look at them. They fouled the traditional grounds where for centuries the people had walked, talked, traded, travelled, and lived. Government House, set off to the side of the Legislative Building, housed the defining human symbol of the people's defeat, the lieutenant governor, the "white mother" personified. The Legislative Building, constructed of massive Tyndall stones taken from the people's land, sat on sacred land, and was sited there purposefully to taunt the people and to remind them every day of their defeat. Tourists marvelled at the fossils captured in the stone, symbols of the ancient land. But where were the true symbols of the land, the natives? Nowhere.

The building, designed by a French architect, was a majestic monument to Western mythology and prejudice, and was decorated with the white man's superstitions, including, as with the Union Tower downtown, scores of weird Masonic symbols.

Even the one nod to the New World was, for natives, filled with bitter irony. Two giant bison guarded the grand inside staircase. Two giant bison, designed by Europeans and built in the United States, emblematic of the mindless greed and destruction Europeans brought to the prairies. Did these treasonous metal beasts now guard the settlers against the ghosts of their kin, slaughtered without reason or mercy? Were they here to guard the whites against the return of the native? Or were they secretly waiting for us to come and right the wrongs done to them as well as us? Alex wondered. And then there were the sphinxes. What were symbols of Egypt's ancient culture doing here? Were they put there deliberately to offend us?

His eyes drifted upward to the Golden Boy, the crowning insult. Another European disgrace, designed and forged in France, the pride of the local worthies, it depicted an idealized white man who gazed serenely over the grasslands and the meeting place of the peoples, dismissive of their spirits and traditions. Gold, Alex thought. What more telling symbol of white settler values could one imagine? The people had not scraped away the fertile land for shiny metal of no value except that given to it by Western money-lenders and, today, advertising moguls. This statue was the perfect symbol of the three C's of European conquest—Commerce, Civilization, and Christianity—cast in metal, coated in gold, imported from a bastard foreign culture, raised up high, alone, dominating the skyline. Nothing bragged so loudly of the white settlers' pride and values. Nothing stood so high out of reach, a striking symbol of the people's unending defeat everywhere. But we're coming for you, Golden Boy, warned Alex.

A recce of the legislative grounds would be, Alex suspected, a tricky affair. He was sure he could get away with simply walking the perimeter; a scruffy native wandering along Broadway or the riverside walk wouldn't be noticed. But touring the interior of the building in these shabby clothes might tempt a guard to let loose the dogs and possibly compromise the entire operation. Unfortunately, time was in command here. Alex needed information and details and he needed them now.

He stopped in a bus shelter to straighten his shirt, comb his thick black hair with his fingers, and tuck in his shirt; he stuck the tractor hat in his pocket. He pondered his map and notebook for a moment, then arranged them into a neat bundle held in scholarly fashion, right hand angled upwards across on his chest. I'm a student, he thought, dressing on a budget but with a perfect right to the legislature, not some shambling, confused street bum. Here his habitual military bearing was a distinct asset. Back straight, eyes forward, he strolled deliberately to the front, north-facing entrance.

On his way in, contemplating Queen Victoria on her throne outside the grand entrance, he automatically recorded the completely open approach to the doorway. Even a light truck could drive directly in from Broadway without reducing speed too much; that would allow it to keep up momentum to get up the grassy embankment and onto the wide staircase. In any case, the short curved driveway presented no obstacle to crashing up the entrance staircase in vehicles. Now, he told himself, let's test the interior security.

He walked up the staircase, pushed open the tall glass door, and stepped into the deserted foyer. The whole building seemed quiet, nearly empty. A bored custodian glanced up from behind his curved, polished desk. "Is the legislature open for tourists?" asked Alex, wishing he'd thought to bring wide-rimmed glasses. "Actually, I'm a history student, not a tourist, and I'd like to take a look at the architecture and decoration."

The little grey-haired man behind the desk mechanically thrust a clipboard at Alex. "Sign here. There's no tours till later, but you can walk about if you want. Just don't touch anything."

Alex signed in as "Dagwood Bumstead" and walked through the open door to the base of the main staircase. Maybe I shouldn't have done that, he thought. No time to get cute. But the custodian returned to the sports page of the *Free Press* without a further look at the form or the man who'd signed it.

For the next forty minutes, Alex walked freely about the building, covertly measuring key distances by counting footsteps and recording the numbers and their tactical consequences in his little book, periodically adding a sketch of some carving or vista to maintain his cover just in case someone checked. No one did. He walked up the grand staircase past the great bronze bison—a security measure at least as effective as the old man at the desk—and right up to the doors of the legislative chamber, unchallenged. The massive doors were locked now. But someday soon, he mused, one of my people will stride through those doors and take control of the ornate blue room beyond them.

As he walked back to the main entrance, Alex measured the distance from the desk to the chamber again just to be sure. A mere skip and a jump, he thought; a good warrior could make it through the outside door, up the stairs, rake the chamber with fire, and withdraw in literally a matter of seconds, before the guard could make a phone call for help. So much for increased security against terrorism after 9/11, he thought. As a soldier I used to worry about that. Now I'm glad of it.

"Thanks for the visit," he said as he passed the guard. "Beautiful place. You can be sure I'll be back someday soon." No answer. This guy wasn't even going through the motions.

Back outside, Alex walked around to the side of the building and sat on the west entrance steps to make some notes under the stony gaze of General Wolfe and Lord Dufferin. Appropriate somehow, he thought. I'm still fighting the guy who took the people's land with a gun and the one who took it with false words.

The rest of his walk around the grounds was a routine check for surprises or new barricades. There were none. On the east side only La Vérendrye and Lord Selkirk, two other celebrated robbers, stood watch. For what—invading native hordes? "Well, gentlemen," he said out loud, "wait no longer. Here I am."

Alex strolled out across the east lawn onto Kennedy Street, circling the lieutenant governor's house as he went. I probably could walk in for a drink, he thought, but then added, no need to tempt the spirits. I'll need all my luck and shouldn't behave arrogantly. Leave that to the whites. He limited himself to a military estimate—the house was unguarded and tactically simple, with a greenhouse at the side that offered a covered approach to the south entrance of the Legislative Building. Again, no surprises, no new features. That was all he needed to see personally. The rest of the details he could get from government-supplied maps and the Internet.

Alex walked out to the south-facing riverside promenade. And there, suddenly, stood Louis Riel. Alex put his notes away, ran a hand through his hair, and stepped up to look respectfully at Riel. The great leader, mystic, politician, untutored soldier, rebel, and traitor, symbol of his people, in life, now in bronze, he stood facing the Assiniboine River, back to the legislature, a political man yet apart from politics.

Even today, he was too politically costly for white leaders to ignore, but too powerful a symbol of native rights for them to allow him a place inside the legislature, so they put his statue here. Riel in life and death, the rebel and the ironic symbol of white power and white guilt, hanged on a rope by a distant Sir John A. Macdonald. Three times elected to the House of Commons but never able to take his seat, thanks to the white man's democracy. Alex stood for a while, contemplating the man. Riel the victim, symbol of the victims, the outsider, standing darkly shrouded, separate—forever outside.

Alex studied the statue. It was a revised Riel, he knew, unveiled in 1996 and meant to be respectful, unlike the tormented nude 1971 version now safely tucked away at the Collège Universitaire de St. Boniface. But the conventional style of the new one—moustache, neat city clothes, long, wind-blown coat—made him look more like a Washington senator of Lincoln's time than a prairie catholic evangelist. He held a scroll, perhaps his demands, and under his arm, a book. Of what?—laws, a Bible, his own work? But it was exactly the boring style of the boring statues of prime ministers on Parliament Hill. Where was the man? Maybe the sculptor meant to be polite, but by denying his essence, he had only made him respectable. There wasn't even a plaque, Alex noticed. It was as if Riel didn't need to be explained. As if Riel couldn't be explained. What would a plaque say? "The true spirit of the people and their Métis brethren, he died for liberty"; or "Mad traitor, threat to the settlers' gold"; or "Patriot who died to save the power of the Rome church." Why not all three, stamped in brass in three languages?

Alex turned uneasily away. Riel, the romance of a lost cause left behind. But were the Métis and aboriginals better off for what he did? A zealot, arguably half-mad, incapable of compromise, he led his followers and his people into disaster, twice! Is that what you're doing? Alex asked himself as he boarded the Main Street bus heading back to the Aboriginal Centre. How was Molly Grace different from Riel?

The yellow-and-orange bus coughed to a sudden stop at Main Street and Higgins Avenue on the outskirts of the rundown Point Douglas community. Alex stared out the grimy bus window. He could see nothing clearly.

Wednesday, September 1, 1410 hours
Ottawa: Integrated Threat Assessment Centre

Eliot Quadra tapped his pencil on the shiny table with increasing impatience. In front of him, down both sides of the table in the most secure conference room inside the ITAC, sat the best intelligence officers he could assemble from the Canadian intelligence community. They had been assigned to the analysis section because they were both experienced and intuitive. Each of them had the rare ability of being able to extract the essence of a security problem from masses of data. They all possessed that rare and vital analytical quality, insight—the capacity to find the hidden truth in complex situations. Yet here they sat, after an hour of discussion, with no clear idea of how the Native People's Movement was organized and, more to the point, what their leaders were planning now that they had openly attacked Canadian Forces bases and armouries and collected a worrying range of deadly weapons.

Eliot had to get something out of them. As the chief of the Integrated Threat Assessment Centre, the ITAC, it was his job—a job that was both routine and highly classified—to collate for the prime minister and the cabinet intelligence reports from most, if not all, the government's snooping, listening, and watching agencies. His staff gathered information from Canadian organizations like the Border Service, the Communications Security Establishment, the Canadian Security Intelligence Service, the military, and the RCMP and other police departments across the country. They used the information to produce regular assessments of threats facing Canada from sources inside and outside the country. Today the only questions were about internal security, and the prime minister was asking the questions. "I want," he had told Quadra directly, "some solid, credible intelligence on the threat facing the government from the so-called aboriginal radicals. And I want something other than what the military is telling me."

"Let's go over it again," Eliot said to the assembled intelligence officers. "We have a sketchy idea of who's who in the Movement and where they're mainly located. We know they have cells operating on many reserves and in some cities, especially on the Prairies. We assume, and let's go right on assuming, that these raids were not spontaneous, but part of a deliberate plan to destabilize the government and encourage native uprising in various parts of the country. We assume also that the main area of interest is Quebec. And we know that getting inside the Movement and developing intelligence contacts is difficult, to say the least, so we don't have and aren't about to get reliable new information from that direction. Agreed so far?" Heads nodded around the table.

"Okay, let's review what we don't know. And if anyone has any Rumsfeld-style thoughts on 'what we don't know that we don't know,' please chime in. Otherwise, Maggie, give us the assessment in the West for a start."

The lean, intense blonde woman to his left swept the table with her eyes as she began a staccato recital. "My people think there's something big, maybe a type of *intifada*, building in the major cities across the West. A couple of my officers believe it's even bigger, possibly a large-scale, well-organized uprising aimed at governments at all levels. What's particularly supportive of both these ideas is the presence of senior members of the Movement in the West, especially in Winnipeg, including a couple of experienced ex-military officers, including at least one deserter. We've identified, for instance, ex-Special Forces Colonel Sam Stevenson, and we think a deserter—he may very possibly have commanded the Petawawa raid—a former captain named Alexander Gabriel, who served under Stevenson, we think he's there too.

"We don't know anything about their plans, but—worst case—they actually might organize natives in the northern communities and invade the south. Stevenson's service record shows a consistent pattern of thinking big, moving against established ideas, and getting his opponents to look one way before coming at them from another direction. That argues for us looking in that other direction, outside the major cities. And also, let me emphasize, this intelligence suggests we're wrong to assume the main area of interest is Quebec. There certainly seems to be trouble brewing there too. And folks, if something significant is happening in Quebec and out west, we can't avoid the conclusion that what's happening is very big and well organized."

Eliot looked first to Mike Liu, a long-service operator and the oldest member of the team. "Mike, comments?"

"Well, I agree with most of Maggie's assessment. But she suggests a great deal of sophisticated planning and coordinated operations, and I don't see it, at least not yet. If the regulars in the Movement are in charge, which I admit we're not sure is true, then this isn't a military coup, it's a political movement. If we think they are planning what Maggie suggests, or that someone else has taken charge and is planning something that big and that military, then we ought to try to imagine answers to the why, what, and how questions. I'm thinking why the West; with what possible objectives; how would they carry out the operation? We haven't been able to answer these questions, and since these people aren't stupid, I assume it's because they're not planning that type of activity."

Wednesday, September 1, 1435 hours
Winnipeg: Colonel Stevenson's Headquarters

The usual afternoon ops staff team sat around the large map table, note-books at hand. Colonel Sam stepped up to the map. "Okay, let's go over the outline operation to make sure we're clear on objectives and how we're going to reach them.

"The Western strategy is uncomplicated: control Winnipeg and we con-trol the region. The Red River Brigade is assembling battle groups across the province; Alex Gabriel's Group Riel is assembling in Winnipeg. Group Winnipegosis is being activated in Flin Flon and The Pas. Group Métis is still undercover but ready to form-up on short notice for action at the Winnipeg airport. And in the east, near Kenora, and farther west, in Sas-katchewan and Alberta, other contingents are increasingly ready. The assault teams and columns in each group are commanded by cadres of seasoned, ex-regular Canadian Forces officers and NCOs who've hastily trained their civilian 'warriors' to handle small arms, work as teams, and, usually, follow orders." Light-hearted banter and smiles eased the tension.

"Nevertheless, we need to keep things as simple as circumstances allow. In the first phase, and on my command, three mobile columns from the north and east will take the offensive in Manitoba. Column Cree will move from The Pas on Highways 10 and 60, then rapidly along Highway 6 to an assembly area spanning Warren on Highway 67 to Stonewall. Column Pelican will follow from Flin Flon via Highway 10 south to threaten Bran-don and block western approaches along Highway 1 and southern routes into Winnipeg. Column Ojibwa will move from its assembly area near Kenora and move to block Highway 17 at the junction of Highways 17 and 44. Alex Gabriel's Battle Group Riel and his combat teams will capture the centre of Winnipeg. In the second phase, we'll threaten the real targets."

Wednesday, September 1, 1450 hours
Ottawa: Integrated Threat Assessment Centre

Eliot Quadra looked around the table. "Okay, we have two different concepts. Any others?"

Walter Boudria joined the conversation. "Eliot, I'd like to go back to the question of the aim. Let me throw some kind of random thoughts on the table. I'm assuming a bold operation. We have all the tapes of Molly Grace's public speeches and the secret electronic intercepts as well, and I don't see any compromise in any of them. She's not in this to win some treaty benefits. I think she wants the whole cake. So how about this: the Movement is going to try to grab control of all the ungoverned spaces in the West and hold them for negotiations about aboriginal sovereignty over the West. In which case, Maggie's right: the Quebec thing, at least south of James Bay, is a decoy. And, by the way, I'm convinced they're going to move soon."

The assessment team looked to their boss, but Quadra deflected the group-think invitation and refused to endorse or reject Walter's ideas. Instead, he continued evenly, "Okay, Walter, tell us how they'd carry out this bold plan of yours."

"Well, the speculation factor expands with imagination, but I assume that they will use their main advantage, which is people. In other words, they'll assemble large groups of natives across the North, move south suddenly, and simply overwhelm the local security forces, then sit on the ground until we quit or negotiate. We don't have the resources to handle such an eventuality and Stevenson knows that. So I bet on his playing to his advantage. Besides, it's simple, and he can't manage anything but a simple strategy with the forces he has available."

Mike broke in. "Sure, nice plot for fiction, but where's the evidence? We would've seen some indication of this. Maybe not the overt preparation for an assault, but other things, changes in the routine in the community, things that are hard to hide. There simply aren't any such indicators—no training camps, no rallies, no hostile movements, nobody of interest disappearing and then suddenly popping up in the community again. Things look normal."

Maggie jumped to Walter's defence. "But that's the point, Mike. My assumption—our assumption—is that they've been successful in keeping things normal and that means they have to go for something simple. And for simple to be effective, it has to be big. If you were Stevenson, what would your plan be? Normal today, uprising tomorrow. We won't see anything until we see the whole thing blow up in our faces."

Elena Morales joined the sceptics. "But then what's the rest of his plan? Why would the government negotiate, even if large numbers of natives moved south and sat around Winnipeg and Regina? We could wait them out. It's true that Stevenson could get a pretty large number of angry people to do something simple on a large scale, but the other great weakness of amateurs, besides inability to coordinate things, is they don't stick it out when things get tough.

"We're nearly into autumn and you know there's a good chance most of the region will be snowed in by Hallowe'en. Besides, who's going to feed these people while they sit there for months, even if they don't get bored and wander off? We agree on one thing: Stevenson can't manage complicated logistics. So the government stalls until the natives go home, or we reassemble a strong military presence in the West. And Stevenson, or whoever's really in charge, must be able to see that far ahead too. So what have they got, or what do they think they've got, to make us give in?"

Wednesday, September 1, 1510 hours
Winnipeg: Colonel Stevenson's Headquarters

Stevenson looked around the table. "That's the bare-bones outline. So what have we got to back it up? First, there're our troops, the active people and the supporters in the background. There're more than 70,000 native people living on reserves in Manitoba alone, and more than 100,000 in Saskatchewan and Alberta combined. We need only a small fraction of them to carry out this mission.

"Remember, all of Ireland and the bulk of the British army were held in fear and in check for more than twenty years by a few hundred Irish Republican Army radicals. The hard corps was not much more than a thousand men and women, but the real strength came from the silent supporters, ordinary citizens, who provided safe-houses, food, and so on, and who carried messages and kept an eye on the Brit soldiers and the security forces. We've got enormous strength there too. Not from everyone, not from all the elders, but more than enough to get the job done.

"Now let's review phase two and the real targets."

Wednesday, September 1, 1525 hours
Ottawa: Integrated Threat Assessment Centre

"So, what have they got, or what do they think they've got, to make us give in?" Eliot turned to Hugh Jones-Winsor. "That's your cue, Hugh. Everyone, Hugh and I discussed the vulnerability factor earlier today with the defence minister after the CDS and Ed Conway softened him up with an outline version. I'd like Hugh to run through the assessment his section has developed from that meeting."

"Thanks, Eliot. Just for background, I explained to the minister that the threat isn't where we should be concentrating our attention. Rather we need to look to our vulnerabilities; you all know the argument. I'm assuming the native leaders understand our weaknesses and that they'll be going for them right away. Remember that Manitoba chief who said in 2007, 'The white man only worries about two things—his possessions and his money. Well, we're going to take both if that's what it takes to get his attention. If we have to use guns, well that's the way it's going to be.' He was immediately shut up by the Movement's strong-arm guys, but I assume that's because he reflected their thinking, not because he didn't.

"So, let me put our vulnerabilities on the table and then we can link it to Walter's bold-move option. I brought some copies of the charts we used to brief the minister. Would you pass them around please?

"You all know it's a big mistake to underestimate your adversary or to assume he won't think of things because you can't handle them or it screws up your plans. I'm going to start by assuming that the native leaders see our vulnerabilities the same way we do, and that they are going after them the way we would. Thus, raids on the cities will be dramatic, but the big Western target, because it is Canada's great economic vulnerability, will be the resource industries, especially the gas and oil pipelines running to eastern Canada and south into the U.S. I believe the Movement leaders think that if they can threaten these, it will bring the federal government to the table quickly, and if the government hesitates, the destruction of a few key sites will bring them around even quicker. That's why we don't agree and can't assume that the government can simply wait them out. And the Movement knows that too.

"It's not a matter of some Indians squatting in the bush shouting slogans. Canadian natural gas and petroleum industries deliver the lifeblood to North America's economy. They're the critical components of the well-being of millions of Canadians and Americans even if we don't always notice them. They're especially important to the northeast, northwest, and west coast American markets, and they have to operate constantly or we're in trouble fast. And it's not just us. Ninety-five percent of Canadian natural gas production is exported to the United States through six great pipelines; that's a full fifteen per cent of U.S. requirements, and that number is growing fast.

"The loss of gas or oil supplies, even for only a few days, would have a devastating and cascading effect across the entire United States. A long interruption in the West could, according to some estimates we have seen, plunge the United States into an irreversible depression.

"But the dependence and thus the vulnerability do not reside only in the American West. A complete loss of natural gas and oil supplies would cripple the economies of Ontario, parts of Quebec, and particularly Montreal. Furthermore, quite apart from the indirect impact of economic collapse in the far western American states, significant disruption of the pipelines would starve Minnesota, Wisconsin, Michigan, New York, and Connecticut, and likely shut down manufacturing industries in Detroit and across the northern states as well.

"Should these interruptions occur any time between early October and May, a man-made winter disaster of enormous danger would engulf the entire northern tier of North America. Our vulnerabilities here are enormous.

"The four main pipelines—the Duke line to British Columbia, the TransCanada line from the northern and central Alberta fields to the eastern United States and Canada, the BP line into Washington State and California, and the TransGas line from Alberta and Saskatchewan—are the easiest and softest targets. In all, 38,000 kilometres of natural gas pipelines snake out of the Alberta/Mackenzie River valley western sedimentary basin, moving eighty per cent of Canada's gas production to markets in Canada and the United States. The system includes not just the pipes above and in the ground, but also more than 115 large, complex compressor stations that drive the gas through the lines to its destination. There's one about every 330 kilometres along the whole system. The compressor stations are the weakest link in a weak system.

"And you can add to this maze another 70,000 kilometres of oil pipelines. They aren't guarded and there's no way to guard them. I'd bet the mortgage that Stevenson will go for a few compressor stations first as a warning, creating damage easy to fix if we give in promptly, but he'll start smashing up the whole system if we try any systematic attack on the native forces."

"Surely we've done something to protect the system, especially after 9/11," said Maggie. She pointed to Hugh's maps and charts. "I can't believe that we've just sat on our collective asses and hoped for the best."

"Well, Maggie, the government did move quietly after 9/11 to enhance security at vital points across the country, but serious measures were taken only on military bases and at particularly vital points in Ottawa and major financial computing centres in Montreal and Toronto. Elsewhere, only 'get ready' warning orders have been passed to police detachments and to the Canadian Forces Reserve units. Even then, the prime minister in 2004 ordered that no overt actions be taken anywhere for fear of worrying citizens and disrupting investments."

Eliot rejoined the discussion. "Nothing of consequence has been done to protect the energy transportation system. Not that anything really can be done to make the system perfectly secure.

"Sorry folks, but this situation is really bad and we have to assume the Movement knows it. I think the politicians are the only ones who don't, or won't, accept it. If we can't protect our vulnerabilities, we have to reconsider countering the threats to them instead. That's why we're here.

"So, these are the answers to our initial assessment questions. Where will they strike? In the West and in a big way. How? With a large, dispersed amateur force moving rapidly out of the north. At what targets? The cities, to distract us, and the energy network, to bring us to the table on our knees. Where are we most vulnerable? The oil and gas pipelines, and, I might add, the railway and highway infrastructures.

"So, ladies and gentlemen, that's the hypothesis. Now get to work and disprove it. If we can't disprove it in five days, we take it to the government as the gold-embossed assessment. I only hope we have five days. In the meantime, I want a warning sent to the RCMP operations centre here in town, and to NDHQ, stating that we believe small groups of aboriginal radicals may be concentrating in Winnipeg and surrounding areas and that they might be planning some kind of demonstrations in the city or elsewhere in the province. But make it clear that there is no evidence of any immediate threat to national security. Thank you all."

Wednesday, September 1, 1545 hours
Winnipeg: Colonel Stevenson's Headquarters

"Right, phase two. We've identified three main target groups: the initial production centres, oil fields and the like; the infrastructure, pipelines and auxiliary systems; and the end-base production and storage facilities. They're all wide open to simple interference, like long-range rifle sniping, and all easy to attack and essentially impossible to defend. Furthermore, repairing even moderate damage, especially to the transmission or storage facilities, would take weeks if not months.

"In the second phase of the operation, once we are in the south and in control of the cities, we move on these targets. The natural gas compressor stations are the weak link in the system and are basically undefended, as you can see when you look at the images of a few of the targeted stations in Saskatchewan and Alberta.

"I had an old army staff college classmate, a white guy named Beamish MacDonald, a good man who saw the truth about Canada's vulnerabilities long ago. He confirmed our new assessments for us last year. According to his calculations, and I trust them, merely to guard the 115 compressor stations on the TransCanada pipeline would require a force of more than a hundred army platoons of about thirty people each—3,000 soldiers plus command staffs and logistical units. Besides the compressor stations, there's all the pipelines and all the other vital points to be defended at the same time. No such force capable of all these duties exists in Canada. We simply have to move our trained teams around, feigning attacks, spreading rumours of attacks, and sniping at people and sensitive equipment. We'll freeze the defenders wherever they may be and move to where they aren't, because they can't be in all the places all the time. Of course, we can dramatically change the tempo with a truck bomb in a station any time we need to, but I hope that feints and small unit attacks will do the trick."

The burring telephone interrupted the meeting. Stevenson's chief of staff took the call and immediately handed the phone to his commander.

"Yes," Sam said, and scribbled a few letters on a pad of paper. He snapped the cellphone shut, walked across the room to a locked cabinet, dialled the combination, opened a small steel locked box, and took out his code book. His fingers slid down a list to the three-letter code Alpha-Foxtrot-Whiskey and read across to the next column: "Go to twenty-four hours notice to execute the plan."

So it begins, he thought to himself; too bad for everyone.

Wednesday, September 1, 1720 hours
Ottawa: Canada Command HQ

As Canada Command staff officers watched and assessed the situation in Quebec and elsewhere after the raids on the ammo compounds, the growing hints of wider trouble suggested that their worst planning scenario, "a prolonged, coordinated challenge to the government of Canada" by armed militants in the native community, was unfolding before their eyes. The operational staff at NDHQ believed the trouble was confined to Quebec, a rerun, some said, of the 1996 Oka problems, and they meant to keep it there.

Lieutenant General René Lepine, appointed Commander CANCOM some months ago, wasn't so sure. He stood quietly away from the staff as he surveyed the centre's large electronic map of Canada. He let his imagination play with the computer simulations as it developed the situation in front of him.

He was responsible for the conduct of all military routine and emergency operations in Canada. The few politicians who even noticed the CANCOM mission statement assumed "operations" meant fighting floods and fires and snowstorms and searching for lost souls. They were wrong.

The new post-cold-war cohort of senior officers, trained and conditioned by more than a decade of messy experiences in the Balkans, Afghanistan, and now in Zimbabwe, worried a great deal about the eruption of similar types of conflicts at home. Senior officers and RCMP officers worried especially about convergence of native grievances and nation-subverting criminal gangs. Canada Command's real purpose was to prepare for just such a disaster. No plans for this eventuality were committed to paper and no one spoke outside the family.

That is not to say that General Bishop, RCMP Commissioner Jean Richard, and officials from CSIS and their predecessors had not tried repeatedly to bring their concerns confidentially to cabinet and its various committees. They had. But every attempt to point to dangerous activities on reserves, even clear evidence of the open defiance of the law by native groups involved in smuggling, stockpiling weapons, and cooperating with organized criminal gangs, was rebuffed.

Nevertheless, the staff at CANCOM continued collecting and cataloguing indications of a growing threat as they saw it. The filing cabinets in HQ CANCOM overflowed with computer assessments and anticipated consequences of "serious domestic disturbance scenarios." The most dangerous to anticipate and control involved challenges to the civil authority beyond the means (or willingness) of provincial or federal police to control; interruptions to trans-Canada oil, natural gas, or central electronic economic information systems, including all or part of the national transportation infrastructure; and finally, a prolonged, coordinated challenge to the government of Canada by armed terrorist movements, criminal gangs, or any other "resident population."

Lieutenant General René Lepine, a hard-nosed infantry officer, was one of the first senior officers to recognize the Petawawa raid for what it was—the opening move in a significant native challenge to the government. René knew that it was the product of radicalized natives, and he recognized also the professional army fingerprints all over the operation. After all, he was "of the people," Ojibwa, born on the Grassy Narrows reserve in northern Ontario. He understood the grievances and problems on the reserves and the power the radicals had over many of the young people.

"Excuse me, sir, sorry to interrupt your thoughts." Lieutenant Colonel Erick Brandon approached Lepine carrying a handful of notes and his own wrinkled map. "You asked me to go over the scenario files. I did that and I remembered an exercise Bill Coupland and Doug Harrison and I did, a computer game, so to speak, some time ago. We thought you might like to see it—it's all unofficial, but a bit too close to today's event to let slide."

"Thanks, Brandon, what have you got?"

"Well, sir, perhaps you remember, some time ago Roméo Dallaire— after his retirement as general—well, he was speaking in a Senate committee meeting, and General Dallaire asked what would Canada do if the native people found a leader and got organized. He answered himself and suggested that they could cause problems all across the country."

"Yes, I recall something like that. No one seemed to notice the exchange, though."

"Yes, sir, it seemed to pass in the night, so to speak. But Bill, Doug, and I, we were working then on some staff college computer simulations and in our spare time we worked up a sort of war game one weekend to see what might happen in the Dallaire scenario."

"They must be getting slack at the war college in Toronto if you guys have time to play games not in the curriculum. So what happened?"

Brandon, blushing slightly, shuffled through his notes and unfurled a large marked-up map, and put it on the table in the centre of the ops room. "Well, sir, we did, more or less, mark out all the vulnerable points across Canada that rebels might take over and use as negotiating chips with the government. Then we tried various ways the native radicals could best bring pressure to bear on the government, and we came up with three options."

"Okay, go on."

"Here on the old map I saved, sir. Option one. Grab a vital resource or target, like Montreal or Highway 401, and hold until the feds negotiate. Option two. Really seize a lot of territory, Northern Quebec or the communications lines across the North Superior routes, and stop Canada's economy. The weakness in these options is that the army and the police and so on could easily concentrate against the natives and take them out in time, like at Oka. To be really effective, the native leaders would have to go for a third option: distract the army and strike all the vulnerable points at once. But to do that they would need lots of weapons and lots of organization. We concluded that they don't have either."

"So Brandon, how did the game play out?"

"Stalemate, sir. The natives got themselves in a box, scattered all over the place in small ineffective operations, and the feds got into the same situation by reacting to the native moves. The outrider in the game was the idea that if the natives moved faster and smarter than the army commanders—they would move us to all the wrong places."

"I see. Not a very happy scenario in any case. Why would they do this? What's their aim?"

"That was the tricky part, sir. We kind of followed the news we've heard over the years and thought they would be looking to settle their grievances we've heard about all the time from native national leaders. But I wasn't convinced. I thought if that were the case, they wouldn't be radicals. Radicals always go for, well, radical ideas and objectives. They might want something we never contemplated."

"I assume you played the game to the finish. So, who won?"

"That's interesting too, sir. When the natives selected options one or two, they lost, sometimes slowly, but they lost nonetheless. Actually, in some cases—we ran the computer options several times—their units, as we called them, mostly just disintegrated over time. When they used option three, however, they always won or the situation blew up into chaos."

"Which option did the feds assume at the beginning?"

"That's the strange part. As we played it, we all began and persisted in assuming the natives would go for small local or regional operations, options one and two. And when we did that we always lost if the natives actually chose the cross-Canada option or surprised us by switching to it later on.

"When we forced the computer program to go on probabilities—we took what we knew about the capabilities and the organization of the natives from our intelligence data bases and applied them—the high probability was that the natives would use a local or regional strategy and that we would defeat them. The analysis stands so long as our data is correct and logic prevails on all sides."

René Lepine stood motionless for several minutes. He ran his fingers over Brandon's map, jabbing lightly here and there across the country.

"Here's what I want you to do, Brandon. Develop this winning scenario. Let your mind run with it. Give me a native aim. Give me a strategic framework to achieve it. And then do a task-to-mission analysis—you know the drill, add up the things they would have to do and then see if they have the resources to do them.

"Get some help from whoever you need and brief me later this evening. We'll go from there. Oh, keep this work inside the headquarters. No need to spook NDHQ with computer games at the moment."

Lepine turned back to the map. He re-read his notes, then went back over the intelligence file on the National People's Army, re-read Molly Grace's public speeches and declarations, as well as analysis from think-tanks in Canada and the United States. He checked the CSIS files and found them to be, as usual, well behind rapidly unfolding events. Finally, he let his imagination roam once more. The obvious scenario, another Oka-style problem in Quebec, seemed too pat, too predictable. It was, he decided, an unacceptably ordinary explanation for the entirely extraordinary set of skilfully coordinated raids on Canadian Forces bases that had started whatever was happening.

I hope to God we make the right choices, he thought. There's no road back once we deploy. Where can I find a reserve to hold ready for the surprise Molly Grace has for us? He closed his eyes, breathed three times slowly and deliberately, clearing his mind. And then the words of Sun Tzu, the ancient Chinese strategist, flashed across the ages. *All warfare is deception. March by an indirect route and divert the enemy by enticing him to a bait.*

Lepine called across the operations room. "Comms!"

"Yes, sir?"

"Get me General Bishop on the secure phone as soon as you can, please."

Wednesday, September 1, 1800 hours
Akwesasne: The Complex

Bill Whitefish sat thinking about the upcoming meeting, one that he was sure would sap him of most of his energy. And he thought about Molly. Molly had called the meeting that morning. She wanted to meet with the Native People's Council to, as she said privately to Bill, "straighten out some policies and some people." Nothing unusual there, Bill thought. Molly watched everyone and commanded everything. She relied on a few trusted workers, like Bill, and some others tasked directly by Molly to watch and listen for her. As the operation began to unfold, Molly's insiders informed her that several members of the Council were openly questioning her judgement and the whole operation. Bill knew that Molly intended to confront the doubters before they infected the entire compound.

Bill expected the next few hours would be rough, but he knew Molly and understood who would come out on top. Yet as he prepared for the meeting he wondered, as he had occasionally, if perhaps Molly's fierce determination to lead the people, the very thing that held him to her, might not be too determined and too fierce to hold everyone else to her and to the cause.

He had seen her magic effect on people before and couldn't help recalling the time in Winnipeg when he was confused and worried about himself and his people and the aimlessness of most of the talk he heard from the usual aboriginal leaders and chiefs. It was the accidental collision of that state of mind and his first encounter with Molly Grace that brought him into the movement some four years ago.

Winnipeg
Four Years Earlier

Bill Whitefish was Cree, born and raised on the Norway House Cree Nation reserve on the Nelson River north of Lake Winnipeg. Life for the boy, and the young man, had been rough, save for his mother's warm and protective embrace. Other families may have suffered from neglect, but Suzy Whitefish was determined to raise her six children right and get them out of the reserve life into a more promising future. And she did.

Bill grew up with few belongings except those provided by the vast lake and forest at his door, storehouses few Canadians appreciate. But he escaped the temptations of mischief and booze that led many of his friends to career into delinquency, a brush with the law, then a dead end of lost possibilities. Bill didn't just finish high school, he did well enough to earn his teachers' recommendation for university in the south. When a provincial program for higher education for native people landed on his principal's desk, Bill was the chosen candidate and was immediately successful. In September 1995, he took his first flight, in a small, noisy, commuter plane up, out, and over the great shining lake. He never came back.

The University of Manitoba campus, a sprawling architectural jumble thrown together on the twisting banks of the Red River, was the most frightening enclosure Bill Whitefish had ever encountered. He struggled every night to keep from running away, flying home to the sanctuary of isolation. But he won those struggles and stayed on. He spent his time studying, socializing with his class as he found it, only taking time away from classes and the library to walk on weekends through the strange blaring streets of "the Peg."

Bill was an academic success. He made the Dean's List in his first year and decided to major in economics and commerce. He graduated with high marks and was offered positions in graduate programs, and employment in the university's administration and in several local businesses run by wealthy UM alumni. He elected to pursue graduate studies, in politics and commerce, and continued to impress his professors and peers.

Along the way Bill also found a calling, as he termed it, helping drifting native kids in Winnipeg's forever drab north Main Street warehouse
district, a massive accumulation of block buildings, old and new. His voca-
tion came about pretty much by accident. In his undergraduate strolls off
campus, Bill had often walked through the dingy area from Portage and
Main down to "The Forks," where the Assiniboine River flows finally into
the Red. He strolled occasionally north on Main Street, then west along
Higgins to watch the great freight trains being assembled in the vast CPR
railway yards.

He first visited the area soon after he got to Winnipeg, partly to see
the native museum, but mostly out of curiosity sparked by stories he had
heard in the university dorms about wild Indians and easy women, characters unlike any he had seen at home. It was a fine fall evening when he
stepped alone into that world for the first time. He'd taken a bus north
from campus right after dinner and wandered up Main Street, noticing
rough-looking natives begging or just standing around the entrances to
small hotels—they were really just beer parlours, in fact—and some girls
obviously in the business.

He'd hesitated at first to head west off Main into the scruffy streets
north of Notre Dame. He thought he looked too prosperous, neat, tidy—
basically like a tempting target. Hang on, he thought. It's still daylight, I'm
native, the rumours are just rumours, and so he took the plunge, heading
randomly west off Main, then north along King, to Logan.

The streets were dusty, dirty, a litter of paper and beer cans scattered at
every turn, like much of the older parts of the city, Selkirk Avenue or Sher-
brook Street south of Broadway. Winnipeg is, after all, an industrial city,
and in the autumn, the harvest adds grain dust from a thousand combines
and smoke from burning stubble to the city's polluted air, giving the older
sections a desolate Third World drabness.

The immediate image was exaggerated by cold, greying buildings,
"accessorized" with ubiquitous urban costume jewellery—litter, parked
cars, toppled empty garbage cans rocking click-clack, click-clack in the
wind, dog shit, and newspapers left to fly, spreading the news about the
streets. Everywhere, wind-blown plastic bags raced each other down
the streets or wrapped around lamp posts and hopeless, naked trees,
before finally ending up crowded together in doorways, out of the wind,

uninvited. Partners to the discarded plastic bags, too many natives, foreigners in the white man's cities, ignoble savages, drawn from the shining forest to become living accessories, dangling, dishevelled forms that
crowded the area's mean alleys and the cold, chain-link fences around the
buildings. And always the wind animating the bleakness as sunset's shadows settled over the streets.

That evening, Bill headed back to Main, then south, passing the old
Occidental Hotel and a small band of rough-looking natives leaning
against the wall. Somehow the sight made him feel out of place and alone,
longing again for home. Others on the street, native and white, mostly
passed him by unnoticed.

He walked a long way, sometimes jeered by small gangs of young men
and once, frighteningly, by a loiter of older, menacing men and women
standing across the street, all in jeans and beaded leather jackets, hair in
braids. "Hey, white Indian," they called and laughed. "Want a girlfriend?"
Bill moved on. Another time a police car cruised up silently from behind
and the officers looked him over, sneered, and moved on. Worthless, he
thought, even to the police. It was, he would say later, the night he began
to grow up, to find his purpose.

The north Main Street's drifting "at risk" native kids became Bill's purpose.
Even before he finished university, he volunteered to work as a part-time
counsellor at the First Nations Family Office in the Norquay Community
Centre in the South Point Douglas district off Main Street. After graduate
school, Bill had taken a permanent position there and worked with kids
and families for several years. After a while, however, he felt increasingly
overwhelmed by the endless flow of broken lives that stepped though his
door every day.

One day had been more frustrating and depressing than usual. He had
just spent another long, difficult afternoon arguing with some local cops
at the King Street and James Avenue station about a young delinquent
Bill wanted to send home to the Sandy Hook First Nation. The beat cops
wanted to throw the kid into the system. Finally, around 4:00 p.m. the boy
was released into his care and custody. But as soon as they stepped out of
the police station, the boy promptly ran off with a gang leader who had

been waiting for him most of the afternoon. Bill stood in the street humiliated and defeated before the cynical cops he'd just convinced to let the boy go. Dejected, he scolded himself, "Why even try to help these kids? I'm just wasting my time. I'm getting nowhere and neither are they."

He decided to walk home; no sense in going back to the office only to face some new disaster. He headed down Main Street to the Assiniboine River, intent on following the Riverwalk below the Legislative Building towards Maryland on his way to his small apartment on Fawcett Avenue. A slow stroll home along the riverside promenade was always calming, even at rush hour.

As he reached the river an old friend from university who lived in the same neighbourhood caught up with him and reached out a hand. "Hi, Bill. Thought that was you walking ahead of me."

Alan Lathlin was Cree too, born on the Opaskwayak Cree Nation, a thriving, well-managed reserve just north of The Pas. He worked for a downtown law office where he specialized in matters dealing with aboriginal people and the law. He and Bill had cooperated occasionally on juvenile cases that had gone off the rails. "Out of the office early aren't you, pal?"

"Bad day, Al. You know, another kid gone over to the gangs. Thought I had him in hand, but what do I know, really?"

"That bad, eh? So what now?"

"I don't know actually. Don't even know if we're on the right track at all. You know how it is. The kids come in or are picked up, then they're counselled and returned to the street only to continue their descent into hell. It's always the same: crappy, low-paying jobs, or aimlessness, unemployment, petty crime, prostitution, booze and drugs. And you know what's behind it, Al? Loneliness. These kids feel a kind of loneliness in big crowds that they can't deal with. It's not the same for white urban kids.

"Most of these kids come from small communities, like you and I did. Sure the reserves may be isolated, and sure they may often be in quite miserable places—I know mine was—but they also provide a tight, even, clannish society. You know how it is, we grew up in it. Everyone in the community is everyone's extended family. Sure, booze and drugs are problems—and the problems are getting worse—and they destroy families. But the kids still feel rooted in the land and secure among the people, their extended family.

"In the big city, these kids are no more rooted in the community than the dead leaves or the heaps of garbage all around them. A native kid arriving in Winnipeg has to find a way into an alien urban community and few have the necessary skills. White kids, immigrant kids even, everyone else grew up in a community of strangers, so they weren't traumatized by moving among them. For native kids it isn't the same.

"I tried, and you and the rest of the community here tries to help them by teaching skills, explaining how to get a job from a stranger, how to make friends with strangers, how to live in a building with strangers, but these aren't things you can learn from a book. And the more we tell the kids they need to change, the more they feel like outsiders, and the more anxious and alienated they become. Meanwhile, the loneliness festers, turns to depression, and then to fear and desperation. They become attracted to gangs, not to be gangsters, but like wild geese are lured to decoys. The gangs look like home."

"But you've accomplished a great deal Bill," said Al. "Saved a few kids. I know. I've seen you in action helping us in the courts and in our dealings with native families. They trust you."

"Yeah, sure, of course, Al, we win a few. But just as often the gangs get the kids, because they give the kids what they need so desperately: a community where they fit in, with familiar faces, where they can hear their mother tongue, where they can find 'elders.' Not real elders, of course. Some of these gang leaders may be not much older than the kids they recruit, but, you know, they're substitutes for the elders. We help but we can't be with the kids all the time, or even most of the time. And when we aren't there, then the gang leaders set the pace and almost always it's destructive."

Al nodded. "Yah, I see it all the time too, but from a different perspective than you do, Bill. Sometimes I think it's impossible. Assimilation, say through native businesses and urban reserves, simply can't fix the problem, especially for lonely kids from far-off, small reserves. It takes years of education, socializing, and group-think to prepare a white urban kid to fit into the great economic society. How can we expect to do the same thing for a native kid raised and poorly educated in an isolated, remote community?"

The friends walked in the shadow of Riel's statue without giving the old leader a glance, and followed the walkway under noisy Osborne Street. They stopped and sat on a thin green bench in Mostyn Place Park, silent for a few minutes as they watched the shrivelled, late-summer Assiniboine trickle by below on its way to the Red River a few blocks away.

"You're right, Al. Countless native kids have tried to follow the 'just go to a city and get a job' idea but the transition is way too difficult. And after they fail in the cities, they go to jail or drift back to the reserves stripped of any sense of worth they might have had before they left. Back home, the grievances multiply as the road to the future narrows to a dirt trail then peters out entirely. These ruined kids become bad examples—complaining about governments and the whites and on and on—all the unfairness caused by everyone but themselves and their native leaders. Their bad-mouthing contaminates the next generation."

Bill stood up to walk on. Al held him by the sleeve of his coat and motioned for him to sit down again.

"Actually Bill, she's here; your native ideologue. Tonight, at the United Church hall on Westminster. I've seen her before, spoken with her, in fact."

"Who's she? A local politician, I suppose?"

"No she's from out of town. Come to think of it, she never told me where she came from. Kinda vague, back east from one of the big Mohawk nations. But Molly Grace is the real thing, Bill. I do some work for her and her groups out here. *Pro bono*, of course. Let her use my offices for meetings with the local chiefs and manage some of her, ah, well, her files and deals with the government here in Winnipeg and in Ottawa. Nothing big, really."

"I recall the name now, Al. Heard of her a couple of times when I was working with community groups over in the Douglas Point area. Saw her the television too. Some of the young people there are all charged up about this person, though no one had ever met her. Just another fiery radical as I see it. Out to excite the crowds and make some money, I suppose."

"Not at all, Bill. Not at all. Molly Grace has a message, a very real message. Why don't you join me? That's why I'm out of the office early. Come on along."

"I'm kinda tired, Al. A long disappointing day…"

Al stood up and offered Bill his hand. "Come on, Bill, she's the answer the people have been praying for, but I am sure not the answer the whitemen and the Ottawa chiefs want to hear. Come on, you're not that tired and I'll buy you a beer after the meeting's over."

Bill smiled, accepted the hand, stood up, and patted Al on the back. "Well, okay. Maybe I need a change of scene. I know I could use a beer. You always were the smooth-talker in class, Al. Guess that's why you're such a success as a lawyer now."

Four Years Earlier
Winnipeg: Westminster Avenue

Bill and Al walked up to the base of the church steps and stopped. A large, round man dressed in jeans, a deerskin jacket, and a war bonnet waved to them. "Hey you guys in the nice suits, come on in, you'll learn something. Maybe you'll even come back to your people. Come on, nothing to fear here."

They moved towards the steps, pressing themselves lightly through the crowd of last-minute smokers gathered on the sidewalk. The crowd cheered and heckled happily as Bill and Al made their way up the steps and into the church.

The long, brightly lit church hall was nearly full. Bill motioned Al towards a pair of chairs up front, just two rows back from the low platform. "You go ahead, Bill. I've got some business to attend to with the organizers. I'll look for you afterwards near the main door."

"Sure, okay. Don't forget, you owe me a beer too. If I can't find you in the crowd, I'll meet you at Sonny's." Al waved and walked into the crowd.

Bill, excusing himself, squeezed past friends, neighbours, strangers and a couple of "streets" more interested in warmth than enlightenment. The quiet chatting of people around him raised a loud incomprehensible hum in the little hall that unified the audience as they waited for the speaker to appear. Bill suspected that many, like him, were eager simply to see in person this radical native debater made famous by television—an outspoken, uncompromising critic of nearly every public leader, native and white. Here tonight the "talking head" would finally become a real, live person. Would she, he wondered, seem smaller than she appeared on the tube? He expected little from the evening except a diversion from his immediate worries: a review, now two weeks late, of a case study into how the media distorts the reality of urban native life.

Molly Grace strode through the door and down the long aisle, reaching for hands and nodding to familiar faces. The cheers grew louder and louder as people looked over their shoulders, trying to catch a glimpse, then joined the welcome with claps, whistles, and shrieks. Bill turned and observed that she seemed more ordinary than on TV. Almost embarrassed by the thought, he searched for some distinguishing feature. Molly looked to be mid-thirties, dark hair worn in a long braid, a classically native, strongly featured face. Okay, Bill confessed to himself, she had a bold, captivating smile, and there was something very alive about her eyes. As she walked, her coat flapped open, revealing a slim figure under a simple dress. Both the woman and the dress were attractive, but she was not, to Bill at that moment, remarkable.

Protected by two large native men who stepped firmly in front of those who pushed too eagerly out from their chairs to touch the lady, Molly reached the front, climbed the three steps to the platform, dropped her coat casually on a chair, and stood before the lectern. Bill felt a surge of eagerness sweep the crowd. Chairs suddenly stopped scraping on the old hardwood floor, and the hall went dead silent and everyone there leaned forward, eager to listen. The evening had somehow become an event and Molly had not yet uttered a word.

"Our people," she began in a melodious, compelling voice, then repeated the phrase more strongly, pointing round the room. "Our people, you and me, we own the land! We own the land, not as a mere asset, but as the people of the land, a part of the whole. We own the land as the wind owns the prairie grass, the geese the sky, the wolves the forests. We are one people, the living and the ancestors, the spirits and the future. But we have been torn from the land, stripped of our heritage. We have surrendered our ancestors and ourselves. And for what?"

The congregation, utterly silent in the dim light of the crowded hall, waited breathlessly for the word. "We surrendered our land, our place in the land, to aliens, white settlers, and their destructive ideas of land as property, land as profit. Land, the whites say, is without real value, except when it is exploited, given a price. We allowed them, and yes, our so-called leaders continue to allow them, to lock up our bodies on reserves, our rights in their courts, and our spirits in a never-world, abandoned to wander far from our homes. We, the people, have become, as the land is in the white mind, without real value except as workers to be exploited, worth money or worth nothing."

The faithful in the crowd, already converted by a message they had obviously heard before, joined the speaker. "Yes, they have!" "Yes, we have!" "No more!" "Never again!" "We own the land!"

Others listened, rapt, hearing the true sound of their own existence for the first time. Inside them the same cries sounded. "Never again!" "Shame on us!" "We own the land!"

Bill shifted uneasily, wanting to turn and look at the transformed crowd, so ordinary five minutes ago and so impassioned now, but unwilling to break contact with Molly's eyes, fixed, it seemed, on him alone.

On she went, speaking without notes, not missing a beat. "White academics provide new shackles, new reasons to dismiss our people. We're the 'fourth world,' people lower than any East Indian 'untouchable' or outcast in darkest Africa. They say we're trapped in dependency, unable to escape because we are too weak. We are doomed to indignity because we are too few. Our so-called native leaders join this self-serving white nonsense, repeating their humiliating words: 'You are too weak...you cannot replace the alien community...you cannot free yourselves.' These men are no longer natives like us, they are white Indians, sniffing for scraps from the settlers' tables, working to hold us in check, preaching accommodation and delivering despair.

"We are trapped, the white academics declare, between being ourselves—unattainable because the traditional ways are gone—and being members of the community—unattainable because the white settlers won't accept us. But it gets worse...they say we can't even follow the example of the blacks in old British African colonies who destroyed white imperialism long ago. We're too weak, too few, too disconnected from the 'modern' economy, so we're stuck in soul-destroying dependence on the settlers' welfare cheques.

"Well, my brothers and sisters, their arguments are false and their motives are racist. The blacks and the Vietnamese and the Algerians and all the others escaped from the white settlers' grasp because they fought their way to freedom. Why can't we be ourselves and rule ourselves? Size doesn't matter—the white government gave half the North to a few of our Inuit cousins. We don't seek a share in the white man's booty and we don't seek to become their mirror image. We seek to become ourselves! So we'll recreate our fathers' space and be ourselves when the time comes. And that time is soon, my people. Soon!"

Her last, soaring shout brought the audience to its feet cheering and shouting support and determination. Bill was startled and then impressed to find himself clapping first politely, then vigorously. Almost in spite of himself, he was captured by the mood and the woman on the stage.

Molly visibly drew power from the crowd's embrace. "Soon, my people. Soon we will have freedom from the shackles of government. Freedom from self-serving native leaders, lackeys of the white settler government. Our supposed leaders!" She changed her pitch and cadence, suddenly, from high, fast, and exalted to deep, slow, and methodical.

"Think about this: 600 chiefs representing 900,000 people. That's about one chief for every 1,500 of us. That's like having 21,000 members of Parliament in Ottawa." The crowd snickered.

"And just last July these same chiefs travelled first class to Calgary to stay in a fine hotel and play golf. Imitation settlers, that's what they are, golfing, dining, and enjoying whisky and cigars in the lounge while deploring dependency among the savages. All of them bought for a green fee and a dinner tab. Our kids don't have clean water and these fat-assed chiefs play golf with your money. No more, my people, no more." The crowd erupted in hoots and cries, jeers, and whistles.

Molly rode the wave, picking up the rhythm and raising her voice with every sentence. "We want freedom from the self-imposed destructive life of the reserves. We must help each other. You are the people. You own the land. Chase away the devils of booze and drugs. Educate yourselves. Care for your children. Provide for the poor and the sick. Respect the elders. Remember dignity is earned, not given to you by governments, white or native."

Molly worked the stage and the crowd, repeating her message again and again, preaching hope based on dignity, not given but earned. On she went, crossing the stage, speaking to all at once yet to each one alone, reaching out to hearts and minds—fifteen minutes, thirty minutes, who knew? The crowd by turns silent, loud, polite, and boisterous. The rhetoric free and even funny, poking at the "chiefs" and white stereotypes of the noble savage and the drunken one. This was no savage, Bill thought; there was nobility in her vision, in the images her words conjured up in his mind in succession too rapid for contemplation, demanding his full attention with each change in theme and delivery.

"Recently," she said, dropping in cadence and pitch again, as a priest might to alert the pews that an almighty message was forthcoming. "Recently, the settlers' courts condemned one of our great leaders and humiliated him in public, saying his words were 'intemperate.' The words he spoke, the white judge said, 'were racist.' The judge was forced to take back these lies and yet the whites missed the message. But we didn't.

"My friends, the message is this: it's not words that define racists. It's what the white courts and white politicians do to us that define racists." Her voice became rhythmic, almost lyrical, and the crowd began to clap in time and cheer with each phrase.

"I will tell you what's 'racist' in this country. Racist is a home without hot water or electricity. Racist is cold food, poisoned water, and hungry children. Racist is crapping in an outhouse in February." Young women blushed, giggled, eyed each other, and covered their mouths with cupped hands, cold memories of pain and shame dissolved by the warmth of unspoken sharing.

"Racist is Third World schools for us and every advantage for their spoiled brats. Racist is an abundance of beds for us in their prisons, but none in their hospitals. Racist is unemployment, drugs, and alcohol. Racist is the white man's sicknesses—TB, measles, flu, syphilis, whooping cough, and AIDS.

"Racist is the white man's lust for our young women, as toys for sex and murder. Racist is violence and buggery disguised as religion. Racist is suicide for our kids and our nation."

At every phrase, the people shouted back, "Yes, that's it. That's right." "Damn the settlers." "No more!"

Molly stopped, breathing hard, her anger seemingly spent, letting the crowd vent, waiting for silence. When the room was once again quiet, expectant, she resumed softly, almost whispering into the microphone. "Racism is an unexpected slap in the face. The settlers' top politician gets to choose a deserving Canadian to represent us all to the world. So who does he pick as the English queen's governor general? A black foreigner, a person so unsuited to the position that even the white settlers notice. And then he declares, 'This person is what Canada is all about.' Well he got that part right." The crowd gasped, but Molly raised a finger. "Both he and this lady do represent what Canada is all about. Never a thought for a native, not even a white Indian. Well, Jack Hemp, you can start thinking about us. We are the people and WE … OWN … THE … LAND." Silence, then wild cheering. Bill noticed that he had joined in.

When the crowd again fell quiet, Molly beckoned to someone standing in the shadows to the right of the stage. A tall, elderly Indian stepped slowly forward, his long white hair tied back, his brown face wrinkled by age and weather. He was dressed simply, in jeans, sweater, and boots. He waved softly, almost shyly, to those in the crowd who recognized him and called out.

"Here," said Molly, "is Martin Fisher, the Ojibwa shaman known well to you from Kenora and Grassy Narrows. Martin travels among you, a faithful leader of the people, a man of peace and love for all. He is our memory, and memory is the people's true soul. He is shaman to the people. Martin lives in the world between dreams, connecting we the living to our ancestors, who speak to us in our dreams. Come Martin, speak to us. Tell us what they say."

Martin paused before the microphone, put his hands forward, and braced his thin body against the lectern. "Greetings to you all from the people of the land of the Ojibwa," he began quietly. "I have a simple story of the days many years ago when the white settlers came to our land north of Superior. They made treaties with us. Only nations can make treaties with each other. So we spoke with them as a nation, one to the other.

"We were not beaten savages or some lost tribe of Israel. We had no need of the settlers. They needed us. So we made a treaty, equals to equals, to share our land with them in peace and to let them take from the forests and streams and lakes what was of use to them. We were given promises, a fair return on what was taken from our land—they promised hospitals and doctors and schools. What Ottawa and Toronto gave us instead was disrespect, whisky, reserves, helplessness." Martin paused, motionless, the crowd held as tightly by his gentle manner as by Molly's passion.

"Each day, even now, as we see the lumber trucks carrying our trees to give profits to someone, the people cringe and hide their faces in shame. We sit in our miserable homes while the settlers use our resources to build cars and grand houses for themselves and blame us for our downfall."

Martin Fisher was neither angry nor animated. His grandfatherly voice soothed the excited crowd. But this was not the passive calm of apathy. It was the intense, balanced calm of a man pulled by two mighty, exactly opposite forces: the ancient spirits and his worldly life. Bill knew at once that Martin, too, was always aware of the white man's outrages but never crushed by them.

Martin Fisher walked away from the microphone towards the front of the now darkened stage, the one remaining soft light directly on him. He was chanting, seemingly lost in his own world of dreams. Then the melodious sound stopped, and he opened his eyes and released his fearful vision in the same calm voice.

"Early in the spring, when the ice had just gone out, I took my canoe and paddled north, following the first geese. I stopped for many days beside a fast river where it emptied into a fine lake. I was alone and happy. Then one day, as I sat by the river and watched winter melt away, I had a terrible dream. I was awake, but I had a dream." He moved ever so slowly across the platform and into the shadow of the curtains, the soft light following him.

"I was in a village of my people. There were no men left there, just children and women and dogs. The village was a blasphemy in the pure forest. Houses were dirty and unpainted, garbage littered the ground, the water smelt foul. The children stood in rags, eyes glassy. The people had forgotten how to hunt. The fish that once happily gave us life now tried to poison us."

Martin began to chant softly to himself again, perhaps summoning back this terrible dream. Then he spoke again. "The village had no elders or leaders. The people sat as always in a circle in the centre of the village, but instead of the council fire or the elders' dance, they sat around the large rusting, leaking drums holding the fuel everyone used to heat their homes and run their machines. White men and white Indians paid by the settlers sat with them and talked with them about what they were to do about the leaking fuel. They talked for days and months and years while the fuel leaked and the ground was soaked in gas and the village smelt of gas.

"The village was surrounded by the forest and the forest was burning everywhere. It had burned for as long as most of the people could remember. Smoke filled the air and choked the people, but they paid no attention. The white men and the white Indians paid no attention."

The hall was still. Not a word or a cough, only an occasional low, choking moan. Martin moved back across the stage to the lectern. "In this dream," he said more loudly, "two young men, men of the village, walked out of the burning forest. They were ugly. Their hair was long, untied, and filthy. They wore animal skins, but of the lowest animals, ragged and dirty. They stared at the villagers and shouted abuse at them. But neither the villagers nor the white men nor the white Indians could see them. Only I could see them. They had left the village as boys and returned as devils." The crowd shifted in their chairs, appalled, some terrified, all eyes fixed on the shaman on the darkened stage.

"The two wild men walked through the burning bush, deliberately circling the village. They snarled and watched for weakness like wolves. Then they stopped and each of them picked up a burning stick and waved it in a circle over his head. They called out again, but this time with the voices of young boys. 'We want to come home,' they wailed. But no one heard them. The villagers were listening only to the white men and the white Indians from Ottawa. The devils beat the ground with their sticks and howled. Then they began to walk out of the fire and into the village." The crowd stirred. A woman gasped.

Martin's hypnotic voice grew louder. "The devils walked right up to the circle and shouted foul words at the villagers and the white men and the white Indians from Ottawa. Still no one saw them. No one heard them. But I saw them and I heard them and I was afraid. I trembled as the ugly men jumped into the circle and struck the fuel drums, knocking them over, then hit the gas-soaked ground with their burning sticks. Now the villagers and white men and the white Indians from Ottawa jumped to their feet, for at last they saw the devils. But it was too late. A great flame burned up the village and all the people, and all the white men and all the white Indians from Ottawa, good and evil all burned together."

He closed his eyes again and his voice sank low. "Look about the world, my people, and see this warning. Enter these times with dread. We cannot, will not, go back to sleep. We elders hold the circle together and speak for peaceful ways, though we are losing the arguments in the lodges of the people. But the young devils are returning. Can no one see them? The settlers must keep their promises or suffer with us if they do not." Martin walked quietly into the shadows off stage. No one clapped or cheered. Some wept quietly.

Then abruptly Martin turned around and stepped back towards centre-stage and faced the crowd. He stopped and held up a hand as if to say a final word. "Beware the wild leaders on the prairies and in the forest," warned the shaman Martin Fisher. "They'll only take you down their path, not yours." But no one in the church on Westminster Avenue heard Martin's warning because, inexplicably, his microphone had gone dead and the light had drifted away from him as he spoke his final words from the shadows of the stage.

No one heard Martin's warning passed him by the spirits of the land. No one noticed as Martin disappeared behind the stage curtains.

Instead, Molly stepped up to the lectern and the lights sprang back up. The mood in the room changed abruptly from fear and sorrow to anger as she spoke harshly, ruthlessly, taking the crowd along a deadly path.

"There is," she said loudly, raising her arms, "a third way. A way free from the oppression of the white capitalist, free from the white pretence of self-government, free from 'the Ottawa men.' A third way, free from native leaders on the take, free from those who lure us into mimicking white ways that would keep us forever torn from the land and our ancestral heritage."

People rose to their feet, ready for the word and the way.

"Take back the land!" Molly shouted. She paused, letting startled silence pass for consent, then struck fast and hard. "Take back the land," she shouted again, "and rebuild the rightful heritage of our people. Remove the intruding society from our land. Provide for all the people the gifts the spirits gave to us alone. The people, masters in their own land, but masters over no one."

Molly stepped back from the lectern and raised a clenched fist. "We the people must now decide: change the world or perish here in the white man's dirty cities far from the land that is our soul and necessary destiny. It is time for each of you to decide in your own minds. Will you act? Will you join me?"

The room hesitated, the majority wavering, inspired, excited, but this was too bold, too demanding. Then, with exquisite timing, her followers started shouting, promising, rushing to the platform...“Me!” “You can count on me!” “Yes, we're with you.” “Our land, our people, our way!” Molly's raised hands waved over them, blessing all together and everyone individually.

Bill, too, hesitated, and then stepped forward. He'd heard the message: unambiguous, forceful, filled with hope and purpose. Part of his mind called out. The words, a combination of the sadly familiar and absurdly extreme, are words he would dismiss immediately if anyone else had said them. But his native soul realized that the words weren't the message. It was Molly. Molly Grace was the message.

He flowed to the platform, aware that he was moved not by the crowd or the rhetoric but by the image before him. The messiah? He felt devotion and commitment overwhelm his usually cautious mind. He told himself he intended only to touch her hand, to say thanks. And then he was there before her and stammered unprepared words. “That was wonderful. My name is Bill Whitefish. Thanks.”

Molly crouched towards him, knees bent, balanced on her toes, legs together. She looked at him and only him, as if they were alone in the room, and clasped his hands in hers. “Yes,” she said, “I know who you are, Bill Whitefish.” She smiled and looked right into the depths of his soul. “We've been waiting for you. Welcome to the cause.” For a couple of seconds Bill could hear nothing else in the room, while other outstretched hands waved around them silently, disembodied, as if from a great distance.

Bill stood transfixed, not knowing how or whether to respond. Then Molly stood up slowly, letting Bill's hands slide out of hers, her fingers lingering briefly, maintaining contact at last only with her deep brown eyes. Then she was gone, swept off the stage and down the steps and through the grasping crowd to her car, and the clamour and chaos of the hall flooded back into his ears and eyes.

Bill stood blinking, searching for her, longing to say words full of meaning he still couldn't find even now that she was gone. His face felt flushed, his pulse raced. “I know who you are, Bill Whitefish.” On paper it sounded like a politician's cliché. But he hadn't doubted, and still didn't, that she really did know, not just his history but his essence. Then what? "We've been waiting for you. Welcome to the cause." What could this mean? Who was this woman? What cause? I came here only to listen, he protested feebly. But it was no good and he knew it.

The answers to his many questions would only come months later, in bits and pieces. But from that moment, there in the hall, swaying under the bright lights as people pushed past him, Bill knew he was committed, that he had to find Molly, ask her how he could help, and by helping, help himself and the people. He pledged to do whatever she asked him to do.

For the first time in years, Bill longed for home. At last he knew who he was and what he had to do. Molly knew him, and through her he finally knew himself. And he would follow her without question.

Wednesday, September 1, 1815 hours
Akwesasne: The Complex
Native People's Council

Two weeks after Bill's first encounter with Molly Grace on that evening four years ago, he had joined the cause. He quickly began to understand the vastness of the Movement and its network. His view at the time of specific details was restricted, of course. Security was paramount, discipline was tight, and the leaders looked for RCMP moles under every bed and inside every mattress. People were followed even after they were cleared. Those who followed them were followed, and everyone was interrogated time and again. "Need to know" was the watchword—only those who absolutely needed information were given it, and then they were only given as much as they needed to do their jobs. Careful attention to other revolutionary organizations in other countries and in other times had persuaded the leaders that strict compartmentalization plus strong-arm methods were the keys to keeping the Movement and its secrets safe. So far it had worked.

Bill had been placed initially in the Financial Unit, a logical choice given his education, but it was also a training position from which he could get a deeper sense of the Movement. "Follow the money" is a venerable investigator's adage for a reason. In the Financial Unit, Bill learned the nuts and bolts of irregular financing and, in the process, came to understand the Movement's broad reach.

Even to an MBA in commerce, it was eye-opening to see how easily money could be moved from place to place and program to program in Canada, and how simple it was to launder not just the proceeds of crime but also "legitimate" money from governments.

The Movement was extremely adept at getting money from governments. Of course grants and subsidies were solicited by legal, bureaucratic means, but these funds were then cleverly redirected. Elections offered prime opportunities for more aggressive tactics: politicians keen to be photographed making grants and frantic for campaign money presented a natural coming together of interest and opportunity. It was dead simple—get a grant, kick part of it back as a political donation, minus a "commission" for the Movement and the helpful fixer. After the election, pick up another grant with the assistance of the grateful member of Parliament. Round and round and round she goes. And who in any Canadian government wanted the press to catch them aggressively auditing a native organization?

For the same reason, there wasn't much scrutiny of how grant money was spent. And in an emergency there was always bribery, or blackmail, of government officials manoeuvred into compromising situations over money or women, especially with native women conscripted for that particular duty. Bill had learned such tactics and had learned them well. But his main contribution was finding ways to move and use funds efficiently once they were raised and cleaned, a role that earned him the respect of the Council and Committee's leaders and, most importantly, Molly's trust.

Within a year, he was transferred into, and soon directed, the Information and Intelligence Authority, where with an accountant's mentality he carefully reorganized operations based on a cost-benefit basis, ruthlessly assessing intelligence needs and information sources. Systematic targeting of native people in the Canadian Forces and the militia as ready sources of important information was his major coup. His network spread quite rapidly through all branches of the armed forces and rank levels, though, of course, there were few native officers in the regular forces. The militia also became a vital way to train Movement members in the basics of soldiering and a key source of military-style weapons, especially thanks to the government's hurriedly re-engineered Equality and Diversity Program for bringing more native people into the military. Rooting out government informers was an unpleasant but necessary part of his job, and Bill was as ruthlessly efficient in this duty as he was in all the others.

Efficiency, brains, imagination, attention to detail, a degree of cold-heartedness, and Molly's growing trust carried Bill ever further into the Movement's organization and plans. In time, he was given the lead role in drafting the "grand strategy." And soon after he was accepted by the Committee, Bill was promoted to chief of staff and became Molly's confidant. Outside the inner circle there were naturally rumours that he was more than a trusted advisor, but those closest to Molly knew that her entire life-force was directed into the Movement, that she had neither time nor inclination for conventional pleasures of the flesh or comforts of the soul.

As Molly's chief of staff, Bill held all the reins in his hands, and while Molly and the inner Central Committee might provide direction, it was Bill who turned ideas and orders into actions and outcomes. His role gave him considerable power; though he never openly selected a policy option for the Committee, he frequently shaped the choice of choices, the range of options, from which the Committee decided. He understood very well that he who defines the problem chooses the solution. But whatever his power to lead the Council and even the Committee in a desired direction, it depended entirely on Molly's trust. In any case, his loyalty to her was so absolute that he never sought to shape, only to implement, her will.

Bill Whitefish walked to the small lectern at the front of the long table and dropped his notes on it. Although meetings of the Native People's Council were often a bit tense, today Bill expected serious trouble. Having the initiative in war is desirable, but it includes an unpleasant source of stress. When you attack, you must make decisions; on defence, commanders most often simply react, in ways largely dictated by unfolding threats. Now the Movement was attacking, which meant the chiefs on the Council had to make crucial, frightening, fateful decisions. Very possibly, they would decide to run away. For however full of bravado they appeared on the outside, it was obvious to Bill that on the inside they were timid, ready to bolt like nervous rabbits in a low bush.

Bill had sensed when he left Molly's office a few minutes ago that she too expected a confrontation with the dozen chiefs who made up the Council. They had, they told each other, "let Molly decide matters" when things were routine. But today it was immediately evident to Bill as he entered the room that the mood had changed and that the Daily Operations Briefing would be the stage for a showdown.

The ops briefing was, however, a poor place for the chiefs to try to show some backbone. The briefings weren't actually open forums where equals discussed business and took decisions. Rather, the briefings, like the Council itself, were really just another of Molly's concessions to the chiefs' vanity. Molly took the important decisions in the seclusion of the Central Committee, and Bill and the few trusted others who made up the Committee understood this fact even if the chiefs on the Council did not.

Molly and her disciples had seized the leadership of the Movement soon after the failed Days of Protest in 2007, and began to implement their grand strategy in earnest after the second violent Caledonia crisis of 2008, which had evolved from a dispute over the illegal sale of cigarettes by a local native family. After these failures, Molly realized straight away that the leaderless Council of "equals" was infected with a serious, potentially fatal weakness, and its bouts of indecision threatened to wreck the entire organization and its plans. "It's past time to detach the Movement's centre for decision and move it far away from the old squaws of the Council," she had told Bill, "especially as hard decisions and tough battles are coming our way." So Molly, with Bill's help, simply usurped the gossiping, do-nothing Council's authority and established the Central Committee, which she advertised to the chiefs as "necessary to assist the Council's deliberations."

In fact, the Committee assisted only one person, the leader, Molly Grace. Yet Molly understood there were moments when fiction and fact had to coincide—when the chiefs needed to be reassured that they had some control over the Movement, if only to forestall an internal rebellion led by the chiefs. The decision to accelerate the grand strategy was one of those fateful times.

This morning, Molly needed the Council to endorse the grand plan without, in fact, knowing what it really was. They all knew something about the Quebec scheme and the raids, if only after the fact. But that diversion was meant to deceive them as well as the federal government. The real plan, the grand strategy, was locked away, safe, in Molly's mind, its major elements developed and charted in rigorous detail in secure compartments trusted only to cells within the Central Committee. Nevertheless, she needed the Council to give her the green light for what had to be presented eventually to the people as a very major operation, the one bold chance they'd all been hoping for and working towards. The operation was in reality a huge gamble, a throw of the dice. If Molly didn't maintain control of the Council the chiefs might balk and the people might go with them.

The mood at the table confirmed Molly's suspicions about the chiefs; they looked nervous and gobbled exactly as she had warned Bill they would: "Like fat turkeys the day before Thanksgiving."

"Sure, the raids were successful, but perhaps now is time for an operational pause," said one fat belly, mimicking some "Pentagonese" he'd heard on CNN or somewhere. Others grunted in agreement, trying to look wise.

"Look," announced another chief, without looking at Molly as she entered the room, "the Quebec government has asked to parley, to call an inquiry into native grievances and to consider land claims and self-government in the north…We might get what we want without any conflict and I think—"

Archie from Wikwemikong interrupted. He had never been keen on the Movement anyway. He had lots of cash and investments in and around the reserves, and like a good capitalist, he was for the raids if they brought business north, soldiers with money to spend now and more grants to buy peace later, but not if they might harm his position and his sweet deals on the reserves. "Yeah, that's the thing, ah… the rest of Canada, you know, is on our side and the politicians in Ottawa are shit-scared of Ontario and the Maritimes and the do-gooders at the CBC…"

Alain Selkirk spoke up. He was the only member of the Council who Molly feared, and she feared him because she respected his brain and his dedication to his people, the large Blood band in Alberta. Alain wasn't scared or dishonest; he was smart and careful, which carried weight even in this crowd. "It's really a dangerous gamble," he began, his familiar cau-

tious refrain. "The government is powerful and it's not going to lose—
there's the army and everything. Even if we win local control, we lose
because the people will be harmed and prejudice will grow. We'll become
the Palestinians of North America, despised, rioting without aim against
an unbeatable force, walled off from their cities, burning our own businesses, split into little factions of self-hate, and for what—a few acres of
snow and bush?

"Do you guys really think the soft-hearted liberals and socialists in
Toronto will support us if they think we might actually demand part of
their rich lives? Have you ever seen tourists at the grizzlies' cage at the zoo?
They ooh and ahh and admire them and feed them...but if the bears get
out...BLAM! They're dead.

"I agree we should frighten the whites into concessions. But the rope is
very short. If we pull too hard they'll just cut it, and then what? We're fighting for a chance to negotiate, not trying to win a war. This is just politics.
How many families and homes are you willing to see destroyed simply to
get heard, to get a seat at the table?

"Well, listen to me. If you get enough families and homes destroyed,
and they'll be our homes mostly, it won't get us to the table, it'll smash the
table and we'll end up with nothing. Never doubt the whites' ferocity. They
aren't on our land and most everyone else's in the world because they run
away from a few angry natives. They hanged Riel, remember? They'll do it
again. The Sioux got Custer, but the U.S. Army got Montana."

Bill knew the crucial moment had arrived. He had listened without
comment to the chiefs, but now he watched Molly. She stood silently, jaw
clenched, eyes furious, arms tightly wrapped around the notebook she
held across her chest.

"Backsliders!" she said in a loud icy voice. Her fury swept the table,
startling the chiefs.

"Alain, who elected you to lead a retreat?" She moved sternly, commanding the room from the doorway like a teacher who'd surprised a
class of little boys throwing spit-balls around the room in her absence. She
stalked to the table, banged her ever-present notebook down, and glared at
the chiefs, all older than her, and some twice her size, yet all cowed by her
presence. Bill Whitefish stepped quietly back from the lectern and stood,
admiring her, arms folded, as Molly threw herself fearlessly at the chiefs.

"Snivelling whiners! You're ready again to take a promise over the facts of our history. What happened to last year's speech, Archie, your great empty speech outside Parliament? 'We never gave up our lands, we never signed a treaty, we never agreed to give up our system of government.' Great stuff for TV, you made page one on the *Globe and Mail*. But your father did all those things too, and he went home as empty-handed as you did. Don't you lecture us about dealing with the government or anyone else."

She looked round the table, then right back at Alain. "I know *and you know* that the only possible end of negotiations is defeat and assimilation. Everything they refuse, and everything they grant, drives another little wedge into us. You know this. You know that if we let them treat our community as a community of individuals, our best interest as individuals means abandoning native reserves, getting assimilated into the Canadian economy. Is that what you want, half of us selling our heritage and the other half dying drunk in some alley in Winnipeg, or Saskatoon, or Edmonton?

"And for what? To join a 'me first' society where the white middle class in the suburbs with their SUVs and their Big Macs and their healthcare and daycare are as dependent as anyone, wards of the state on the Etobicoke reserve.

"Is that what you want? Should we throw away our advantage, our cohesion, and slide unnoticed into Canada? Alain, Canada doesn't even exist! Just a bunch of fake subsidized multicultural groups. Look at those proud separatists in Quebec, sucking billions a year from the federal treasury. Should we aim to be like that? What community will we belong to if we don't belong to the aboriginal community...the French-Canadian community; the Muslim-Canadian community; the Japanese-Canadian community? Maybe we should all become red-skin-Canadians?

"No. Never. We've decided all these questions. We're going to be free of both reserves—the government reserves and the welfare reserves. That's our plan and our salvation: finally, a united, sovereign nation free from social welfare and free from 'the great white mother' in Ottawa. We call ourselves sovereign, don't we? First nations, we say. Government to government, we say. 'We never gave up our lands, we never signed a treaty, we never agreed to give up our system of government.' That's what you said too, Alain. And you meant it, didn't you? And you had better still mean it! I do!

"Our duty is to help the people free themselves from reserves built on welfare, and recapture our land and a society built on dignity and self-reliance. We're not going to get there by negotiating away our inalienable rights. We're going to succeed by holding to the grand strategy and by holding this Council together.

"Look at yourselves. Leaders?" Molly's eyes swept the room, lopping off upraised heads, forcing down-cast stares onto the table. "Canada still treats our people as the churches treated them for so long. Today, the system is like a giant, modern version of the residential school, where now the bishops are politicians and civil servants are their priests. But you don't have to be the choirboys in the great church of the holy handout. The traitors like that self-styled Grand Chief Onanole and the others claim they're singing their own tune for us, but they're really in it for themselves. They're mere missionaries for Ottawa. You're not. We're not. I'm not!

"No more endless talk, negotiating over … what? Our birthright? They divide the people with a land grant here, a fishing treaty there, a school, a few houses, toilets. Toilets? We beg the white man for a fucking toilet? Praise 'the father,' the prime minister, from whom all blessings flow. He gave us a potty? Well, bullshit!

"Look at yourselves. Leaders?" She mocked them again. "Do leaders take commands from new Canadians fresh off the boat? The so-called minister of aboriginal affairs is a Sikh, for Christ's sake. Here we are on the lands the Creator gave us; he got here ten years ago and he's in charge. Do you want to go back home and explain that to your kids?"

Molly paused, caught her breath. Her silence cut as sharply as her words. "Let the people suffer. Drive the kids into the cities to rot. You're all children before 'the father.' For how long?"

She fastened her glare on Alain again. "Tell me, Alain, for how long will you live this lie?" Before he could speak, she resumed. "No longer. We never gave up our system of government. You said it, and it's true, and it's time to act on it. The people are sovereign in their own land. We're not going to ask permission from the whites or anyone else to live on our own land. Not having to ask, that's what the word 'sovereign' means, Alain. That's what sovereignty means."

And then Molly gave these men and the two women on the Council the word. "Look up. Look at me! Raise up your faces! You are the people. You are proud. You are leaders." She drove the words hard into their eyes. "You will take—back—the—land!

"Say it in your mind," she commanded. "'Take back the land.' Once you pledge that sacred mission to yourself, nothing can change it, nothing can pull it out. Take the pledge in your mind or leave us alone." She looked again at Alain. He nodded, just perceptibly, and it was done.

Molly, flushed and breathing hard, stepped back from the table, looked away and whispered just loud enough to be heard, loud enough to take command: "There will be no backsliding."

Silence.

"Ladies and gentlemen," Bill said after a minute, "real leaders of the people, let me bring you up to date." Molly dragged a chair noisily up to the table and dropped her glasses on her notebook.

"Yeah," said a voice from the table. "What's whitey up to?"

Molly asked calmly, "Any movement in the army?"

Bill flipped open his notebook and scanned through his carefully sorted notes. "Yes. They think something's up. There's a great deal of planning and pre-deployment underway, almost all aimed at Quebec. Our people in NDHQ report that the headquarters is on a 24/7 emergency manning posture, although there seems to be a lot of confusion in the headquarters about what that means. The place isn't really organized for war or operations. Frankly, it's not really organized at all. But the CDS has told CAN-COM to go to short notice to move and has 5 Brigade in Valcartier ready to move into Montreal as early as tomorrow if necessary, and you can bet your bottom dollar that 5 Brigade is organized." He turned a page.

"Meanwhile, the Special Service Regiment in Trenton is assembling—leaves cancelled and the unit is confined to the base, and the base is locked down. Their air transportation squadrons are preparing too, though the aircraft commanders are struggling to get enough aircraft serviceable to deploy in any useful strength. Clearly, the paras are getting ready to go somewhere and it looks like an airborne operation. But we don't know where they might go; could be James Bay or they might simply fly into Montreal. It will take some time for us to get either confirmation or details, so we'll watch them as best we can."

He turned another page of notes. "CSIS and the RCMP are pretty worried about Quebec. They think 'radical elements,' as they call them, will probably try to disrupt traffic and business across Quebec soon, but they see the problem as 'a civil action demonstration,' mostly political and mostly in the big cities. However, some of our staff people say a minority in both organizations, junior guys who really know the files, are more worried and have even used 'rebellion' in their reports. But the bosses aren't willing to support these assessments for now—just too 'politically loaded.'"

Molly scoffed. "Just wait for the inquiry the government will call in a few months to cover up their stupidity and inaction. They'll blame these same guys for not bringing them the word—they'll call it 'an intelligence failure,' that's a given." Around the table there were snorts of derision and approving nods.

"Well," Bill said, "it's a kind of intelligence failure, or I suppose, more accurately, a failure of intelligence. Just not by the people who'll get blamed."

"Yeah, okay. What's happening in the West?" Molly's tone returned the meeting to a more serious frame of mind.

"Much as we had planned," Bill replied. "Our operations—the assembly of forces and so on—are proceeding quietly under various covers. Stevenson reports that his forces are ready, weapons and supplies stockpiled in safe houses, leaders have been briefed in detail and confined to safe locations. It's the same in the rest of the areas. Canadian Forces bases have gone on alert, but the guards and so on are of low quality—the combat units are mostly deployed or getting ready to deploy. The only exception is the 3rd Patricias in Edmonton.

"It looks like they're being held for operations in the West. It seems the CDS and some of his senior officers agree that something more menacing than a political disturbance in Quebec might be happening. He's getting some support from CSIS and the RCMP, but they're fighting each other, the usual turf wars. At today's cabinet meeting…"

Alain Selkirk butted in. "How do we know all this? How do we know what was said in cabinet?"

Bill glanced at Molly, who smoothly stepped in. "Listen, Alain, all you guys, you know how important security is, but we're asking you for a big decision and you need the facts. No one lets this out, right? No talk to staff, wives, girlfriends. We have sources in Ottawa, you know that, a lot in the military including people who handle briefing papers. We also have…I really mean it, no blabbing. If anyone talks, they'll find the source but you need to know this is right from the source…we also have people on the Privy Council Office translation staff. Bill got this report from someone who was right in the cabinet room during this discussion." A couple of people whistled. Alain nodded at Molly and sat back, 'Mollyfied'—Bill Whitefish's private quip for Molly's amazing ability to neutralize people, even strong-willed, sensible people like Alain Selkirk.

After a brief pause Bill resumed. "At today's cabinet meeting, the PM flatly refused to acknowledge any problem in the West. At which point his kiss-ass chief of staff, Eddie Geldt, jumped in and suggested noise in the West was a ruse to keep the army out of Quebec." Again chuckles ran round the table.

"In any case," Bill continued, "the PM refused to allow any overt actions in the West. He warned the RCMP to stay a safe distance from native assemblies so as not to provoke the people. The meeting broke up with some very hard feelings around the table. Finally, while our sources inside the Quebec government are limited, the premier is said to be in a panic and may call for federal troops at any time."

Bill paused. But Molly sat silent, head down, eyes closed. The chiefs waited for several long, quiet minutes. Suddenly, she sat up, alert, seeming refreshed and sure. "Our so-called native leaders in Ottawa are unwittingly helping the cause by reassuring the government that they are in control of the people and nothing is going to disrupt the country. And the government and the media are so conditioned to this fable that they're reporting as usual what these fools are saying rather than the facts in front of them. Fine. But this charade won't last past the first real trouble in Quebec. We have to move fast, before these weasels see what's happening and try to change sides and usurp the leadership of the people's movement away from you chiefs at this table—our real leaders."

Reaching for her notebook, Molly started reading off the operational plans and put them into operation. The chiefs, nodding, admiring, didn't even notice that somewhere along the way she'd somehow skipped the bit where they were asked to say yay or nay. "I want the Mohawk radicals at Kahnawake and others in Quebec ready to move into the streets in overwhelming numbers by 0600 hours Friday morning. They're to shut down Montreal centre and all routes through the city, north and south, right away; occupy parts of Montreal and Quebec City permanently; and Sherbrooke, Trois-Rivières, and Hull for as long as they can. Blockade streets, close businesses, stop car and foot traffic, but nothing more, no spontaneous, overt hostilities, no provocations, no gratuitous violence, and no unnecessary killing of civilians. The police and the army are another matter."

Whitefish and the others scribbled to keep up with Molly's fire-hose flow of directions.

"The special teams," she continued, her voice quivering slightly as her excitement grew, "are to conduct demonstration attacks in the cities to show the government we're serious. As many major police stations as possible will be harassed and isolated. When the army moves out of Valcartier, I want several demonstration roadside bombs exploded—ahead of the troops. Just demolishing the roads; we want to avoid large casualties that would turn the rest of Canada against us—but we can't be pussyfooting around either. We'll move on James Bay at first light on Friday before the army gets in there. I'll speak directly with our top guy there as soon as we're finished here.

"Bill, I want the intelligence staff to drop all their other work and get answers to these three questions: Are any CF units in the West moving, and if so, to where? Are we holding units deployed in Quebec in Quebec, and if not, what additional pressures should we exert to hold them there? Based on these assessments, when should we launch the main effort in the West? Keep on top of these questions and update the info continually and let me know of any significant shifts in any area." Molly Grace paused abruptly. "Tomorrow," she declared, "is history right now."

She surveyed the table, looking into every face and asked each member of the Council in turn, "Any questions? Now's the time to speak up." Some shook their heads in a silent no. Others more determinedly replied, "Let's go."

The unchallenged leader stood up. "Remember we're in the right. Remember that you are leaders. Remember: take back the land."

In the hallway after they left room, Molly whispered to Bill, "Put some-one on Selkirk. He can't be trusted."

Bill hesitated. "Is that really necessary, Molly? You can't bring them all along without giving them a chance to contribute to the operation. Per-haps you should delegate some authority to the brighter chiefs—especially those from the bigger nations. We're leaders of a federated movement, aren't we?"

Molly stopped, turned, stepped in front of him, and locked her eyes onto his. Bill shuffled awkwardly a half-step backwards. He tried, but couldn't look away. He saw only the captivating face he remembered from the first night in Winnipeg when she clasped his hands in hers—a "laying on of hands," some would suggest later—and drew him into the Move-ment.

"Look, Bill," she said softly, "our people on the Prairies lost most every-thing in the last uprising in 1885 because the leadership was divided. But I don't mean the defeat was caused by the divisions of clans or between the Métis and the Indians or between them and the Red River French elites. Even if these groups had formed some kind of alliance, it wouldn't have had a spiritual centre to hold the people together at the critical points of the war. Anyway, the whites would have broken such an alliance with brute force that the people could never have matched physically. But John A. and his government would never have defeated the people if they had been joined together under the Great Spirit. What the people didn't have and needed was a leader, a messiah, an emissary from the Great Spirit to bring the fighters and the chiefs inseparable together.

"The divide that did them in was the divide between the messiah fig-ure, Riel, and the fighter, Gabriel Dumont, and, the lonely unifier of the people, Chief Great Bear. They failed because they never coalesced into one being. They were just individuals. None could fulfil that role for all the people, none could be the Spirit of the rebellion. That's where they failed the people, Bill.

"We mustn't be too hard on them, though. They were, after all, just men. But we need to remember the lesson—unity under the Great Spirit will terrify and defeat the whites because it is something their violence and weapons can't reach. With the help of the Spirit, a strong fighter, and a clever unifier, we will win back the land for the people." Molly turned and walked away slowly, content in the moment.

Bill let out a deep involuntary sigh. His edgy voice called after her, "So which one of the three are you Molly? Tell me that at least."

Without pausing Molly answered quietly over her shoulder. "I'm all of them, Bill. All at once, in one soul. The people won't come for money, Bill, but they will come for me."

DAY FIVE

Thursday, September 2

Thursday, September 2, 0735 hours
Ottawa: NDHQ, North Tower, Thirteenth Floor
Office of the Minister of National Defence

The defence minister's chief of staff, Ray Wallis, knocked and entered the minister's office, interrupting Jim Riley's private meeting with the CDS. "Minster, the prime minister has asked for you and General Bishop to meet with him immediately. Seems the PMO is finally concerned about the situation." He hesitated, glanced at the CDS, then to the minister. "In fact, the PMO is in a total panic with a bunch of political staffers making war plans and drawing up press statements at random. Everyone's in charge as usual. Plus the Quebec premier has been on the phone to Eddy Geldt most of the morning demanding action against the Indians. Oh, and the media is circling in, hoping for a scandal, I suppose."

Riley looked at the general. "Andy, I think you better come along and bring whomever you need to brief the prime minister. I mean *really* brief him. It's time for us to head off these politicos before they get us into real trouble."

Bishop winced. What the hell, he asked himself, did Riley think they were in now?

Thursday, September 2, 0910 hours
Ottawa: Langevin Block

Jim Riley, General Bishop, Vice Admiral Marie Roy, and Colonel Ian Dobson arrived at the Langevin Block to find a disorganized meeting underway with Eddie Geldt, Hemp's principal secretary, Harry Southern, and the clerk of the Privy Council, Eileen Doyle, all wrestling to chair a quarrel of bureaucrats and PMO staffers. As Riley and his party stood inside the door waiting for someone to acknowledge them, RCMP Commissioner Jean Richard arrived with three senior Mounties, followed immediately by the head of CSIS, Heidi Gunter, and her deputy. The professionals surveyed the amateurs with dismay.

Finally the prime minister walked in, tired and on edge.

Jack Hemp had been leader of the new Progressive Party of Canada, the PPC, since its founding convention. He had won the top PPC job by ruthlessly running over his rivals in a no-holds-barred campaign of smears and misinformation, and with a Bay Street-manufactured "business-friendly" image. Hemp then won the federal election by promising to spend every loonie he could find on things that would make voters' lives pleasant and risk-free. The press and his political rivals had ridiculed the strategy as outdated, but Hemp proved that he knew the Canadian electorate better than anyone else.

On the other hand, Hemp knew nothing about national defence and security issues and made no effort to understand them. His speeches were full of joyful noise about "Canada making a difference in the world," to which he added the slogan, "We will stand on our own feet, because the world needs more Canada," something that voters loved so much. He always got an especially loud cheer from the crowds and the media when he puffed himself up and declared, "Let me simply say this. There is no more important matter than defending our wonderful nation and taking our example of peace, order, and good government to less fortunate people around the world."

The stuff about defending our nation was, of course, empty rhetoric even by his standards; for Jack Hemp, every evil in the world was a social problem to be fixed by reasonableness, dialogue, and handouts. And his advice to the United States was a patronizing, "When you're the big guy on the block, it's the time to be nice. Give in once in a while, lose a few for the good of the world."

Canadian voters loved this stuff, it made them feel special. And Hemp's philosophy for political success was simple. "Pat a Canadian on the back," he lectured his staff, "and he will follow you anywhere." So Jack Hemp patted every back he could reach in his campaign to get to the government benches in Ottawa. His platform was carefully tailored to appeal to political cronies, special interests in the cities, women and minorities, and especially to the loudest of the multicultural communities, which also happened to be the ones best organized to turn out the vote on election day. His outreach program for aboriginal Canadians amounted to trading votes for promises of more money and less accountability. Hemp thought he was using all these special interests. The Movement saw the matter in a very different light. Blinded by cynicism, Hemp couldn't see what Molly Grace saw plainly. She knew that Jack Hemp's shallow promises would one day devour Hemp's career.

The prime minister brought the meeting to order with a rambling announcement of his priorities and strategies. General Bishop stared at the table, thinking grimly that nothing in Hemp's experience had prepared him even remotely for the reality of this moment. "We have the initiative in this situation, folks," Hemp blithered. "The ordinary native person is with us ... the native leaders will come around given a few concessions ... nothing major ... The chiefs just need to give the people an impression of success to get elected again ... I understand that. We're all politicians. Perhaps more seats at more federal conferences or just more money, you know the Kelowna thing? Just bigger. So let's hear ideas. Where's that election night go-get-'em spirit? Where's the 'A hundred days of decisions'? Now, that was slick."

Eddie Geldt joined in. "Yes, sir, prime minister. Glad I thought of it. Okay people, you heard the PM. Who's first?" Hemp frowned at Geldt and the room sank into an embarrassed silence.

Finally Riley spoke up. "Prime minister, we could review the latest intelligence first. It'll take about ten minutes and then we'll know where we are and where we might go." Hemp hesitated and looked to Geldt, but Riley pressed his point. "It might be useful, prime minister. You really should hear this."

Hemp shrugged, and without waiting the CDS motioned Ian Dobson to the head of the table where, without notes, the colonel began the briefing.

"Prime minister, as of six o'clock this morning"—Dobson was in civvy-speak, no twenty-four-hour clocks and no acronyms—" the situation is as follows: the leaders of the so-called Native People's Council have issued a declaration of rebellion against the federal government, and against Quebec in particular. I believe you saw the tape from the Native People's Television Network where Molly Grace, the apparent head of the Council, made certain declarations?

"Within a few hours after her declarations, several disturbances took place in and near Montreal and Quebec City. They were aimed mostly at blocking traffic and commuters at bridges and major highways, and they succeeded. Traffic is now at a standstill in most of Montreal, Quebec City, and on the highways between these cities. The SQ has put pickets—sorry, I should say guards—at the various sites, but they refuse to try to break up the demonstrations because they reported natives in masks, carrying weapons, at every site. Without robust rules of engagement and military backup, they are, well, formally they're advising caution but essentially they're refusing to risk any kind of escalation."

Hemp stirred in his chair, picked up a pencil, and began doodling on a notepad. Dobson paused briefly in case anyone had questions, then continued. "Outside this Montreal-Quebec City core area, we have reports of large gatherings of native people at Oka, Akwesasne, and Kahnawake. So far, they're basically just milling about, but there are indications that they may be preparing to move to support the barricades. This secondary movement isn't coordinated on a large scale, but it's not entirely spontaneous either. Intelligence reports indicate that several groups of armed natives from the 'warriors' society' are travelling from other parts of Eastern Canada and the United States to support the uprising. You may recall, prime minster, that the same thing happened at the railway blockages at Deseronto in the spring of 2007 and summer of 2008, and on a larger scale at Caledonia when the situation turned ugly there later that year."

Geldt interrupted sharply. "There's no uprising, colonel. We're not using that word." Hemp nodded in agreement, but Bishop, regarding Geldt with open contempt, snapped, "Carry on, Colonel Dobson."

Ian Dobson shifted focus. "We've also detected what we think may be hostile activities in the James Bay-Radisson area. The information is fragmented at the moment, but local police have noted several non-residents in the area, including a former Canadian Forces warrant officer who has been seen with native leaders suspected of subversive leanings. Other indications of threats in the province are being analyzed at the moment."

Hemp was suddenly fully alert. "Wait a minute. Are you suggesting that there is a threat to the James Bay facilities?" He looked around the table at his cabinet colleagues. "Surely, one pissed-off ex-soldier isn't going to blow up the great dam. General, I don't want anything like this type of alarmist statement reaching the press or the Quebec premier. Or anyone, in fact. Honestly, you people..."

Andy Bishop cut him off. "Prime minister, we can only respond to the information we receive, and prudence must be the watchword until we can confirm the facts. But the facilities at James Bay are themselves vulnerable and would be very difficult to rescue if they were suddenly attacked. The power lines that run from there to the south are even more vulnerable and are extremely difficult to guard. A few 'pissed-off' ex-soldiers, or for that matter just a few angry citizens with some dynamite, certainly could interfere seriously with the power supply."

Hemp blinked at him. "So what are you suggesting we do?"

"What I'm already doing with the units we have—basically issuing preliminary orders to bring units and aircraft to a higher degree of readiness—to give you as many options as possible. There aren't that many. But since you ask for my recommendation, I advise the cabinet to consider a three-point deterrence plan: first, a preventive deployment of small combat units to the James Bay region; second, bring the combat brigade in Valcartier to readiness to move into Quebec City and Montreal to support the SQ; and third, I also recommend that we begin to alert reserve unit headquarters to prepare, and to start recalling their people, for vital point protection duties.

"I make these recommendations understanding, of course, that such measures would certainly reach the media. With all due respect to the, uh, public relations side of things, prime minister, as chief of defence staff, I am formally advising you that it is critically important that the government move to deter any violent disturbances before they occur. The hesitation of the SQ has already emboldened the native rebels and things are likely to get badly out of hand in short order if we don't act."

Hemp reached for a glass of water. "Well, Christ, we can't go sending the army all over the place. I don't want any obvious moves, and we can leave James Bay to the Quebec authorities. I assume they have the same intelligence that you have? So, General Bishop, you do whatever you need to do to ready your troops, but do it quietly, behind the scenes. Also, get somebody talking to the SQ, but I don't think we can just walk into Quebec. It's a bit tricky, you know." Hemp hesitated, actually worse off for the information Dobson had given him, which had lessened his ignorance without increasing his understanding. "Okay, I see the big picture, thank you, colonel."

The "bit tricky" part Hemp referred to had also been a problem for Prime Minister Brian Mulroney during the 1990 Oka crisis. As a rule, Canadians tend to be sympathetic to native protestors, and recoil from any use of force against them—so long as the trouble isn't in their own backyard, of course. Moreover, many English Canadians, fatigued at being called the oppressors of Quebec, were eager to side with natives crying "oppressor" at Quebec City. They were especially agitated when the Quebec premier, Madeleine Commeau, a separatist by conviction and a ruthless negotiator by nature, went on television crying for blood. "Les sauvages must be put down now and hard ... Quebec will not put up with another Indian blockage of Montreal or attacks on the highways."

"Listen," Hemp said to the room, "here's what Commeau said to me this morning. 'Jack, there'll be no more Okas. You get these Indians under control or I'm going to let the SQ sort it out. If that doesn't work, I will call in the army and you know I can do it without your permission.'"

Actually Hemp didn't know anything of the sort. He was as ignorant of the laws governing civil-military relations in Canada as he was of anything else to do with the military. In his entire time in office, he had only talked to the CDS once, at a reception for the Secretary General of the United Nations.

"So someone tell me what she's talking about," Hemp said, getting to his feet and pacing around his chair, a sure warning to his staff that he was greatly frustrated. He spoke to no one in particular. "I can't go shooting Indians in Quebec or anywhere else. The rest of Canada wouldn't put up with it for a minute. What does she expect me to do, satisfy Quebec's demand to fight their old battles with the Iroquois and tell the rest of Canada they don't matter?"

He turned to the CDS. "General Bishop, what does she mean by saying she can call on the army without my permission? They're federal troops, after all." Hemp sat down and all eyes turned to the CDS.

The CDS hardly knew where to begin. A complex answer would befuddle the prime minister, but he decided to keep it simple for the moment; there was enough confusion in the room as it was.

"Prime minister, according to the National Defence Act, the provinces may request what's called 'aid of the civil power' from the chief of the defence staff, who would then be compelled to provide armed forces whenever the provincial authorities believe they cannot control a riot or other threat to public safety." Bishop watched heads turn around the table, including the prime minister's, who shot a sudden questioning glance at his chief of staff. Then he continued.

"In other situations of this sort, the FLQ crisis of 1970, for example, the problems at Oka and so on, the chief of the defence staff has, of course, informed the minister of defence and the prime minister of the request and his plan to respond and consulted with them. But it is his call whether he sends in a corporal's guard or a brigade."

The prime minister stared at him and snapped, "So you're telling me if Commeau calls you and asks for the army, I just have to sit here and let her take them and use them as she sees fit?"

"In the starkest terms, yes, that's the law, prime minister. If the premier of Quebec were to make a formal request, then I would be obliged to make some kind of response. But I hasten to add from what we know of the situation at this moment, there is as yet no need for an overt deployment of troops and I am prepared to tell Premier Commeau that in person."

Everyone sat waiting for Hemp to respond, but the prime minister just sat fiddling with his pencil. Finally Eddie Geldt broke the silence. "Well, we could let her make the request, and if anything bad happens, it really isn't your fault, prime minister. You could distance yourself… the government, I mean… pretty easily from any, uh, untoward incidents. I mean, if we have no choice, then the media would point to Commeau or the army."

Hemp glared at Geldt, who fell silent. The PM did his best to look thoughtful as he replied, "Eddie, the military is under my control and I don't want anyone thinking it's not. And of course we're not hanging the guys and gals in uniform out to dry, not this government. Plus the media wouldn't let us just blame Quebec. No, I think we have to try to get to the native leaders and find a deal. Eddie, you get on it right away. Haven't we got a couple of those people on the payroll? And get that old fart Labbé, my so-called Quebec lieutenant, tell him to get on the phone and tell Commeau to cool it."

He turned to Bishop and Riley. "General, if you get a request from Quebec, you hotfoot it to Riley's office; he'll speak with me and we'll give you the game plan. Thanks. I really appreciate your attitude." Turning to the rest of the room, he continued in the familiar Hemp bluster, "Okay, guys, we can handle this. Remember, there's no crisis if we don't admit to one, right?"

He got up, and Eddie Geldt followed him out the door. Hemp grabbed Geldt's elbow and hissed, "Good suggestion Eddie, but damn it, you should keep that stuff to yourself. You just pissed off the military guys and you know I don't trust them. Bishop is worse than the rest of them—they're not team players. He says something, then the rest of them all say the same thing. It's worse than dealing with union bosses.

"Anyway, have your guys draw up a couple of statements just in case. You know, 'I deeply regret the actions of the armed forces and the loss of lives, heads will roll, etc.' How do I fire Bishop? Check that out, but keep it quiet, for Christ's sake. And get a meeting organized with Al Onanole, just him and me. We're going to need all the strange bedfellows we can round up."

Thursday, September 2, 1050 hours
Ottawa: Office of the Grand Chief of the First Nations
Federation

Chief Al Onanole, Grand Chief of the First Nations Federation, had played native politics in Ottawa his whole working life. For the most part, he was successful at the game, at least as these things are normally reckoned, which accounted for his recent election to a third term. He kept the money flowing, kept native concerns on the public agenda, and kept the status of his organization intact—meaning that in the minds of the non-native public the FNF was the legitimate and sole arbiter between the native community and the federal government. Politicians listened when he demanded "a place at the table" beside the prime minister. In return, Onanole acted as the helpful fixer, making sure native issues never became a significant political embarrassment for the major politicians and their interests.

Alan Onanole was born in 1950 on the Sweetgrass First Nation reserve in Saskatchewan, the middle child in a family of two brothers and six sisters. Along with his brothers and sisters, he had been raised by their maternal grandmother, who had taken over the job because his mother and father had both been "incapacitated most of their lives," as Alan later remarked, by "serving hard times in residential schools." Thanks to his grandmother's steady hand and his own unyielding determination, Alan managed to graduate from high school, the only one in his family who did so. He went on to study law at McGill and Native Studies at Trent, but his fast-growing involvement in aboriginal politics prevented his graduation in either program.

During a rare visit home one summer, the band elders came calling. They needed someone to manage the band's land claims, and as a bright, young, educated person, he had been deemed the perfect person to deal with the white government and its confusing rules. Alan was only twenty-four years old and had had no thought at the time of winning such a post, but he attended the band's meeting in the reserve's community hall that evening. As he often later liked to recall, it was there that he gave his first political speech. He told a story of a far-off day when the band and all native people would be free and prosperous, when the white man would apologize for the evils they had poured on the people, and how he would try to lead the people to that day.

Al Onanole won that election and many others over the years. He was now an unassailable Grand Chief. But Alan was tired. Too many fights, too many challenges from young native radicals, too many new problems— drugs and gangs and so on—that sapped his energy and resolve. The comfortable life in Ottawa had its costs and distractions as well.

He watched with growing dread the storm he could see gathering over the people. It was a great danger, if it were allowed to grow, that might bring the whole weight of an angry, vengeful country down on the careful consensus of moderation he had constructed with Canadian politicians. He knew that they would turn to him eventually to solve "the Molly Grace problem," even though Alan wasn't sure he could placate native demands this time. Nevertheless, in the circumstances, the call from Jack Hemp's office wasn't unexpected

"Could Chief Onanole," purred the ever-so-courteous PMO staffer, "stop by to meet with Prime Minister Hemp in the Langevin offices this evening at seven o'clock?"

"Yes, certainly," came the reassuring reply. "And the topic?"

Courtesy hesitated slightly to avoid any hint of a demand rather than a request. "The prime minister's office suggests that Chief Onanole might like to discuss the current, ah, situation in northern Quebec."

"Yes," said reassurance. "I believe Chief Onanole would be pleased to do that."

Thursday, September 2, 1130 hours
Akwesasne: The Complex

Molly and Bill walked into the main ops room at the Complex. Her planning staff sat eagerly anticipating the opening moves of the campaign they had devised over the summer, rehearsed on paper so many times, and dreamed of for years.

As usual, Molly offered no pleasantries, just dropped her notebook on the table and said, "Right, what are they up to?"

Bill clicked on his PowerPoint displays. "NDHQ is collecting information and holding meetings with the RCMP and CSIS. They have picked up the situation we set out for them, including the fact that Boucanier is in Radisson and talking to Neetha and other 'discredited Rangers,' as the security forces call the dropouts. The agencies are suspicious of these meetings, but haven't done much about them ... seems the SQ doesn't want to play. So, basically no resources have been sent to the region; they're nibbling the bait but haven't taken the big bite yet. The situation in Montreal and Quebec City also has them very worried, but at present they think the SQ can hold on. Units in CFB Valcartier have been assembled and are ready to move, but the prime minister has the brakes on, so our sources tell us. Some Western units are on stand-by to fly east, and aircraft are being positioned for that effort, but no one has moved, except a few advanced recce parties. However, I think they'll go if we push them just a little bit more."

"Is there any hint that they suspect the Western strategy?"

"No. One junior intelligence staff officer at NDHQ did write a memo pointing out the vulnerability of the West if everyone were moved east, but our man in the headquarters intercepted the memo and managed to misplace it in the files. I wouldn't underestimate Bishop and his staff, and we can't penetrate the Armed Forces Council. But my assessment is that any warning voices will be ignored by the politicians if we turn up the heat in the East just a little at a time. Besides, the more we give them to think about in Quebec, the less time commanders and their staffs have to think about other contingencies."

"So," Molly said, "where are we and what comes next?"

"We're more or less where we thought we would be, kind of a hang-fire. The media are covering the blockades and are predictably split—the French press are against the natives, and the CBC and Toronto papers, except the *National Post,* of course, oppose any action by the feds. What next? I think it's time to go to phase two and put more cheese in the trap."

Molly looked around the room, inviting comments, but everyone just nodded. "Okay, let's move. We want a few small car bombs near military targets, the complete closure of the Montreal transit system and bridges, a few non-lethal attacks on rural SQ stations to intimidate the cops, and put the James Bay plan into operation—D-Day early morning Friday.

"Tell our Ottawa sources to keep an eye on NDHQ and our eyes out west to set up a watch at the military bases. They're to tell us immediately of any movements, even if it means taking a security risk by sending the message in clear. At this point, their cover matters less than our getting timely information. Finally, get some leaks out to the media suggesting that 'the Indians' are going to kidnap politicians, rob banks, and set off roadside bombs if the army moves out of Valcartier. Questions?"

No one stirred. Molly glanced at Bill. "Is the Winnipeg campaign ready?"

Whitefish closed his notebook. "Yes. Stevenson spoke to me a little while ago to confirm the change of readiness status. He's confident that he can pull it off, but he warned that several local bands and some gang toughs—the Warrior Posse, for example—are excited by the Quebec situation and ready to do something rash. Sam is taking steps to control them and has several band leaders making appeals for calm. They're harmless and don't know the plans, so it's all good. They sound sincere, and they *are,* actually, and the local white leaders who think the band chiefs are in charge are of course reacting like this is the worst time to do anything provocative, so they're adding to the paralysis."

Molly pushed her chair away from the table and stood up. "Fine, do it. We will meet later this afternoon to gauge the results."

Thursday, September 2, 1455 hours
Ottawa: NDHQ, Thirteenth Floor, Conference Room B

General Bishop was in a stern mood. He'd called this operations meeting of the Armed Forces Council—to which no civil servants were invited— soon after leaving the Langevin Block with the shaken defence minister. He set out his intentions as soon as he stalked up to the table.

"Ladies and gentlemen, no notes please. I believe the nation is threat-

ened and that the difficulties in Quebec may not be the most serious matter before us. René Lepine and I discussed the possibility of a feint in the
East as a lead-up to an attack in the West. There is scant intelligence to
support this notion, but in a brief conversation with RCMP Commissioner
Richard, he reported that his detachments in the West, though not in B.C.,
and on the East Coast were reporting gatherings of young native people,
increasing hostility to the police, and minor outbreaks of violence in some
towns against non-natives and on some reserves against some residents.
We both concluded that we need a much more detailed intelligence picture from these regions and he has taken the lead in developing a collection plan with CSIS.

"However, we can't wait until we get more intelligence. We have an
immediate problem in Quebec and I anticipate a request to aid the civil
powers from the premier within days, possibly hours. I want to tell you,
and you will keep these remarks to yourselves and not discuss them, even
among yourselves, that I intend to interpret my powers as CDS in the
broadest possible way. I intend also to take full advantage of the prime
minister's vague directions to bring the Canadian Forces to a high stage
of alert. When the politicians wake up and say jump, we'll be more than
ready to go.

"To review: the CDS, as you all know, is appointed by order-in-council
and holds the appointment at pleasure. The prime minister under normal
circumstances can relieve me any time he wants to. But these are not normal circumstances. I share with the government a responsibility for the
defence of Canada, a fact well established in law and custom. I am also,
like everyone in uniform, subordinate not to the prime minister but to
the governor general, who constitutionally appointed me to this position
on the advice of the government. I think the distinction was left in place
for times like these."

Bishop paused to let the message settle in his commanders' minds. "I
will visit the governor general tomorrow morning to discuss affairs of state
and the conditions and circumstances of the Canadian Forces. Under the
circumstances, it is critically important that the governor general be kept
thoroughly, and immediately, informed of our situation, our decisions,
and our thinking."

The CDS paused again, then flipped open his briefing book and continued in a more normal tone. "Now you can take whatever notes you need. First, Benjamin, I would like a briefing on my constitutional situation for my conversation with the governor general for tomorrow morning."

The judge advocate general—the JAG in military parlance—a studious, balding, military lawyer in thick glasses, took a note. "I presume in two copies and marked secret?"

The CDS nodded and turned to René Lepine. "René, you work closely with the DCDS to build a plan to move units of Canada Command into Montreal and Quebec City in support of the SQ, but, uh, I mean support according to our directions. Once I give the order to execute it, it's yours. But I want you and your commanders to be nimble. Feel uneasy about this situation, that's the best way to avoid surprises. I also want a full update of the operational plan by tomorrow evening, again supporting the SQ to reinforce security at the James Bay sites if they're threatened and to retake them if they're captured by criminals or terrorists. We need in that plan some ideas on how to protect the power grid as well.

"Let me know your assessment of the force requirements, but for initial planning purposes you can count on at least 5 Brigade from Valcartier, an infantry battalion group from out west, and the Special Service Regiment from Trenton for operations in the James Bay region. The force is to be given robust rules of engagement and the JAG will help define what that means for operations inside Canada. Not quite the same for operations against foreign irregular troops, of course."

Bishop looked to the chief of the air staff, Lieutenant General Scott Hamilton. "Scott will get the necessary aircraft assembled to move your units and support them once they're deployed." General Hamilton nodded his acknowledgement of the CDS's orders.

An unspoken message passed between the Bishop and Lepine. "Yeah, René, I know what you're thinking," Bishop said, "but what I gave you is what we've got until I can get the prime minister to call out the reserves. So what you see is what you've got. I am worried about the West too, but without any clear signs of trouble, I want as many troops on the ground in Quebec as possible and at the first opportunity presented to us by hostile native actions, at the barricades, for instance. I want the situation resolved forcefully, and quickly, as an example to the rest of these so-called warriors elsewhere.

"That's all for now, ladies and gentlemen. I don't have to remind you, but I will. Hold this information and these plans and intentions very closely. Need to know only. Questions?" Bishop paused and looked around the table. "No? Good. See you later this evening."

As he left the conference room, Bishop turned to his executive assistant. "Vince, call the Pentagon. I want to speak with the chairman of the Joint Chiefs of Staff, General Leonardo, at his convenience, of course, but, uh, I do mean at his *earliest* convenience."

Thursday, September 2, 1640 hours
Outside Radisson

Will Boucanier clicked off his cellphone and stowed it in his pack; next stop for it was the bottom of the river. He had followed the drill—made his recce, completed his plan, given his orders—and now he sat waiting for the word to deploy. Army units don't simply jump up and go into action; at least, not those that win battles, Moving into operations is, or ought to be, like performing a well-rehearsed grand ballet.

So many things need to be done in a coordinated way to bring the many elements of a combat operation to the right place with the right resources at the right time. Troops must be warned; plans made at each level of command; weapons, ammunition, and supplies assembled; and units moved into position to attack or defend an objective. Time is always fleeting, and to the badly organized it is always a menacing foe.

As a leader, Will knew it was also his duty to prepare his troops, not just by reminding them of the details of the plans, but by reminding them of their mission and of the cause they were fighting for. "Remember always," he had told his Ranger leaders, "we're the Native People's Army. I want you to remember not just the people bit but also that our cause is their cause and it's a worthy cause. I want you to believe that you're going to win, because you're the people's army. It's 'People's War, People's Army' as the great Vietnamese commander, Vo Nguyên Giap, described the essence of revolutionary warfare. We're a revolutionary army, and if we're going to win, we need to act like one. The people and the army are one, and our people are counting on their army to help win their freedom."

Boucanier knew it wasn't enough to give speeches, something he rarely ever did. If he expected his junior leaders to follow battle procedure drills, he had to keep on top of them himself. And ordinarily he'd have been on the ground moving from one patrol to the next, checking and coaching and checking again, as he had in the Canadian Forces.

Instead, here was the coded message sooner than expected. Time, the pitiless, aggressive opponent, was at it again. No matter. Battle procedure was nearly complete, and he had enough time, just enough, to sort out and allocate the "special goods" and deploy his troops. He had told his patrol leaders to expect eight hours notice before they had to move anywhere. Now he began the steady, deliberate reduction in warning times.

Will walked outside, down the street away from the hotel, found a cool, shaded corner, and pulled out another, as yet unused cellphone. He dialled; a suspicious voice said, "Yes?"

"Racing Rabbit. Meet me in three hours at the place. Put your people on three hours notice to move from eighteen hundred hours tonight. I repeat, three hours from eighteen hundred, that's six p.m. for the clueless. Remind them they're going hunting. A truck will arrive tonight at your shed. Off-load the equipment and pack most of it. Use the items I told you about to give your people a quick refresher course. Once they're assembled, no one leaves the area, no phone calls, no beer. I will get back to you once your people are set. Any questions?"

On the other end Joe Neetha paused, startled by the "go" code word. "No, don't think so. It's really going down, eh?"

"You bet. Just do as you were told and things will go okay. And again, no beer. No beer. No beer. Got it?"

"Yeah. We're ready."

"Good." Will hit the off button, dialled again, then repeated the code word and the message to the other cells in turn: be ready to go on three hours notice as of tonight at 1800 hours. He warned the leaders that they too could expect "a package" from the south, and told one cell to be ready to meet a special team later that day.

Calls made, he unfolded his map case and rechecked the chart of the main area of operations, the La Grande Rivière corridor from the airfield at Chisasibi to the Hydro works at Radisson. The cells on the road southward and along the Hydro-Québec installations there were mostly in place to support Operation Thunder. His mission was to isolate the Robert-Bourassa generating facilities and literally turn off Montreal and New York City. But the mission behind the implied mission, the one he kept to himself, was to support operations elsewhere about which he knew very little, except that they had targets somehow much more important than the La Grande.

That wasn't his problem. His problem, and his plan, was quite simple. At H-hour his A Team of thirty warriors, under his command, would seize the main operating room, plant explosives near the turbines, detain the workers in a secure location, and establish a security perimeter around the site and on the roads leading to it. He assumed the local police would react first, probably carelessly, in which case he intended to capture as many of them as he could. The SQ was bound to show up eventually, but he'd been warned that the Committee would issue a statement and ultimatum to the premier of Quebec as soon as the action started, which meant the SQ might come running early. He wasn't worried if they did.

Will had placed his C Team under one of his best leaders, and gave her his strongest warriors and orders to take control of Radisson, bring up the trucks to join Will's A Team once they had secured the generating station, and then to guard the town and the approaches to the station. The team would ambush the SQ without warning if they appeared on the roads any-where near the town or the station. But Will expected the SQ to behave like their comrades had in other fights with the warriors. At Oka for instance. SQ tactics were very simple: "They came, they saw, they ran away." But if by chance some stayed to fight, they'd lose. There just wouldn't be many prisoners afterward.

While the A and C Teams were securing the La Grande and Radisson, his B Team under Joe Neetha would take Chisasibi and environs, blocking the road to Radisson and capturing the local police. Neetha was to hold the town and surround the airfield, securing the approaches and key firing positions, but leaving the airfield open to lure the army onto the field. The idea was to keep his guys out of the obvious target areas during the initial landing, but as soon as a few Hercs were on the ground, they were to open up harassing fire, disable the planes, and pin the troops on the airfield. If that failed, or to be honest even if it worked initially, he was to fall back along the road to Radisson, join C Team and hold the road, or at least delay the army's drive towards the La Grande as long as possible.

Will knew this was a big gamble for several reasons. Not only was almost half his force exposed at Chisasibi, far from the crucial power complex, but he couldn't be sure the army would even try to fly in a force to retake the La Grande from the ground; they might get bold and just parachute straight onto the site at Radisson. He was betting on an air assault on Chisasibi airfield, then a forced march up the hundred kilometres to Radisson, even though it was slower, because jumping into the La Grande site would be a hard-assed tactic. If they did go the para route and took the station, he had a nasty surprise ready for them. One way or another, the army would eventually have to take Chisasibi, if only to support the operation. And Joe Neetha's job was to make that necessity as costly as possible.

The reality was that Will had to count on the fifty warriors at Chisasibi to hold the airfield area for several hours and then withdraw slowly up the road to Radisson and pin down any rescue force on the road, with luck, for several days. The thirty warriors of C Team would take the Radisson police station and radio station, and control the population, and then on his order move a section down the road to Chisasibi, to meet up with Neetha. Will was sure the importance of the target and his obvious actions, which he expected the army to track on satellites, would force the politicians and the army commanders to stick their heads deep into Molly's noose.

And it was quite a noose. On his southern flank, his cells would knock down transmission lines and towers to add considerably to the problem caused by the stoppage at the generating facilities themselves and heighten the risk and anxiety for government planners and rescuers. Once rescue columns moving from the south—he assumed first the SQ and then army units from Valcartier—were committed on Highway 109 from Val-d'Or through Matagami, his teams along that route would create havoc by blowing bridges and beaver dams and cratering roads. The more noise and action, the bigger the reaction in the East. And that, though he didn't know the details, was a key part of Molly's game plan.

Planners at the Complex had initially worried that it would be too difficult for inexperienced members of local cells to break up the transmission system. But Boucanier, with the aid of his ex-army engineers, had quickly showed them just how simply it could be done. The towers supporting the transmission lines came in two kinds but both could easily be disabled with three simple C4 plastic explosive charges in a standard configuration. All you had to do was put cutting charges on two legs and a third "kicker charge" higher up the structure on the opposite side rigged to an equally simple delaying fuse, a pre-made "ring-main" of detonating cord. When you set the thing off, the two cutting charges would sever the two legs, and a second later the kicker would twist the whole structure without bringing it down. That was actually important, because it meant repair crews would have to take down the damaged towers before they could get new wires in place, which was much more time-consuming than pulling aside a tower already on the ground, even if you didn't have to worry about booby traps. Which, of course, the cells would make sure they did.

Just to be absolutely sure, Will had tested the procedure a few months earlier in a raid on a transmission tower in the Eastern Townships, deliberately mounted by an amateur group that had been mentored by a veteran explosives expert. The evident sabotage was news for a day or two, but NPC disinformation tactics led investigators to blame disgruntled union members, not native radicals. The demonstration, however, convinced the Committee to give Will the resources and the specialists he needed for the real show.

Of course, knocking down towers takes time, and there was always the chance that an assault team could be surprised and shot up by a patrolling helicopter. There were enough cells that one or two such mishaps wouldn't matter. But again, to be safe, there was a backup plan to pull down power lines without destroying towers. It wasn't nearly as effective because it was much simpler to repair, but it was easier and faster and could be done even by a totally amateur idiot with minimal practice. It was a technique taken off the Internet from a pamphlet for the ultra-low-tech "counter-revolution in military affairs."

All it took, according to the pamphlet, was an all-terrain vehicle or, in winter, a snowmobile, some heavy nylon line attached to a stout plastic rope and then to a steel cable, and a bow and arrow or, though it lacked a little symbolism, a new-model crossbow. At the lowest place between two towers, you attached the nylon lead line assembly to the arrow or the crossbow bolt and fired it over the lines. Once it was over, you pulled on the light line until you got the stronger plastic rope in your hands, which you then hooked to the ATV or snowmobile, and you drove slowly away. The plastic rope pulled the steel cable over the transmission lines, shorting them out and destroying them in a great flash of sparks and fire. The plastic rope would melt and perhaps even catch fire but it would insulate the vehicle from the electric shock. Job done, the crew could then race home or to a new site miles away. This technique had also been tested, and, fortunately, the Hydro-Québec authorities had concluded it was either some kind of weird prank or another isolated piece of union mischief.

Satisfied with his review of the terrain and his plans in each part of it, Will closed his map case and strolled to the nearby coffee shop. He might not beat the army, but that wasn't the real mission. He was absolutely confident that he would accomplish the vital, covert mission of drawing enough forces to northern Quebec, and keeping them there long enough, to denude the rest of the country of its few defenders.

He stepped into the coffee shop and greeted Constable Bob Ignace, who was enjoying his daily doughnut. "Great day for doughnuts, Bob. Gotta watch the waistline, though."

Ignace shifted in his chair and growled a reply. "I thought you were fishing. Maybe you need a lesson after all. Or perhaps you're up to no good with that asshole Neetha." His tone softened a little. "Why don't you really open a lodge, Will? You're a good guy. Why hang around making trouble? What kind of example do you think you're setting for the kids? We don't need radicals around here; we need guys with jobs and families, guys who stay sober five days a week, put food on the table, and don't hit their wife or kids. Where is Neetha anyway?"

"Can't say, Bob. You know the fishing business, 'need to know' only." Will ordered coffee and took it to a seat at the other end of the shop, watching out the window as his tail, SQ or more likely RCMP, crossed the street and hung around trying not to be totally obvious while Will slowly drank his coffee.

Thursday, September 2, 1720 hours
Akwesasne: The Complex

By late that afternoon the staff in the Complex were clearly excited. No more drills, rehearsals, fits and starts. It was really happening. But when Molly walked in she was as cool as ever. "Okay, what do we know?" she asked without preamble.

Bill Whitefish glanced at his notes and said, "We know the armed forces are at a high state of alert and have reinforced their bases with a few reserve personnel. The Patricias in Edmonton are assembling, but have no order to move, although the supporting Herc squadrons are on alert and the crews are sleeping on the base. CFB Trenton has recalled all air crews and search-and-rescue teams, and all aircraft on training and domestic flights, and put them on short notice to move. The Valcartier brigade is the most active. The troops have reported to their units, vehicles are loaded, and commanders have tentative plans to move to Montreal and Quebec City. But no one is going anywhere right now.

"Significantly, the Valcartier units are on light ammo loads—just small arms weapons and not a lot of ammo in the lead units. Seems they're preparing to suppress a riot rather than fight a battle. But the Western units and the Special Service Regiment are going heavy, lots of heavy weapons and ammo, which suggests they're going to be the backup if things get nasty. There are few indications that anyone is much worried about the West, though local RCMP detachments near The Pas have asked for reinforcements because of the big rendezvous there. They have also reported conversations in bars about a scheme to 'get whitey' but they think it refers to the usual local chatter by the Warrior Posse." Bill paused, inviting questions.

"Go on," Molly ordered.

"According to our sources in NDHQ, the prime minister is in a sweat. He's placed restrictions on the CDS, no moves without orders from him, even if Quebec asks for assistance. Apparently his main concern is to avoid suggesting to the public that there's a crisis out there." The staff looked to Molly as Bill folded his papers.

"Right," she said, stepping to the front of the table. "Let's give the boy a few hints. Are the Quebec teams ready, and what about Boucanier and the Western columns?"

"Warned and ready as planned," confirmed the chief of staff.

"Okay, then, let's put the ball in play. Remember, nothing's going to go as planned. You all have to think ahead and expect to get half the results from twice as much effort as you thought you'd need. Any number of circumstances can throw plans into disarray. Everything's hostage to uncertainty. Only a fool believes that rotten chance evens things out over time. You can't count on getting half the bounces your way. You're here to worry and to anticipate the next right move, especially if what you just did didn't work. I want to outpace the government's ability to act, to keep them chasing the wrong rabbit. Don't forget, the guys on the other side have it no better, and in many ways a lot worse than you do."

Molly turned to her notes. "Okay. Give the Quebec cells the order to go beginning at first light tomorrow. I want chaos in the streets for morning rush hour, the police in a panic by noon, and a car bomb detonated against a military vehicle outside the gates of CFB Valcartier at the first sign that they're responding. Bill, you get hold of the moles in NDHQ. We want to know immediately when the Western units get the go for Quebec and how many are on their way to Radisson." She paused to let the fast-scribbling staff catch up.

"Op Thunder at James Bay is to begin at first light tomorrow, Friday. We'll judge the federal reaction tomorrow night and expect the main event to launch thirty-six hours later in Winnipeg. Right, there's lots to do, so everyone do your part."

Thursday, September 2, 1810 hours,
Ottawa: Canada Command HQ

Lieutenant General René Lepine sat alone at the long conference table waiting to begin a secure video conference call to his base commanders. He had at hand an ordered jumble of data provided by his staff in Canada Command headquarters. This situation looked like a complex, nightmarish game of Clue where there could be any number of villains and losing wasn't an option. One of the main villains identified by the CSIS and one of Native People's Army's best leaders was Sam Stevenson. Imagine, Lepine thought disgustedly, my once friend and RMC classmate Sam Stevenson in Winnipeg with the radicals. What tricks, Lepine wondered, has Stevenson devised that we haven't considered? What would I be doing if I were him?

As Lepine and everyone else in the military knew, the Canadian Forces had been running on empty for years, depending on the courage and can-do attitude of dedicated volunteers. They were a fearsome lot, well experienced in the wars of the twenty-first century, but while good people are necessary to military capabilities, they are not sufficient. Without logistics, soldiers, no matter how good, get hung out to dry.

Lepine had too little equipment, too few supplies, and the one thing he had lots of, too much in fact, were under-manned, under-equipped bases maintained across the country—many solely for partisan, political reasons. Today, they were vulnerable targets. If he protected them all with real combat troops, he wouldn't have any units left to deploy. If he left them to the best efforts of the cooks and supply types, the "base defence force," he might lose the bases and the people left to protect them. The correct military answer was obviously to evacuate those bases of little operational value and concentrate his forces on those of high value. But he knew, before he even hinted at the idea to the CDS, that the prime minister would faint at the suggestion. So you do what you can.

The video screen at the end of the room snapped to life. After the commanders had checked in, Lepine opened the meeting directly. "Ladies and gentlemen, we haven't a lot of time. So I'll give you the outline and depend on you to protect your bases and support my operations. You're all aware of the situation and you have the latest intelligence report issued this morning.

"You are to assume that your bases will be attacked by lightly-armed groups intent on disrupting your operations. I want maximum efforts to secure base perimeters, post armed guards and patrols, and otherwise severely restrict access to the bases. High-value targets on the base, like aircraft parked outside and communications and fuel sites, are to be protected with sandbags and steel barriers and armed guards of the base defence force.

"Essential civilian employees are to report to work, but you have to expect that some of them might not show up, especially if there is a deadly incident at any of the bases. Soldiers' families on bases are a particular worry, and without ordering any formal evacuations, you are to encourage members to send their families elsewhere. My words of the day for you are: 'Dig in and get serious.'

"A major concern is the safety of the scores of aircraft stationed on wide-open bases across the country. They're highly vulnerable, thin-skinned, and must be protected. At the first hint of real danger, we will concentrate the aircraft on one or two bases. Jim," Lepine said, indicating the commander at CFB Bagotville, "I want you to prepare to send your squadron of CF18 fighters to Cold Lake. I'd rather hold them in the East, but no base there has the resources to maintain and ready these complicated machines for operations."

"Sir, we've anticipated this move and have made some arrival arrangements with Sandra at Cold Lake. I sure could use a few Herc flights to get some equipment and tech personnel moving."

"Yes, so could I. Unfortunately, many of these forty-year-old aircraft are unreliable and will be needed to move the combat units wherever. I'll see what we can do, but we have to ration the aircraft.

"In any case, I want the Hercules fleet to be concentrated at Trenton. It's the safest base and close to the action in Quebec; the remainder will be moved to Edmonton. We will waive most of the usual safety restrictions and use aircraft currently grounded for precautionary reasons if the situation becomes critical.

"Transportation plans are ready to use railway trains in place of aircraft for short hauls and even cross-country deployments if necessary. But as I am sure you all appreciate, road and rail transportation could rapidly become problematic. The worst situation I can imagine is having an entire combat unit on a train somewhere north of Lake Superior trapped by the sudden destruction of the line before and behind it.

"Even in southern Ontario, previous scattered native blockages of railways have effectively shut down major transportation routes. But I assume in the developing situation local and provincial police will be given authority to clear the routes. That order may increase their demands on us for assistance. One encounter with my infantry, however regrettable, will, I think, rapidly clear radicals off the tracks, not only at the offending site but also for kilometres down the line. Let's hope it doesn't come to that, though.

"As you harden your bases, I want you to look carefully at your stocks of essential supplies and fuel lines into the bases. You should anticipate that power will be cut and prepare on-base generators to maintain essential services.

"Okay, I want my principal staff officer to say a few words and then we can take questions."

The commander of operations, Colonel Stan Owens, spoke first. "Hello to everyone. Most units are at least at eighty per cent effective manning. The major training has been halted and your people on course and some new trainees are on their way to their units. New recruits who have at least completed basic training are being sent to various units. Commanders will have to whip them into shape in a hurry. The military schools are being combed for essential trades and specialist officers and so are the reserve units. A discrete but urgent call-up of reserve unit commanding officers is underway; we're trying not to alert the press but either way we'll get the guys in place. Basically, we're pretty good to go.

"All brigades are reporting op ready or near op ready. The airborne commandos of the Special Service Regiment are concentrated in Trenton and completing readiness drills with the aircrews. CFB Valcartier is at three hours notice to move, since we expect it to be called out first. The other units in the East are at twelve hours notice as of right now, and the Western units are at twenty-fours hours notice, mostly waiting for aircraft arrivals and rigging."

He turned things over to J2, Intelligence. "Gentlemen and ladies, I'll be brief. There really isn't much new to report. The police have some persons of interest under surveillance in Quebec and Winnipeg, and they're watching that so-called rendezvous in The Pas. The only new development involves natives in the James Bay Hydro area booking off work in unusual numbers. They all say they're going hunting, which their bosses find hard to believe. But anyway, they're gone. Oh, and a local constable keeps bugging the SQ about this one retired soldier, Will Boucanier, who he thinks is definitely stirring native trouble. Anyone know this guy?"

A lieutenant colonel down the table broke in. "Is that the airborne Warrant Officer Will Boucanier—Medal of Military Valour? Sir, I served with him in Afghanistan in JTF2. We should tell the SQ or Mounties to watch out. Boucanier's one tough, smart cookie. I hope he's still on our side."

The J2 looked to his commander. "I'll check it out, sir. See if we have a positive ID on the guy. That's it for now."

Lepine took comments and situational updates from the base commanders and then closed the meeting. "Okay everyone, thanks."

He stood up and beckoned to Commodore Miller, his chief of staff. A serious officer, nicknamed Shiny John by his colleagues, he was already pegged by them as the navy's next candidate for CDS. "John, let's get to the Ops Centre. I want to go over the James Bay plan with you."

Thursday, September 2, 1840 hours
Ottawa: Canada Command Operations Centre

The Canada Command Operations Centre was completed in early 2008 and was the most sophisticated, fully integrated and interactive intelligence and operation facility of the Canadian Forces. The situation room, though not large, provided each staff officer with access to secure computers and a wall full of electronic screens on which they could flash up maps, charts, and real-time images and operational data produced by remotely controlled, unmanned drones, high-altitude aircraft, satellites and communications intercepts in whatever dimension required. Officers could track forest fires and floods and follow the course of search-and-rescue, or SAR, aircraft minute-by-minute.

A powerful, flexible database made it possible to determine the whereabouts, activities, and strength of each unit in the command almost instantaneously. CCOC was supported by an intelligence staff, specialist teams of RCMP, Coast Guard, and emergency measures personnel permanently seconded to the Canada Command, and each team had its own place and specific duties in the centre.

The centre's vast communications network, with connections to the Canadian Forces NDOC, subordinate command headquarters, provincial emergency centres, RCMP headquarters, U.S. Northern Command in Colorado, and the Canadian Forces attaché in Washington, provided René Lepine and his staff with almost instant, correlated information. The staff might have been the brains of the command, but the "comms network" was its indispensable nervous system.

No one took much notice of the commander as he walked into the CCOC with his chief of staff. His people were used to the commander's habit of wandering in at any time of the day or night and appreciated his easy style around busy people. Commander Nick Pew, the CCOC director, put down his phone and walked over to greet the general.

"Afternoon, sir, anything special I can do?"

"Not yet, Nick. Anything unusual going on?" Lepine asked as he scanned the current ops display.

"Just the changing readiness status of the para unit in Trenton, sir. That's on time, although the Hercs are being bitchy as usual. We'll have an op-readiness state in a couple of hours. NDOC did report a short while ago that things are heating up in Montreal and their sources tell them the natives are planning a big show in town tomorrow morning. The SQ says they can handle it, and have put their so-called riot cops on standby. But the CDS expects an aid-of-the-civil-power requisition from Quebec at the first sign that things are getting out of hand."

Lepine settled into a chair. "Yeah, especially once the premier realizes she can have our guys for free and save SQ overtime payments. I'm not sure the politicians get it, Nick, but we need to be ready. What about James Bay?"

"Well, sir, thanks to USNorthCom, we have a satellite over the La

Grande, but everything there appears very still. Of course that could mean nothing's going to happen, or that everything's ready for something big to happen."

"Fine, Nick. John and I just need to view the region up close. Put it on screen three, please."

Nick Pew returned to his station, clicked a few computer keys, and sat quietly while his commander absorbed the information.

John Miller knew better than to interrupt Lepine when he was in this state. Instead, he took advantage of the boss's momentary distraction to shuffle through his notes and this morning's bundle of e-mail messages looking for items related to a suspected code word, Op Thunder. CSE listeners had picked it up a couple of times in the last few days in different cellphone nets in the Radisson region and near Montreal. What points of conversation in the ether, he wondered, connected these dots?

The J2 staff and CSIS were trying hard to break into the cellphone nets, but each contact vanished quickly because, evidently, whoever these guys were, they were smart enough to discard compromised cellphones, exchanging them for new ones working on new networks quite frequently. Still, they couldn't be carrying fifty cellphones each, so there was some hope of nabbing some of them. The chase through the airwaves continued.

After several minutes, Lepine interrupted his chief of staff. "John, give me the staff attack options once again please. On the wall charts if you can."

Miller put his notes on the table, turned with a laser pointer to the satellite-enhanced map to Lepine's left, and delivered a characteristically crisp, logical summary of the mountain of details in his head.

"The main features in the area are the village of Chisasibi and its airfield, the generating station at Radisson, the highways between them, and Highway 109 here, running south to Matagami and Val-d'Or. The terrain in between is too rugged for us, or the bad guys, to move through fast, and frankly there's nothing of interest anywhere in it. The generating station is the probable main target of any raid—the other Radisson facilities, the fifty-three-storey-high dams and so on, are simply too massive to attack successfully. The other glaring vulnerability is the five main transmission lines running some 1,400 kilometres south. They are wide open to attack and the only way to defend them would be saturation aerial surveillance spotting and neutralizing threats before they reached the lines."

He flicked the pointer's red dot onto a smaller side chart. "The population in the northern region, including about 3,000 natives, is displayed here. Mostly, it's a peaceful community." He turned back to the main map. "The facilities aren't really guarded, just locals with flashlights. NDHQ has tried to get the SQ to beef things up, but they say there's no need and it's too expensive."

Lepine deposited his pen grimly on the table. "Wait till the lights go out."

Miller paused briefly, then continued. "We conclude, obviously, that the generating station is the main vulnerability, the transmission lines are next, and if the attack is on a larger scale than quick sabotage and retreat, that the civil authority, police and officials will be scooped up and held prisoner, possibly as hostages. The attacking force would have to come from local native people—bringing in enough outsiders to do the job would be impossible to hide in a community this size and we've seen no sign of it. Therefore, we assume from the data and close intelligence, that the bad guys have about 100 young men and some women, lightly armed and poorly trained but led by ex-Rangers and some ex-Canadian Forces people who have moved back into the area. That's about it, sir."

The general walked to the map and ran his finger thoughtfully down the Chisasibi-to-Radisson road. "Okay. So what're our options, John?"

"It's not much of a combat challenge, once you're on the ground, sir. There's no way the bad guys can put up a fight against any kind of regular force; the only real issue could be taking back the generating station without damaging it. Getting there is the real trick. Here there are three main approaches we could use. First, we could drive up Highway 109 with a couple of companies with air support and take the area. But there are two problems there. First, it's a slow way in, even if unopposed, and we can't expect that. Given ambushes and obstacles, and we have to assume there would be both, it could turn into a slow, miserable crawl north, giving the opposition ample time to destroy the facilities, even cripple the dams as well as the station if they want to, then get away. Second, the obvious units to use from 5 Brigade will probably be busy elsewhere, in the south—in Montreal, for example."

Miller shifted his pointer to Chisasibi and the airfield. "Option two. We take Chisasibi and the airfield with guys from Trenton, use it as a base of ops, then drive or march up the road from there to Radisson. Two problems with that one also. First, it's also slow; we might have some opposition on arrival, and certainly have to expect it on the road. Second, the village is small and so is the airfield. We're doing a staff check at the moment with the air commanders, but you can see from the map that there's only one runway and it's so small we could only get one Herc in at a time. Then we'd have to turn it around, taxi back, and take off to clear the runway for the next one. That's very slow and very open to attack. And if one Herc were disabled on the active runway, game over. Unless the bad guys are idiots, they know that too—and whoever we're up against are not idiots."

He switched the map to Radisson and zoomed in close to the facilities. "So, option three: a para-op directly onto the site. At least this one has clear advantages: speed, surprise, direct action against the high-value target. It also has one big disadvantage: crappy dropping zones, with broken ground, boulders big as cars, deep ponds, and scrub trees all over the place. In fact, by the book, there aren't any dropping zones in the area. When we passed the close-up photos around a meeting of the para commanders, they all sucked in their breath. They said if it's the only way, they'll go, but they predicted lots of casualties on landing and considerable difficulty assembling the troops. If it were an opposed landing, they said, all bets on reaching the facilities before they could be damaged were off, so this one isn't that quick either. And when I asked if we could go at night, I thought for a moment that they were going to throw me out the window.

"A secondary disadvantage is that it's hostage to the weather. Wind and fog are the main worry and even if we were to go in at very low altitude, high winds over the DZ would scrub the operation."

Miller looked at Lepine, who asked quietly, "Can we do it by helicopter?"

"Not with the crates we own. They're too small, don't have the legs, and aren't reliable. We'd have to hip-hop all the way north, at which point we might as well go by road. Our attaché at the Pentagon, at the express direction of the DCDS, sounded out the U.S. army for a taxi fleet of Blackhawks. The U.S. Army chief of staff was keen to help, but the request would have to go through the White House and then CNN would know. So, no joy there."

Lepine looked over the maps once again. "Okay, here's my outline. My aim is to take and secure the generating station with minimum chance of serious damage to the site. We will drop right on it, grab it and the Chisasibi airport to support a second stage assault later in the day." Miller was already taking tidy notes.

"I want all three airborne commandos on the mission. Two drop on the generating facilities and initially the third stays airborne as a reserve. Once it is clear that the first drop got on the ground without serious opposition, the third commando goes to Chisasibi, drops on the airfield, secures it, and holds it for the Herc landings to follow. If the attack on the generating station is in serious doubt, then the third commando will drop there to support the first two. In that case, we'll sort out the Chisasibi airfield assault as the situation develops.

"The whole force should expect to be on the ground until relieved by the Quebec authorities, but it must be self-sufficient for at least one week. If the operation continues beyond that period, plan to relieve the para companies with units from 5 Brigade. As soon as the paras are on the ground, I want a major unit from 5 Brigade up the Matagami-Radisson road as fast as they can move to take over the mission from the airborne. I want the Special Service Regiment pulled back into reserve soon as possible. I think we may need them somewhere else, sooner than most people expect."

The general stood up and faced the wall map. "Next: rules of engagement. The operation is to be conducted as an air assault into a hostile environment. It's not an aid-of-the-civil-powers operation. However, commanders are to use minimum force until engaged by armed forces and then only enough force to stabilize the situation at hand." Lepine noticed Miller had stopped writing and was looking at him.

"I know what you're thinking, John. It's a bit ambiguous, but I don't want any prep-fire plans or overly aggressive engagements. I love them, but dammit, this is inside Canada and we have to keep the paras on a short leash. Shortish. We fight wars as we have to, not as we would like to…didn't some old general say that?"

"Yes, sir," Miller replied without hesitation. "Lord Kitchener, during the First World War. Not the most encouraging precedent. But I'll have the draft order for your review in a couple of hours. The staff have the preliminary details in hand. Anything else, sir?"

"No. Just get the CDS on the secure line in my office. I'll give him the outline and look for timings and we'll check the political temperature.

Then send the attack warning order to the CO of the Special Service Regiment as soon as possible. Best to give the young Colonel Rusty Campbell as much time as we can to get his people ready."

**Thursday, September 2, 1845 hours
Ottawa: Langevin Block**

Chief Onanole and his ever-present, strikingly beautiful executive assistant, Martha Kokohopenace, walked in off Wellington Street, up the dark steps, and through the wooden doors of the Langevin Block to the commissionaires' desk. Even though they knew Chief Onanole by sight and addressed him by name, they walked Al through the security routine. The Manitoba legislature wasn't the only place in Canada where the appearance of security mattered more than the reality.

"Photo identification, please, sir. Sign in here. Please step back and through the detector—no coins or metal objects in your jacket? Thank you, sir. The escort will take you up to the office."

Following his guide through the familiar passageways, the grand chief made his way down the wide, blue-carpeted halls into the prime minister's outer office. Jack Hemp's private secretary, Heather, stood up to greet him, offering to take his buckskin jacket. Al declined. He knew today was a day for buckskin, not Harry Rosen. "Please have a seat, Chief Onanole. The prime minister will be with you in a few minutes. Coffee?"

Before he could answer, Jack Hemp, hand extended, strode briskly out of his private office. "Grand Chief Onanole, Al, thanks for coming in. Beautiful fall day, eh?"

Martha smiled, accepted a lingering handshake from the prime minister, then sat down as Onanole and Hemp walked into the prime minister's spacious inner office. Although the chief had been in the room many times, the wall covered with scores of newspaper cartoons of Hemp, and the shelves lined with dozens of gold-framed photos of the PM with political celebrities, still made Onanole pause. The only things missing, he thought, were a few glass-eyed, political trophy heads hanging on the wall.

Hemp might be a white man, but he was Al's favourite kind of political white man.

"Chief," Hemp began, "you saw the Molly Grace thing on television, I assume?"

Onanole nodded. "Of course."

"Well, it looks like she's not kidding. I'm going to level with you, Al. We've also had serious raids on our military bases and it seems now we've got a difficult problem developing in James Bay that I'm sure you're aware of. The Quebec government is going wild. The media is in full indignation mood. The opposition is on the warpath—ah, poor choice of words, I guess. Anyway, I thought you might have some ideas, suggestions really, about how to resolve this matter before it gets out of hand."

Al shifted in his chair. "Well, prime minister, I'm going to level with you, too. It seems to me the matter is already out of hand. I suggest that you open negotiations right away. Perhaps over the grievances we've discussed over many years. The Federation will do what it can to help, but this is a matter for the local nations to discuss with you and perhaps the premier of Quebec."

"Come on, Al. You know I can't negotiate with a gun to my head. We need a return to civilized behaviour and then we can call a meeting with all the players. You could co-chair the conference with me. That'd give you the lead... show Canadians you're in charge... put these radicals in their place. I'm sure the government would appreciate the gesture... in the future, I mean."

Al knew exactly what Hemp meant and how the PM expected the minuet to develop. But he had a problem the white man opposite didn't fully appreciate. Al and the Federation didn't have as much influence outside Ottawa as they pretended to have, and the current crisis had revealed that they had even less influence than they'd thought. As a matter of fact, Al Onanole didn't really understand what was happening. The James Bay bands had long ago stopped acting on his direction, and the band leaders had been getting damn well uppity and disrespectful at Federation meetings. Lately, he wasn't even getting information from his usual sources in the area, and he wasn't about to risk his status by getting into a fight with band chiefs just to save Hemp's political skin.

Still, a smart man keeps his options open, so Al decided to rag the puck.

"Civilized behaviour, prime minister? Who's civilized in these matters? If Canada and Quebec had carried through on the fair deal the FNF nego- tiated at Kelowna, we wouldn't be in this mess. Most of the chiefs were happy with that outcome and there wouldn't be this trouble if we'd gotten the increased benefits, reasonable land claim settlements, and freedom to hunt and fish without interference from your game wardens that we were promised. But no. Instead, as you may recall, the meetings I put together broke down because a few rednecks from out west and the Ontario Hunt- er's Association didn't like a few of the bits about hunting, and you didn't have the guts to face them down. Now you've got a real armed rebellion on your hands and you want me to walk into the middle of it. No thanks!"

Hemp took the hit. He didn't like being hustled but he'd done enough hustling of his own to know when a man had to eat a little dirt. "Okay. What's the deal? What do I need to do to get this thing off dead-centre?"

The opening came faster and more directly than Onanole was antici- pating, but he was ready to explore it seriously. Hemp's position was weak, but Al knew his wasn't very strong either. He was up against the NPC and Molly Grace, and if things escalated too far too fast he'd never get back his authority or at least his reputation for authority in the native community. He knew also that Hemp was as ready to throw him overboard as he was to chuck Hemp, namely in two puffs on a peace-pipe. But if they could find a way out of this together, Al would take that too. He was an unsentimental man, but Hemp was going to have to give him quite a bit to pull the trick off this time. So it was time to throw the guilt card on the table and then offer to make peace on "reasonable grounds."

Al played his trump. "End the oppression of the people. Not just in Quebec, but across Canada. Do it and I'll deliver the people."

Jack Hemp stood up, leaned over his great desk, and glared into Al's black eyes, his voice rising. "Don't give me that crap, Al. That's just bar- ricade rhetoric. I can't 'end the oppression of the people' and I can't go out and tell Canadian taxpayers that the people to whom we give eight billion dollars a year are oppressed. Bullshit, Al. Give me something better."

"Oppression is a lot more obvious to the victim than the perpetrator," Al snapped back. "You try putting on my skin and walking around Winnipeg, or Ottawa, or Regina, or live on a reserve for a year and see how you like it.

Jack, I've been warning you for years that things were very bad. You want my help now, the first thing you do is listen."

"Yeah, right." Hemp paced in a quick circle around Onanole and returned to his desk. "Let me tell you something, Al. 'The oppressed': that's just a handy label for an assumed collective you guys trot out when you're at the table with us. But the really oppressed natives aren't in that room and you know it. They've got lawyers, politicians, zealots, your band leaders bartering for them, in their place, in their name, but we both know who gets most of the gravy. Those who don't like what's left after their 'brokers' take their cut, well, they're free agents, kinda like hockey players. They're stuck out on the fringes and if they're too pissed off to play by the rules, now I think you're at least as responsible for it as I am."

Hemp warmed to his arguments. "I agree with you, Al. Oppression is more obvious to the victim. It's all the fault of 'the system' or the free market or what's it … the 'generational effects' from those, I admit, dreadful residential schools—it's always something other than self. We apologized, Al, and what do we get: the fatalistic notion that nothing can change the evil effects of the past in the future. You know something that I find strange: the residential school effect, I mean the negative ones, seem only to show up in the reserve population. All those native families who moved off the reserves and into cities seem to have prospered while those on the reserves continue to suffer from the past. Someone should do a study on those effects too.

"Anyway, Al, the rascals who represent the downtrodden prosper and the rabble continues to suffer. Had a whisky and local tap water at Kashechewan up on James Bay lately, Al? No? Well, ever since the Conservatives signed that deal in 2007, governments have spent enough money on that reserve to make tap water flow in a desert, and you guys are still complaining and the saps who don't have titles and cellphones and expense accounts also don't have water their kids can drink.

"I know who frightens you, Al—the radicals, that's who. They've got your number. To tell the truth, I can't separate out the motives behind the radical native movement in Canada. You tell me. Did they come from the oppression of the whole community, or from the way a few individuals lined their own pockets at the expense of that community? Sure, there are grievances, and abuses in the community and of the community. There always are, in every community."

Onanole shot back, voice rising. "So what? You think the symptoms of oppression—listlessness, irresponsibility, depression, drunkenness, suicide—that stalk native reserves are just things I make up?"

"No, of course not." Hemp took a deep breath and, calmer, sat in his chair. "But real, head-busting oppression is about cruel treatment, fear of authority, prohibition of choice, murder and mayhem. Where are they in your people's case? As likely as not, I'd say its oppression arises from your traditions or from the culture on the reserves. Al, you can't convince me that unsatisfied want is oppression. Are there unequal outcomes? Sure, but is there oppression if it comes from failing to better oneself? If someone doesn't take choices when they could, where's the oppression? Can a person or a community be self-oppressed? Probably. The hawkers of grievances may be damaged adults, or rabble-rousers, or crazy, like Molly Grace perhaps. But if people buy what they're selling, it's not always somebody else's fault." Hemp stopped abruptly. He usually knew better than to express such thoughts, even to colleagues. But now that he had made his point in private it was time to offer a compromise.

"All right, Al, suppose I grant your claims for the sake of discussion. Native Canadians are downtrodden; they have dozens of grievances, and seem to discover new ones all the time, by the way. Sure they're way down the Canadian scale for receiving rewards from our economy, and those on the reserves suffer more than most—more people in jail, more suicides, more disease, lower life expectancies, and so on. I'll buy for now the argument that these problems, especially combined with a booming population of unemployed, often unemployable, young people, are the ingredients for an explosion. It just needs a spark, an egomaniac for a leader, and boom!

"These aren't new arguments nor are they unique to natives in Canada. And I know that it's this picture—which is badly distorted in my opinion, but we won't argue that point now—that outsiders and trouble-makers point to when they say 'Canada's native community is a Third World country within a first-world country.' Well, let me tell you, Al, I've been to Africa and I'm telling you middle-class people in a lot of Third World countries should have it so good.

"Anyway, that's the argument in a nutshell, is it not?—poverty, past injustice, and unequal present distribution of land and wealth and opportunity create grievances and breeding grounds for crime, social unrest, even terrorist recruits, and it's our fault, and if we don't fix it they're going to come and murder us in our beds. I get it ... don't necessarily believe it. There're lots of situations where you don't get these kinds of results. There are no bad communities, Al, just bad leaders. But that's the argument and God knows I've heard it often enough.

"Even Jean Chrétien, to his great discredit, used the same tripe in one of his more-than-usually confused and offensive statements about the 'root causes' of the 9/11 attacks. I'll never forget the insensitivity of that CBC interview—it was all our fault, 'the Western world is going to be too rich in relation to the poor world. And necessarily, you know, the poor, they look upon us being arrogant, self-satisfying, and greedy and with no limits. And the 11th of September is an occasion for me to realize that even more.' Such crap—I have a grievance so I'm justified in killing indiscriminately. And it's just what we're getting. In fact, now I'm hearing this argument offered by some native leaders. So what is it, Al, an iron truth of history or blackmailers' threats?"

Onanole leaned forward in his chair. "It's neither, none of the above. It's a statement about truth and consequences. You don't need to be a professor to see the relationship between grievances and violence. You're right that it's not new. And it's not just in Canada either. The really galling thing, though, is that Canadians, your voters, even your caucus, are all for citizens in other countries rising up against tyrants. We encourage it. We exploit their grievances to suit our interests or to make us feel better about ourselves. But when the stream flows the other way, when it's directed against us, well, then it's an unjust threat and their leaders are all terrorists.

"Anyway, you can't argue away the facts sitting at the table with us this afternoon, prime minister. The world has a huge mass of disadvantaged people who may someday storm the Bastille. It doesn't matter where the grievances came from and who's at fault. I take your point that history furnishes too many grievances and sometimes they're exploited by unscrupulous people. But there's lots of things about the world we can't change sitting here yakking, and that's one of them.

"And here's another: when you're hungry and completely frustrated and led to believe that there's nothing much to lose by fighting and much to lose by not fighting, violence becomes your best friend. Don't get me wrong. These people need to understand that violence is a fickle friend at best. She gets you killed and others benefit or, more likely, other violent people win out and you're in a worse place. What do you think I spend my days telling the hotheads and the angry kids? We at the FNF think—and *I* think, prime minister—that especially in Canada's situation, we can make reasonable changes and demonstrate that there is another way. But we're sitting here now having this discussion because we didn't do it. We failed to move in any useful direction to win that argument with the radicals and the maniacs, and now we're all going to pay the piper unless we come up with something convincing and do it soon, really soon—like now, in fact."

"But Al, that's my point. Look, things are so perverted, corrupted in most real Third World countries—we even invented a name for them, 'failed states'—that they're beyond redemption. Even if Western countries sent ten times as much aid—a hundred times—to places like that, and we somehow made sure the money actually reached the people there—fat chance, and you know it—we still couldn't rescue every state. No matter how they got that way, they're such an economical, cultural, political, and, between you and me, often a religious mess, they can't reverse their own decline, no matter how much money we give them.

"Al, the idea that if we create a booming economy in every wretched Third World hell-hole the social problems and terrorism will disappear— and the idea that we can create such an economy—is simply doomed by reality. They need a revolution in social concepts that we can't engineer and apparently they can't either. But Al, this is Canada, not southern Afghanistan. Here we have the choice. So what's it going to be?"

Onanole bristled. "Are you suggesting you *can* turn the supposed aboriginal Third World nations here into First World nations, prime minister?"

"It's not quite the same, that's true. But the dynamic is very similar, and we're talking mainly about the reserves. What do we do—create stable communities where kids go to good schools, where drugs and booze are taboo, where health and safety in communities are inherently a community responsibility, where private ownership of property is the norm, where people have work habits suited to the modern Canadian economy, and then expect social peace and prosperity? Or, do we pour in money, create artificial economies where everyone's subsidized, unemployed, or both, and wait for a spontaneous social transformation? That's the present concept and it's not working."

"Prime minister, who said we need a social transformation? There's nothing wrong with our traditional culture except we got robbed and run over by the Europeans and had our rights taken away. What we want now is a fair deal from the Canadian government and we'll take care of ourselves. We'll run our communities on our land and distribute our resources according to our social norms. That's why we call ourselves nations. Once the economic grievances are settled, the harmful social conditions in our communities and the threats to your people will disappear."

"Okay, great, let me buy that for now. You sound like that Molly Grace on the TV, but never mind. Just tell me this: what do we do until that grand day arrives? In Canada, we have the wealth and the motivation and the education, and the native society has the brains to handle the complexities of change. But what are we going to do with the—what's the politically correct thing to call them—the 'lost generation'? And before we even get to that, what are we going to do right now? It's a damn wicked problem, Al, and one most Canadians are content to ignore. I know what you're going to say: that we political leaders ignore it too because of the dangers and threats to our interests in the situation—it's just too politically incorrect, too outrageous to mention in public. I know that's true. Well, I guess it looks like we're not going to be allowed to ignore it for much longer, but I'm worried that it might just be too late to do much except let the bad blood flow.

"So, Al, that's the situation we're in. We've let—yes, for now let's blame both of us and let's both of us find a short-term answer—we've let the native community situation evolve in such a way that the thugs have control and lots of restless, poorly educated native kids to recruit. Now the mere problem of glue-sniffing kids and street gangs has morphed into a political movement that's threatening the country, or at least threatening 'peace, order and good government.'

"I need an immediate solution, an immediate strategy. Now. Today! Not some long distance, dreamy, untested thesis on social re-engineering. You and the lefties can go around crowing 'we told you so.' And we can reply that all you ever told us was you were seeing the same things we were seeing, that you had nothing useful to say about how to get out of this tailspin, the social equivalent of what pilots call a death-spiral.

"To tell you the truth, Al, I don't think there is a solution—this isn't a puzzle, you know. I tell you one thing, for the immediate future, John A. Macdonald's homily is changed: it's going to be order first, and good government and peace later. That's how it always was anyway. That's why John A. sent the Mounties to the West: order first, then good…well at least reasonable government, and then peace. If the world needs more Canada, then after 9/11, Jean Chrétien should have put that slogan on the table: order, good government and peace. Remember John A. fought Riel and the Métis after they hanged that Orangeman, Thomas Scott. The prime minister settled things down by hanging Riel, and after that they worked out the other stuff."

"Is that how you're going to handle this situation, Jack, by hanging people?"

"I'll do what's necessary, Al. Just watch me, as Trudeau said."

Al sensed an impasse building that wouldn't save either of their skins. "Jack, we're grown-ups. Let's get a grip on ourselves. These radicals are renegades and I don't support them. In truth, I have little control over their actions. We do have some of our people trying to get at the leaders, but this thing isn't originating in Radisson. There are others involved and I bet your intelligence snoops have told you that already.

"Anyway, here's what I propose. The media is on to this meeting. We should make a joint statement to the effect that the government recognizes that some grievances have not been handled well—blame the civil service if you want, previous administrations, failure to communicate, I don't care. Then tell them that we're working to resolve the issues, we'll settle some major issues with the community. I'll stand beside you and support the notion. On the condition, prime minister, that you clearly acknowledge me and the Federation as the rightful spokespersons for the native community, now and in the future. Oh, and also that you keep secret, to the grave and beyond, the source of any information on radical leaders and so on you get from us."

Hemp moved cautiously toward possibly accepting the formula but his guard was fully raised. "I like the idea, Al, but first explain this. What am

I getting into if I say you and you alone speak for the native community? I've got a half dozen other people who tell me that they speak for the native community or big parts of it, and some damn reporter will certainly point that out."

"That's a strange question, prime minister. It's obvious I do, I mean we do; the FNF speaks for the native community and we have for years. We're the responsible voices and we're the elected ones. What do you mean, what are you getting into?"

Hemp smiled. He loved when the other guy asked these types of questions. It meant he'd got his adversary—or partner; in Hemp's world they weren't really different—arguing from his agenda, which gave Hemp control.

"I'll tell you what I mean, Al. I don't think there is a 'native community.' There are just bunches of natives of all shades who say they belong to one group, and then they say they also belong to another group, or belong to several. There're natives, meaning Indians, and natives, meaning Inuit, and natives, meaning Métis, and natives, meaning on-reserve and natives off-reserve, and natives, meaning women, who are disenfranchised by all the other natives, and natives, meaning people organized under the so-called 'friendship centres.' If we recognize the FNF and things go smoothly, it makes sense, but when something like this happens, other people ask questions. I need to be ready for that, even if I'm not asking them myself—which I'm starting to. Mainly, who are we Canadians supposed to deal with and how do we know which community and which leaders are legitimate?"

Onanole countered smoothly. "That's so like a politician, you know. Trying to divide and conquer all the time. You know well that the FNF represents the largest and the most needy and the most representative group of First Nations. We've worked hard to find a place on the government's agenda and a place in the structure of government so we can communicate with the system in Ottawa. Just because you didn't listen to our warnings and demands, uh, suggestions, doesn't mean we weren't legitimate in putting them forward."

"Yeah, sure, Al, but let me finish. The FNF says only forty per cent live off-reserve at all. I have the government bean-counters giving me thirty-seven per cent off-reserve, which is pretty close to your number, but lots of other people say lots of other things. There's lots of confusion about the numbers for all the other groups too, and I need to have answers when the reporters start asking questions, which they will. And then we have quarrels about who's in charge and how they get that way. Remember the federal government, supposedly out of cultural sensitivity but really to avoid a squabble with the natives, caved in to the 'traditional chiefs,' as they call themselves, of the Mohawk nations…"

"That's the Six Nations Confederacy, prime minister."

"Yeah, whatever. It's just another example of the native leaders arguing with each other. Anyway, it recognized the authority of these non-elected chiefs on the grounds, not entirely unreasonable, that elections are a European institution. And just the other day the traditional leader from the Six Nations, a Mr. Brant, said 'We're sick of them,' meaning the band chiefs, Al, 'selling us out.' So who am I to deal with, Al, the hereditary chiefs and their families, or the elected band councils? Someone will ask me that."

"Prime minister, you have Canadian soldiers all over the world fighting for liberal democracy, or so you say, and that means to me that people should have the right to elect their own leaders and not be forced to follow some divine right of chiefs. Or have I got it wrong?"

"Touché, Al! Touché indeed. So I should let the army have a go at these people and you'll back the move? Because if I recognize your unchallenged authority and then you don't back me, I'm totally screwed and you know it. So what I need to know is, who speaks for whom, and how I explain it and what they're then gonna say in this crisis. Oh, and I should also ask, since I'm sure it hasn't escaped your notice, who's supposed to get what from the federal treasury once this mess is all over?

"We don't want any more 'failures to communicate,' Al, especially not ones that lead to uprisings and meetings like this one. So let me ask you for some more clarification. You were quoted in the newspapers the other day and, unless they misquoted you—they do it to me all the time—you said, 'The myth was that there's this tremendous migration into the urban communities. Actually, the reverse has happened. We believe that there should be more emphasis on off-reserve initiatives. We don't disagree with that… but not at the expense of one or the other.' Now Al, where does this leave me? There's only so much money to go around. Does it go to reserves or off-reserves or what? And if we pony up, do you back us on that too and say we made the right funding decision, or do you pocket the cash and keep on yelling?"

Al Onanole chewed his lip and spat back, "You can't play that game with me, prime minister. We have understandings with a lot of governments. They've agreed for years that the FNF represents the Indian community in this country and we're not going to fall back on that hard-won ground. The band chiefs are behind me and they're going to demand that we get what's coming to us under current arrangements. Do you and the cabinet really want even more trouble?"

Hemp dropped the document on the desk. Point made. "Well, Al, it's hard to imagine more trouble, but no, we'll stick to the deals. But—and it's a big but, Al—but your Federation had better deliver. Because admit it or not, there's another player at the table and she, this Molly Grace and company, are not going away soon. If I have to negotiate with someone, who's that to be? I'll tell you who.

"I'm going to negotiate with someone who can bring this situation back to normal. In fact, I'm inclined to suggest to Parliament that we bypass all the community lobbies, including yours, and go directly to the native people—one-on-one, the federal government and the natives themselves, no intermediaries, and just cut a deal for all times. Now might be the time to do it, seeing how your leaders have overstepped the boundaries by a very long margin."

"I wouldn't recommend it, Jack. We will fight tooth and nail. Besides, if we don't represent the community, who will? I speak for the band chiefs and you can't do anything with them. And are you really going to negotiate with Molly Grace? I don't think so. She's not exactly the negotiating type, and you haven't got time to find new friends."

"Not so sure, Al. Seems Ms. Grace has by-passed the chiefs and gone straight to the people, and you've got to admire her political savvy. At least, I do. Anyway, remember, when we fix Grace and her bunch, we can still go around you guys—there are lawyers out there who'd sell their mothers into a brothel to get a cut of the aboriginal file—the grievance file of the century."

Al Onanole just glared. Was this fool ready to make a deal or not?

Hemp swivelled in his leather chair and looked out over Parliament Hill, his back to Onanole. He sat still for a moment, calculating, then swung around abruptly and spoke decisively. "Okay, deal. We'll announce together this evening. When this thing is settled, you get action on a number of grievances, serious action with money attached, and you get credit for getting it from us. But now you get me some names and places and you come down hard on these bastards, and when they're swinging from a rope, you join the cheering section. Got it?"

Al hesitated briefly. He wasn't at all sure he could deliver but he knew this was the best offer he could get and it was the one he'd come in looking for. Might as well look enthusiastic. "Right! How do you want to stage this?"

Hemp was way ahead of him. He wasn't just thinking of the upcoming press conference or the gathering crisis. He was already looking for a strategy for afterward that let him take credit if things worked out but would stick someone else with the responsibility if they didn't, a strategy that left plenty of doors open for him. If Onanole's demands were unreasonable, he could blame the Indian leaders for having misinterpreted his position once things were quieted down. If they were manageable, he could make a show of generosity. In any case, he thought, I should have given myself more options. He was going to find some aboriginal friends outside the FNF at the first opportunity.

Hemp smiled at Al. "Done!" he said, tapping the knuckles of his right hand lightly on the desk top, as a used car dealer might signal "deal" by tapping the hood of a old car. "We need something to offer reasonable, average First Nations people. What do you think they need to get them not to back Molly Grace and these other lunatics? What makes sense to promise and how do we make the promise immediately credible?"

"Prime minister," Al began without a moment's hesitation, "they want all the things all my people want and have been asking for all these decades: respect for treaties, settlement of land claims, fair payment for resources taken from our land, education and social assistance programs that fit our society, a protocol to protect our sacred sites, safety from the police and the courts, and, above all else, respect for our inherent rights. This violence comes from Canada's continued frustration of our rightful demands. That's what they want."

"Al, save it for the media and the academic conferences. The natives at

James Bay are as well off as any on-reserve people in the country. They sold their land to Quebec long ago. Besides, I didn't ask you here to solve every problem in every reserve across the country. I just want you to help us solve the James Bay problem. You saw that TV clip from Molly Grace; she wants sovereign control over the whole damn place.

"You know, you guys could choke yourselves trying to eat the whole pie at one sitting. You should have learned by now that Canadians will give up lots of cash—what's it at this year, eight billion dollars—and we'll give up land that's far over the horizon, but no one understands what we're meant to give up when you demand that we 'respect your inherent rights.' Christ, that could mean anything. I don't think you even know what it means. So we aren't going to deal on that, especially not now."

Onanole moved to interject, but Hemp held up a hand. "Just let me finish. I had that guy from the Inuit Association, what's his name...?"

"Walter Agloohuit, Jack. Walter Agloohuit." Onanole couldn't resist pronouncing it slowly, patronizingly. But his contempt stung Hemp into a rant.

"Yeah, that's it. Well, he was on about living off the land and the sacred relationship with animals and how the 'land' provides for the people and that's why they demand seventy per cent of resource incomes and so on. And, oh yeah, several million a year for his organization, out of which he'd get plenty to buy his rifles and trucks and snowmobiles and other traditional artefacts from the good old days before the white man came.

"I should've had the Mounties throw him out. Instead, I pointed out to the gentleman that according to our figures—and he had none—Inuit don't eat seals or bears or fish or caribou any more. Know what they eat, Al? Sure you do. They eat popcorn, French fries, processed food. They drink more soda pop then they eat seal meat. Their diets are terrible. They don't live off the land anymore; they live off the Hudson's Bay store.

"People can't make a twenty-first-century living shooting seals and trapping foxes, even with metal tools and gasoline engines and radios. It's hard work and it pays next to nothing and it costs a hundred dollars an hour to have someone fix your Skidoo up there. It costs a month's good wages to buy food for a couple of people living close to a settlement. Al, I'll pay good money to train someone in a technical trade or to work in the oil fields, or to come south to go to law school, but I'm damned if I will pay somebody to go duck hunting. I might as well pay a farmer to plough his fields behind a horse and an iron ploughshare.

"Look, Al, we bring some two hundred thousand immigrants into our economy every year. Most of them are less adapted and used to Canadian ways than some Inuit watching sitcoms on a satellite TV on Ellesmere Island. But the immigrants, and especially their children, soon fit into the economy because they have to. Imagine the calamity if we said, 'Come to Canada and we'll support your native way of life.'

"You've got four hundred thousand people, more or less, living on reserves. Why in God's name can't we create an internal immigration policy to bring all those people who want to come into the economy into it over the next five years? And don't tell me they don't want to come in off the land. Because I'll say that's because you and the other chiefs refuse to provide the leadership to inspire the people to give up the ancient ways for a more prosperous, sustainable way of life."

Chief Onanole held his temper. This was definitely not the place for this conversation and he was surprised at Hemp for losing the thread. It was time to make a deal, not score points. High time. "Prime minister, you're getting off the subject. Our people are not immigrants in their own land. We need a practical solution here. We have a press conference to manage."

"You're right, Al, you're right. This crisis, that's what it is, this crisis is taking us over the edge. It's getting way beyond our control. But listen. If you think your people are frustrated, just wait until the dollar consequences of Grace's activities hit the markets in downtown Toronto and other places, where no one's even seen an Indian except on TV. We can't talk to them about 'respect for inherent rights.' We need a solution that makes sense and doesn't involve a blank cheque.

"There's an iron rule in political conflict, Al, 'Radicals beget radicals. Violence begets violence.' We absolutely don't want to get ourselves into a situation where we can't make peace or defeat one another, an interminable, unwinnable warfare on the Israeli/Palestinian model. I'm really afraid that's where we're heading. Is that what the native community and Canadians want?"

Hemp leaned over his desk. "No. It's not what they want, and it's not what you and I want. Chief Onanole, I need all the help you can muster to get us out of this before my radicals rise up against your radicals and a lot of people get hurt as a consequence. If you don't believe me, think back to the 1990s Oka crisis. A few hot-headed Indians jumped on a golf course and within days a bunch of Québecois, white savages, stoned a convoy of Indian women and children trying to leave the area. Give some people any excuse and they'll quite willingly kill each other."

Chief Onanole stood up and walked to the window, where he stared quietly over Wellington Street for several minutes, struggling to compose his conflicting thoughts. "Prime minister," he said, still gazing out the window, "the truth is, I'm not much in control of what's going on. I don't know much, probably less than you do, about Molly Grace and the so-called Movement. I know they've been very active on the reserves and with the street gangs in the West. But not much more. I'm not even sure who in the FNF to trust any more."

He walked back to the side of the prime minister's desk. "I do know this. The majority of the native community from coast to coast, and north to south, are loyal Canadians, and they want nothing to do with these radicals. But they're afraid, afraid of more empty talk and broken promises and another generation of young people going down the goddamn drain. I can't negotiate with Grace and her gang because it would have little effect, it would ruin the reputation of the FNF, and it would be the wrong thing to do—it would ultimately harm the people."

"Yeah, Al, I know that. But I think we need to offer to deal with them, for appearance's sake. If they agree even to talk, it undercuts their radical appeal, and if they refuse, it shows how unreasonable they are. We make it sound all solemn, and if anyone who matters panics, we can quietly tell them it's all BS."

Onanole smiled despite himself. "Prime minister," he lied, "I'm glad you're on my side. I can negotiate with you, and if we get a meaningful deal, I can do a lot to undercut these radicals. But I need something positive, something really important, something we announce today. If I have it—I'm not trying to twist you here—it's a matter of having something real on these problems we both know about. If I have it, I can rally the people against the Movement by exposing its destructive intent.

"My strongest card with the loyal chiefs, and that's most of them, is the ability to bring the power of the elders to the meetings. You may not have much time for our traditions, but in our society, people with grey hair still get respect. We should at least be able to move the majority on the reserves into a position of neutrality by putting the elders between the people and the young warriors. That I will try to do. But you have to give me something the elders will be willing to endorse. We can't trick them and I won't try. I need, say, another billion a year for education on reserves and another billion for community economic development. For the rest, a few kind words about respecting existing legal obligations would be great."

Jack Hemp sat still and then smiled and stood up, extending his hand. "Chief Onanole, you're offering me a great deal indeed. I thank you for the effort and as one grey-head to another, I appreciate your wisdom. So we're on for a press conference later this afternoon?" Onanole nodded.

Hemp hit the button to the outer office. "Heather, would you please ask Harry Southern to join us in the office and ask Chief Onanole's assistant, Ms. Kokohopenace, to come in. And book the National Press Theatre for an important joint statement by myself and Chief Onanole for later this afternoon." Hemp looked to Onanole, who nodded again in agreement.

The prime minister switched off the intercom. "Well, partner," he said with a wink, "welcome, as Don would say, to the rock 'em, sock 'em of prime minister's politics. Molly Grace and company should know better than to corner a couple of old grizzlies like us, shouldn't they? After all, they're native hunters, aren't they, Al?"

Southern and Kokohopenace walked in. Hemp waved them towards his desk. "Chief Onanole and I have reached an agreement. We will make a joint public statement immediately, reinforcing our determination to cooperate and condemning the disturbances as harmful to all Canadians. In the strictest secrecy, I have asked Chief Onanole to approach Molly Grace and her people to suggest that we open non-committal, secret discussions to see where grounds for negotiations might be available. Harry, I want the government, acting only in a small group under your direction, to provide the contact with Chief Onanole and to shepherd this initiative forward between my office, the chief, and the, ah, other side. Once we see where that goes, we can plan the next step."

Southern moved as if to question the strategy. Onanole asked unpleasantly, "Problems, Mr. Southern?" Harry shook his head and backed off.

Hemp regained control. "Fine, then. Chief Onanole will act in his own stead and as my unofficial emissary to Molly Grace. The offer is open only for a short period, so let's get moving. I want a press conference in three hours. Meanwhile, Harry, you can set up a secure hotline with Chief Onanole's office. He and I are going to solve this thing together and I want him to have immediate access to me any time he needs it, any time of the night or day."

Everyone shook hands and then the chief and Martha Kokohopenace turned and walked towards the door, Onanole holding his assistant lightly by the elbow, speaking quietly into her ear.

When the door closed, Harry Southern turned to Hemp. "Are you out of your mind? If the natives think you're going to deal, they'll rise up all across the country. What the hell do we have to deal with anyway? How am I going to keep this a secret in this town? You let that young woman in on the idea. Christ, she may be a spy for Grace for all we know." Southern dropped into a chair.

"Look, Harry, I'm playing for time. If things get out of hand, I want to say, 'I tried to keep every avenue open, keep the talk going, not my fault that other governments failed to act,' etc., etc. If this thing blows wide open I'm gonna hang it on Onanole and at least bust his fat ass. I hope I can at least keep the James Bay facilities working as an opener, and I'll give that Molly Grace something she can have control of, well, let's try Winnipeg—kind of. You know, we'll support that dumb-ass idea the late mayor had for urban reserves. Such BS, a great way to spread the problem, that was. We'll let the barriers stay up and Grace's mob can pretend to act as customs guards, have special places on the city council, something like that. She can be bought, she's just like any of us—she's a politician, isn't she, Harry? You give me some ideas later. Okay, Harry?"

Southern looked sourly at Hemp and after a long silence got up and headed for the exit. "Sure Jack. Freak'n' great. Thanks a lot." The door slammed shut behind him.

Thursday, September 2, 2130 hours
Ottawa: National Defence Operations Centre

Colonel Dobson gathered his notes and reviewed the briefing he was about to present to the CDS and the defence minister. Operational briefings were now scheduled for every twelve hours in the Ops Centre, with extra situational briefings whenever significant events and incidents warranted. All these sessions were now restricted to the CDS, the minister and his chief of staff, the senior officers who together made up the Armed Forces Council, the department's deputy minister, Steven Pope, and the principal members of the joint operations planning staff.

Dobson knew this evening's briefing would be tense. His boss was deeply concerned that, although intelligence reports and deployment schedules clearly demanded the immediate movement of his units from their home stations closer to the expected "disturbances," his political masters continued to ignore the CDS's advice and stalled in the hope that the whole thing would somehow just go away.

Ian had listened to General Bishop describe from experience how when crises erupted, Canadian politicians would expect instant military responses despite their neglect of the armed forces over the years that made timely, comprehensive responses next to impossible. And he knew also that by the time politicians did act, it might take a lot of effort, and bloody effort at that, to restore the peace. That was the sure lesson from the "bungle in the jungle," the unprepared mission to Zaire, launched on a whim by the Chrétien government in 1996. Dobson, however, was confident that the message he now held in his hand would force this government to move quickly, and perhaps, if they were lucky, just in time.

Dobson stood ready at the lectern when the CDS and the minister walked in and took chairs facing the national situation displays. Although General Bishop had been briefed earlier by Dobson and the deputy chief of defence staff, Lieutenant General Gervais, Dobson started at the beginning for the benefit of Jim Riley. The CDS was determined that the minister would convey the full seriousness of the matter to the prime minister that same night, and Dobson understood that his job was to make sure Riley got the message loud and clear.

"Minister, General Bishop," he began. "This briefing is based on information as of seventeen hundred hours today. In brief, the national security situation is deteriorating rapidly. Intelligence sources, including those at CSIS and the RCMP, conclude that significant threats to civil order exist in Quebec, particularly in the major cities of Montreal and Quebec City and at the James Bay facilities. They conclude also that conditions exist for significant unrest across the Prairie region and in northern Ontario. The main threat arises from militant native groups led by, supported by, or affiliated with the Native People's Movement and backed by the so-called Native People's Army. I have outlined these organizations before but if you have any questions I would be happy to elaborate."

Dobson paused briefly while the staff adjusted the situation maps and displays. "Gentlemen," he resumed, "these displays illustrate the current Canada Command deployments. Of particular importance are the reinforcement of airborne troops and supporting units to CFB Trenton, the reinforcement of 5 Brigade with troops from CFB Gagetown, the deployment of the CF18 squadron from CFB Bagotville to Cold Lake for security reasons, and the increased readiness of all regular and reserve units across the Canadian Forces.

"We have received two Significant Incident Reports since the last briefing. Last night at about zero-two-hundred, one of the main Hydro lines from James Bay to Montreal was severely and intentionally damaged, resulting in a power outage in the city which is still affecting approximately 50,000 customers. The Hydro-Québec crews refused to go to the damage site without a police escort, and that escort couldn't be arranged until this morning. We're waiting for a report on the repairs at this moment."

"Well," Riley interrupted, "I can tell you that the PM and his Quebec lieutenant, Mr. Labbé, are mighty pissed off at this attack and they want to know what the army is doing to prevent another one."

"Minister, you can tell the PM, or I will, if you prefer," replied the CDS icily, "that we can't assure the free functioning of every kilometre of transmission line, especially not if we sit in the barracks. Carry on, Colonel Dobson."

Dobson looked directly at Riley. "The second SIR involves a penetration of the security perimeter at CFB Bagotville around first light this morning by a small party, we suspect less than a dozen natives, riding around in three pickup trucks and three or four all-terrain vehicles. Shots were fired in the general direction of the hangar lines. The base defence force returned fire. The marksmanship on both sides prevented any casualties to anyone and the raiders disappeared immediately on taking fire.

"Minister, we appear to be in a preliminary phase but not a static one. Native groups in Quebec seem to be forming larger parties, maybe even some units, as we understand the term, and they're acting more aggressively. The Canadian Forces are deployed as best they can under the prime minister's guidelines, but…" Dobson slowed down, pronouncing each word clearly and distinctly. "But we are not deployed in sufficient numbers or in the right locations to pre-empt or deter hostile actions that we can now anticipate." He paused for effect, then resumed more rapidly. "The premier of Quebec, however, seems about to force the government's hand."

Riley sat up straight and stared at the CDS. "What's this? What does she mean?"

"She means," said Bishop, raising a finger in Riley's direction, "that we have been informed in the last hour from Canada Command that the solicitor general of Quebec is preparing a requisition for aid of the civil power on the grounds that, as we understand it, Quebec is facing 'an apprehended insurrection' mounted by militant native groups from within and without the province. I anticipate that the requisition will hit my desk in the next few hours or early Friday morning, and if it does, I will have to respond immediately as the National Defence Act stipulates. Therefore, minister, you and I had best get over to see the prime minister as soon as Colonel Dobson is done here so that I can explain to him how I intend to respond if and when the requisition arrives."

The defence minister opened his mouth, and then without a word closed it again. He swallowed hard and blurted, "Well, this could blow the whole thing into the press. Do you have any idea how the PMO is going to react to this, what's it you call it, a requisition?"

"That's right, minister, a requisition under the National Defence Act. I have no doubt that the press will eat it up. But that, minister, is not my concern, and I don't think it should be the prime minister's first concern either. If he tries to downplay the seriousness of the situation, that tactic will soon bite him in the ass and you can tell him I said so. Better yet, I'll tell him myself. Minister, let me be clear, and Colonel Dobson, I want this statement in the briefing record: should I receive a requisition from the solicitor general of Quebec, I will act with dispatch and deploy an appropriate force of well-armed units to assist the SQ in Quebec.

"And minister, I will also deploy a force into the James Bay region to deter if possible and to snuff out if necessary any threat there before we lose control of that situation too. Furthermore, I will make what arrangements I think are necessary to protect Canadian Forces members and assets in other regions and to make a show of strength in the West to deter any group that thinks it can take advantage of the situation in Quebec."

Jim Riley moved to speak.

"No, minister, please don't interrupt. My concern here, my very great concern, is that Canada's governments, including yours but not only yours, have left the situation unattended for so long that we may be too late to avoid a long and costly struggle. You and your colleagues, including the prime minister, must understand the situation and prepare yourselves for bloodshed. It's no longer a question of bad publicity. It's a question of struggling to avoid a massive and irredeemable breakdown of law and order."

Riley took a hunted look at the wall of brass around him, flushed, then struck back in classic political style. "Okay, look here, General Bishop, the government will decide what is to be done, National Defence Act or no National Defence Act. If the situation develops as you think it might, and I don't disagree for a minute with the assessment, then it becomes a national defence problem and not an aid-to-the-civil-power problem and we will do what we think is necessary. Now, am I right in this distinction or am I not?"

"Yes, minister, you're right. The federal government, meaning practically, the prime minister, has the power to declare a national defence emergency and to deploy the Canadian Forces whenever and wherever in the country it decides. In fact, I would welcome such a decision as it would clear the air and open up many other so-called order-in-council avenues for action. However, minister, in the absence of such a declaration, I am not legally permitted to ignore a requisition from Quebec. Once it's in my hands, I am obliged to respond. I could stall briefly, but the prime minister will either have to leave it in my hands as a Quebec problem and live with the consequences, or pre-empt the premier of Quebec by declaring a state of emergency. And it's something he will have to decide very soon, so he'd better understand what's happening."

Riley seemed almost relieved. "Well, in either case, I expect your cooperation and I assure you, you'll get mine. I'll see the prime minister immediately and pass your message along. If he wants to talk with you, I'll let you know. But there are other things civilian authorities have to think about, you know. The military doesn't have all the answers all the time. We need realistic advice. We have to consider the facts of national life. You guys don't."

Bishop turned to face Riley squarely. "Fine, minister, you speak with the prime minister, but I advise you to state the case in very clear terms. You and the prime minister will have my cooperation, but I must decide where my duty lies as circumstances unfold. If the prime minister decides that he can't accept my advice, then I'll recommend a candidate to take my place, unless, of course, he wishes to become his own CDS in the midst of this crisis."

Without waiting for a response that Jim Riley was, in any case, in no condition to give, Andy Bishop turned to his staff and said, "Thank you all. We'll reconvene after the minister has returned from his meeting with the prime minister, if that suits your purpose, minister?"

Riley, gathering up his papers and notes, stammered, "Ah, sure, Andy, we'll, ah, let you know."

Thursday, September 2, 2312 hours
Ottawa: NDOC

It was close to midnight when Ian Dobson returned to the NDOC and found two worried-looking staff officers waiting for him. The senior duty officer handed him a couple of pages of notes. "The latest int reps are just in, sir, and they don't look good. Actually, I think the shit's hit the fan."

Dobson glanced through the assessment. "Have you verified this with CSIS and the Mounties?"

"Yes, sir. They agreed that something big is developing tonight and they have their people on it right now. We also asked the Ranger commander here at NDHQ to make some inquiries among his units in James Bay. He phoned around then told us that everyone in the units has gone hunting. When he asked a couple of the women why the men were hunting at this time of year, they clammed right up and refused to talk to him any further."

"Okay. Keep on the other sources. Jimmy, secure fax this to Canada Command ops. Get the senior duty officer on the line for me ASAP and call the DCDS and ask him to come down here. Everyone, staff doubles up tonight."

DAY SIX

Friday, September 3

Friday, September 3, 0625 hours
Radisson

The peaceful September morning dawned over Quebec cool, crisp and clear. In Montreal, stark reds and brilliant yellows splashed across Mont-Royal's hillsides. Early commuters walked along Peel Street, coffee in hand, *La Presse* under arm. Backpack-laden students propelled by first-term eagerness hurried up the hill to McGill's learned halls. In Quebec City and across the province, unexceptional citizens began what they expected would be another unexceptional day. They were wrong.

Will Boucanier knew the day would be exceptional as he checked his watch at 0630 in the pink and gold pre-dawn glow. Behind him, crouched in the hollows and scrubs, the thirty "warriors" of his A Team anxiously awaited his call to move forward and enter the Radisson generating station. Everyone knew his job, drilled into them in rehearsal after rehearsal and in repeated sessions over simple sand-table models Boucanier had constructed in a garage just outside town.

Another dawn raid, Will thought. Another start-line. But this one's at home. He took a deep breath. Time to go to work. He glanced at his young radio operator, Simon. One last check that the boy had control of his satellite communications gear, the key to Will's control of the extended operation about to unfold under his command. The sophisticated equipment had been delivered to Will and his distant team leaders days before in the "special packages" sent from the States through Kahnawake and Akwesasne. But the radios were not on their most secure setting. The aim was to alert the feds, to bait the trap, so they were deliberately going to let the Communications Security Establishment, the national electronic snoops in Ottawa, pick up snippets of their conversations. Will took another deep breath then reached for the handset.

"Two alpha, this is two, over." No response. A second call. No response. "Bloody amateurs," he muttered softly to no one, prompting a nervous grin from Simon. "Two alpha, this is two, where the hell are you. Over?"

This time the radio crackled into life. "Ah, Two, this is two alpha. Over."

"Two, you get someone on that radio and you stay connected!" Will snapped. "Got that? Over."

"Two alpha, ah, roger. Over."

"Two, Op Thunder begins. Move your team into position as planned. Take the targets, but stay off the airfield. I repeat, stay *off* the airfield. Move at 0830 and report your progress to me as you take your objectives. And Joe, keep your people under control. Remember the locals are on our side and I intend to keep them there. Over."

"Two alpha. Just as planned. The guys are keen to go and they know the rules. I'm out of here at zero-eight-thirty on the nose. Over."

"Two, roger. You'll do fine. Out."

Next Will checked in with C Team leader Mary Tessel and repeated the orders he'd spent hours explaining and checking with her. Mary reported her team in position and repeated back her instructions. They'd had the local leaders in Radisson under surveillance all night and they would pick them up first. But they would leave the police, and especially Bob Ignace, to the last, giving him time to raise the alarm in the south.

The plan risked a gun battle with the alerted cops, but that was a risk worth taking. Will reminded Mary one last time that in such a situation C Team was to take cover and simply pin the police down. The idea here was to bait the trap. There was no need for a massacre on either side. The remainder of the team, moving into position on the Chisasibi-Radisson road, would play their part much later, and it might be deadly. But for now the key was to lure in a major rescue operation, and for that, police officers taken hostage or under fire were arguably more compelling than police already dead.

Finally, Will gave the "Go" to his transmission-line saboteurs. They were to begin with a few "demonstrations" down the line once the generating facilities were in Will's hands. If the SQ or the army moved north, they would then turn their attention to the roads and ambushes. Sabotage, harass, and withdraw—that was the drill. The ex-army pros with the teams would handle the major demolitions and direct the road operations. But Will knew that hit-and-run tactics on a small scale are difficult, even for well-trained teams, in such exposed terrain.

Frankly, he assumed that after a few successes, his teams of moose hunters would be eaten alive by the regular army units once the latter understood that the game was for real and took off the gloves. Will knew well the cost of war. His young men and women for the most part were innocent. On several nights in different locations he had explained as best he could the situations the teams were going to face, and they had seemed content with his explanations. Everyone trusted him.

Everyone, that is, except an uninvited elder who at one meeting sat and listened and then scolded young people. "You should all go home and mind your own business and your families. We were a warring people once long ago before the whites came here and all the blood we spilled then only brought more blood and tears into the lodges and starvation to the children. We don't need to go there again."

Will realized that the old man understood the realities of warfare and recognized the consequences that would descend on the innocents caught up in its horrors. Months before, Will had promised himself that he would try his best not to carelessly expose these young people to the dangers that were coming their way, but he knew that after this mission was over—win or lose—there would be tears in the lodges. Now, however, was not the time to allow reality to invite fear into his meetings.

"Remember when you were a young, hot-blooded warrior, old man," Will praised the elder. "These young warriors have your blood in their veins. They'll be fine and live to have many children, just as you did." The young warriors laughed at the hint of a future paradise.

Boucanier checked his watch again. He stood up, looked over the few waiting faces he could see in the growing light, then glanced at the generating station some 500 metres away. "On your feet, up. Prepare to advance."

He listened as the order was repeated down the line, then watched, satisfied, as his little company shook itself out, each warrior finding space and extending the formation off to the left exactly as Will had taught them to do. Pride and adrenaline surged through Will's heart. Holding his rifle at the trail in his left hand, he stepped out several metres in front of his troops, faced the station, and made a chopping motion with his right hand forward through the air towards the danger. "At a walk," he commanded, "follow me."

The sun touched the horizon and the new nation moved forward upright, confident, and proud. However briefly that might be, Will celebrated the idea nonetheless.

Friday, September 3, 0715 hours
Montreal: Peel Street

It is a rule that contented citizens, comfortable in the peace and prosperity of civil society, react to sudden violence just as pastured cattle react to the sudden appearance of a wolf in the distance. They stop and stare, curious, gawking, heads turning and twisting for a better view of the odd interruption to their routine. The rushing sirens, the crunch of fenders, the loud shriek of some crazed, street person, they're all just grist for early morning office gossip. The disturbance over, commuter strolls on. The wolf gone, the herd returns to the pasture grass.

At 0715, a small bomb in the mailbox outside the Peel Street subway exit in downtown Montreal exploded, breaking windows, setting an illegally parked car on fire, filling the windless street with a towering plume of black smoke. The unlucky few too near the blast sat on the sidewalk, dazed. Some were bleeding. Others, across the street and in the next block, stopped to gape. A few came to help the injured. What the hell was that? Was that a bomb?

Then came a sudden screeching of tires and gunshots in the air, as a disordered convoy of pickup trucks and cars roared onto the streets. Men, mostly, waving rifles and shotguns. In what seemed only a moment, other groups of vehicles appeared across the inner city. Everywhere, piles of tires thrown from the trucks soon barricaded Peel at Sherbrooke over to St-Denis, south to René-Lévesque, and for several blocks in other directions. Cars and small trucks parked nearby were commandeered, pushed across into the traffic, and overturned, adding to the barricades. "Warriors," some in native costume and some in second-hand fatigues, most sporting Mohawk haircuts or long braids, nearly all wearing kerchiefs over their faces as masks, mounted the barricades and fired a few brief, deliberately harmless shots over the crowd.

The once merely curious commuters froze, incredulous. The warriors, too, stood still, seemingly unsure what to do next. Then the crowd stampeded. In a moment, chaos filled the downtown streets of Montreal. Paper coffee cups, newspapers, bags and cases hit the pavement as the curious scattered outwards from the bomb site. Then, by some primordial signal, they became a crowd, a mob, surging this way and that in a pack. A few more bullets buzzed overhead, and people began to duck near cars or dash into shops and office buildings, breaking windows and doors in their panic, some accidentally slashing themselves on broken glass, spreading blood and mayhem. Others froze in the middle of streets, crouching, hiding their heads beneath coats and sweaters. A whining noise, faint at first, then growing intense, filled the air.

The first police car, lights flashing, siren wailing, slid into the intersection at Peel north of Sherbrooke, and warriors, standing carelessly along sidewalks or in pickup truck beds, riddled its bumper and front tires with bullets. The police officers threw themselves out of the car and scrambled for scant shelter behind the vehicle, radioing frantically for backup as they did so.

Within seconds, various first-responders—fire-fighters, paramedics, other police officers—alerted by a babel of 911 calls from dozens of terrified pedestrians, rolled into the area only to be caught in the ambush. A few were wounded immediately. Most escaped their vehicles and ran for cover. Eventually, as the police force grew, cops regrouped in the shelter of various buildings and organized themselves to return fire on the barricades, but they were massively out-gunned by the warriors. The centre of Montreal became Baghdad for a day.

The same scene was repeated in other parts of the city, at Highway 10 and University Avenue and Rue Guy, and on the major roads into the city. The Victoria and Jacques-Cartier bridges over the St. Lawrence were instantly closed down. Barricades appeared to drop from the heavens onto the roads. Heavily armed warriors took control of the city's core.

The media soon picked up the theme—*intifada* had come to Quebec as the native storm swept over other cities and towns from Sherbrooke to Chicoutimi. The major border crossings into the United States were barricaded on the Canadian side from Akwesasne in the west through Fort Covington, Highway 15, and at Abercorn, Stanstead, south of Coaticook, and at Woburn and east to Highway 173. Scattered bombings, the most serious near the front gates of CFB Valcartier, took place in various regions. And in some areas, as the day wore on, spontaneous attacks on government offices and the SQ broke out.

Molly Grace and her staff had anticipated a violent reaction from *les Québécois* once trouble started, and as soon as it did, their agents contacted various native leaders, most of whom were as shocked and opposed to the uprising as any other citizen, advising them to block access into their communities and organize armed forces to protect themselves from "retaliation by the French." Such attacks were not long in coming. By late in the day, there were reports of violence, burnings, and sieges at dozens of native villages across the province.

Friday, September 3, 0715 hours
Radisson: Outside the generating facilities

The attack on the generating facilities at Radisson by A Team was literally a walkover, different from a tourist visit only because the warriors came early, stayed late, and carried weapons. The staff, though not welcoming, weren't overtly hostile. Will Boucanier's team forced the unarmed guards to open the doors, making sure—unintentionally, it seemed to the staff—those further inside the station had time to alert their supervisor, who in turn had time to call Montreal. Then the A Team rounded up the workers, locked them in the tourist reception area, and prepared to defend the site.

The Bay Bombers, as they informally called themselves, went first to the generating rooms and wrapped short-fused detonating cord around critical panels and larger electrical circuit lines. At the same time, others wired the vital control room machinery so the complex could be put out of action for days, maybe weeks, simply by setting off those few charges.

While they worked, Will carefully surveyed the site inside and out, looking for security devices he might have missed on his recce earlier in the week. Except for a few new alarms connected to the Radisson police station, he noticed nothing of significance. While Will completed his rounds, his second-in-command organized a makeshift command post in the main administrative offices and hooked it into land lines to Chisasibi and Akwesasne. Then they confirmed their radio contact with all the teams and the cells down the road south, and told them to stand by for a message from Boucanier.

At the same time, outside the facilities, team leaders began to fortify the site. The road to Radisson was blocked after the attack by trucks brought up to the site by C Team. The trucks also carried equipment not needed in the assault, which the warriors now used to build camouflaged firing positions. A larger party of warriors walked back along the irregular winding paths between rough mounds of stone and deep ponds they had used an hour before, stringing simple barbed-wire obstacles at knee height or lower. Where they could, they drove short stakes into the hard ground, then loosely stretched the wire from stake to stake. Where the ground was too hard, they used rocks, bushes, or anything else handy.

This low wire entanglement was meant to delay, exhaust, and confound troops trying to rush the facilities. As they advanced, they would trip, fall, and with luck become briefly entangled. And if they avoided the traps, soldiers would tend to fall into single files as they found lanes through the wire, creating bunched-up targets. The warriors had only what wire could be brought up in small trucks after they captured the station, not much by military standards, but enough to complicate the enemy's expected attack.

After Will finished his recce, the other teams checked in as ordered. B Team at Chisasibi had accomplished all their objectives by ten hundred hours. The town was under control, and the authorities, such as they were, had not only surrendered, most had quickly joined their relatives in the team. With the town secured, Joe Neetha sent a small patrol in a confiscated police pickup to make contact with C Team on the road to Radisson, and assigned others to blockade the streets at key intersections. He reserved for himself the duty of leading half the team to set up observation posts overlooking the airport. Once they were in place, a few shots fired well over the control tower convinced the employees to take a sick day and the airport quickly went quiet. Then Neetha and his team sat down to await whatever might come their way.

The town of Radisson was secured by C Team almost as easily as Chisasibi had been, except for a brief skirmish near the police station. Bob Ignace himself was captured early on, not far from the generating station, as he responded to the silent alarm there. The rest of the on-duty police spotted the intruders and put up token resistance, but they were taken prisoner after a couple of nervous, inaccurate shots were fired by both sides. The rest of the small off-duty force was simply rounded up in their homes and locked up in their own jail. Other town officials and the radio station were taken without any difficulty by C Team members walking through town with long guns in their hands and murder in their eyes, just as Boucanier had anticipated. No one was killed or even injured.

"I knew you were a terrorist, Boucanier!" shouted Ignace as he was led into the generating station office locked in his own handcuffs.

Will looked at him quietly for a moment. "Well then, Bob, you should have done something about it. Right? Now we're going to detain you, and unless the army goes crazy when they get here, you and the others should be okay. Behave, and when this is over I'll recommend you for a medal."

"Yeah, well, the army will be here soon enough, you bastard. You can count on that."

"You're probably right on that too, Bob."

Will turned to the guards. "Lock him in the supervisor's office. Take off the handcuffs and give him a ration pack."

His men led the unhappy police officer into the office, unlocked the cuffs, and, on their way out, threw a military meal pack carelessly at his feet. Ignace kicked angrily at it. Will chuckled. "Don't blame you, Bob. Kinda nasty, that army stuff... until you're hungry, that is." He nodded, and his men closed and locked the door.

Will turned to the map his guys had tacked to the wall. Op Thunder, though the Hollywood ring of the nickname embarrassed him, had gone well so far. But he needed a response from his old comrades in the Canadian Forces to make it a complete success. He nodded a couple of times, deep in thought, then turned to the site supervisor, who stood, visibly shaking, between two large members of the A Team.

"Okay, son," said Will in a soft but commanding voice, "I want you to turn off the power, now."

"Well, uh, sir, I, uh, that takes some time to do safely, and, uh, I need some help from my people you've locked up."

"Take your time, but don't screw with me. Find the people you need and get the job done. By the way, the system is going to be interrupted by other means soon anyway, so let me know if there are some technical issues we need to deal with here." The supervisor licked his lips, glanced around, then stammered, "No, sir, I, uh, a couple of hours, uh, we can do that, it uh, yeah, we can do that."

"Well, then, get to it," said Will. He gestured toward the tourist area where the staff were held prisoner. The supervisor nodded and walked down that corridor followed by his escorts while Will reached for the radio and called each sabotage team leader in turn. The message was brief. "Bring down the first sets of wires and towers and report when the job is done."

Friday, September 3, 0905 hours
CFB Trenton

Lieutenant Colonel Campbell stood before the planning boards comparing the maps of the James Bay region with the satellite images he had just received from Special Operations Forces Command. He was interrupted by his operations officer, Captain Maggie Harkness. "Here it is, sir, the warning order in hard copy." She handed the formatted message to her CO and stood aside as he read the order in silence.

SECRET
0855 HOURS
SOFCOM OPS 023
DISTRIBUTION LIST A
WARNING ORDER—OPMERCURY

SITUATION:
Enemy Forces: A force estimated at near 100 persons, some former CF *Rangers and* CF *soldiers, have attacked the Hydro-Québec facilities at James Bay/Radisson region and the roadways into the area. The force is believed to be lightly armed, but well organized. A detailed int assessment will be forwarded by secure means later this day.*

Friendly Forces: At present, the community and the facilities are guarded only by local police and a small detachment of SQ. *Hydro-Québec employs approximately 20 unarmed security guards of unknown reliability. Other national communication security assets are active in the area. Their information will be made available to assist planning as security procedures allow.*

Attachments and Detachments: Special Service Regiment is placed under OPCON *to Comd Canada Com as of 0930 hours.*

8 Wing, CFB *Trenton, is place under* TACCON *to Comd Canada Com as of 0930 hours until completion of Phase I of Op Mercury.*

MISSION:

Special Service Regiment will mount a regimental combat airborne assault on the James Bay Hydro-Québec facilities at Radisson to secure and protect the facilities.

CONCEPT OF OPS:

The operation will be conducted in three phases. Phase I—airborne assault to secure the Radisson facilities; Phase II—airborne or ground assault to secure the airfield at Chisasibi; Phase III—the relief of the Special Service Regiment by other CANCOM *units at the direction of Comd* CANCOM.

Phase I will be mounted from CFB *Trenton and completed when the facilities are secure. Phase II will begin EITHER concurrently with the assault on Radisson facilities or later depending on the* CO SSR *assessment of the situation at Radisson after the initial airborne landings. Phase III will begin on order of Comd* CANCOM.

TIMINGS:

Phase I: Airborne landings no later than Wednesday 0630 hours. Phase II and III on order.

Timings for aircraft loading, air approach plan, and dropping zones to be coordinated by CO, SSR *with Comd 8 Wing.*

All units on six (6) hours notice to move as of 0930 hours today.

ALL ACK.

Rusty Campbell looked over the maps and turned to his regimental ops officer. "Okay, Maggie, let's get the drills moving. Draw up a warning order for me along the lines we discussed last night. Add in the timings. O Group here at …" He checked his watch. "… at ten hundred. Ask Comd 8 Wing if he and his air ops officers could join us and tell him that you and I will be at his office in thirty minutes to go over the outline. He's on the distribution list of course, so I suspect he's moving on his own battle procedure as well. Any questions?"

Maggie looked over her notes. "No, sir. I'll have the regimental warning order out ASAP and then join you here once I confirm the meeting with 8 Wing."

Friday, September 3, 1003 hours
Washington, D.C.

The White House National Security Advisor held his red phone, waiting for the president. "Ms. President," he began as she answered, "we may have a major national security threat to the United States developing in Canada. I recommend that you convene immediately the full National Security Committee at the White House and increase the armed forces alert status to State Orange."

Friday, September 3, 1015 hours
Ottawa: Prime Minister's Office

General Bishop left NDHQ by the Mackenzie Street entrance, hardly acknowledging the salutes of the soldiers passing him in the doorway. He stepped into the back of his waiting staff car, while Colonel Dobson slid into the front seat beside the driver. For the first time in his appointment as CDS, Bishop had accepted a military police escort, even though he was only travelling the short distance to Parliament Hill.

The prime minister had called a meeting in his office to plan the government's response to the crisis in Quebec. As he entered the room and looked around the table for his allotted seat, Bishop noted that the gathering was unusually grand. The deputy prime minister and the five cabinet ministers of the Defence and Security Committee were huddled in a corner; their deputy ministers stood about or consulted hurriedly with the clerk of the Privy Council, the government's chief bureaucrat and their real boss. Three senators from Quebec joined the meeting and moved uninvited to the head of the table. Bishop nodded to RCMP Commissioner Jean Richard and the director of the Canadian Security and Intelligence Service, Heidi Gunter. Several lesser bureaucrats sat in or hovered about the chairs lining the conference room walls. As the CDS set his notes and files in front of his allotted seat at the table, Jack Hemp strode through the door and motioned everyone to their places.

Standing behind his own chair, gripping the seat back, Hemp began speaking. "We are facing a damn serious national crisis. I intend to show that this government is fully capable of resolving this matter and that we will not allow lawless actions by anyone to direct the affairs of the country." He turned his chair back, sat down, and leaned forward with his elbows on the table. "Having said that, however," he continued, "you know that in international affairs I'm a peacekeeper—talking is better than fighting and all that. But that's for domestic consumption and it keeps us out of difficult commitments and, General Bishop, the army out of the treasury." A few politicos at the table and around the room snickered, but Bishop ignored the laboured and inappropriate joke.

"All right then," said Hemp, going into his gruff, theatrical, take-charge tone, "what do we know for sure? Perhaps, General Bishop, you could bring us up-to-date on the military situation."

"Thank you, prime minister. First, I would like to say a few words to you all about my directions to the Canadian Forces and my intentions over the next twenty-four hours. As you know, significant, well organized, and violent attacks have occurred, and continue to occur, in cities and towns across Quebec, the most serious of these being in Montreal.

"A second very serious, and, we are convinced, coordinated event—the attack on the James Bay facilities and surrounding area—has effectively shut down power transmission from the region, resulting in widespread power outages across the eastern seaboard of North America. These events, and others that we anticipate as part of what appears to be a carefully planned campaign, have prompted the government of Quebec to declare the situation beyond its control and ask for the aid of the Canadian Forces. The requisition came to me at nine o'clock this morning, and the Canadian Forces, under the authority and responsibilities vested in my office under the National Defence Act, has already begun a large-scale response to these violent attacks. And, prime minister, for the benefit of others at this meeting, I should stipulate that my actions were discussed with the minister of national defence and he has, so I understand, your concurrence with our preliminary deployments."

Hemp nodded. "Yes, that's right—for the preliminary deployments."

Bishop let the remark hang in the air briefly then continued. "I have ordered the Commander Canada Command, Lieutenant General Lepine—" Here he looked directly at the senators from Quebec. "He's the commander responsible for domestic security and emergency management—to deploy the 5 Brigade from CFB Valcartier supported by troops from CFB Gagetown to aid the civil powers in Quebec. That deployment is underway. I have also ordered the Special Service Regiment, our airborne battalion now assembled at CFB Trenton, to retake the James Bay facilities and to secure the region. That operation will begin this evening, and other units from the West are being readied to move into Quebec as transport assets become available."

Bishop was intentionally vague on these deployments simply because he had no way of knowing who in the room he could trust. He paused, looked around the table, then raised a pointed forefinger. "I must warn the cabinet," he said solemnly, "that these are combat operations and although I have issued stringent rules of engagement, we expect to meet resistance in all sectors and to take casualties and to inflict casualties on the renegades."

Hemp smiled and held up a hand. "Whoa there, general. The CBC will never allow the word 'renegades' on air. We'd best think of something neutral."

Eddie Geldt took the cue. "I'll work on it."

Andy Bishop frowned and closed his notes. "Thank you, prime minister. As soon as your staff finds a suitably polite word to describe the people who are attacking the country, disrupting our economy, and killing our citizens and soldiers, please let me know and I'll incorporate it into our next briefing."

General Bishop's assistant flipped on a projector. "Prime minister, ladies and gentlemen, the Canadian Forces are deploying the appropriate units available in Canada to the most threatened and dangerous areas in Quebec.

"The Canadian Forces with the assistance of CSIS and the RCMP estimate that upwards of 300 members of the Native People's Army, the NPA, are active in Montreal. A less reliable figure places from 150–200 so-called warriors in Quebec City, Sherbrooke, and Trois-Rivières. Another 100-

plus warriors and supporters are probably on the reserves ready to join the operation. CSIS, on information from their own sources and as yet unconfirmed information from American sources, estimates that as many as 700 Canadian and American natives and sympathizers are moving from the United States towards Quebec to join or support the rebellion."

Bishop noticed the prime minister twist in his chair, but continued before his term "rebellion" could be challenged. "Further spontaneous activities by aboriginals across Canada may also occur, but that's our estimate of the hard-core people actively coordinating their activities at the moment."

The CDS nodded to his aide and the projector shone a wide-angle, very detailed, satellite image of the Radisson area then zoomed in on the generating site. "This image, prime minister, taken at about eight o'clock, shows the main building here ..." He indicated it with his laser pointer. "... and the barricades on the road, here, and here. Each barricade is guarded by approximately ten armed people in covered positions. These more recent images pointed to several small figures in the fields surrounding the site, who appear to be mining or stringing wire in the area to guard against any attempt to retake the facility."

Hemp interrupted. "I didn't think we had satellites like that."

"We don't, prime minister. We don't have *any* sophisticated ways to monitor Canadian land and sea spaces. The project that was to come on-line last year is still in the government's procurement decision stream. The images you see were provided to us by the Pentagon after I requested the chairman of the United States Joint Chiefs of Staff to position a satellite over the region, as is permitted under the North American Command Arrangement signed by our government two years ago."

"The Pentagon?" Hemp yelped. "I don't want the bloody Americans in here."

Bishop pointed to the screen. "This is a source of information critical to our operations. We are going to send units into the area and I am not prepared to send them in blind. Besides, prime minister, General Leonardo, apparently on the direction of the president, told me directly that the attack on the James Bay facilities and the cutting of the hydro transmission system into the United States made the matter a vital concern for United States homeland security. He was preparing to put the satellite over

James Bay whether we asked or not. At least now we know about it and can use this very valuable resource."

Bishop returned to the screen. "Prime minister, we estimate that some fifty warriors, mostly Canadian Forces Rangers, are in the Chisasibi area and that the town is in their hands. The airfield in the town of Chisasibi itself, which is vital to our mission, seems to be out of operation, but the satellite images show no one on the airfield and no obstructions there either. Another group of natives is on the road between Chisasibi and Radisson and appear to be digging defensive positions on the road."

The next image clicked onto the screen. "To the south, there are no obvious barricades on the single road leading to Radisson from Montreal and Matagami, although native groups—we are not sure how many and in what numbers—have knocked down transmission lines here, here, and here, and two actual transmission towers are down here and here. The natives in this area are lightly armed, basically rifles and shotguns, but have enough firepower to keep police and repair crews out of the area.

"Now for friendly forces. Units from Valcartier and Gagetown are moving into the most difficult spots in Quebec. The first convoy out of Valcartier was attacked by a roadside car bomb on the road near Quebec City. Two vehicles were destroyed, but no one was injured. This event has slowed the deployment, but we are now using our few serviceable CF helicopters, as well as aircraft requisitioned from civilian sources, to move light infantry companies into Montreal. These units will clear the renegades out of the cities and destroy the barricades on the main roads. This operation may take several days.

"At James Bay, we are mounting a major airborne operation that will retake the Radisson site and the Chisasibi airport and the town and restore the connection to Radisson. A second force forming now in CFB Valcartier will move today to a staging base at Matagami, here, and move north on Highway 109 and clear the road to Radisson.

"Let me add, prime minister, that logistical challenges make this a very demanding operation regardless of the enemy's strength and tactical abilities. It's more than 500 kilometres from Valcartier to Matagami, and then some 620 kilometres from there to Radisson. The road north is limited, isolated, and filled with potential obstacles. Just driving a large military convoy to Radisson unopposed would take time. If the force has to fight its way north, the operation will be difficult, to say the least, and it will be slow.

"Those are the main points, prime minister. Are there any questions?"

Hemp looked around the table as if to gather support for his outburst, then shouted. "Are there any questions? Jesus Christ, general, you're telling us that there are just a few hundred natives on the loose and you're going after them with the whole army, but it's going to take days, I suspect you mean weeks, to put them down?"

General Bishop spoke calmly. "That's right. In fact, prime minister, the government had best prepare itself for a long, drawn-out security problem that will disrupt Quebec for months. And if we can't contain the uprising to that province alone, which we won't be able to if they've made similarly careful plans on a similar scale elsewhere, it will disrupt the rest of the country for many months as well.

"Let me remind the cabinet that the Irish Republican Army at its worst had only some 500 full-time, hard-core fighters, but with the tacit support of a significant section of the population and by frightening the rest into silence, it kept thousands of British soldiers occupied for years and put Britain on a virtual war footing for three decades.

"Whoever these people are and whatever their immediate plans, they too are widely supported, or feared, among the native community. I want everyone in this room to understand, really understand, that we are facing a very serious national threat here, not a temporary inconvenience. Our country is vulnerable partly because it is an open society and partly because we have been reluctant to see the internal dangers lying openly before us."

The CDS paused and looked slowly round the table. No one dared speak up. He turned directly to the prime minister for his final words. "My advice to your government, prime minister, is to bring all the power of the state down on the heads of these renegades. And begin by acknowledging the facts before us. As we start to bring the present situation under control, the government should prepare plans to occupy the reserves most responsible for this outrage and to remove the sanctuary the native rebels now enjoy there. We need to invoke the strongest provisions of the Emergency Act and I demand your authority to call out the reserve forces on active service.

"I cannot emphasize strongly enough that this rebellion must be stopped in its tracks before a perception of national weakness encourages hundreds, perhaps thousands, of native people to join the small force we are now facing. If that were to happen, prime minister, I could in no way ensure the defence of the country, nor maybe even the safety of our scattered military establishments."

Frozen silence filled the room. After the longest fifteen seconds any of the civilians present had ever lived through, Jack Hemp found his voice and tried to regain control with a show of resolve. "Yes, well thank you, General Bishop. I apologize for the unnecessarily harsh tone I just used. Your tough, uncompromising advice is exactly what the cabinet needs and has come to expect from you, and it's the kind of advice I want from everyone these days."

It was Hemp's turn to look around the table. "Any other critical information we need to air right now?"

Aaron Hays, member for Halifax-Dartmouth and minister for foreign affairs, raised his hand. "Prime minister, I would like to say a few words on the situation prompted by the international, and especially the U.S., reactions to the situation." He opened a slim file marked "Secret: Canadian Eyes Only," and, without waiting for leave, he began. "Two issues need to be considered by the cabinet. First, our ambassador in Washington reports that he is under considerable pressure from the American administration and Congress to explain what is happening and what we are doing, in the blunt words of the White House National Security Advisor, 'to end the conflict.' The secretary for homeland security was on the phone to our ambassador twice today asking essentially the same questions. He said his department will try to intercept any natives travelling to Canada, but he can't assure us he'll be successful. Even more worrying, the Senate majority leader, speaking on a morning TV news show carried nationwide, said words to the effect that 'if the Canadians can't protect themselves, then perhaps the United States will have to help them, even if they might object to the help.' The president has not said anything in public about the matter, but she is decidedly anxious and may act soon.

"Second, our ambassador to the United Nations met with the French ambassador who told her that, quote, 'the French people have had a long and mostly mutually beneficial relationship with Canadian Indians and that France encourages Canada to deal fairly with the matter,' unquote. He then went on to say in effect that, 'French citizens have a special relationship with Quebec and they expect France to aid in the protection of that distinct society.' He ended by offering our ambassador his good offices to help negotiate an end to the conflict. Prime minister, I have to report that some senior members of my department suspect that the premier of Quebec may be having conversations with French officials in Ottawa or even in Paris, but we have no hard evidence of such goings on. I hardly need to tell you all that both these developments represent a threat to our sovereignty, and—"

Hemp cut him off. "Well, our lady in Quebec City better have told that French ambassador bastard to get lost." The prime minister turned and glared at his chief of staff. "Eddie, get their ambassador here on the phone right after this meeting and tell him that."

Hays looked directly across the table at Hemp. "Prime minister, it gets worse. A proposal is being circulated at the UN General Assembly by the 'African Francophone Coalition,' which includes a number of states we have criticized in the past few years for their failure to protect minority populations. They are trying to get a Security Council resolution condemning Canada for its failure to protect the native population. They're also looking for support for their idea that a UN peacekeeping force be sent to Canada to guard the natives from, quote, 'white abuse,' unquote. It is unlikely at this point that the Security Council would even agree to debate the proposal, and anyway we expect the Americans and the Brits to veto it if it gets there. But the French ambassador said he was awaiting instructions from Paris."

"Sonofabitch!" Hemp slammed his palm on the table. "They're just getting back at us for backing the Americans in Sudan. I'm accused in the Quebec separatist press of being an American lapdog and in the *National Post* as a French poodle. But I assure you, folks, I'm going to show Canadians I'm neither."

When he was finished, Hays concluded his remarks by saying, "Prime minister, we're working the corridors in Washington and at the UN, but I agree with General Bishop. This matter requires the firmest and most immediate attention of the government."

"Thanks, Aaron." Hemp turned to his chief of staff and said, "Eddie, record these directions." Then to the CDS he said, "General Bishop, I understand your concern for your bases and the limits of the Canadian Forces and your desire to have a reserve if things go wrong in other areas, but there are no overt signs of trouble outside Quebec. Therefore, the government of Canada directs you to continue with the deployment of units now under orders and further directs you to move into Quebec all other appropriate units necessary to make a convincing show of force and bring this situation under our control. Please prepare a robust set of rules of engagement limited only by the constraint to use only lawful force at levels appropriate to the circumstances and only for so long as such force is required. Through these instructions you are formally relieved of the requirements under the National Defence Act respecting the 'requisition for aid of the civil power' you received from the province of Quebec. The matter will now be managed by the federal government as a defence of Canada concern.

"General, your priorities are these. First, secure Montreal and Quebec City and restore stability in the province, and second, secure the Radisson facilities and transmission corridors. This is a 'whole-of-government' operation. You are, therefore, authorized to deal directly with all departments and agencies of government. The cabinet ministers will get the word immediately. Are these directions clear enough?"

Bishop looked directly at Hemp. "Yes, sir."

"Okay. Aaron, first, get a message out to all your posts. They are to tell anyone who raises the subject, and vigorously defend the message, that the situation is under control and the government of Canada is acting to restore order where necessary. The so-called 'root cause of the disturbances' is a dispute and struggle for control between rival native leaders, led mostly by radicals. The native population, by and large, is loyal and peaceful and is not rallying to the radical message.

"Second, get our UN ambassador on the phone and give her the word in the strongest tone—she is to protect our interests and lean on the Africans if necessary. I want you to arrange a telephone conversation for me with President Ricardo—we are in control and she should have no worries and we expect her support in the UN. Tell our ambassador in Washington to get with the House and Senate majority leaders and pass them the same message. Jim Riley will speak to his colleague, the secretary of defence, and General Bishop will pass the same message to the Pentagon.

The prime minister turned to Howard Pentergast, the justice minister. "Howard, get your people working with DND on this aid of the civil power thing and you call Madam Commeau to explain the decision. If she has a problem, which she will, of course, tell her to call me later. But give her a big, fat hint that Quebec is to stay in its own yard. Have your department draw up the necessary papers to enact provisions of the Emergency Act and prepare a briefing on the Act for today's cabinet meeting."

"Okay, everyone. Full cabinet meeting in two hours. Remember what the old man said during the last, uh, apprehended insurrection, 'there're no bleeding hearts around here.' We'll get through this thing and we don't need, nor will I allow, any outsiders to interfere with this internal national matter—no one."

Hemp instantly softened his tone. "General Bishop, Andy, thanks. Watch over your guys. I'm coming to NDHQ when that airborne thing goes in. Please have someone give my office the details."

The CDS pushed back his chair. "Thank you, prime minister. I suggest that you come to Canada Command headquarters. That's where General Lepine is commanding the defence of Canada operation. My staff, Colonel Dobson, will arrange the meeting with Mr. Geldt."

Friday, September 3, 1020 hours
CFB Trenton

Lieutenant Colonel "Rusty" Campbell looked at the warning order in his hand and then out at the full regiment of paratroops standing easy in order of their commandos on the floor of the giant hangar that usually housed the enormous C17 transport planes the Canadian Forces had acquired in the spring of 2007. Two of the aircraft were outside the hangar on the tarmac being readied to lift the Western units and their vehicles to Quebec. The other two were in Zimbabwe, prepared to bring elements of the Canadian battle group home if the native uprising got out of hand.

The hangar doors were open on this warm September night, and guards patrolled the area to make sure Campbell could speak to his unit without interruption. He intended, as was his habit, to give everyone a very general briefing about what the regiment had been asked to do before he called together the officers commanding the commandos and his HQ staff to give his detailed orders.

Regimental Sergeant Major Skip Martin, senior non-commissioned soldier in the unit and a real warrior who had seen combat service in Eritrea, Afghanistan three times, and more recently Zimbabwe, raised his deep commanding voice: "A—ten—tion!"

The hangar reverberated with the sound of 374 pairs of boots simultaneously hitting the deck. "Steady up and keep quiet." He turned smartly to salute his commanding officer. "Three hundred and seventy-four soldiers on parade, sir."

"Thank you, RSM. Stand the regiment at ease and gather them around the podium please."

The orders given, the paras mingled forward and formed a wide semicircle in front of Rusty Campbell. He tapped the microphone in front of him and spoke directly to the unit.

"We have been warned to prepare for a full-scale airborne assault..." The soldiers shuffled about, speaking to each other excitedly, before Campbell could finish the sentence.

"You people quiet down and pay attention," the RSM commanded.

"As I was saying... a full-scale airborne assault on the power generating facilities at James Bay. A large group of native warriors..." Laughter and several shouts of "yeah, really!" broke out here and there in the ranks. "... have seized this important hydro facility. Our job is to conduct an airborne assault to take the facilities back and secure them from harm.

"This is not a training exercise. The natives, about a hundred armed people according to the int reports, are determined and willing to fight. But then so are we."

Shouts of "Airborne!" swept across the floor followed by a deep, cadenced chorus, "Hur—rah! Hur—rah!"

"We are on six hours notice to move from midnight tonight. I want every one of you to fall in and under your officers, and NCOs begin the battle procedures we have practised so diligently all summer long. This one's for real, folks, and the terrain in the target area is rough and weather is worse. We're going to make a mass drop, two commandos together and a third commando on a separate target. It will be difficult, but I know you're more that up to the task.

"Officers to remain behind. RSM, fall out the regiment and let's get cracking."

More hurrahs filled the air.

Friday, September 3, 1130 hours
Akwesasne: The Complex

The Complex was a hive of anxiety. Military plans before active operations begin are tidy, rational abstractions. Operations, on the other hand, are chaotic. A regular army—the double meaning of the term exposes the problem of the peacetime profession—thrives on order, predictability, neatness, and established drills. But great commanders and their armies are comfortable in the midst of disorder. If you wish to win a war, citizen, find a scruffy, brilliant radical to command your armed forces.

The leaders of the Native People's Army were discovering the disorder that is warfare and not everyone was handling the opening day of the battle for Canada very well. Staff officers in the Complex were at a loss as to how to deal with the rapidly evolving situation, and panic was beginning to creep into the room. Bill Whitefish sensed the crisis as soon as he arrived for the morning briefing.

His chief of operations, Eric Longstreet, a middle-aged resident of Akwesasne who taught business management in a local community college, stood looking at the maps of southern Quebec, seemingly not sure what he should do as the Movement's well-laid plans seemed to unravel around him. He turned, relieved to find Bill standing behind him.

"Christ, Bill, the Montreal police seem to have gotten over the surprise of this morning's attacks. Their SWAT teams are moving all over the downtown area. We don't know how many there are. I didn't think they could move that fast.

"Our warriors at the downtown barricades, some of them I guess didn't see the early calm as just the police getting into position. The guys standing up in trucks waving weapons at the police really got it. The survivors are telling me that rather than being in control of the streets, they're trapped like fish in a barrel. We think an army sniper team has arrived from some- where ... the guys saw a helicopter come in low and drop some soldiers on a high building near the barricades. We've had six warriors down in the last half hour and we can't get anybody out, even the wounded."

"Sure, Eric, but we do have the police and the first army units fixated on Montreal and now Quebec City, too. And that's what we aimed to do. How are things going outside the cities?"

"Well, the momentum there is shifting too, but not as quickly. The police and some soldiers are trying to isolate Akwesasne and the other border reserves. I don't know much, seems we have a bunch of firefights along the back trails and waterways along the U.S./Canada border. Some- one reported that they think the Canadian JTF2 and U.S. Border Services patrols are ambushing the warriors and weapons convoys heading into Quebec. I don't think so; could be our own guys firing at each other or just locals from the reserves taking shots, or maybe the drug smugglers are mixed in there somewhere.

"Everything's all fucked up. I'm not sure what to do next. What do you think we should do, Bill?"

"First thing is you take a couple of deep breaths. Get your people here to help you. They can handle the minute-to-minute events and get them to put a picture together. Doesn't have to be perfect. You just get a sense of what's really happening and where we have resources and where we can best use them. Okay?"

"Ya, sure. That's what we practised all summer, but it's not unfolding like we thought it would. I hardly get done with one problem on my plate and then two more show up."

"Well, Eric, from what I've read over the months, and from the few pro- fessionals we have around, that seems to be business as usual. But look on the bright side: the James Bay operation seems to have gone off without a serious hitch. That counts as a success. And the attacks on the power grid have produced the response from the government that we counted on.

"Eric, understand this. Molly Grace knows what she's doing. You have to believe that all of this will work out in the end—that the grand strategy will be a success. It takes imagination and resolution to command this type of operation and Molly Grace has all those qualities in spades."

Bill began to organize the staff for the morning briefing, then he walked down the hall to speak with Molly and alert her to the jitters, or as he described it, "a collective case of the runs in the ops room." Molly didn't see the humour in Bill's description of events. She only saw a threat that had to be stamped out.

"I'll get rid of Longstreet! I don't want anyone around who can't stand the heat."

"No, Molly that's not the answer. You can't fire everyone who isn't as cool as you are. The team just needs a bit of encouragement, some reassurance. Perhaps you could say something like that before the briefing." Molly wasn't comfortable comforting others, but she took Bill's suggestion, if not to heart at least as a practical way to handle "this problem of weakness" for the moment.

As Molly entered the ops room for the morning planning session, Bill gathered her panicky staff together. "I want everyone here," she began, "to shake off the excitement and distress of the last day and a half. You may have expected we were in some kind of bloodless sport, where everything goes our way and you're not in any danger. Well, welcome to the revolution. Things are unfolding in the chaotic way you should have expected, but they are unfolding in our direction. If you think we are playing events as they occur and not to some automatic schedule, you're right. That was the plan. This is reality. But think of the other guys in Ottawa and Quebec City. They have no idea what's going on. They're just reacting to our game plan. Things are just as chaotic for them, but they're losing and they don't even know it yet."

Murmurs and affirmations passed around the table. Molly looked to Bill Whitefish who took his cue, glanced at his notes, and turned to the wall map.

"I can confirm Molly's assessments. The disturbances in Montreal and Quebec City have been rougher than we expected, or at least the authorities and the army have reacted quicker and more violently than we expected. They let the separatist goons go free and shoot our people, including women and a couple of kids. Typical. But listen: the barricades have attracted almost all the province's police SWAT teams and the army is being drawn into the cities as we planned.

"Outside the cities, the countryside is at our mercy and the army is having a tough time getting from Gagetown and Valcartier to Montreal in any numbers because the car bombs have slowed their convoys to a crawl. Even our 911 hoax bomb calls are giving them fits. Their bomb squads are scurrying all over the place and the army is investigating every vehicle they see parked on the roads."

He pointed to the map. "Our barricades at Oka, Akwesasne, Marieville, Barrington, Berthierville, and at several points along the U.S. border are still effective and are not under much threat. Spontaneous barricades are popping up between Quebec City and Montreal and are at least forcing the SQ to guard other places far from the main areas that concern us. The sites in Montreal are in trouble and we might withdraw the people from there tonight under cover of darkness and open new sites in the city during the night. We don't really need many of them in Montreal any more, thanks to the James Bay raid. Will Boucanier's operation has been very successful and is on schedule. Okay, any questions so far?"

People shuffled in their chairs. Molly alone spoke up. "How long can the downtown Montreal barricades control the streets if we ask them to hold?"

"I'm not sure," Bill replied. "I spoke with Sylvain and Lenny a couple of hours ago and they sounded defiant as usual, but they are low on supplies and have several casualties that need to go to hospital. They might be able to stay until morning—that is if the army doesn't try a night attack, which I think is very likely. But daytime sniper fire is murder and I don't think they can hold out past noon tomorrow either way."

"Okay, go on. What's the other side doing?"

Bill returned to his seat and his notes. "Our sources tell us the prime minister held a high-level meeting this afternoon and argued with the military. The CDS wants to save some troops for other operations, but the PM put all the eggs into Quebec. The PM is also pissed off with the UN and France and wants to put on a big show of control to keep them out of the situation. The hard news is that the airborne are committed to James Bay soon, maybe tonight, but I suspect they'll move in the daylight tomorrow. And the prime minister ordered the military to bring more units into Quebec, basically everything they've got. All the CDS gets to keep out west is one battalion in Edmonton and a bunch of militia.

"Oh, and the American president, of course, is really getting raked over the coals in the media and in Washington. A *New York Times* report says the Senate majority leader called her a 'do nothing president,' but then he would since he's in the race for her job."

Molly sat quietly for a moment. The staff anxiously searched her face for clues to her mood, but Bill, unconcerned, gathered up his notes. He knew Molly would break the silence when she was ready. And he figured her brand of revolutionary theory in practical matters meant direction, not discussion, would follow. It did.

She stood up, as short people tend to do to make a point. "We'll play to our strengths and their fears and expectations. Let me recall for you the principles of our campaign. Remember months ago we talked about Lawrence of Arabia's 'revolt in the desert.' Like his, our aim is political, not military. The enemy prizes his material things—the cities and the streets within the cities, the oil wells and the power lines. We don't, but that doesn't matter. We will attack them because he does value them. We'll force the enemy to spread his units to the breaking point. He will uselessly guard countless material things, his 'vital points,' even though we'll never seek to possess them, wouldn't take them if they were given to us. The enemy will be strung out in small detachments and vulnerable. The Canadian army has great technical strength, but everywhere it's immobilized by the need to protect goods, even to the point of sacrificing the essence of the country."

Her voice raised, wavered just a touch. "Our weaknesses, our poverty, our lack of formal military skills, these we'll turn, have turned, into our greatest assets. Like Lawrence's Arabs, we're tough, we're self-assured, we know the land, and we have on our side courage borne of righteousness and despair. We'll use our inexpert force with economy. We want the army to go after James Bay and fight in Montreal and Winnipeg. We want them to hold these places in large numbers. We want their vital systems to work, but just enough that the governments think them worth defending.

"White greed will keep them sitting on their possessions while we take the empty land when, where, and as we like. As the master wrote, 'This pride in his imperial heritage will keep the enemy in his present position—all flanks and no front.' Lawrence wrote that for centuries the whites believed they deserved what they could assert. Well, we believe that now too, and we'll act on our belief."

Bill, standing aside from the group, watched apprehension disappear. He saw confidence stand up once again, steady and sure beside Molly's pride and purpose. He watched Molly, the messiah, grasp her devoted followers.

Not for the first time, however, he felt a stirring of apprehension. Despite all the time and effort he had devoted to the Movement, and despite his admiration for Molly, he found himself uneasy when he saw the effect of Molly's words on her followers. He wondered, if only for an instant, whether Molly's heroic rhetoric and her vision were not in truth just another brand of dangerous Western nationalism, an imported settler doctrine dressed up in feathers and buckskins.

How, Bill thought, does declaring that native bands are, in fact, nations defend the native tradition and native way of life? Isn't it all the rhetoric, like "the declaration" from the First Nations Federation and the Grand Chief about "an aboriginal creator who gave us *distinctly unique* laws that govern all our relationships and *distinctly unique* traditions which we have followed from time immemorial," a declaration that is thrown to the wind by all the native leaders and their followers who crave the European, Enlightenment traditions of the nation presumably given to the settlers by their creator?

Bill shook his head. He couldn't think about it. Not now. That discussion, he told himself, was for another day. Now was the time for unflinching loyalty and for action. Which meant it was too late for "another day." He chased the thought away and focused on the present crisis. Molly was talking to him.

"Bill," she was saying, "this is what we'll do in the next phase. First, I want the lawyers to launch a widespread legal challenge to everything the governments are doing. Tell them to use their imaginations, and if they haven't got any, tell them to buy some. With the fees they charge, they can afford it." Laughter around the table eased the tension. "Seriously, we can challenge the use of the aid of the civil power laws and the Emergency Act against native people. We can challenge the threat to our treaty rights from the blockade of our reserves and the imposition of restrictions on our movement over borders which we don't recognize. And so on.

"Second, get our media machine working. I'll give interviews by radio and TV to the CBC and to our network this evening—the message is that we want to negotiate without conditions, but insist on our rights. The CBC will broadcast whatever I say in the name of balance. I'll give interviews to the *Star*—white guilt stuff, they'll eat that up. And to the *Globe and Mail* on 'the need to be reasonable and negotiate' and 'root causes,' etc. The *National Post* need not apply ... no, actually, if they are interested I'll give them something to fan the flames, pump up their editorial line 'Enough With the Apologies.' That should do it."

People sat around the table and listened as Molly spun out her plan to spend lives for a cause few outside the room had had any chance to discuss, and, whether they had or not, had little comprehension of how it was meant to improve their lives.

"Third," Molly continued, "I want our champions in New York to demand a chance for me to appear before the UN Security Council to explain our position and express appreciation for the African initiatives. The Africans owe us help for supporting their ambassadors at our Vancouver conference. Including ... what'd they call the girls? 'Room expenses?' If necessary, someone could remind them about the videos. Oh, and we could try for a meeting with the French ambassador in Ottawa. I'll bring up both diplomatic possibilities in my media interviews, if only to distract the government.

"Fourth, on the home front, we'll use Saturday to consolidate our gains and repair weaknesses. I want everything ready for the big event next week. So, I want you to send the imported backup teams to infiltrate Montreal and reinforce the downtown teams if they can. If not, no point just getting them killed or trapped. If it's too hot downtown, they should join the highway barricades. They're to use their own judgment once they get close to the action; no point having us guessing what they're seeing.

"Alert the Round Lake Algonquin cell to move ASAP to open a new front in Hull. Specifically, they're to occupy the bridges over the Ottawa River coming in from Quebec and engage any police or army units sent to remove them. Make it convincing. Don't just fold up or run away when they return fire. But tell them not to sabotage the bridges. We want to push the government to move the army out of the West and into Quebec. Let me know when the Round Lake cell is moving.

"Fifth, warn Will Boucanier about a possible airborne raid. He's to react as planned if it happens. If the paras drop in during the night, he's to make a hasty exit. If they come in the morning as we expect, he knows what to do. The best we want is for him to hold the paratroopers there in a kind of stand-off for as long as he can.

"Finally, put the Western units on notice to move as of tonight. Timing is critical, but let's bet on a full-scale operation beginning in the West on Monday.

"Stevenson is prepared to take operational command of the NPA if the government raids the Complex. You all know the drill. If we get word of a raid, as we expect from our moles inside the PMO and DND, then the headquarters and the Committee, but not the Council of chiefs, bugs out for the American side and moves to Manitoba. If we get boxed in here, or worse . . . well, the operation continues from Stevenson's alternate head-quarters.

"Any questions? No? Thank you. Keep your peckers up and let's get to work."

DAY SEVEN

Saturday, September 4

Saturday, September 4, 0610 hours
Radisson Generating Station

Will Boucanier was up early as usual. Shaved, tidy, prepared. A half hour before first light, his leaders kicked their warriors into full alert, morning stand-to. The satellite radio babbled with wake-up traffic: radio checks, code changes, coded messages, and sit-reps—situational reports. A morning wind was rising in the half-dark sky. Too windy for a peacetime drop, Will told himself. But no matter, they're coming.

His orders to his leaders left half the force on stand-to and sent the rest to pack the vehicles, orders that surprised and confused his warriors. They hesitated briefly, but then responded without questions. As they worked, Will, coffee in hand, binoculars around his neck, stood outside the facilities facing west, the growing breeze at his back. The grey dawn light cast no shadows. He continued to watch and wait.

Simon Knewac, his seventeen-year-old radio operator, stood behind him. Mike Maloney walked up and told him tersely, "We're ready to go, boss. But I thought we were going to fight."

"We are, Mike. Just not here." Will shook the coffee grounds out of his tin cup and stowed it in his rucksack. "Okay, call in your patrols. Move everyone and the vehicles about 500 metres down the road towards town. Then gather them around the vehicles and I'll brief them there. Leave the explosives in place and put those warning signs we made—'Danger: mines'—on the front door and around the building."

Will walked to the tailgate of his truck. He pulled back a plastic tarp covering a medium-sized, khaki-coloured metal box; it looked like the heavy-duty tool boxes you'd find at the local Canadian Tire store. He slid the box to the end of the truck and unlocked the lid. Simon, curious as ever, tried to look inside. "What's that, Will?"

"Never mind, Simon. Just go get Joe Neetha on the radio. Tell him to stand by for a message."

Will reached into the box and tested the switches and lights on the top of the electronic device that took up most of the space in the box. Then he raised a small shiny antenna, pushed a button, and another light bleeped on. Next, Will reached farther into the box, into the narrow space beside the main device, took out a small red-coloured cellphone, and dialled in a set of numbers. The box bleeped again and more lights came on. Satisfied, he switched the phone off, zipped it into a side pocket in his jacket, closed the lid, locked the box, and lifted it from the truck. It was heavy, but Will managed it by himself, as he always had since putting it in the truck the day of the attack.

The station manager stood in the doorway of the generating station. "Good morning," Will called out. "Hope your night wasn't too uncomfortable. We're leaving in a while, but you're going to have plenty of company soon enough. We've collected all the cellphones and disabled them. Don't do anything stupid. If you do, the army just might blow this place to pieces.

"I want you to get Ignace. Put these handcuffs on him so he doesn't do anything stupid either, and take him with you. The two of you walk down the road, a kilometre or so. There's a little chair and table there with a big white flag on a stick. You sit there and hold on to that flag. When the paratroopers arrive—yes, the paratroopers, they're on their way—you wave the flag high and often, and when they land, you ask to see the commander.

Introduce him to Bob Ignace. I'm sure they'll have lots in common. Got it?" The manager, worried but relieved, nodded mutely.

"Okay, off you go." The manager walked a short distance into the station, then stopped and called "Good luck" over his shoulder. Boucanier smiled and nodded.

Five minutes later, after the manager had left with a subdued but snarling Ignace, Will walked into the building carrying his metal box. Twenty minutes later he returned, jumped into his truck, and drove away from the power station to join the little convoy he had sent to park down the road to Radisson.

There he checked the trucks, briefed his warriors, then walked away, thinking about his next moves. It was 0650. The sun peeped over the horizon. Will relished sunrise in the autumn, remembering the good days hunting with his brother and uncles, and the exact moment when the snow geese would rise in their great flocks off the bay and head for the mud flats on the shoreline and his homemade, feathered decoys.

He looked to his troops and then again to the east, and his heart jumped. There, already, coming fast out of the rising sun, Will spied four CF18 fighter planes on a low attack run. He sprinted toward his men, who were standing around the vehicles all brilliantly reflecting the morning sun against the dark western sky. Will waved his rifle in the air, warning them.

"Don't shoot! Don't shoot! Get away from the trucks!" Will yelled frantically. The warriors stared at him, uncomprehending. "Fighter planes! Get down! Don't shoot!"

Far down the road, another crew bumped along the road heading back towards the station from their night-time post near Radisson, too far to hear him, even without the engine noise. The warriors spotted the fighters and raised their machine guns and opened fire, a blaze of muzzle flashes betraying their position while tracers flashed skyward nowhere near the planes.

Will watched in horror as the lead jet slid off its line toward the convoy in a low, soft horizontal arc—a little too far to the left, correcting to the right, then settling on the proper line. A soft burr in the morning air, and the wayward truck was engulfed in smoke while bodies cart-wheeled through the air or flew across the road in chunks. The smoke cleared around the truck, which rocked gently then burst into flames.

The lead jet rejoined the formation which roared low over the convoy, then split into pairs left and right, climbing in high arcs, clearly preparing for another run with doubly lethal crossfire. Will yelled at his leaders, "Get out of here! No firing, just get the bloody trucks into town. Rally near the cop shop."

A cloud of dust covered the disorganized departure. The warriors, some vomiting over the sides of the trucks, sped past charred fragments of what minutes before had been their cheery friends. The CF18s unexpectedly circled off north and south instead of coming in to finish the job. Looking to the western horizon, Will saw why.

In the far distance he spotted the high-tailed silhouettes of three C130s turning on line for the generating station. Dark exhaust smoked out behind them as the Hercs lost altitude and formed into an inverted "T"—the third plane trailing some distance behind and above the first two. Warriors in the speeding trucks pointed, waving at the two lead planes.

Will watched too and even at this distance he could see the aircraft bounce and slide in the stiffening easterly wind. No fun in there, he thought. Definitely no fun. He waved the rest of his convoy on to Radisson and told Simon to pull their truck over to the side of the road. There, Will dismounted and watched the Hercs on their run-in drop to 400 metres. He could imagine the scene inside the planes. The jumpmasters yelling over the noise of the engines and the wind rushing past the two open side doors. "Three minutes!" The second and third pilots watching the lead aircraft while fighting the turbulence and their instinct to pull up and abort the drop. Troops, their drills completed, standing, hooked up, overloaded with gear, and every one of them airsick.

The wind threw the planes out of formation, forcing them to buck and drop, before recovering sharply. Inside the planes, several troopers slipped and fell onto the vomit-covered floor. The jump might be dangerous, but by now everyone was eager to get out of the stomach-churning aircraft, no matter what waited below.

Three hundred metres. Will looked up as the first two Hercs, struggling to stay in position, flew over his truck. There they were, "his boys." Pride and envy choked his throat. "Careful, lads," he whispered involuntarily.

The jumpmaster, almost falling over, shouted the command. "One minute. Stand up!"

The soldiers stood together, caught their balance, flipped up the canvas bench on the side of the plane, and turned to face the jumpmaster as he and his crew slid open the two rear doors, one on each side of the Herc.

"Hook up!"

Marcus Wright took the steel hook, a locking clip at the end of the static line leading over his shoulder and back to the parachute harness bag, and snapped it onto the strong cable that ran on both sides of the cabin from the front to just past the rear doors. Once the hook had clicked onto the line to the cable, he tugged it to make sure it was secure and then looked to the jumpmaster for the expected words and signals.

"Check your equipment!"

In a well-ordered and practised procedure, Marcus and the other paratroopers checked their parachute harnesses, in front and down their legs, tightened their helmets again, and double-checked the heavy cargo packs at their feet and the weapons strapped to their sides. Each then reached forward and checked the parachute pack and harness of the comrade standing in front, roughly pulling on the equipment to make sure it was absolutely secure.

The jumpmaster shouted and signalled, "Check static lines!"

The troopers yanked on the hooks and lines, their last connection to the aircraft once they stepped out the side door. Then each reached forward and pulled hard on the static line of the soldier in front.

From the rear of the Herc came the order: "Sound off for equipment check!"

And in order from the rear of the two lines, the paras assured themselves and their comrades in front and the jumpmaster that they had checked and found no fault with their gear or that of their buddies.

"Fifteen okay!"

"Fourteen okay!"

"Thirteen okay!"

Marcus hit the shoulder of the paratrooper in front of him and shouted, "Eight okay." And so the drill continued down the lines to the stick leader, "One okay."

Satisfied, the jumpmaster ordered the lines of troopers to the doors. "Stand in the door!"

The paras shuffled towards the windswept and still-dark doorway. Eyes up and forward, one hand on the static line hook to move it along the cable. They moved awkwardly, one foot forward and the other slightly to the rear, pointing into the arc of the forward foot so as to arrive at the door positioned to step away from the Herc.

The stick leader in each door stopped, eyes up, looking outside. He could feel the jumpmaster's presence on the other side of the doorway, knowing that his eyes were concentrated on the red and green lights as he listened on his headset to the air force navigator counting the seconds waiting to hit the "Go" light.

"Green light. Go!"

And the stick leader stamped his foot on the doorway and launched himself into the dawn. He immediately assumed the jump position: legs tight together and straight out; hands tightly holding the sides of the reserve chute clipped around his stomach, the better to keep his arms close to his body; his chin pushed forward on to his chest to avoid the risers snapping out of the parachute harness—one careless position and the lines would skin the jumper's neck, creating a painful riser-burn.

Without hesitation, jumper eight in the stick, Marcus Wright, his eyes up, right hand on his static line, almost running to keep up with the fast exiting paratroopers, stomped himself through the doorway. The wash rushing alongside the aircraft carried him away and downwards. The static line slipped behind Wright's head, and he rolled slightly to the left. As the twenty or so feet of static line played out, it snapped tight, stringing the soldier out in the air behind the aircraft. In an instant, the carefully engineered system of lines and straps separated in order: the static line pulled away from the harness and ripped open the parachute bag, pulling the long, packed parachute out in a smooth line.

Multiple sticks of ten men each sailed out the doors in order, individuals rolling, twisting, falling fast in the wind.

Marcus Wright counted fast, "One, one thousand, two, two thousand… Check your canopy. Check your position, Check your landing. Remember to drop the bundle. Legs together, knees bent."

Will, too, turning to follow the aircraft, silently talked the jumpers through the drill. "Too fast, you're dropping too damn fast!"

The wind forced Marcus straight down. No side-slipping glide. Just straight down into the rocks, trees, and ponds. He let his heavy equipment pack go at what he hoped was 200 metres. It dangled below him on the tight strap. He could see the large boulder coming up at him and tried to slide downwind to the left—no luck. Then, as he braced for a hard landing, his pack caught a slim tree and snagged him just enough to pull him clear of the rock. He hit the ground as he drifted backwards and tumbled ass over tea kettle into a low shrub.

He could clearly hear the grunts and heaves as his mates hit the hard ground. He watched as the wind grabbed some chutes and dragged awkwardly loaded men and women hard across the unrelenting granite.

Most got their balance quickly enough to roll and pull their chutes down into the wind, collapsing them in a pile of cords and risers. Several, however, landed hard and didn't move, or were dragged limply along until someone else stopped their skid. Leg bones stuck through combat pants. Arms jerked, tangled and maimed in harnesses. Some lay silent, others cried in pain, unable to move damaged limbs. Some writhed convulsively.

As he scrambled out of his harness, Marcus looked for his platoon commander. Nowhere. No, over there—still in his harness, parachute billowing, the young officer's body wedged between two large boulders. Wright dropped his gear, grabbed his weapon, and rushed to knock the chute down. Lieutenant McFarlane was unconscious but breathing. As best Marcus could see, his leader had got his left leg tangled in his parachute risers and landed on his back at full speed. He needed help now.

As the companies assembled, those medics who were not injured hurried from one casualty to another across the broken ground, stopping bleeding, bracing limbs, or simply giving pain-killers. Marcus grabbed a medic and pulled him over to his platoon commander.

"Ya, okay. I've got him. You get going," shouted the corporal.

What was he talking about? Get going? Marcus wondered. The lieutenant was the leader. He was supposed to mark the rallying point for the platoon and get us pointed in the right direction.

Marcus looked around at the confusion on the ground, troopers all mixed up in the mad landing. Right, do something, Marcus told himself.

He stood up, grabbed through the platoon leader's kit, and found the radio and marker flag each platoon in the commando had been issued to mark their rallying point. "Okay. Lieutenant's taken care of … mission first!"

Marcus Wright flipped on the radio as he drove the flag into the hard ground. "It's Marcus," he signalled inexpertly. "Everybody rally to me, at the red on yellow flag." Heads looked up from across the DZ. Soldiers called to one another, "Over here, to the left." "Behind us, over there." The scattered little unit began to move together.

"Where's the lieutenant?" asked one of Marcus's buddies as he slid in beside him.

"He's over there with the medic. Have you seen the sarge? Someone has to take charge. We have to get to the objective, the station. I can see it over there to the right, but I'm not sure if we're in the proper line with the other platoons."

"Beats me," answered his friend. "Tommy said the sergeant's down too—broken leg."

Other soldiers stumbled into the little gathering platoon. Marcus had the radio and the flag and they looked to him for the next move. "Call the commando HQ," someone called from a fold in the ground. "Yeah," others encouraged. "Right, just call the CO, he'll tell us what to do."

Marcus tried. No luck. What to do? What would the platoon commander do?

"Look guys, there's no one on the radio, and people are all over the place. Remember, our job is to get to the right side of the station over there and secure the flank for the platoon going in the door at the front. So, that's what I'm going to do. Who's coming with me?"

The soldiers, several older and more experienced than Marcus, just looked at him. No one moved.

"Well, I'm going now." He stood up, shouldered his pack, ran a bullet into the chamber of his rifle and stepped out. "Come on guys, mission first, follow me. We can't let 2nd Platoon get all the glory." Marcus Wright's little command watched him move out, then hesitantly, one by one, they stood and walked and jogged to join him in the assault on the Radisson generating station.

Will stood boldly in the distance beside his vehicle and his increasingly anxious driver. The first two Hercs climbed steeply southwards for home. But the third pulled up without dropping its paras and began a long sweeping turn south and then westward. Will grabbed for the radio. "Joe, Joe, come in. Over."

"Two alpha. Over."

"Two—Joe, you got company coming, fast. At least a company of paras. Two Hercs dropped here, one didn't and is headed your way. They should be on you in fifteen minutes max. Expect them to drop right on the airfield. Over."

"Two alpha, roger. We're ready. I'm going to harass the landing then pull back into town as we planned. A bit more harassing fire then we'll work our way onto the land and head for the road."

"Two, roger that. But look out, there're CF18 fighters in the area and they'll gun you down if they see you interfering with the drop. I think the paras will be happy to secure the approaches and outskirts of the airfield and wait for the next wave before they enter the town. That phase is probably on the way but I'd guess an hour out. Anyway, make trouble but don't get trapped and chopped up; we need you and your guys later. I'm going into Radisson now as planned and we'll join you on the road eventually. Over."

"Two alpha. Roger that. Uh, we have a Herc in the distance now. See you later. Out."

Will took one last look through his binos at the paras about a kilometre away. They were shaking out, preparing to move quickly over the obstacles to the generating station. Well, he always said he'd have a surprise for them.

He turned his binos across the field and there he saw, he was sure, the para commander looking his way. Will smiled. "Poor lads. The army accepts an invitation to a war and the host doesn't show up to fight." He gave the para officer a long wave with his rifle then walked casually to his truck. Simon hit the gas and they disappeared down the road to Radisson.

Saturday, September 4, 0610 hours
Ottawa: Canada Command Headquarters

Jack Hemp walked into Canada Command headquarters early Saturday morning, bright and cheery, followed by a couple of aides who looked as though they were just coming home from a long night out. The prime minister greeted the CDS and Lieutenant General René Lepine warmly, then walked about the busy operations centre speaking with apparent interest to the officers and soldiers on duty. The generals waited patiently, respecting the politician's instinct to campaign.

After a few minutes, Hemp walked to the seat offered by René Lepine and sat down. "Well, general, everything going as expected, I hope?"

"So far, yes, sir. The airborne force is in the air supported by four CF18s out of the forward operating base at Trenton." Lepine motioned towards the electronic displays and pointed to a large-scale, animated electronic map of the Radisson area and the aircraft approaching the DZ. "The paratroopers should be dropping just outside the Radisson facility, here, any minute now. They'll land here, assemble quickly, and then move to take control of and secure the generating station. Once that task is complete, they will move into the town of Radisson and secure it as well. A secondary mission from the same force is to secure the airport and village at Chisasibi, and open the runway for a small, air-landed support force currently preparing to take off from Trenton. The two sites should both be secure by noon today."

"Yeah, interesting. What about the natives, are they going to resist, and if they do, what are the rules for your guys?"

"Prime minister, the native forces have dug in and settled down at both sites. We have satellite surveillance over them day and night, but there is very little activity. At Radisson, a few vehicles are moving back and forth between the town and the facilities, probably making supply runs of food and so on. They've put some minor obstacles on the road and near the sites. The rules of engagement are straightforward enough. The troops will secure the objectives without any preparatory firing. They are under orders to move in, fire on targets that engage them first, but cease firing once the resistance stops."

General Bishop interrupted. "You must understand, prime minister, that these are the initial rules of engagement. The natives are well-armed and we suspect that they have air defence weapons that could bring down a Hercules aircraft. The CF18s are in the area to protect these vulnerable transport planes. If we start losing Hercs our options get really limited. Once the force is on the ground, they will, as General Lepine said, take their objectives. The amount and ferocity of any fighting initially, and I emphasize initially, will be determined by the native force. If they open fire on our troops, our commanders are instructed to use their units and weapons according to the ways they have been trained to act and over- come the native force by all necessary means. That doesn't mean, of course, that they'll act indiscriminately, but it does mean that they will take the initiative from the native force once the fighting begins and not give it back."

Hemp looked at Geldt, sitting beside him, then at the man next to him. "Well, I understand, but I don't want Jim, my press secretary here, having to go on Canada AM later this morning to explain away a bloodbath. I hope everyone understands that deadly force is the last resort."

"The troops, prime minister, are well trained and under the control of some very experienced officers. But we can't lose. If we lose at James Bay, or in downtown Montreal, the government of Canada has no other recourse."

General Bishop paused and looked directly at Jack Hemp. "Explaining to the Canadian people and to the president of the United States that the Canadian Forces were defeated and the natives are in full control of the James Bay region because we lacked courage and resolve when it was needed would be, I suspect, a much more difficult thing to do on tele- vision, for your press secretary or you personally. We'll do our job care- fully, prime minister, but the native leaders decide when and where we reach what you call the 'last resort.' After that, we make the decisions and we won't lose."

As the CDS was speaking to the prime minister, a staff officer passed Lepine a note, then whispered something into his ear.

"Prime minister, CDS," Lepine interrupted, "a few minutes ago, as the CF18 flight approached the Radisson site, they were fired on by a native truck convoy. The lead pilot took evasive action, then engaged the vehicle from which the fire was coming. The truck was destroyed with casualties to the people on board. The firing ceased immediately and the other vehicles, about ten or twelve, moved on down the road towards Radisson.

"The CF18s are giving protective cover for the airborne unit now dropping on the target. The weather is very poor for this type of operation, the wind is much stronger than we like. But the unit CO gave the go-ahead and should report to us in the next little while as his people assemble on the ground. There was apparently no firing on the Hercs or on the paras as they dropped in, and none as the first soldiers are on the ground."

"Thank you, René." The CDS turned to the prime minister. "It'll take a little while for the operation to unfold. Perhaps, prime minister, you'd like a bit of breakfast?" Andy Bishop stood up and pointed Hemp towards a small room off the back of the operations centre.

"Thank you, Andy. I need a cup of coffee. Jim, here," Hemp waved at his press secretary, "will organize the media gang with your people. But I would like to follow events until the facilities are secure and then we'll face the media."

He took his press secretary by the arm and they headed towards the little breakfast room. "Look around," Hemp hissed as they walked alone. "Here we are, Canadian airplanes have just fired on Canadian citizens, paratroops are falling out of the sky with deadly intent, the media is gathering outside the door and likely to howl for my balls and this place is as calm as a call-in centre.

"Look at them—officers quietly answering phones, signals flashing on the boards. And the generals ask me to breakfast. Where the hell do these people come from? Who produces them? You know, Jim, we politicians don't know enough about these guys and how they work, and we hardly ever even ask. And we're supposed to be the ones in charge."

Hemp joined General Bishop, who offered him a coffee. "Well, Andy, tell me, where'd you go to school—at that military college, whatever, in Kingston, I suppose?"

Saturday, September 4, 0655 hours
Dropping Zone Radisson

Lieutenant Colonel Rusty Campbell struggled out of his parachute harness in the half-light and looked around, checking his unit as his commando commanders assembled their troopers. Billowing parachutes marked the injured and those still caught in the wind. As medics responded to people motionless on the ground and to calls from soldiers kneeling over their comrades, Campbell's small headquarters section gathered around him, checking radios and weapons and orienting themselves towards the objective. Officers were already directing their troops to the start-line, ready to advance as rapidly as the skirmish line of engineers and snipers could clear a way forward through the barbed wire and any booby traps or mines. The operation unfolded smoothly, thanks to the drills rehearsed time and again over the last week.

On the western horizon, Campbell saw the third Herc carrying his third commando platoon approach the dropping zone. He waved his radio operator over and grabbed the mike to speak with the aircraft commander and to Major Brad Hinton, the commander of the platoon, who was on the flight deck and plugged into the Herc's radio. "Shotgun Three, this is Shotgun Leader. We are secure on the ground. Break off and go to Objective Romeo. Brad, report when your commando is secure on the ground. Over."

The pilot's flat, impersonal voice crackled through the air. "Shotgun Leader, this is Shotgun Three, breaking off now." Hinton acknowledged his orders. "Three wilco. Out."

Campbell watched the C130 continue on track for a moment and then gracefully bank into a long sweeping turn to the southwest, then he returned to his immediate concerns. A few kilometres to the west he saw black smoke rising from the truck the CF18 had shot up. Rusty raised his binos for a fast look at the wreck and the surrounding area. As he scanned the horizon, he spotted another vehicle, stationary on the road. He swept back for a closer look, fingers spinning the focus wheel. He saw clearly, bold and unconcerned, a tall man in uniform beside the truck, a weapon hanging from his shoulder, binoculars to his eyes. The man was watching Campbell watching him.

The distant soldier lowered his binoculars, turned to watch the third Herc going west, then seemed to speak into a radio held by a smaller person who had come up beside him. Replacing the mike, the soldier moved towards his vehicle where he suddenly, inexplicably, stopped, looked back towards Campbell, raised his rifle in his right hand, and waved—a long, arm-over-the-head, side-to-side wave. A second later he turned, jumped into the truck, and was gone.

Rusty Campbell kept his eyes on the bold soldier's truck as it disappeared down the road to Radisson. Then he lowered his binoculars and spoke absently. "Will Boucanier. They said he might be here. No doubt about it now. I watched him do the same thing to a bunch of Yugos who fired at him time and again without effect. Cheeky son of a bitch. Never changes."

Ignoring a baffled look from his own young radio operator, he continued speaking to no one in particular. "All right. Back to business." With that, Rusty came back into sharp focus, reached for his radio, and tersely ordered his waiting paratroopers to "Move out." In an instant, camouflaged soldiers appeared out of the ground and stepped towards the silent building in the distance.

Saturday, September 4, 0710 hours
Ottawa: Canada Command Headquarters

Jack Hemp sat off to the side in the Ops Centre chatting with his staff, going over the draft of the remarks press secretary Jim James had sketched out for his meeting with the media who were growling outside. The themes— the spin, as some would call it—were predictable and upbeat: the operation was in fact a peacekeeping mission; the aim was to free the local people, natives and all, from these radical terrorists; only necessary force in response to the radicals' use of weapons was authorized; this was not an action against native people; we have no quarrel with the ever-helpful FNF;

the situation in Quebec should soon return to normal and we have already seen a reduction on threats in the south; the Canadian government is in complete control; we salute our brave men and women in the Canadian Forces—then segue to the CDS for the technical points.

Hemp frowned at James, took his pen, and scratched the reference to the FNF out of the text. "There!" he said as he handed the paper back to James. "Good. All neat and tidy. They'll eat it up."

General Bishop's aide-de-camp interrupted the prime minister. "Excuse me, sir, General Bishop asked if you could join him. The staff report on the para operation is ready and he thought you would be interested."

Hemp, coffee in hand, walked over to the briefing area and reached for a chair. "So gentlemen, what's up?"

René Lepine stood at the small lectern before the situation screens. "First, prime minister, let me bring you up to date on a recent incident in Montreal. It appears that a car bomb was used a few minutes ago to attack one of our convoys moving into the city on Pont Champlain. It appears it was a suicide bomber; if so, it's the first we've seen. At least three soldiers are dead and several injured. An unknown number of civilians in the area were also killed or wounded. The barricades in the centre of the city have been taken down after heavy fighting and a few dozen casualties, mostly insurgents. However, other barricades are being set up in Montreal, in other parts of the province, and in Eastern Canada by what we think are random groups of natives acting on their own in sympathy with the organized insurgents. They certainly don't seem to be coordinated with them ahead of time or even after setting up."

Eddie Geldt interrupted. "Prime minister, I have a text message here that says the premier of Quebec spoke this morning with the French ambassador, who, it is reported, offered to send aid to the province if it is requested by the government. Commeau apparently thanked the ambassador and made no other comment. But she was quick to leak the conversation to the press."

Hemp, clearly agitated, snarled at Lepine. "Well, go on general. Any good news?"

Lepine returned to his prepared notes. "The situation at James Bay has taken a surprising turn, but in this business we expect surprises. The initial landing operation developed somewhat as we expected."

"Somewhat?" Hemp stared at Bishop.

"Prime minister," the CDS said, "military operations are flawless only in Hollywood. We expect and train for uncertainty. Anyone who expects military operations to be surgical strikes must have had surgery done with an axe and a chainsaw. René will bring us up-to-date."

Lepine continued with his briefing. "Prime minister, as you saw earlier this morning, the insertion operation went well. The unit at Radisson unfortunately suffered six serious injuries and ten disabling injuries, broken bones and so on, on landing, but met no resistance at all. None. And that was a surprise. When they advanced to contact, they found the facilities undefended; in fact, there was no one there at all other than a couple of people, including a local police officer, sitting on a bench waving a white flag. The native force had deserted the site minutes before the airborne force arrived. The site is now being cleared of mines and explosives and should be secure in a few hours. The unit commanding officer has sent an envoy, a doctor, to the town under a white flag to ask for permission to bring his casualties into the local hospital for treatment and he offered some of his medical staff to help there. We're awaiting a response."

The maps and charts flipped on the screens in precise harmony with the general's script. "Weather conditions for the airborne landing at Chisasibi were rough as well, but the ground was far better and landing casualties were light. There was some resistance but it was not very effective. The force commander reports that he's in control of the airfield and its approaches and has patrols out clearing the few renegades and snipers operating near his force. The follow-up air landing operation will begin within the hour and we are readying a ground force to make contact between the unit at Radisson and those at Chisasibi using the road here." Lepine pointed out the various sites and the highway with his laser pointer.

Hemp brightened up. "So I can tell the media that the facilities will be up and running as soon as the local workers get back to work. Good."

Lepine shifted his notes, glanced at the CDS and turned back to the prime minister. "Well, sir, not exactly. We hold the generating station and its immediate area. But the native force is still intact and has withdrawn to the town, which they hold. Our reports from inside the town indicate that it's barricaded and upwards of forty to fifty armed people are on the streets. It also seems that many unarmed natives are cheering the radicals on and are out in the streets. We are in no way in control of this situation and may not be able to gain control without reinforcements and the risking of a lot of casualties in the community if the natives stand and fight. Presumably most of the sympathizers will get under cover if shooting starts, but there's a substantial risk of civilian casualties, especially if the radicals deliberately fight in such a way as to invite them.

"Also, we hold the airport at Chisasibi but we don't know for sure the situation on the road from there to Radisson. We do know it's a basic road with lots of places where it can be broken up, and lots of ambush areas. And we estimate that thirty to sixty native warriors may be waiting for us along the road. It's not going to be a simple drive from one place to the other. In fact, I'm concerned that the native forces may concentrate on the road to keep us out of Radisson. There really isn't any way we can get in there otherwise. Our airborne capability is spent. So the road is now, as we say, the key terrain in this operation and the place where our superior firepower and training translates into a smaller advantage than in a pitched battle in the town or especially at the airfield. And whoever's organizing the bad guys is clearly swift enough to figure it out."

Lepine flashed up some high-resolution satellite pictures of the Radisson facilities. "These images were taken at the Radisson site itself an hour ago, after our people entered the buildings. The commanding officer spoke by telephone to some Hydro officials in town and reports that the civilian operators are unharmed, but uncooperative. The native workers in particular are being unhelpful but the others seem frightened and some have quietly reported that the natives—their colleagues, not the radicals—threatened to harm them if they went back to work at the site. We checked with the Quebec authorities, who stated that they would not expect their people to be put in harm's way and that they would not send anyone to the town or from the town to the site until it was completely safe."

The prime minister looked at his press secretary and then to General Bishop "Well, general, when will that be? What am I going to tell the media?"

The CDS was stern-faced. "Prime minister, we cannot predict that moment. The operation will proceed by stages as outlined and we will keep you informed of its progress. We have secured the airport at Chisasibi and the surrounding area. An infantry unit with armoured vehicles is on the way too, and it is ordered to clear the road to Radisson, but that will take time. At the same time, we will divert troops on security duty from the cities in the south and send them by road north to secure that access route, and, as best we can, the transmission corridors. But that operation will take some time too—we estimate at least a week of rough going if the native force resists and we must plan on that eventuality."

"A week?" Hemp banged his coffee cup on the table. "You're the army. I thought you said just a few minutes ago that we were winning. Now you're telling me it could take a week, maybe more. I don't have a week. Quebec is in an uproar. If you move troops out of the cities and the Indians come back and burn Montreal—we'll all be out the door. The Americans aren't going to stand for a power blackout for much longer. Where are your troops? Get some more into James Bay!"

Bishop stood up. "General Lepine, please ask your staff to leave the room. You stay." No command from Lepine was necessary. The military staff got the message and without comment or expression shut down the microphones and projectors and swiftly, silently, vanished out the door.

Meanwhile, the CDS collected his thoughts then stepped to the front of the room. "Prime minister, we have told cabinet time and again that the Canadian Forces were overstretched and under-equipped. We warned, and others in universities and in Parliament warned, that Canada was on the verge five years ago of having no useable armed forces at all. We have struggled to prevent this collapse in the short run, but at the expense of wearing out our people and our equipment. What you see deployed and deploying is what we have. We can't go to private contractors and ask for reinforcements. There isn't anything else."

The room was still. Bishop paced away from the lectern and continued almost distractedly, as though unaware of or unconcerned about the prime minister's rapidly growing discomfort. "We also warned the cabinet, as did CSIS and the RCMP, that failure to address the rising violence from gangs and radicals in the native community on the reserves—a group clearly alienated from Canadian society and from the majority of the native community outside the reserves—was a neglect of national security. Nothing was done.

"You ask, 'Where is everyone?' Well, 'everyone' is not many in any case, and they are where I already told you they were. Our best battalions are patrolling the bush and farms in Zimbabwe and the streets of Haiti, and it doesn't matter where we wish they were because we can't get them here in time. And it doesn't matter what other troops we wish we had because we don't have them. We're moving the last of the regular troops from the West to Montreal as we speak, and they'll either open the highway to Radisson or patrol Montreal—your call, prime minister. But they can't do both. And I warn you again, I don't think this thing is going to end here.

"I think today shows us this native force is not some ragtag bunch of bucks. We are committing ourselves to this one region, Quebec, and we may very well regret it. So what should you tell Canadians? Tell them we are in the midst of an organized assault on our society and we will have to expend some very serious efforts to overcome that threat. Tell them the truth and they'll respond. Duck and dodge and you're dead."

Silence. No one but Bishop looked at the prime minister. Hemp the politician looked desperately for room to duck and dodge. Seeing none, he began struggling to find a way to do the right thing against a lifelong habit of self-serving compromise.

"Okay, general, okay, I get the message. But your top priority, your best troops, go to secure the cities. I'll get you as many civilian police as I can weasel out of the provinces. The RCMP will drop their other duties to help out. If you need the militia and the army reserves called out, give my staff the procedures for that and we'll think about it. But that would scare the pants off the electorate. Clear out the James Bay region and use whatever force you need to do it after your secure Montreal. We can handle a few native casualties; after all, they asked for it.

"I'll back you, beginning this morning in front of the media. That should give you room to move the troops and toughen up the rules of engagement in the North. I want you and General Lepine there to lay it on hard: maps, charts, casualties, the NPA stats, the works. We're going to turn this thing against the radical natives.

"The message is still we have this thing under control and I don't want anyone, especially any soldier, talking about an unfolding threat. I repeat, we have control. That's what the people are going to hear and that's what the Americans are going to hear. My staff and I will take the coffee room to organize ourselves for the briefing."

Hemp stood up, reaching out a conciliatory hand. "Thanks, General

Bishop, I'm sure your guys can handle this. They always do, even if things are not always perfect. Their can-do attitude saved other governments and it'll no doubt save this one."

Andy Bishop watched the prime minister walk away. He had Hemp's political directions, but his mind was clear. He knew where his duty lay and what he must do—was obliged to do—to try and save the country.

Saturday, September 4, 0915 hours
Akwesasne: The Complex

Molly walked down the hall with Bill Whitefish. "Well, so far so good. The feds are moving east as we hoped they would. But we can't command the next phase from here; it's getting too hot and too close. So, Bill, Sunday evening we'll move this headquarters west to Manitoba as we planned. I want you to get in touch with the U.S., let the Lakota Syndicate know we need the private planes and pilots as we arranged at the meeting last year. You and I will go first from here and cross the U.S. border inside the Akwesasne reserve, and then to the Massena airfield. We'll hopscotch cross-country on the U.S. side to International Falls, move just south of the border to near Highway 90, and then directly into the St. Andrews airfield north of Winnipeg, just as we planned. The remainder of the staff can follow in later shuttles and join us at the Peguis headquarters."

Bill jotted some lines to his notebook, then stopped writing, pursed his lips, and spoke up. "You know how I feel, Molly. Leaving our guys in Quebec on the hook is unfair and may endanger the whole operation. They're doing what we asked them to do and they've taken a big gamble. Once they see us shift the focus out west, and pretty much abandon them, it won't take long for the operation here to fold. They're going to pay a big price, and word is going to spread fast that we used them and left them in the lurch."

Molly hardly broke stride. "And as I told you before, the academics are partly right. We can't take the whole country. That was never my aim ... our aim. We're going to take what we can—we deserve whatever rights we can assert, remember. The natives here have lived well off the present system. You never saw them raise a finger for the West. They're just like central Canadian politicians."

Then she stopped and faced Whitefish squarely. "Bill, most of the staff and leaders here are our people, imports from the West, not Easterners. The Mohawks are in it for the money and local power. The James Bay Cree are different; they're our true allies. They'll have to take care of themselves for now, but we won't forget them later. Meanwhile, depend on Boucanier. No matter what, he's not leaving James Bay again. He's certainly not about to hand over power and his little army to just anyone. I said depend on him, Bill, not trust him. Today he's an ally; I'm not sure about tomorrow.

"We'll find a place for the Quebec Cree at the negotiating table. But it doesn't really matter. The point is, they're going to benefit from any agreement we make with Ottawa. Once we get our rights, the settlers won't dare deny them theirs. Maybe they can organize a separate north-south confederation with an independent Quebec. The *separatist* politicians have been edging that way for years—it'll be history repeated. The French and the natives allied against the English. We'll see. But once we win, their position improves enormously over anything they could get otherwise. The thing is, we have to win, which means we follow the plan. So let's get ready to move. I assume the advance headquarters team is in location and setting up?"

Bill turned away. "Sure, Molly, as you ordered."

DAY EIGHT

Sunday, September 5

Sunday, September 5, 0745 hours
Akwesasne: The Complex

Molly hurried to prepare the few belongings that she would need for the next phase of the operation. She stuffed essentials and her warmest jacket, sweaters, and extra cords and jeans into her large black-and-red backpack. Her most precious belongings—her notes, diary, letters from supporters, the strategy, and the scrapbook filled with Louis Riel's essays, letters, and poems—she kept in her bulging, tattered leather briefcase. It was never far out of reach.

Today was the day of the big move—the day before Molly would spring the trap on the federal politicians and the white Indians and all the wishful, naive, white do-gooders across Canada and around the world. Today, the bold strategy to take back the land would begin. But first, there were several critical decisions to be made and details to review. Molly flung her backpack onto the small bed in the room that had been home for the last several weeks and walked down the long hallway to the last meeting in the Complex at Akwesasne.

As usual Molly asked Bill Whitefish to bring everyone up to date on the events of the last few hours and his assessment of the developing situation.

"The situation in Montreal," he began, "has become untenable for the warriors at the barricades. They are actually caught in a trap of their own making. The barricades have themselves been barricaded by hundreds of police and soldiers now arriving from outside the city. Moreover, the deployment during the night of army sniper teams from Valcartier means that there is no way for the warriors to expand their positions and no way for us to reinforce them. Any exposed movement brings a fusillade of shooting from the police, and even when our guys think they're under cover, every careless exposure is punished by a sniper's bullet. However, the fact that the barricades are still standing has forced the police and the army to concentrate their scarce resources there, and the police at least are getting tired.

"Other barricades, mostly spontaneous outbreaks that appear and then disappear when the police arrive, are popping up all over the cities and in some other regions across Quebec. Some helpful idiots from Ontario are blocking the 401 from Cornwall and the 417 from Ottawa, acting they say in 'solidarity with our native brothers.' All these actions are helping to spread the police reserves to the breaking point. The question for the Council is this: should we hold the barricades in downtown Montreal in place or allow the warriors to make an honourable withdrawal or even surrender?

"In the eastern U.S. states, and especially in New York City, things are a shambles. Power is out most everywhere, traffic is snarled, airports are closed to all but emergency traffic, and the stock exchange has suspended operations until it can get some kind of emergency power. That closure, of course, has rippled across the country—and the world, in fact. The president is under all sorts of pressure to do something, but it's hard to figure what the politicians are up to. The situation in the country is the only news in the media—CNN and especially Fox News are in full howl with 'blame Canada' stories one after the other. They seem to think we're Iranian terrorists or at least that we're working for them. The FBI is reportedly moving to arrest American native leaders on suspicion that they are in on the attacks somehow, or maybe as a deterrent in case they try to piggy-back on our operations. Frankly, Molly, I'm getting worried about a serious American countermove."

Molly waved the comment to the side. "We can worry about the Americans later. They can't be so stupid as to not see that we hold the keys to the hydro power and other resources they need. Anyway, in my next media interviews I will make it clear that we can do business with the U.S. administration provided they treat us peacefully. Bill, see if I can get a spot on an early CNN broadcast today."

Members of the Council had never in their lives had to make real life-and-death decisions or, as in this case, had to decide to spend lives to accomplish their aims. Everyone hesitated. Evan Boyce spoke up. "Seems to me a needless loss of life to leave those guys in Montreal if they can't accomplish much more. They did get the police to move and the army too. So what's the point of continuing there?"

The other chiefs around the table nodded in agreement or sat silently; some looked to Molly. She said nothing for several minutes, letting the inconclusive chatter die out.

"The logic of the barricades," she began quietly, "is to draw and hold the police and the army in the city. We are attacking what the enemy holds dear. We don't actually want to occupy Montreal or any other city. We want our land back. The provincial police and the army can't hold both, so they'll hold the cities. So long as the warriors on the barricades can hold the attention of the security forces and, most importantly, the attention of the public and the politicians, then they are fulfilling their mission. We expected casualties. The spirits of the land will reward the dead and wounded. The barricades stay up and the warriors stay there. What next, Bill?"

Bill flipped though his notebook. "The raid on Radisson and Chisasibi went off without a hitch. Will Boucanier is a real warrior commander; we're lucky to have him."

"I agree, Bill. We're lucky he's on our side, at least for the moment. Go on."

"As you all know if you watched TV lately, the Special Service Regiment from Trenton dropped in for a visit to Radisson and Chisasibi early Saturday morning. They took both sites without any real opposition, much as we'd planned. Unfortunately, the fighter jets that covered the operation killed several of our people. Nevertheless, we seem to have met our aim. The facilities at Radisson are disabled, our 'persuaders' in the community have made sure no worker, native or non-native, is going to work there any time soon.

"Along the Radisson-to-Montreal corridor the transmission lines are down on each route, and Highway 109 is effectively closed. The government is in an uproar and the breakdown in the electricity system along the American East coast is the only story in the U.S. media this morning. I don't expect anything in the North to change much in the next twenty-four to forty-eight hours, simply because Boucanier's warriors are too strongly situated and the paratroopers are too weak to take them on right now.

"There was talk in Ottawa and in the army headquarters of sending a second wave of troops to Chisasibi to open the road to Radisson, but that action appears to have been put on hold by the prime minister, who wants all attention and troops concentrated in the south. I think we have a few days in the north before the army sends a unit up Highway 109; even then, there's going to be whole lot of long cold nights for southern Quebec and the American East."

Several members of the Council chuckled and elbowed each other, seemingly pleased with their apparent successes. Molly cut them off. "The man who matters is General Bishop. Hemp may have the authority to give orders, but Bishop controls the guns. What's he up to?"

"The army is more or less and reluctantly following the government's directions for the moment. It seems strange to me, though. The CDS is more than a little suspicious of things in the West and so is General Lepine, the commander in this operation. I'm not sure, but I think Bishop has something big yet to play. He might not be as subservient as Hemp thinks he is. I just have this uneasy feeling that Bishop isn't going to simply roll over and play dead, or if he seems to be doing that, we had better watch out."

The chuckles and banter around the table disappeared abruptly. The chiefs looked first to Bill Whitefish to continue, and when he stood silently and dropped his notes on the table, they looked to Molly Grace.

"Okay," she said. "As we discussed last night, the operations in Quebec continue, and where we can we'll intensify them. Get as many barricades up as possible; it hardly matters where they are. Reinforce success. Second, get our special teams of marksmen to begin sniping at the police and at police stations. Two can play that game.

"Finally, we're moving the headquarters west as we planned. Bill, I want you to check carefully our HQ deception plan. I want lots of fake radio traffic and other electronic noise coming from here while we deploy, and afterwards. The left-behind HQ team is to keep it up for as long as possible, even after we're set up in Manitoba. The more confusion for the feds, the better for us.

"The Council is suspended for the time being. The Central Committee of the revolution will command for now. Once the operation is successful in the West, we'll meet again. You'll all get your instructions later; for now, you should try to rejoin your nations and be as helpful as possible to the grand strategy. Any questions?"

Shock and silence in the room.

"I don't get it, Molly," said a startled Brian Tessier. "You're bugging out, leaving us here to fight the whole army?" Other worried chiefs joined the growing noisy reaction to Molly's directions.

"Yeah! I've got a whole bunch of people on the barricades, and they trusted me when I said this thing would be over quickly and then we could negotiate a new deal. What the hell am I to do now?" Chief Fred Pitchenesse pushed his chair hard against the wall.

Leo Nattaway echoed Pitchenesse's angry tone. "So we just stay here and take the heat while you and Whitefish here fly away to safety. Well, I'm not about to go to jail for some idea and some decisions that mean nothing to my people in New Brunswick. If the army attacks my people, I'll surrender and negotiate at the first sign of serious trouble. Mark my words, Molly Grace."

Alain Selkirk, the usually argumentative Blood chief, waved a hand across the table. "Why are you guys surprised? Don't you get it? Molly Grace is for Molly Grace. She used you people in the East as decoys. Now you're surprised. Remember, all of you, you gave her the power to run things. You sat back and hoped for something for nothing. So don't cry on my shoulder.

"Molly, you snookered most of us well and good. Congratulations. Well, I'm willing to go another round, like it or not. We actually do have the feds in a terrible situation. They're losing control, even if they don't know it yet. Maybe we can get something out of this mess after all. Anyway, no sense in just throwing in the towel and letting all the blood we've spilt go down the drain for nothing.

"Molly, you go out west. If the others agree, I'll run things from here as best as we can. In the meantime, I think we should play it as if we're all in this together; otherwise, as always, they'll just crush us one at a time. But Molly, this Council is not dismissed. It's going to be your real partner and we'll take a hand at running this revolution too. I think we should play good cop, bad cop with the prime minister. I'll lead the good tame Indians and seem to offer a deal; you keep the heat on them and see what we can get out of the barrel of a gun. Deal?"

Molly simply reached over and stuffed her notebook in her briefcase. "Deal. You give this rabble some backbone and we can make a historic arrangement with the white settlers. You keep this complex running and I'll support your position as best I can. We'll see where the road takes us. But you're right on one count, Alain, now's not the time to run away.

"Bill and I are not running away. I'm taking the fight to a whole new plateau. We're going to take Canadians to somewhere they never dreamt in their worst nightmare was possible, no matter how shamefully they treated our people all these years. Bill will handle the details with you, Alain, before we leave."

Molly turned away and left the room and the Council in confusion.

Sunday, September 5, 2025 hours
Near St. Andrews, Manitoba

In twilight's evening haze, several small, multi-seat aircraft arrived over the course of an hour, apparently separately, at the community airfield on Highway 8 near St. Andrews just north of Winnipeg. Each plane was met by a few nondescript SUVs that took the passengers off north towards

Selkirk. Molly Grace and the major elements of the Central Committee from Akwesasne were on their way to the Peguis alternative operational complex from which she would establish the "native people's provisional government." Louis Riel, somewhere, smiled.

The cars left the airfield unmolested, in fact unobserved, by the local RCMP who, Molly surmised correctly, had all been drawn into the uprising in Quebec or into the surveillance of the growing unrest in the north. As the convoy approached the south side of Selkirk, she pointed out the window with grim satisfaction to Lower Fort Garry, the white man's shrine to the subjugation of the native people, the very place from which the RCMP set out to capture the West for Canada. She had marked it for a special humiliation later—a suitable place, perhaps, for the settlers' government to accept her terms. For now, however, the task was to get reorganized in the new headquarters and reinforce her authority over Stevenson and the other senior military commanders in the West.

The cars continued through Selkirk, north on Main Street, and out of town. Now the road ran right beside the Red River—that traitorous waterway that had carried the whites into the heart of the native domain. At Peguis, an unremarkable junction of dirt roads on the ancient boundary of the once-prosperous Peguis Nation, the convoy cut west for a few kilometres towards Clandeboye, then turned north at a farm just short of the village, where they paused at a steel gate guarded by local warriors. After some distance they stopped in front of a set of new-looking farm buildings.

The Western complex was safe from police prowlers because it was on native land and far enough off the township road to remain under cover. The buildings looked too new and rich for a native community and immediately attracted the interest of the federal narco-police. But the First Nations Federation had advertised it as a model modern farming operation, the beginning of the resurrection of the Peguis Nation, rhetoric the provincial premier was keen to adopt, and take credit for, during the last election. The police were told to back off and they did.

In fact, the new, expensive but otherwise typical farm buildings enclosed not a grow-op but a sophisticated command centre. Outside it was made to look like a working farm, with a large collection of utility buildings and a pleasant house with a wide west-facing verandah decorated with rocking chairs and benches. There was also a small car garage,

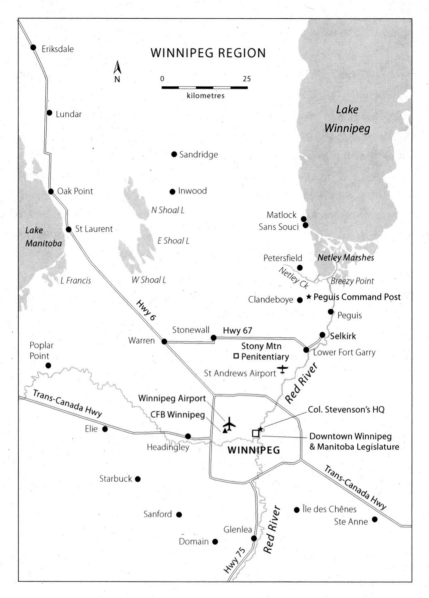

set apart from the working buildings. The barn and tiny corral sat farther down the lane, east of the house, to let the prevailing westerly winds carry the scent of manure away from the house. Not that the farm had many cattle; it was mostly a wheat farm with just a few animals for family consumption. Seven grain sheds, small conical outbuildings, ran in a line out towards the ploughed fields, and a pair of corrugated-tin Quonset garages, each about ten metres long, held a collection of machinery, the most expensive and important investment on any farm.

The only oddity to an experienced eye was the absence of toys, swings, and bikes, and dogs playing with children. For all any stranger knew, it might very well be run by a group of keen twenty-somethings with community college agriculture degrees. Anyway, passers-by on the road to and from Clandeboye took little notice. The farm was set far back from the road and partly hidden by the typical prairie farm barrier of tall pines and scrub oaks meant to break the ever-blowing winds. It was Indian land, after all, so who knew, the locals said, what had brought the sudden wealth and strangers to the old homestead. The only answer, they guessed, was government handouts.

DAY NINE
Monday, September 6

A bright cool Monday morning greeted downtown Winnipeg. A light haze from prairie harvest dust and acid smoke from distant, burning stubble fields covered the city. Stan Przewoznik pulled his bus into the intersection of Portage Avenue and Memorial Boulevard as he had done hundreds of times before. With his seniority he could have had a later schedule, but he liked the early morning shifts and his regular passengers. They talked about the same things—seasonal things: the damn, cold winter wind; the damn, hot summer wind; the Bombers—"Maybe this year"; "Not like the old days"; "Bud Grant. Now, you know, there was a guy who knew football"; "My grandson's playing for Kelvin. Looks like a real college prospect"; "You don't say."

Out the corner of his eye Stan saw the speeding pickup cut across the intersection into the Portage eastbound lane. He swerved expertly, avoiding the truck but bumping hard over the curb and up onto the sidewalk. Passengers cried out, grabbing for support. Przewoznik stood on the brakes hard, stopping his bus a metre or two from the big Hudson's Bay store windows. An old woman slid off the front bench seat and thumped onto the floor, her thermos and her salami-and-onion sandwich lunch rolling into the door-well.

"Bloody, drunken Indians!" Stan shouted. He saw the men in the back of the truck waving at him, but didn't notice their weapons. He got up, checked that the old lady was awake and alert, patted her shoulder, and said, "Stay here, ma'am, don't try to move." He then began to walk back down the aisle checking his other passengers. Most were collecting their senses and possessions, but a few, including the old lady, probably needed medical help. Stan headed back towards his seat and his radio.

"Don't touch anything," a masked warrior commanded from under Stan's side window just as he sat down.

"What do you mean? I need an ambulance here." Stan still hadn't realized what was happening. He reached for his radio again.

The shot through his windscreen shattered the glass into his face and onto his clothing. The bullet, meant only to get his full attention, passed harmlessly out through the roof of the bus. For a moment, no one on the bus spoke or moved.

The mask shouted an order. "Get the people off the bus and tell them to walk back across the street and keep moving. You stay there." Stan pulled the lever, opening the doors, looked back over his shoulder and shouted to the rear of the bus.

"Okay, folks. End of the line. Just get off, someone help auntie here, and just walk away. Come on, get going." Slowly, then in gathering panic, the twenty or so passengers walked, pushed, and, once on the street, ran from the men now commanding the intersection with rifles and shotguns. Stan looked down the aisle, checked that the bus was empty, and moved to get up.

"Hold on, Pop," growled the mask. "You back this rig up and get it across the street. I want you to block the eastbound lane. Got it?"

Stan nodded to the warrior, who pointed as he gave directions. Other natives were hurrying along the street and through the intersection, stopping cars and buses at gunpoint and getting them moved into the intersection to block it. In a few minutes, no traffic on Portage Avenue could get past Memorial Boulevard or up or down Colony Street. Drivers and passengers were ordered out of vehicles then pushed, prodded, and threatened west along Portage and down Memorial. A crowd began to assemble and traffic snarled in all directions. More drivers, unaware of what was happening in the intersection, honked their horns, yelled, or stepped out of their vehicles to try and see what was causing the delay.

Then a police car, responding to a message about a bus accident in front of the Bay, sped down Vaughan Street, out onto Portage, and skidded to a stop. Constable Pat Maloney looked in bewilderment at cars jammed together and people walking and some running up the side streets and in both directions on Portage Avenue. He stepped out of his car and was speaking into his shoulder radio when he suddenly spotted two warriors with rifles aimed at him. They fired together, their bullets smashing the windshield of the patrol car, knocking the roof lights into twisted wreckage and taking the driver-side mirror off the car. Maloney dropped to the pavement, grabbing for his pistol, and yelled into the radio, "Shots fired! Shots fired! I need assistance, now!"

A Dagmar Station fire truck, responding to a 911 report of a bus accident, inched down Colony Street, siren blaring, and stopped at the edge of the intersection. Warriors, now standing high on the strengthening barricade, promptly put two rounds into the truck's front bumper. Their comrades rushed the truck, pulled the startled crew from the vehicle, and forced the driver to crash the massive vehicle into the jumble of cars and buses already jamming the street. When he'd forced the truck as far into the clutter as it would go, the warriors ordered the driver out, then matter-of-factly shot out the tires and holed the gas tanks, setting the fire engine and surrounding cars ablaze. Once gas tanks started exploding, no further orders were needed to move the crowd or disperse the curious commuters caught in the traffic jam.

Meanwhile, the second warrior team smashed its way into the Hudson's Bay store, raced up the escalators, and climbed the emergency stairs onto the roof. Other groups with hunting rifles did the same at the Arts Centre on Memorial. Together they commanded the intersection in all directions. In the distance they saw smoke rising from Main Street and heard gunshots echoing between buildings from the direction of the legislative buildings. Their attention, however, quickly focused on the police cars and trucks trying to ring their area of Portage and Memorial. The riflemen settled into position and began to shoot at and disable the police vehicles just as they'd practised on old car wrecks on the reserves. The snipers cheered and jeered each other as their spotters called out the targets and indicated hits and misses.

Thirteen blocks away to the northeast, Alex Gabriel followed his team as it stormed city hall on Main Street. It was not much of an action. The building was empty except for a few startled, unarmed security guards. The warriors quickly bound their supervisor, stripped the others of radios, handcuffs, and other useful gear, then shooed them out the door with a choice of options: get lost or get hurt.

In minutes, the building was "under new management," as a large, hand-coloured sign hung on the front door would later announce. Warriors with rifles took positions in the high windows and on the roof. Alex's staff moved into a large interior office, set up their maps and communications equipment, then turned on the TV in the corner and flicked through the channels to Canada AM.

His other teams began to call in. Alex had originally expected to launch the raid in the late afternoon, but the change to an early morning operation had several distinct advantages—fewer civilians to deal with and less traffic in the barricade area. He watched out the window as Team Juba secured the area around James Avenue and another team moved north on Main to fortify the Ukrainian Cultural and Educational Centre and barricade the junction of Main and the Disraeli Freeway three blocks north.

His staff reported that they were in radio contact with all the teams and with Colonel Stevenson, who was getting ready to make his way to the airport. Most of the teams reported having captured and settled into their objectives without much difficulty. The civilians they encountered weren't sure how to react at first. In Lombard Square, at Portage and Main, most people had apparently thought the warriors with their trucks and the guns were just another movie company using the downtown streets as a suitable "roaring twenties" backdrop. When police cars screeched into the area, many commuters stopped and craned their necks to watch the action—until bullets began to rattle off the buildings and burst the windows around them.

The shootout around Lombard Square was violent, but short-lived. The cops had neither the firepower nor the inclination to engage in urban warfare. As soon as police dispatchers began to grasp the extent of the challenge in the downtown core, and small, on-scene SWAT team leaders reported in that they couldn't control the area, officers in central headquarters pulled their teams back to regroup while they assessed the situation across the city. Everywhere, police radios and civilian 911 calls reported armed natives were building barricades, chasing people off the streets and out of the city core, and, more ominously, freely shooting at police and other first responders. Casualty reports started coming in.

The chief of police, Stan Cohen, later famously remarked that his people were there "to serve and protect, not to get shot in combat. That job was an army job and I'm not a general." Alex didn't hear the chief's remarks, but he felt the same way. In fact, he was wondering when the army would show up.

Alex had little tactical intelligence to go on now that the operation was underway. He could speak with Colonel Stevenson but his sources were limited too. Alex's best bet was TV and radio news. He suspected, however, that eventually someone in the police or Canadian Forces command centre would shut down electric power throughout the area to prevent fires and cut off his TV. Although Alex and the other leaders had battery-powered radios, once the authorities alerted radio stations to stop airing information useful to the insurgents, their main source of information would be phoned in from warriors and their families detailed to watch TV reports from places outside the battle zone. However, he couldn't rely too much on that: TV news wasn't always totally reliable. He'd just have to play it by ear, and by eye.

For the moment, Alex consolidated his successes, reinforced weak areas while it was still safe to move through exposed ground, and began patrolling aggressively. During the staff checks and rehearsals for the operation, he and Stevenson and the other planners had decided that it was likely that at some point the battle would become a stalemate, and as the police regrouped, that's what appeared to be happening. His teams controlled the buildings they occupied and the streets they could cover with rifle fire. The police held the other areas, but more or less conformed to the deployments Alex had established. In other words, he was confined within a rough circle and the police were content for the time being to sit on the outside.

The "battle for the legislative buildings," as it would later be known in the popular press, quickly became Alex Gabriel's main worry. The stubbornness of the defenders and the ongoing firefight in the area surprised him. Militarily speaking, the legislative site was important but not critical to the line of defence he and Stevenson had devised for the inner core. But politically it was a critical target, since it was the symbol of the crusade. In planning the attack on the building, Alex faced a common though unpleasant field commander's dilemma: if winning the battle at the legislative buildings became too costly in people and resources, then tactics demanded a withdrawal; strategy, however, demanded an advance. The Golden Boy was the central symbol in this war for justice. Alex understood well the power that would flow from the native people to the Movement once they saw on their televisions the image of the Golden Boy in native hands and the warriors' flag flying from the top of the grand building. So he was prepared to spend lives to take it. The trick was to take it while he still had lives to spend.

It was proving difficult. The raid on the legislature went off-track early, not because the plan was faulty or the warriors weren't rehearsed and determined, but because damn circumstance, the friction of war, intervened. Professional soldiers train for and expect things to go wrong. The best officers and tacticians live naturally in disorder and when the plan goes awry, they invent another one on the spot. Irregular soldiers, especially those in their first engagement, often come apart when the plan does. They might fight bravely together in small groups or they might run. But very few of them will adjust to changed circumstances in any orderly, logical way. This inability to read the battlefield accurately had defeated many rebellions and now it threatened Alex's.

The plan for the main force of Team Dumont—named for Gabriel Dumont, the principal military leader of Louis Riel's Indian/Métis rebellion of 1885, and a keen tactician—had been to literally drive onto the grounds and up the steps of the legislative buildings, rush inside, overwhelm the amateur guards, and take possession of the buildings. Other sections would occupy Government House, capture the lieutenant governor if possible, chase her family away, and take the captive or captives back to the main building. A third team would then select positions from which to command the area, including the junction of Broadway Avenue and Osborne Street and the Osborne Bridge, then patrol eastward to link up with the team attacking HMCS Chippewa barracks. Once in position, Team Dumont would hold the area until relieved by the columns advancing from outside the city. Straightforward enough.

Unfortunately, as the secondary raiding party's pickup trucks dashed onto the grounds from Kennedy Street to hit the lieutenant governor's house, they ran into two RCMP cars right by the gate. Reconnaissance patrols only days before seemed to confirm that the RCMP would not be in that area at that early hour. Nor had the Mounties changed their plans. Instead, by sheer coincidence, the constables had rolled into the grounds simply to gossip and share a coffee.

When they saw the speeding trucks and the natives, the surprised constables thought they were dealing with a few drunk drivers. But they had been warned of possible problems caused by the Quebec situation, and as soon as the trucks got close enough for them to notice the weapons and the pickup's direct, clearly deliberate route toward the house, they realized they were in trouble. One constable jumped from his car, grabbing his shotgun, and shouted a warning at the lead truck. The other constable rammed the gear shift into drive, hit the gas, and skidded her cruiser into position to block the main entrance to the house. She fumbled for her radio and called for backup. As soon as she got acknowledgement, she, too, jumped from her patrol car and drew her pistol.

The raiding team hadn't expected to find anyone near the house except, at most, a solitary commissionaire. When instead they saw two police cars in the lane and found armed constables confronting them, the trucks rolled to a slow halt and their boisterous crews fell silent. Green troops invariably hesitate and some freeze on first encountering the enemy. Besides, these were Mounties. All their lives, these young natives had considered the redcoats more or less part of their own villages. The elders had taught them the "Horsemen" were fair and helpful friends. Every instinct told the younger natives to back away, even though they were only facing two isolated constables, crouched, half-hidden, behind their cars. For a moment nobody moved.

This brief pause was the constables' only advantage and Margaret Shelly took advantage of it. She stepped out to the rear of her car, weapon at the ready but pointed at the ground in front of the lead truck, and commanded loudly, "Put those weapons down. Turn off the trucks and everyone dismount and lie on the ground." A traditional, gutsy Mountie bluff, but this morning, tradition and guts were not enough.

A shot from the leader in the back of the first truck barely missed Shelly and sent her diving back for cover behind her car. Then other warriors joined in, blasting away randomly at the cars and the constables behind them, all to little effect. The Mounties returned fire. Constable Paul LeBlanc blew out the lights and windows of the first two trucks with shotgun pellets and, in a shower of glass, wounded those natives too inexperienced to duck for cover. Margaret Shelly forced the drivers to abandon the other two trucks with a couple of careful rounds from her pistol. The firefight was uneven; despite their better fire discipline, the outgunned Mounties quickly withdrew, crawling and dodging, to the somewhat better cover of Government House. Warriors jumped from the truck. A few continued shooting at the now-abandoned, crippled patrols cars, while others fired indiscriminately around the area. In the distance, sirens announced the approaching response to the constables' call for help.

Within ten minutes, a running gun battle had developed around Government House and in the grounds south of the legislative building. At first the natives had the upper hand as they ran about rabbit-hunting Shelly and LeBlanc in the bushes and long shadows thrown up by the rising sun. But then two RCMP patrol cars slid in behind the empty trucks and blocked the exit. They were quickly joined by several other patrols and then a strong RCMP SWAT team held ready for trouble in the city. Fifteen minutes after that, RCMP Superintendent Daniel pulled his mobile command post into the parking lot and began an organized, aggressive defence of the grounds.

Neither Stevenson nor Gabriel knew that days before, the RCMP and NDHQ had received a warning from the Integrated Threat Assessment

Centre of "a possibility of the presence of radical native elements in Winnipeg" and a further warning of "possible local disturbances developing in the city." The RCMP divisional commander responsible for internal security in Manitoba took the warnings seriously and his orders for increased surveillance of known radicals and gang leaders soon produced weak signals from native informers that something big was planned for Winnipeg. When this information was matched to ITAC analysis and other electronic intelligence, the divisional commanding officer began to assemble plans, police teams, and other resources to protect, at the very least, federal interests and properties in Winnipeg and surrounding areas.

Their preparations were somewhat sketchy. Weak signals are hard to decipher and not always trustworthy. Plus there'd been extremely frustrating internal competitions and conflicts within federal agencies and between the feds and the provincial authorities. Every detail was chewed over by departments and agencies, chewed over again by political hacks, and then bickered over by both.

The best that could be decided was that the city police would maintain their regular routine, the RCMP would assemble a small ready-response team in Winnipeg, and the Canadian Forces would stay in the background. In reality, the federal plan was driven by the prime minister's determination to wish away any assessment suggesting native trouble in the West. The usual socially conscious provincial and city leaders cheered on the refusal to make any "provocative" preparations.

Despite these internal quarrels, the RCMP responded well to the situation once trouble started. The SWAT team, though better armed than the regular patrol constables, was still outgunned by warriors carrying Diemaco C7A2 and M-203A1 assault rifles stolen from Canadian Forces armouries and the militia. But these officers were tactically trained and soon turned the tables on the warriors, causing the native plan to evaporate in the heat of unexpected resistance, and allowing the Mounties to take the initiative away from them.

The warriors scattered, acting increasingly as individual fighters, firing randomly on police reinforcements or just bushes rustling in the wind. Those natives still able to form plans tried to work their way towards the south side of the legislative buildings, while the police cautiously tried to contain their adversaries and push them into the open areas along the

Riverside Promenade and the strong point their colleagues had established on the north side of the Osborne Street Bridge.

The tide suddenly turned again as the second part of Team Dumont showed up late and, as chance would have it, caught their adversaries from behind. Just as the RCMP thought they had the upper hand in the southern grounds, the four trucks carrying the remaining two dozen members of the team raced onto the grounds from the north, through the Broadway Avenue entrance, aiming for the front steps of the building.

As they entered the grounds, two warriors manning light machine guns, stolen from Petawawa by Alex Gabriel's raiders, smuggled into Winnipeg, and mounted on the cabs of their pickup trucks, riddled the police cars blocking the entrance. Two constables died in their cars before they knew what was happening; the others, caught unprepared—facing south towards the building, the anvil on which the SWAT team was planning to hammer the insurgents already on the grounds—scattered under cars and into bushes without time to return fire as the native trucks roared past them and up the legislative steps.

Queen Victoria's long, uncontested guard over the front steps ended abruptly. The obviously vulnerable entrance, undefended except for a lone, unqualified guard, stood open because the Speaker of the legislature had decided in 2008 that a barrier of any kind would be "unsightly and too much an American overreaction to so-called terrorists."

Patty Leduc had been terrified when she gave the order for a "through the mud and blood" mounted attack from Broadway, across the legislative grounds, and into the buildings. Like most of the warriors, she had never shot at a person or seriously injured anyone in any way. Yet here she was, against all instinct and tradition, shooting at the Mounties, screaming her head off, rough-riding in her pink-and-black truck over the grass and right up the legislative building steps. Strange way to make a first visit, she thought even as she threw herself out of the truck and joined a dozen or so of her troopers in a race for the great front door.

They burst into the grand hall. A few warriors paused in awe, then rushed to join the others as they scrambled to clear the area of startled, frightened security guards. There weren't many and after their commander decided that escaping alone out a low window was the better part of valour, they put up no resistance.

A couple of police in the legislative building, however, had been alerted to the battle outside and opened fire on the raiders from the balcony above the entrance, ricocheting rounds off the walls and floor. Some warriors ducked for cover along the walls under the balcony, others found protection from the white men's bullets under the great metal bison. First one, then several, and finally most of the warriors recovered from their surprise and filled the balcony with automatic rifle fire, driving the police far into the building interior. As the police retreated, four or five warriors, dodging from pillar to pillar, scrambled up the stairs and occupied the balcony.

Patty took out her cellphone and with shaking hands dialled Alex Gabriel. "Alex, we're inside the hall," she gasped, nearly breathless with excitement and pride.

"Good job, Patty. Good job. Well done. Now secure your position. Your guys have done well, but it's not over yet. It's just started. Are you with me? Take a couple of deep breaths."

Patty did, and, calmer, responded, "Yeah, I'm here."

"Good. Now listen carefully. You need to secure your position. Block the doors with desks, chairs, filing cabinets, to keep them closed and soak up bullets. Put some people by the windows, but be careful. The police are bringing in sniper teams and they'll shoot anyone they see. Tell your guys to keep their eyes peeled but their heads down. The bad guys can really shoot and they will.

"And listen. Our other team is held up near Government House and around the grounds outside the back. They're having a lot of trouble with the cops out there. If you can get a few people in the high windows on the southeast side, looking over the Assiniboine River, and give our people some support by firing into the rear of the police positions, do it now. But watch out for snipers. I'll get around to you eventually. I knew I could count on you, Patty."

She put down the cellphone and called to her team. "Eddie, John, Pierre—get up to the next floor, on that side, see if you can see the other team and the police, and if you can, start shooting to help them out. If you can't see them, go higher till you can. Got it?"

Eddie nodded, waved the other two towards the stairs, then scrambled, half stooped, after them up the stairs, past the blue chamber, and out of sight. Patty Leduc, now a real warrior, ran in the same half-crouch across the hall, putting her people in position, warning them to watch, shoot at easy targets, and keep their heads down. She settled near the door waiting for ... what next? She wasn't sure, but she could feel her team's command of the building. She felt alert, clear-headed, keyed up, yet serene. Successful command in battle, that elusive combination of tactical insight, imagination, and coolness under fire, was hers by nature.

Monday, September 6, 0645 hours
West Winnipeg

Colonel Stevenson checked his wall map for the last time. The confusion of the morning seemed normal to his experienced military mind. He knew for sure that Alex's teams had succeeded in most areas and that the strong points were secure for the time being. Lombard Square was more or less under control, but the warriors were battling a traffic jam and a swirling crowd of commuters and office workers trying to find shelter or escape the area. Oddly, the warriors and the police caught up in the confusion were hard-pressed to find open chances to engage each other. But the team leader reported that he held the high buildings and had the police pinned down as far as he could see. The most important good news was that he controlled the underground pedestrian tunnels. Patrols were also out along the banks of the Red River, gradually linking the strong points to each other. The only real fight and the only place where the outcome was doubtful was on the legislature grounds and within the buildings there.

Stevenson knew that Alex would follow doctrine and common sense which, Sam had often explained to staff college students in earlier days, ought to be the same but rarely were. But in this situation he expected Alex to use his tactical sense to secure his core positions, then widen his control of the city centre—Memorial Boulevard at Portage down to The Forks, up Main Street to city hall and the CP station. The legislative buildings might stand or fall, but with the police, and possibly the army, concentrating there, Alex knew better than to spend lives trying to reinforce that attack now.

Colonel Sam, too, had the operational aim fixed in his mind. Take the city to draw the police and the army into the area, thus allowing the second phase of the operation to succeed. Holding the legislative buildings or any other specific position was not the aim. If the police and the army wanted to fight for bricks and mortar, so much the better. Alex and his people would accommodate them. Once the city was in their hands for good, the Golden Boy would be thrown down. Stevenson at the moment had another objective in mind. Right now Winnipeg, like Quebec, was a diversion.

Sunday evening before the attack in the city centre, Peter Dubé had quietly settled Battle Group Métis into the Winnipeg communities of Garden Glove, Silver Heights, Brooklands, and Weston, as well as in the western outskirts near Headingley. It was prepared to move boldly and with speed onto Winnipeg International Airport and the Canadian Forces air base located across the runways from the civilian terminal. These early deployments in white neighbourhoods were risky, gambling easy access to the targets against discovery by a curious resident or suspicious police patrol.

The teams took care to park their trucks separately, one here, another there, in shopping malls, industrial lots, and on quiet streets within their assigned sectors on the western side of the city. The warriors slipped into safe houses near the parking places and stayed quiet, careful to give the locals no cause to call the police.

Considerable caution was needed because in Winnipeg the mere presence of a bunch of Indians anywhere outside the usual areas—North Main Street, Selkirk Avenue, St. Matthews and Memorial, or along Sherbrooke and Maryland—might trigger a complaint. The order was no beer, no parties, no loud noise, no groups of young men, just quiet, routine family activity. Some fighters brought along their women and children while others "borrowed" families for camouflage. The plan worked well enough, and discipline was tight enough, that they attracted nothing more than a few hostile stares from a handful of residents and the occasional police cruise-by of one or two of the houses. When the kids waved to the cops, they drove on, and a quiet evening calm settled over the city streets.

Half an hour before first light on Monday, a few early joggers were puzzled by people in open pickup trucks rushing through the western sections of the city. Drivers picked up their assigned trucks and met warriors arriving from the safe houses, carrying covered cases and small boxes containing weapons and ammunition that weeks before had been stored in the safe houses, garages, and U-Store depots rented by the NPA.

The assembly phase was an especially worrying time. Chance might easily put a police car near an assembly point with a suspicious cop at the wheel. A nervous driver might miss a rendezvous or, worse, cause an accident. Even a minor fender-bender involving a truck full of natives with boxes and duffle bags would mean a call for backup, resulting in either an impromptu shootout on a city street or a search of the truck, then an alert to police and even military authorities about natives with rifles, rockets, and grenades.

But nothing of the sort happened. The west end was quiet as the dawn sky turned to daylight, and as they began to move out, the raiders started hearing faint distant reports of weapons downtown and police sirens answering frantic calls from the chaos there. At that point, Battle Group Métis turned its attention to its duties, knowing almost every police car in town was heading away from them and their target as fast as it could go.

Meanwhile, Colonel Sam was wending his way through the streets towards the airport as his driver and escort had practised many times. His tactical headquarters group, seven bright, young native militia officers, all graduates of militia staff courses in Kingston, travelled along behind him in two specially constructed cube vans. Their job was to scan news stations and police radio frequencies and to monitor the battle groups' actions until they could establish secure communications at the new airport HQ location. Stevenson checked his watch. Time to let the teams loose.

"Métis," he barked into his tactical radio set. "This is Steel. Over."

The radio crackled back immediately. "Métis. Over."

"Steel. All set? Over."

"Métis. Roger and eager. Over."

"Steel. Okay, make your move. I'm on time and will follow the first team onto the objective and meet you there. Over."

"Métis. Roger. On the way. Out"

Stevenson sat back and gazed out the open truck window at the faces of citizens at bus stops. Strange, he thought. There they stand, complacent, caught up in petty private worries. Their world is about to be turned upside down, and they have no more control over their lives than if a huge hurricane suddenly swept down the street and smashed their ordinary lives to pieces. Which, in a sense, was exactly what was about to happen to them all. Their chance to avoid the gathering storm and control their fate was long since lost to ballots not cast or fools carelessly elected.

Monday, September 6, 0720 hours
Ottawa: NDOC

Warrant Officer Steve Mack, NDOC comms chief, blinked at the message. "Sir!" he called to the duty officer. "A flash SIR from CFB Winnipeg."

Lieutenant Colonel Rick Lemieux scanned the page and actually jumped. "Jesus Christ!" he said, very loudly. Then, recovering his composure, he turned to Mack. "Comms, call Colonel Dobson across the road at the Westin. Tell him to get over here ASAP, then get me Winnipeg Ops on the secure means. Jessie, make sure CANCOMOPS has acknowledged the message and then click over to CTV Newsnet and see what they're reporting."

Lemieux read the message again more slowly. "Police report heavy firing and native attacks in downtown Winnipeg. RCMP SWAT teams deployed and in a gunfight near the Legislative Buildings. The base defence force is deployed and moments ago reported gunfire from the area of the civilian terminal. We have gone to full alert. I have ordered ROE, 'Shoot to defend.' Base Commander sends."

The duty signaller handed Lemieux a secure phone. "Sir, Colonel Dobson is on the way. Colonel Christie at Winnipeg is on the line."

Lemieux put the phone to his ear and jumped again. "Jesus Christ! Paula, what's the situation? Is that automatic weapons fire I'm hearing?"

"Affirmative," Colonel Christie answered crisply. "We've got a full-scale assault on the airport and the base underway, Rick. It looks like Kandahar in the bad old days. The city's in turmoil ... Indians with lots of automatic weapons have control of downtown, looks like from the Hudson's Bay store to city hall and up Main Street. The reserve barracks, HMCS Chippawa, is out of contact, maybe lost, we don't know with what casualties. There's a big fight at the legislative buildings. Seems the natives have the main building, but have got themselves trapped inside. The RCMP claim they have the situation in hand there, but I'm not so sure.

"The base is secure at the moment, but we've got a real firefight developing all around us here too as I speak. The BDF commander, good boy, had everyone at 'stand-to' at dawn—too much Gagetown army training for a pilot. They intercepted three pickup trucks loaded with wild Indians driving onto the runways from the north. The Indians came in firing on the parked Hercs and I'm afraid they damaged several aircraft, but they drove right into one of our ground defence points and the girls and boys let them have it. No casualties on our side, but we are still counting the others—looks like four KIAs, a half dozen wounded, and two trucks knocked out. Just a minute...

"Rick, we've got reports right now of other raiders coming in on the south end and though the base gates. Gotta go. I'll get back to you. We've sent another flash message to you and CANCOMOPS, but check for me to make sure they got the message—we're under attack, repeat we are under attack."

The phone went dead and Lemieux turned to the duty staff. "Flash up the Winnipeg city and base charts on the centre boards. Jessie, call the backup staff in pronto, then locate the DCDS. If he's inbound, ask him to come directly to the Ops Centre. If he's still at home, get him to activate his secure cellphone and keep it clear for an urgent, repeat urgent, call from Colonel Dobson. And get me the CDS's EA on the phone."

Monday, September 6, 0735 hours
Winnipeg: Inside the Winnipeg Airport Control Tower

Stevenson looked at his watch. The Winnipeg operation was going as well as could be expected. The growing chaos in the city centre was causing as much disruption by now as the warriors' direct actions. As best anyone could tell from reports by moles within the police services and militia units, the government side was attempting to organize a counterattack to retake the city, but, not surprisingly, the various governments' so-called "inter-agency command arrangements," long discussed in useless bureaucratic committees, were near nonexistent. The RCMP was fully engaged on the legislative grounds while the militia was clumsily trying to assemble a small force that, if it moved as Stevenson's sources reported it was planning to, would soon be caught up in the centre town melee. And nobody was talking clearly to anybody else. The emergency forces and the various police services didn't even have compatible radio equipment.

Colonel Sam's main worry was the regular army units in Shilo, 200 kilometres west of Winnipeg. The Shilo combat units had been deployed to Zimbabwe in the early summer, but the garrison units—mostly "loggies" and technicians—might be enough to upset the natives' timetable at least. As best he could see, that little unit, too, seemed to be mobilizing and heading for the city. If so, the bait was attracting the coyotes. And if Stevenson's and Molly's luck held, the native columns dropping down on the city from the north would trap the government forces in the city as planned and the NPA could shut the door, bolt it, and negotiate from a position of great strength.

Stevenson flipped open his secure cellphone and called Tommy Twoskins, the commander of Cree Column, 800 kilometres to the northwest. "Tom, expect an H-hour time to go for early Tuesday morning, the seventh. Begin now to assemble your leaders for final orders and make quiet preparations to move. When I give you the word, secure The Pas, then call me once you have reasonable control there. Remember, it's critically important that you get out of The Pas and get your Column Cree down Highway 10 and past the junction with Highway 60 before Column Pelican from Flin Flon arrives or there will be a bugger's muddle on the road south from The Pas."

The young commander responded eagerly. "Roger that. We'll have the town under control quickly enough, don't worry. I have people loitering near all the targets and ready to go on my say-so. We've already coordinated the plan with Pelican so they can move through The Pas unhindered by the RCMP or anyone after we leave. And I have patrols on the highways to guide the columns south. I'll give you the word once I'm on the way. Not to worry, sir, we're going to move south like shit through a snow goose."

Stevenson acknowledged the message and turned to more immediate worries.

Monday, September 6, 0740 hours
Ottawa: CANCOMOPS

Lieutenant General René Lepine tossed his beret and coat on a desk and took the Winnipeg base commander's SIR from the Ops Centre's director, Colonel Nick Pew. After a silent minute he asked, "Okay, Nick, what's the latest?"

"Bad, sir. Looks like the base might go down. The civvy side is out of action, tower's out, and the Indians are driving up and down the runways. They seem a bit confused best we can tell. Seems they don't know what to do now they are on the objective. They're driving around shooting at buildings and aircraft, but the BDF is holding them away from the base for now. But there's a lot of them, heavily armed, and the base commander confirmed a few minutes ago that there are other raiders coming in from the south end."

"What's the chance of reinforcing the base from local units?"

Pew pointed to the maps. "Bad to worse, I'm afraid. The local units, such as they are, are in action downtown and mixed up with the city police and the RCMP. It would be difficult to remove them and get them to the base. Besides, that move might only result in the loss of positions in the city core without helping the airfield. And, sir, we don't know who might be waiting for us to try and drive out Portage Avenue. From the scale and coordination of their plan so far, I suspect they've set some ambushes on the likely roads into the base."

"And," said Lepine pointing to the provincial map, "moving an ad hoc unit from Shilo would take time to organize and Highway 1 could be blocked in several places. So, not much there either."

The commander turned abruptly to ponder the maps, with half an ear on the background noise of messages from CFB Winnipeg describing the faltering situation there. Equally abruptly he turned and pointed at Pew. "Don't we have a subunit of the Patricias in a Herc moving from Edmonton to Quebec? Are they in the area?"

"Yes, sir, I'll check their exact location, but that flight's the last one out, and luckily it's carrying most of an infantry company." Nick looked over his shoulder to the log desk.

"Jamie, where's that Herc with the last load of Patricias?"

"Checking, sir." The staff officer turned to his computer and tapped in the codes. "Sir, she's just south and west of Winnipeg. Passing the city about twenty kilometres south in fifteen minutes."

Again Lepine stood apart, quietly grinding the factors and sifting them into options and then a solution. Deep in thought, he shifted closer to the Op Centre's dynamic, high definition wall maps and ran his fingers slowly over the detailed display of the city and the changing deployment of his units and the enemy force.

"I'm afraid time commands, here," he announced suddenly. "We move or we lose, and we may lose anyway. Okay, Jamie, get the pilot on the radio for me."

The C130 Hercules carried a light load—an infantry company with their immediate gear and supplies, and two G-Wagons, a type of armoured SUV, tied down nose-to-tail in the centre of the aircraft. There is no hospitality class on a Herc. The eighty-plus soldiers sat crowded together on the simple canvas sling seats that folded down from the sides of the aircraft. A few tiny portholes here and there along the fuselage provided a dim light and no view at all. It was nearly impossible to read by the faint, overhead lights high up in the roof.

Major John Lewis, first pilot and mission commander on this flight, listened intently to the unexpected message from CANCOMOPS. He looked to his right to his second pilot, Captain Mary Ferguson, her concern clearly evident on her face as she took control of the aircraft. Lewis acknowledged the message, switched to the Hercules' intercom, and called the loadmaster. "Jason, would you ask the company commander, Major Kempling, to come up to the flight deck now, please?"

Within seconds, Kempling, a young infantry officer but veteran of two combat tours in Afghanistan and one in Haiti, poked his head up the ladder and climbed onto the deck. The "nav" passed him a headset as he took a seat on the bench, blinking as the bright light of the clear blue high sky struck his eyes. He flicked the mike on and said, "What's up, John?"

"Change of mission, I think," replied Lewis. "General Lepine's coming on." He changed frequency, checked in and paused, then said, "Yes, sir, you're on, and Major Roy Kempling commanding the company is listening."

"Gentlemen," Lepine announced, "we have a change of course and mission. Major Lewis, you are to divert immediately to Winnipeg. The base is under attack by at least two Indian raiding parties. We count so far about twenty-five to forty attackers, some in pickup trucks and most armed with automatic rifles and shotguns. They're riding around the airfield causing damage and it looks like they intend to stay. The base commander is holed up in the hangar line and the base defence force is holding its own there and around the aprons and parked aircraft. However, more natives seem to be coming in from the south, from the Portage Avenue area. So I'm obviously concerned for the safety of our people, but also I'm worried that if we lose the base, we're going to have a tough time getting units into the city at all.

"Major Kempling, you are to take your company into the base and reinforce the defence force and then, once you've had time to assess and stabilize the situation, I want you to take command of the defences and clear the west side so I can get some other units in. It's not an easy task, but I think we can surprise them if we get in fast and low. Major Lewis, that's your job.

"We think you can make it in from the southwest, the wind's right, and drop on the runway right along the hangar line with the ramp down on approach. We'll get the base commander to give you all the support and cover fire she can as you come in. Just make sure to give her a warning when you're a few minutes out. I assume you have the flight maps of the area?"

"Yes, sir, the crew's breaking them out as we speak."

"Good. And Kempling, you know the area too, I think?"

"Yes, sir, served some battalion time there."

"Okay." Lepine put the mission in his young commanders' hands. "You guys work out the approach. The staff here has some other details for you, I'll put them on. Once you've got it worked out, we'll give Winnipeg the word. But head straight in. We've got to get in before the natives bring in more trucks and block the runways or overrun the BDF. Good luck."

Lewis spoke for both officers. "Thank you, sir, we're on the way and dropping on approach now. Out." He took control of the Herc as the flight crew worked on the approach.

Kempling climbed down the cargo deck, called his platoon commanders to the rear area, and warned his sergeant major to rouse the company. Fortunately, they had their weapons handy and a full load of ammunition ready for a hasty deployment once they reached Quebec City. In minutes, the groggy company jumped to action, finding and hooking on their flak jackets and helmets. The loadmaster and his crew grabbed the cargo chains, tightened the load for a hard landing, and rushed to the rear to stand by the ramp. The Herc cut a sharp curve in the air and turned north and west towards the city and the airfield already visible on the horizon.

Monday, September 6, 0820 hours
Ottawa: CANCOMOPS

René Lepine sipped at his coffee as he followed the radio conversations from the base, waiting intently for the first reports of his own little surprise. A sudden commotion at the ops desk disrupted the centre's habitual steady order.

"Oh shit, oh goddamn." The desk officer in direct contact with the base ops turned and handed the headset to Colonel Pew. "You'd better take this, sir, it's Colonel Christie."

"Yeah, Paula, I…" He froze, listening, then swayed forward, bracing himself against the desk, eyes closed. All eyes were on him as he opened his eyes again and spoke softly into the headset.

"Yeah, okay. Sure. You hang in there, Paula. We'll get you some help as soon as we can. Yeah, you too." Pew placed the headset gently on the desk and turned towards René Lepine who, from across the small room, read disaster in his face.

"Problem, Nick?" he asked unnecessarily.

"Yes, sir. The base commander was talking Major Lewis in on his run into the base. As the Herc swung over Fort White and dropped into its final approach, it took ground fire, perhaps a Blowpipe missile. The pilot reported the left outside engine and wing were damaged then burning. He pulled it up and got it under control for a few minutes, but they were low and fast. He struggled and lost it over the Tuxedo Golf course, clipped some trees, and banged hard into Assiniboine Park and scattered wreckage over the Assiniboine River and up the bank on the other side as far as Portage Avenue. There're no survivors. Almost ninety people, sir ..." Nick's voice sank.

General Lepine scanned the faces in command centre. The staff stood or sat silently, looking at their commander, ignoring the flashing boards and buzzing computers and telephones demanding their attention.

René had been in a lot of tough fights and had spent soldiers' lives for mission success before. But the shock never really went away. Instead it grew, inside, held at bay by training and duty. He had long feared that shock and her comrade, depression, were accumulating in the dark recesses of his mind, waiting to ambush him some dark day when he was tired or old or grown unsure of what he'd done to satisfy "mission first." Not today, he told himself sternly. Not today, of all days.

"We'll settle the score later," he said quietly. "Right now, you people shake it out and find me some other resources. We're going to give the base commander as much as we can find and that includes breaking off the downtown operation if we have to. The base and the airfield have priority. Get me Colonel Christie. While they're doing that, Nick, would you get the CDS on the line. I don't care where he is or what he's doing." Nobody moved.

"Listen," he said, "these things happen in war and there may be worse to come. We'll grieve later. Right now we have a job to do." Lepine paused. "You're all good people. It was my call, not yours. Remember that."

Monday, September 6, 0840 hours
Outside Flin Flon

Tommy Twoskins was the eldest son in the latest generation of an ancient Cree family. His people had lived in the headwaters area of what is now called the Nelson River basin for countless generations. Tommy had travelled out of the region only for schooling and a fairly successful but not entirely happy military career. In 2001, "Toques," the nickname he acquired in the army and carried home, had left the Canadian Forces honourably, a captain with six years service as a special operations infantry officer. But he left in frustration.

In part, he left because of what he saw every day: disrespect for aboriginal soldiers and ignorance of their rightful needs. But he left, too, because he was ashamed of the image, the reality, of his people he saw most every day on TV in the south—failed native parents and leaders in his native communities who allowed their children to wander unattended and uneducated through their early years. But in his heart, Tommy was ashamed of himself—unreasonably so, an army counsellor had once told him. He was ashamed of his army successes, achieved only, he believed, because he had deserted his people. "You think I'm a success? I ran away to save myself when I should have stayed home to help my mother and my younger brother."

He had tried while he was home on leave to relieve the guilt by pleading for responsible behaviour and setting an example for the kids in his village, but when he left again, his uneasiness returned tenfold. Tommy knew he could never make a difference if he travelled between his two worlds. He had to choose one or the other. Finally he decided the true call of duty was to leave the world beyond the village and return home to the Athapap First Nation south of Flin Flon—to stay and make a difference.

Tommy Twoskins was a fine example to the young people in his village and indeed throughout the region. Tall, fit, and sober, he attracted the attention of many young women in the area. They told one another they were eager to meet the big, good-looking hunk with the short, thick hair and big black eyes. But in their hearts they knew he was far more than just a handsome bachelor. He was a rare catch—a responsible working native with whom they might some day not just have children but really raise children.

Not everyone who noticed the difference could put it into words, but Tommy was unusual more than anything else because he was positive, even optimistic. He attracted boys and girls to his side because he led by example. Disciplined and honest, he worked for the community without material reward, listened sincerely to the elders, and less than a month after returning home simply began on his own to clean away the debris and fix the reserve's rundown school. Within days, others, mostly kids, began silently coming along, carting away junk and carrying in lumber and supplies.

In time, a kind of community team was born, without direction, subsidies, or regulated help from governments. Tommy Twoskins later joined the small native staff trying to teach and organize the hundreds of young people on the Cree reserves. In every one of them, though he never spoke about it, he saw a reflection of his deeper reason for trying to help save these kids: a part of himself that was locked away in a white man's prison far to the south at Stony Mountain.

Try as he might, Tommy soon discovered that even with the best will and habits in the world, one man could not overcome the pathologies of an entire community deprived of hope and responsible example for decades. Tommy needed the willing cooperation of the "lost generation," the twenty-something child-adults who until his return had set the example, mostly bad example, for the village kids. Few of the lost generation, however, were willing to come to his side; most only jeered at him in the streets, and those who did join him soon fell away again, drunken and ashamed.

Tommy also needed the help and cooperation of the resident chiefs and band leaders, but they saw him as an outsider and a challenge to their privileged authority. As for white government officials and their programs, he saw them as worse than useless, undermining his efforts by rewarding dependence and suffocating initiative with unearned welfare. And they reciprocated his dislike and actively worked to frustrate his initiatives. In time, though he tried to hide it, Tommy started to feel despair creeping up on him.

He had, of course, been approached by the National People's Army when he was in the Special Operations Forces Command. He was exactly the sort they went after. But he had ignored the recruiters' probes while nurturing his dream of coming home and changing his village. By the time they came calling again, three years after he left the Canadian Forces, he was more receptive. The problem was more deep-seated than he had realized, and the NPA had a more radical remedy, one that seemed to be based on the same values he cherished, and one he knew the kids needed: discipline, purpose, organization, pride based on real achievement, and, not insignificantly, money with which to get projects done.

Even though Tommy at first had little time for the aggressive rhetoric spouted by some NPA junior leaders, he endured it because it brought him the money he needed for his own programs: the clubhouse with its squash court, the lacrosse field, the little library. Later, when his work in the Athapap First Nation faltered under the weight of government and band chief interference, not to mention a deep sense of alienation from the adults in the community, he gave in to temptation. Tommy finally admitted that, exactly as the NPA leaders in the region had said, "it's not 'the system and the situation' that are the problems, it's the delinquent leaders, white and native. And Tommy, your good deeds can't beat them. Our people are drowning and we have to drag them to a safe shore. You're just treading water and losing."

Waiting for the word to go into action on the roads to Winnipeg that sunny September afternoon, Tommy Twoskins thought back to another early September day two years earlier, and his first meeting with Molly Grace. She had come one day in the fall to tell the people of the Cree First Nations in northern Manitoba about her vision of self-help and responsibility and freedom from white governments and corrupt white Indians, the very ideas he was trying to build in his own community. Toques was happy to listen to her, but he had his own ideas. After her speech at the Opaskwayak Cree Nation near Flin Flon, she asked to see him and they talked for three hours.

"Sure," he told her, "we should take the land and scare the feds into some new kind of arrangement. But how can we make it stick? We can't even depend on the white Indians and the politicians to settle land claims and other grievances for us, and we can't take political control from the provinces even in Manitoba and Saskatchewan where we are the majority. How are we to win anything?"

Molly eyed him carefully and said quietly, "Go on."

"My friends and I can point to example after example where some contentious matter put our people up against the Canadians and the outcomes were predetermined in favour of the whites by their laws and the constitutional arrangements they set in stone long before the native people became politically aware. What's come of all the years of agitation and days of action and even rioting? Nothing! So what's the use in negotiating now or ever, from weakness or strength, calmly or in anger? What's the use of anything, Molly?"

She sat quietly for some time after he was done. Then she said, "You're right, Tommy. What's the use in negotiating? None. The game is hopelessly rigged against us. Just look at the provincial boundaries. They're nothing but arbitrary lines on paper maps. Try telling your ancestors or mine that some straight line running from horizon to horizon separates something called 'Manitoba' from something called 'Saskatchewan.' They're white man's lines. Just lines on paper. But they divide the native vote and the native traditions on the land forever. If we negotiate on the settlers' terms and with settlers' governments and their impregnable positions, not just legal but intellectual positions, you're right, there isn't much use. But we're not planning to negotiate. We've planning to take back the land and then redraw the maps and the land deeds and everything else.

"Imagine this, Tommy Twoskins, a land with no boundaries between Sault Ste. Marie and the Rocky Mountain divide, as it was in the time of Riel and before him. A wide-open range under native laws and traditions. A new region where our people can live in peace, with the settlers we might allow on our land—but only on our terms. Where the people decide who gets what, according to our traditions. Where the people decide who goes to jail and for what crimes and when they are released.

"Imagine how whitey would feel if the settlers had from the beginning been forced by us to conform to our laws and ways, if they'd signed treaties we wrote and later we told them: 'Sorry, you didn't understand our laws, you're just savages. The fine print says we get everything.' Well, I know how they would have reacted, and you know too—they'd have killed us and taken the land! Which is what they did anyway, just took the land, made a few phoney treaties to cover up the theft, and killed our culture and our spirit.

"Well, Tommy, no more. No more negotiations with an occupying nation over something that is our inalienable right in the first place. It's time we treated them the way they treated us, the way our ancestors would have treated them if they'd been able to imagine the horror that would follow their being trusting and peaceful and honourable. That's the difference between the Movement and all the other failed native and government ideas at reconciliation. Tommy, we're changing the logic of the argument. And I want you to help us."

Tommy had stared at Molly, appalled and fascinated. He'd never thought of the problem like that before. He'd always assumed he was in the wrong and required to negotiate, strike a deal, give away something essential to get back some of the things that he knew were his in the first place. And yet somehow she was speaking his own inner thoughts, the ones he'd never known he was thinking but recognized as she spoke them. He knew then that the frustration and anger he'd felt didn't come from the loss of material things, however important, but from the humiliation of having to go hat-in-hand begging the settlers for what was his by birthright. No, not having to go. Agreeing to go. Not being beaten, being suckered.

The logic of the white man's negotiations gave the settlers presumptive possession of what was by nature and tradition Tommy's and his people's. Obedience to the logic of rigged negotiations, he thought suddenly, with terrible clarity, is the habit that gives the white man his power over us. The counter-logic is to not ask, but to take—take back the people's land! It's ours, not theirs.

He was startled to see how simple it really was—change the logic. Isn't that, he thought, what Martin Luther King did in the States so long ago? King didn't ask for freedom. He didn't negotiate or trade something else of value, for a morsel of freedom. He didn't beg or whine. He demanded what had always been his, what was his inalienable right: unconditional freedom.

Molly sat patiently while Tommy sorted out the thoughts racing around inside his head. After a few minutes he stood up and put out his hand, knowing why she had won him over completely to the Movement. She hadn't convinced him of her ideas. She had shown him his own.

Later that year, Molly introduced Tommy to Colonel Stevenson, a legend he'd known only by reputation during his regular army days. That was the day he became not just a fervent supporter of but an eager soldier in the NPA. And it didn't take Stevenson long to promote this remarkable young man; within months Toques had command of the major north Manitoba columns, code-named Cree, that would move south with the other major column, Pelican. Tommy's duty was to train, prepare, and lead his column south in the attack on the white man's government in Winnipeg.

Now, glancing again at his watch, then pulling out his secure cellphone, willing it to ring, Tommy reminded himself of the strategic importance of his mission, first revealed to him in the spring of 2009 when Stevenson came north with his small staff and armloads of maps, and secretly assembled Twoskins and the other commanders who would lead similar columns from northern Saskatchewan south to Regina, Saskatoon, and Yorkton, and from north-central Alberta into that province's oil fields. On the first day of the meeting, the colonel laid out the general concept of operations.

"The vast area north of Easterville-Grand Rapids in Manitoba, west to Cumberland House in Saskatchewan," he began, pointing to the large map pinned to the wall, "is our secure, safe haven. We're the majority here and we can and will control the entire region easily. We will move from here on to Winnipeg, Brandon, Regina, Yorkton, and Saskatoon in four columns moving down Manitoba highways 6 and 10, and Saskatchewan highways 9 and 6. These roads will be code-named to avoid confusion, since there are two '6's, as well as to baffle eavesdroppers before we get rolling. The operation here in the centre will be supported by other columns originating in Kenora in the east and a separate operation under my command that will undertake special actions against specific targets in Alberta.

"The columns," he explained with the aid of charts and small plastic toys, "will be organized as light units to move quickly down the long, open highways from the north to the south. They will be sufficiently well armed to make fast attacks on any police barricades or strong points they encounter on the road, but not to engage in pitched battles with military formations.

The success of the operations depends on leaders' ability to outpace the enemy's thinking and to get south rapidly before the army or major police units can intercept the columns."

Stevenson drew a quick sketch. "Each column will operate like a long spear with a sharp point probing the way, followed by the main weapons and best fighters as a larger, stronger 'blade' behind the point, and a logistics shaft in the rear." For Toques and the others, all ex-soldiers, it was a basic "advance to contact" tactics refresher course.

"The columns," Stevenson continued, "will move with reconnaissance groups leading, followed at some distance by the main combat body and finally the supporting logistics group. As the country opens up as you move south, you will deploy 'flank guards'—fast outrider units—to protect your columns from surprises. But in the early going, nature will protect you with forests, rivers, and wetlands. And we've organized an important bonus capability for each of you thanks to the wide array of light aircraft, float planes, and so on that our people control in our home region. They'll provide eyes in the sky ahead, behind, and on flanks down the routes south. These aerial scouts will supplement your ground recce troops in daytime and as the weather permits."

Bill Kelly of the Whitefish First Nation in Alberta, one of the Saskatchewan commanders, was eager but sceptical. "Where," he challenged Stevenson, "are we going to find army trucks, heavy weapons, and things like that to beat the Mounties if they try to stop us? Won't they bring out the big guns as soon as they see us move? Besides, I only can count on twenty-five guys right now and that's not going to cut it against anything bigger than some isolated RCMP outpost."

Stevenson put down his pointer. "Good questions. Generally, we're going to depend on you, each of you, to find the equipment for your columns from local resources. Our communities have hundreds of light trucks, SUVs, heavy trucks, and ATVs. They'll provide the wheels, the mobility, for the mission. Your homes are full of hunting rifles and shotguns—all properly registered with the government, I hope."

The meeting cracked up. "Yeah, sure thing, colonel. Want to see my carry permit?" More laughter.

"Good," Stevenson continued. "But I'm going to supply you with some 'special weapons' to give you a decided advantage over the police and even the militia if they show up. We're taking our time, being careful here, but you'll have them in plenty of time to train your best guys to use them the right way. As far as people are concerned, there's over 180,000 natives on reserves across the Prairies and a lot of them are young men. Even if we only recruit five to ten per cent of the total and concentrate them in a coordinated plan, that's more than enough to overwhelm all the police and army in the region. And that's what we're going to do.

"Yeah, I know," he said, forestalling objections, "a lot of them won't know squat about fighting and you can't turn them into an army without someone noticing. That's okay. The point and the blade units in the columns need to really know their business; the rest just have to provide numbers.

"Now, let's talk about the point and the blade. I'm depending on you not just to direct the columns but to find leaders, our junior officers and NCOs, to make them work. You've all been in the army, so you know what to look for. The rank and file will be recruited locally too, but you don't need to rush at that just yet. First, train the trainers and then we'll get the troopers. Remember, the NPA has the resources to back you, and we will."

Stevenson paused and quickly laid out his dollar store toys in a model column on the floor, then pointed to the little trucks at the front. "First, immediately, I want each of you to organize and train two recce groups, the eyes and ears of the column. You'll need about half a dozen light trucks and small SUVs for each group, and twenty people in all. Their primary job is to get out in front, about ten or fifteen kilometres ahead of the main body, to find obstacles and police barricades. If they find any, they're to scout around them looking for soft points and bypasses. Of course, outside of towns there's not much way for the column to bypass anything blocking the road, but remember we're in a hurry, so if the cops are blocking the intersection with flashing lights in some Podunk town, we're just as happy to go down a side street.

"Anyway, the recce groups will send a description of the contact and the bypass if there is one to the column commander, and if the barricades are minor they'll keep right on going south. If the opposing force is large or well dug in, the recce groups are to picket the site and guide the follow-on blade from the main body into the attack, then get back on their way. The blade will slice through the obstacle and the column will move forward again. Speed is of the essence here. But remember, the police are few and far between along these routes..."

"Yeah, colonel, but what about the city cops and the army and the Mounties from the south? They'll come storming up that road and there'll be lots of them once we get south."

"You're right, Stan, that would be a very difficult problem, but it's actually not likely. All I can tell you now is that we have plans, very sophisticated plans, to prevent government units in the south from coming north. I'll describe the plan closer to the event. For now, let's concentrate on getting your columns trained and organized." Such was the reputation of "Sam Steele" that the group nodded, satisfied.

The colonel resumed his presentation. "As I was saying, the recce groups will carry an assortment of equipment besides their weapons—walkie-talkie radios, wireless laptops, and cellphones for communications, for instance. They'll be armed with mostly light weapons—rifles and shotguns and pistols—but each group will have at least one team of grenadiers with RPGs—those are rocket-propelled grenades, in case you've forgotten—a couple of light anti-armour missiles, plus a few medium machine guns mounted in the trucks just in case they need to blast their way through something. Their job is not to fight, but it's also not to get trapped by unexpected trouble.

"I expect you to put three or four warriors in each scout vehicle. And I want you to train three or four of these sections as truck-mounted assault troopers to make rapid attacks on small targets along the road. Finally, each recce group needs two flatbed trucks carrying four ATVs each to give leaders a quick cross-country capability for scouting and bypassing enemy positions. Okay, any more questions so far?"

Stevenson stood back and took a drink of his now-cold coffee while he waited, but no hands went up. "No? Okay, let's go on." He swung his pointer back to the model column on the floor and indicated the larger group of plastic army Jeeps behind the recce trucks.

"The main bodies following behind the recce groups will be larger organizations of about 100 to 200 warriors each. They're to be mounted mainly in light and medium trucks and armed with heavier weapons and heavy machine guns which we'll provide from our sources, mostly in the States and on the reserves in Eastern Canada.

"The main body provides the real punch in the force, the strong 'quick attack capability' to clear any obstacles the recce groups can't brush aside or that we can't bypass. Again, try to push your units around any minor roadblocks and small police detachments if you can, but roll over them if they're blocking a vital point like a bridge or the main highway south. Your headquarters staff should be with the main body, but I want you personally to be well forward with a small tactical HQ near the front of the blade. These guys aren't regular forces—they need to see you in action or they'll freeze.

"Behind the blade, I want warriors mounted in trucks and buses. Get together some engineer teams, guys with construction, logging, or mining experience, with chainsaws, front-end loaders, ropes, chains, and stuff to make hasty repairs to bridges and overcome craters that might be blown in the roads to slow the columns."

"Colonel," Tommy asked, "these engineers, we'll need some explosives, and how about some kind of air defence and anti-armour weapons teams in medium trucks?"

"Yeah, Tom. I'm depending on you to find the explosives. There's lots of it in mining camps, and in a pinch use fertilizer and diesel—we'll give you the formulas later. Think IEDs—improvised explosive devices. Some of you know all about those from bad experiences in Afghanistan and Darfur. On the heavy weapons, I'll have something to say later in the year. But again, I assure you we're taking care of it. We know what we're doing."

"What about logistics, colonel?" Bill Kelly asked.

"Logistical planning for the columns will be pretty basic. Bring three days' rations of food and a day's extra load of fuel and light loads of ammo. Then make do. You're going to scavenge the countryside for additional food and gas. We expect that there will be plenty of gas along the routes as each farm holds large quantities for its machinery. By the way, beer is not a food ration and stop your guys scavenging it. Be tough about it; I mean really tough. This is a military operation, not a Saturday night brawl." Stevenson paused to let them all imagine the squalid dissolution of their column in alcohol. Then he lightened up. "The good news, of course, is that the columns are going to be moving towards the supplies they need all spread out before them in the richer, more populous southern towns.

"The Manitoba and Saskatchewan plans are simple—drive south, bypass contacts, isolate or capture RCMP detachments along the way, and seize key terrain to surround the major cities. Getting there is the main challenge. We'll organize a recce of each route for you later in the spring."

The room was hushed. Mary Otter raised a hand. "Sir, what do we do with the wounded and other prisoners besides the Mounties?"

"Good points. We'll have some paramedics joining us, in the lead elements and the support units. We'll have also a couple of native doctors who have agreed to join the columns, but we're depending on the local hospitals and doctors along the routes. They're not on our side, but they're doctors—they're not on anyone's side, they always say. So I expect they'll treat anyone who's hurt. Hey, folks, it's going to be just like real native life: all the essential services get better as we get farther south." The remark broke some of the tension and prompted a few rude jibes.

Stevenson took control again. "Listen up. As for prisoners, we'll keep the Mounties in the jails. If we need to hold someone else, it will be because they committed a crime, or hurt someone, or won't go away when ordered to. We'll hold them and when you get a chance, put them in with the Mounties. Later, we'll put them before native courts and we'll round up white village leaders and use them to carry out the new provincial assistance policies." More laughter. "I hope we won't have any of our own people become discipline problems, but if they do, make an example of them." That remark didn't provoke laughter.

"Any more questions? Okay, let's get down to details and make some map appreciations and so on. Over the next couple of days, my people who came here with me will help me put you through some tactical exercises on paper and help you sort through some of your own training problems."

Monday, September 6, 1435 hours
Outside Flin Flon

Tommy understood Stevenson's orders—drive south fast, surround Winnipeg from the north and west, then be prepared to enter the city—and he knew why they mattered. But he had a personal objective Sam didn't know about. Tommy looked at the map and stabbed his finger at the spot marking Stony Mountain Institution, the fortress-like federal penitentiary sitting on a high hill overlooking the plains twenty-five kilometres north of Winnipeg. When Stevenson assigned it to him as a primary target, Toques' heart had jumped up into his throat.

Stony Mountain, the prairie prison, had become an important symbol of white justice's prejudice and repression against the aboriginal community. Stevenson didn't care about that at the moment; he wasn't interested in using his scarce resources to attack symbols. Rather, he worried that Stony Mountain could become a rallying point for federal troops, so he wanted it surrounded and all the routes leading to it blockaded, at least initially. Tommy went after the target with great enthusiasm, pushing his planners relentlessly, probing and questioning every assumption and idea about the prison. "Who do we know on the inside? Which guards are native and can be trusted? Who can be intimidated? Who's locked up for petty crimes against whites? Who's crazy, dangerous? What's the structure of the jail?" On and on, day after day, he honed the plan for his assault on Stony Mountain.

A lot of it was surprisingly easy. His planners scanned the web and easily found essential, unguarded details of the institution's layout, rules, and procedures. They carefully contacted native gang leaders inside. The prison guard union helpfully, if unwittingly, provided information on the guards' routine and patrol numbers for each shift. Eventually, Tommy's plan took shape: his column would lay siege to the fortress from outside, but he would essentially take control from within. The arrival of the column would be the signal for the prison population to take control and open the gates. Tommy thought it a fitting irony that incarcerating too many aboriginals would prove Stony Mountain's downfall.

Colonel Stevenson reviewed the plan as it came together during one of his flying visits to Tommy's headquarters and expressed pleasure at the diligence the young commander had exhibited on this part of the operation. But it worried him a little too.

"You're really focused on the Stony Mountain, and I'm not sure why," Stevenson had remarked. "It's a sideshow, Tom. I want you to keep your eye on the mission outside Winnipeg; the prison can wait until we are secure on the ground north of the city."

"Yes, sir," Toques had replied. "It's a sideshow... provided we don't let the other side turn it into a major problem for us. I don't intend to let that happen." It was a good answer. But it was a lie.

What the colonel didn't know was that Toques had a very personal grudge against Stony Mountain. Of course Stevenson knew all about how Canada's notorious justice system treated natives. Prejudice had produced a system of "quick justice," hasty convictions, and long-term incarceration. As Canadian government reports highlighted again and again, the worst examples of "disproportionate severe punishment" in Canada shone brightest on the Prairies.

Tommy Twoskins also knew the statistics well: aboriginal people represent 2.8 per cent of the Canadian population, but account for eighteen per cent of the federally incarcerated population. On the Prairies, aboriginals account for thirty-six per cent of federal prisoners and the numbers in the provincial system are far worse—in Manitoba jails, sixty per cent of the prisoners are native and in Saskatchewan an astonishing seventy-six per cent. But one of that number mattered more to him than all the others—too much in fact. Brian Twoskins, trapped in the statistics and hidden away in Stony Mountain.

Brian had been the pride of his large family, even more than Tommy. Bright, polite, and quick to learn, he left the reserve at eighteen for university in Winnipeg. One early fall evening in his first year, he had wandered into north Main looking for a few lost friends and found some of them sitting on the sidewalk outside a rundown house drinking beer. Brian joined them, cracking a beer and taking his turn loudly recalling stories from home and school.

It was all fun and games until a couple of patrolling constables approached the group, ordering them to ditch the open beer and move on. Kids plus beer led to smart remarks, a few obscenities, then a not too gentle boot from a cop, and then a scuffle. Brian, sober and worried, jumped in to break up the trouble he saw coming, but inadvertently pushed a cop who stumbled and dropped his nightstick. Backup for Brian and his buddies arrived quickly, resulting in more natives yelling at and shoving the outnumbered, frightened constables, and then three squad cars full of angry cops arrived. Brian, caught up in the melee, pushed his way to the edge, trying to find his bearings; a policeman fell past him to the pavement, bleeding from the head. Immediately, the cop's partner grabbed Brian and hurled him against a cruiser, where two other cops pounded him with their batons then threw him roughly into the back seat. Charges: assault with a weapon; assaulting a police officer; resisting arrest; carrying a concealed weapon (a beer bottle); drunk and disorderly. Defence: an overworked government lawyer. Trial: as one of a group. Sentence: three years in Stony Mountain federal penitentiary.

Stony Mountain was infamous for good reasons, Tommy knew. The 130-year-old medium-security institution, built to hold 500 prisoners, was overflowing with 600 offenders, nearly half of them native. When Brian arrived, 163 gang members were incarcerated either at Stony Mountain or the smaller, minimum-security Rockwood Institution on the same grounds. And almost all new native inmates were immediately recruited into one of the two Stony Mountain "branch offices" of the dominant Winnipeg aboriginal gangs, the Manitoba Warriors and the Indian Posse. As Brian told Tommy, the occasional recalcitrant native prisoner was "beaten in," smashed about until he saw the value of membership. Once in the gang, inmates entered a graduate program in gang culture and methods, and Tommy knew that once they were released, most graduated to full-time gang-related employment on the outside. The conditions were bleak for anyone, but for Brian, who was young, small, slender, and attractive, it was a nightmare from day one.

Tommy Twoskins knew all about what was happening to his kid brother, and it tormented him. So it was no wonder he eagerly accepted

Sam Stevenson's direction to take Stony Mountain. He'd been getting close to doing something desperate anyway. In the last year, he'd visited his brother almost every week, encouraging him, talking about his attempts to get a legal review. Eventually, though, Tommy saw the subject depressed Brian, then, worse, bored him. Week after week, Tommy's concern grew as Brian seemed to grow more comfortable, almost at home in prison. At first he'd complained about the gangs and "Big Fred," the leader of the gang that conscripted him, but now he avoided the topic, putting off Tommy's questions and cautions with "you don't understand." Last August, Brian hadn't appeared when his brother came to visit him. At that point, Tommy had started sketching plans for a desperate rescue attempt. And a month later, Stevenson gave him an amazing, unexpected opportunity with his assignment to command Column Cree.

His phone jolted him back to the present. "Tommy, Colonel Sam here. The situation is developing here more or less as we expected. Your H-hour to move is zero six hundred tomorrow, that's Tuesday, September 7. Can you make it?"

"Yes, sir. Zero six hundred tomorrow it is. Anything else?"

"No. I know you can do this. You're in command, so command. Got it?"

"Got it and thanks. See you in Winnipeg."

"Roger that. Keep me posted with thirty minute sitreps."

The line went dead. Tommy dropped his phone into his pocket and turned to his chief of staff.

"Gerry, pass the word to commanders and get a personal acknowledgement. H-hour 0600 tomorrow morning. Orders group here at 1500 today. They're to place their units on thirty minutes notice to move as of midnight tonight and begin assembling all their personnel at their base camps now."

Molly and Bill stood near the back of the closed-in and now fully functioning Peguis operations room near Clandeboye. The data and reports transmitted in code from Akwesasne indicated continuing disruptions and chaos in Montreal, Quebec City, along the border areas, and along the St. Lawrence River valley generally.

"So," Molly demanded from the duty officer working at the operations desk, "what's going on in Quebec right now?"

"Well, a weak SQ attempt to make a police raid on the Compound at Akwesasne failed early this morning, thanks to an alert from our mole in the police HQ. There were casualties on both sides. Alain Selkirk seems to have handled that well, and he is doing a great job, in my view, with the defence of First Nation's communities. According to reports, he's organized the moving of small bands of warriors under cover from area to area whenever he sees a police build-up suggesting an attack. His resources, however, are running low and his control of the situation slips away more every day.

"The bomb squads you organized last year with the American advisors are also working well. Our teams detonated several IEDs near critical facilities and that's proving of immense value to the Quebec-based warriors. Even the small weapons the warriors have are panicking the local population and, more important, the politicians. They've ordered police and the army to rush out to guard the damaged sites. Little by little, federal and provincial resources are being wasted in attempts to protect everything—as they say, it's 'all flanks and no front.'

"I'm amazed, really; we've created an enormous amount of chaos. And, it's achieving what you asked for, Molly; it's drawing in and holding large numbers of police and army units in Quebec, not to mention causing lots of confusion for the prime minister and his crowd. They're not going to be able to bother our operation here any time soon.

"At James Bay, the standoff continues. Boucanier is holding his own and the army paras don't seem ready to try and force him out of the town. He told us last night that he sent a warning to the army commander saying he would harm the Hydro workers if the army attacked him and then there would be no one to run the operation. Pretty good-sounding idea, but not really necessary. As we know from our other sources there, the workers, even the non-native ones, aren't likely to go back inside the facilities until all of the buildings have been combed clean for bombs and so on."

"Okay, thanks, Bob. Keep me posted if anything changes greatly."

"Sure thing. We'll have another report ready near noon. One thing though, Molly. Seems we're getting interference on our signals and data links from Quebec. Kinda subtle, hard to say what's causing the noise. I checked with our electronic jammer boss, and he's checking the system. He said nobody in Canada has the equipment to get into our system. The Americans do, but they're not here. We'll sort it out and let you know."

Molly walked with Bill to the door and out across the shadow-filled yard. He was anxious and bothered. "Look Molly, we've talked about this before, but I'm uncomfortable with leaving the people in Quebec to their own devices. Even if you don't care much for the people there, it's a threat to this operation—if the feds break into the Compound, they will have the whole plan."

"Not really, Bill. The demolition devices we planted under the buildings and in the area will take care of that problem. Selkirk knows what to do."

"Yes, but we could harm a lot of our own people too."

Molly pointed to a circling flock of white pelicans high overhead. "Beautiful aren't they, Bill? Just sailing and circling in the sky, hardly moving a feather. I remember them from my grandfather's home, long ago, when I was a child and everything seemed calm and orderly." She walked on.

"Sure people are going to be hurt, Bill. That's what happens when you tackle the government. You can't be a leader or accomplish anything worthwhile in this business if you're not willing to spend a few lives to make progress. You signed on to that idea a long time ago, Bill."

"I signed on to make the people's lives better. Sure, I knew it would be costly, but we're getting to a point in Quebec were the costs are not rational, not fixed on achieving anything. Things there are spinning out of control. I just thought you might want to give Selkirk the option to organize a type of ceasefire."

"A ceasefire? And let the government turn its troops around and come and get us...just as we're making the essential moves here? Think again, Bill. At the first sign of any movement from east to west, I'll send Selkirk the word to launch random bomb attacks all over the province."

"What about Will Boucanier? He on his own too?"

"Boucanier, Bill, has always been on his own. I suspected something long ago. I never told you, but one of our secret intercept systems has picked up odd message traffic from the Radisson area...from way off in the North. My man with Boucanier, Joe Neetha, has two jobs. He works for Boucanier on the outside and for me on the inside.

"Oh don't look shocked, Bill. You always hedge your bets in this business. Neetha has told me that he thinks Will is working with a group of Cree and Inuit who have their own plans for the North. I mentioned this before, you know that. So don't shed any tears for Will Boucanier, Bill. I won't.

"Come on. Let's walk a bit more, watch nature. Act like regular people, Bill."

Monday, September 6, 0930 hours
Washington: The White House

The National Security Council, the President's principal forum for considering national security and foreign policy matters, was assembled in the White House Situation Room at the direction of President Ricardo immediately after her secure teleconference with the U.S. Ambassador to Canada, James Laforge, and her National Security Advisor, Murray Segal. The usual attendees, the vice president, the secretary of state, the secretary of the treasury, the secretary of defense, the newly appointed secretary for homeland security, Jim Fields, the chairman of the Joint Chiefs of Staff and his colleagues, and the director of National Intelligence, were settling into the small conference room as the president and Murray Segal walked in.

President Carla Ricardo, a fifth-generation California Latino, was in her second year in office and had a well-deserved reputation as a "tough cookie." She had fought her way to the president's office as she was fond of saying, "by conquering on each rung of the political ladder the double prejudices of being a women and a Latino." That battle had sharpened her political and debating skills—her detractors called her a "combative, sharp-tongued harpy." But many opponents had learned the hard way the result of underestimating her, and even her worst critics had to admit that she'd proved herself as a leader. She seemed, to those old enough to remember, an American Margaret Thatcher: in-charge, well briefed, and unhesitatingly confident. No one ever crossed her a second time. Though she carried the scars inflicted on her ancestors by America's racial history,

Carla Ricardo was an unfailing "America-firster," as anyone she believed was acting to harm the nation's vital interests through reckless actions soon discovered.

"We are here," the president began immediately, "to discuss the surprising situation developing in Canada over the last few days. I don't need to tell you that the United States has several important pokers in the Canadian fireplace and we cannot allow insecurity there to disrupt or interfere with our national security, economic security, or the safety and well-being of Americans. I asked the director of National Intelligence and chairman of the Joint Chiefs of Staff earlier today to prepare a short briefing on the situation in Canada from their perspectives, and after they make these remarks I will provide you with some directions based on my conversations with Ambassador Laforge earlier this morning. Murray, would you begin, please."

"Madam President, ladies and gentlemen, the National Intelligence staff has been routinely following various situations in Canada—mostly in cooperation with our Canadian colleagues—dealing with external terrorist threats, foreign espionage cases, illegal drug traffic, and illegal money transfers, transnational criminal organizations, and so on. We, and the Canadians, have also been watching the activities of aboriginal gangs, increasingly so over the last couple of years, but almost always in the context of these illegal drug and other smuggling matters. Beginning about three years ago, we learned of and informed the Canadian authorities about certain aboriginal radicals who had visited the United States and met with American aboriginal leaders and discussed various types of cooperation.

"These incidental events prompted a wider interest in the intelligence community from an internal American perspective and a Can-U.S. perspective. I won't go into the details, except to say most of these activities were low-level, not related to the legitimate leadership of native communities on either side of the border, and dealt with ways these various loose, radical factions could help each other's causes.

"That scenario changed recently, in the past year, when we began to see significant increases in the flow of illegal weapons from the United States to Canada and a significant increase also in the illegal transfer of money from third-party nations through the United States and into Canada. All these transfers were confirmed by us and the Canadians as going to clandestine aboriginal organizations in Canada. Unfortunately, we assessed that the transfers were made in the context of ordinary criminal activities—drug running especially—and we therefore assumed also that the threat they might pose to the United States was low-level and concerned matters best dealt with by the FBI and state authorities. What was not well followed up was the fact that once these weapons and money crossed the border, they simply disappeared—in other words, there was no clear connection between the weapons and the money and run-of-the-mill criminal activities."

A series of charts and maps opened on the screens lining the sides of the Situation Room and Segal swung his chair to point to them.

"As the events of the past few days clearly indicate, these resources are in the hands of well-organized ... and not well known to us ... armed radical native bands in Canada, at least in Eastern Canada so far. The attacks of the native bands on Montreal and lower Quebec, as the electronic map on this wall indicates, seem pointless. The natives do not have the numbers to immobilize southern Quebec for very long. But I must warn the Council that neither our intelligence agencies nor the Canadian agencies fully understand the situation we are facing and where it will lead. We are, of course, watching the situation carefully, and we have manoeuvered a number of satellites into position to help us collect data on an hourly basis. We have also launched Predator UAVs to maintain a 24/7 surveillance patrol on both sides of the border region, facts, I say in confidence, of which the Canadians are not aware.

"The attack on the northern Quebec hydro facilities, as everyone here is personally and painfully aware, I assume, is having a very serious impact on the economy and welfare of business and Americans all along the eastern seaboard and well inland as well. Major transportation systems in Washington, Baltimore, New York, and so on are in chaos. Air traffic is disrupted across the country. The weather is predicted to worsen this week, with a cold front moving over the region, and that event will increase hardships everywhere. We are trying to patch the East Coast electric system into other domestic systems, but that effort is not going well.

"Finally, there are indications that the Canadian native rebellion is spreading west, and if that happens, we can expect some interference with our commerce, transportation, and, maybe, our energy supplies from Canada."

Segal nodded to the president who turned to General Leonardo. "What do we know from your side, general? And what preparatory measures do you recommend at this time?"

"The Defence Intelligence Agency is, of course, working closely with the CIA, the FBI, and with Murray's people. I concur with his assessment and admit too that this situation has caught the Joint Chiefs by surprise, not that we ever pay much attention to the military security of our northern borders, except in the Arctic, where we know the Russians and others are sometimes active.

"I spoke briefly with my Canadian counterpart, General Bishop, and he is very worried about the situation and the hesitancy of his prime minister to act forcefully. But Madam President, Canada simply doesn't have appropriate or capable forces to deal with even a small internal security problem and this problem isn't small.

"We have, obviously, military attachés in Ottawa and other ... ah, sources of information, in the country, so we will of course continue to collect as much information on the situation as possible. But, in the short term at least, I advise that we avoid any overt activities for the time being and watch how things develop and how the Canadians handle matters. If they were to come to us for military assistance, use of satellites, and so on, then I would recommend we provide them as the circumstances dictate. I recommend, however, that the Joint Chiefs develop some options for your consideration in case the Canadians prove unable to redress the situations that concern our national security—in the James Bay hydro region for example.

"I have placed appropriate military units near the border region on increased alert, restricted our operations in Canadian air and sea spaces, and asked the Joint Chiefs' operational staffs to build for us a computer-generated scenario from information as it is assembled. There is, Madam President, no military threat to the United States arising from this situation at the moment."

"Thank you both. I have asked the secretary of energy this morning to gather separately from this meeting all and everyone from government agencies and the private sector to a confidential meeting to discuss our energy situation. From that meeting, she is to provide me with a clear, current assessment of our energy vulnerabilities that might arise from a widespread and prolonged internal conflict in Canada. It's no secret that we are dependent in a major way on Canadian energy sources—oil, natural gas, and electricity—and that our economies are inseparably linked also.

"At this time, I will say only that we cannot and I will not allow internal disruptions in Canada to endanger our economy or our national interests. I hope that the Canadian government will find a peaceful way out of the mess, one, in my opinion, they created for themselves. We will offer as much aid to them as is reasonable in the circumstances. Nevertheless, I told Ambassador Laforge that his main responsibilities now are to assess and gauge the stability of the Canadian government and to keep me informed about his assessment of Canada's likelihood of regaining control of the situation and when that might occur.

"These, too, are the responsibilities I have asked Murray to manage for me as an urgent task. What is the situation in Canada? How vulnerable are our energy sources of all kinds? What contingencies ought we prepare for and what national responses should we consider in each case? I ask you all for your full cooperation in these assessments.

"General Leonardo, I would like the Joint Chiefs to consider the necessity of securing our vital energy resources. Let me be clear here: I am not interested in securing Canada for Canadians. I believe they can do that themselves. However, I will not stand idle if things get out of hand and pose a threat to the United States. Obviously, I hope these assessments will remain highly confidential in this leaky city. In any case, the press line is that we are watching the situation closely and encouraging the Canadian government to restore order and so on. There will be no hint of any American action and I don't intend to launch any—yet. I hope and pray that good sense will prevail.

"Murray Segal will tie up the details with you and we will meet again later today or as the situation necessitates. One last thing, Murray, would you have someone, Library of Congress, I suppose, prepare for me a brief history of the aboriginal situation in Canada. You know, the history, their demands, government policies, the current players, and so on.

"Thank you everyone."

Monday, September 6, 1600 hours
Southwest of The Pas

Tommy Twoskins' O Group—the orders meeting with the column commanders, their senior subordinates, the special-hit detachments, the logistical commanders, the air detachment CO and his main staff officers—sat
waiting in a large barn near Young Point, out of sight of the curious just
outside The Pas. The key staff, full-blood Cree and Ojibwa, along with a
few Métis, mostly in their twenties, sat on rough folding benches arranged
in a semicircle before the map board, with maps and field message books
on their laps. No one spoke as they shuffled along the benches, making
room for latecomers. One or two tardy warriors stood at the main wall
map, hurriedly tracing control lines and nicknames of villages, roads, and
places onto their personal maps. Jimmy Payuk, the force communications
officer, handed out sheets of paper bearing the operational radio frequencies, cellphone numbers, and passwords they would use to control the
move south.

When the room looked more or less settled, Tommy stepped in front of
the large wall map, pointer in hand, without notes. "Ladies and gentlemen,
tomorrow we move out to free the land."

The young leaders shifted about on the benches, trading glances and
nervous smiles. Finally! They knew from TV reports all about what was
happening at James Bay and in Winnipeg. Some of them were getting worried they might miss the war, or lose control of their warriors, who knew
almost nothing of the plan, other than that they were going south someday, "to make demonstrations on the legislative grounds." In the circumstances, it was obviously a slim cover story, but it was allowed to circulate
to explain the increasingly frenetic and detailed preparations over the last
three weeks. Nevertheless, it was becoming increasingly difficult to hold
the warriors in town and keep their attention now that the geese were
moving and the scent of the fall hunt was in the air—until news of the
trouble in Quebec filled the airwaves and told them this year the game was
different and more dangerous than usual. And now it was difficult to keep

them from heading south on their own. No wonder the room was buzzing with the news that the wait was over.

Tommy rapped the side of his table hard three times to get their attention. "Your attention please," he said. "You all have your orders and I've gone over them with you individually several times. You know what I expect of you and I know you can do it. But we're gonna review the general situation as of today and then go over the outline of the operation one more time.

"First, the friendly forces. We know that Colonel Stevenson's assault teams more or less control downtown Winnipeg and have captured most of the airport. They have firm control of city hall, the area around Portage and Main, the Hudson's Bay store intersection, the approaches to the city centre from north Main Street, south from Pembina, west down Portage, and along roads and streets leading to the Forks. The situation is less clear around the legislature. Some buildings are burning, and the Mounties seem to have some of our people surrounded. I think some of the warriors from the city centre are moving to help our comrades, but remember, our victory doesn't depend on taking over Winnipeg. The aim of our comrades there is to create confusion and trouble and draw as many police and army units as possible into the centre of the city so they can't interfere with us. And I can report that our brothers and sisters from other First Nations have blockaded the city from the south, west, and east. We'll complete the ring and join up with them as soon as we can."

Toques looked around the room. Most of his warriors had been head-down, busy scribbling notes to pass to their teams or looking intently at their maps, but the news that Winnipeg was partly blockaded already brought all eyes up. He paused briefly, then resumed his briefing, following the military format he had learned at the army staff college in Kingston.

"Next, the enemy forces. The James Bay operation is going as planned and significant army units are tied down there. You will be glad to know the elite Special Service Regiment is trapped on the ground there, even if they don't know it yet." A nervous chuckle ran through the room.

"Other major Canadian Forces units are moving to their rescue and are of no concern to us. Quite the reverse: as we planned, the military has committed almost all its units and transport aircraft to Quebec and they can't get back here anytime soon. In Winnipeg, as I said, the RCMP SWAT teams are fully engaged in the city. The city police are hanging around the action, but, according to our brothers on the force, they don't want any part in the fight. The militia has been called out, but they're no problem for now. The main worry is the remainders of the regular units on CFB Winnipeg and from Shilo, but again most have gone to Quebec and those remaining are non-combat personnel.

"Now pay attention! Just because most things are going our way at the moment doesn't mean we're going to walk through this unopposed. The Canadian Forces are pros. They're experienced and proud. They're not going to let us run away with this thing. They may be off-balance right now, but they'll be back and they'll be pissed off. So stay alert and keep your wits about you if you want to keep your heads.

"Along the road south," Toques continued, returning to a low-key, O Group cadence, "we can expect to meet RCMP detachments, some concentrated at important road sites. They still have access to air patrols, unarmed of course, but the air force might put lots of fighters in the area … which they may use. I doubt it, but they might, so keep your air sentries alert. You can also expect some of the local rednecks to take potshots at the columns, but unless they're really effective, just give 'em a few return shots then bypass 'em. You can let the column commanders know the location so we can deal with them later. We're not getting into a firefight with a bunch of duck hunters, not because we wouldn't win, but because our strategic task is to move south smartly and in good order.

"So that's the situation. Now, one more time, the outline of the operation. Remember this when you have tactical decisions to make. Our strategic aim is to take effective possession of Manitoba down to and including all areas north of the Perimeter Highway outside Winnipeg. This is a two-phase operation. In phase one, we advance in three columns to surround and isolate Winnipeg. In phase two, we join the main forces already in the south and move on the city to relieve the warriors there and hold the city during negotiations for a ceasefire. The orders I've covered today are for phase one only. We'll have time to assess the phase two situation once we're down south, and I'll hold another O Group at that time.

"But here's the big picture. We will, as a consequence of this operation, surround Winnipeg to prevent any reinforcement of the local armed forces and police. And the combined effect of the Winnipeg operation and ours will lead to the surrender of southern Manitoba to the Native People's Army."

Tommy stopped talking and let it sink in. Once all eyes were on him, he gave them the word loud and clear. "This is the real thing people, H-hour, zero six hundred hours tomorrow morning."

The room burst into gasps and cheers.

"All right. Some of you have a long way to go to rejoin your units, so look over your notes, check details with the staff, make sure if you have any questions you ask them now, then go brief your people. See you all down south."

The O Group immediately broke up into small meetings—column commanders checking and cross-checking routes and phase lines, radio details and code; logisticians explaining specific supply arrangements and refuelling points. Half an hour later, with high-fives and handshakes, back-patting bravado and good-byes, the commanders and staff moved to their trucks and sped off to their rendezvous with history.

Tommy stood by the door as they went, observing their demeanour, giving encouraging goodbyes to his young leaders as they hurried off. He was confident that he'd done what he could, but he knew this operation would really depend on how his leaders reacted to sudden, unexpected situations on the road. The plan, as he knew from Afghanistan, wouldn't last far beyond the first contact with the enemy. The more important question was whether his inexperienced troops would.

Monday, September 6, 1640 hours
Ottawa: NDOC

Ed Conway, his necktie slack and shirtsleeves rolled up over his wrists, strolled into the Ops Centre with a collection of papers in his hand. Dobson looked up from his desk. "You look like hell. Bloody awful hours we're spending here, old friend. Remember the fun days of the Cold War: all we had to worry about was the U.S. and the Soviets trying to blow up the world."

"Yeah, and I remember at the end of the Cold War, when was it, 1990 or something? The media talking heads were all going on about now there would be nothing for the armed forces to do, and for guys like me just starting out in the intelligence game, nothing to look for. Well, welcome to the new world order—I have some of it here in my hand."

"What's up, Ed?"

Well, it seems Molly Grace and her main guys are on the move. SIGINT has been listening to her HQ at Akwesasne all the time, and all of a sudden on Sunday night the intercepts from there began to change. Same kind of message traffic, about the same volume, but the voices and language style in e-mails and the timings started to change.

"I took the liberty to call my contacts in Washington—the Defence Intelligence Agency and the FBI and some people in Homeland Security. They deny it, of course, but they know that we know they've been listening to native radicals here and in the States for a long time. So, I asked them what they're hearing from Akwesasne."

"And?"

"Same thing. Something's changing. Changed patterns like I noticed. All they would admit to is that they think the headquarters there is moving—actually, they think that it moved sometime on late Sunday or early Monday. FBI says they missed the physical move, but think it was assisted by radicals natives from outside the New York area.

"Good news is that we have both begun to pick up some traffic from Manitoba, but it's scattered, lots of background noise—can't tell if it's the local bands on the air or if it's something new. Our guys and communications security here in Ottawa will keep an eye on it.

"Okay, thanks, Ed. I'll put you on the agenda for the next special briefing."

Monday, September 6, 2035 hours
Flin Flon: RCMP Detachment Office

Staff Sergeant Jessie Edwards closed the station door behind him and walked past the patrol desk into his backroom office. He was very worried. Things in the street just weren't right. It might not stand up in court, but this wasn't some vague intuition. The mood out there was wrong, strange, and bad. None of the usual banter from the natives, not the "Hi Jessie, how's it going?" from the nice ones, or rude remarks from kids trying to impress their friends by "dissing the Mounties." Instead, everywhere a strange, dumb wariness, exactly the look he'd seen countless times from a suspect afraid to say anything because he was obviously busted.

"Peter," he called out to the desk officer, "why are you still here? Where's Frances?" Frances Siggins was one of his auxiliary constables, a native trained as a police officer and employed mostly around native communities. First the mood on the street, now the auxiliary hadn't shown up. What the hell was going on? "I thought Francis was on tonight so you could take your kid to the hockey game," he added.

Constable Peter Ainsworth, an older guy, but a rookie right out of the Regina training program who had only been with the detachment since April and was still finding his way around the town and the people, leaned in through the doorway. "She suddenly booked off. Said she was sick. I got Martha to take Connor to the game. I'll hang on till the next shift. Besides, there's something going on—lots of native traffic moving about."

"Anything else?"

"Yes, sir, there is. Rachael just called in from her patrol and said there are odd convoys of cars and trucks driving about. Seems there was some kind of warriors' meeting on an old native farmstead down near Young Point. She said she tried to drive in, but the natives wouldn't let her; they blocked the lane. While she was trying to chat with them, she noticed several rifles and guns in the truck. The guys said they were going hunting in the morning but she didn't like it, thought they were lying. She's still in the area and wants to know what you want her to do about it."

"Peter, you call her right away and tell her to get back here. Right away. Lights and siren, if necessary. Don't panic her, just tell her to come in now. I want to concentrate the detachment here. When you've got her, call our other patrols … and get the off-duty guys in, too. We were warned by HQ to look out for trouble after this Winnipeg thing started, and I think it's found us. I'm going to call around and see if there's trouble in the other detachments in the south. Oh, and Peter, double-check the door locks and open the weapons lockup. You can kick Sam out of the cells; we don't need a drunk in here tonight."

"I'm on it, boss."

Ainsworth scurried off to his desk as Edwards spun to face the computer and opened a blank secure e-mail. He hesitated for a minute, thinking. What other explanations could there be? Nothing fit. It's not a bar night. There hasn't been trouble somewhere, no stabbing, shooting, domestic murder, getting people on edge. In fact, there were no disturbances on the street, no house calls—that's unusual in itself. There's the rendezvous, but that meant natives should be heading into town, not out. Hunting, that's bullshit.

He started tapping at the computer.

To: Ops - HQ, North Service Area
From: Det. The Pas
Subject: Unusual Activity Report

In and around The Pas we note sudden and considerable native vehicle traffic and concentrations of natives moving south of the town and concentrations of known warriors near vital points in town and the surrounding area. Suspected radicals of NPA we have been watching have, according to sources, gone underground. I think more likely they are in distant band locations. My auxiliaries are mostly available, but two have not reported in today and cannot be located. We have at the same time an unusual concentration of native people from several bands who are in town, supposedly to attend the government-sponsored rendezvous but as discussed in RCMP intreps this week, that explanation might be a cover for other activities.

Would appreciate any info on like activities elsewhere. As a pre-

*caution, I am calling the detachment to duty and restricting all patrols
to immediate area.*

Edwards sends.

He clicked the send icon then began tallying the assets he had at hand. Ten rifles, three riot guns, assorted ammunition; the weapons in the cars and the constables' side-arms; not much food; adequate water for now; a generator for power, at least until the gas runs out; radios, cellphones, two computers, the TV networks until the antenna goes down. It wasn't much but, Jessie Edwards didn't feel that he could call on the white population for support—it might trigger a riot or worse.

Ainsworth knocked on the open door, walked into the office, and spoke over Edwards' shoulder. "Rachael is on the way in, and by the way, she reported a steady line of cars and trucks moving all over the highways, including several loaded with equipment and ATVs, with natives driving. The whole detachment is on the way in. Oh, and Sam thinks God freed him from jail ... I confirmed the fact for him. Anything else I can do?"

"Not right now, Peter. Stick to the phone and the e-mail ... I'm looking for a response from the other detachments and from Winnipeg. Just trying to add up our supplies and so on. Not much really if things get bad."

"Well, maybe our reputation will save us from the radicals. Sounds corny, I know, but you've had years of good relations with the native community, so they tell me, and besides, most of the people are peaceful."

"Sure, I know that. But it's not 'most of the people' I'm worried about. It's the others, who aren't peaceful. Something's up and it's got the regular folks spooked. So I'm going to prepare us for whatever the kooks might do. If the peaceful majority wants to help us, fine. But don't count on it. Folks try to get along, Peter, but there's a lot of bad history in these parts, a lot of mistrust. Things could get mighty lonely for us here."

DAY TEN

Tuesday, September 7

Tuesday, September 7, 0626
Ami Bay, Manitoba, on Highway 60

Tommy Twoskins pulled up behind the convoy's leading element, stepped from his Jeep, and walked towards the barrier across the road. He found the column commander in an animated conversation with Chief Eleanor Ami. "What's going on here?" he barked. "What's the delay?"

Muriel Breton shrugged her shoulders. "The chief wants to join the column and go to Winnipeg and present a petition to the government to settle her band's land claim. And I'm not too sure she'll let us pass until we agree to take her along."

Tommy resisted an urge simply to ignore the old woman and tried a little "peacekeeping technique" first. "Okay, Chief Ami, give me your papers and petition and I'll deliver them myself to the government people, whoever they turn out to be."

"No!" the chief said, her voice flat, her face impassive. "I must go or the people here will say we'll be tricked again."

Tommy glanced east at the brightening sky, anxious to get moving before the army or the police could organize a counterattack. "Okay, Muriel. Load the chief in a truck. Take her along. Watch out she doesn't take command. Now get this convoy moving." The old chief, delighted, scrambled into the cab of the nearest truck, waving her people off the road. Column Cree roared to life and leapt forward.

Tommy was determined to make St. Martin Junction on Highway 6 by midday and to clear the way to Ashern before evening. If everything went well, they would be on the stop-line at Stony Mountain by early Wednesday morning at the latest. By that time too, Column Pelican on the other side of Lake Manitoba would be on the doorsteps of the good settlers of Brandon. Once on line, Column Cree would secure the prison, then concentrate near Warren and send patrols east to Highway 9 to make contact with patrols at Fort Garry moving from Kenora. Tommy would send other patrols west a few kilometres north of the Perimeter Highway to meet the Pelican patrols coming east around the south end of Lake Manitoba to Poplar Point.

The Pelican patrols at the same time would slide southwards to contact the native barricade already in position on the Trans-Canada Highway at Elie. By noon on Wednesday, September 8, Winnipeg would be surrounded and effectively cut off from the outside world.

Tommy checked his maps and his timings yet again, and called the Pelican Column commander to confirm the outline and his progress down Highway 10. Everything confirmed, everything fit. Ashern, Warren, and then move east and west and close the circle around Winnipeg. That was Stevenson's plan.

But Stony Mountain was Tommy's target; he had his own plan and his brother was the prize. Tomorrow everything for his family and his people would be different.

Tuesday, September 7, 0717 hours
Ottawa: NDOC

Inspector Steve Mackintosh, seconded to the NDOC from RCMP headquarters in Ottawa, hung up his phone and watched an e-mail flash onto the
screen in front of him. He printed it immediately and took it to Ian Dobson. "More trouble, Ian. Looks pretty ominous, although the details are
sketchy." He offered the message to Dobson but the colonel raised a hand.

"Go ahead, Steve, you read it, I'll listen while I check these sitreps from
James Bay."

"Well, let me give you the highlights first." He scanned down the printed
e-mail, skipping the preamble and stopping at the main section.

"Right. Quote: 'In Manitoba—significant and sudden unrest in the
streets of Flin Flon, Cranberry Portage, and The Pas. Large, well-organized
groups of armed natives in vehicles have taken control of these centres.
Our Flin Flon and The Pas detachments are under siege and we have lost
contact with the Cranberry detachment. Several police patrols on the
highways between Flin Flon, The Pas, and as far south as the junction
of highways 10 and 77 have failed to report in or are reporting that they
are under some kind of assault by organized native gangs. The intersection of highways 60 and 6 is blocked by a large group of natives with long
guns. One report identifies this group as mainly from the several local
First Nations.' Unquote. There's more."

Dobson swivelled his chair to face Mackintosh. "Christ! More? Okay,
go on."

"Quote: 'We have indications that several large convoys of natives,
all armed, are at this moment moving southwards on highways 10 and
60. The convoys are overrunning the few small roadblocks local RCMP
detachments tried to erect and that might account for the loss of contact
in the area. Reports from some native elders and others indicate that a
very large-scale force organized by the NPA is intent on advancing into
southern Manitoba to, quote "take back the land." Unquote.' Shall I go on?"

By this time several staff officers had turned from their work and were listening intently to Mackintosh's brief. Dobson nodded, the James Bay sitreps laid aside.

"Quote: 'In Saskatchewan, similar disturbances are underway and convoys of armed natives are advancing southward from areas near Flin Flon and branching out along highways 38 and 9 towards Yorkton. RCMP detachments in the area report loss of contact with their patrols and blockades of detachments in the towns. None is secure.

"'Comment: A highly dangerous event is forming across the northern Prairies. The convoys are not, repeat not, spontaneous gatherings, but appear to be working from a well-conceived plan. Our detachments cannot be concentrated in time to intervene north of the line from Arborg-Eriksdale-Mulvihill-Dauphin in the east along Highway 5 to Yorkton in the west. However, we cannot, repeat cannot, hold that ground if the native groups are determined to advance. Southern Manitoba and Saskatchewan to the Winnipeg-Regina line are wide open to assault.

"'Commissioner requests immediate Canadian Forces support to locate the convoys, determine their strength and direction, and to reinforce RCMP detachments. He anticipates a request to provide combat support to the RCMP if the convoys continue to advance and do not unilaterally stop.' Unquote."

Mackintosh let the note drop to his side. "Well, colonel, now what?"

Dobson grimaced. "Do we have a secure line to Christ Almighty?" No one laughed. "Okay then, get the Pentagon and let's get some satellite confirmation of this stuff. And pass this report to Canada ComOps immediately."

Tuesday, September 7, 0810 hours
Ottawa: NDOC

The RCMP report was soon confirmed by satellite images beamed into NDOC from American sources. Moreover, CFB Cold Lake was already under attack and just holding its own, but the base was virtually useless for aircraft operations in the circumstances.

Colonel Dobson and Colonel Ed Conway, NDHQ director of intelligence, stood watching the moving columns on screen with a certain detached admiration for the way they moved around the hasty barriers thrown up by the police. "I think they've got soldiers directing traffic, Ian," Conway muttered. Dobson nodded.

"Nothing but a determined military force can stop these columns reaching the outskirts of Winnipeg, Brandon, Regina, and Edmonton. What do you think?"

Conway nodded. "Yeah, I agree."

Just then General Bishop strode through the door with the DCDS, General Gervais, in his wake. "Well, Ian, what's the latest report?"

Dobson, Conway, and Mackintosh quickly reviewed the situation, and Dobson offered the pessimistic assessment that the Canadian Forces would have a very difficult time intercepting and halting one of the columns, never mind them all.

"And General Lepine, what's his estimate?"

"Grim, sir. He has all his forces tied up in Quebec except a few thrown-together units in the West, cooks and bottle-washers mostly. Even if he could muster a few companies to block the columns, he doubts we could get them into place before the natives are in Winnipeg. He doesn't have the aircraft, and after this morning's Herc crash, he is assuming the approach into Winnipeg airport isn't secure. He thinks we'd lose another, maybe several, aircraft and units trying to get in there. He's checking the possibility of bringing any units and Hercs he can round up into small private and community fields north of Winnipeg and in to Brandon and Yorkton, but there's a significant risk here too—we don't really know the situation on any of the likely fields. And once on the ground, the Hercs might not have enough runway to turn around and get out again.

"There is one alternative, and that's to call in air-strikes, use CF18s and hose down the columns. It would be pretty messy and we're not sure it would work. We have to remember the Petawawa raiders took several Blowpipe anti-aircraft missiles and we have to assume they're with these columns."

"Well," said Bishop, taking a chair in front of the displays, "I just spoke with the prime minister. He's understandably overwhelmed. I mentioned an air strike and he almost threw up on his desk. 'We're not in goddamn

Lebanon!' he shouted. So that option's off the plate for now. Carl, what will the Americans give us to help hold the fort?"

The DCDS, looking tired and frustrated, closed his notebook. "Not much, it appears. The Commander NorthCom said he's tied to the president's direct order not to engage any native people north of the border. He said he'd like to help, but other than satellites now in place and a few aerial drones, he has nothing for us. If the natives from Canada or the United States were to attempt to cross the border or hit the pipelines to the U.S., well, then it's a different ball game and he'll let us know what he's going to do. Sir, I emphasize, he only promised to let us know once he decides, not to consult with us. It was not a happy conversation."

Bishop looked at the screens for a minute but found nothing helpful on them. He sighed. "Okay, I'll have a go at the chairman of the Joint Chiefs of Staff, but I expect the same answer. So much for 'there's no threat and if there were one the Americans would save us,' the slogan that's passed for Canadian defence strategy and policy ever since Wilfrid Laurier's time, the world wars excepted, I suppose.

"All right, bitching won't help. Carl, orders to General Lepine: he's to deploy all available forces in the West not currently engaged on critical duties to assist the RCMP in blocking the columns. He has my authority to use whatever helicopters he can find to attack, repeat attack, the columns once they reach the Interlake region and points along that line westwards and eastwards. He is to try to extract a couple of high-value units from the East and move them, risks and all, into Manitoba. He can call out any militia units we have left in the West to form home guards around their towns and villages. The ROE is 'shoot to defend.'" He paused and rubbed his temple.

"Oh, and Carl, have René develop a command structure for the Western theatre. We're going to be at this for a long time. And you keep at the U.S. commanders on the ground and weasel out of them as much info and support as we can get."

The CDS turned to Steve Mackintosh. "Well, inspector, what can the RCMP offer? Perhaps you should bring me up to date on your organization in the West. I assume it's rather skimpy, given the area and the demands of normal police duties."

"It's skimpy in these circumstances, sir, that's for sure. Let me put up the current display and the detachment organization for the North West Region—that's the one that includes Manitoba, Saskatchewan, and Alberta." Mackintosh hit a few keys and a new map filled the screen. "It's a huge area, as you obviously understand, larger than most countries in the world. And in total we have about 4,100 regular RCMP officers in the three provinces. You understand as well, sir, these officers are essentially trained to police small towns and the highways outside the major cities, much like the Ontario Provincial Police does in Ontario. They're good officers, but we don't have 4,100 urban SWAT team members out there."

"Yes, of course. I know these guys well from my time commanding Moose Jaw and Cold Lake. Go on, and let's concentrate on the Manitoba situation for now. If the NPA gets control of the area south of the lakes and boxes in Winnipeg, they'll effectively cut the country in two."

"Right, sir." Mackintosh grabbed the mouse, moved the cursor, and clicked twice to zoom in on northern Manitoba and the central Interlake region. "The RCMP has three districts in Division D, a.k.a. Manitoba, that interest us right now. The Northern Service Area covers all the territory north of the lakes. We have nineteen detachments there with about 210 officers. The East Service Area, here, has fifteen detachments of 250 officers responsible for a large area with a population of about 180,000 people, including thirty-three native communities of various sizes. And over here, west of Lake Manitoba, the West Service Area has another 250 officers operating out of thirteen detachments. In total, forty-seven detachments and 710 officers. Not all available, of course, some are sick or away, but in this kind of emergency eighty-five per cent, say 600 officers.

"Our main worry right now is the East Service Area, and, obviously, the Interlake area. We're pretty thin here, unfortunately. A small detachment at Lundar on Highway 6, here, is held by ten officers. Their nearest support in the area is Gimli, here, on Lake Winnipeg, which is about eighty kilometres away, and that's over a maze of back-country roads. The nearest detachment south on Highway 6 is Stonewall, which normally has eight constables, but some of them have already been sent to support the operation in Winnipeg.

"Over on the other native convoy route here, we have a detachment on Highway 10 at Swan Lake—fourteen officers—and in Winnipegosis, ten officers.

"Finally, sir, the immediate problem in the north. The Flin Flon detachment, about 650 kilometres northwest of Winnipeg, is responsible for some 10,000 people, including a large native population, and for that it has one staff sergeant, one sergeant, and eight constables. The detachment commander is also responsible for a so-called host detachment at Cranberry Portage, here, about sixty kilometres by decent highway, where we have a corporal and three constables.

"The detachment at The Pas, about 120 kilometres south of Flin Flon and directly on Highway 10 south, has another staff sergeant, a sergeant, and fifteen constables. These are again all very large patrol areas, though I suppose right now control of the highways is the main thing.

"General, the numbers in Manitoba might look helpful if we could concentrate the detachments, but I'm afraid that is just not an option now. They are too scattered and isolated, and if they move anywhere, we risk having them snapped up at NPA roadblocks—'use them one at a time, lose them one at a time.' In fact, sir, in the north and in the Interlake region, we're, uh, counting on the army to rescue our mission, not the other way around."

"Thank you, Steve. Would you please call Commissioner Richard and ask him to call me as soon as possible? You can tell his staff that I want to talk to him about concentrating an improvised force on the most critical highways to block the native convoys in Manitoba. I'm aiming to have them in place early this afternoon if possible.

"Okay, everyone, that's it. The country may be going down, but we're going to try to save as much as we can."

Tuesday, September 7, 0832 hours
20 kilometres north of the Gypsumville Road on Highway 6

Tommy Twoskins checked his map and drew a small blue arrow at the spot overlooking St. Martin Junction, where the leading recce troop leader had last reported his location and situation. He was surprised by how fast they were moving and how little resistance they had met so far. But, he cautioned himself, it was early going; the road from The Pas to the north end of Lake Manitoba ran through mostly empty bush country, and the army and the police hadn't had time to react yet.

All summer, Stevenson had been busy setting up native lookouts along the highways the convoys were now using. Basically they were just a few people with cellphones sitting near critical junctions and in villages ready to warn the convoy leaders about police movements or anything out of the ordinary. So far they weren't very busy. It was just another normal September morning in the Interlake region.

At the moment, traffic control was Tommy's biggest problem. As always, there were dozens and dozens of big transport trucks, the main carriers of supplies into northern Manitoba and Saskatchewan, moving north and south on the single highway, and they were breaking into his convoys and disrupting movement everywhere. We should have anticipated that problem, Toques told himself. I guess it was too obvious. He reached for his radio handset.

"Comms, Toques. Get on the cellphone net and instruct the highway watchers in the south to set up some way to stop traffic coming north. They can stop the trucks and tell them they might get hurt if they go north and suggest they pull over into some parking place in the villages. The lookouts should try to act like helpful citizens warning the drivers about problems up ahead. Don't have them go threatening people and attract police attention. We need their eyes on the road. I'll get on to the logistics groups at the north end of our convoys and have them drop off some people to stop traffic coming south; they can be a little rougher if need be. You call Flin Flon and The Pas and tell the commanders there to block the roads south once we're clear. Nobody moves on the roads south without permission. Over."

"Toques, comms. Wilco. They're doing that already in The Pas, but I'll pass the word again and get on to the others. Oh, you should know the TV networks are reporting an 'uprising in the north' and seems like they've set off a panic in some of the southern towns along our routes. People are loading up their cars and trucks and heading for Winnipeg. Good news is it may block the army from getting on the road—bad news, it may block us as we get closer. Over."

"Toques. Yeah, maybe. But we'll know in advance, and spontaneous roadblocks just north of the Perimeter Highway are okay. If our blockades get mixed up with big civilian traffic jams, so much the better. The feds aren't likely to attack us with guns blazing through a horde of confused civilians. I'll get back to you as we get south and see if we have a traffic problem. At the rate we're going now, we should be near the final objectives by mid-afternoon. But we'll see. Out."

Tuesday, September 7, 0845 hours
Five kilometres north of St. Martin Junction

O'Reilly Keith, a self-described "Irish French Cree Métis," had been a warrior from the first days of the NPA and, at twenty-three, now commanded the recce troop motoring down Highway 6 towards Winnipeg. He stood in the chopped-out cab of his four-wheel-drive pickup, which he had painstakingly painted a mottled green, tan, and black. Reilly, as he called himself, never wore a hat, but today his long dark hair was corralled by the headband of the goggles that were shielding his eyes from the wind and dust flying about the open truck. Binoculars hung around his neck and his map fluttered in the wind as his driver sped south. He was excited, joyful—a soldier, in command, leading his small team into action in the early morning sunlight, doing what every man in his heart would like to have done at least once in his lifetime.

He looked back at his small troop strung out in the distance behind him. His group consisted of three patrols, his and two others, each of two vehicles. St. Martin was the first village where they might find police, so he decided to go over the recce tactics one last time.

"All stations, Reilly," he shouted over the wind into his radio. "Like I told you at orders, my patrol with Stan will lead, followed by Martin's patrol, then Lucy's. We'll continue to drive south and only start moving tactically in single patrols once we get to St. Martin or we make first contact. I expect our air patrol off to the east will see any roadblocks before we get to them and I'll give you radio heads-up and orders when they do. But just follow the drills if we unexpectedly find the, ah, enemy." The odd word caught in his mouth.

"As we practised, we'll approach the village quietly, scan the position, and then I'll decide whether we go through or I send one of the patrols to look for a bypass. No shooting unless we have to protect ourselves. Remember, we're the eyes and ears, not the muscles. Keep a steady pace, not too fast, stay spread out as we practised, and watch for aircraft. Out."

At about 0910 Reilly's recce troop rolled up to St. Martin Junction, a typical hamlet on Highway 6—gas station, convenience store with post office, a few small houses and outbuildings, and not much else. Just a few honest people making a living selling goods to local ranchers and farmers, and transport drivers stopping at the last pee-break north and the first coffee shop south. Not a place kids stayed once they got car keys.

Today for Reilly, however, St. Martin was a tactical problem and his troop's first test. He ordered his driver to pull over to the right side of the road as soon as the village came in sight, and called Stan Higgs in the second truck in his patrol.

"Stan, Reilly. Okay, like we practised. It looks normal from here. I'll cover you, so move along just off the left side of the road to that red garage at the edge of the village. Take a look and if it's clear, wave me forward. I'll cover you from there to the next bound into town. Over."

"Stan. Roger. On my way. Out."

Reilly checked back down the road and watched his four other vehicles pull off the highway and take cover. "All stations, Reilly. Okay, once I move you, follow along and take my place here. Stan and I will leapfrog into town and you follow along. As I move forward, you move too. Keep your distances and keep your weapons loaded, but locked. I don't expect any trouble, but if there's a problem, you can cover us as we pull back. Out."

Reilly radioed his commander leading the main body. "Toques, Reilly. Sitrep—just outside St. Martin, no contact. Moving in for a look. Over."

"Toques, roger. Take your time, we're okay for time here. Let me know once you're clear of the village and moving on. Out."

Reilly watched Stan roll to a stop just to the rear of the garage and lift his binos to search the way forward. After a minute, Stan waved his arm over his head, all clear, and Reilly told his driver, "Go."

The recce group had practised this drill time and again, and Reilly's driver, Mary Bearpaw, didn't need any other orders. She sped up to Stan's truck then braked hard, and Stan pulled out immediately to the next bound, to the junction near the convenience store about 200 metres ahead. Reilly covered Stan's advance, then as he moved forward under Stan's cover, the troop behind him moved into the area he had just vacated. And so they manoeuvred forward—"fire and movement" was the most elementary tactic on the battlefield, though for the recce unit it was actually "search and movement." Visual inspection rather than suppressing fire, making it safe for your buddies to move forward while acting as a kind of screen to warn the main body about trouble on the road.

Stan and Reilly were in and out of the village in three bounds. The only thing to report was four or five truck drivers and a clerk standing at the gas pumps staring blankly at the strange antics of the natives in pickups on the highway through town. Once the village was clear and his troop had passed through the village, Reilly radioed them to take it slow till he caught up, then he circled back and stopped at the gas station. He called to the men standing around the trucks, one still holding the gas pump nozzle, discussing the weapons they'd seen the Indians in trucks carrying.

"Morning, gents. I want you to just go about your business here. But park the trucks and shut down your radios and cellphones and stuff. If you're peaceful, this will all be over in a few days. There're a lot of our people heading your way from up north and they mean you no harm. But they are coming through and they'll not be stopped. If you've got any guns around, bring them out and pile them over there across the road. Someone will pick them up."

"Screw you, redskin," said the man with the gas hose. "John here's got a contract to deliver this load to Flin Flon and I'm making an honest living here and I'm not letting any Indian parade ruin it. So you just get the hell outta here before I call the cops."

No one had ever accused O'Reilly Keith of being aggressive and he let the merchant's cheap insult slide. Waving back the two warriors in the truck bed who were raising their rifles, he said "Steady, boys, the gentleman is just confused."

He turned to the other men standing near the pumps. "You guys just settle down. You take this loudmouth aside and do as I said. If you move from the station, your trucks will be destroyed and the station burnt to the ground. I think it's better for everyone if you just stand aside and let the convoys pass, that way no one gets hurt. Okay? And, by the way, don't bother calling 911 or the Mounties. As of today things around here are under new management."

The men at the pumps stood still until the store owner moved to speak again. A trucker touched his elbow. "Come on, Wally. This isn't our business. Besides, I saw three cop cars pull out of here about an hour ago heading south at high speed. So let's have a coffee and sit it out. The Mounties or someone will sort out these buggers soon enough.

"Come on, everybody, let's go inside. And Wally, you just fetch me that shotgun hidden under your counter that none of us knows about, right, boys? You just give it to me and I'll put it across the road." He took Wally's arm more firmly and pulled him away from Reilly toward the gas station store.

The other truckers turned away too. "Yeah, Wally," said one, "let's go get your secret gun." With a forced laugh, the truckers dragged the fuming Wally to the shop door.

Reilly reached for his radio. "Toques, Reilly. St. Martin is clear. You may want to detain the shopkeeper at the convenience store." He looked over his shoulder. "That's Wally's Gas Bar. He's hostile and needs watching. Otherwise, all is good to go; the truckers here agree it's not their problem, and we're going to move south of the village. Over."

"Toques. Good show. I'll take care of the problem there. You keep to the schedule. Get to the bridge at Fairford. It's the obvious place to block us, so dash for it and hold it until I tell you to carry on south. The colonel told me something might be building near St. Laurent down south, but he said it's hard to tell for sure so he'll keep us posted. I'll let you know well before you're in the area. Out."

Mary gunned the truck out of the station parking lot in a spray of grit and gravel, driving fast and confidently, passed the two rear patrols, and fell into place a tactical bound behind Stan's vehicle. Reilly dropped down into his seat, patted Mary on the shoulder, refolded his map to show the next section south, and circled the Fairford bridge with his red marker.

Reilly had never been very far south of The Pas before, and as he ran his finger down along Highway 6 searching for St. Laurent, he sang out the names. "Fairford, Steeprock Junction, Moosehorn, Ashern, Camper, Eriksdale—" The start of Icelander country, Toques had told him. "—Deerhorn, Lundar, Oak Point, ah there it is, that's a long way south." Doesn't look too important, he told himself . . . unless we get stuck there. He shifted his map back and forth trying to see the town and the roads near it. "Damn thing would be right in the fold in the map," he growled.

Tuesday, September 7, 0850 hours
Ottawa: NDOC

Inspector Mackintosh handed General Bishop the secure telephone. "Commissioner Richard, sir."

"Thanks, Steven. Jean, good morning. Yes, well as good as we can expect under the circumstances. I assume you've seen the int report from our people and the satellite images we sent you on the secure net? Yes, very disturbing. I have my people working on a plan to find and assemble a force to get up Highway 6 in Manitoba as far and fast as they can to block the approach from that direction. If I can pull it off, we might just split the natives into several smaller groups before they can concentrate outside Winnipeg. If they get past the Interlake area and out onto the open plains we'll have a devil of a time rounding them up. Worse, they might be able to make contact with the warriors south of the city and even infiltrate large groups into the urban core as well. I'm going to try to put a cork in the bottle as far north as I can."

The CDS gestured to Ian Dobson to activate the speaker phone. "Yes, Jean, but just a second, I've got the speaker on here, just so you know, bringing my staff in—thanks, please go ahead.

Richard's strong, accented voice filled the room. "As I was saying, Andy, I think your idea is the right one. I would like to help as much as I can. My problem, I'm sure you understand, is that my force is scattered all over hell's half acre. My police detachments in the Northern District are essentially out of action. I've told the commanders there to try and stall the natives, but not to get into a shootout except in self-defence. We just don't have the people, even for a small-scale counterattack up there. I took, unfortunately as it now appears, a lot of people out of the Eastern District and some from the Southern and Western districts and sent them to reinforce the teams in Winnipeg. Now I'm guarding the front door and the natives are coming in the back door."

"Yeah, Jean, I fell into the same trap. Most of our units are in Quebec, and what's left in Manitoba is caught up in Winnipeg, either downtown or at the airport. I was trying to get the remains of the Shilo garrison near Brandon into Winnipeg, but now I need them to protect Brandon and the Trans-Canada Highway around that city.

"Well, at least I can help there, Andy. My detachments near the highway and Brandon and Portage La Prairie can take care of the highway area for now. For what it's worth, they could also set up a roadblock near Westbourne to cut off easy passage east around the south end of Lake Manitoba, though I take it most of the trouble is coming down the other side of the lake. But they're already in the region and know the roads and the locals, so if that might help we can do it."

"That would help a great deal, thanks. Here's what I intend to do, Jean, in broad strokes. General Lepine is cobbling together a Manitoba combat team as we speak. He's placed a militia colonel, Dick Slate—ex-regular force, Patricias—in command, and we're together bringing in as many militia and regular soldiers as we can find. There aren't any units left in the province so this ad hoc unit will have to do.

"The new CO is on his way to Stony Mountain. He'll set up an HQ, probably in the village, then deploy whatever armed forces they find as they arrive. If you can find some members of the force, strip the detachments in the south maybe, I would appreciate you sending them to Stony Mountain and putting them under my command for a few days. I think this thing is going to be decided in the next few hours, or a day or two at the most, unless my private conversations with the Pentagon bring us a miracle, or, actually, several miracles."

"Yes, okay, Andy, I'll see what I can do and let Steve Mackintosh know the details. He has my authority to coordinate RCMP operations in the West with General Lepine. Unity of command is what we need here, Andy, and you have my permission to assume command of the detachments in the West until we bring this thing under control. Have Steve sign anything you need him to sign, got that Steve?"

Mackintosh nodded at the phone. "Yes, sir, got it."

"Good," came Richard's voice. "Why we had to wait until we had a major emergency on our hands before we practised combined operations is beyond me. Politics, I guess. Anyway, if you agree, we can start to do it now."

"Thank you, Jean. That's just what we need. I'll have my staff arrange the details with Inspector Mackintosh and I assume he'll put the word out to the appropriate detachments as soon as he can. I'll try to organize a situation briefing for you at Canada Command headquarters for later in the day if you're available."

"I'll check the timetable. Right now I'm off to see the prime minister— his invitation. I'll explain our arrangements and plan to him, if you agree, and debrief you at this afternoon's meeting."

"Certainly, that's great, thanks. Talk to you later."

Bishop hung up, gestured to Dobson to close the speaker system, then spoke to the colonel and Steve Mackintosh. "You heard the commissioner, so make it happen. I'll be in my office; let me know when you're ready with a full update."

The two men acknowledged the general's orders and simultaneously reached for telephones while Andy Bishop walked over to the display board covering Western Canada, where thin red, electronic arrows marked the native convoys as they crept steadily southwards. He swore quietly to himself.

Tuesday, September 7, 0855 hours
Winnipeg: Winnipeg International Airport

In his makeshift tactical HQ at Winnipeg airport, Colonel Stevenson was also watching the convoys moving on the map, though in a much less sophisticated way. He was limited to coloured-pencil marks drawn on paper maps that indicated his columns and patrols. The maps were updated based on radio and telephone messages, TV broadcasts, and reports from his lookouts along the routes.

His staff had hurriedly improvised the command post in a room recently taken by his warriors in a brief skirmish with the base defence force. Speaker and handset lines, run in from his truck-mounted radios, dangled from the windows. Large-scale maps covered in plastic sheets were tacked to the walls or balanced on large easels.

His young chief of staff, Don Coutts, was busy changing the map displays to show the reported positions of friendly and enemy units in the city and on the roads south towards Winnipeg and Regina. Other staff officers moved chairs and tables into place around the map boards or hastily re-established contact with Stevenson's subordinate commanders across the West and with Molly Grace near Clandeboye. The set-up was primitive by modern standards, but the old system had always been at least adequate... and it worked when the power failed. Stevenson was confident that he had a reasonable degree of control of his units and that his plan was unfolding much as he had intended, at least as far as he could tell in the midst of combat confusion.

But Colonel Sam knew full well that he could see only part of the battlefield, and tried constantly to extend his information and his intuition to anticipate what might be happening "on the other side of the hill." He was sure of one thing: General Bishop and the Mounties weren't about to let his little native army motor south without a response. The questions were where, when, and how they would move to counter his plan, not whether.

"Don, have we anything at all from our sources on the army's response to our move south?"

"Not much, sir. They seem to be trying to organize something. But our militia contacts in Winnipeg say that so far the only hard indication is a 'warning order' sent to the units in the city to thin out their lines and bring a number of people back to the Minto Armouries. We could guess that it is one of three possibilities—a move out of the city, a strike inside the city, or they could be just trying to rest some people.

"But one of our guys overheard a message about 'a change of mission' and 'be prepared to move to a new location northwest of the city.' And we have scattered reports that the Mounties are up to something. Scouts near

Langruth and Gladstone and MacDonald tell us a lot of police cars and vans are on the roads west and south of Lake Manitoba. I put the reports together and it looks like they're all travelling south and east, but it's hard to be sure."

"Okay. Get back to those Langruth and Gladstone and MacDonald guys and our people on the roads near the Delta and Poplar Point and tell them to report every sighting, everything, no matter how small it seems to them. If a cruiser parks, tell us. If he stays parked five minutes, tell us that too."

Stevenson stepped up to the map of southern Manitoba, working out the logic of the situation, talking to himself. "If I were Bishop or Lepine, what would I try to do? CF18 attacks on the convoys? Maybe, but 'a slaughter of natives on a peaceful rally' might really excite the international press and bring the UN down on the government. Ground attack on all the convoys at once? Not enough troops. Concentrate what I have and fight a major engagement to disrupt our plan by reversing or smashing up one of the convoys? Hmmmm. What would I do? Probably start with a blockade in force to stop the most threatening column from moving farther south."

He stared at the map, waiting for the information Don had given him to form a pattern in his mind. "What did Napoleon say? 'Begin by attacking what your enemy holds dear.' What do their generals and politicians hold dear? The transportation routes, infrastructure, and oil and gas lines in the south—and keeping the people in Winnipeg from panicking. Hardly anything north of the Trans-Canada matters, at least in the short run.

"So, which of my convoys presents the greatest risk to what the government holds dear? None in Saskatchewan north of Regina. The convoy heading west of Lake Manitoba down Highway 10 is a problem, but not immediately critical. Nor is the one coming from Kenora. Twoskins and his Cree convoy, they're the problem. If Toques gets out of the Interlake area and south to Stony Mountain, then Bishop loses and he knows it. So that means a blockade on 6 north of Warren somewhere."

Stevenson finished talking to himself and spoke instead to his chief of staff. "Don, where is Twoskins right now?"

"Checking, sir." Don spoke briefly into the radio, waited, spoke again, waited again, then signed off and walked over to Stevenson by the large map. "His lead elements are about here, on 6." He pointed to the narrow neck of land between Lake Manitoba and Lake St. Martin. "They're safely across Fairford Bridge. The local band chief, though no friend of Molly Grace, had already secured it on his own initiative and just waved the Cree convoy's recce troop through. The convoy's making good progress—hardly any resistance—just a few transport trucks pulled across the roads by rednecks with CBs. But Toques anticipated that and has a couple of heavy tow-trucks up front in the main body yanking them off quickly enough so he doesn't get backed up. He thinks he'll be near Stony Mountain as early as late afternoon if things keep going the way they are. We're way ahead of schedule."

Stevenson spoke without turning his head, as if afraid that looking away from the map would disrupt the pattern that had formed in his mind. "Yes, well," he said distractedly, "things in battles rarely keep going well. You and Toques should know that after your Afghan dust-ups."

Suddenly his focus and his tone sharpened. "Tell me this, Don. Along Highway 6, Twoskins' route south, where's the natural defensive position where a small force could hold him up and maybe block his advance for a longer time? If you had to stop him with, oh, thirty guys, or sixty, where would you do it and how?"

Don put his papers aside and stepped closer to the map board. He ran his hand through his long hair, thinking, then pointed at the red arrow marking the lead elements of Column Cree and let his finger slide down Highway 6 to St. Laurent which he stabbed with his fingertip. "Here, sir. Right here. I'm still for St. Laurent just like I was during the map exercises we did together in the spring. Maybe even more so now since the feds haven't responded much at all farther north."

"Okay, go on. Why?"

Christ, Don said to himself, army staff college again. To Stevenson he said, "Well, sir, the town and really the whole area here is a natural defile, a bottleneck—Lake Manitoba on the west side, the Shoal Lakes in the middle and Lake Winnipeg on the other side. It's really difficult to move east-west in that area. The roadways, other than Highway 6, are mostly gravel tracks, narrow, and easy to block. The ground's flat and covered with scrub oak and rocky pastureland near St. Laurent, but nearer the Shoal Lakes it gets pretty wet and rough, slow going for a wheeled convoy. There aren't any natural defensive features, but the village could be made into one. It's on the highway, more or less stretches from there to the lake on the west side, open fields of fire to the east. So if you were to fortify the houses and so on, you could take a stand. It might be a real problem for, I assume, a small force without much skill in fighting house-to-house to clear a way through it.

"Besides, where else? Even if they could get farther north, the defensive possibilities are worse because it's wider, and farther south, ditto, plus Tommy—you know we served together in a couple of hot spots, sir?"

"Yes, Don, I know that and I understand how you must feel right now."

"Well, sir, Tommy's an aggressive commander and kind of secretive, he likes to surprise people. So, as I was saying, the column could cut east on 415 or even back-road it south of the Shoals to 322 around the village if the army let them. But that would be me planning for the enemy to do what's easiest for me to handle. A strongpoint in the village, that's the easiest thing for them and the worst for us. So, St. Laurent, sir. I'd bet on it."

"Yes, that makes sense. So what do we do?"

"Well, Tommy could take 415 all the way to Teulon on Highway 7, then south to Stony Mountain. But that's a big sweep, and it might allow the enemy to push him up against the Shoal Lakes and trap him there, leaving Highway 6 north wide open to a counterattack. But if they've got that kind of strength and dig in at St. Laurent, a frontal assault by our guys won't get through fast enough.

"Sir, if I know Toques, I'd bet he'd be looking at pinning the enemy with a fire base to the north of the town and then going around, a kind of end run, to the east, along, uh, here, Sherrington Road, to 415." He led Stevenson's eye to the highway. "And then I'd cut down 518 and back to 6 east of the village and take them in the flank. 'Fix and flank,' sir! As you well know, the oldest offensive tactic in the book.

"Anyway, so an end run makes more sense. Probably the other side will try to get some kind of force covering 415 too, but, again, if their forces are limited, they'll concentrate on St. Laurent and concentrate on bottling up Tommy between Lake Manitoba and West Shoal Lake and let him run east if he dares." Don stepped back and looked at the colonel.

"Good, Don, thanks. That's how I see it too. Get Twoskins on the radio for me, please."

Tuesday, September 7, 0857 hours
Ottawa: NDOC

Lieutenant General Lepine walked into the National Defence Operations Centre and caught the eye of the CDS, who was speaking on the secure telephone. While he waited for General Bishop to finish his call, he got a coffee and looked over the sitreps and int displays with Ian Dobson. There was not much changed in the last three hours, that is if you consider a full-scale native uprising and internal invasion of Western Canada as not much change.

"Sorry, René, that was Commissioner Richard," said the CDS as he walked over to the ever-changing displays. "He's moved his detachments to support you, and he hopes to find others from B.C., the Maritimes, and his headquarters staff too. The problem is moving them west; we can't take them through the States, not yet anyway. How are things shaping up? Bad or horrible?"

René Lepine put his coffee on the table and walked to the map display of southern Manitoba. "Just bad, I'd say. We're very thin and mostly ad hoc, but I have a small unit forming to block Highway 6 at least. The RCMP is a great help and local cooperation is fine. My chief worry is that we're still in a very serious, quite precarious situation in Winnipeg, and extracting units from there is difficult and endangers that mission.

"Nevertheless, and with or without moving people in significant numbers from Winnipeg, I'm confident that we can slow down and significantly disrupt the convoy that's moving south on Highway 6. If we can create enough casualties and confusion, we may even be able to stop them in their tracks long enough for me to find a major unit to bring from the East into the West. If I just had a couple of regular infantry companies to go after those convoys ... But, of course, even if I could free one from Quebec, I couldn't get it west in time to stop the convoys on Highway 6 from spilling out into the prairie around Winnipeg."

"Yes, I understand René. But it gets worse, I'm afraid. Richard just told me that the Flin Flon RCMP detachment held out for several hours but has been overrun. We don't know what happened to the officers. But in his last report, the detachment commander reported that the mood in the native community had swung to the NPA. He said the elders had lost control and the young people, women as well as men, really believe Molly Grace is going to make them all rich.

"In his last message, the staff sergeant wrote, uh, here it is, quote, 'dozens of trucks and buses, including school buses, are being assembled in the towns and villages around the north to bring hundreds of cheering, excited natives south tomorrow morning. Many of them are armed, and while these actions are largely spontaneous, many of the armed natives are now being grouped into ad hoc units by NPA leaders here and elsewhere. We assume they...' The message ended abruptly at that point.

"René, we've got to stop the lead convoys and do it convincingly if we're to put an end to this spontaneous eruption in the north. Stevenson's NPA units under mostly ex-regulars officers is one thing, but mobs are something entirely different and decidedly more dangerous to the farmers, ranchers, and even the native population in the north generally. They're also a lot harder for us to deal with once we regroup."

"I was afraid this might happen, sir. I don't suppose the prime minister would let loose the CF18s?"

"Not a chance. He's already under pressure from, of all places, the UN. Some committee or other has declared the Native People's Movement as leading a 'war of national liberation.' Our friends in the UN, and there aren't many outside our original NATO allies in Europe, plus the Americans and the Aussies, of course, are trying to block the most radical resolutions before the Security Council, but it's a losing cause so far. God knows why the PM cares, but apparently he does. So, no fast air and no artillery either. What have you got going otherwise?"

"Not a lot in numbers, but a fair deal in quality. The force commander, Dick Slate, the militia colonel I mentioned to you yesterday, is on his way to recce St. Laurent. He rustled up an industry-owned helicopter based on a private field outside the city from one of the militia's 'honorary colonels.' I'll never question their usefulness again. Slate will use it to check Highway 6 and the area south of the Shoal Lakes once he has enough light, in about thirty minutes.

"The second-in-command he appointed himself..." The CDS raised an eyebrow. "I know, sir, I know, a tad unusual, but these are unusual times. Anyway, he's another retired militia colonel. During the night he rounded up and prepared a truck-mounted, mixed force of about thirty to forty militia personnel and he's about to leave the city any time now and drive north to St. Laurent too. He'll meet Slate there and they'll be joined by whatever the local RCMP detachments can provide—I hope we may get another thirty people from them.

"However, the best news is that during the night I was able to extract a small Special Operations team from Quebec, put them on a civvy aircraft they 'borrowed' —" Lepine held up his hand as Bishop was about to speak. "Don't ask, sir, that's what the team leader told me, but it's working and they're on their way."

Bishop smiled. "Okay, René, we'll wait for the inquiry."

"Yes, indeed. I wonder who's going to convene it, us or Molly Grace … In any case, this team gives me and Slate greater leverage. They can do a lot of damage in a short period, but there's only a dozen of them. I expect them to arrive at the airfield near Selkirk …" Lepine glanced at his watch. "… in a few minutes actually. They'll have to 'find' a couple of ground vehicles as well. I expect them to be in the St. Laurent area in an hour or two.

"Once Slate completes his recce, I'll confirm his plan. But I ordered him to find a defensive location based in St. Laurent to cover Highway 6 so he can set up a blocking position to keep the native convoys away from Winnipeg for at least forty-eight hours. It's a tough assignment, but I think with luck we can do it."

Bishop turned to the map. "Okay, so show me the outline plan for St. Laurent—it's a strong Métis community, you know."

"Yes, sir. Slate and I agreed that St. Laurent, here, is the place. It's the best choke-point on the route south. Slate knows the area and he's confirming the layout now. Given the circumstances, and the native and Métis population in the area, we need to look the place over before we go waltzing into trouble."

"Zoom in on that town please, Corporal Brown." Andy Bishop turned back to the map display as the technician punched her magic buttons and instantly displayed a large-scale image of St. Laurent and surroundings, with a sidebar listing everything anyone might wish to know about the town's vital statistics.

"Thank you. Could you give us a look at the area east of town, around the bottom of the Shoal Lakes?" The display zoomed in for a highly detailed sweep east, south, and back toward the bottom edge of the town.

"I'm pretty sure it's defensible, sir," said Lepine, "and I'm absolutely sure it's the most defensible spot we can find. I know the area pretty well, actually. I usually go out there each fall to hunt ducks and geese with a friend of mine. I pity anyone who tries to drive those back roads in the dark, especially if they don't know the country. I tried it once and was lost until noon. I only wish we had a company of LAV IIIs to put there."

"So do I. Okay, good! Keep me informed as things develop. I think the estimate said we have about six hours before the convoy reaches that area. When will the new unit be in position?"

"In about two hours or so, with luck. But I'll hurry them along. Mind if I use a flight of CF18s to buzz the convoys at a distance every so often? It would probably slow them down quite a bit, and any time I can get is helpful."

"Yeah, okay, we'll call them photo-recce flights. We need to run some in any case to back up the satellite images. No gunfire though, René, because despite my high regard for you, if some pilot lets loose, I'm afraid I'll have to hang you in the morning."

"Well, sir, I don't want that. I told Marie-Ann I'd be home in a couple of weeks and we could go on vacation. I'll notify you as soon as Colonel Slate reports contact."

Tuesday, September 7, 1100 hours
Lundar, Manitoba

Toques expected trouble now. O'Reilly's recce troop was moving towards Oak Point and the main body had pulled over along the highway north and south of the Lundar Hotel. Thirty minutes earlier, Tommy's command had had their first real skirmish outside the village when the recce troop got into a short and sharp running gunfight with the Lundar RCMP detachment, which Reilly's guys surprised as the Mounties were moving out of town. There were wounded on both sides. Fortunately, the villagers stayed in their homes and shops, leaving the Mounties to fend for themselves. But the natives had fired on the cops, and word of that action would soon reach their police colleagues farther south. It would be "shoot first and ask questions later" from now on.

After the action, the RCMP roared off south on Highway 6 and O'Reilly stopped briefly to care for his not-too-badly injured warriors and prepared to move south again. Meanwhile, Tommy rested his convoy and reorganized for the real battle that both he and Stevenson anticipated farther down the road. He'd used the pause to send O'Reilly's troop to Oak Point, then off to check the eastern flank as far as North Shoal Lake. But the real worry was St. Laurent and Tommy wanted the recce troop to start probing the village from several directions.

"Reilly, this is Toques. Over," Tommy said into his handset.

"Reilly. Over."

"Toques, I want you to get back to the highway and prod south to the outskirts of St. Laurent. Get a patrol down 6 to Sherringham Road then swing around and look the place over. Get your patrol out near Shoal Lake to head down Ideal Road and circle in towards the town from the east. Max tactical movement. I want you to see them before they see you. Over."

"Reilly, roger. Moving now. Out." Reilly switched frequencies and gave his patrols orders while Mary Bearpaw followed Martin's truck as the patrol moved tactically by bounds along Highway 6.

"All stations, this is Reilly. We'll move ahead carefully by bounds to recce St. Laurent. Martin, your patrol takes the lead on 6. Be prepared to hold up short of the junction of 6 and 415 and give the village a very good look from there.

"Lucy, you take your patrol on Wagon Creek Road—go east to Ideal Road by the lake and then down to 415. Once you get there, cut southeast cross-country towards the town and check the east side from a distance. Try to stay under cover in the edge of the bush.

"Everybody check your weapons, round in the chamber. And take the smoke grenades out of the crates. But remember, 'sneak and peek.' I want to see what's there and we'll let the main body deal with any trouble. I'll follow Martin's patrol. Over."

"Martin. On the way. Out."

"Lucy. Turning off 6 now. If we make contact in the east, what next? Over."

"Reilly. Take cover and report. If necessary withdraw and report. Don't get stuck and don't get shot. Be prepared on my order to probe around the east side of town, or, and this is important, if it's quiet in St. Laurent I'll give you the word to go east on 415 to the junction of North and East Shoal Lake to see if the route's clear. Over."

"Lucy. Wilco. Moving now to Ideal. Out."

Tuesday, September 7, 1100 hours
Highway 6, on the outskirts of St. Laurent

St. Laurent, a village of about 200 citizens some eighty kilometres northwest of Winnipeg, sits by the zigzag of asphalt where Highway 6 turns to the southeast. Most of the village's low whitewashed houses and garages are scattered along the gravel roads on the west side of the highway. Just south of the junction of Highway 6 and the main street, Lake Francis Road is occupied by the district high school and a small strip-mall containing a *dépanneur*, the Aboriginal Head-Start Centre, and a temporary, now empty, RCMP lock-up. Behind these low buildings, a mean settlement of a dozen look-alike white stucco bungalows sits forlornly in the prairie grass. Down the road to St. Ambroise, a frame house sports a crooked sign that declares "Métis Power," and farther on, an ill-kept sign identifies another house as the "Manitoba Federation of Métis Inc."

What is now St. Laurent had been for centuries an important aboriginal fishing settlement on the shore of Lake Manitoba. In the 1800s, priests and French trappers and hunters moved into the region, a history that is marked today by the local Catholic church, the neatly kept cemetery, and the still predominately Francophone community. The village is quiet most of the year, except in summer when cottagers and tourists head for the lake's long white-sand beach. It's also pretty peaceful for a village sitting on the divide between the prosperous, urban south and the poor, rural north.

Occasionally, minor squabbles between the natives or the Métis and the late-arriving white settlers disturb the tranquillity of the town council, but the leaders of these communities have always found reasonable ways to settle their differences. But today was different. Ironically, the national crisis, long brewing elsewhere because the so-called leaders of these communities faraway from St. Laurent could not decide to get along, was about to explode in the middle of this ancient village that had found ways to get along.

Tuesday, September 7, 1115 hours
St. Laurent

Colonel Slate's little company had only moved into town two hours ago. He had first got his soldiers busy building hasty fire positions near the white houses to cover the road and approaches from the north, and other positions in the strip-mall to cover the eastern approach across the highway. Slate then rounded up the few citizens who hadn't already fled to Winnipeg, explained the situation to them, and ordered them to pack essentials and get out of town, "to move south, within thirty minutes." Most everyone did. Most everybody except George Hamelin and Pierre Parenteau, Métis activists known to the RCMP as NPA radicals, who angrily refused to move.

"We're not going nowhere. This is our land. You take your soldiers and get back to Winnipeg or wherever you came from. There'll be no trouble here if you're not here. So bugger off," Hamelin snarled. Meanwhile, Parenteau walked to his dirty brown pickup truck without a word and started to pull out of the parking lot beside the highway, apparently heading northward. A couple of soldiers jumped in front of the truck and, facing the driver's window, levelled their weapons at him and motioned him out of the truck. He braked but didn't cut the engine. No one moved.

Slate motioned his guys farther left to keep a clear field of fire then walked over to the cab window. "Can't let you go right now unless you're heading south. Is that where you're going?"

Pierre glared at the soft-spoken colonel.

"Come on now, sir," said Slate, "what'll it be? You get out of town, going south, and don't come back, or I'll lock you up and you can take your chances with us."

Parenteau leaned out the window and spat on the ground. "Yeah, okay, I'm gonna get my family and I'm out of here, okay? Come on, George." He gunned the engine and once Hamelin had jumped in the cab, made a fast, dusty U-turn onto the highway and drove southwest back into the village followed by a couple of young soldiers in a civvy-style Jeep.

As they went, George pulled out his cellphone and dialled an emergency number. "Yeah, hello. Who's this? Okay, it's me and Pierre at St. Laurent. The army's here. I could see about thirty or more militia." He looked at Pierre, who nodded agreement. "No, no big vehicles, but they look like they're blocking the road and moving into the houses facing the highway." He paused. "Okay, we know where that is, but they're watching us so we'll go south and then circle back along a tractor trail on the east side of 6 or along Gaudry and north to 415."

Fifteen minutes later Pierre, his wife and son, and George were southbound on Highway 6, escorted by two militia soldiers in a Jeep. At Duchene, the Jeep turned around, satisfied, and a couple of minutes after that, Pierre's brown pickup was racing east on Gaudry Road.

Tuesday, September 7, 1145 hours
Highway 6, overlooking St. Laurent

Reilly directed Mary to pull their truck into a position overlooking Martin's patrol, hidden in a low tree-line along Sherringham Road at Highway 6. He was about to radio Lucy when the *crack—thump* of rifle bullets passing overhead made him duck behind the dashboard. His radio squawked.

"Reilly, Martin. We're under fire. My window's out and Moe's cut. Christ, they just shot out my front tires, two shots! We're bailing out. Shorty, cover us, throw the smoke."

Reilly peered over the dash trying to pinpoint Martin's patrol. The sudden pop of a phosphorous grenade sent a burst of dense white smoke billowing across the road. Shorty's truck reversed into the cover at high speed; seconds later it came roaring back out of the cloud down the Sherringham Road with Martin and Moe crouching on the rear bumper, scrambling to get over the tailgate.

"Shorty, Reilly. Good work. Get into cover towards the lake as soon as you can. Stay off the highway."

Another round passed high over Reilly's truck. Snipers searching for him, hoping the rounds would make him respond or move and expose himself. He knew the tactic from Bosnia. It meant soldiers, not duck hunters, were doing the shooting. Okay, we have contact. Reilly grabbed Mary's arm. "High reverse! Cut her over across the road and try to get that General Store on the east side of the road between us and that group of houses."

He yelled into the radio again to the other truck in his patrol. "Stan, Reilly. Open up with the light gun on those houses just off the road, then move back out of there as soon as I'm under cover. Out."

Stan's machine gun began chattering as Reilly's truck bounced across the highway and he gave more orders. Chunks of white paint flew off the houses as Stan swept the area with his machine gun looking for the unseen snipers.

"Lucy, this is Reilly. Over …" He fought for his balance as Mary bounced backward over the ruts in the field, then turned sharply, smashing a fender as she shot the truck over the ditch and across the road and in behind a scrub of trees. Ernie and Russell in the back steadied their rifles as best they could and fired a couple of wild shots in the general direction of the town before they were thrown to the floor of the truck bed.

"Lucy, this is Reilly. Over," he repeated. "Where are you? Watch out for snipers."

"Reilly, Lucy." Her voice was calm. "We're just north of the junction of 415 and 518. No contacts, but we kicked up a lot of dust and…Wait out!"

Mary jockeyed Reilly's truck behind a low shed and stopped. In the distance, she could see Shorty with Martin's crew piled into the back, speeding west on Sherringham towards the beach as the last of the smoke drifted away. Luckily, a fire, caused by the phosphorous grenade, billowed in the long, dry grass, adding another layer of cover from the sniper fire.

"Reilly, this is Lucy. Contact. Infantry in the mall along the highway are firing on our vehicles. We threw some smoke, but they seemed to find us through it. My truck's hit several times, but no one's hurt. Looks like Sean's driver's down—they've stopped and seem to be changing round. I'm opening up with the machine gun. Over."

"Roger, that. Cover Sean as best you can, then pull back east on 415. Over."

"Lucy. Okay. But hang on, there's something strange going on over across the field, about half way towards us and in the fields north of Gaudry Road, I think. A black truck is parked in the scrub and two guys are behind it, firing across my front at the infantry in the mall. Whoever those guys are, they're drawing fire away from me.

"Oh shit! One of them's down, looks like. The other guy's in the ditch, but he's still firing. Over."

"Okay. Locals freelancing. Can't hurt, but we can't help them. Get back down 415 and try to winkle around on the east flank of town to look in from another direction. I'll get Martin's patrol to drive down the beach road to check for openings on the west side. See if we can develop the situation. Stan and I will try to spot the army's positions from here. Time for Toques to come up. Out."

O'Reilly called his commander. "Toques, this is Reilly. Have you been covering my frequency? Over."

"Reilly, Toques. We're on it. I'm just coming up behind your location now to take a look. Don't risk your people beyond 415 and Ideal Road. Hold your positions there unless fired on, and keep me informed as you spot enemy positions.

"The main body's on the way. The first platoon will come in on the west side from the highway and along Sherringham and take a firing position somewhere near the beach and Chartrand Road to give flanking fire from around there on to that group of houses and across the front of the town.

"I'll take the other platoons east on Wagon Creek Road, then down Church Road for a mounted attack south of the village from a start-line on 415. Have Lucy guard my left flank as I turn towards the village. Roger so far. Over."

"Reilly. Roger. Over."

"Toques. I want to cut the army unit off, so we're aiming to punch through somewhere south of town at Bruce Road and Highway 6. As we move across the start-line, Lucy can move. Get one of your patrols along 518 and cover my flank. Over."

"Reilly, roger that. A classic 'fix and flank' attack off the line of advance, boss—right out of the book. Anything else we can do to help? Over."

"Toques. Keep firing on the village as I move. Also, I put our three mortars in the gravel pit, just north of Gravel and Stony Roads. When we hit the start-line, I want you to control their fire—smoke the east side of town first and then drop some high-explosive bombs on Francis Road and Highway 6 and walk a few into the mall. Over."

"Reilly, wilco. Call the start-line and I'll send in the smoke. Good luck. Out.

"Lucy, this is Reilly. Move your patrol east to the junction 415 and Ideal, and set up an observation post. Be prepared to move down 518 as flank observer. Move now and watch for the main body coming down Church Road and stay out of the way. Over."

"Roger, on my way. Out."

Tuesday, September 7, 1245 hours
East of St. Laurent

Tommy Twoskins glanced out his side window. The four trucks of Three Platoon were roughly spaced out to his right, driving as fast as the ground would allow as the unit turned west off Church Road at 415 into the field and prepared for the charge to Highway 6. On his left, One Platoon was just then making their way around a small oak copse and out into the open facing St. Laurent, about five kilometres across the field. Toques was in the centre, slightly behind the platoons. His combat team, once in position on the start-line, stopped momentarily; the commanders looked and listened for Tommy's word to advance.

"Reilly, Toques. Good show on the smoke rounds. Now six mortar rounds high-explosive, rapid fire centred on the mall and Highway 6. Over."

"Reilly. On the way. Out."

"All stations, this is Toques. Two, begin your harassing fire on the right. One and Four, advance in line for your targets on the east side of town, crash right in, dismount, and chase the militia back to the beach, then hold the town there. One, once we're in the village, move your people to cut off anyone trying to get out the back door, the west side of town.

"Okay, see you all on the objective. Let's go get 'em! Out."

The trucks jolted forward, dashing and crashing down the roads and across the fields. Warriors standing in the back fired wildly towards town, lucky to hit even the buildings hiding the militia. Bullets fired from unseen weapons in town cracked the air around them, mostly harmlessly. Some scored a hit on a fender here, a cab there, but their speed, their erratic movement—a result of their approach over uneven ground—and the screening from smoke from the mortar bombs and grass fires, all assisted the fast-approaching warriors.

Tuesday, September 7, 1310 hours
Ottawa: CANCOMOPS

Suddenly, the ordered routine of messages, assessments, and commands flowing about the Ops Centre changed. Several officers grabbed for their radios, calling operational units to alert, and Nick Pew called to Lepine across the room. "Sir! You need to hear this. I'll put it on the speaker system. It's Slate's sitrep—they're under attack."

The map displays angled to various aspects of the area around St. Laurent showed the native convoy picking up speed and then breaking off into two forces—the smaller one heading off the highway, westwards towards the beach. The red square, the computer version of the platoon deploying off Highway 6, shot along Sherringham Road, stopping short of the beach road; twenty or more red markers dashed into the field towards the village—native warriors seeking cover in the overgrown ditches. Flashes on the screen indicated the same firing audible on the speaker as Slate began speaking, calmly and directly.

"OPS, this is Slate. We are under sustained fire from several locations, mostly from the northwest. We are getting sniper and machine-gun fire from the area near the highway. Visibility is limited due to phosphorous grenades and some grass fires north of us, possibly started by the grenades. My scouts on the east of town report a lot of dust to the northeast, probably from vehicles approaching 415. We're still getting sporadic machine gun fire from the recce vehicles in that direction. I took about five casualties when the enemy recce trucks rolled into town and surprised us as we were trying to get into position.

"Most of my force is spread out in a line north of the town roughly in the houses north of the village and west of Highway 6. I'm trying to anchor my right flank on the mall southeast into the buildings and the church and the cemetery on the west side of the road and facing northeast."

Pew spoke into his headset mike. "Roger, we can see you. It looks like a platoon-size unit is making its way to your left; they might be trying to flank you along the beach. Another larger unit seems to be moving to your right—that's east—now turning off Wagon Creek Road and south on to Church."

"Roger that. We saw the move to the beach. I sent one of the sniper detachments over there. I think they can give me lots of warning and with a bit of luck they might stop any movement down that road. Depends how gutsy the natives want to be and how many casualties they're willing to take."

"Dick, General Lepine here. I'm concerned about that movement on your right. They may be flanking you and planning to bypass your position, or they may be heading off east on 415 to Teulon or Stony Mountain. Or they may be coming after you head-on. We'll keep watch and let you know as soon as we get a better idea. But I don't want them to pin you there and then get down south. If you can, get some heavy weapons sited to cover the fields and, if you can, 518; try to take out as many trucks as you can. The trucks are the key, without them, the natives aren't going anywhere.

"I'm bringing a mixed RCMP/militia unit around west and south of your location to help you—they're trying to get into position west of the highway near Lake Francis, the town not the actual lake, and then they'll make contact and arrange to move north and link up with you."

"Right, sir, but I think they might be late for the party. Looks like the answer to your three enemy options is coming straight for me around my right flank. I've got incoming mortar rounds on our heads. Damn it! You guys didn't tell me they had mortars! Gotta go."

From his little command post in the St. Laurent *dépanneur*, Dick Slate tried to spot with his binoculars the enemy north of the town on Highway 6. He swept eastwards across the highway and, startled, pulled back from the doorway and ducked for cover as he grabbed for his radio while calling out to his militia soldiers nearby. "On the right, in the fields, engage the trucks, stop the trucks!"

Then he radioed warnings to the rest of his small platoons, which were scattered across the north edge of the village covering the approach north down the highway: "Jamie, hold your guys at the corner, keep that building no matter what. Harry, get your people back, keep low, and try to get over here, around behind me, and then over to my right flank facing east. Get them into the ditch and houses on the highway. Move now and fast."

Slate hadn't finished speaking when high explosive mortar rounds started crashing into the pavement and buildings around him. Glass flew over his head and shrapnel whined though the walls. His signallers and riflemen learned an instant lesson—don't ask why someone shouts, "Get down!" Just get down. Private Sandra Knight, standing near a window, had asked first, and now she sat crumpled on the floor, back against the wall, her guts in her hands.

Even before the smoke from the mortar attack drifted out across the village, rifle and machine-gun fire from the warriors near the beach road cut through the village, hitting soldiers trying to fall back from their forward lines on the north end of town. Slate rallied those he could find from the northern platoon, but their sergeant told him that his platoon commander, Second Lieutenant Harry Mills, had been shot dead trying to help a wounded man. "Right, then," said Slate, "you follow me and we'll put your people down there, guarding the south end of the village."

As they jogged, hunched over against the bullets snapping off buildings and ricocheting through the streets, a corporal high in a window shouted a warning. "Look out! Trucks and Indians coming across the road!" He opened up with his assault rifle as Slate waved his riflemen back into the village, all chance of taking a defensive position south now lost to the urgent, determined speed of the warrior attack.

Tuesday, September 7, 1345 hours
Winnipeg: Winnipeg International Airport

Stevenson listened to the familiar sound of a battle building on the radio. Short, staccato messages back and forth, flat and factual: units moving; weapons firing; people trying to kill each other. From the sharp end, choppy messages—"I'm taking fire on the left"; "Jimmy's down"; "Get over on the right ... now!"; "Okay, on my word, everybody up and forward. Follow me in!"

From HQ, experienced staff officers recorded, questioned, and responded to the battle unfolding on their wall maps, gathering and distributing information with quiet urgency.

"Roger, two-six, say again your contact. Over."

"Three-two, you have five trucks, locals, coming up on your right, southeast of Highway 6. Watch for friendly fire. Over."

"Toques, can you confirm your lead elements are clear Chartrand Road on your right. Over."

The battle for St. Laurent unfolded as battles always do—confusion, moves and counter-moves, confusion, orders, counter-orders, and more confusion. Disembodied slices of reality passing from radio to radio. In Stevenson's primitive HQ and Lepine's electronic citadel, comms ops technicians and duty officers traced what they thought they saw and heard onto maps and charts, screening out the sounds of fighting in the background and the thought that one of these might be a friend's last message. Command, as always, was running long minutes behind events in the front line. Later on, scholars would assemble an orderly picture, literally make sense of what happened that day, generally giving credit to commanders for a degree of control, reason, and order that honest and sensible officers never claimed to have exercised.

"Stevenson, this is Toques. We have the east side of the village. Casualties are light, but several trucks are out of action. I'm pushing the militia west and south towards the beach and we'll try to trap them there. Over."

"Stevenson, roger that. Be aware, there is some kind of RCMP force moving your way along 411 from near St. Marks. They may be trying to cut you off from moving south. I want you to push the militia out of town, as you're doing, drive them back towards the beach or marshy fields to your southwest, then put a small force in the area to keep them pinned down. Then, reorg your units and get going for Warren as planned, just as fast as you can. We'll turn St. Laurent over to the mob that's coming south. I've got them under control … well a kind of control. But three hundred natives should be more than enough to hold the town long enough for our purposes. Over."

"Toques, roger. I could swing back onto 518 down to Woodlands and stay clear of 6 for a few kilometres. Over."

"Stevenson. No, it's not necessary and too slow. Build a guard position at St. Francis as you planned, then shoot for Warren before dark. You'll get past 411 before those Mounties get there, but once you do, keep a sharp eye out on your ass end. Let me know when you're moving.

"I'm going to get you some help from Pelican Column. They've had a pretty easy time of it and are now just approaching Dauphin on Highway 10. Once they get south to Neepawa, I'll order the commander to split off a strong detachment and send it along Highway 16 to Gladstone and then around the lake on 227 to come up behind the army and RCMP positions. With speed and luck, we might trap a good catch between the two columns. I'll keep you posted on the move. Over."

"Toques, roger. Tell them to call their approach as soon as they cross Road 430 and that we'll use orange smoke to mark our positions. Over."

"Stevenson, wilco. Out."

Tuesday, September 7, 1435 hours
Ottawa: CANCOMOPS

"OPS, this is Slate, sitrep. Over."

"OPS. Send your sitrep. Over."

"Slate. We've been pretty much chased out of St. Laurent. Highway 6 is open north and south. Enemy forces are in the east side of the town and along Highway 6 south in large numbers. I estimate that a hundred to a hundred and fifty natives supported by machine gun and mortar fire attacked us in, I must say, a finely executed rapid attack off the line of advance. Someone there took the combat team leaders course in Gagetown, that's for sure.

"I've pulled back into the west side of town and am trying to reorg and consolidate my platoons—really sections now. We took several casualties for sure, but the main difficulty is that the warriors overran our scattered positions before we could react. I suspect many of my missing are POWs.

"I'm going to be pushed into the lake unless I can cut out south across country. Request permission to move in that direction. Over."

General Lepine took the radio handset from Nick Pew. "Dick, René here. Unfortunately, we got you in there just a little too late. But you slowed the native convoy, which gave me time to find a small reinforcement group to help you. We'll give you the contact details later.

"I want you to move south along the ..." He glanced at the map display. "... the St. Francis Road area and head towards Road 87 north. The RCMP detachments are heading your way from St. Marks. Once you link up, it's your command. I want you to get people in position to take the south edge of St. Laurent and Highway 6 under effective fire. The aim is to harass and block, if you can, native movement on or near the village and the road. At least I hope to slow the movement of any follow-on units they may have coming south and if necessary force them east into the Shoal Lake area. Over."

"Slate. I confirm the mission continues to be to block the area, but now from south of the village. I think that's possible, but it's going to take me about an hour to get into a new position. Most of my vehicles are still in St. Laurent and I have to get together with the Mounties. I'm sending a liaison officer in a Jeep to look for them as we speak. Can I have some air support to get after these natives and hold them away while I reorg? Over."

"OPS, Lepine. I'll get some fast air, CF18s, to at least buzz the area at low level. I've ordered the two helicopter recce flights from Portage to get with you, but I'm not sure how we're going to support them with fuel and so on once they leave the base. I'll worry about that; you get to work. Commander Nick Pew here will give you the contact frequencies and so on—I assume you brought a wireless laptop with you, because that's how we're going to run this thing now. Out." Lepine held out the handset for Pew.

"Some goddamn defence policy!" he spat out. "Some goddamn army I've got! Order the soldiers to go to war and 'Oh, yeah, don't forget to bring your own equipment.'"

Tuesday, September 7, 1520 hours
10 kilometres south of St. Laurent

Tommy reached for his radio handset. "One, this is Toques. Orders. Over."

"One. Send. Over."

"Toques. I want you to move forward cautiously along the beach road and then into the north side of the village. The militia are mostly gone. You round up the rest, treat the wounded, and hold any prisoners—officers in the RCMP lockup, everyone else in the school gym. You're to hold the town as we move on. A follow-on unit will arrive in the early evening. You brief the incoming commander, then join us. Call once you're in contact with the follow-on guys, then call me again for directions once their commander is ready to take charge. Over."

"One, roger. Out."

"All stations, Toques. We're moving on. Reorg your people and bring up the vehicles. O'Reilly, take what's left of your recce troop and get out on the right flank, west of Highway 6, and watch for that RCMP unit that's supposed to be there.

"The rest of us, Two Platoon leading followed by me and then Three Platoon, we'll get down Highway 6 and keep going past Warren. If we get fire from the RCMP off on the right, we'll just cut to east off the highway and keep going. When we get to Grosse Isle on 6, a slight change of plans—we're going to Stony Mountain to bang on the door. Over."

No one answered immediately, then after several seconds Toques' senior platoon commander buzzed into the radio. "Toques, what about Warren? We were supposed to go there and stop. Why Stony Mountain? Over."

Radio procedure fell away. "Change of orders. These are my orders. Our people are locked in that place and we're getting them out first. I've got it organized from the inside. We can't risk the bad guys using it as a rallying point so we're taking it. Everyone do as I ordered and we'll be in and out and back in Warren, and in Stonewall, in a few hours. Anyone not willing to do as I asked can sit it out until later."

"What about the colonel, does he know about this plan?"

"Gerry, you leave the colonel to me. Are you going or sitting?" The radio hummed to itself, unconcerned with the discussion at hand.

"Toques, Gerry. I'm in, moving now. See you at Stony Mountain. Besides, I haven't visited that no good father-in-law of mine for years. Guess I'll just go to his cell and say hello. Out."

The other commanders acknowledged their orders one by one, partly because they trusted Tommy but mostly because of their deep, unspoken reluctance to break the bond of loyalty that held the unit together. Their decision wasn't about the mission, or the colonel, or the Movement, it was about belonging and holding tightly to their buddies. It was the Three Musketeers thing, though none of them had ever heard of the strange French cavaliers or their universal soldier's pledge.

Tuesday September 7, 1610 hours
On Highway 6 south of St. Laurent

Crisis past, Twoskins took out his cellphone and punched in a number. Three rings and a rough response. "Yeah, who's this?"

"Toques! Get me Fred. Now!"

Silence, harsh voices in the background, then, "Fred here. What's up?"

"I'm thirty minutes from your location. What's the situation there? Are things going mostly according to our agreement?"

"Yeah," Fred lied. "Things are going surprisingly good. Your info was right on. So we're in the yard, in the pen and in Rockwood yard, too. The guards who were on duty inside are locked up. The warden is trying to negotiate, and the other guards are on the walls and outside trying to hold things together, but they're shit scared. They know the Mounties and the army can't help them. So now what? When are we getting out?"

"You'll get out when I let you out. Here are the rules again. You separate the natives, all of them—don't give me any of your 'our gang only shit.' You put the gang members in the yards and keep control of the prison from the inside. You put the whites and others in their cells—keep out only those who are useful or trusted buddies. You harm no one. Believe me, we'll shoot anyone who gets rough. There's to be no revenge. Got it?"

"Yeah, sure. Like lambs. Beside, if you're serious, no one's going to risk a chance to get out by punching a stupid guard."

"We're serious. So you make sure the guys stay in line or you're the first back in cells when we arrive and the guards can have you. Where's my brother?"

"He's safe," Fred lied again. "He's in the yard here, sitting by the wall quiet as can be. That's one real little leader, your brother. A few more years in here and he'd have taken my job. Anyway, I'm controlling the cell bosses in the yard. They're separating the natives and the gangs and putting the guards out of harm's way, just like you said. So, when are we going out and then what?"

"You'll be out before morning if all goes well. Screw with me and you're not getting out. I'll make a deal with the warden. Once you're out, you're going to work for us. Remember, and tell your guys, my warriors aren't working to the justice system rules. Everybody gets one chance to follow orders, but there's no parole, no Club Med here. Stand by for orders and keep things quiet and calm inside."

"Right you are, brother. You're the boss."

"Partly right, Fred. I am the boss. But I'm not your brother." Toques clicked off the phone.

Tuesday, September 7, 1610 hours
Ottawa: CANCOMOPS

"Colonel Pew, there's a strange movement by the Highway 6 convoy. Looks like they're turning off the road and heading east." The duty officer flashed his laser pointer at the display. "There's one small group of vehicles here in the north; another larger unit, a couple of platoons I'd say, here on 6; another bunch here—look they're just turning east now too, at Grosse Isle."

"Strange." Nick watched the display as the little red computer-generated squares traced the units in the convoy. "They're going for what, Selkirk? We had them pegged for Warren, then the Perimeter Highway. It's wide open. Why would they expose their flank? There's nothing else over there, except…" His stomach cramped. "Bastards! Stony Mountain! OPS, flash up that TV report from a couple of hours ago. The one about a 'disturbance at Stony Mountain.' Shit, that's all we need."

Pew and his duty ops officer watched the rerun: "… disturbance, guards in trouble, warden negotiating, asking for help, but 'no cause for alarm in surrounding communities' as the prisoners seem content to remain inside."

"Okay, get me the warden and the RCMP deputy commissioner in Winnipeg. And have someone flash up the assistance-to-civil-authority plan for the prison. We need some maps and details, pronto."

Tuesday, September 7, 1615 hours
Winnipeg: Winnipeg International Airport

"Toques, Stevenson. Send me a sitrep. Are you approaching Warren? I want patrols on the Perimeter Highway by dark if you can. Over."

No response.

The colonel turned to his ops officer and the technicians tracing the called-in locations of the units flowing south on the wall maps. "Where's the Cree column?"

"It's supposed to be here, approaching Warren, sir, but I haven't heard anything from Toques. He could be moving too quickly and nothing might be happening, nothing to report."

"You know better than that!" Stevenson snapped. "Don't guess, find out. Start by trying to get him on the radio."

After several calls the duty officer flashed a thumbs-up and clicked on the speaker phone on the table near the wall map. "Toques, Stevenson. Why haven't you reported Warren yet? What's holding you up? Over." A noticeable pause followed and the technician reached to fiddle with the radio dials, but Stevenson brushed his arm away. "It's not the radio."

"Toques!" the colonel demanded once more.

"Sorry, colonel," came the reply at last. "Change of plans. I'm clear of Warren, but I have other business in the area and I'm taking my units to take care of it now."

Stevenson, his orders and authority openly challenged and his whole plan in sudden jeopardy, paused and then coldly, quietly asked: "What other business, son? Talk to me. We've come a long way to chance losing it all now."

"I'm going to take the natives out of Stony Mountain, that's my other business. Colonel, I owe you an apology. You know I'm committed to the Movement and its grand plan, but I have a chance to get my brother out of prison—he shouldn't be there and every lawyer we talked to on both sides knows it. So we're going to secure an extra strong point, pick up some more very determined people, and while I'm at it, right a wrong. It's part of our tradition for a man to look after his family, sir, and I'm the head of my family."

"Well, Tommy, that's a great letdown, especially that you lied to me. But, okay, what do you plan to do? Perhaps we can salvage something here."

"I made arrangements of a sort a year ago with the native gang leaders on the inside to stage a big prison bust. I didn't let them know what you were up to, but I just made, you know, a kind of informal side-order. It worked; the prisoners are in charge of Stony, and Rockwood as well, so now I'm going to convince the warden and the other guards to open the gates. Then the native prisoners, no one else, will walk out. The deal is that they, under their own leaders and in their own gangs, will more or less act as auxiliaries for my column, stand guard on the road, and so on. They're not trained soldiers but they're harder than the mob following us in buses."

"Son, why would the warden and the guards agree to open the gates without a fight?"

"Several reasons, sir. First of all, they've lost control of the situation and they'll rightly leave it to the RCMP and the military to restore control rather than have us attack from outside and get a lot of people killed, mostly them. Second, they'll open the gates immediately when I tell the warden I have his family in custody. Third, the guards will do whatever the warden says once they hear their kids and wives on the phone. We're rounding them up now. I trained what I called 'special detachments'; they moved south a week before the big advance and got near their targets. We had them pegged months ago. It was easy to confirm where everyone lived near the prison and in Winnipeg—get a list of union members and click into 411.com and, presto, an address list.

"No one's going to get hurt. I'll take the prisoners out, clear the site, lock the doors, and then we're back on the plan."

Stevenson groped for words. "Tommy, Tommy, think what you're saying. Those natives in prison are no good, you know that. They're mostly gang members. You can't make soldiers out of them. Put them back in the population and they'll just prey on other natives. Put them on guard duty and they'll start raping and killing whites.

"Look, here's another idea. Give me time to speak with the Mounties and the warden, and maybe we can arrange to get your brother out in return for keeping the others inside. Molly has a plan to review every case of every native in prison and then go from there—in native courts, Tommy, real courts, with real justice. We can make it work."

"Maybe you can, colonel. But what if the feds come back and beat us before I get him out, then what? We can't sit around here while the white man talks us to death."

"All I'm asking for is a chance to try another way. Give me a couple of hours. Put your platoons in position, make a demonstration—don't hurt anyone—and I'll see what can be done. But I want you to put a platoon on

Highway 6 at Warren right now and send a small patrol to the Perimeter Highway to link up with the southern units. Will you do that?"

Tommy Twoskins hesitated. Loyalty and honour and his word to free his people from history's abuses scraped across loyalty and honour and his word to his mother to free her son from Stony Mountain. "I'll give you two hours, colonel, then I'll take the prison. You can tell the warden that I've got three mortars and enough ammo to blow the walls down. I'll put the patrols out as you asked, and when the deal's done, I'll pass command to O'Reilly Keith, my recce commander; he's best suited for the rest of the mission."

"Okay Tommy, deal. Watch your back. And don't trust the gang leaders, not for anything."

Tuesday, September 7, 1630 hours
Inside Stony Mountain Penitentiary

Big Fred put away his cellphone and turned to his warrior companions— his range leaders and enforcers. The competition, the prison leader of the Winnipeg Posse, Eddy Paul, stood to the side warily, waiting to see what Fred had to offer.

"Okay, here's the deal. Twoskins and his gang have the Mounties and the army on the run, but it seems they need more guys. That's us. He's going stage a break-in..."

"Nobody's tried that since I've been here."

"Ya, well if you don't keep your mouth shut, I'm going to leave you here, Mike. Like I was saying, he's coming in and we're to help, but nicely. So that's what we'll do—until we get the keys. Paul, we need a truce. If we're going to pull this off, we can't be fighting each other. Deal?"

"Ya, sure, so long as my guys work for me and we keep our side of the pen and the yards and, you know, we all get out too. After we get out, the truce ends."

"Oh, well, look fellows. Eddy Paul, still the same big man BS. Look, do you want in on this or you want to blow your mouth off? Anyway, in or out, the thing's happening. My people are rounding up the white prisoners who aren't in the gangs and locking them in the cells. We have a bunch of the guards holed up on the ranges and in their lockdown areas. But the yard is ours and so are the main areas here and in Rockwood too. I want you, Jerry, to take some brothers and get to the weapons lockup, bring a couple of the guards and the guns we took from them with you, and tell the others we'll shoot their buddies unless they open up. Got it?"

"Ya, sure."

"Okay, where's that little shit Twoskins? He's our ticket out of here."

It was the Warrior Posse leader's turn to drive a bargain. "We have him. Thought he might come in useful sometime today, so we snatched him in the exercise yard at noon."

Fred grabbed Eddy by the shirt. "You snatched him, you bastard. He's mine. Where is he?"

"Well, that's the problem, Fred. We had him and the yard guards came running, and in the scuffle, they grabbed him and took him away."

Fred scoffed. "Real tough warriors you are."

"Hey, they had their shotguns out. So they took him away, they said for insurance. He's not far, we have them cornered. They locked themselves behind the security fence near the main block, but they can't go anywhere. Our guys control the yard and the block.

"So Fred, here's the real deal. We'll get the Twoskins kid whenever we want and we'll hold him as our insurance. Soon as we're out, you can have him and trade him with his brother or the police, I could care less. Oh, and I want a fair share of the guns for my people too."

Fred tramped the ground and pushed Eddy across the yard. "You little prickhead Métis bastard. You hurt that do-gooder wimp and the whole thing goes down the drain. That happens and I'll personally cut your throat for starters. So you had better get over there and make sure he's safe, and tell the guards if they get careless, we'll grab their girlfriends and share them with our friends in here."

Eddy walked away. "Let me know when to deliver the prize, Fred, all gift wrapped. Outside the gates, of course."

After Eddy Paul had pushed through Fred's gang leaders, Fred turned to more immediate things. "There's a shiv in that prick's future, I guarantee that. The rest of you, get moving and round up the boys. Johnnie, you make sure we keep a close watch on the warden and see he stays in his office. I have some business with our guys on the outside. If the guards don't want to cooperate, we have some homes here and in Winnipeg to visit later this afternoon. The rest of you, stay cool, got it?"

Tuesday, September 7, 1640 hours
Ottawa

In Ottawa, in the midst of the accelerating disorder, events gradually slipped away from the government's hands. A torrent of disconnected pieces of information tumbled through the prime minister's office. Ministers, bureaucrats, politicians, and party hacks stormed the Langevin Block, demanding decisions and pushing advice. Decisions fell far behind events. No choice, no pronouncement was secure from assault by new facts and issues. "Order, counter-order, and confusion" ruled the bureaucracy.

The best officials could do was to try to summarize for their leaders the course of events and find resources to match demands. But Molly's strategy provided no respite for anyone. No government had anticipated such a calamity, and none, therefore, bothered to provide for it. There was nowhere a national security plan, a functioning modern operations centre, or a cadre of officials trained for the inevitable day when the country would need clearheaded thinking in an emergency. An expectation of reasonableness in all circumstances was the policy. Hopefulness was the plan.

Tuesday, September 7, 1700 hours
Ottawa, CANCOMOPS

Colonel Nick Pew busily verified the command's situation report due to be sent to NDHQ that evening. He scanned the brief operational paragraphs:

Op Quebec: Situation in Montreal and Quebec City and other major cities is under control; CF units are preparing to hand over responsibilities to the SQ and to deploy into the province to suppress disturbances in the outlying areas. Major efforts are underway to take control of Kahnewake and Akwesasne. Movement of battle group on Hwy 109 is delayed and slow due to enemy actions and obstacles.

Op Radisson: SSR is in control of the Hydro facilities and outskirts of Radisson. Road Radisson-Chisasibi is closed due to enemy actions. Contact in all areas is moderate. Facilities are inoperable and transmission lines in all areas are down or otherwise inoperable. Expected date/time for opening of facilities unknown. Link-up with Hwy 109 battle group expected within the week.

USA comment: The senior American military attaché in Ottawa reports that "his superiors are under increasing pressure to encourage the CF to move quickly to clear the Hydro facilities." He reports also that conditions on eastern seaboard of U.S. "are critical, hospitals and other public facilities are failing due to lack of reliable power and cities are dangerous with significant criminal activities increasing every evening due to lack of lights, etc."

Op WestCan: Major operations to begin today to halt/delay Hwy 6 advance on Wpg. Detailed sitrep to follow after engagements expected this afternoon. Wpg is not secure.

Commander's Comment: Units engaged in *Op Quebec/Radisson* in need of replenishment and relief in the line. I have no reserves should the enemy initiate operations in other areas. Disengagement of deployed units and formations would be difficult and slow. In the West, attempts to halt the columns advancing out of the north in all areas are dangerously slow. Ops this day and tomorrow in Wpg and in the outlying regions will be critical indicators of future success. I cannot assure protection of local populations or vital national transportation routes or energy infrastructures across the West or around Lake Superior.

Tuesday, September 7, 1710 hours
Washington: The White House
The National Security Council

President Ricardo looked up from her briefing note and across the table to Murray Segal. "This is incredible. Are you telling me that the entire nation, Canada, is coming apart at the seams?"

"Well, that seems to be the case. All the indicators we have suggest that the Canadian government has or is in the process of losing control over large regions of the country. Of special concern to the United States is the reliable delivery of natural gas, petroleum, and electrical power. We, of course, depend on the extensive trade networks we have between the countries and, thus, any serious disruption there is going to disrupt our economy."

"Thanks, Murray. Ambassador Laforge, glad we could get you down here from Ottawa on short notice. What's your assessment of the Canadian government's mood? Has Prime Minister Hemp got a grip on the situation?"

"Madam President, I would recommend that we stand on the side of caution in this matter. I do not have confidence in the prime minister's ability to manage this national emergency to a successful, peaceful outcome. The machinery of government in Ottawa is creaking under the strain of this very widespread attack by the so-called Native People's Movement.

"These events are particularly difficult when the country has over the last ten years or so become so fragmented—provinces battling Ottawa, separatists in the West and in Quebec, and in Newfoundland, all sparring for an advantage. As one columnist in a major newspaper commented some time ago, 'If there is nothing tearing us apart, there is nothing gluing us together either.' Well, I have to say that now there is a very serious native rebellion effectively tearing Canada apart.

"Madam President, my advice to you is to take care of America's interests first. If the Canadians can pull it together at the last moment, well, fine. I would not, however, bet our welfare on such an unlikely future."

"Thank you, James. General Leonardo?

"I agree with Ambassador Laforge, Madam President. The matter is clearly running against the Canadian government. Their armed forces are too small, not to mention the fact that they are recklessly scattered worldwide, to overcome this attack, and their police forces are likewise incapable of recovering the situation outside of a couple of major cities, perhaps. If the native columns referred to in your briefing note move on to the transportation lines and into the energy-producing areas as seems likely now, then our vital interests will be threatened.

"I believe Murray has informed you that I have spoken informally and in secret with General Bishop ..."

"Yes, I am aware of these conversations and approved them."

"Thank you. My information is that the Canadian Forces are so deeply committed to the defence of the eastern areas of the country and trying to recover the James Bay facilities that they cannot effectively defend the vast, open transportation and energy system the ambassador mentioned. I concur in that assessment.

"Furthermore, Madam President, I believe that there is little time left for the Canadians to reverse the situation. My assessment is that the native columns—very large numbers of people—will be in position in the next few days to intercept and disrupt the flow of vital commodities into the United States."

President Ricardo sat quietly for a moment, glancing through her notes. She looked up. "General Leonardo, do you have ready the requisite forces to secure the national resources that flow into the United States and to protect them from harm?"

"Yes, Madam President, we have adequate forces for such a mission. Senior commanders have been alerted to the situation in Canada and its consequences for our national security, and they have at my direction taken a number of preliminary steps as a result. We would need a few days to bring their formations and units to the final stage of readiness."

"Your NSC note mentions some of the insurgent leaders. What do we know about this Molly Grace person?"

Gene Tedder, the director of the FBI spoke up. "We know very little about the native movement in Canada and only pay attention to their leaders when we find them in communication with our home-grown native radicals. We have very little on Molly Grace, a person who has drifted in and out of our files.

"We first noted her some years ago when she entered the United States from Canada on a student visa—claiming to come from a native reserve in southwestern Alberta. Nothing really unusual in that visa application. She travelled to Chicago and began a graduate degree in economics, and then switched to Afro-American studies, at which time she became involved with university politics. We began a file on her, but then she simply vanished before completing her degree. We picked her up again in Nevada in the company of one Hector Diaz, a defrocked Catholic priest working among local native bands."

"Is he American or is he one of those so-called liberation priests from South America?"

"Madam President, we believe he's a native Mexican. According to church reports, he was excommunicated for 'preaching sedition' in indigenous communities in southern Mexico. He was also accused of preaching that ..." Tedder checked his notes. "... the 'white man's version of God is a false God' and then he went about ordaining female aboriginal priests on his own hook."

"Yes, indeed. That'll get you the boot in my church. What's the connection to Grace?"

"Well, they seemed to travel together for some time, and then they both disappeared. We understand from reliable Mexican sources that Diaz was abducted and taken to Mexico. We assume he was murdered there, on whose orders we don't know. About the same time, Grace vanished, and the next information we have on her is some sketchy references from Canadian security authorities. But we had no reason to be much interested in her at that time."

"Thank you, Gene, that was useful. Right, ladies and gentlemen, my directions to you are these: Ambassador Laforge, please join the secretary of state and draft a statement on the Canadian situation and the growing international and UN reaction to it for use by my office. We'll need a policy position soon, I suspect. James, I want you to then return to Ottawa and send me a detailed update on the stability of the Canadian government. Stand-by for instructions I intend to issue tomorrow or soon thereafter.

"General Leonardo, please continue your conversations with the Canadian commanders. I believe we have certain options open to us under the Defence of North America Agreement and we should explore these carefully. You will continue to provide the support you have already provided to the Canadians, but no more than that for now.

"Murray Segal will begin immediately, with your assistance and advice, to draw up a draft Presidential Directive which will include actionable options for my consideration. We will continue to assess this dreadful situation overnight. However, we will decide on a definite course of action to defend America's national interests. The Canadians will eventually have to fend for themselves; they're not my concern, thank heavens.

"We will reconvene when the directive is ready for review. Thank you all for your advice and candour."

Tuesday, September 7, 1820 hours
Ottawa: CANCOMOPS

"General Lepine, sir, it's RCMP Deputy Commissioner Bill Garry in Winnipeg on line two."

Lepine picked up the phone. "Yes, hello, Bill. So what's the situation at the prison?" He paused, then Nick Pew heard him say, "I see. How many hostages are they holding? Are we certain? Yes, dreadful. We can't have hundreds of armed criminals out on the street." Another pause, "Stevenson called you ... Really! How did he find you? Of course, dumb question on my part. I expect he has all our numbers. What's his deal?"

Lepine listened intently, jotting down notes in his nearly illegible handwriting. "Well, that sounds reasonable in the circumstances and about what I would expect from Sam Stevenson. I mean, he can't be behind a plan to let these dangerous people out on the street. If we can resolve this prison problem by simply releasing someone's brother, why not do it? So you arranged a conversation between the warden and Stevenson—under some kind of truce, I suppose? How did that go?"

Pew saw Lepine rise slowly from the table, his free hand clenching into a white-knuckled fist. "Oh my God! Just what we need: another stupid act, especially when so many people are in danger. Does Stevenson know yet? Perhaps we should try to cover it up, play for time." He slammed his fist on the table. "They did what? Those irresponsible damn assholes. Yes, you try to placate Stevenson and keep the line to him open. I'll see if there is anything Ottawa can do, but I think we just provided an excuse the radicals will jump on to inflame the entire Prairies. Doesn't anyone understand that we have hundreds, maybe thousands, of natives coming south, and no one, not Molly Grace, not the federal government, no one, is in control of this situation?" He paused again, his face flushed with anger. "Sure, Bill. We'll be in touch as soon as we have any news. Thanks." Lepine passed the telephone receiver to the corporal standing by the desk.

Nick Pew looked at his commander. "More trouble, sir?"

"Incredible trouble, Nick. The natives took several of the Stony Mountain penitentiary guards' families hostage. Some of them got roughed up in the process—not seriously, thankfully. But word got back by cellphone to the guards in the prison. They know Tommy Twoskins is one of the native leaders. It's been all over the news all day, and the guards know his kid brother's in Stony Mountain.

"So, at the first sign of trouble they took the kid brother out of his cell and hid him, and when they found out their families were hostages, they tried to use young Twoskins as a hostage to get themselves out and get to their homes. Somebody got stupid, a prison yard riot broke out, fighting between guards and prisoners and between white prisoners and natives.

"It got ugly, sticks and knives, some serious injuries. At some point, the guards holding Twoskins' brother took him into a secure part of the yard behind some locked gates, apparently to negotiate their own release. Well, things went badly and a bunch of native prisoners tried to break down the gates to get at Twoskins; in the confusion, a couple of guards shot him. One story is they stood him against the wall and executed him. Who knows? Maybe they did.

"At that point, the rioting went totally nuts. Guards on the wall started shooting, some of the guards captured in the yard were killed and scalped. All that happened more than an hour ago. The warden tried to keep the killings quiet, but someone called the 'breaking news' program at the CBC—and those jerks just broadcast the horror to the world about five minutes ago."

"Sir," Nick began, "we've got more than the hostages at Stony Mountain to worry about. Christ, we've got hundreds of unprotected citizens on farms and villages in the path of the native mob coming out of the north—" A duty officer interrupted Nick and his commander.

"Sorry, sir, an urgent message. Our special ops patrols near Stonewall report heavy weapons fire from the area of Stony Mountain. They're all reporting mortar fire and rounds impacting inside the prison walls. The natives are shooting the guards off the walls. They say the prison's burning. The Stonewall patrol reports several natives in trucks attacking and burning houses and stores and cars all around the prison. They want to know what orders, sir?"

Nick Pew turned to René Lepine. "Sir?"

Lepine shrugged. "How should I answer anyone? We could have talked our way out of this situation. But no. Not us. Nick, tell the special ops leaders to take out those mortars immediately. They're to use whatever means they think appropriate. Have we got anything else in the area? Are the CF18s still in the air?"

"Yes, sir. There's a combat patrol—four aircraft—in the vicinity, fully armed, of course." Nick hesitated. "Orders, sir?

"Get the CDS on the secure line and confirm our contact with the aircraft."

DAY ELEVEN

Wednesday, September 8

Wednesday, September 8, 0634 hours
On Highway 109 to Radisson

Nature joined in the struggle against the units pushing north towards Radisson from Matagami to rescue the airborne units and restore the generating stations. As Will Boucanier had anticipated, the battle group deployed from Valcartier was at the moment strung out along Highway 109 between Matagami and the Rupert River, and found themselves fighting bugs, swollen rivers, and tight country, as well as small native ambush units and saboteurs the whole way along the two-lane road.

Lieutenant Colonel Marc Leblanc was sitting in the rear hatch of his command post checking maps and reports when he spied Jim Willis from *The Metro Star* walking towards him, recorder in hand. Marc wasn't a fan of embedded journalists. He had to admit most of those he'd encountered in the field during his tours in Afghanistan and Zimbabwe had tried to be fair. But too often their bosses demanded "balanced" reports, which meant interviewing the usual self-anointed "experts" who made a living criticizing and second-guessing whatever officers at headquarters said and whatever the troops in the field were doing.

So far as Marc could see, the media and these experts were in bed together—both thrived on controversy, real or invented. The more outrageous the expert's opinion, the more often he was interviewed, enhancing his usefulness to reporters and leading to even more interviews. Reporters cultivated these easy sources, who knew why they were being interviewed, and publishers and broadcasters were thus assured of that day's controversial headlines, the lure that sells television news and newspapers.

There was, the colonel had noticed, no balanced investigation of that phenomenon in the daily press. Willis had bluntly explained the facts of life to Marc a few days earlier over a ration-box lunch at the side of the road, ironically specifying that he was doing so "off-the-record."

"It's like this," he said. "We know that everyone in government spins his story and that a lot of real experts, especially academics, are too, ah … measured and too long-winded to give us some headline-grabbing quote. So we go …" Willis made quotation marks in the air. "… for 'balance' to someone from an impressive institution or, failing that, an institution with an impressive-sounding name, to give us something quotable. I have to pay the mortgage at the end of the month, too, you know."

The conversation hadn't improved Leblanc's opinion of the press or the usefulness of trying to explain things to reporters. But he'd promised Willis an on-the-record interview the night before; it was part of his job in the modern army, so he resigned himself to repeating what they'd talked about earlier in the week, but with more care and a good deal less bluntness. He greeted the journalist civilly and Willis settled into the folding chair next to the young commander, clicked on his recorder, and flipped open his notepad. "Okay, all yours. Why don't you tell me what you're doing here and we can go from there?"

"Okay, from the top. My mission is to relieve the parachute companies, secure Radisson, and open the road to Chisasibi. Once that's accomplished, then the SQ and Hydro-Québec will get the power running. It's a fine, simple plan. We drive up the road, break through the native lines near Radisson, and take back the area.

"I command the battle group composed of my own First Battalion of the Royal 22e Régiment—that's the Van Doos to your readers—plus a squadron of combat engineers and a heavy mortar platoon, all mounted in various versions of the CF standard LAV III—that's Light Armoured Vehicle; as you can see here, they have tires, not tank treads—plus an armoured recce squadron, uh, reconnaissance squadron, and we also have four helicopters on call deployed on local airfields along the way."

"Tell us something about the operation itself," Willis said. "There's not much room to manoeuvre here, and the enemy are, as your soldiers say, 'just a bunch of Indians with guns,' so for professional soldiers this must be a rather straightforward operation, no?"

Leblanc set his map-case aside. "Well, the reality is different. And first let me say that nobody here has referred to the enemy as 'just a bunch of Indians with guns.' We are dealing with armed insurgents challenging the fundamental authority of the government of Canada. Second, my troops are dedicated, highly trained professionals, but we're on a bush-covered road which restricts our movement and in some ways affects the functioning of our high-tech instruments and weapons. Also, we're strung out in one big snaking column and the bad guys have the initiative—they can strike at any part of the column they choose and we can't crawl along protecting everything or we're not going to get to Radisson before it's too late. So this is a difficult mission.

"Our column has encountered determined opposition ever since we left the assembly area at Matagami. Sniping from the woods, scattered roadblocks, and real and suspected IEDs—that's improvised explosive devices or, if you prefer, homemade land mines—have slowed our advance to a few dozen kilometres a day. Movement at night—movement by the main body I mean—though possible, rapidly proved sufficiently dangerous that I restricted night ops to aggressive patrols out ahead of the next day's advance. The column itself advances only in daylight."

"Colonel, what are the tactics you use when you hit a roadblock or some such obstacle?"

"Well, at each obstacle, infantry sections dismount from their LAV IIIs and with the aid of combat engineers, check, clear, and secure the area. Then the battle group moves on. It's standard procedure but it's slow, basically a leapfrogging exercise—move forward, encounter the obstacle, conduct the obstacle drill, clear the way, then shove the next company forward to do it over again a few kilometres up the highway."

"I've noticed a lot of helicopters buzzing around. Are they armed and what are their orders?"

"I'm not going to tell you their exact orders, you understand. But I can tell you they're not just doing reconnaissance. We were initially trying to unsettle the rebels and gain some speed and surprise by sending infantry sections forward in helicopters—three-dimensional warfare, if you will. But after two instances where helicopters were fired upon and one returned smoking from gunshots, I abandoned the tactic as too dangerous and not very useful in any case. We'll give it another go once we get clear of this bush country. But we are not engaged in indiscriminate firing that might endanger non-combatants, even in this sparsely inhabited region, a restriction that I might add does not affect our adversaries."

"So are you winning, can you get up the road to save Radisson and the Hydro facilities?"

"Let me explain the results so far. My soldiers have surprised some saboteurs on the roads and around transmission towers, and killed one or two. We've also killed a couple of snipers and captured several more. But this is truly a 'war in the shadows.' The kind of guerrilla war you hear about but never thought would come to Canada. I'll tell you frankly, Jim, most of the local residents are at best neutral and it's increasingly difficult to identify the bad guys. Our adversaries almost always have the initiative, as I said, and we have suffered casualties. My guys are edgy as a result, and we've had to emphasize the ROEs—the rules of engagement—to prevent us shooting friendlies, uh, civilians to you civilians."

"Colonel, I spoke with Mr. Steve Sapp of the Elgin Institute in Ottawa. He says you personally and your soldiers might be charged with war crimes if this mission turns into, in his words, 'another Afghanistan detainee crisis.' His research, he says, indicates that five out of every ten soldiers on this mission are poorly trained and experts don't think they are qualified to deal with this kind of warfare."

Leblanc forced a smile and repressed a strong impulse to tell him what he thought about Sapp's so-called "research."

"I don't know the man, and he's free to say what he likes and make up what he likes. But I hope you asked for the data on which he based that assessment, if he even has any, and that you interviewed some other 'experts' on the subject of Canadian Forces training and discipline, and on international law, so you could verify his story before your editor gives Sapp another free ride into your paper."

"So you deny that your soldiers are ill-prepared?"

"Yes, I damn well do. My soldiers are fine professionals and I'm proud to command them; furthermore, they're a lot better prepared for their duties and a lot more responsible than some so-called expert prattling about this operation from the safety of some Ottawa office. And you can quote me on that. Maybe someone should invite Mr. Sapp to come up here and help us clear some IEDs under hostile fire and see how he likes it." Leblanc winced. He shouldn't have said that. Then again, he reflected, why not? Let the man come.

"Colonel," Willis went on, "you and other commanders were criticized yesterday by opposition politicians and the 'politics' crowd on the television shows for, and I quote, 'moving too slowly.' What do you say to that?"

"Well, the people on those shows are, in my opinion, talking as usual about the politics of the situation and not the actual situation. I appreciate that you came here to actually investigate the situation before you decided we're moving too quickly or too slowly. This is not Hollywood.

"My objective is the Radisson area and the generating station, but the generating station without secure transmission lines is of little real use to anyone. The area near the road giving access to the transmission system is key to winning control in this situation. And control means neutralizing as many insurgents as possible along the way.

"Some kind of helicopter assault directly into Radisson is simply out of the question because the Canadian Forces has no such capability—'too expensive,' said successive governments. And again, anyone who thinks we're moving too slowly can come up here and walk over a possibly mined area to let us know if—"

An urgent voice from inside the vehicle interrupted the colonel. "Sir, contact. Suspected IED. They're investigating now." The senior duty officer inside the command post pointed to the danger on his map.

"Okay. Keep me informed. Sorry, Jim, it's been a pleasure, but as you heard, I've got to go to work... later perhaps."

"Sure thing. Thanks, colonel. Mind if I make my way forward to see what's up at the obstacle?"

"Nope, go ahead. Keeping your body parts connected isn't my concern." Leblanc paused and stood up. "Sorry, Jim. Guess I'm getting rude in my old age. Actually, I appreciate your willingness to go take a look; it'll help you tell the real story to Canadians. Better grab your protective gear, though."

Wednesday, September 8, 0743 hours
4 kilometres forward along Highway 109

Warrant Officer Daniel Dubras, leading an engineer recce section in the battle group's vanguard, stopped to check a large water-filled culvert running under the road. He slid carefully down the east side of the ditch, looking out for anti-personnel mines as he went. Master Corporal Jean Granville followed his boss several metres behind, out of range of a mine blast...he hoped. "One man, one mine," was the rule.

Dubras checked the exterior of the culvert on one side for signs of buried wires, recent digging, or grass and bushes disturbed by an intruder. Then he approached the edge of the shallow, fast-flowing stream cautiously, shaded his eyes, and stared into the iron-coloured water. He grunted non-committally, then waved to Granville. "Jean, grab my arm and hold on while I try to take a look into the culvert." The corporal took his left arm and Dubras took a couple of careful steps, then called over his shoulder as he slid sideways in the loose gravel beside the stream. "That's it. Whoa, hang on now. Don't you drop me in the cold fucking water or I'll kick your ass all the way up the road to Radisson."

Jean smiled. "It's tempting, Warrant, but have no fear, I've got you safe and sound."

"You better," Dubras grunted, then turned his head to look up the culvert. As his eyes slowly adjusted to the dim interior he saw on the water a small raft loaded with explosives floating near the centre of the culvert, long wires hanging in the water down to the streambed below.

"Aw shit..." he said, just as the first explosion blew the culvert to pieces, tearing a hole ten metres wide through the middle of the road. Chunks of tarmac, twisted metal fragments, rocks and debris rained down for a hundred metres around the site while dirt and water shot out of both ends of the culvert, stripping nearby bushes of limbs and leaves. When the debris settled, there was no sign of Dubras or his corporal.

Seconds later, the next explosion blew a gaping hole in the large beaver dam fifty metres away, deep in the bush off the right side of the road, sending a muddy brown wave six feet high down the streambed into the wreckage that had been the culvert and roadway. The wall of water tore away gravel from under the remains of the road, causing more of the tarmac to collapse into the stream. In a few minutes, a small lake several feet deep covered the whole area where Granville and Dubras had died.

Slowly, people in the vanguard picked themselves up off the ground or stumbled from their mud-spattered vehicles. The recce section commander, Captain Gilles Morin, his ears ringing, sprinted up the road looking for his engineers while the supporting infantry section ahead of him, recovering fast, reversed their LAV IIIs into cover and opened fire on the bush on both sides of the road around the crater. The section leader waved his riflemen forward, but away from the immediate area of the explosion.

Morin grabbed his signaller. "Gimme the radio, son. Zero, this is two. Contact. Grid reference zero, two niner—six, one, five. Roadblock and explosion. Road cratered and flooded. Two friendlies likely KIA. No enemy. Moving to secure the area. Over."

"Zero. Roger," came the command post's even reply. "Helicopter bravo four three on the way. ETA, three minutes. Out."

Jim Willis, who had wandered up to the scene, was himself grabbed by the section leader and shoved unceremoniously to the ground. "Get down, you idiot! We don't know what's out there. They might have planted a second IED to get the rescuers. Got a wish to be sent home in a body bag?"

Thirty minutes later the area was secure. Foot patrols were past the crater and searching the wood-line for possible bombers or snipers aiming to attack the engineers once they started repairing the road. It was a standard tactic in all such cases, and in this case Morin and his engineer commander had concluded that the mine in question, a large one, wasn't on a tripwire but had been command-detonated, probably by someone using a cellphone and hiding nearby watching the column approach. Perhaps they had hoped a vehicle would be on top of the culvert when they blew the charges, and changed their plan when it looked like Dubras would find their trap. No matter. It had done its deadly work, and delayed the rescue operation again.

Captain Morin was sure about a couple of things. This was no backwoods *habitant* with a few sticks of dynamite. The guys who built this trap were highly skilled and clever. His engineer's guess was that the explosives had been high-grade *plastique*, with the detonating cord and fuses expertly knitted together and timed on some type of ring-main so the two explosives would support each other with only one command from the bomber. They had floated the charges down the stream so as not to disturb the grass and soil around the culvert, but still get it in the middle of the road. "Sir," the engineer sergeant said, "this wasn't the work of your average rebel. Whoever did this was special forces trained for sure."

As Lieutenant Colonel Leblanc walked up to the site, a young soldier, pale and shaking, approached him and held out a helmet. "That's it, sir. That's all we can find on this side of the road."

"That's okay, Gagnon. You just leave the helmet here and go over and talk with your buddies. We'll get the guys who did this." That was feeble, Leblanc told himself as the kid wandered off.

He looked at his engineer, who waited until the kid was gone then said, "We found two boots over there, sir. Both left feet. I called it in as two KIAs. The follow-on sections will police up the area for the bodies once the water drops."

"Okay, Gilles. Let me know. We're moving on as soon as you can rig a span across the good section of the road on the left there."

Two hours later, the column resumed its hide-and-seek run up the road to Radisson. Contact was sporadic but persistent. Obviously, the enemy's game was to keep the battle group on edge and slow its move to Radisson. And it was working.

The Van Doos were mine-wary, pissed off, and tired, a bad combination at any time, but especially so when soldiers are working among civilian populations. Roadblocks and snipers continued to harass the column. IEDs and mines set off behind the vanguard and between sub-units in the main body split the column into ragged bunches of vehicles and men, trapped on or near the road, fighting small, brief battles on their own against an enemy who vanished infuriatingly whenever riflemen deployed to hunt them. This, Leblanc reflected grimly, was not the time or place for a gun-toting moose hunter to wander dopily onto the road. Given the unit's mood, he'd likely end up as road-kill.

Wednesday, September 8, 0850 hours
On the outskirts of Radisson

Stalemate ruled at James Bay. The paras held their objectives at the Radisson generating stations and the airfield and had a tentative hold in Chisasibi, but the commandos were stuck on the objectives unable to break out or join forces. The government in the south had too few resources to help, let alone control events around Radisson. As a result, the paras held the generating stations, but no power flowed south.

To be fair, turning on the power wasn't the army's objective. The assumption in Quebec City and in the prime minister's office had been that once the army was on the ground, resistance would collapse and the station manager would throw the "on" switch or whatever it was engineers did in situations like that. Regrettably, it was one more case of politically self-serving thinking. The plant staff simply refused to return to work, some out of sympathy with the uprising—this was especially true among the young natives—some out of fear, some from a mix of the two. All declined every invitation, and inducement, to return to work under the army's protection, even when the elders pleaded with the native workers to reject "these bad troublemakers."

The workers and management spoke with one voice: "No dependable security for me and my family and my home, no electricity for you." So Montreal and New York sat in the dark.

There was not much either side could do. Will Boucanier held Radisson for all practical purposes and his small unit from Chisasibi controlled the road between the towns. He had the classic military advantage of "interior lines." His forces were inside a rather irregular circle so he could rush troops to any threatened point on the perimeter faster than the para commander could force-march his guys around the outside to mount a raid or full-scale attack on one of Boucanier's positions—especially in this unwelcoming terrain. Besides, Colonel Campbell didn't have enough people to guard the station and the airfield at Chisasibi and mount any kind of assault on the natives. So he sat in position waiting for relief or reinforcements.

Will, too, was basically reduced to standing pat. The last thing he wanted was to give the forces already in place against him any chance at a decisive battle. He was the decoy trying to lure the government into committing more troops into the rough terrain that multiplied the efficiency of his small force. The more troops committed against him the greater his success. This time the Indians were inside the circle of wagons and the cavalry was riding around firing from the outside.

Wednesday, September 8, 0850 hours
Ottawa: NDHQ, Thirteenth Floor, South Tower
Office of the CDS

Naval Captain Vince Webber, General Bishop's executive assistant, knocked once and entered the chief's office. The CDS stood, hands clasped behind his back, watching the morning rush hour traffic jerk and idle its way across the Laurier Bridge. Bishop had been in the building all night and, after a few hours' sleep, was up early ready for another grim, endless day. He had always valued the few moments he was allowed each morning to contemplate his own world and never more so than now. He waited a couple of seconds then, without looking around, said "Yes, Vince?"

"Pentagon, sir. General Leonardo's on the secure line." Webber started to leave but Bishop, turning now, stopped him.

"Sit down, Vince. Take some notes for me. Just for the record."

Andy Bishop had known General Anthony "Tony" Leonardo III, the chairman of the Joint Chiefs of Staff, for many years, and under the circumstances welcomed his call. He reached for the telephone marked "Secure" on his desk, and, still standing near the window, said "General

Bishop. Yes, thank you." He waited, gazing still at the commuters on the streets below.

"Good morning to you too, Tony. Yes, a fine sunny morning here too. A bit cool, but you know Ottawa in September. Plus we're in the middle of an uprising. And unfortunately, the security situation has taken a turn for the worse, as I suspected it would. I assume you're on to the problems in Winnipeg? Yes, and that it's become much more serious with what appears to be a general spontaneous uprising of native bands on the Prairies?" Webber waited, pen poised, as Bishop listened to the JCS chairman. After a minute the CDS responded.

"Yes, that's it. I think our politicians are very surprised by the events in the West, even though I warned them. And at this point we, and they, need to think about the very real economic problem for both our countries, namely the very real threat to the gas and petroleum networks."

Bishop paused again for what was evidently a long detailed explanation from his American colleague. As he listened he sat at his desk and motioned to Webber to start writing.

"I see, Tony. Okay. Presidential Directive 186 of yesterday, Tuesday, at twenty-three hundred hours." Bishop glanced at Webber, who nodded while continuing to record the details in his notepad in the tidy but idiosyncratic stenographic style he had long ago devised for his own use.

"Yes, of course," Bishop added after another pause. "But for the record, I did call you first and suggest the United States take action under the CANUS 2008 Defence of North America Agreement, and particularly the section that allows the military chiefs of staff to use, quote, 'all necessary means to protect the continent in an unusual critical situation,' unquote. Tony, the prime minister isn't aware of my request to you yet, and that's the way I'm going to play it here. I'm going to try to convince him and the cabinet that it's the best way for him to characterize the situation as well, and I'd rather not be seen to be twisting his arm. Unless I have to." Another pause, and Bishop again looked at Webber, who was recording the gist of the side of the conversation he could hear.

"Yes," Bishop replied after listening intently for several minutes. "I understand. Of course, the president will have to couch things in terms of U.S. interests. When will she call the prime minister? Eleven hundred, okay. Fine. Can you give me a few hours before you move? Okay. I see, of course, on the president's orders. I will alert the prime minister to be in his office by eleven. That's right."

At that point Bishop jotted an additional note to himself, then said, "It would help me if your staff could send us by secure means copies of your op orders, especially the timings for immediate deployments. I need to be precise on these things as you understand—we can't have any clashes on the ground. Yes, thank you."

The American spoke again.

"Yes, sure," Bishop responded. "I sent a reinforced operations team to the embassy in Washington last night. The leader is Major General Tom Fisk. He has my complete authority to assist your people in the coordination of the deployment. I will arrange for him to brief your staff on our situation and deployments at any time today convenient to you and your staff." Webber again nodded, acknowledging the chief's implicit directions, and resumed writing.

"Okay, fine. Who's commanding your operation? Ah, yes, Lieutenant General O'Neill." Bishop emphasized the name and rank for Webber's benefit. "That's John O'Neill? Commanded the NATO force in Darfur? Sure, I met him there last year and again at the UN meeting on multinational force operations in mandate states. Yes. I agree. A complete waste of time, but necessary to keep the UN true believers happy.

"He's a good man—has lots of experience with our officers and units. Cavalry, isn't he?" Bishop nodded, listening. "Yes, appropriate, at least as history. But let's just keep that association to ourselves for the moment."

Another long pause followed, during which Bishop frowned as he listened intently. Finally he spoke in a way that suggested to Webber that he was interrupting his colleague.

"Sure, sure, I ... sure. But let me say again, it's important that we declare from the outset that your forces are under Canadian operation command—I know it's notional, but it's a serious political point. O'Neill must be 'op-com' to me. Yes, I agree, that's the right level."

Bishop looked at Webber and raised a finger. "Yes, sure thing. Your command liaison team will be housed in Ottawa. We have a special hangar set aside, and I believe our comms and int people have been working with your attachés here and your advanced headquarters group for the last few days to get things ready." Webber again nodded confirmation, this time of arrangements already made rather than instructions received.

"That's right," Bishop continued. "I have not considered it necessary to inform the defence minister or any other politician about these contingency matters."

Bishop again made some notes to himself as he listened to his American counterpart. "Sure, as things develop, but I suggest we discuss the future stationing matter once we have stabilized the situation on the ground. Yes, of course." Another long pause.

"Okay. Sure thing. Finally, Tony, would you please have General O'Neill alert our ops staff once he is inbound? I'll meet him and take him to meet the prime minister immediately as he and his personal staff arrive in Ottawa." A shorter pause.

"Indeed. I agree. Sure. I agree. We can certainly restore order in a few days and then ... ah, assist the prime minister in planning his next political moves. Thanks—I'll be with the prime minister when the president calls. Well, no guarantees, but I hope she'll get a calm response. Yes. Okay, thanks for all your cooperation. Yes, I'll speak to you in a few hours."

Bishop hung up the phone. "Okay, Vince, let's get things moving as planned. We have less than two hours until the president calls and you don't keep that lady waiting."

He stood up and picked up his notes. "First, alert Admiral Roy. Ask her to send the arranged codes to the principal commanders. They can forward their op orders to their subordinate commanders but not before twelve hundred." Webber flipped a page in his notebook and looked up at Bishop.

"Then ask her to assemble a senior orders group in the Ops Centre for twelve hundred. Make sure General Lepine is there. The U.S. op order, as you heard, is on the way—keep on it and let me know immediately it's in. Then ask the DCDS to prepare a display of the U.S. plan for the ops meeting, and to give us his impression of it and lay out some options for my response."

As Webber wrote, Bishop paused to check his own notes. "Okay, after that, call the clerk's office at the PCO and warn Ms. Doyle directly that I will be calling on the prime minister at ten thirty; Doyle should be there—don't disclose anything other than it's about urgent national affairs. But do not allow her to argue about the time or anything else. Then call the PMO, get the chief of staff on the phone, and tell him that I must see the PM with reference to a 'matter of the gravest national concern,' and that President Ricardo will be calling the PM at eleven hundred this morning. That should light a fire and get him moving for a change. Again, do not allow him to argue." Bishop paused, looking through his notes and reflecting on his conversation with General Leonardo.

"Okay. That's enough for now. Except get the defence minister on the phone right away and tell him that I'm on my way to his office in fifteen minutes…Thanks, Vince. It's going to be a busy day. Would you see if Jimmy can rustle up some coffee, please?" Bishop turned away then abruptly turned back.

"By the way, you heard my remarks to the chairman on the initiation of this operation under the defence agreement. No one—no one, you hear?—needs to know differently. Someday the academics can argue with each other and come to their own conclusions about what's going to happen today. Our version is we asked first."

Webber smiled. "Aye, sir. I'm sure one day one of my friends will write 'the unexpected story' and make a bundle."

"I'm sure you're right Vince—'the unexpected story' indeed. I wonder who they'll tag as the villain. It'll be difficult to blame an entire society, don't you think?"

Webber left the office without answering and closed the door, leaving the CDS to his last few quiet moments. Bishop turned and walked back to the window.

Wednesday, September 8, 0855 hours
Peguis Farm, near Clandeboye

Rex Himmler, a former air force electronic counter-measures (ECM) instructor, stood back from his bank of computers and radio. He was proud of the communications centre he'd built; it contained just about every conceivable transmission and reception device on the market and some that weren't. With help from the Movement's surprisingly generous foreign friends, the room was like a grand "revolution-in-military-affairs" command post, as Rex liked to call it.

The guts of the system, a high-powered generating processor, was able to keep the electronics communicating with itself *and* with the outside world. It was, however, an electricity power hog, so it was programmed to diffuse the input power so as not to register on computers at the source, Manitoba Hydro. Its real-time displays of information and large data bank and search engine were as good as anything the Canadian Forces had.

As Rex had told Bill, the big worry came from the Canadian Forces ECM, but Rex had some tricks of his own—an ECCM—to mess up their detection systems. The Internet systems he had built, for instance, were wireless to the world, and had buried wires linked to instruments and antennae some distance from the compound. So, Bill had learned from Rex, even though the spooks might be able to hear them, they didn't have much chance of locating them. Still, Bill liked to be sure.

"We're into the critical phase of the strategy now. Are you sure our communications are safe, Rex?"

"Sure I'm sure. I'd be a little worried if we were up against American 'black ops' types, but they're not here ... are they, Bill?"

Bill didn't answer, but instead pointed at another operating station. "What's here?"

"This is the apparatus that we expect to not only block hostile interference with our comms-network, but that should be able to bounce attacks on us back onto the hackers and complicate their lives big time."

Himmler walked to another desk. "Another major concern is electronic jamming missiles, and electronic and radar searching missiles. If they come looking for us, we haven't got much to go on except the dispersed wireless system. We'll use some standard tricks, changing frequencies, silent periods, and so on, but I'm counting on the fact that the Canadian Forces have only limited frequency attack capabilities and none that could penetrate our good stuff, especially the new things."

As Bill and Rex talked, the int staff reconstructed the operational situation from information taken off the Compound's network. Meanwhile, messages flashed to and from Boucanier at James Bay, Stevenson at the

Winnipeg airport, and the subordinate commanders in Saskatchewan and Alberta, asking for their situations and dispositions. Staff relayed the responses to the operators, who keyed them into the large bright map displays across the room. Gradually, a picture emerged of strong-points, moving columns, quiet occupations, and headquarters locations. Other machines recorded casualties, logistical states, engineer reports on roads, obstacles, and electronic systems.

The intelligence staff also monitored Canadian Forces and police deployments and movements, and noted on large electronic wall charts the changing status of each Canadian Forces base across the country. But Whitefish was most interested in knowing which Canadian units were moving towards which bait and where the chronically under-strength C130 Hercules transport fleet was deployed. Each plane his forces could damage, and each one sent off on some distant mission, meant one less plane load of infantry that could be moving his way.

Once he'd checked out the new ops room, Bill went to fetch Molly Grace from her small office bedroom in one of the grain houses in the tree-fringed farmyard. He knocked, entered at her invitation, and gave her a worried look. "Did you get some rest? Want something to eat? There's smoked duck and goose breasts and barbecued hamburgers in the kitchen hut."

"No thanks. Let's get the briefers together and find out where we are. We need to get a communiqué out today to get the negotiations underway."

Bill frowned. "You really should eat ..." Her hard look made him turn away and mutter, "Okay, have it your way, as usual."

Molly followed him back to the ops room, where, all traces of fatigue gone, she took charge as usual, rattling off questions and directions. She wanted in the next hour a complete situation report of the deployments and operations of the NPA, and details of Canadian Forces plans, with credibility assessments on information derived from various sources. But most of all she wanted to ready the declaration to be issued by the provisional government.

"Bill, you prepare the sitreps. It's time for me to get the announcements ready. I have a few calls to make to Committee members."

Molly, alone, now directed the media strategy, feeding disinformation to credulous national media and decrying the "racism" that lay behind "cruel attacks on native people by the government, the police, and the Canadian Forces." She offered interviews and sound bites, even photo ops, deftly suggesting willingness, even eagerness, to negotiate, but always on terms impossible to define or fatal to accept.

In sum, her strategy aimed to disarm the government by seeming reasonable, offering conciliatory gestures that the government could not accept without ceding the country to the Movement, but could not reject without casting itself as the villain. It was a masterful exploitation of the Canadian chattering classes' image of themselves as "peacekeepers" and the owners of peace, order, and good government above all else. At this crucial moment, Canada's governments were trapped by decades of fatuous rhetoric, unable to negotiate meaningfully but incapable of attacking their tormentors even rhetorically.

Bill was amazed, despite everything, by how rapidly Molly and the Committee seemed to be building an impregnable bastion from which to negotiate Ottawa's and Winnipeg's surrender. Soon they would be supported by Quebec and the Eastern provinces, who were eager to trade peace for economic stability, and who were reflexively contemptuous of the West as always. The CBC had capitulated early, taking the unusual step of airing an editorial on both television and radio asking, "Does it really matter who rules the West, if we can have order in return for merely acknowledging native people's legitimate grievances?" Meanwhile, the Committee was pushing the UN and European Union moralizers hard for irresponsible statements overfull of indignation and devoid of responsibility. The federal government, which was increasingly isolated, must be getting ready to concede, Bill thought.

Wednesday, September 8, 0900 hours
Peguis Farm, near Clandeboye

In front of Molly, now alone in her tiny office, sat the great book of independence, containing background documents, especially Riel's letters and notes, and, in her own tiny, precise script, the constitution she had prepared over many years. Few people had actually seen this document, though Molly had spoken to many leaders about the idea of a constitution and the traditional principles it must contain. Soon, very soon, she would present the document to the people of the West and to Canada, announcing at the same time the provisional government of the new nation, Assiniboia.

Bill walked in unannounced. Molly closed her book deliberately. "What's up?"

"Nothing immediately important, Molly. We've all been really busy and I thought I would look in on you to see if you needed anything."

"No, thanks. I have my own ways to relax, you know that. Work, the mission, the operation; getting the next step ahead of the prime minister."

"I know, Molly, I know all about your work. I wonder sometimes how you keep it up. And where you get it all from. Is it all in that big book you haul around everywhere? I've always wondered what's written in there. Do you have the magic answers all spelled out in there?"

Molly hesitated. A brief sense of distrust and annoyance crossed her mind. "No, not the answers, Bill, just the heart of things for me in many ways. I've kept these since, oh, before I was an aspiring priest in Chicago." She smiled quietly at Bill's stunned stare.

"A priest? You? I don't believe it."

Molly didn't elaborate on this tantalizing, entirely unexpected hint about her mysterious past.

"I record important ideas, passages from our people's records, diaries, stories, fables, and poems in the book. They're my guides. This one is especially relevant. A Catholic priest, a scholar and my mentor, he called himself 'self-excommunicated from the church,' gave it to me at a very important time, when I had returned home to the remains of a ruined culture. It's a poem of sorts by Riel. It goes like this." She began to recite in a quiet voice.

"*The people ... are contrite for their sins, but too late do they, as suppliants, beg for pardon from the bottom of their hearts, weeping. God looks down upon them. But the judgment of heaven must first be fulfilled. The flames increase—a third city now looks like a huge funeral pyre.*

"They're powerful words, aren't they, Bill?"

Bill nodded. Molly went on. "But Louis Riel, though he was close, you know, he almost understood, he never shook off the white man's God. I read that poem and I thought about it, and then one day I wrote under it in my notebook in capital letters: 'THE PEOPLE HAVE WEPT ENOUGH.'

"Our people's situation then wasn't God's revenge for our sins, and the call was not to repent but to rise up. Riel was almost inspired, poor man, and when he wrote those words he didn't understand them. It was the spirits of the land who wept for the people lost in the shadows of the white man's church, as lost there as when they knelt before the white man's laws and governments. The white man's God was a knife at the throat of the native people. Louis could not escape the white man's snare because he had ensnared himself in it. He died trying hopelessly to find freedom while he drew ever tighter the white God's cords about his neck."

Now Molly's eyes were blazing, her voice rising just a little; she held Bill spellbound as she spoke to him alone, as she had seemed to that first night in the church hall.

"The people's true God, the spirits, exist in all living things at once, in an interlaced hierarchy of being. The land supports and sustains all things. Without the land, there is no ceremony and without ceremony no messages can be passed from generation to generation. The hunter has no sign to read to find his food or his way.

"We will return the land to the people and thus the people to their true God: not the white man's God, God the father, 'maker of heaven and earth.' But to the spirits of the land and the water and the sky with whom they once lived, whole and complete, and will live again. Then, soon, the weeping will end."

Molly closed the notebook abruptly. The fire went out. She turned away from Bill and looked out the window.

Wednesday, September 8, 0915 hours
Ottawa: The Prime Minister's Office

"What the hell do you want?" Jack Hemp snapped at Harry Southern. The prime minister was annoyed and increasingly anxious as events visibly slipped out of his control. Southern stepped back from Hemp's desk and delivered a message he knew would not improve the boss's mood.

"Well, prime minister, it seems General Bishop's staff called the clerk of the Privy Council and Eddie Geldt and told them President Ricardo is going to call you at eleven this morning. Bishop insists on seeing you beforehand and he's called half the cabinet to the meeting without telling us. The clerk's in a lather—turf and all that. But your meeting with Bishop is set for ten-thirty. Bishop's shiny boys only said it's 'a matter of the gravest national concern, and that the call from President Ricardo is at her initiative.'"

Hemp slammed his desk. "What the hell is this? I'm the goddamn prime minister. I set my own schedule. I've got that stupid meeting this morning at ten with Bob Halley from the *Telegraph*; he wants our response to that group of lunatics from the... what's it called? 'The Action Committee for an Independent Toronto'? That's all I need, separatists in T.O.? They're just some bunch of idiots, nobody's ever heard of them, but they've been telling the *Telegraph* that because Toronto hasn't had any trouble, they can strike a separate deal with the Indians so the city can get back to normal, take care of itself. They even said they want to act as negotiators between us and the damn Indians! And now the goddamn newspapers are gonna print it or some bloody thing. I don't know what's up Bishop's ass, but it better be good."

Hemp glared at Southern for a couple of seconds, breathing hard, then continued a bit more calmly. "Sorry, Harry, I know it's not your fault. Look, have someone tell Halley something's come up and we'll meet later. Get him a drink and promise a one-on-one meeting—that'll look like investigative reporting—he'll like that. Then we—"

Eddie Geldt barged into the room and interrupted. "Sorry, prime minister, but Jim Riley's on the phone and he won't take 'later' for an answer. He said it's about Bishop."

Hemp gestured helplessly at Southern, then waved Eddie to a chair. "You both sit down! Harry, turn on the speakerphone and the tape machine."

He grabbed the phone, dropped it, swore, and scooped it up. "Yeah, Jim, what the hell's going on down there? What's Bishop want now—permission to start World War Three?"

Riley choked back the first response that came into his mind with some difficulty and answered in a tense but level tone. "Look, Jack." Hemp grimaced; he'd asked ministers not to use his first name. "We have a very serious situation here and I'm not sure that I'm in charge anymore. Bishop would only tell me that he has an issue of grave national interest to talk to you about. He says he's exercising his right 'to speak directly with the prime minister' and he sure wasn't asking my permission. His actual words were polite enough but it sounded like an ultimatum to me."

"Well, Bishop can cool his heels for a while. I'm not taking orders from the generals."

Riley coughed. "Jack, that's not a good idea. I think something is already happening. Since early this morning the military staff has really clammed up. My military staff officer and his guys left the office for a meeting early this morning and never came back. I can't get anyone on the department phones. The deputy minister says he's out of the loop. I sent my chief of staff, Ray Befus—you know him, a Winnipeg militia colonel, usually gets on well with the regulars here—I sent him to the CDS's ops briefing we heard about. The guards in the hall pushed him and blocked the way, and some military police captain told him to go back to his office. Ordered him, in fact. Christ, Jack, the guy was wearing a pistol, and Ray says when he tried to get past him, the guy put his hand on the gun. It's 'uniforms only and need to know day' here, and I'm pretty sure that they don't think I need to know. Me, and I'm supposed to be the damn defence minister!"

Hemp hesitated, looking to Southern and Geldt for an approach, a hint, even. They both just shrugged. "Damn it, Jim, I made you minister to get a grip on those people. Ever since that young radical was CDS, what's his name, the Newfie? Never mind. Ever since he was in the chair, the generals have been telling everyone they're in charge. You go to that meeting yourself and find out what's going on and call me back!"

"Won't do, prime minister." Riley's instinct for political self-preservation, given his long experience with Hemp, was screaming at him to watch his back. And then, suddenly, its shrill alarm died out and another, deeper voice from the back of his mind warned him sternly that this appalling man was not fit to make decisions when Canada's destiny hung in the balance.

"General Bishop is an honourable officer, prime minister," Riley found himself saying. "He has vested rights in the Defence Act to do what he's doing if he believes there is a serious threat to the nation. I'm in no position, political, constitutional, or moral, to tell him he can't meet with you. If you refuse to listen to him, it's your call. But as minister of defence, sir, I strongly advise you not only to meet with General Bishop but to follow his advice while there's still time … *if* there is still — Just a minute, sir. Ray Befus just came in and he's speaking in my other ear." The phone beeped as he put Hemp on hold. Ten seconds later it beeped again and Riley was back.

"Prime minister, my chief of staff informs me that the vice chief of the defence staff just stormed past him without saying a word. He said, quote, 'It looked like she was carrying the devil's wife on her back,' unquote.

"Prime minister, I'm advising you formally to meet with the CDS this morning and to have the principal cabinet ministers present. I repeat, the president is going to call and Bishop is the only one the Americans are talking to, apparently. You need his information and advice before the president calls. I suggest also that you clear your calendar for the foreseeable future. I am seriously worried about our government's capacity to control events of vital importance to the future of our nation, and I think you should be, too."

Searching desperately for a way to get through to this hack, Riley switched abruptly to political language. "Jack, either you take control or Bishop is going to run over you and look good doing it. And you can't take control without getting him onside."

Paralyzed silence followed this blunt declaration. No one stirred in Hemp's office and no one offered a word. Hemp stared at the speaker-phone, then at his staff, then back to the speaker, chewing his lip and clenching his fists. Finally he exploded. "Okay, okay, ten-thirty! But I'm not putting up with any military bullshit! I'm the prime minister. I'm in charge. You tell Bishop that, just in case he forgot. You calm down and take charge or you're toast, Riley. Got that? In fact, you tell Bishop the meeting's for ten and don't be late!" Hemp pounded the off switch on the speakerphone and Southern hung up the headset, carefully checking that no connections were left on.

Hemp threw himself angrily into his chair, leaned forward, and swept a pile of papers aside, sending several folders tumbling to the floor. No one moved to retrieve them. "Disloyal bastards!" he yelled. "How do these generals get their jobs anyway? Chasing a few ragbag gangs of shepherds around Afghanistan, mouthing off to the media—Christ, then I go and make that old fart general from the Yugoslav days governor general and he spends his time giving his buddies medals. You know, we should make these arrogant show-offs stand for election. That might put their 'truth, duty, valour' BS to the test. Make them live in the real world like we do, where slogans like that don't mean anything. They're just that, slogans." Hemp knocked another pile of papers to the floor.

Wednesday, September 8, 1037 hours
Ottawa: Langevin Block

Andy Bishop completed his briefing, stepped away from his PowerPoint computer, and walked to the cabinet table. "Any questions, prime minister?"

Jack Hemp sat speechless. Ministers, incredulous, glanced at each other, then to the prime minister. Another dazed silence filled the room.

Finally, the prime minister broke in, his voice rising in pitch and volume, quivering. "Any questions? Any fucking questions? Bishop, are you out of your mind? You just gave away the country and now you come here and ask, 'Are there any questions?' You listen to me, damn it. You get your arrogant brass hats out of here and you go and call the generals in Washington and you call this whole thing off. I'm the prime minister, not you. I'll decide who invades this country and when!"

Ministers looked at the table or out the windows, stunned, horrified, furious, and embarrassed.

"Prime minister," Bishop repeated quietly and firmly, "the president of the United States will be on your phone in ..." He checked his watch. "...twenty-three minutes. You can tell her yourself that the Defence Agreement you signed last year is defunct ... that you have things in Canada fully under control ... that she need not worry about America's vital national interests or that half the U.S. economy is about to go down the drain. You can try to persuade her to call off her armed forces. But I don't think she will listen and I do not see how you can make her believe such statements."

Bishop reached out and dropped his laser pointer onto the table, pointing toward the prime minister. "The brass hats, as you call us, we didn't do this—you politicians did it. You got Canada into this situation. So now the Americans are coming, as they put it, 'to help us.' And we have, in the classic phrase, no 'defence against help' of this sort.

"Your choices as I see them, and I use the term very loosely, are to fight the Indians and the president and the United States army—and they'll win—or try to get out in front of this thing by announcing that it's your idea. The 'spin,'" Bishop spat the word onto the cabinet table, "is that you asked for assistance, temporary assistance, and that measures are in place to put all U.S. forces under Canadian command. We are acting, you can announce, to secure our interrelated economic interests, restore order, and arrest the leading rebels as a step towards negotiations and reconciliation."

"Yeah, well, general, I've got a better idea," Hemp snarled. "I can relieve you and find a loyal officer willing to carry out the directions of the duly constituted, elected government." That's telling him, Hemp thought to himself, and puffing out his chest, he grinned at his colleagues.

Bishop flushed and clenched his teeth. "If that is your decision, prime minister, I can offer some recommendations for a successor, right now if you like. I cannot assure you that any of them will accept the post if it is offered. But I can assure you that, in any case, if you refuse to speak with the president and to speak to her reasonably, I will announce my resignation and the reasons for it to the nation by this evening.

"As we speak, the American military is opening a central command headquarters at the Ottawa airfield—with our assistance. Lieutenant General John O'Neill, United States Army, will be arriving very soon and has asked to meet with you to describe the U.S. operation and his orders from the president. I suggest we make that for around noon."

No one stirred. Hemp looked around the table. Again, silence.

Finally, Jim Riley spoke up. "Prime minister, we don't need an internal government crisis on top of everything else. Perhaps you could get the president to agree to a type of 'early-in, early-out' strategy—" Hemp's contemptuous gesture cut him off.

"Bishop," the prime minister said, pointing a menacing finger at the CDS, "are you threatening me? If I think you are, you're gone."

Before Bishop could respond, Privy Council Clerk Eileen Doyle put her BlackBerry down on the table and interrupted in a quietly firm voice. "Prime minister, the White House, the president's national security advisor, Murray Segal, is on the phone to ensure their connection to you. President Ricardo will come on the line in a few minutes. Do you wish to take the call?"

Hemp stood up. "Everyone wait here. Eileen, Harry, some note-takers, come with me." He stomped out and down the corridor to his office trailing a babel of bureaucrats. For a moment those left outside in the hallway could hear Hemp as he began to speak—bold, even chipper. "Yes, Murray, I hear you loud and clear … Certainly." A long pause. "Good morning, Ms President. Yes, it is a damn serious business …" Harry Southern slammed the door.

Wednesday, September 8, 1118 hours
Ottawa: Langevin Block

When Jack Hemp returned to the cabinet meeting, he was visibly deflated. "Ladies and gentlemen," he announced quietly, "as you know, I just spoke with President Ricardo about the situation in Canada. She described her concerns and especially the impact the, ah … disturbances are having or may have on the American economy. She spoke about the significant pressure she is under from members of Congress and the governors of California, New York, Washington, Michigan, and from those across most of the eastern seaboard. She asked about our reactions to the threat of attacks on the Prairie oil pipelines and the possibility of serious damage to the James

Bay power grid. I told her of our deployments and progress, giving her the unvarnished story as we know it. I suspect she knows as much as we do, maybe more.

"I won't mince words. President Ricardo was calling to tell me that she has decided to act and to send U.S. armed forces to help us in this situation. Let me tell you, her determination to act is rock hard. I protested and tried to assure her that we had plans, but to no avail.

"What we did agree to is a joint statement of purpose to be broadcast simultaneously this afternoon in Ottawa and Washington—and Eddie, I want your people on this right now. Eileen has the contact numbers. We will say that this temporary action is being taken after assessments by the president and myself, based on our mutual consultation, under the North American Defence Agreement.

"All U.S. forces in Canada will be operating under the direction of our officers, under General Bishop, although American officers will have operational command of their units. All forces will operate under minimal rules of engagement. All U.S. units will have Canadian officers attached to their headquarters to deal with local governments. She seemed a bit vague on arrangements for the withdrawal of U.S. forces from Canada, but I understood her to say the withdrawal will begin as soon as essential services and stability in the regions are restored.

"There's really no choice here. General Bishop's right. There's no defence against help, we simply don't have the resources to be everywhere that's required. Are there any questions?"

"Prime minister," Eileen Doyle interrupted. "Molly Grace a few minutes ago made a 'special breaking news' statement on CTV. She repeated some of the 'history of racial terrorism' rhetoric she has used before and hinted again at dealings with the UN and France. She certainly has a well-oiled cyberspace team. They pick up on every development and get her statements out on the Internet and so on before we can get ours drafted. This morning, for instance, she 'welcomed the implied understanding of the righteousness of the aboriginal cause by the Action Committee for an Independent Toronto, so long as that committee recognized native claims to most of southern Ontario.' We have the tape if you would like to watch it later."

Hemp lurched to his feet but said nothing. His cabinet stared at him briefly, and then Finance Minister Jim Finlay—who openly harboured leadership ambitions of his own—leaned over the table, gathered up his documents, and said coldly, "Prime minister, you shall have my resignation within the hour." Without waiting for a reply, he pushed back his chair, stood, and marched out of the room. Four other ministers silently rose, gathered their own papers and followed him through the door.

Hemp, stung into action, snarled, "Well, you can tell the state of the ship by watching the rats! Okay, those of you with something on your minds other than saving your own hides, let's make the best of this. Where's General Bishop?"

Vice Admiral Roy spoke up from the end of the table. "The CDS has gone to meet the arriving U.S. commander, Lieutenant General John O'Neill. They should be here promptly, and with your permission, prime minister, I'll have members of the staff set up the room for General O'Neill's briefing. General Bishop's aide called me from the convoy a few minutes ago. The CDS should be here within fifteen minutes."

Hemp waved Eddie Geldt, Harry Southern, and Jim Riley over to a corner of the room and asked his aides to set up, within the hour, a conference call to the premiers, and draft a separate announcement that he had asked for the resignation of "the five traitors" who just walked out on him. He turned to Riley and said, "Jim, are you still with me?" Riley nodded. "I'm still here, prime minister."

Hemp actually managed to look grateful, then beckoned the minister of revenue to join the group. "Pierre, this is going to be a bloody day for the markets and the dollar. Things are bad enough now, but when this news gets out, the bottom might fall out of everything. I want you to take over finance too and help us hold things together. Can I count on you?"

"Of course, prime minister," Pierre Jordan replied smoothly.

"Good. Thanks," Hemp said. "President Ricardo has assured me of American support for the dollar; after all, they're in this with us. But I want you to go now, right now, to see the governor of the Bank of Canada and put in place whatever emergency currency controls she thinks necessary to halt or at least control a run on the dollar. We're gonna need an announcement from her right after the press conference with the president. Then I want you to take complete control of the situation with the governor—that's your only job until we get this thing under control. Okay?"

Jordan nodded. "Yes, I understand completely."

"Good. You go ahead now. And Pierre, I'm counting on you."

Hemp turned to the others still seated at the table and spoke quickly. "This is going to require some very slick manoeuvres, ladies and gents. But don't get discouraged. We're going to play the Americans to our advantage. We've taken enough guff from them; it's time to get a bit of help back from the American eagle. They can come in and do the dirty work for us. After all, a lot of the weapons these radicals have were smuggled in from the States. In the end, they're going to leave and we'll have fewer native problems and, if we play this carefully, we can all be heroes."

Smooth, Jack, he told himself. You've still got it. Play this right and you'll be a new father of confederation. Kinda like John A. when he hanged that traitor Riel.

"Okay, people, let's get to work."

Wednesday, September 8, 1157 hours
Ottawa: Langevin Block

Before anyone could actually go anywhere or do anything, they were interrupted by a commotion at the entrance to the committee room. General Bishop had arrived with a glitter of Canadian and American brass. An American officer in starched and sharply pressed fatigues emerged from their midst and without needing directions, walked straight towards the prime minister. Lieutenant General O'Neill, commander of all the U.S. forces to be deployed in Canada, was evidently as well-briefed as senior American officers generally are.

O'Neill extended a hand. "Mr. Prime Minister, it is a very great honour to meet you. I bring you greetings from my commander-in-chief, President Ricardo. And I look forward to assisting you and General Bishop in our joint mission to restore peace and order to the North American continent."

Jack Hemp could never figure out why he was so uncomfortable in front of generals, but they irritated him a great deal. Perhaps it was their self-assurance or their air of control, or perhaps it was because of his belief that they didn't just kill people for a living but that they liked it. Whatever it was, Hemp invariably had to make an effort not to let them put him off his game and it was especially hard at the moment.

"Welcome to Ottawa and to Canada, General O'Neill," he responded with forced heartiness. "Been here before?"

"Only on study trips, Mr. Prime Minister. Although back in the bad old days of the Fenians, my family visited here on occasion." O'Neill smiled at his family joke, but Hemp had no idea what he was talking about. "Well, general, or should I say generals, I understand you have a briefing for us, to bring us up to date on your operations so I can decide how we will proceed."

General Bishop and O'Neill exchanged a very brief glance, then the CDS said, "Yes, prime minister. General O'Neill will provide you with a complete description of his orders and operational concept, with the assistance of his technical staff and mine. I will say a few words afterwards and then we'll be happy to answer any questions you and your colleagues may have and to note any modifications to the plans that you might suggest. General O'Neill?"

John O'Neill wasn't the sort of guy you'd notice right away in a line-up or a mall: about five-seven, slender, his orange-red hair trimmed U.S. Army "white-wall" style with only a close-cropped flattop under his beret. But then you'd spot his eyes, emeralds in a tanned face. And once he began speaking, with a hint of Texas twang—the result of years serving at Fort Hood—overlaying a Boston-Irish base, a potent current of experience, purpose, and resolve beneath his easy manner invariably commanded attention.

"Prime Minister Hemp," he began softly, while an aide placed an open laptop computer on the desk in front of him, "I am here in Canada under the direction of the president of the United States. My mission, Operation Talon, is to secure the hydro facilities and transmission lines running into the United States from James Bay, the natural gas and oil facilities and pipeline corridors flowing from Canada into American systems, all transportation networks vital to the American economy, including the St. Lawrence Seaway, and to disarm or otherwise render harmless all hostile forces in and about Canada that might threaten these facilities, my mission, or my command.

"Operation Talon is under my national command, as officer commanding the newly established United States CANUS Command. USCANCOM, as we call it in the jargon, is a unified command of the armed forces of the United States created specifically for this mission. As commander, I report to the president of the United States through the chairman of the Joint Chiefs of Staff, General Anthony Leonardo III.

"My concept of operations is simple. My command will rapidly and immediately deploy units and formations to seize control of the targets indicated in my mission statement. We will remove threats to these facilities, secure their operations, control the surrounding territory, and maintain continuous security until the president relieves me and my command of these duties. I have been assigned various units for this mission, which in this open briefing I will identify only as infantry, airborne, air cavalry, and naval and air force units and squadrons. Other units of a more classified nature will be described to you, Mr. Prime Minister, in other briefings later in the operation.

"As we speak, my command is deploying to carry out the orders I have received from the president. If I could please draw your attention to the video and computer slides on the screen General Bishop's people have set up for this briefing. Thank you."

The audience watched as a large, animated diagram showing all of Canada flashed onto the screen and then dissolved into detailed maps of Montreal, the Eastern Townships, and eastern Ontario. O'Neill glanced at the screen on his laptop, synchronized to the giant screen at the front of the room.

"The Tenth Mountain Division, stationed at Fort Drum, New York, just south of Kingston, Ontario, has two missions. One brigade will secure the border area and all routes leading into east-central Canada. This includes the occupation of all native reserves on the border and in the Montreal region. A second brigade will liaise with the Canadian Forces units on the road to James Bay and take over this operation. Specially trained and equipped heliborne engineer units supported by gunships and infantry will secure the transmission lines and stations through aggressive use of 'free-fire zones' along the lines. We are now broadcasting this information to all residents in the areas of the lines and informing them that the free-fire policy will go into effect at fifteen hundred hours this afternoon. The division's third brigade will be held in reserve to control Montreal and the James Bay operation.

"The 196th Airborne Brigade, from Fort Benning, Georgia, will conduct an airborne assault on the James Bay region ... uh, on my order. Battalions will drop on Radisson and Chisasibi supported by USAF fighter squadrons and attack helicopters. We are confident that your troopers on the ground have secured the facilities and, as General Bishop has arranged, once we're on the ground, they will hand them over to our commanders. The airport at Chisasibi will be attacked at the same time and, once secured, will serve as the airhead for this part of the operation."

He tapped a key and the big screen zoomed out, then dissolved to a map of Western Canada. "In the West, the Seventh Air Cavalry Regiment will secure Winnipeg, relieve Canadian Forces units in the area, and patrol the pipelines that pass through Manitoba and Saskatchewan. Two brigades of the First Infantry Division will deploy into Alberta—one to secure the tar sands facilities and the second to relieve the Canadian Forces at Cold Lake and to secure that base as an American airhead in Western Canada.

"Farther east, where the threat is less acute at the moment, a brigade each from the Maine and Vermont National Guards will secure the border areas of New Brunswick and Quebec's Eastern Townships to prevent native reinforcements and weapons from entering the fight. A United States Marine Corps Amphibious Combat Team will be stationed off Halifax as a reserve. Three armed vessels of the U.S. Coast Guard will enter the St. Lawrence River this afternoon to patrol the Seaway to Montreal.

"On the West Coast, another United States Marine Corps Amphibious Combat Team will take up station at sea to protect Vancouver's merchant traffic in cooperation with three U.S. Coast Guard vessels.

"These units will, of course, be supported by combat air force squadrons and several auxiliary units and headquarters, the details of which have been given to General Bishop. My headquarters will be located initially in Ottawa and then I will likely move west.

"That, prime minister, is the outline plan. I would like to acknowledge that our ambassador to Canada, Mr. James Laforge, who I am sure you know well, has just joined us and he will explain the authority he has been given by the president to work with your diplomatic and legal folks on the international niceties. Are there any other details you would like to know at this time?"

The politicians looked to Hemp, who stared slack-jawed and bug-eyed at O'Neill, unable even to frame a question. After a dreadful pause, he half-shouted "My God, general, you've brought in the whole U.S. army; we're dealing with a few natives, mostly unarmed and disorganized."

"Well, prime minister, as we learned in Iraq, you 'come big or stay at home,' and you're the beneficiaries of that lesson. We don't want the natives to think they have some chance to overcome us, wear us down, start a lot of small-scale uprisings the day after we're deployed. I want them to have exactly the reaction you just did, that the whole damn U.S. Army is after them. This time when my president says 'major combat is at an end,' major combat will be at an end."

"Okay, general," Hemp responded weakly. "So, how long is this going to take? What's your … how do they call it, exit strategy?"

The little general hit another key, then walked over to the big screen now showing the original map of all of Canada and pointed to Quebec. "I believe we will wrap up the Eastern situation rather smartly, within a week. After all, that's not the native leaders' target. As I am sure you understand, the attack in the East was made to draw your forces away from the West, the real target—truly clever, a real classic if I may say so." He turned and pointed at Winnipeg.

"The West is different," he continued. "I hope the surprise of our arrival in such force will knock the stuffing out of the warriors, because I don't want to get into a fight in the streets of Winnipeg. Urban warfare is not pretty. But even if it does, the warriors will start to fight back outside the major cities. There is little doubt they will attack the pipelines and other critical infrastructure, we must anticipate, with some initial success. I think I can grab Alberta in a few days, but fighting in Manitoba and Saskatchewan may go on for a week, maybe two."

Hemp breathed a sigh of relief. "So in two weeks, you'll have the natives all back up north—kinda herding them back to the reserves. I can live with that. Good. Yeah. And then your units will move back over the border and General Bishop's people can take over. Yeah, okay. Got it." Hemp looked around the table and actually smirked.

O'Neill gave Bishop a puzzled look. "Perhaps General Bishop hasn't had time to lay out the full plan for you and your cabinet?"

"I'm afraid not, John," the CDS replied. "The president's directive only got here a bit before you did. I just briefed the cabinet on the details we had from your phone and text messages. I think you had better spell out the follow-on actions."

O'Neill nodded grimly and returned to his laptop. This time he clicked several times and flashed up four maps and charts, all clearly marked in red, "Secret: U.S. Eyes Only."

"Prime minister, I'm going out on a limb here a bit; these are diagrams used yesterday to brief President Ricardo and they are not meant for... well, foreign eyes, as you will understand. Nevertheless, in the interest of building support and trust within this alliance, I was given permission to show them to you and your colleagues if I thought it might clarify the U.S. position. I am instructed to secure the zones of occupation of concern to the vital interests of the United States. I will—"

"What's that you said?" Hemp hollered. "What's that—'zones of occupation'?" He flushed scarlet from neck to hairline.

"If I may finish explaining these details," O'Neill responded calmly, "I think the scenario will become quite clear."

Jack Hemp tried to take a sip of water and spilled half the glass onto the table. No one moved to assist him—all eyes were on the American general standing before them.

"Prime minister, as I was saying, the United States is acting to protect its national interests, no more and no less. We will deploy troops to solve our problems, but not to solve yours. I'm sure you would agree that to do so would be a violation of Canadian sovereignty. Moreover, the president is under strict directions from Congress not to engage in some drawn-out campaign in Canada. The Congress believes that Canada can and must pay the cost of its own defence and, thus, I am absolutely restricted to my mission. However, that mission is to solve our problems and solve them decisively.

"Therefore, my forces will establish, in the East, zones of occupation approximately ten miles wide on each side of the international border, from Nova Scotia to Lake Ontario. We will establish another zone encompassing the entire James Bay power generating region and extending out five miles on either side of the transmission lines. We will station troops near Montreal and use the Citadel at Quebec City as our regional headquarters. All native reserves within these zones will be occupied and controlled by our units. Outside these zones, your armed forces and police will assume whatever responsibilities Canadian authorities see fit to assign them.

"In the West, we will control all the transportation routes across the top of Lake Superior and into Winnipeg. Here it will be necessary to drive native bands north of that zone, which, I think, for the most part means back to their reserves. Here again, activities outside the zone will be a Canadian responsibility.

"The Prairies are a major problem as they contain so many resources and energy infrastructure critical to the u.s. economy. Winnipeg will be liberated and we will seek your assistance in forming, for a short period, an interim government structure that may include some native leaders—not the renegades, of course, but other, reliable leaders. Otherwise, my orders are to push the natives north of a line roughly from Kenora to Dauphin to north of Yorkton, and then extend the line northwest, north of Saskatoon, to join up with our forces at Fort McMurray. In other words, we will establish a zone of occupation encompassing all the existing oil and gas producing regions and the pipelines to the u.s. We see no need to station troops in British Columbia or in the northern region at this time.

"Finally, prime minister, I want to highlight an important but to some an unpleasant aspect of my mission. On the direct orders of the president, I am to find the main leaders of this so-called Movement and eliminate them, or otherwise take them out of the picture. We'll capture them if the opportunity presents itself. But in reality, prime minister, we're going to, as we say, 'decapitate the leadership' of this bunch of radicals."

"You're going to what? No way. You're not coming here and arbitrarily shooting people you think are radicals. No murders on my hands. No indeed."

"Sir, what do you think we're going to do with all those natives and others who resist my orders? Look at it this way. If we can snuff out the leaders, then maybe, just maybe, the others who joined in for the hell of it, or because they hadn't give the consequences much thought, will back away and go home. In any case, prime minister, I have my orders."

O'Neill glanced at Bishop. "What I can do—rather, what I will try to do—is give General Bishop a heads-up when and if we find them. But I have to say that the finding and the decisions are mostly out of my hands. These are matters for the White House, and the Joint Chiefs; they'll give me the word and confirm this part of the mission once it's necessary to act."

John O'Neill paused. Hemp sat measuring his options and escape routes.

"Okay, general—for now. We'll decide this matter when we have to. There's enough on the plate as it is. Go on with your briefing if you must."

"Thank you, sir. That's what I have for now. However, prime minister, Ambassador Laforge has with him this afternoon a Status of Forces Agreement, a SOFA, much like those we have used in other countries like Iraq." Hemp flinched but O'Neill took no notice. "The SOFA document spells out the arrangements and legal status of our armed forces, and how we will deal with 'incidents' and so on in the months to come."

Jack Hemp stared at O'Neill then at Laforge, looked around the table for someone to shout at, someone to blame, and finally fixed on Bishop. "This is your doing!" he shouted.

"No, prime minister," the CDS replied firmly. "This is our doing as a nation. But I've said my piece several times and I'm not about to repeat it here." Bishop turned away from the prime minister and gazed across the table at no one in particular.

"All right! All right!" Hemp gibbered. "Fine. Splendid. So, members of my cabinet, esteemed colleagues, ministers of the crown, what do we do now? Who's for giving up? Who thinks on our watch it's a good time to carve up Canada between the Americans and the native people? Or maybe there's someone else who'd like a slice? Maybe an African Union peacekeeping force or the Danes in the north or Patagonia?" he concluded in a strangled voice.

The room sat silent, half the cabinet contemplating grabbing their files and fleeing, until Jim Riley spoke up. "Sir, I don't see it that way. We have an alliance with the United States, that's well known. We do need help, and reasonable people will see it that way. After all, the populace is sufficiently frightened that the restoration of order these actions may bring will probably be welcomed, at least initially. Afterwards, there may be a lot of criticism of how we drifted into this crisis, but not of the fact that we acted decisively with our American friends to bring it to an end."

Harry Southern joined in. "I think Jim's right, prime minister. We spent a lot of time getting this 'perpetual treaty' signed in Washington three years ago. It's not as if they forced it on us. I recall how you...I mean we...were all cheerily saying, 'Well, we put one across on the Yankees, now they have to protect us.' I mean...uh..." Southern gave Ambassador Laforge an embarrassed glance across the room. "Ah, well, ah, no disrespect ambassador, just talk among colleagues, you understand."

Laforge took the opening with diplomatic finesse. "Yes, of course. Know the situation well. And prime minister, you know American politics well, too. After the outbreak of civil war in Iraq, most Americans lost their enthusiasm for 'campaigns for liberty,' especially those led by the United States. You know the 2008 Democratic campaign had an 'America First' theme. This administration isn't in the 'saving failed states' or 'responsibility to protect' business, and neither are our people. From now on, someone else can do the job if they think it worthwhile.

"Frankly, sir, we took a lot of grief over the past twenty years from our allies, Canada and France very much among them, for being too active in the world. Some of us were a bit surprised, therefore, and resented the loud complaints from your cabinet and other governments when Congress announced our new strategy and our policies to withdraw from other people's problems and to only become involved in matters that we decided might harm our national interests, narrowly defined, of course. We're looking after ourselves first now. But the strategic arguments don't matter here today.

"So here we are, ready to guard America's interests, nothing more and nothing less. That's what our allies wanted and that's what you're going to get. If criticizing us helps you politically when it's all over, I'm sure that's what you'll do, and I expect we'll all survive somehow.

"But prime minister, ladies and gentlemen, the president doesn't see this as a surrender—perhaps General O'Neill's term 'occupation zones' was a bit...hum, shall we say, overly military. I think we can call them, say, 'zones of mutual defence cooperation,' or some such. Our diplomatic staffs can wordsmith the communiqué for us. Remember, the real occupation of Canada or even small parts of it wouldn't be popular in Congress. Insulting as it may seem to some of your more vociferous nationalists, taking over Canada hasn't seemed worth the effort to most influential Americans for well over a century."

Murray Coates, an Atlantic Canadian politician as quick to speak as he was slow to think, indignantly spat out a few words defending Canada as worthy of annexation, until Hemp shushed him.

"I assume, ambassador, that the president is set on this course of action and that the troops are on their way?"

"Yes prime minister, correct on both counts."

Hemp sat quietly, checking his notepad, doodling a bit. Then he stood up, back in control of his emotions if not his destiny. "Thank you General O'Neill, ambassador. General Bishop will continue the coordination of our military operations in Canada with your, ah, assistance along the lines General O'Neill outlined. My foreign minister, Aaron Hays, will meet with you, Ambassador Laforge, in an hour to draft a communiqué to the effect that we, the cabinet, asked for American assistance under standing treaty arrangements. The U.S. deployments will be temporary—without specific dates—they will be under Canadian military control, formally speaking, and they will be restricted to the protection of vaguely worded 'facilities vital to our mutual interests.' Where necessary to restore order, American officers will be granted 'special peace officer status' in Canada, under control of members of the Canadian Forces. As you suggested, Ambassador Laforge, the staff can develop, uh, suitable wording immediately afterwards. Agreed?"

Without responding, Laforge took O'Neill quietly aside to confer as privately as circumstances allowed, and a few minutes later stepped back to the table. "Prime Minister Hemp, I think we can draft a statement along the lines you suggest if we could borrow an office with a secure phone and take half an hour or so to speak with the White House national security advisor and the chairman of our Joint Chiefs of Staff. Meanwhile, I'm afraid the deployments are too far advanced to delay or alter them now. But of course we can explain the interval between the troop movements and the communiqué announcing them as a 'necessary security precaution.'"

Hemp looked to the CDS, who nodded. Others around the table said nothing. "Fine. Ms. Doyle will take care of your communications needs, secretarial support and so on ... General Bishop and Mr. Hays will assist you in writing the communiqué. I would like to speak with President Ricardo for a few moments just before I sign the note."

"Thank you, prime minister," the ambassador responded smoothly. "I'm sure we can work out a mutually satisfactory arrangement."

Hemp stepped back from the table, ending the meeting. "Mutually satisfactory arrangement? I think not, ambassador, but we have no other choices left, do we? One thing I insist on, though," Hemp looked directly at O'Neill, "general, you just make damn sure you conduct this operation swiftly and completely. If I'm going to take history's censure for this decision, at least leave Canada without an Indian problem afterwards."

O'Neill adjusted his beret and returned the stare. "Not to worry, Mr. Prime Minister. The United States Cavalry knows how to deal with Indians."

Wednesday, September 8, 1243 hours
Ottawa: NDOC

Colonel Ian Dobson returned to the Operations Centre directly after the briefings at the PMO. As he walked into the op room, his signals clerk handed him a coffee and a folder of classified notes. In the far corner, Ian noted the new desk space and work area established for the American liaison officers who had moved into the headquarters during the morning to help coordinate U.S. operations in Canada.

Dobson took a few minutes to look over the morning's sitreps, deliberately ignoring the American colonel who had walked up to greet him. After thus carefully marking his territory, Ian looked up, read the officer's name off his shirt tape, and extended a hand. "Morning, Colonel Armstrong. Are you being taken care of properly? Anything you need?"

The crisply-turned-out army colonel grasped Ian's hand firmly. "Thanks, Colonel Dobson, we're well situated. Your staff's outstanding. I'm here to help and I have some new info for you. We've loaded General O'Neill's concept of ops video orders meeting with his commanders this morning if you'd like to see it."

"It's Ian, colonel—it's the Canadian fashion here. And yes, I'm very keen to see what you have."

"Sure, of course. Mine's George ... George Armstrong. I was directed to be sure that General Bishop saw these orders as soon as possible."

They walked together to the American desk area, hierarchy now properly confirmed. Dobson flipped through the pages, sipped his coffee, and beckoned his senior duty officer to join them. "Danny, the chief asked for a full staff briefing for 1430. My compliments to General Bishop, see if we can move that meeting up to 1330. He needs to see this new info and to meet Colonel Armstrong, who has the latest orders from General O'Neill."

Wednesday, September 8, 1330 hours
Ottawa: NDOC

General Bishop settled into his chair in the briefing room and watched his principal staff and Lieutenant General René Lepine take their places. Bishop had already spoken to General O'Neill an hour before and discussed with him their views on the joint ops plan O'Neill had received from the Pentagon early that morning. This staff meeting was meant to put his mark on the plan and make sure the staff and commanders understood that the operation was to be conducted rigorously all the way to its conclusion and that he and O'Neill were in full agreement on the concept of operations and the rules of engagement.

Andy Bishop was under no illusions—he would carry this operation with him to the grave and beyond via the history books. He would be, through history, the CDS who "allowed and encouraged the American incursion into Canada." Few would acknowledge the context of his advice and decisions, but there wasn't anything he could do about that now, so he wasn't going to waste any time worrying about it.

There also wasn't a whole lot he could do about what his American colleagues were going to do. So his main concern at the moment was trying to influence how they did it. He was determined to salvage as much as possible from the disaster unfolding before him, beginning with preserving as much honour and respect for the Canadian Forces as he could. Among other things, that meant avoiding, wherever possible, conflicts between natives and his soldiers. He was especially concerned to avoid injury to native communities caught in the cross-fire of competing renegade and Canadian ideologies.

His regular troops had learned from years of combat in stabilization and peacekeeping campaigns in the Third World how to navigate the complexities of competing factions. But applying those lessons at home might be very difficult, as well as painful. It also wasn't something to which American commanders would necessarily attach high priority. In fact, Andy Bishop even worried that in some circumstances, Canadian troopers might turn on their American allies if the latter interpreted "free-fire zone" too enthusiastically.

It was a mess that left him no time to think about his reputation in the history books. He was going to do his utmost to protect the nation, the innocent, and the reputation of the Canadian Forces, in that order, with all the authority he held in law, in custom, and in the present circumstances. His personal plan for the cease fire was, in fact, an exit from public life. But until then he would answer the call to duty—starting with another briefing. "Okay, Ian," he said, "what do you have?"

"Sir," Dobson responded with habitual clarity, "my purpose here is to summarize the situation across the country as it was at 1300 hours today to make sure we're all working from the same information as the situation develops this afternoon.

"As you know, sir, the big actions were in the West on Tuesday evening, and they continued through the night. The fight at St. Laurent in Manitoba was surprisingly tough, with significant casualties on both sides. The Slate militia combat team, which also now includes about twenty Mounted Police constables, was driven off their position blocking Highway 6, but they weren't overrun or chased far, and they're being reinforced with more militia personnel as we can find them—some, militia and civilians, are just showing up in small groups on their own. They're not all combat trained, but there're a lot of hunters out there and still lots of rifles behind farmhouse doors too. We're also bringing some small units in from Gagetown via the U.S. air base at Minot, North Dakota.

"Colonel Slate's team is holding a position southeast of St. Ambroise along Road 411 here." He pointed to the map. "He's pretty much in the open, but we have some makeshift helicopter gunships in the area to give them some support. He can threaten and harass the native traffic on Highway 6, but he can't stop it."

René Lepine broke in. "Excuse me, Ian, but I reviewed the int from our radio intercepts and my other sources, and spoke with Slate as I was driving here from my headquarters. Perhaps I can add to the detail you have.

"Slate's position is not secure. The large native force coming down Highway 10 west of Lake Manitoba swung off that road just south of Dauphin and onto Highway 5. We're watching it now, and it looks sure they're heading for the Trans-Canada just north of Carberry." He pointed to the map Dobson had called up. "But the column broke up at Neepawa, and a significant force is now heading east on Highway 16. Its lead elements are already through Gladstone, here. I think they're going to keep going east." Lepine traced the route on the map. "If they do, they'll get behind Slate and cut him off, and then he'll be in serious trouble.

"The column on Highway 6 that attacked St. Laurent and Stony Mountain is in Warren, and has control of the area across to Selkirk in the east, but their rear elements are still a threat to Slate, especially if he's attacked and forced east." He turned to direct his comments to the CDS.

"In my view, sir, we either reinforce Slate's command or withdraw him south to reinforce the police in Portage La Prairie, but that move might get him into a running fight with native groups near Highway 1 regardless of whether they come in west via 26 or south down 240. Besides, his people aren't trained well enough to make a withdrawal under stress and he doesn't have many vehicles, so if we move them and anything goes wrong, we could lose them all."

"Well, René, recommendation?"

"Sir, I recommend that we hold them in position, get some air cover over them, and use it if necessary. My guess is the column at Gladstone wants to move south, not east anyway, but Slate where he is helps complicate that choice for the natives and simplifies our planning somewhat. Slate's still a threat, or at least a nuisance, to the bad guys in Warren, which I propose to exploit. I will use his position as a hard core, a place to rally and regroup, and once it's reinforced, we can move it either toward Warren or to the south ... and meanwhile give our old friend Stevenson several things to worry about." Lepine paused. "Frankly, sir, those are our options with our own forces, but I'm essentially banking on the U.S. army to get me out of this fix. I've given Slate a warning order to strengthen his position and prepare to hold it until relieved, pending our discussion here."

"Okay, René, confirm your orders and we'll see how it develops. Change in ROEs. The CF18 squadron has authority to attack any targets that attack or look like they're preparing to attack Slate's positions. That means 'danger-close air support' only, not a freedom to gun down the columns at will. But with that stipulation, René, I'm passing fire control there to you. If we can get some troops in by helicopters to support Slate, do that too ... Now, Ian, how are the other operations proceeding?"

Ian Dobson returned to his script and electronic maps. "Sir, the native attack at St. Laurent and the advance south turned into a confused, seemingly spontaneous attack on Stony Mountain penitentiary. We don't know why it happened or how, but the whole thing apparently got out of hand and turned into a riot inside and outside the facilities, with various groups attacking each other without much direction from anyone. The casualties were high and the prison is damaged beyond use for some time to come; in fact, it's still burning. Apparently some of the attackers had mortars and knew how to use them.

"Unsurprisingly, there are prisoners wandering all over the area. Some have surely made it to Winnipeg or are heading that way alone or in small groups. Others were rounded up by the native warriors and they seem to be sorting them in a worrying way ... separating out the natives from the others. Some prisoners stayed in the cells and others have tried to turn themselves in to the police when they come across them ... they say it's safer in jail than out.

"We have no sure count of the inmates: casualties, in custody, or missing, either escaped cross-country or gone over to the insurgents. But thanks to the native leaders, especially Colonel Stevenson, we were eventually able to arrange a kind of local truce near the prison and gain the release of the civilian hostages and the wounded.

"The int staff believes that some kind of breakdown occurred in the Manitoba native leadership during the fight, or that night, right after the prison attack. In any case, our electronic intercepts have been tracking a commander named Toques or Tommy Twoskins, ex-captain, special forces, who was the leader of the whole Highway 6 column and the St. Laurent attack. He's now disappeared from the radio traffic. He may be dead or wounded, but it was his brother, Brian, we think, who, we can now confirm, was murdered by the guards. We believe Twoskins has been replaced by another commander or commanders, named O'Reilly or Reilly. Or both. We're not sure whether we're dealing with one individual or two. Time and careless radio security on their side will give us the answer eventually.

"Generally speaking, the convoys that came from the north have settled here along this line north of the city and linked up with other native warriors deployed south and now west of Winnipeg. The city is more or less surrounded, but the native control is not strong or well disciplined … our special ops teams are moving in and out of the city at their discretion.

"The bigger problem is the thousands of natives flowing south without any control by anybody, with nowhere to go, nothing to eat, too many guns, and too much booze. In our truce talks with Stevenson during the Stony Mountain event, he said the NPA was trying to organize and control these mobs, but he wasn't sure anything would happen soon. Oh, and by the way, our truce with him ended at 0600 hours this morning."

Dobson switched to a new set of charts and maps. "In other locations, the base defence force is still holding a section of the Winnipeg airport, but they are under heavy pressure from remarkably well-directed native forces. No lack of discipline there; obviously they put their best people here, a lot of ex-military, ours and American. The centre of the city is in native hands, except at the legislative grounds where a nasty fight is still going on. The RCMP and militia are concentrating their efforts there, to the extent that they have any freedom to manoeuvre."

Dobson moved his laser pointer to the detailed provincial maps. "Sir, as I mentioned, the native columns that attacked out of the north have moved almost without interruption or interference, except at St. Laurent, to an east-west line from here to here across the Interlake area north of Winnipeg, and on a more ragged line extending west through Saskatchewan. As you see, they seem to be surrounding the main cities and towns there. From the aerial and satellite images I've seen, the columns, in Manitoba especially, look like classic staff college exercises—well ordered and disciplined, led by very mobile recce units that know their business. When they come up against police and small militia barricades on the roads, they adroitly bypass them, and where they can't do that, they bring up speedy assault units to take them out. It all looks pretty textbook to me, sir."

Bishop shifted in his chair. "Glad to see our attempts to bring native people into the forces and put them in advanced training positions has been such a success." This uncharacteristically abrasive comment surprised every officer in the room.

"Yes, sir," Dobson managed to continue blandly. "CFB Cold Lake is secure, but out of action due to hostile sniping. The base defence force, in a sharp action of cooks and clerks, fought off a determined truck-mounted attack yesterday that continued for some six hours. We had three KIAs, including the base defence force commander, a female logistics lieutenant shot leading a counterattack, and six others wounded, two seriously. Four native trucks were knocked out and it appears six natives were killed. The rest withdrew in disorder to the outskirts of the base and seem content to stay there. Some decorations will be due there, sir... if we're ever in a position to present any.

"The oil fields in all locations are virtually shut down because workers refuse to go to work without guarantees of safety, which nobody can give. The pipelines have not been attacked, and our small special ops detachments in the area are trying to locate threatening native parties but, as I am sure you understand, sir, the protection of these lines is an enormous task. We've asked General Lepine to concentrate on the compressor stations... they're the most obvious targets.

"The West Coast is relatively calm, just a few spontaneous eruptions the local police are watching. In a word, sir, the situation is very critical. We have troops deployed in the wrong places, in the East, when the obvious key fight is in the Prairies, and in Winnipeg, when the real threat is to the energy infrastructure, and we have very little capability to redeploy our units."

The electronic charts flipped eastward across Canada. "In Quebec, outside the James Bay region, native activities have slackened off and civilian police are returning to duty in Montreal. It's relatively calm there... no significant incidents have been reported in the last few hours. Electronic intercepts from CSE suggest that the native units operating in the area are withdrawing from the cities and redeploying to the border areas and the reserves, apparently to protect them. CSE says there seems to be real concern about that in the radio traffic. They may have got wind of what our American associates are doing, at least in part.

"On Highway 109 to James Bay, the Van Doo battle group reports continued small-scale contacts. The battle group is holding in place awaiting orders and the arrival of U.S. forces. At James Bay, the paras continue to patrol the area defining native positions and guarding the power generating plants and facilities. The natives, for their part, are generally passive; they seem content to hold the roads between Radisson and Chisasibi, and the actual towns. Again, comms intercepts by CSE suggest that the natives will take no offensive action in the next twenty-four hours.

"The para commander, Lieutenant Colonel Campbell, has arranged a local cease-fire to care for the wounded on both sides, and he's trying to speak with the native commander, who we can now confirm as retired Warrant Officer Will Boucanier, a decorated, very competent soldier, well known to and much respected by the paratroopers.

"Going back west a bit, sir, all transportation routes over Lake Superior have been completely compromised. There is no train or through road traffic in the area. The towns and cities along the route north and west of the Soo are more or less on their own. All civilian airline flights are, of course, grounded. Essential non-military air traffic has been diverted south of the border. Small civilian aircraft are flying all over the place, mostly helping communities that are organizing their own defences and resupplying critical items. Nobody's filing flight plans, though.

"Finally, sir, I know you've spoken with General O'Neill directly, but Colonel Armstrong—he's the ranking U.S. liaison officer—is here with orders to ensure you've seen General O'Neill's concept of ops and his mission directives to his units."

General Bishop turned to acknowledge the American's presence. "Welcome, Colonel Armstrong. Could be better times for you to pay us a visit, but welcome. As Ian says, I did speak with your commander a few minutes before I came in, but I suggest you give your report to the senior staff. I think it's a good idea for you to bring them up-to-date."

Armstrong stepped forward. "Thank you, General Bishop. I'll arrange the briefings with Colonel Dobson later."

General Bishop stood up. "I want to emphasize to everyone in this room that General O'Neill and I are entirely agreed that everyone's interests, including especially those of innocent native citizens, will be best served if we get this over with quickly. Ian, please send immediately the coded warning order to senior commanders outlining the U.S. operation. General Lepine, would you join me in my office, please?"

As the two officers walked towards the chief's office, Bishop took Lepine's elbow. "René, assure me that our own plans, the ones that you and I discussed earlier, are in place and ready."

"Yes, sir, they are. I have deployed into the West every special operation team I could get my hands on. We even managed to bring several home from Afghanistan and Zimbabwe over the last few days, thanks to the Brits and Aussies. Most are already operating under cover, prepared to track the U.S. teams to gather whatever information we need to ensure our...uh...mutual cooperation. We also have a few teams tracking the native columns in Manitoba and Saskatchewan, identifying leaders to be hit whenever you give the order.

"We managed to assemble that ad hoc airborne company you asked me to throw together—it all came together quite quickly, I'm happy to say— and it's now on the ground and ready at Cold Lake and Edmonton. They jumped secretly into the area last night using one of our black ops Hercs. I expect them to make short work of the natives in the area and be able to take control of the bases before the Americans arrive. That should help us to secure our sovereignty in the area, and also protect our CF18s at Cold Lake.

"The SSR at James Bay has been instructed to hold the generating stations and Lieutenant Colonel Campbell understands that he is to take the lead in negotiations with the native leaders in Radisson and elsewhere. As you directed, the word has been given that in all situations we want to make U.S. commanders work through our officers. The Van Doo battle group commander on Highway 109 will be ordered to relieve Radisson. He will receive an 'eyes only' order this morning. Basically, he'll be told to stall the Americans on the highway—'problems' with the handover routine, concerns about IEDs, and so on—for long enough to let the fast combat team he's organizing now make a dash up the road to make contact with the paratroopers outside the town. It's a risky operation, but I think everyone understands that we need to take control of the road and the area around Radisson as soon as we can or we're not going to get it back.

"I have to warn you, sir, this is a tricky business. My main problems, as you know, are lack of troops and transport, and lack of confidence in the American's truthfulness in all this. We've got a few things going we didn't mention to them, and I expect it's mutual. In fact, my feeling is that they have some significant operations in the pot aimed at James Bay for after the operations that they haven't told us about."

Bishop stopped in the doorway to his office. "Thanks, René. You do your part and I'll do mine. We have to square a large circle. We have the legitimacy in this affair, but the Americans have the guns. And, oh, don't forget Molly Grace and the natives get a vote too. I'll speak to you once we see how the first few hours unfold tomorrow morning. By the way, neither the prime minister nor his office is on Colonel Dobson's distribution list for the outgoing operations message. Wars are too important to trust to politicians … especially this one and these ones. Join me for breakfast tomorrow, say 0500?"

TOP SECRET
FLASH MESSAGE
NDOC/CANFOROPS 058/1358 HOURS EST
COMDS EYES ONLY

SUBJECT: OP TALON—IN EFFECT FROM 2300 HOURS EST. SIGNIFICANT US OPERATIONS TO BEGIN IN CANADA TOMORROW AT 0600 HOURS EST. MAJOR US COMBAT UNITS WILL ADVANCE IN AREAS OF MONTREAL, QUEBEC CITY, JAMES BAY AND EASTERN TOWNSHIPS, SOUTHERN MANITOBA AND WINNIPEG, AND IN THE AREA OF THE RESOURCE FIELDS OF ALBERTA. MAJOR US NAVAL COMBATANTS WILL ENTER CANADIAN WATERS DURING THE SAME PERIOD. USAF OVERFLIGHT RESTRICTIONS ARE LIFTED AT 2330 HOURS EST.

DETAILED DATA, CODES, AND MAPS TO FOLLOW BY SECURE ELECTRONIC MEANS.

TOP SECRET DIRECTIVE 'CDS OPS 112' OF 0730 HOURS EST TODAY IS EFFECTIVE IMMEDIATELY.

ALL ACK.

DAY TWELVE

Thursday, September 9

Thursday, September 9, 0710 hours
The Red River just north of the Canada/U.S. border

Wayne Rymerchuk walked around his dusty John Deere combine. He'd harvested a quarter section and stopped for his morning "pee and tea break," as he liked to call it. But these days the pee part came a lot more often than the tea, as his wife repeatedly and worriedly reminded him. Anyway, he had to wait for his son-in-law to bring the grain truck back from the morning run to the elevator in Letellier, twenty kilometres up Highway 75. Young Jeff might not be everything Wayne had wished for his daughter, but he knew the land, worked hard, and he had a new truck. Rymerchuk was as attached to the land as anyone could be. His family had been in the wide flat valley of the Red River for almost a hundred years, straight from the great plains in Ukraine, where they'd been since who knew when, and it meant a lot to him that Kathy would farm it after him.

In the distance, he watched other machines beat clouds of grain dust into the air across the stubble fields. The early September sun cut low and bright across the sky, angling southwest in the morning blue. Long skeins of geese rose along the Red River, heading for the grain fields. Wayne checked his watch. Just past seven. Right on time, every autumn day, every year. Out here there were things a man could count on.

And for all his young failings, Jeff was one of them. Wayne reached a hand to the rail to climb the ladder into the cab as, a kilometre away, his son-in-law's big grain truck turned off the highway and into the field. He'd be alongside in a few minutes to take another load as Wayne harvested the long swaths of Durham wheat. Sure, there was a hard day's work yet to come, and sure, he felt it in the evenings a bit more now than thirty years ago. But there was nowhere Wayne would rather be on a fine September morning: a man on his land reaping the benefits of generations of proud work.

Wayne could not recall later what caught his attention first. But something made him stop, one foot on the ladder, and look skyward just as six fast, sleek helicopters roared past overhead, northwards, just a few hundred feet off the prairie grass. He didn't know he was watching a U.S. army Cobra and Black Hawk gunship team clearing the way for the following assault force. They flew in a loose side-by-side formation, crews scanning forward and to the flanks for any sign of trouble.

Rymerchuk stepped back from his combine and walked a short distance into the open field to watch the machines fly off north. An even louder noise made him spin round just as an even larger flight of twenty or thirty troopships prop-washed their way across his field, also heading north, chasing the recce flight fast and low to the horizon. Each ship was loaded with air cavalry troopers, the elite "Air Cav." Some troopers sat facing out the side doors, feet braced on the skids, weapons across their laps. Door-gunners swung their machine guns over the fields and for a moment Wayne thought they were aiming at him directly.

More helicopter flights of twenty or thirty machines each ripped the sky, scattering flocks of complaining geese. Jeff had stopped his truck at the edge of the field and jumped down, and walked slowly in a circle watching the show. Helicopters seemed to be everywhere at once. Here and in the distance, over the river and to the west, helicopters streamed north. Jeff held his hand to the peak of his tractor hat and squinted into the sun; yet more helicopters heading north from the American border, unimpeded, over the autumn harvest.

Everywhere cars and trucks stopped and parked on the highway, and farmers jumped down from their trucks and combines to stare into the sky. None of them, as they needlessly told one another later, had ever seen the like. Few, as it happened, saw the large, dark-coloured fixed-wing aircraft high in the cloudless sky above the helicopters, slowly tracing a course northwards in large overlapping circles. But inside this USAF C17 Globe-master III, an entire airborne headquarters was busy tracing the course of OP Talon and passing a steady stream of information and messages to the commander of the Seventh Air Cavalry Regiment, who was comfortably settled into his onboard command post. Satellites floating far above in space provided his staff with minute-by-minute details of the disposition and situation of every U.S. army unit in "the Western Area of Operations," and marked the location of every enemy unit as well.

A sudden, odd flash from one of the last troopships rushing over his fields caught Wayne's attention. A trooper sitting in the side door, feet dangling, waved his rifle-empty hand high across his body. As Wayne stared, the trooper repeated the wave, then brought his rifle hand up alongside his body, chest-high, and mimicked a steering wheel with his weapon, making several quick turns to the left and right. He then lowered his rifle and gave an exaggerated thumbs-up with his empty hand.

Wayne gaped, surprised at life in the death machine. He stepped forward, obviously meaningless and invisible in the vast flat prairie, but responding with a natural gesture of greeting nonetheless, he waved his John Deere hat slowly, high overhead as he turned to follow the aircraft as it sped away. The trooper waved back.

"A farm boy, no doubt about that," Wayne said to himself. "Some kid out of Minnesota or the Dakotas ... and he'd probably rather be down here covered in combine dust than in that infernal machine."

Now Jeff bounced his truck across the rough ground, braked hard, and jumped to the ground beside his father-in-law. He yelled excitedly, "Hey, Pop, did ya see that? Wow, must be going to an air show or something in the Peg."

Wayne paused again with his foot on the combine ladder and looked over his shoulder at his excited son-in-law. "Jeff, you and your friends have gotta start reading the front part of the newspaper. Those Yankee troopers are after the Indians, you just mark my words." As he looked up to his cab, he saw the large, strange, dark plane circling high overhead. "There'll be an air show all right," he muttered, "and no money for the grain this fall either, I'll bet."

Thursday, September 9, 0735 hours
Southern Manitoba: On the Highway 75 approach

Eighty kilometres north of Wayne's farm, the Seventh Cav gunships pounced on the casual Indian roadblock at Glenlea on Highway 75, the main route from the border to Winnipeg. Mary Collins, the warrior squad leader, heard the helicopters approaching, but couldn't locate them. Several kilometres south, the pilots had dropped down to ground level, flying "nap-of-the-earth." Two Cobras skimmed up a low fold in the field and over a slough about 800 metres from the loose gathering of trucks, cars, and wandering warriors. Unlike Mary, the pilots knew exactly where to look. The satellites had pinpointed every single native position between the border and Winnipeg and passed the information to the command C17. From there, airborne weapons controllers gave detailed directions to the assault force rushing toward the natives.

The first missile hissed out of its tube, its companion close behind. Seconds later, a bright red pickup truck rolled flaming into the ditch while a neat, brand-new blue Toyota Tundra simply disintegrated, raining debris across the fields. The few natives still standing looked about briefly, stunned, until machine-gun bullets whirred from the Cobras, beating up the roadways and slicing them into corpses. Mary Collins was dead on her feet.

Six Black Hawks, noses down, chattered across the field from opposite sides, guided to their objective by pyres of black smoke. At 400 metres, two of them slipped off to the west flank and at 300 metres opened fire, hose-piping the area with copper-covered bullets and small-calibre depleted-uranium rounds that swept away the remaining vehicles at the roadblock.

At 100 metres, the four other sky-chariots pulled their noses up and flared into a hover two metres off the field; thirty troopers leapt out and dashed forward in practised bounds—squad firing, squad moving—leap-frogging to the objective. The few natives who'd found cover in the ditch from the first assault and who didn't spontaneously throw away their rifles and shotguns and thrust their arms into the sky, were shot where they lay. Two who foolishly dashed for the open fields were cut down by the circling gunships before they got fifty metres. The classic covering force tactic was over in less than ten minutes.

The following squadrons slowed their advance only long enough to allow the gunship recce teams to remount and lead the way towards Winnipeg airport. The C17 hummed in a westerly arc toward the north. Officers inside the aircraft's belly working the "comms-net" and the glowing green computer screens reported the engagement and the forces' progress dispassionately to the command base in Fargo, North Dakota, and the newly established USCANCOM headquarters in Ottawa, as well as to comrades winging north on their mission "to secure and occupy Winnipeg and southern Manitoba."

Meanwhile, other combat recce teams, covering other assault companies to the east and west, replicated the Glenlea tactics at Ste. Anne, Île des Chênes, Domain, Sanford, Starbuck, and as far west as Elie on the Trans-Canada Highway between Winnipeg and Portage La Prairie. In each location, warriors were surprised and overwhelmed by the speed and violence with which the sky opened up on them. Four Air Cav companies converged on Winnipeg along Highway 1—the Trans-Canada—from the east; up the Highway 75 corridor from the south; northeast across country passing west of Sanford; and farther west over Starbuck, aimed at Headingley. No word of the approaching menace reached Stevenson or Molly Grace from the smoking, silent roadblocks.

Thursday, September 9, 0830 hours
On the road to Radisson

Lieutenant Colonel Marc LeBlanc took off his headset and looked at the notes he'd made during his secure conversation with Lieutenant General Lepine, a surprising direct transmission of orders bypassing all his normal chain-of-command. He reread the orders and stepped out of his command post to join his ops officer, Captain Denis Fournier, who stood waiting for directions.

LeBlanc ran his fingers over the map Fournier had mounted on a tripod in the sunshine, then said, "Denis, change of orders. Apparently, the Americans are coming, big time. We're to step aside, let them take the lead, then fall back on Montreal. Rather a big piss-off if you ask me, but of course, no one asked me."

He pondered the map. A "passage-of-lines," in which one unit in an advance allows a follow-on unit to pass through its lines to take the lead, isn't an easy manoeuvre, even on favourable terrain with units that are used to working with one another. And here he was expected to make it happen on a narrow road in rough country with foreign troops he had never seen before, against guerrilla adversaries. Well, he thought, that's why they pay me the small bucks.

"Okay, Denis, issue a warning order to the battle group as follows: halt in place; secure units and locations; no movements on the road except for medical or operational necessity. American helicopters, fighters—fast air—and combat vehicles are expected in the area within the next two hours. Therefore, 'weapons fast,' no firing unless ordered otherwise. O Group this location in thirty minutes. Feed the people and fuel and service the vehicles. Everyone on one hour's notice to move as of right now. Got it?"

Fournier checked his notes. "Yes, sir. I'll get the order out ASAP. Do you want to check it first?"

"No. Do it, then get the command post ready for orders."

As Fournier headed for the CP, LeBlanc felt a sudden, deepening despair. He stepped across the road and sat by himself on a fallen tree trunk. What the hell, he thought. We grind our asses way up here, lose six good guys, then they want us to stand aside and let the Yankees charge in, bugles blowing, and save the day. Then at the same time General Lepine calls and personally orders me to prepare as if I'm to return to Montreal and in the next breath secretly orders me not to. "Your ears only for now, Marc ... stall the handover." Yes, sir. I, Lieutenant Colonel Marc LeBlanc, will personally stall the United States Army here on this road. Oh, and while I'm at it, I'll also rush a small combat team to Radisson, which I couldn't reach in a hurry with my entire battle group. This operation's going to get screwed up, big time. Men, stand by to screw up. Oh wait. The generals and politicians already did that.

None of the subordinate commanders at the O Group were in a better mood than the CO once LeBlanc gave them his orders. Of course he put up a professional front, neither questioning nor criticizing the orders he had just received. So the job changes—that's warfare. Their basic operational instructions were to concentrate their units, secure them in place against surprise attacks, and get some rest without letting their guards down.

George Arnolt, the officer commanding the artillery troop, spoke for the others. "What do we tell the soldiers? It's the 'reason why' question, sir."

"Well, George, you tell them that the Americans are coming, but that they need a whole mountain division to do what we are doing with a battle group. You can suggest that we may still have to stand by to rescue them anyway." Cynical laughter relieved the sombre mood.

"You tell them just what I said. You can also tell them we're on stand-by to return to the Montreal area to assist operations there. But among ourselves, have no doubt, ladies and gentlemen, we'll be back here again and probably for a long time. Okay, lots to do. Shake out your people and get ready to move when we get the word."

As the O Group broke up, LeBlanc's deputy, Major Bob Arsenault, pulled him aside. "Sir, the U.S. column commander is on the way to our location to confirm details for the advance through our lines. Last message gives his ETA as thirty minutes, and they want a landing zone. I have a party opening an LZ in the clearing just down the road. Do you want to meet him there or here?"

"Send a vehicle to pick him up and bring him to the CP. Best we look over our int and situation maps here. I want you, the Ops O, the RSM, and

OC headquarters company to join us. Let headquarters know we're in contact once the helicopter arrives.

"But Bob, here're the real orders." Marc pointed to his map. "While I'm briefing the Yankees, I want you to get the recce platoon and Bravo combat team moving north as soon as you can. Send them up the highway and across the bridge on the Rupert and have them establish a strong combat outpost at the junction of 109 and the road from Chibougamau. Tell them to keep an eye out for booby traps, but hustle. They're gonna have to take some risks that way. Once they're in position, they're to prepare to move fast up the road under my orders. If we can get beyond the bridge, we hold the key terrain. Once they're in position there, let me know and I will give them their next objective. If the Americans ask anything, the word is that we're just adjusting the column."

Arsenault gave his CO a baffled look. "I don't get it, sir. I thought we were going back to Montreal."

"You don't have to get it, Bob, and neither do I. Between you and me, we're not going back to Montreal any time soon. There's something going on that I don't know about, but it seems the CDS wants us to beat the Yankees in a race for Radisson. It's above our pay grade, so get recce and Bravo moving, and someday we'll tell 'war stories' about it over a beer at the Legion. Oh, and take that bloody embedded reporter and embed him somewhere else far down the line. A bog would do nicely. Better yet, offer him access to the American commander. It'll keep them both out of my hair for a couple of hours. And Bob, have someone ask the cooks to rustle up some coffee and something to feed our guests. I intend to string out the briefing over lunch."

As LeBlanc turned to his maps, the radio crackled to life on the brigade HQ net. "All stations, Op Talon is active. Enemy force in Quebec seems to be dispersing, but if reconstituted may present a continuing threat to area and to communications on Highway 109 north from Matagami. All ack."

The CP duty officer looked to his CO just outside the vehicle's rear hatch. LeBlanc nodded and the young signals officer pressed the microphone switch. "Romeo Juliette, this is Mike Whiskey. Ack. Out."

Marc LeBlanc pulled out his field message pad and jotted down the date then wrote, "Enemy force may present a continuing threat," circled it, and added, "A military understatement to remember."

Thursday, September 10, 0912 hours
Outside Radisson

Will Boucanier was uneasy. During the last several nights, para patrols had probed his position, made off with a couple of idle native sentries, and spooked the rest of his people. Joe Neetha reported similar activities in Chisasibi and on the road to Radisson. Little by little, the para commander was dominating the area, especially at night. Will knew from his experiences in Bosnia and Afghanistan, where his JTF2 patrols had scared the crap out of the Bosnian militia, that once the shadows get the best of a man, he's finished. Boucanier could feel the same thing happening around him, and there wasn't much he could do to change the situation. His Rangers could never beat the paras in a war of patrols. But when people wake up in the morning and find little messages left on their gear by the other guys, they stop sleeping at night and start firing at every rodent rooting around in the weeds and bushes in the dark. Then they desert.

This morning, though, Boucanier had other things on his mind, and they weren't better things. Since dawn he'd been watching the paras moving about, clearly adjusting their deployments. They had established some new ops around the town and abandoned others. Their normal patrols had slacked off very early, but just before sunrise, a black Herc had come in low and made a drop on the station, mostly supplies but also about a dozen soldiers. The aircraft seemed odd, from its completely black paint job to its unusual wing pods. Will didn't like it, but he didn't have much time to think about it.

Joe Neetha had also reported unusual activity in his area. The most worrying was that the paras there had somehow silently cleared the runways in Chisasibi during the night, a clear sign of trouble on the way. Will's Rangers still held the local roads and had time to plant plenty of mines and obstacles along the roads from Neetha's positions. And the natives still controlled the land. So as long as everyone was on foot, the battle could only proceed in slow motion, despite the ominous pressure from night patrols. Will still had the advantage over the paras and could hold out for

some time if his guys' nerves held. The best news was that his patrols on
the road north from Matagami had been more successful than Will had
expected, and at last report, the Canadians were crawling along somewhere just below the Rupert River bridge. No immediate threat there. Yet
the dawn sky brightened menacingly.

Will had spent the morning walking through town, encouraging his
Rangers, moving up to the barriers to make sure people were alert and
careful about para snipers, who he knew would be scanning his positions.
He called Neetha several times. "Any changes? Anything going on?" There
wasn't. Everywhere the little battle sat suspended, or so it seemed. Will
stood up, tossed his now cold coffee on the ground, and told himself,
"Time for another walk-about."

He left the east barricade and strolled briskly towards the centre of
town. He stopped, stretched, looked south, and froze. The sky was suddenly full of Hercules transport planes just a kilometre south of the town.
Boucanier had seen mass drops before and had even jumped in some at
Fort Benning, Georgia. But the view from beneath the aircraft was stun-
ning. At least twenty Hercs in four widely spaced rows hummed across
the town, doors open, troopers at the ready. Will scanned the horizon and
saw red smoke suddenly rising from at least four places north, east, and
southwest of the town. Now he understood that strange early morning
supply drop. It was actually a U.S. pathfinder team coming in under cover
of a resupply drop. And now they were in place, popping smoke grenades,
marking at least four separate dropping zones.

Will sprinted for his truck, far down the road, as the Hercs began dis-
gorging hundreds of airborne soldiers, backpacks and weapons dangling
below their legs as they descended. His Rangers stood mouths open, arms
slack, weapons hanging at their sides, watching the spectacle.

Boucanier began screaming orders to his bewildered section leaders.
"Get moving out of here, head out of town, but keep clear of the road to
Chisasibi! Don't go down the Matagami road! Call in once you're out of
range of here. Once you're clear, ditch the trucks, take your people, and
head out on the land. But watch for the paras; they're going to try and cut
you off and ambush you."

The leaders jumped and one by one pulled themselves together and
started rallying their people to dash for the trucks, throwing their gear

and themselves pell-mell into the vehicles. Will jumped into his own truck and waved off Simon, his young driver. "Kid, get out on the land and make your way home. You've done a great job here; now stay alive and get to your family."

The boy protested. "Hey, I'm going with you. "I'm your guard, remember. Don't treat me like a kid and don't call me one. I'm a soldier."

Surprised, Will paused, looking at the boy. He had a point. Will had brought him this far. It wasn't fair to pat his head and send him home. "Sure you are, son," he said. "Quick now, get in. We have a job to do and then we'll both head out on the land." Simon scrambled into the passenger seat. Will gunned the truck, spun it around, and headed towards the generating station as more paras sailed down in the distance, followed by bigger chutes dangling larger equipment and small vehicles on platforms. As Boucanier wrestled the truck down the road to his target, he muttered, "Where did all this stuff come from, Simon? We couldn't bring all this to one spot if we tried."

The boy, grabbing for his seat belt, ignored his leader's odd question. But Will got his answer seconds later, when a low-flying Herc cut a tight turn over the road, its big black-painted stars and stripes plainly visible. "The Yankees—the bloody Fort Benning boys are here," Will yelled. "Good Christ. Simon, quick. Get Joe on your radio, quick now."

Pale and shaking, Simon managed to follow his instructions and held out the mike. Will jerked the truck suddenly off the road onto a little trail and, with one hand on the wheel and the other on the radio, called out, "Joe, we've got U.S. paratroops coming down in hordes. What's happening at your end?"

The reply came in pieces between bursts of static. "Will...in the same shit here...parachutes all over...and fighter planes buzzing the town... moving out. I'm just...road...to the Radisson barricades. I lost contact with...few minutes ago...there, then silence...a lot of fighter planes... lots of..."

"Joe!" Will hollered. "Get off the road! Get off the goddamn road! Don't go making dust towards Radisson or anywhere. Joe, did you get that?" Back came nothing but static.

"Damn it, Simon. God damn it, I should've seen it coming. But we've still got a few tricks."

The boy looked to Will, his eyes wide with excitement and dread as he clung to the door frame while the truck banged and jolted down a little trail his leader had chosen days before. In the distance, they could see the transformer yards of the generating station and soldiers running across the fields, hunched over. Recognition flares shot into the sky as the Canadian and American units linked up.

As Will raced along, young Marcus Wright, now in his own eyes a veteran combat paratrooper, stood gawking at the fleet of aircraft passing overhead. Everywhere he looked it seemed like parachutes filled the air. He had no idea who they were or what they intended to do.

Around him Canadian paras were standing up in their combat positions looking skyward. Marcus recovered and stared down at the prisoner he had captured during the night—just a kid, he told himself, not much more that sixteen, he guessed. Wright motioned with his rifle for the captive to get up and get moving towards the prisoner lockup outside the generating station.

"You'll like it there," he said. "We've got a dozen of your friends waiting for you. Next time you go to war, idiot, stay awake after dark. You're lucky you didn't get yourself killed."

As he pushed his frightened captive along he knew that suddenly he was in the middle of a whole new battle and he wasn't sure where it would take him—could be anywhere, but certainly not home.

Boucanier spun the truck off the trail into a small depression behind a bush and slammed on the brakes. Before it skidded to a halt, he had grabbed his jacket and yanked out the small red cellphone that never left his side. He jumped down from the cab, frantically punched buttons, pulled the little antenna up, and held the phone towards the station. Cool and deliberate now, his fingers found one, one, two, one, eight. He looked up, inhaled sharply, and pressed "send."

A couple of kilometres away, inside the generator room, the metal tool box he had carefully hidden after the initial assault exploded violently, tearing the machinery to pieces.

On his "tourist" visit to the station, Will had spied a disorderly collection of spare parts, instruments, and furniture, everything from old computers to filing cabinets, stacked carelessly in a corner of the room near the main switching station. It offered a classic opportunity to a skilled saboteur. His people had left obvious explosive devices in obvious places, to be found and disarmed when the airborne EOD guys checked and cleared the building they believed had been booby-trapped by "amateurs." Meanwhile, the only one that counted, Will's surprise, was hidden in plain view, just another beat-up box in a pile of beat-up stuff right out in the open. It cut the heart out of the facilities in a flash. All the presidents' horses and all of her men couldn't put this Humpty Dumpty back together again any time soon.

The damage and resulting fire flashed deep inside the building and there was little evidence of a problem other than the muffed sound of the blast. Will focused his binoculars and could see the soldiers who had gone to ground at the noise slowly standing up. A couple of leaders walked forward, checking soldiers near the doors. No one seemed seriously hurt—yet. But Montreal and New York City were going to feel a lot of pain soon and for a long time.

Will jumped into the truck, backed onto the trail, and drove carefully along it to another rough road that led to a distant copse of skinny, stunted, black spruce trees. There he parked and scanned the sky for fighter planes as he pulled Simon from the truck.

"Come on, soldier. We're done here. Grab your pack and rifle. Time to get out on the land. It's going to take a while to reorganize this place properly, Simon, but I've got a little plan and some friends and a few good caches laid up that will see us through. Besides, the walk will do us good." He reached as if to rub the boy's head of thick, black hair, paused, slapped his back instead, and sent him on ahead.

Will looked back and saw smoke starting to seep out of the depths of the inner building. American Blackhawk helicopters, just arrived from the south, circled the site, then began to chop around the area. The lights in New York will stay out for a bit longer, thought Will. But for what? If the Americans wanted our electricity, why didn't they just ask us instead of dealing with those fools in Quebec City and Ottawa?

Ah well.

He humped his pack high on his shoulders and turned away, once again, from his homeland. But he would be back.

"Tell me, Simon," he asked as he caught up with the boy, "ever heard the story of 'the man who would be king'?" Simon shook his head and struggled to keep up with his strange chief. "No? Of course not. Well, I'll tell you the story as we walk along."

Thursday, September 10, 0940 hours
Ottawa: NDOC

The American staff officer dropped his headset and hurried over to Colonel Armstrong's desk. "Sir, a flash message from General O'Neill's command post. The Pentagon intercept stations have apparently found the central native command and communications location. They think several key leaders are inside. It's just north of Winnipeg; one of my guys is pulling up the satellite images of the area. General O'Neill has orders to call a Predator strike on the whole place, but as a courtesy he wants to check with General Bishop first. I'm informed by, ah, sources that General O'Neill is restraining the Pentagon; they want to shoot without consulting the Canadians. Looks like the first big test of cooperation, sir."

Armstrong took the message and stepped briskly to Ian Dobson on the other side of the centre and repeated the news. "Well Ian, what do I tell General O'Neill's eager staff?"

Dobson typed a hasty e-mail, then reached for his phone and hit the speed dial to Bishop's executive assistant. "Vince, I need to see the CDS and DCDS right away. Yep, now. Look at my e-mail, I just hit send." He paused, then said, "Yep, okay, you have O'Neill's number. Okay, on the way."

Dobson put down the phone and turned to his American partner. "Okay, George, you with me to the CDS now. Bring your direct phone to O'Neill's HQ. But I suspect the CDS will be in touch with him by the time we get there." And indeed the two officers arrived at the CDS's office just behind the DCDS to find Andy Bishop on the phone to O'Neill.

"Of course, John," he was saying. "I understand completely the view from the chairman, but we're dealing with a matter of national sovereignty. Besides, if we take out Grace, we risk creating a martyr—we did it before with Riel—and fomenting spontaneous uprisings across the country. Plus if she's burnt toast, who'll we negotiate with? The prime minister has got to be the one to make the call. But if you're forced to shoot, I suggest you shoot to miss."

Bishop listened briefly, then said, "Yes, exactly. Let's assume the target will stay in place, at least the complex will. I'm fine with a strike on the complex so long as we find some way to warn off the principal occupants. Can you get a special forces team there quickly?" The CDS waved the waiting officers to his office's small conference table. "Okay, I'll see what we can do."

He paused again, writing notes. "Right, John. I'll see the prime minister immediately and get back to you. I've got your Colonel Armstrong in my back pocket now. Again, my recommendation is to scare off the leaders, then destroy the complex." Another brief pause. "Okay, you do that and I will speak with you presently."

Bishop clicked off his phone and turned to his visitors. "Right, you know the story, gentlemen, and you heard my remarks to General O'Neill. Vince, please call the PMO and tell them I'm on my way to see the prime minister. I don't care if he's having a bath, I'm seeing him immediately. Carl, tell René Lepine to get a special ops team onto that target as soon as he can. Ian will give you the details. You know my standing orders in these cases.

"Colonel Armstrong, if you please, I'd like you to join me on the PMO visit, but first please call Ambassador Laforge and ask him if he'd please come to the PMO immediately too. I'm sure the prime minister would like to speak with him directly on this matter. Oh, and Vince, I suppose we should call Minister Riley and get him over there as well."

Thursday, September 9, 0945 hours
Peguis Command Post

Rex Himmel, system manager for the Committee, was uneasy. Outstation reports were suddenly intermittent. Odd bits of messages were popping up on the secure net. Random hackers? He didn't think so. No one had the equipment and software to penetrate his system. Nobody, that is, except American spooks. And what would they be doing here?

His chief techie had installed a decoy system when they arrived at Peguis. It was sending and receiving messages and junk to attract Canada's cyber spooks and seemed to be doing exactly that. So what was this new disturbance on the real network?

Rex tapped into system control. Or tried to. Not much happened except an unmatched set of characters flashed across the screen and vanished. He tried chasing the sequence through the computer. No luck. As he got close to the source, his computer locked up.

"Whoa! Trouble. Big trouble." Himmel turned to his duty officer. "We've got spooks. Everyone minimize. Pass the 'compromised' code to the stations if you can. Those who can are to report on land lines. The others are to use their disposable cellphones. Boot up the backup decoy system and run it for an hour, and activate the dummy antenna. Time for me to see the boss."

In the main boardroom, Molly and a half dozen trusted Central Committee members and staffers sat around the pine table drinking coffee. They were calm, almost triumphant. The plan had unfolded perfectly. Federal troops were trapped in the east and in Winnipeg, while the real target, the rural West, sat before them unprotected. The federal government was already hinting at negotiations—"hints can be made into terms," Molly declared. The issues on the table that day were how to consolidate the gains in the West; what extra measures if any were needed to hold the army in the East; and how to follow up "the proclamation," the declaration of Assiniboian independence. Molly, as usual, controlled the discussion.

"The critical factor," she declared, "is to gain recognition from two groups, our own people and influential foreign countries. On the first point, what counts is the acceptance in the minds of a majority in our community that they belong to a nation and that the Council is the lawful authority in that nation. It's not that difficult because everyone, natives, useful idiots, provincial governments, and the feds have accepted the bands as nations long ago.

"Personally, I think it was an absurd idea, at least on an individual band level—especially with the smaller groups—but the old chiefs of the association kept hammering away at the message and eventually the white politicians conceded the argument. Now they're stuck with it—these once-disparate and scattered bands are a nation, like France and Japan. Settler governments certainly can't start trying to take it back now. If our people declare loudly that Assiniboia is a nation, a federation of existing nations…nothing new…the average Canadian will accept it and, presto, we win.

"It's also important, early on, to get foreign nations to recognize Assiniboia as a nation. We've got a bunch of Third World dictators onside, but some of them, like Iran and Syria, are iffy, and the half-dozen Africans who want us to recognize their illegitimate regimes in return may be poison pills." Snickers and sneers ran around the table.

"On the whole, though, as long as we get a chorus of Third World voices, it doesn't matter all that much how many they are or who. But we need one or two major states as well; if we get that, we're on our way to the UN. It looks like France might extend 'conditional recognition' as a ploy to get involved in the negotiations. At least that's the coy message I got from the ambassador through the Quebec separatist backdoor. Strange bedfellows. The separatists are no friend of the people, just the opposite. Even if we get only conditionally recognized initially, well, that's like being conditionally pregnant, or conditionally dead. What foreign ministry is going to reverse itself from a conditional offer? None. Okay, let's get the latest sitrep and map out our negotiating points for the—"

Rex Himmel stuck his head into the room and interrupted her without ceremony. "Sorry Molly, but I think we've got a major problem." No one spoke, so he stepped into the room. "The computers are recording hits from some outside sources. Serious hits. Someone out there is looking for us and I think it's only a matter of time before they're into the net. They're breaking into the system a bit at a time, chewing up our defences as it were. Worse, they may be getting a physical fix on our location."

Molly looked up icily. "You said the system was tamper-proof. What's happening?"

"I'm not completely sure, but someone's tap, tap, tapping at our window. Somebody big, strong, and scary." He hesitated, looking for a cue, but got none so he took the plunge. "I think it's probably the Americans, the Pentagon or worse. I also think they're going to break in eventually and disable the whole works. In fact, I can't guarantee that we haven't been compromised already."

"So," Molly barked, "now what?"

"I've stood down the system, gone to land lines and secure cells. But that's not my chief worry."

"It's not? Then what is?"

Rex hesitated. "If they're clever enough to break in, I'm not sure they'd let me see it this easily. I think maybe what they're doing is tracking the electronics and the message traffic, trying to pinpoint our location, and didn't realize it would cause this kind of disruption in our displays and messaging. If I'm right, and they know what they're doing, the Mounties or JTF2 could be on our doorstep any time. There's no way I can tell for sure. Since they're still hunting and got sloppy enough for me to see them, they may be messing up. Tricky business, though. But something's sure as hell happening that shouldn't be, and it can't be good and it's probably very bad."

Molly sat silent, thinking. Just as she raised a hand to speak, Bill Whitefish, pale and breathless, intruded on the meeting. Bracing himself against the door frame with one hand, a clutch of papers in the other, he panted, "Molly, we've got serious problems. We lost contact with Will Boucanier. His last message was that he was under some kind of attack in Radisson and at Chisasibi, something about paratroopers, lots of them, then static. And now Stevenson just reported that he's lost contact with all the detachments south of town, every single one, but his 'eyes' near the roadblocks are reporting the sky is full of helicopters and smoke and gunfire. He's put his people at the airport on alert and gone to ground. I think we're under attack, but I have no idea where the troops are coming from—unless the Americans are coming in. You remember we talked about that possibility."

"Yes," said Molly coldly, "and you all remember our reaction. If they're coming for us, then we're going to burn the place down."

Thursday, September 9, 0955 hours
Ottawa: Langevin Block

Bishop put down his notes and let his reading glasses drop and swing from the cord around his neck. "Prime minister, this is your call. We can take a shot at Grace and company, who we assume are on the farm, or we can try and scare them out, then destroy the building, and, I believe, her ability to conduct operations. The American choice is to decapitate the leadership … as usual."

Jack Hemp was no war leader, but he wasn't squeamish about destroying an enemy. "What's your advice, Andy, thumbs up or down?"

"Prime minister, I think we want the devils we know on the run and in sight. We should get them to bolt, then destroy their main HQ, which will, I assume, make them increasingly vulnerable to electronic intercepts as they try to communicate in the open. We have our own means of tracking them now we have them located, and I'm moving people there as we speak. There's an American liaison officer in the outer office and I think Ambassador Laforge will be here soon too. We should, you should, decide, then I'll pass the message through U.S. military channels and your office can send the same message through the diplomatic channel."

"Okay, Andy. Boy, I'd like to take a shot at the whole gang… But you're right, it's better to finesse this one…and it helps show the world we're the good guys here. So yeah, you get a message to O'Neill; I'll speak with the ambassador. But make sure we keep a tight line on where Grace is and what she's doing. How long before we can scare them out and take out the farm?"

Before Bishop could answer, a knock at the door brought Hemp's secretary, Heather Bright, into the office. "Excuse me, prime minister, but Ambassador Laforge is here. He has an immediate urgent message for you. And the American officer is excited to speak with the CDS."

Hemp looked to Bishop who shrugged. "Okay, show them in."

Ambassador Laforge walked straight up to Hemp's desk, forgetting for the moment his polished formalities. "Prime minister, the secretary of defense has ordered an immediate strike on the native compound in Manitoba."

Bishop looked to Armstrong, who simply held out his hands and shrugged again.

"The secretary of defense," Laforge continued, "has decided that it is in the interest of the United States that these people be put out of action. As I understand it, the action will begin in a few minutes."

Bishop turned tensely to the American officer. "Well, Colonel Armstrong, what can you tell us?"

"Me, sir? Not much. But General O'Neill is on my phone and wishes to speak with you." He handed his cellphone to the CDS. "Just press and talk, sir. It's secure."

"John, it's Andy," Bishop snapped. "I thought we had a deal."

Everyone fixed their eyes on Bishop and the phone as if by staring hard enough they could hear the other end of the conversation. After some time the CDS responded much more gently, "Yes, I know, politics. I see. Yes, right. If you can sell it, it's a clever, ah ... assessment. Okay. I'd like a post-strike report as soon as you have one. Thank you." He handed the phone back to Armstrong, who switched it off.

"Prime minister, General O'Neill has reported to the Pentagon that he wishes to delay the operation for thirty minutes because, as they say in the jargon, 'the target is reshaping.' That means in English something is happening and they need to figure out what it is before they start shooting. It appears that a convoy might be forming up, so General O'Neill has, uh, taken the precaution of asking the Pentagon whether he should engage the farm or the convoy."

Colonel Armstrong coughed.

"Prime minister," Bishop continued, "General O'Neill informs me that the American chain of command can sometimes be slow making up its mind. He thinks he may have to question the satellite watchers' interpretations of what they see from space and correlate it with his special forces detachment's interpretation of what they see on the ground. Regrettably, by the time it's all sorted out he estimates with a high degree of probability that the leaders will elude the missiles, but the farm will almost certainly be destroyed. We'll know presently."

Hemp nodded solemnly. "Yes, well, bureaucracy can be a problem sometimes, but what can you do? General Bishop, I look forward to your report. Thank you, gentlemen. Good day.

"Ah, Ambassador Laforge, perhaps you could stay for a few minutes? We'll have coffee. I would like to discuss with you the ... well, the protocol, shall we say, if we encounter such an incident again. You know, sovereignty and President Ricardo's assurances to me and all that. Just a little chat ... promote clarity ... if you have time."

Thursday, September 9, 1005 hours
Winnipeg International Airport

The pair of "fast air" fighter jets burst over the airport and crossed the runways diagonally from southeast to northwest. At the centre of the field they hit their afterburners and in perfect formation sat on their tails and bolted skywards, two menacing rockets gone before any warrior could raise a weapon in protest. While Stevenson's troops on the ground stood, transfixed, staring after the departing jets, two more pairs came out of the west, low and fast, banked sharply overhead and screamed off towards the city. In the wake of their roaring engines the once triumphant natives ran in all directions seeking cover.

Sam Stevenson dashed to the doorway of his makeshift command post in time to see the F16s disappear in a low curve over the civilian terminal building on the other side of the runways. He had expected trouble, but not from the Americans, at least not so soon. "Damn it," he muttered, and then Harry Kidd called him back inside, urgently. "Colonel, colonel, quickly, the patrols in the south are reporting dozens of army helicopters all over the place and the guys at Elie on Highway 1 see smoke and hear machine guns firing over near Starbuck."

"Can you raise the other stations there?"

"No, sir. Not a word."

Stevenson reached for the radio, trying to alert but not panic his small units. "All stations, take cover immediately. Get off the runways. Spread your vehicles and get your people into the ditches. Repeat, get off the runways now. You may be attacked by helicopter gunships. Our mission here is completed. Look for a chance to break out towards the city, but then head north to the RVs as planned. Do not go into the city centre and stay off the main roads. Travel as individual vehicles, if you can. Do not engage the helicopters unless you're forced to protect yourselves. And no dumb heroics. We need you for other work outside the city. All patrols on the runways move into the building areas. Those on the north end head for cover in Brookside Cemetery. If we lose contact, scatter, head out, and join our patrols north of the city. RV at Stonewall. Out."

He clicked off the mike and barked, "Harry, get me Molly!" Kidd twisted a few dials and said, "Go, sir." While Sam briefed her, another deafening roar of fighter jets right overhead.

Thursday, September 9, 1008 hours
Peguis Command Post

A duty officer rushed up behind Whitefish. "Bill, Stevenson's on the line. He's really excited … wants you or Molly Grace on the phone right now. I transferred it in here, line two."

"Put it on the speaker," Molly said. "What's happening, Sam?"

Stevenson's voice, steady, matter-of-fact, cool, came over the line. "We are about to be attacked, I think by very significant forces. A minute ago several pairs of F16s shot across the runways very low, then hit their afterburners and rocketed straight up into the stratosphere. Not Canadian CF18s—these were F16s, USAF. They didn't fire on anyone, but they meant to let us know they were there. Then a flight of at least four fighters, looked like more F16s, came in from another direction and peeled off north and south. I think they're coming around again. They're trying to frighten my kids and, truth be told, they did a good job. Lots of firing in the south. I have no contact with anyone … radios are out."

"What do you make of it?"

"What do I make of it? Well, Molly, welcome to the big show. I didn't think the Americans would move without a lot of talk first, but I guess we pulled too many of the eagle's feathers. They're coming here fast and in force. I'm going to pull my people off the open areas and prepare to fall back north. If they're bringing what I think they're bringing, we'll be chopped liver if we stay here...Wait a minute..."

A sound like a loud burr came down the line, followed by the unmistakable roar of low flying jets. It was like a 747 in full takeoff. But this time the roar was, in fact, mixed with cannon fire from the jets.

Kidd looked out the window. "Jesus! Our guys got slaughtered. And look, sir, over the south end of the airfield. Helicopters! Lots of them!

"Molly, Sam. We've just been strafed. At least four, maybe six jets flew in from different directions and hit every truck in the open near the runways. Looks like Uncle Sam has declared war for real. Our guys are running everywhere, but there are casualties for sure and I'm out of here as soon as I can get some order. We can't stay here. I'll keep in touch as best I can, but the airport's a goner. My bet's that the Air Cav is just outside town and we're the target."

"Sam, what happened to the Blowpipe and other missiles?"

"No use here. We can't swing them fast enough to get on the fighters, especially when they come over at rooftop height and drop anti-aircraft flares as they cross the airfield."

"All right, do as you think best. We only wanted to suck the police and army into the city and we've done that. Get as many as you can out and head north, and we'll hold there for the moment. Can you get your people out of the downtown areas?" Molly looked to Whitefish as she spoke, perhaps, for once, seeking reassurance.

"I think so. I'm going to head for Stony Mountain area as we planned. My guys are moving off the airport and into the housing areas for protection, then they'll cut north and west. I spoke with Alex Gabriel before I called you. He's got things under control downtown for now—we're going to lose the legislative grounds soon, but he's holding firm elsewhere. I ordered him out of the city. We need his units later, and I need him especially; he's the future."

Again Molly looked to Whitefish. He nodded vigorously. It was time

Molly listened to her top military guy. Or anybody other than herself. "Okay, Sam," she said. "You get moving. Pull the Winnipeg units out of the city and rally your forces north of the city. Keep me informed. And oh... ah, thanks, good luck."

"Right. On the way. I've got reports of another large helicopter formation near Fort Whyte, coming north low and fast. Talk to you later."

People seemed stunned, looking helplessly to Molly for direction. "All right," she said, "we anticipated this in the plan. They get rough, we retaliate. Bill, where are our special units? If Hemp wants to play dirty games, offering negotiation while bringing in Custer, I'm going to kick in his oil and gas lines... for starters."

The words were hardly out of her mouth when Rex Himmler ran back into the room, nearly breathless. "We've got to get out of here now! Just before the computers locked up for good we ran a scenario program and it told us that we were being tracked by military computers linked to weapons systems that are normally set to lock and fire automatically. In, ah, about three minutes. I managed to get a fix on the antenna probes and whoever it is has us fixed within twenty metres. Must be remote drones— Predators, UAVs, or something. They've got missiles that can take down the entire compound. We've got to abandon the buildings and fast. Now!"

Molly stared at Himmler then at Whitefish. People were getting up, twitching, ready for a dash to the door. "Bill," she said, almost calmly, "what do you make of it?"

"I think we had best move out of here. If they're going to shoot, some kind of ground force is probably close behind. If they've got drones up there, they'll see us and might go for us, so get outside and head for the trench shelters in the bush as we practised. Molly, I think we better activate the leaders escape drill, just in case."

At that point Rex took off without waiting for formal orders, shouting down the halls, "Evacuation, evacuation! It's not a drill. Out of the building and into the shelters. Everybody out!" Most of the staff followed him.

Bill turned to Molly in the nearly empty room. She slammed the table and yelled. "Bastard Onanole. We're negotiating, aren't we? Where are these troops coming from? The Americans can't be that stupid. All they had to do was make a deal with us, not the feds. We're going to decide if the gas flows south, not somebody in Ottawa. Doesn't anyone in Washington realize that they can't negotiate with the feds? The feds have no credibility anywhere. We're the people who control the land, not Ottawa's politicians!"

Horrified, Bill grabbed her arm and dragged her out the door, shouting "Now, Molly, now. We have to go. We need you."

They raced down the corridors and into the yard, where other critical members of the staff were jumping into vans and trucks lined up, engines running. "All right," she agreed. "Let's go." She leaned out the car window and spoke to Himmel, who was standing scanning the sky.

"Okay, Rex," she told him. "We're doing the leaders evac thing like we planned. Get to your back-up comms vehicle and computer gear, find a safe spot to hide it and yourself, and follow us to Tango One as soon as you can. We can't afford to have all our command and control people and equipment in one convoy."

She looked to Eric Jackson, who had overseen the construction of the farm. "You're in charge of everybody else here, Eric. Keep them safe, get them out of here, and move what you can and join us at the alternate HQ at Shoal Lake. We'll let Stevenson and others know we're moving to Tango One. You can be sure our special teams will send our own messages to Ottawa soon enough."

For his part, Sam Stevenson hadn't waited around to see what it was like to be on the wrong end of a high-tech assault. The moment Harry Kidd alerted him to the helicopters, he'd rushed his small team out the back door into waiting trucks and a couple of vans. They tore across the parking lot, squealed along East Street going north, then west through holes cut as a precaution in the fences at the edge of the base to get on to Saskatchewan Avenue. From there they moved north to Sturgeon Road and under the Perimeter Highway, where they split up, some going east to Highway 7, some west to 6, and Stevenson over to 236, driving steadily for the rendezvous with the Cree Column near Stonewall.

As he escaped from the base, the Air Cav recce flights buzzed into the field, hose-piping every person and every vehicle on or near the runways. Trucks loaded with warriors caught in the open field zigzagged hopelessly before exploding or crashing, reduced to burning disabled wrecks manned by dead and dying natives. A few reached the shelter of the terminal out-buildings, and a handful from the edges of the tarmac burst out of the immediate target area unnoticed as the helicopter crews circled for another sweep of the runways. The machines took no return fire from the warriors. "Shock action tactics" had overwhelmed them. They fled or died; they did not fight back.

Within minutes, a second wave, this one of Black Hawk troopships, chattered onto the field. One section of about ten machines headed straight for the civilian airport facilities and hovered low over the main terminal building while troopers expertly slung ropes over the side and rappelled onto the roof, unclipped themselves, kicked open doors, and rushed inside. Eight more helicopters headed for the military side of the airfield and flared near selected buildings a metre above the ground as riflemen jumped out and ran forward.

Door-gunners in the helicopters covered them as they executed their obviously well-rehearsed plan, dropping in front of and on the roofs of the buildings where the beat-up remnants of the base defence force had barricaded themselves in and fought off the warriors. The fight for Winnipeg International Airport was over in minutes. Other squads began the systematic securing of the surrounding buildings, looking especially for any sign of Stevenson's headquarters.

Sam hoped others from his scattered and beat-up little force would meet him at the RV, but he knew well enough that many, perhaps most, were dead, or prisoners, or too shocked to function. As he looked back to the airfield as his truck approached the Perimeter Highway, he could just see a dozen transport planes, giant C17 transports and smaller Hercules, entering a landing pattern over Winnipeg. The main force would be on the ground soon with heavy weapons and vehicles to pursue the warriors.

He wondered, though, why the helicopters had not chased the scattered native vehicles fleeing north from the city and tried to finish the business as the trucks raced away into the open prairies. Were they that squeamish about possible civilian casualties, either collateral or because they'd targeted the wrong van? Maybe. But Stevenson felt strangely uneasy about the fact that he wasn't being chased and shot at.

Thursday, September 9, 1110 hours
Breezy Point, on the Red River

After leaving Peguis, the Committee's convoy had bumped across the farmyard onto a gravel road headed northeast along the west bank of the Red River. The team leader had already sent a code word by land line, alerting a special warrior team that had been waiting near the Lake Winnipeg hamlet of Petersfield to rescue Molly and her staff, just in case this type of situation arose.

When they got the word, the team jumped into their flat-bottom river boats and headed for Breezy Point, a small boat landing on a broad, curved stretch of the Red River where it flows into the lower reaches of the great Netley Marsh.

The quiet riverside park was suddenly alive with people as the convoy of cars, trucks, and SUVs pulled into the landing. Almost immediately, five fast boats, roaring down Netley Creek from the west, turned sharply, cut their motors, and coasted to a landing, running up the gentle, sandy riverbank.

A warrior jumped from the first boat and waved Molly and the rest of the group across the beach. "Quick now. The message for us to meet you said there may be Predators about. If they find us, it's going to be rough. We'll get moving up the river as fast as we can. Spread yourself out in the boats. Molly you come with me."

He turned to the vehicles. "You drivers, get back down the road ... stay separated. Move in and out of the cottage lanes. Try to look like local traffic. Get into Selkirk, park the cars in the shopping centre—not together— then go to the safe-houses. Don't hang around here or a missile will get you for sure."

The man jumped into the last boat and helped push it into the current that carried it out into the Red River. The five boatmen cranked their motors to full throttle and swept in a widely spaced column north into the main channel leading to Lake Winnipeg, ten kilometres away. The little fleet raced downriver through the marsh-lined channels. One by one, the boats broke out of the channels through the narrow coastline of sand dunes, high grass, and twisted trees that guard the marshy estuary where the Red River finally spills into Lake Winnipeg.

Minutes later, the boats pulled up to the docks and landings watched over by the empty sprawl of low summer cottages that was Sans Souci in early autumn. Trucks waited there, and more warriors, openly armed, grabbed the passengers and hustled them into the vehicles, which hurried off through the nearly deserted afternoon streets of Matlock. The scattered convoy headed west past Inwood, finally turning down a prairie gumbo track and stopping where the track faded to a single lane on a native homestead southwest of the village of Sandridge—the new central command post of the native resistance.

Thursday, September 9, 1125 hours
Peguis Command Post

The Peguis compound had been reduced to flaming rubble a scant fifteen minutes after the central staff got away. On the tails of the third wave of missiles, helicopters and U.S. army special forces troopers rushed in to finish the job. They searched the ruins and a few small outbuildings still standing, then fanned out in pursuit of any warrior who might have fled into the low bush and marsh grass north and west of the compound. When the special forces soldiers flew away an hour later, empty, shattered buildings smouldered in the bright prairie sun and no living person remained.

The volunteer fire brigade from Clandeboye arrived at the Compound, alerted by 911 calls from farmers kilometres away who saw smoke and helicopters and assumed some terrible accident had occurred. As the farmer firefighters pulled into the ruined compound, they let their trucks and sirens idle into silence and stood staring uncomprehendingly at the splendid, silent wreckage before them.

In fact, the seemingly clumsy pre-attack on the compound's communications system had given the staff time to evacuate the farm complex. Most of the warriors and their supporters had scattered before the Predator attacks began, finding shelter in the deep cattail wetlands lining the south end of Netley Marsh. But it was a temporary solution. Eventually, they had to move back onto dry land and find shelter with natives in the area or find a way to join Molly and the others near North Shoal Lake.

Rex Himmler was among those now face-down in the marsh grass. He had stayed behind to patch the communications system into the Shoal Lake alternate command post, and, fortunately for him, the first missile had narrowly missed him, taking out another building. Once clear of the area, he had made a quick call on his satellite phone to Molly.

"It's Rex," he barked. "Don't talk, just listen. The complex is destroyed, most everybody got out before the attack. I still think that for some reason they let us know they were coming. I'm going to move in your direction after I gather up some stragglers. We'll move at night. Stay off the system. Use our other means as I showed you. Stanley, I hope, is with you... he's got the gear and knows what to do. See you all later." He turned off the now compromised phone and hurled it into a marsh-lined slough.

Molly took the message without expression as the big SUV bounced towards the evacuation rendezvous several kilometres north of the Peguis compound. "Bill, get Stevenson on the cellphone. We need to know what's happening in the south before I send in the demo teams."

"Look, Molly, I want to talk to you about that plan before we do something rash."

Molly stared at Bill, her face stony, emotions detached from the narrow escape they had just survived, voice raised just enough to confirm her authority. "Not now, Bill. Not now. Just do as I ask!"

Thursday, September 9, 1130 hours
Winnipeg: Perimeter Highway

Sam Stevenson snapped his cellphone open and hit the op number for Alex Gabriel. He could hear occasional bursts of gunfire from the direction of the airport, and not always just from there.

"Come on, Alex, answer the phone!"

Alex clicked in, cool and assured as usual. "Yes, sir. What's all the excitement out there? There's nobody on the radios."

"Look, Alex, we've been cleared out of the airport. U.S. Army Air Cav, I think. Lots of gunships and USAF fast air. They really meant business. I'm moving the headquarters to the alternate location as we speak. I'm bugging out to the RV north of town to link up with the northern units. We'll re-org there and see what develops. I want you to pull your people back into the centre of town near your HQ, and then if the army makes a push on the city, disperse your guys into the streets. Tell them to clear town and you make your way up north to meet me. Got it?"

"With respect, colonel, I'm not too keen on cutting and running. My guys in the legislative grounds are pinned down and hurting. I don't want to leave them there alone."

"Alex, your orders were to suck the police and the army onto your positions and to hold until relieved. You're relieved of that mission! I need you for other operations. Call the section commander on the grounds—that's uh ..." Sam searched his brain for the name of the young commander he had selected and tutored for command.

"Patty Leduc."

"Yeah, of course, Patty. Good girl. Tell her to stop the action and surrender. I'm sure they'll be treated according to the rules and there's not much else we can do now. There's no point getting her and her people killed. Tell her to surrender, then you get the rest out of the city as best you can. Mission accomplished. You hear me, Alex? Mission accomplished! Now get clear and meet me."

"Yes, sir. I'll get moving. Out."

Stevenson had hardly dropped Alex when his cell buzzed again. I better get rid of this thing pronto, he thought, and flipped it open. "Yeah, Stevenson."

"Sam, Bill. We've been shot out of Peguis. Stay clear of that location. What's your situation?"

"Glad to hear your voice. We're out of the airport. I just escaped being overrun by Yankee troopers. I'm on my way to the northern RV with whatever I can assemble. I gave an evacuation order to Alex and the others, ordered them to scatter and get north as well. As planned, we'll link up with Cree Column and hold the line there, take advantage of the local population and the villages for shelter. If we get pushed farther back, north of Stony Mountain, we can fight it out in the low bush as planned. It'll take months to get at us and then we'll have the winter on our side. Should be enough to force some kind of international cease-fire." He paused. "Bill, how's the boss?"

"Boss is good, Sam. She's here with me. Actually, she's mad as hell and after blood. Sam, she wants to use the demo teams *now*."

Stevenson held the phone away from his ear, as if questioning it. "Bill, we can't do that. That plan was only meant to stop a full-scale attack without limits, a genocidal attack. If we use it now, we're only going to lose all international sympathy and enrage the American public. The plan was meant to avoid that."

"I know. I tried to hold her back, but she's pissed." Molly glared at Bill, but he kept right on. "I'm going to try again when things calm down—if they calm down. You get in the clear and then call. It would help if you could show a little victory here or there. Truth is things are falling apart all across the country. We have CNN to help, but info is vague. Looks like James Bay is gone and our people around Montreal are being rounded up and put in cages and camps south of the border. We haven't heard from Alberta since last night's stupid attack on Cold Lake."

"Okay, Bill. Try to get some order there. I need to meet with the boss, perhaps later tonight. I want to get my people gathered up. If Alex gets clear, tell the boss I want him deployed to take over the west flank, the west shore of Lake Manitoba. He's a great and clever fighter, just like Gabriel Dumont. Bill, we have to use Alex's tactical skills to fight an irregular campaign and not let Molly make Riel's mistakes all over again and try and fight these regulars on their terms. I've got to go before someone gets a fix on this phone. Speak to you once we break clear. Don't use this number again."

Sam snapped off the phone and sat back. We're in a tough spot, he thought to himself. We miscalculated the American response. So now what? We're probably still okay, so long as we can convince the world that we're the victims and that the uprising is led by righteous, united people. Now's not the time for bravado or overreactions to the enemy's opening moves. Lord, I hope Bill can stop Molly sending out the demo teams.

Thursday, September 9, 1142 hours
Winnipeg: City Hall

A cold wind and dark clouds swirled in from the east marking a typical sudden change in the city's prairie weather. A little steady drizzle soon settled the dust in the street. Alex shoved his phone into his ammo-pocket and thought for several minutes about his conversation with the colonel. Then he turned to his driver. "Get our truck ready for a dash to the legislative grounds. I've got something to tell Patty, and I need to tell her in person."

Then he called each team leader still in control of a vital point in the city centre and relayed Sam's instructions, ordering them to pull back in short bounds until they could break contact with the police and the militia, then get clear. All, that is, except the team at the Hudson's Bay store. They were to prepare to support his move to the legislative building and then away again, sniping at any police or army units that might mess with him. Once they saw that he was clear of that site, they were to split up and take off for the north end of town. The other teams were to follow the evacuation plan he had laid out for them at the beginning of the operation and withdraw in small groups—"exfiltrate," as military language put it.

As Alex confirmed his orders and the evacuation, his driver and other members of the headquarters team quickly and quietly loaded the trucks, two in the cab and four or five heavily armed warriors in the back of each vehicle. Waiting for their leader, they stared up Main Street, empty and wet, all relatively calm after three days of intermittent fighting—an easy run north out of the downtown, then a zig and a zag to the Perimeter Highway and north to sanctuary among their people. They all knew what was happening to Patty Leduc's team. But they also knew Alex was planning to ride to her rescue alone.

Alex walked out the door to the trucks and pointed to the street. "Okay, you guys cut up Main to Inkster, then Brookside and 7, then cut west and north to the rendezvous near Stonewall. Spread out, be individual trucks, not a convoy, watch out for the attack helicopters. Yankee helicopters with big guns. You'll find our people at the RV. Report in and get settled. Good job. I'll meet you there later with Patty and the others."

No one moved. "Don't think so, boss," grunted big Rob McCain.

Rob was older than the others and older than Alex, too. Age gave him influence with the others and made him a bit unruly. He sat on the running board of his flashy, emerald-green pickup truck, legs outstretched. "Think I'll go with you. Kind of back up, you know? Lots of time to get up to Stonewall, but I wouldn't want those guys to think I left Patty to the Mounties."

The other drivers and crews shuffled about, embarrassed but clearly determined to follow Rob's lead, not Alex's directions.

Gabriel looked at them, undecided. "No use giving you orders, I suppose?"

The remark was met with a collective shaking of heads.

"Well, at least do as I say on the way." Alex pulled out his gas-station map of the city.

"I just called Patty. Her people are in trouble, but holding their own. She has them concentrated on the lower floor near the grand staircase. A couple of snipers are in the high windows, but she can have them downstairs quickly. This is a bit of a gamble, so speed and surprise and guts will have to get us through it. I'll lead, with you, George, close behind. We'll take Main to Broadway and just drive straight at the building entrance near Victoria's statue. Rob, I want you and Mike to distract the Mounties on the south side—go down Main ahead of me and cut up Assiniboine... here." Alex pointed.

"When you get near the Mounties' position, pull the two trucks into cover and open up with everything you have. If they give chase, fight your way back down Assiniboine then try to hide in the streets and get back here and take off up Main Street—got it? If they don't, come back and annoy them until they do. You still have a few smoke grenades for cover?"

McCain nodded. "Yeah. And you can count on us. We'll make it hot for everyone."

"Of course I can, that's why you're all here with me. Okay, Jimmy. You take Rick and his guys up Portage and get in behind the Bay. The guys there will give you covering fire, so you make it down Kennedy here ... and try to hit the junction with me at the same time. Hold one truck as a fire base here at Memorial and Broadway and send the other to support me and get Patty's people out. If anything goes wrong, you're in charge. When we're done here, however it turns out, anyone who can heads north to the RV. Okay, any questions?" Alex waited a moment for his instructions to sink in. No one spoke.

"Right, then. Check your weapons and radios, plain talk all the way. Mount up and watch for my signal to go. I'll give Patty a fifteen-minute ETA. See you all at the RV."

Alex's heart was already pounding with excitement and from fear. He'd performed bravely in the field repeatedly, in Bosnia and in Afghanistan, but he'd been afraid every time. It was, he believed, the reason he was still alive. He certainly wasn't ashamed of it. Every soldier knows bravery is not absence of fear but victory over it. Alex knew it too. It didn't mean his hands didn't tremble every time he got close to death.

He paused in the truck's doorway, the rain cold and now steady. Alex Gabriel looked back for a "ready" wave from each vehicle. Satisfied, he pat-ted his driver, Howe Pahpasay—a "displaced Ojibwa," his friends in The Pas joked—on the back. "Okay, Howe, driver advance."

The little convoy rushed down Main Street, McCain's truck leading. Alex made another quick call to Patty. "Patty, Alex. Change of plan. We're coming to get you out. Have your guys ready by the front door. It's a dash in and out, no time to screw around or we're all dead. Good. See you."

At Portage and Main, Jimmy and Rick broke away and headed towards the Bay, cutting back and forth through the litter of burnt and abandoned cars and buses, forcing their cargo of warriors to cling for their lives to the sides of the speeding vehicles. Four blocks later, at Main and Broadway,

Alex slowed, waved Rob's crews past and gave them time to make the next block and turn west onto Assiniboine.

With luck, they would all hit the target at the same time and create enough confusion for Alex to rush his "forlorn hope" onto the building steps, grab what was left of Patty Leduc's team, and beat a retreat before the Mounties knew what was up. Besides, Alex told himself, he had pulled off a similar rescue of the embassy staff in Kabul this way. But, he promptly reminded himself, he'd had twenty JTF2 soldiers with him that night. Yeah, but, he rationalized back to himself, my warriors aren't special ops, but the Mounties aren't the Taliban either. Then he forced himself to stop his silly internal quarrel and pay attention.

As McCain's vehicles roared round the corner onto Assiniboine Avenue, Alex gave a holler, pounded the side of the truck and Howie, as he liked to say, put the pedal to the metal and headed west on Broadway, the beautiful tree-lined double avenue. The warriors in the back of his truck and the one behind picked up the spirit and whooped like their Indian and Métis ancestors on a buffalo run. They brandished their weapons above their heads, eager to close with the game and collect the honours that would fuel campfire stories for years to come. "There I was, on the great raid with Alex Gabriel … you should've seen the Mounties run, like stampeding buffalo they were …"

Everyone's eyes were fixed on the road ahead. Alex thought he heard Rob McCain going into action with an intense, prolonged burst of the machine gun fire. No one in either truck saw the two Cobra gunships rising up out of the Red River valley behind them, slipping into low cover behind the grand railway station on Main Street. They didn't see them cutting across the street and dropping down on the little convoy.

The first burst from the lead Cobra knocked George's truck off the street and into one of the graceful trees lining the boulevard. George had no chance to warn Alex, but even if he had, it wouldn't have mattered. A long burst of cannon shells from the second helicopter cut into Alex's truck, ripping through the cab, tearing Howie Pahpasay's left arm off at the shoulder and throwing him over the steering wheel into the windscreen. Blood and body parts from the crew in the back flew right over the cab as Alex, unharmed, grabbed for the wheel. But Howie's corpse slid down, blocking the way, his foot jamming the throttle to the floor.

The vehicle, its left front wheel sheared off, swerved left, bounced high off the curb in the centre of the boulevard, sailed through the air on its side to crash on the far side of the boulevard and roll several times before coming to rest on its top amongst the sweet flowers on the immaculate lawn of the elite Fort Garry Hotel.

Smoke swirled about the street as the noise of firing, crashing vehicles and the engines of the departing helicopters died away. Then Alex's truck erupted in a spectacular fireball. Oily smoke billowed into the air, blackening the hotel doorway and curling the yellow autumn leaves on nearby graceful elms.

Patty huddled anxiously in the large stone doorway watching for her rescuers. All she could see were two helicopter gunships skimming west just over the trees along Broadway then banking north, leaving ominous black smoke boiling up in their wake. No Alex.

She stood up to order her survivors to try to escape while she stayed to cover them just as six Black Hawk helicopters circled in from behind the legislative building and settled on the lawn fifty metres away. Scores of American soldiers jumped out and dashed for the buildings.

Patty shouted her last command over her shoulder: "Defend yourselves!" She dropped to a knee and opened fire on the Seventh Cavalry troopers who instantly returned a deadly volley of bullets and grenades. The battle for the Golden Boy was over.

Thursday, September 9, 1820 hours
North Shoal Lake

Molly paced the floor of the rough, squat bungalow. Technicians noisily scrambled to bring online the equipment they had saved from Peguis. Other staffers pushed the few ratty pieces of furniture into a type of office space. Outside, Joe Koostatak's confused family carried what they could to their rusty truck and headed off to his sister's house across the long, unkempt fields. Joe stayed, not out of any sympathy for these intruders, but to guard his early season muskrat catch hung in the outbuilding.

When things get back to normal, he told himself, he'd skin the 'rats and enjoy himself as he always did this time of year.

Joe's yard was littered with partly disassembled engines of various sorts, wrecked trucks, split wood in heaps, tattered laundry flying like a flag of want from a twisted line—all the usual household accoutrements of rural native poverty. A small red tractor stood abandoned, jacked up, on its one good tire. Two snowmobiles, not new, waited for winter. Dogs yelped and barked around the strangers. Wind blew from the northwest as always, through the yard and out to the horizon of autumn grasslands.

Joe couldn't understand why these wild Indians had to come and bother him. It made no sense and it scared the game. Molly briefly tried to explain "the cause," and Joe listened politely, not wishing to give offence, especially to so many men with guns. But behind his expressionless eyes, he asked himself how he could be the cause of this great national upheaval. Nobody had ever asked him about it before they came and took over his life and home. Nor did anyone ask his opinion once she finished her explanation.

Bill Whitefish stood on the wet, unsteady stoop at the back door. The rain had stopped as suddenly as it had started. He was equally puzzled, unsure what to do or how to reach Molly. The homestead reminded him of the world he had tried to escape. The little family, failing in Molly's eyes if not in its own, brought to life his ambitions to somehow bring Joe the trapper safely into the urban world just over the southern skyline. He had accomplished nothing. Not as an academic, not as a social worker. And now he stood at the edge of two worlds, about to sacrifice Joe in a head-on, bloody collision or else abandon him to this yard full of junk, torn laundry, and smelly rodent skins.

Bill had believed, he was convinced, that Molly offered another way. Now, suddenly, a cold shiver of doubt ran down his backbone. Is Molly truly a messiah or is she a martyr? Bill wondered to himself. Is there a difference? I've helped her all the way on faith alone—belief without evidence. I never asked the essential questions. But I don't know now, he admitted. Feeling desperate and bereft, Bill bowed his head and did something he had not done for a long, long time. He began to pray. "Great Spirit," he murmured, "please guide me now!"

Just then, a chilly gust yanked open the loose screen door behind him then banged it shut. Molly stepped out, zipping up her grey ski jacket, and said, "Let's take a walk, Bill. We need to talk."

Without waiting, she started off down a dirt track leading through the wind-blown grass to nowhere in particular. Bill followed, appalled, sick to his stomach, yet still as mesmerized as when he had first encountered the strong, willowy woman with the big idea. He watched the wind catch her long black hair and whip it around her face, saw her sleek body shifting inside her characterless jeans. Even now, as he wrestled with his conscience, he knew that if she gave him one hint of compromise, one trace of attachment to Joe, he would stay, give in, do her bidding. Even though he knew, intellectually at least, that Molly's concept of the future lived in the past. He knew that Molly wanted him onside, but he knew also that she wanted to occupy Louis Riel's dreams even more.

When the track petered out in the knee-deep, grassy field, Molly stopped and turned to face him. "I don't understand your attitude, Bill. We just got the shit kicked out of us, the white guys are ganging up on us with everything they've got, and you want to hold back. That's not what we agreed on. Bill, we're going to take back the land or else."

"Or else what, Molly? Or else bring the world down on old Joe here and his kids? We got our asses kicked, but we accomplished what we set out to do. We lured the army into Quebec, then decoyed the remainder into downtown Winnipeg, and got a free-ride all across the Prairies. We thought the Americans might jump in. Well, they did, just with bigger boots than we expected. But notice one thing. Stevenson saw it immediately. The Americans attacked him on the airfield, but they didn't follow him over the Perimeter Highway. Christ, Molly, they've got to know where we are and I bet they let us out of Peguis. They have to be watching the columns moving south, but they aren't attacking them."

"Sure, Bill, they aren't attacking them ... yet."

"Okay, then, let's wait and see. The Americans aren't here to save Canada ... they're here to save their supplies of oil, gas, and electricity. If they stop on the edge of the pipelines and leave us alone, you've won. We hold the Prairies and the Yankees will try to defuse the conflict in place. We'll get Assiniboia ... for Joe and all the others like him. If we go for your demolition plan now, it will only incite the Yanks to attack us without mercy and burn everything down."

Molly pulled at a long stem of grass, stripping the seeds from the head and throwing them into the air. She walked farther out into the field. "Bill, I'm not here for half measures. I thought you knew that. We can't let the situation slip back into a three-way negotiation with the Americans dictating the terms to us and the Canadians. What the hell's the advantage there? Negotiating with the white man on the white man's terms under the white man's guns. What's the difference from today? We'll be divided as before. Those old ladies from the Council are already whining, 'Enough.' They can't see the future, the real aim." Molly stared hard into Bill's eyes and then walked even farther into the grass.

"Are you putting me in that camp, Molly, after all we've been through? A whining old lady, because I don't want Joe's shack burned down around his ears? You know I'm in this for more than the bloody revolution. I thought you were, too."

Molly stopped and reached out for Bill's hand. "I am too, Bill, but there's no future in going backwards, for us or for the people. This isn't a novel Bill. There's no predictable happy ending. Right causes and reason don't always lead to peace and a better world. It was a tough choice, I know, but it's one that we would have had to face sooner or later. We've discussed this. The status quo was not an option, and appealing to the government for meaningful change has never gotten us anywhere. To save our people and our culture, we had to reject completely the laws by the whites. You *know* that, I know you do. That's what the work of the Movement has all been about. Well, if they won't accept our determination to throw off their dictatorship of our lives and futures, then we only have two choices. Either we surrender absolutely or we rebel, and then everyone can reap the rewards or suffer the consequences of our decision. They refused to accept meaningful, peaceful change and so we rebelled."

Bill and Molly walked silently together under the gathering clouds carrying the first hint of snow. Lines of grey geese sailed downwind heading for Oak Hammock, or perhaps they were sensing a storm and were heading to the Red River and down into Minnesota and the Mississippi Valley. Bill was sullen, unsure of his feelings or his responsibilities to his people. "So, what's the plan?" he muttered at last. "I don't understand."

Molly dropped his hand. She was leader and prophet once more. "The aim is not to negotiate with Canada, but to destroy it. It's an artificial nation ... a multicultural blob held together by little self-interested mobs of foreigners." She swept her hand across the horizon.

"Look Bill, no one in Toronto or Vancouver or Montreal gives a rat's ass about this land. They care about getting to work on the subway and paying off their mortgages. All this national unity and 'the world needs more Canada' is just slimy campaign rhetoric. For Christ's sake, Bill, the prime minister chases votes in Chinatown by apologizing to Chinese ancestors because they had to pay an entrance fee to get into this bountiful country. He should apologize to us for letting the bloody Chinese take our land!

"Nothing in this land will change simply because we're standing here talking." Molly swung a hand at the tall grass that swayed away and returned undisturbed.

"We, the native people, are a nation with our own understanding of what that means. Ironic, isn't it? The whites break up the nation to satisfy outsiders, and we, inhabitants of small diverse scattered bands, unite as 'nations within a nation' and beat the ass off these rich, powerful idiots.

"Even the horrid white Indians, Onanole, the self-styled grand chief, and the other six hundred chiefs sucking at the feds' tits, they got the message. Create 'nations.' Peddle grievances. Concentrate on white guilt, and, presto, you have all the politicians in Canada at Kelowna trying to outdo each other in giving away tax dollars.

"Bill, I'm not interested in being a monkey performing tricks for bribes. This isn't about me; it's about all of us. We are the land and the land is the people. We cannot survive divided one from the other. You tried—it didn't work. The 'grand chief' isn't leading. The common folk are leading and the people in the street, that's who frightens the white politicians. Most frightening of all are people in the street, natives and whites, who can't be bought off with election promises, money or spin.

"Look, who would have thought that little communities of know-nothings up the Mackenzie River could bully the feds and the prime minister and the big oil companies? Who needs the federal government? It's just an anachronism, rotting timbers trying to hold a lost and abandoned idea together. What I'm doing, what we're doing, is driving a splitting maul through this deadwood. You watch, Bill, once the provinces and the regions see Ottawa's impotence and the threat to their livelihood, they'll race to be the first at our table. Regionalism trumps Canada, every time.

Multiculturalism is the requiem for the country. Too bad for them. Great for us.

"I'm telling you, the whole thing is coming down and it's coming down now. Once the government of Canada is seen to be powerless, the provinces will jump through hoops to negotiate with us separately. Isn't that what Ottawa's been doing for years, backing down at very encounter? Some rag-tag band makes a commotion and the feds and the provinces compete with each other to see who's going to have to pay the bill as the local band keeps upping the price for peace. They can't turn back now. We have them. We're not going to negotiate with the central government. We're going to negotiate with the fragments of a shattered state—ironic isn't it, we've reversed the game.

"Within days, days, Bill, there will just be two powerful political entities in the north, us and the provinces. The weak, discredited provinces. We'll redraw the map of North America. We'll negotiate with Washington, or they won't get any oil or gas or electricity. Then we'll control our lands, with the aid of American industry and a few fiefdoms in southern Ontario and Alberta. No forty-ninth parallel anymore.

"That's what I'm going to do, Bill, and damn it, I need you. You know that. I need you to help me, help us all, in this final act. We're going to let loose some of the demo teams as a signal to Washington of our power. We're going to ignore any hand put forward by Ottawa. We're going to rein in Chief Onanole, give him just one chance to join the Committee or perish. We're going to dismiss the so-called elected chiefs. We're going to open negotiations with the provinces one-on-one once Washington comes onside: no invitation to Canada. The UN is a crowd of hopeless idiots, but we'll use them, so long as Washington doesn't object.

"I want you to be our ambassador in Washington and go there just as soon as our demonstration brings this round of fighting to a stop. You know the native lobby group in the U.S. has a connection to the oil industry and they're already petitioning on our behalf—very quietly, and for a future fee, of course. We need you there to give credibility to the movement. Will you go?"

Bill stepped back, overwhelmed by the power of the idea, its insanity, the very audacity that meant it might work. How could it have come to this? A couple of native people standing in the prairie grass on the edge of a national buffalo jump, yet confident that the hunters who so carelessly drove them here will miss the quarry and hurl themselves right over the cliff into the bone-yard below.

"Is it right what you're doing, Molly? That's the question. It's not just 'let's do what can succeed or we think will succeed' or simple-mindedly doing what we can assert. You're asking me to destroy valuable property and maybe kill a lot of people on your say-so that things will fall into place to suit your plan. There are other options. We have the feds where we want them…which I thought was the plan. Now they have to negotiate hard because we have the upper hand. But why would the Americans and the provinces just give up on the Canadian federal government and deal with us?"

Molly walked in a small circle, quiet, thoughtful, then turned around. "They'll deal with us, Bill, because we can deliver peace, order, and good government in the regions, and the prime minister can't. We just proved that. And, more important to the Americans and the big cities, we can deliver the goods, the oil and gas, and Ottawa can't. We're showing the Americans and the others the facts of national life in North America, and we're going to paint it in stark flaming colours just to make sure it's clear to everyone.

"We're going to proclaim Assiniboia tomorrow and invite the media to meetings with the provisional government, even if we have to do it here in the open prairies. If the plan fails, we'll fall back on the land and keep up the fight through the winter, but first we'll burn every farmer and every villager out of the countryside from here to the Rocky Mountains. And for good measure, we'll keep all those nice Mounties we've picked up and trade them as we see fit.

"You said there were 'other options.' Well, Bill, name a few. Surrender and jail? Wait and see until that slippery bastard Hemp recovers? Wait for more Canadian troops to come home? Let the Americans think they have things under control? Jesus Christ, we fought to get the Americans in the position Ottawa was in last week—hostage to our decisions. Oh yeah, there's another option all right. Servitude. No thanks!

"Come on, Bill, we've got to get back to the command post. There's work to do, and besides there're enough rumours swirling around us as it is. She put her arms around him, pulled him close and spoke softly, her head resting on his shoulder. "Bill, take a deep breath. Come back and join the fight. It's a good cause, the only cause. We can get old together and worry about the mortgage years from now—after we get the Nobel Peace Prize." Molly laughed, took Bill's hand, and turned, confident and unafraid, towards the farm and the war and to Joe and Riel's ghost.

Bill and Molly walked wordlessly back to the crooked house. Once inside, she returned to business. Bill moved to a far wall as Molly tossed her jacket on the floor and pushed back her hair, then settled into a chair behind what was actually the kitchen table but was draped to resemble a desk. Her technician adjusted his camera angles and shifted lights around, evenly illuminating not only Molly's fine features but also the Warrior flag he had hung as a backdrop. He adjusted the small framed photo of Louis Riel on the desk to Molly's right so it didn't reflect glare. Then he clipped a tiny microphone to the collar of her beaded suede shirt.

"Comfortable?' he said. "I'll get you some water. Need anything else?"

Molly shook her head, "No, I'm okay." Molly shuffled her notes, checking the occasional point even though she knew the lines by heart, knew them in her heart. She had worried over them and revised them in her mind for years, rehearsing scenes where she would stand before a great crowd and make this declaration. Countless times she had scribbled in the margins of her creased notebook, adding new lines and amending others, fixing a word here and a phrase there.

The technician fiddled with his machines, checking connections, waiting for the call from the NTV studio that would send Molly's taped message to the major Canadian and American networks in time for their Friday morning network news shows.

The phone buzzed.

"Yeah, hello, Edmonton? Yup, got it. Sounds good, clear." The technician turned to Molly.

"Okay, could you count down a few numbers for me so we can check the sound?" The technician watched his instruments, cupping his headset mike in his left hand. "Okay, good to go here. You okay? Yeah? Hang on."

"Molly," he said, "they'd like you to turn a bit to the right, and put your hands in front without holding up your notes too much...a clean desk looks more, ah...in charge, you know."

Molly adjusted her position without comment, shook the tension out of her shoulders, and said, "Okay? Let's do it."

"Right, you look great. Okay, Edmonton, stand by." He turned to Molly. "In five, four..." He counted down the last three seconds silently with his fingers then pointed to the leader.

DAY THIRTEEN

Friday, September 10

"We interrupt this special edition of *Canada AM* to bring you this break-ing news. In a moment we will broadcast a startling announcement from Molly Grace, the apparent leader of the First Nations Movement. As we understand it, this announcement was taped sometime late last night from somewhere in Western Canada and forwarded to the major Canadian and American networks a few minutes ago. We bring it to you in its entirety without editing or comment. Following the broadcast we will try to get responses to this declaration from Ottawa and Washington."

From a dot in the centre, like a brush fire, the Warriors' flag filled the nation's TV screens.

"Ladies and Gentlemen," said the tenor voice in the background, "people of the Confederation of the First Nations, we bring you, from the battlefields of the First Nations of America, our leader and revolutionary Grand Chief, Molly Grace."

The picture quickly dissolved to Molly, looking straight into the camera, confident and calm, naturally captivating, the flag behind her.

"White invaders, political oppressors, native turncoats, and other enemies of the rightful heirs of this great, wild land, hear these words.

"We will not give peace a chance. Peaceful surrender is the refuge of the weak, the home of our trusting ancestors raised in a community of honour and truth, deceived by the white invaders, who knowingly left generations in servitude and spiritual poverty.

"Peace, as we discovered to our misfortune, is easily achieved—the people have simply to surrender all self-respect and all their history and culture to the overwhelming power of the most brutal, the foreign invaders. Through the generations and still today we live in a dark dungeon called 'peace,' like our brothers and sisters across Africa and Asia and Iraq and Afghanistan.

"Our peaceful nature has given us what? Poverty and a genocidal slide into shame and self-pity. Peace for us is an acceptance of oppression as our natural lot in life, a shackle fastened onto us by the white man, a lying, skulking domination of our people. It is a shackle once willingly accepted, naively, through trust misplaced, but now held tightly to our body by white prejudice and the self-interest of the white Indians who live on scraps at the feet of the oppressor. Peace is not the solution. It is the problem, the curse.

"In 2006, the great Six Nations of the Mohawk Confederacy woke the sleeping giant of native pride. We discovered at Caledonia, as we had not at Oka or Burnt Church, our true power, based not in false peace but in the power of righteous action, of necessary self-defence—a right granted to all nations under the United Nations Charter. We tried to show the justice of our demands in peaceful 'days of action' in 2007 and 2008 and again in 2009, but Canadians failed to listen. Their leaders made false promises and false apologies but their governments failed to act.

"We the peoples of this land are downtrodden because we have argued from the wrong side of history, from the wrong side of justice. Now is the time to counterattack, to expose the ugly face of white oppression and fight back. Why are the farmers and merchants of the Prairies rich? Why does Quebec thrive on power generated in the land of the Cree? Why are immigrants, in Canada no more than five years, suburban homeowners, while our people live in rags and crumbling shacks? These so-called Canadians are rich because they live off the avails of theft from the native people. They live on the profits from the rape of native land and native culture.

"White society prospers and Canada's economy rides with a posse of lies. The white oppressors' invented legality depends on the gross lie that they own the land because they paid chiefs and band leaders to surrender it forever. No such surrender occurred. The chiefs would not and could not give away the land. Any papers that assert these claims are fictions and frauds, bearing the names of ancient leaders too trusting of the white man's deceitful words, or coerced into agreements they did not understand.

"Deceit alone backs the white man's claim to native land. White oppressors own the land, they declare, by right, because of deals made according to their laws between, they say, willing sellers and willing buyers. It is a foul-smelling, ill-conceived lie carried on the stout shoulders of prejudice. 'How,' the settlers asked, 'can we allow a motley band of illiterate natives to own land when we know they will do nothing to increase its value?' So they stole it.

"The white man's concept of the land as inherently valueless unless exploited for some purpose is alien to our culture. The white man's concept of private property is alien to our culture. The white invader invented the self-serving notion that our ancestors sold the land to them, and, then as now, they use this foul idea as a tool to plunder native societies. No native leader and no native nation in ancient days or now thought land was 'private property,' so no leader, then or now, could sell the people's inheritance to anyone. The so-called precedence of land sales is an invented history of no standing in our community.

"Yet even today the deceit continues. And today native lackeys help perpetuate it. White governments offer bribes to the traitorous white Indians, as if they could buy the souls of the people with mere money. They hope the people will accept the white man's notion of land as a trinket to be bartered and bargained over and sold for gain. But it will not be. The people will never surrender the traditional idea of the land as indivisible from the spirits and from the people. The people reject genocide hidden in smiling faces and handshakes in 'photo-ops.'

"From the first day the white invaders set foot on our land, we have been treated as wards of the state—culturally destitute inferior beings, incapable of caring for ourselves. We were treated as mentally defective, in need of direction in every facet of daily life. But our welfare was the excuse, not the goal. Outright eradication or the cultural equivalent, assimilation to the white invader's norms and expectations of 'citizenship,' that was the true and only objective. The settlers believed, and still believe, that because we were not white, grasping, individualistic, and faithful to the white man's God, that we were uncivilized. The white man offered us the three C's of colonial oppression—commerce, Christianity, and civilization—with genocide as the only other choice lurking in the shadows.

"Salvation from savagery, they said, would come from white power and white bribes. They offered extermination, wardship or 'citizenship,' which meant incorporation into the white culture under the white man's terms, the white man's concepts of government and of property.

"Today we reject these assaults on our culture, and we call them by their proper name: genocide. We are not wards nor will we be assimilated. We have attempted in good faith to join Canada as self-governing nations, only to be met with trickery and subjugation, a recognition of our 'nationhood' that left us prisoners in dependent, impoverished communities. Having stripped our nations of their rightful inheritances and ownership of their resources, Canada offered us 'self-government' while stealing from us the rights of sovereignty.

"No more. It is over. We do not need Canada to grant us the rights of nationhood. We are and have always been sovereign in our own land. We will build our homeland, Assiniboia, embracing all the lands from the western shores of Lake Superior to the eastern slopes of the Rocky Mountains, on an unshakable foundation of traditional native values. The first among these values is the sanctity of the land and the oneness of the people with the land.

"The Central Committee of the Provisional Government of the people of Assiniboia, therefore, puts before the General Assembly of the United Nations—*The Assiniboia Declaration.*

Assiniboia is a sovereign nation, the free and independent homeland of the people and the Métis; neighbour to the free Inuit in their northern home; and the confederacies of native people elsewhere in Canada and in North America. We enjoy all the rights and privileges of a nation under the Charter of the United Nations. We specifically declare the right of self-defence of our native lands under that Charter.

A Congress of the people of Assiniboia will meet as a Provisional Government to decide in council its constitution and system of government and we call on the United Nations to protect this Congress and to assist it in freeing the people from the oppression of Canada.

The people of Assiniboia demand reparations from Canada in the sum of $700 billion in compensation for two centuries of abuse and the plundering of the people's inherent wealth and the continuous assault on their culture.

Assiniboia will not be subject to any debt or taxes imposed on Canadians, but will establish its own community of support in which those able will provide for those in need as tradition demands.

The Provisional Government and it alone will determine who is a 'native person,' under terms it alone will establish, and declares that notwithstanding present circumstances, only 'native persons' are entitled to citizenship in Assiniboia as the Provisional Government defines those terms.

The Provisional Government is the sole authority in Assiniboia and it alone will negotiate any and all treaties with the government of Canada and all other nations. Only representatives appointed by the Provisional Government will represent Assiniboia at all international assemblies and in all organizations including especially in the General Assembly of the United Nations.

The Provisional Government has sole rights and unfettered possession of all resources in Assiniboia and the right to collect taxes from all systems of communications and transportation and from all goods— industrial, agricultural and mineral, including water, natural gas, and petroleum—produced in or entering, leaving, or passing through the territory of Assiniboia.

All public and privately-owned facilities once deemed 'owned' by

any foreign government, including those of Canada and of Canadian
provinces, hereby stand forfeit to the Provisional Government.

The official language of Assiniboia is the native dialect of the Cree
nation, but English and French, while subordinated to and separate
from the language of the Cree, shall enjoy equal status in the nation.

The Justice System of Assiniboia will be built on traditional native
customs and practices as the Congress of the people shall direct. The
Provisional Government immediately suspends the authority of all
Canadian officials and officers of Canadian courts in the nation.
Nevertheless, the Provisional Government holds Canada liable to
maintain and finance federal penal institutions until such time as all
native convictions are reviewed by a people's court of reconciliation
and new institutions compatible with native customs are established.

All debts contracted by the Provisional Government and citizens of
Assiniboia in consequence of the illegal war and repressive measures
waged by and adopted by Canadian officials and the armed forces
of Canada to bring about a civil war in our midst shall be paid by
Canada. Moreover, Canadian officials and military officers respon-
sible for the creation and implementation of those measures shall be
subject to investigation by the International Criminal Court of Justice
as directed by the General Assembly of the United Nations. No person
of Assiniboia, nor any ally of the people in other parts of Canada, or
anyone acting for the Provisional Government, shall be held liable
for any of the actions taken to defend the people from the aggressive
actions of Canada.

"We, the leaders of the Provisional Government, attempted for decades
to bring the interests of our people into harmony with those of the white
people and others who have exploited our people and the land. We rejected,
repeatedly, the efforts of some governments to divide the councils of our
nation, knowing it would be ruinous and disastrous to all. Yet the evil
agencies and prejudices of the settler community overwhelmed our efforts.
They excited grievances and self-interest while resisting reasonableness at
every turn. Where once it was impossible to rally our separate nations to
rise up in rightful defence against the hostile attacks and misdeeds of the

white settler community, the actions of these callous governments finally overcame the people's traditional cooperative nature.

"In these circumstances, calls for peaceful negotiations between Canadian political leaders and the white natives of Ottawa were merely traps meant to hold the people in bondage. We will, therefore, fight for our people and our inalienable rights as we define them from our legends, customs and traditions. Whether relations between the separate nations of Assiniboia and Canada develop on fair and friendly terms or in a destructive contest is for Canada to decide. We the people of Assiniboia with our esteemed and courageous native allies in North America and with the moral support of the United Nations will in any case defend ourselves with unfailing courage."

Fade to black.

Friday, September 10, 0730 hours
Ottawa: Langevin Block

Jack Hemp, ashen-faced, slid into the cabinet room with his principal aides. He hardly noticed the haggard faces of those at the table, who, like him, had just watched Molly Grace's "Assiniboia Declaration." The Canadian government was in disarray, and Hemp's claim that all military operations in Canada were under Canadian command had been exposed as gibberish by reporters embedded with American units in the field.

Defence minister Jim Riley's hastily arranged press conference early the previous morning to explain to the international media the operational structure established under the CANUS military relationship had been pre-empted by a Pentagon briefing an hour earlier. Riley had tried his best to recover the initiative, but his effort collapsed when an angry three-way quarrel erupted between Canadian and American reporters and government political staffers. The American representatives of the U.S. cable news networks were openly astonished and angry at being denied interviews with the prime minister and General Bishop, and hurled insults at the government spokespersons. Members of the Ottawa press gallery, unaccustomed to such aggressive competition, tried to shout down the Americans as Jim Riley stood helplessly nearby.

Michael Blast, chief political correspondent for CNN, let his viewers watch several seconds of the aggressive scrum from his "Operations Room" in Atlanta, then sneered, "How long will President Ricardo allow the puny Canadian army and the disorganized political system in Canada to direct military operations while American forces are engaged in a desperate struggle to defend this nation's vital interests?"

The remarks struck a sensitive nerve in the White House, prompting the president's spokeswoman to organize a special press briefing an hour later to "set the record straight." That message cooked Hemp's goose.

"The president," the spokeswoman explained, "has full command of American forces in Canada and dispatched General O'Neill to direct operations there. Furthermore," she announced, "the president yesterday afternoon appointed the former governor of Maine, Stanley Kitson, as special envoy to Canada to assist the government of Canada and Prime Minister Hemp in formulating appropriate responses to native nations' rightful land claims and redress of abuses of their human rights, the neglect of both of which are the root cause of this unfortunate misunderstanding between the native nations and Canada."

All night, the premiers of every province except B.C., Ontario, and P.E.I. had been yelling into the phone at Jack Hemp, demanding troops and federal police to help defend them from organized attacks by the NPA and the even more dangerous spontaneous outbreaks of violence occurring in their provinces. The National Defence Act and the federal Emergencies Act contained ample legal provisions for typical disorders, but Hemp was facing a national defence catastrophe where no rules existed and no resources were left to enforce them if they had. The majority of the federal public service, having resolutely ignored questions of national security on a wide scale, sat mute, without recommendations or direction.

The only Canadian troops not already embroiled in the violence were deployed overseas, and squabbles with foreign states over the native situation delayed their redeployment from Africa and the Middle East. Even when Canadian units were allowed to get to various airports and file flight plans, the International Air Traffic Association and foreign unions, "out of sympathy for the righteous native cause," delayed or cancelled military and civilian flights meant to bring troops home.

The United Nations Security Council was in emergency session at the request of China—acting, rumour said, on the assumption fostered during clandestine meetings with intermediaries for the Native People's Committee that early friends of Assiniboia could expect mineral and oil rights once peace was established. The Chinese resolution had wide support in the General Assembly, though, in fact, its double-dealing authors had also initiated informal "conversations" with Canada's ambassador to the UN on whether a suitable "modification" of their position would result in preferential natural resource trade arrangements with the Canadian government once the disturbances were settled. Their actions, some commentators assumed, were simply tit-for-tat in response to Canada's long scolding of Beijing over China's human rights record.

Alarm in Ottawa turned to panic when ministers learned that the United States was quietly letting it be known that it would not necessarily veto a Security Council resolution, if the General Assembly requested one, for the deployment of a UN peacekeeping force to Canada, provided it was composed of American-nominated contributing nations from the Western Hemisphere and commanded by an American general, presumably John O'Neill.

A steady stream of reports from ambassadors, ministers, and public servants with connections overseas reflected a continuing collapse of Canada's position in foreign capitals and international organizations. Only Australia, which had its own aboriginal problem, argued in the UN for understanding and support for the legitimate government and its honourable record in native affairs.

Under the circumstances, the cabinet meeting could hardly focus on General Bishop's account of the significant military difficulties he suffered, let alone draw comfort from his attempt to encourage the politicians with reports of some quick and nearly bloodless successes over the past twenty-four hours. Especially since, in answer to questions, he could not, he said, "speak for the situation after the American units have reached their arbitrary stop-lines"; and because his attempt to have the Van Doos battle group rush up the highway from Matagami to capture Radisson before the Americans could fully deploy in the region had failed.

General O'Neill hadn't fully explained his plan for an airborne assault on the natives there. By early on September 9, the James Bay area and the villages were in American rather than Canadian or NPA hands, although the Radisson generating facilities were all but destroyed. With winter coming, Montreal would freeze without electricity, and there was none to be had from the north or south. Without electricity from James Bay, Quebec and Ontario would need oil and gas from the West in even greater quantities, and without some accommodation with the native leaders, that supply was problematic.

The news from acting minister of finance, Pierre Jordan, was no better. Winnipeg was a disaster area. Large parts of the city core had been damaged, streets were closed, the economy of the city was in peril, and huge numbers of frightened Prairie refugees were pouring in from the countryside; consequently, much of the harvest would be lost. Saskatchewan was a little less chaotic, but the fighting there was only delayed, not prevented.

Trans-Canada transportation and commerce were dead in the air, on the roads, and along the railway systems east and west. The Toronto stock market had been falling steadily since the beginning of the raids in Quebec. The dollar had plunged to fifty-eight cents U.S. and was still drifting down. Another calamity, the governor of the Bank of Canada warned through Jordan, would send the Canadian economy into a deep, irrecoverable depression.

"Okay, ladies and gentlemen, ideas please." Jack Hemp, wearing a ghastly grinning mask of phony optimism, looked around the table for someone else to state the obvious. "Come now, people, you're the government of Canada, surely someone has a good idea." Noise from traffic up and down Wellington Street seemed louder and louder in the silence that followed. Eyes sought the floor, the desk, the ceiling.

"Negotiate." Softly, then with increasing defiance, Judy Cross, minister of equalization and member of Parliament for Toronto-Rosemont, repeated the frightful word. "Negotiate! We have no choice but to call in the native leaders, wave some sweet-grass and a feather around, and ask for terms. That's it, said and done." She pushed her chair away from the table. "I can't be a party to decisions that let Toronto go down the tubes to save a bunch of sod-busters in Saskatchewan. Better buy out the Indians than kill Canada's golden goose, Jack."

Stan Urlich from Saskatoon slammed his fist on the table. "Goddamned wonderful, Judy. Goddamn Eastern bigots. Who built this country? Not city-slickers like you. My family farmed the West for a century and got nothing but rudeness from Hogtown merchants and their high-society ladies-about-town. Negotiate? Bullshit! I'm not negotiating anything with those layabout Indians. All we do is give them handouts and they bite that hand, too. I say we get the army home and ask the president for more help and we beat the crap out of these renegades. That's my vote."

Hemp smiled, preparing to slide up the middle in this acrimonious political exchange. "Well, Stan, those pesky redskins don't seem like lay-abouts this morning. Eric, you had something, ah, calmer, I hope."

The normally invisible deputy prime minister, Eric Smith, from Vancouver, weighed in cautiously with a question. "Prime minister, will the native leaders negotiate? I mean, why should they? What can we offer that's not on the table now—dissolution of the country, Balkanization? I've got to be honest here, prime minister, the government and the people in British Columbia don't feel threatened right now, so maybe an approach we control might—"

"Well, now we're getting somewhere," said Hemp cutting off his deputy. "So let me suggest that we ask this new U.S. envoy—Kinson, Kitson, whatever—to approach the native leaders as a disinterested third party to create a cease-fire and hold things in place while we make arrangements for discussions, not negotiations mind you, just discussions.

"That'll give us time to get things in order, consolidate our military gains, get the U.S. troops out of sight, sort of, and for General Bishop to bring some people home, under cover if we can. It'll look good in the press, satisfy Congress, let CNN get back to reporting some starlet's drug problem, whatever. Then we can see if there're any cracks in the native camp. Divide and conquer ... that's the plan. It's worked before. We can use the winter too—starve them out in their villages."

"It's dangerous, Jack," Riley warned. "No telling where it might go."

"Agreed. Got a better idea? Anyone? Right, this is a tightly controlled situation. Anyone here, and that goes doubly for the public service, anyone here who speaks without my express permission is gone. We'll have three main action centres: Jim Riley and General Bishop will manage military affairs and get as many troops together as they can. General Bishop, I want General O'Neill on a tight string; you take control of all deployments in the country and make him go through Washington if he objects.

"Aaron," he told the foreign minister, "I want a full-court press at the UN. You tell those bastards on the Security Council and anyone else who looks like a vulture that 'we ain't dead yet.' If they want to gamble over oil and gas, I'll fix them when this is over. Set up a call for me with Prime Minister Wellesley. We need allies and the Aussies are it for the moment."

Hemp pointed his finger at the Canadian ambassador to Washington. "Herman, all out in Congress. If they want assured energy supplies, they better think long-term and remember who has the skills to deliver, and it's not Molly Grace. Remind them also that eighty-five per cent of our trade goes south and we're in this together.

"Harry Southern will handle the media, all the media people! First off, I want this Molly Grace brought to earth. She's no Joan of Arc—surely she's got stains on her skirt somewhere. So find them. Open the secret intelligence files to our select friends in the media if that helps.

"The storyline is this: the so-called Committee are not some happy group of noble savages working for the good of the people ... they're just in it for selfish personal gain. They don't represent the demands and interests of the native people. We were well on the way to opening a new dialogue with the legitimate native leaders and Molly et al moved to destroy this threat to their communist position. Okay?"

Stan Ulrich raised a hand. "Prime minister, you said we were going to negotiate, er, discuss issues with the native leaders. Now you said they don't represent anyone. Won't the press catch on to that? And what about that Onanole grand chief fellow? Where's he fit in?"

"Look Stan, you leave the slippery side of politics to me. You're out of your depth, here. You're too, well, too ... plain-spoken. Nothing wrong with that ... but it's not what we need just now on this file. Tell you the truth, I've already taken Onanole out of the game. Besides, everyone, you know we didn't get into government by being nice guys and—"

The door flew open and Jimmy Fellows, a junior PMO political aide, ran in and yelled, "Prime Minster! The Prairies are on fire!"

Hemp chuckled inanely. "Jimmy, you Ontario nitwit—it's September.

The Prairies are always on fire in September. The farmers are burning the chaff."

Jimmy rushed to the large TV in the corner and started punching buttons. "No, no, prime minister, I mean … damn, where's CNN … there … I mean, the oil fields are burning, everywhere. A gas compressor station was blown up in Saskatchewan, many are dead, and the gas flames are sky-high. Look!"

The cabinet turned to the screen as Fellows fumbled with the volume control in time to get the breathless CNN reporter at the scene, reporting to his equally breathless anchor in the Atlanta Operations Centre.

"Michael, this is a terrible tragedy. Oil derricks in several areas of Alberta, that's Canada's main oil-producing province, north of Montana, are on fire. The pipelines in and out of the vital tar-sands region are burning or ruptured. All across the horizon, the sky is turning black; there's oily, thick smoke billowing up from a dozen fields here and blowing towards me. I'll stay on duty, Michael, in the best CNN tradition, but my crew will have to get out of here soon. I tell you, I haven't seen anything like it since the first Iraq war when Saddam Hussein set Kuwait on fire and did billions of dollars in damage."

"Thank you, John. And now we go live to … ah … Sas-kat-cher-awan where terrorists have apparently driven a large grain truck bomb into a natural gas pipeline compressor station. Joining us from the site by helicopter, Bernie Gates. Bernie?"

A hoarse yell came over the noisy chop-chop-chop of the helicopter. "Good morning, or should I say, bad morning, Michael, because here below me is a scene of devastation. The large fenced compound that once held several buildings and machinery to pump thousands of tons of natural gas through the lines to American homes and industries is no more. Great flames are shooting into the sky. We are flying with caution, trying to avoid being swept into the firestorm that was once a functioning compound."

"Well done, Bernie, and yes, be careful. Tell us: how many people were actually killed or injured there on the ground?"

"Well, Michael, it's hard to tell, but the army had some troops guarding the site and by the looks of it, none got out. There's a story that the natives actually allowed the soldiers and workers to leave before they set off the bomb, but we can't confirm that yet."

Harry Southern stalked over to the screen, waving Fellows off, and looked at Hemp as he turned off the sound. "Prime minister, we have other news coming to us from other sources. Molly Grace was just on CTV, live this time, and gave another press statement." He looked at his notes. "She repeated the bit about the Provisional Government of Assiniboia being established as of today. Then she said the attacks on the pipelines were in retaliation for, and this is an important quote, 'the unprovoked attacks on our native people by the government of Canada. We lay no blame on the Unites States government or its armed forces, who were duped into supporting this outrageous attack on innocent people.' End quote.

"Then she went on CNN to tell all the world that, quote 'the Provisional Government of Assiniboia will not negotiate with the Government of Canada, but we look forward to sovereign negotiations with the government of the generous people of the United States who once fought their own battle for freedom. The NPC is also prepared to discuss future conditions and terms with provincial and municipal leaders in Canada in the hope of building a mutually beneficial and new confederation with all the nations in North America.' End quote. And then a lot of bullshit rhetoric I'll give you later.

"But get this bit. She went on, quote, 'We welcome just deliberations with our friends and supporters in the United Nations and look forward to peaceful and prosperous relations with friendly countries everywhere. In the meantime, we will in the near future send envoys from the Provisional Government to the United States, which has agreed to informal discussions at the level of envoys, and to the United Nations General Assembly, where I hope to present the Assiniboia Declaration to the international community.' End quote."

Southern dropped the notes on the table. "That's it, Jack, she scooped us."

Hemp sat down heavily. "Indeed."

Southern waited for something more useful but in vain, so he went on. "It gets worse, Jack. The CBC and CTV newsnets are reporting the premiers of Quebec, Alberta, and Manitoba have expressed an interest in meeting with the Provisional Government. Premier Commeau said she saw reason to be optimistic that relations could be improved and that Quebec had the right to negotiate its domestic security arrangements without the consent of the government of Canada, especially given the inability of that government to maintain order.

"And just a few minutes ago, according to the CBC, Ambassador Laforge confirmed to a media scrum outside the U.S. embassy that the secretary of state had agreed to an 'informal' meeting of Provisional Government and U.S. envoys, but on condition that oil and gas supplies are safeguarded and flow immediately and without any commitments from the American side. I think these attacks on the gas lines were meant to bring a more conciliatory tone from the White House."

Jack Hemp made one feeble attempt to regain control of the cabinet. "Well, busy day, lots to do. As I was saying ..." But his voice trailed off as ministers ignored him, either speaking among themselves or simply walking out of the room.

"As I was saying, Jack," Judy barked as she left, "you lost the country! Who's going to listen to you out there on the street? You're the undertaker of Confederation, for Christ's sake. I want no part of this."

As she disappeared through the door, Hemp hollered after her, "You can't stick that label on me. I didn't lose the country. Those louts who were in government in the nineties ... they did it! Going on negotiating with gangs, blaming law-abiding citizens for every sin of their fathers. Who ever stood up for Canada?"

Stan jumped to his feet. "You idiot, we Westerners have been warning you and warning you, and you guys in the East just called us bigots. And the police and the security services told us in parliamentary committee meetings and briefings and cabinet committees over and over that a crisis would come sooner, not later. So what did Parliament or cabinet do? Nothing! And the provinces? Eventually the police got so fed up with taking the blame every time they tried to enforce a court order or stop smuggling or gun-running, they just quit. And we all let them. So who's to blame?"

Hemp was scarlet with rage. "Oh sure, Stan. Big man from the West. You were in Parliament for what, twenty years, why didn't you do something?"

"Well, prime minister," Stan sneered, "wasn't it your Liberal hero, Trudeau, who said 'Fifty yards from Parliament Hill, MPs are nobodies,' and then went out of his way to make sure we were? And what did you ever do about it? Can't blame us, Jack Hemp. Did you ever once listen to me about this? Did you ever even talk to me? Noooo. You big shots spent all your time criticizing American presidents for not doing enough to stamp out the so-called root causes of terrorism like poverty, sick living conditions, depression, failed expectations, insecurity all over the world, while you sat in Ottawa and let the exact things we called 'root causes,' to say nothing of lawlessness, thrive in our own backyard."

Hemp clapped his hands mockingly. "Well said, Stan. Well said. But you're a politician, Stan, you know that Canadians didn't worry about the Indians. They might feel sorry for them, but to the ordinary Canadian, they weren't a real problem. We read the polls. So why should we care; we're the servants of the people, aren't we? In the end, Stan, you know you can't blame the government: it's the people's fault—after all, they elected us."

Ulrich, purple with fury, rose from the table.

Harry Southern looked up at Ulrich while gathering his own papers and stuffing them into his leather brief case. "Yeah," he added, "and you remember, Stan, the Indian leaders, the grand chiefs and that lot, they have to take a share of the blame. Those bastards kept the pot boiling, always looking for another grievance, another way to bilk the white guy. Well, Molly Grace is going to skin them too."

Ulrich, speechless, turned and stormed out.

Southern glanced out the window. "Take a look, Jack. Your directions didn't go far. I count five … no seven ministers in various scrums on the street. Want to see a government disintegrating in midair, like that space-ship a few years ago? Bet they're not following the storyline or singing your praises. Perhaps we'd better try to pass the ball to the opposition or go to the governor general and call an election. Hard to tell what good that would do, though."

Hemp, going down for the third time, characteristically clutched at this last chance to blame somebody else. "Guess you're right, Harry. If Canadians don't want a real country, why should we knock ourselves out trying to give them one? Ironic, isn't it? We all ran around the world telling everyone the world needs more Canada and it turns out *Canadians* don't even think they need Canada."

But he was talking to himself, alone in the cabinet room. Over his shoulder, a muted CNN showed a film clip of burning oil fields; streams of refugees driving or walking through beautiful, partially harvested grain fields; smoking, ruined buildings at James Bay; shattered streets in Winnipeg, Yorkton, and Montreal; and RCMP constables in handcuffs in their own jails. As the report ended, the producer cut to the grounds of the Manitoba Legislative Building, where Patty Leduc's bullet-riddled body lay on the wet, cold, concrete beneath Louis Riel's black statue. Rain, like tears, fell from the hero's stone face.

The people... are contrite for their sins, but too late do they, as suppliants, beg for pardon from the bottom of their hearts, weeping. God looks down upon them. But the judgment of heaven must first be fulfilled. The flames increase—a third city now looks like a huge funeral pyre.

"Well," Prime Minister Jack Hemp said to the empty room, "somebody else should have done something about this long before now." He shrugged and wandered away.

THE RICARDO DOCTRINE

Thursday, September 30

Thursday, September 30
Washington, DC: The Oval Office, The White House
The President's Address to the Nation

My fellow Americans:

Three weeks ago, a great danger to the safety and the welfare of the United Sates erupted on our northern border. A native uprising overwhelmed the Canadian government and its armed forces and security services. The wide-scale violence destroyed large segments of Canada's resource industries and infrastructure and as a direct consequence endangered the lives of Americans across the nation. As the situation worsened, I decided to act to protect our citizens and our economy, and ordered the commanders of our armed forces to take appropriate, but limited, actions to restore order in Canada. This they did quickly and efficiently.

For most Americans, the events of the last several weeks will no doubt come as a shock. Canada has always seemed a peaceful nation, blessed in its riches and tolerant of differences. There was something rotten in the state, however. And it seems that we did not see the trouble that was brewing. Nor, it must be said, did Canada's leaders.

Problems long left unattended—problems such as enduring native poverty and unresolved land claims—were the cause of the distressing events that we have witnessed recently. Eventually, when negotiations with the government failed to produce solutions, these problems provided a platform for native radicals and their unyielding demands. Fiery speeches by ambitious leaders meant only to win political support within native communities soon trapped these so-called leaders in positions from which they could not retreat. Or so they thought.

Once radical demands became the norm, and communities' expectations for redress and rich rewards for past "humiliations" and "grievances" soared, a kind of political and sociological "bidding war" began. Demands once made became "rights," impossible to abandon.

A similar process in Canada's mainstream political parties reinforced this dynamic. While attempting to demonstrate compassion for the native community to the electorate at large, Canadian politicians, it seems, made ever more extravagant, but essentially empty promises to accommodate native demands. Even heartfelt apologies for past wrongs given in the House of Commons served only briefly to change the discourse from its dangerous direction. Soon afterwards, radical leaders used these words of penitence as proof that the legitimacy and authority of Canada as a whole had been overturned.

We Americans watched in alarm as the inconceivable situation unfolded—Canada at war with itself. We could not and cannot understand how a country that works could destroy itself in such a horrible fashion. Canadians told us, "You don't understand the seriousness of the disputes."

How could anyone understand quarrels about land in a country overwhelmed by its space; arguments about language between people who rarely spoke to each other; solemn quibbling about which group was or was not a distinct society in a nation that had officially declared itself multicultural? How could anyone have predicted armed conflict in a state renowned for "peace, order and good government"?

But of course, as they quarrelled, no one in Canada thought that Mars, the god of war, would ever come through their door, even though from all sides their leaders' belligerent talk and their stubborn politics invited him into their homes. Speak of the devil and he will come, it is said; the same is often true of Mars.

The failures of Canada's political and aboriginal leaders to address this menace in time has many roots. Politicians felt trapped by their repeated assurances to the public that there were no serious problems in native affairs. Such "incidents" as had occurred were all waved off as random misunderstandings that could be worked out by honest negotiations.

Native leaders, too, must be held to account for the conflict that erupted in Canada, even those who did not directly inspire or support it. Their strident rhetoric created in native communities precisely the beliefs the radicals exploited, that any and every serious crisis would force Canada's politicians to make major concessions to natives everywhere and that there was no downside to militancy, however irresponsible.

The more peaceful chiefs—and they were in the majority—who genuinely were intent on negotiating with Ottawa, from a position of political strength, realized too late that they could not control events when militants in the native community almost effortlessly usurped their authority simply by adopting the chiefs' rhetoric of abuse.

There is, however, a more fundamental cause of the disaster that I must underline here tonight if we are to learn from history and not repeat its darker chapters. That cause is arrogance. Almost everyone involved in leading Canada to this final crisis, native and non-native alike, thought they could control events and assure a favourable resolution of deeply embedded political and social problems without making reasonable concessions to others' legitimate interests. As we now know, everyone was wrong and everyone lost. It is a sad lesson, and one that I know all Americans will want to reflect on as we deal with our own challenges in the future.

This evening, my fellow Americans, I am announcing a new political and international arrangement that will direct our relations with the former state of Canada. The Ricardo Doctrine sets out a broad commanding strategy for the defence of America's vital interests in North America. It is based on two strategic imperatives. The first of these involves the maintenance of our secure access to natural resources, primarily energy—natural gas, petroleum, and electricity from hydroelectric and nuclear plants—

and water flowing (or made to flow) into the United States from the former Canadian territories. The second involves maintaining and sustaining the integrated Canadian-United States industries critical to the American economy.

The United States no longer recognizes the U.S./Canada border which, if truth were told, is already largely irrelevant to Canadian economic, security, and cultural policies. The United States will create in Canada five "Vital Mandate Territories" under direct American administration. They are: the Northern Territory, comprising all of Nunavut, including the Arctic Archipelago, and the portion of the Northwest Territories east of the Mackenzie Valley; the Prairie Territory, including all of the northwest petroleum basin as well as the sections of southern Saskatchewan and Manitoba necessary to protect transportation routes and oil and gas pipelines; the Ontario Territory, comprising southern Ontario and the vital transportation routes above Lake Superior; the Quebec-James Bay-Labrador Territory, which includes Labrador and all territory within the province of Quebec above a line running from south of James Bay to the Gulf of St. Lawrence—this region is a critical source of hydroelectric power; and the Quebec-Atlantic Territory, including the remainder of Quebec, all of the Gulf of St. Lawrence, the Maritime Provinces, and the island of Newfoundland.

The Yukon Territory and the critical Mackenzie River region will be absorbed by the state of Alaska, as will most of the northern half of the province of British Columbia. The southern part of British Columbia for simplicity of administration will be absorbed into the state of Washington.

The Ricardo Doctrine implicitly acknowledges the land claims of the First Nations in Canada, though not in their entirety or unconditionally. Land claims in what will become the Autonomous Aboriginal Territories, which lie outside the designated Vital Mandate Territories, are still being adjudicated, and property rights are being assigned by United States proconsuls. The largest of these territories, the Hudson Bay Territory, encompasses most of northern Ontario, Manitoba, and Saskatchewan. I have directed that all claims and compensations in these territories are to be settled as soon as possible and that the settlements will be binding on all parties. The administration and policing of these territories will be the responsibility of the United States until such time as "agreed national enti-

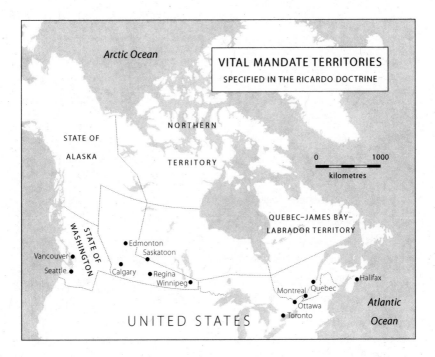

VITAL MANDATE TERRITORIES
SPECIFIED IN THE RICARDO DOCTRINE

Arctic Ocean

NORTHERN

STATE OF

ALASKA

TERRITORY

0   1000

kilometres

QUEBEC–JAMES BAY–
LABRADOR TERRITORY

STATE OF WASHINGTON

Vancouver •
Seattle •

• Edmonton
Saskatoon •
Calgary • • Regina
Winnipeg •

•Halifax

Montreal / Quebec •

• Ottawa
• Toronto

UNITED STATES

Atlantic

Ocean

ties are established for each region." It is difficult to predict when that will
happen.

The principal negotiating party in matters regarding aboriginal affairs
and the United States of America will be the newly established House of
Representatives of the First Peoples, which is to be composed of three
representative bodies—native Indians, Inuit and Métis—membership
of which will be determined by elections based on proportional rep-
resentation. This body's first duty—under the guidance of Washington
officials—will be to draw up a governing constitution for their territory. In
any case, the United States will not be held hostage to treaties negotiated in
the seventeenth and eighteenth centuries between aboriginal peoples and
the British monarchy of the time, the parties to which, for all intents and
purposes, no longer exist.

The aboriginal policy framework of the Ricardo Doctrine is based on
three fundamental, non-negotiable ideas. First, aboriginal people in Canada will be treated as full citizens, not wards of the state or its subordinate institutions. As such, all aboriginal peoples living on reservations on

September 1 will be given title to their residential property, with complete normal legal rights, like any other citizen, to hold, lease or sell real property as they see fit.

Second, land claims will be settled finally and forever once the aboriginal communities establish, with the aid of the government of the United States, the free-market value of real properties.

Third, once the distribution of the property is settled by individual owners, all clans, bands, tribes and so-called nations will cease to have any legal standing in any territory other than in the Autonomous Aboriginal Territories, where legal and constitutional arrangements will be determined by elected representatives of the relevant aboriginal people voting, at least in the initial election, as individuals. Traditional aboriginal associations may, of course, be maintained by private citizens for cultural reasons as they are by a wide variety of other ethnic and cultural groups elsewhere in Canada and indeed in the United States.

Finally, my fellow Americans, despite our long and mostly mutually beneficial relationship with Canada over the past 150 years, it is the opinion of the government of the United States that the safety, security and welfare of America does not demand that we support the continuance of Canada as a unified political entity—quite the contrary, in fact. We have come to believe through difficult and prolonged deliberations that America's interests and the future prosperity of Canadian citizens will be served best by the dissolution of the Canadian federation and the incorporation of its fractious communities under the various arrangements I have announced tonight.

I believe that even without the tragic conflict of September the policy of continental integration that I have announced this evening is a policy that Canadians will endorse, and, indeed, that many have actually aspired to since, at least, the beginning of the last decade of the twentieth century.

We believe that Canadians will soon come to treasure their new association with their fellow Americans and see our announcement this evening as the fulfilment of their true desires.

Thank you, good evening and God Bless America.

EPILOGUE

April 1

April 1
The Washington Free Press
John G. Durham
In Ottawa

A rude April winter storm swept across Ottawa as I arrived in the city. Today, six months after the declaration of the Ricardo Doctrine, Parliament Hill, virtually deserted since the beginning of the United States action, sits covered in snow. No roads or sidewalks have been cleared. No RCMP cars sit idling at the gates. No red-and-white flag snaps in the wind on the pole atop the Peace Tower. The lights are off. The forlorn, empty Hill, now so long deserted, is ignored by those few Canadians who for whatever reason brace themselves against the driving snow and trudge head-down along Wellington Street. The once proud Maple Leaf flag seems of little interest to Canadians these days. Indeed, no one has been sent to ask what became of the last flag that flew over the Peace Tower. Rumours persist that a nationalist public servant secretly took it to his home and locked it away for the day when, perhaps, it might be needed again.

The Langevin Block, home of the prime minister's office, also sits dark and empty, festooned in yellow police tape flapping across the snow-blocked doors and alleyways. Down the street and around the corner, however, the American Embassy is brightly lit and busy. Evidently the ambassador's staff is working overtime dealing with hundreds of Canadian citizens seeking U.S. citizenship so they can take advantage of the new arrangements with the United States.

The embracing of America was certainly on display last fall. On their arrival last September, our soldiers were greeted enthusiastically by those Canadians who had been caught up in the uprising by the native community. As American units rolled into the Eastern Townships in Quebec, and into Montreal, and as they flowed across the great Prairie provinces, they were cheered as liberators. Everywhere, on farmyard gateposts and on the front porches of houses in villages and in the hands of children all along the incursion routes from the border, the Stars and Stripes flew bravely. In Winnipeg, as calm returned and the native armies retreated northward to their reservations, citizens lined the streets to cheer on and welcome the columns of U.S. units passing through the city. In many regions today, and especially in those areas where citizens believe they are still in danger, American troopers are still treated as friends and guardians.

The Ricardo Doctrine was also cheered by many Canadians, native and non-native, who saw it as part of the natural evolution of Canada in North America, and as a lasting guarantee of peace and security.

But others, on both sides of the Canadian dispute, condemned the American actions and the declaration. Although only the native people and their irregular units challenged the American military operation last September, in the past few months there have been signs of organized resistance building in many communities across the country. American military vehicles and encampments have been bombed and harassed. Disturbances and demonstrations are occurring almost daily in many eastern border cities and in British Columbia. As the weather improves, more such protests against President Ricardo's strategy can be expected.

Nevertheless, time is providing opportunities for Canadians and their opinion-makers and business leaders, as well as for natives, to experience the many advantages the new relationship is bringing to their personal lives. In a recent interview, American officials said that they had antici- pated a period of resistance in some regions of the new territories after the end of active combat operations. But they expect that the limited resist- ance they see today will fade away gradually, much as a similar type of post-war hostility disappeared in the southern Confederate states after the end of the American Civil War. As one official noted, "What other options does a disarmed and inherently divided Canada have?"

As well as dealing with the limited resistance that remains in the occu- pied territories, U.S. troops, along with the FBI, are continuing the hunt for those responsible for organizing the native rebellion. According to the Bureau, Molly Grace, the leader of the so-called Native People's Army, and Bill Whitefish, her second-in-command, remain fugitives, and have escaped into the Mexican aboriginal community. Periodic rumours and statements of dubious reliability declare that Ms. Grace is preparing for a triumphant return to the new "freed aboriginal territory" in the northern Prairies.

For most natives, however, the unexpected presidential emancipa- tion of the native people from the clutches of state wardship and the illu- sions of "traditional culture" is rapidly eliminating the socio-economic dysfunctions in the community that nourished the sense of fundamental grievance on which Ms. Grace's revolutionary appeal depends.

According to recent intelligence reports, Colonel Samuel Stevenson, the leader of the native cell in Winnipeg, has disappeared too, along with his main staff, including Tommy Twoskins and other senior leaders. Reports indicate that all withdrew into the northern Manitoba territory, centre now to a true Cree nation, in fact if not in law. They have taken the public position that their efforts last year "freed the Cree nation." But they too are finding that the American-inspired emancipation of all aboriginal people is undermining their appeals for radicalism.

Will Boucanier, another fugitive and now the self-proclaimed "Grand Chief of the James Bay Nation," is carefully consolidating his own organiza- tion of fighters and leaders and holds court somewhere in the far northern reaches of the region. His statements and actions suggest that American officials want a type of "cold peace" in the new Northern Quebec-James Bay Territory. Boucanier appears ready to provide assured electric power to the United States in exchange for a significant autonomy for the Cree in the region and a great deal of money. Sources in Washington will neither confirm nor deny that the government is in contact with Chief Boucanier.

The President in a statement last week praised the many members of the Canadian Forces who distinguished themselves in a last, sadly futile, effort to save the nation they served. Chief of Defence Staff General Andrew Bishop and most of his senior officers resigned together as soon as the fighting was over, unable to support any longer the government and the political class who had, in the words of Bishop's media statement on his resignation, "betrayed the idea of Canada through selfish efforts to perpetuate their own interests."

Individual members of the armed forces were given the option of an honourable discharge or the transfer of their enlistment without preju-dice to the armed forces of the United States. A vast majority now wear the uniform of the United States and stand ready "to fight and win the nation's wars."

The First Nations Federation collapsed soon after rebellion broke out. Many local chiefs fled the reserves and others were captured and jailed by members of the Native People's Army still active in some western and northern regions. The Ottawa office closed after being bombed one night in September—by whom, no one will say.

Grand Chief Al Onanole disappeared the day American units arrived in Canada. He reappeared soon afterwards on a CNN evening talk show where he commended the "forthright leadership of President Ricardo" and suggested that the White House would benefit from his long experi-ence as an aboriginal leader in Canada. Finding no support for this view in the White House, Mr. Onanole retired to his Florida estate to write, he announced, a memoir entitled *Underground Ottawa*.

Jack Hemp was essentially overthrown by the Progressive Party of Canada and flung from office. He left Ottawa and it is reported that he is engaged in negotiations to win the return of his family farm and estate from the local First Nation that "liberated" them at the end of the Amer-ican operation.

The departure of Mr. Hemp did nothing to save the party, which immediately disintegrated in a partisan dogfight. The other federal parties fell into disarray as well, though it hardly mattered given the larger political developments in Canadian-United States relations. Surprisingly, it seems the majority of Canadians have hardly noticed the absence of this community from their daily lives.

Several provincial leaders have been to Washington generally seeking clarification about the type and level of equalization payments the new territories could expect from Congress. They were all informed that the United States government had no such direct transfer policy. Given, however, the realignment of former provincial and territorial boundaries under the Ricardo Doctrine, it is not clear what, if any, residual powers will be allocated to these former administrations.

The Ottawa bureaucracy more or less melted away. It was never formally dissolved and much of it still exists on paper. But sensible people simply stopped going to work. The Bank of Canada is helpfully facilitating an orderly transformation of the Canadian monetary system into the United States economy. Fortunately, the governor of the Bank of Canada had a drawer full of contingency plans for this eventuality.

The economies of the United States and the western areas of Canada have begun to recover as United States military and civilian contractors aided by newly hired Canadian civilian workers begin to put the oil and natural gas pipelines back together. The great hydro facilities at James Bay are still not functioning well, but the forecast is that the transmission lines and roadways into the area will "come online" within weeks.

As the power returns, the attitude of American citizens and their political leaders to this unfortunate situation is clear. People in Canada and all other states who live off America's entrepreneurial skills and ingenuity and the human sacrifices America makes for their defence and security had best remember one fact from this recent history. Never again will America allow any nation to profit from America's economy and its world-wide defence of freedom while at the same time they use their resources to hold Americans hostage to their own interests.

April
Grassy Narrows First Nation

Far from Ottawa, the shaman Martin Fisher sat beside his weeping wife in the smoky desolation of their Grassy Narrows community. "I tried to warn them all, our people and the whites, that night when Molly Grace came to the Westminster Church in Winnipeg. I said to them: 'Beware the selfish leaders on the prairies and in the forest and in the cities. They will only take you down their path, not ours.'

"But no one heard me. My microphone had somehow gone dead just as I spoke these final words from the shadows of the stage. So Molly's war dream overpowered the warning dream that was passed to me by the spirits of the land.

"It's sad how such things just happen. How sad it is too that no one—no Indian or white man, no chief or politician—can tell us how all this destruction just happened. How could they not have seen the future that the elders saw so clearly?"

CREDITS

Having written analytic non-fiction books on *realpolitik*, I imagined writing fiction would be rather straightforward: just create an interesting story with a beginning, a middle and an end, pepper it with drama and romance, and put it on paper—no footnotes, no fact-checking, no peer reviews, no problems. Where facts were inconvenient, just invent new ones.

As it turned out, however, I ended up owing a very great deal to many fact-checkers, editors, copy editors, friends and colleagues—all experts in the style and requirements for composing, writing, and preparing a readable, compelling, (mostly) fictitious story. Brigitte Pellerin and John Robson were among the first to read an early draft of the novel. With great patience they suggested that although some academics seem unable to write a paper without reams of text that follows every side-road of inquiry to the bitter end, and footnote even uncontested statements, most everyone outside the academy might find this style somewhat "turgid." I appreciated immensely their candour, sharp wit, and sharper editing pencils—as well as their continuing enthusiasm for the story and its importance.

Blue Butterfly Book's senior editor, Dominic Farrell, read and edited the story again and brought to it his trained eye for structure and pace, detail and style. In our many personal and on-line conversations we discussed ideas about characters and events. Often in the midst of these conversations and afterwards, I found new insights and ways to better weave complex events into the story. I owe Dominic a great deal of thanks.

When Dominic and I finished our work, Gary Long next took up the grand tasks of detailed editing and designing the book in all respects as a Blue Butterfly title. To keep readers oriented as the story moved into regions perhaps unfamiliar to many Canadians, Gary, a geographer and keen cartographer as well as a graphic designer and typesetter, took up my suggestions for maps and produced clear illustrations to help readers orient themselves. I am truly grateful for the quality of Gary Long's work in the production of *Uprising*, the results of which you can now see for yourself.

At the final proof-reading stage before the typeset book went to the printer, Sonia Holiad graciously volunteered her trained eyes to look for errors. Inta Erwin, Brigitte Pellerin, and John Robson, whom I'll mention again for their other roles in making this book a reality, also provided valuable proof-reading comments at this critical time.

Several other friends and colleagues read the manuscript. Special thanks to my long-standing friend and mentor, Jack Granatstein, who read not one but three versions. David Harris read the narrative with a close eye on the discussions of national security and intelligence.

My friend Kitson Vincent read critically the first draft of the text and reminded me that in many respects the essence of rural, western Canadian culture has not changed much since the early settler days. He reminded me also that no one can understand the Prairies, its people and its history, without understanding the ever-present "spirit of the land." I thank Kitson for allowing me to recapture that spirit during the many times over the last several years we have spent together out on the land in Manitoba's Interlake District.

I acknowledge also many unnamed others upon whom I depended for information and their deep understanding of aboriginal affairs, national defence policy and organization, military tactics and counter-insurgency operations, national intelligence institutions and policing in Canada, criminal organizations and criminal gangs, border security realities, national history, First Nation associations, and government and politics in Canada, among other topics.

My son, a former officer in the Canadian Forces, served from time to time as my "technical advisor," especially concerning airborne training and operations. As soldiers are apt to do, we often debated the merits of the tactical choices characters in the story might make. I enjoyed the warmth of his companionship in this, and in our many other endeavours.

My family followed the development of this project over several years with interest and encouragement. We occasionally discussed the plot and underlying issues behind it at "the roundtable" at our cottage. I believe they will see in the characters and story their individual contributions, which I greatly appreciated.

My wife, Cori, had a special interest in this book and its publication. She was encouraging, and helped me understand life on an aboriginal reserve as she saw it when a teacher on a northern Ontario reserve in the 1960s. We talked about the controversy that might follow from the publication of this novel, and whether the story was worth this risk. In time, we decided the story is worth telling and that, indeed, to keep the book closed might be a great disservice to the aboriginal community and to Canada. Cori came into my life at a special time and we believe for a special purpose.

My executive assistant, Heather Salsbury, helped organize files and information used to develop this story. Her tireless interest and enthusiasm is much appreciated. Melissa Mucci, a bright young scholar with a promising future before her, catalogued the sources used in research for *Uprising* and filed them electronically for future use, and for reference by interested readers.

Patrick Boyer, president of Blue Butterfly Books, is a most patient publisher. Very early on he encouraged me to continue developing the manuscript. When we agreed to publish it, he carefully and enthusiastically guided me through the process of changing a manuscript into a readable book. I admire his great energy and erudition. But I am especially honoured to have become his friend.

Finally, I pay great credit to Inta Erwin, president of Breakout Educational Network. When the first, overly long, rough, and turgid manuscript was finished, Inta demanded to see it. Within three weeks she called me and declared excitedly, "This book is fantastic. I can't put it down." I was not sure it was fantastic or even readable, however, and almost set it aside for other "professional" work. Inta would have none of it. She cajoled me, suggested publishing strategies, introduced me to a publicist, asked Brigitte Pellerin and John Robson to read and edit the draft, and eventually passed a later draft to Patrick Boyer. When I wavered, Inta propped me up and we carried on. I wrote the book, but Inta Erwin brought it into being. Love and many thanks, Inta; there are no better friends in life.

PHOTO BY TAYLOR STUDIOS, KINGSTON, ONTARIO

Born in 1941, Lieutenant Colonel (retired) Douglas Bland served as an officer for thirty years in operational units and senior operational staff appointments in the Canadian Forces. For more than a dozen years since then, as a professor in the School of Policy Studies at Queen's University in Kingston, where he lives, he has held the Chair in Defence Studies.

Over the years, as author and editor of seven books and scores of monographs and learned articles in professional journals, Douglas Bland emerged as one of Canada's most respected scholars and commentators on national and international defence and security affairs.

Often this led to a role in raising the awareness of policy-makers. He became a frequent witness before both Senate of Canada and House of Commons committees, and has served as an advisor to senior Canadian politicians, including former Prime Minister Paul Martin. Now, with *Uprising*, Bland's audience is wider, his message more urgent.

Combining wide-ranging experiences, extensive military knowledge, historical research, travels in strife-torn regions of the world, and his long-held interest in the theory and practices of revolutionary warfare, Douglas Bland now masterfully presents in *Uprising* a chilling national narrative about a future aboriginal "people's war" in Canada.

INTERVIEW
WITH THE AUTHOR

What first triggered your concern that unresolved issues among Canada's First Nations could lead to an armed uprising on a scale larger than already seen at Oka and elsewhere?

DOUGLAS BLAND: One day a few years ago, as I was driving to Ottawa and half-listening to a CBC radio morning program, an elder from a First Nations community north of Kenora, Ontario, described the circumstances of his land and his people. He spoke soberly and quietly about the wasted young people in his community who lived without place or pride. He described how criminals, drugs, and booze had corroded his village.

But mostly he spoke of how disaffected, angry, hostile, and increasingly militant young natives—"the stepping stones to our future," as he put it—were abandoning their families, their villages, and their sense of themselves as a people. He feared greatly not only for his own people, but also for the others, the people of Canada. "I don't think we elders can control the young ones much longer ... they're not listening to us. They're listening to outsiders and those ones are bad people."

Immediately, the scattered symptoms of a growing national crisis—dysfunctional Canadian aboriginal policies, failures of leaders both native and non-native, crumbling aboriginal governance structures, failed schools and failing welfare programs, "days of protest," and occasional violent confrontations between aboriginal people and other Canadians—fell into a pattern for me.

What was the pattern?

BLAND: On the one hand, I could see that the only missing ingredient preventing these loosely connected forces from erupting into a full-blown insurgency was a unifying narrative about injustices, promises betrayed, and rights denied—as extolled by a charismatic revolutionary leader who preached that these crimes provided just motives for rebellion and independence.

On the other hand, I realized that what was missing in the non-aboriginal community was a narrative alerting Canadians to the national danger that failed policies and inept leaders had left waiting on their doorsteps.

It was the prescient elder from Kenora who first pointed me towards this dreadful future. He deserves much of the credit for this story, because it was he who inspired me to write it.

Some people might think it unrealistic that a country could be brought to its knees by the insurgency of a minority group, but your training in strategic defence and terrorist activity suggests otherwise, it would seem. In your view, are Canadians turning a blind eye to reality?

BLAND: Commentators, politicians, and others commonly respond to

any suggestion that Canada could be heading towards a general aboriginal insurgency by remarking that "most native Canadians are peaceful,
reasonable people." And I agree most are.

But I'm not concerned with most of the people. I'm concerned with
the small minority who are not peaceful and reasonable but who are
angry, militant, and hostile to the very idea of Canada as they see it today.

So it is a realistic scenario?

BLAND: It's important to remember that most uprisings are led by a
small hard core of dedicated radicals. The so-called "troubles" in Ireland,
for example, were directed by a hard core of perhaps no more than 500
people, but they succeeded in tying down the British army for twenty-
five years. This small group, moreover, was supported by Irish citizens
who were mostly "peaceful and reasonable," but who in reality were
rarely neutral in the struggle between the British and the Irish Republican Army.

*You said there was no narrative in the non-aboriginal community
to open people's eyes to a similar conflict in Canada—your reason for writing Uprising—but why is this prospect not recognized, given the steady and
increasing flow of news stories?*

BLAND: Are Canadians turning a blind eye to reality? I think most are
just genuinely unaware of the reality out there on the land. Aboriginal
and non-aboriginal leaders, for the most part, seem convinced they can
play safely near the edge of disaster while the underlying problems fester.

For example, after he had left office as prime minister, Paul Martin
was questioned at a Senate hearing not that long ago by Senator Roméo
Dallaire, who of course previously, as a Canadian Forces general, had
headed the ill-fated UN "peace-keeping" mission just before the geno-

cide fully erupted in Rwanda. When Senator Dallaire asked whether he thought a native uprising was possible in Canada, Mr. Martin responded, "I hope not, because hope is all we have."

Of course Canadians take a cue from the country's top political leaders. When one says his policy is to "hope" an uprising won't happen, you can see that citizens might feel justified thinking it's not too serious a matter. Or worse, this suggests that politicians may not have given any thought at all as to how to handle such a crisis if it were to erupt.

You've pointed out that Chief Tecumseh's statement back in 1795, about how one day aboriginal peoples could "win our country back from the whites," today appears on the website of the Assembly of First Nations. Just how strongly do you think that historical awareness is now felt in the aboriginal community?

BLAND: In my research, and in watching the ever-emboldened actions and statements of aboriginal leaders, I believe three aboriginal narratives are coming together and becoming the new single narrative for the aboriginal community.

The first strand in the story is about conquest, theft of land, and false treaties, all crimes committed by deceitful "white settlers." The second strand is a story of shame and poverty and "cultural genocide" that has continued to this day, represented most vividly by the residential schools policy of former governments. The final strand, which arises from the first two, is that aboriginal people are and always have been independent, sovereign people who carelessly allowed themselves to be exploited and who traded their dignity for government handouts.

So is this integrated narrative taking hold with Canadian aboriginals?

BLAND: Their leaders today are telling their people, and Canadians generally, the new story: Never again will we be exploited, and furthermore, we can take back the past to redress the future. In my view, these leaders are increasingly disassociating themselves and their people from Canada and the idea that they are citizens of Canada.

Is that a precondition for an uprising?

BLAND: There is a theory of insurgency that postulates that once a person has, in his or her mind, turned against a dictator or a regime and said to themselves, "No! I will no longer accept my unjust situation," you cannot force him or her to recant that decision. You can beat them and rob them and take the lives of family and friends, but they will silently defy the dictator forever. They may be silent for long periods, but given the right circumstances they will suddenly rise up and rebel, and most often do so violently.

Planting that seed of defiance in the minds of a community is the first duty of every revolutionary leader. It is not at all odd that many of these leaders "preach" the gospel of historic wrongs to their congregations and promise to lead them to the new "promised land." Nor is it odd that along the way they produce much grief and many martyrs.

Even before publication of your book you've had strong responses from people who heard about Uprising, *or read drafts of the manuscript. What are people saying?*

BLAND: People, and especially people well acquainted with the history and present circumstances of Canadian/aboriginal relations and insurgency tactics, seem immediately taken with the underlying idea of a coordinated uprising.

What is more interesting to me is that most informed people, non-experts included, can almost immediately sketch out the plot line as I coach them along by asking, "Yes, and so what do your think will happen next?"

It is most interesting of all, however, to see how obvious the dangerous sequence of events becomes—if one begins the story with the assumption that aboriginal people could come together under one leader and then bring the country to a standstill.

Do you personally have friends and colleagues in Canada's aboriginal community?

BLAND: My connection to Canada's aboriginal peoples developed over the years as I moved about the country and as I changed professions and so on. I went to high school in Winnipeg's north end and in River Heights in the late 1950s. I witnessed native Canadians in the inner city, for the most part in very sad circumstances.

My brothers and I hunted in the marshes north of the city, where we saw another side of the native story, one much closer to nature. One autumn day we met an old man—you would call him an elder these days—who let us use his tiny boat landing to get into the vast Netley Marsh. He lived in a decaying ancient log cabin and some days we sat with him after the hunt and shared our day's experiences with him. He would describe where we should hunt as the seasons changed. In time, we developed a cheerful relationship based on a common eagerness to be "out on the land."

That old Indian is long gone, of course. But to my amazement my brother, entirely by chance several years ago, came across an ink-and-pencil sketch of the very cabin where we used to sit with our friend. It now hangs on my wall beside me as I type these words.

Other experiences?

BLAND: Later I met and worked with many aboriginal people during my life as a Canadian soldier. They were fine comrades and some might recognize aspects of themselves in the pages of this book!

As an academic, I am privileged to count as friends several distinguished First Nation Canadians who continue to make significant contributions to our universities and to public life.

I have also been honoured to share the podium with aboriginal leaders and to speak at public meetings where the main topic dealt with aboriginal affairs and relations among our various "multicultural" communities. These meetings often developed into candid, and even at times blunt, conversations. But for me they were invaluable experiences. In such sessions I met and conversed with aboriginal leaders, including Chief Phil Fontaine and others.

Of course in my military service I travelled our northern and Arctic territories, meeting both native and non-native people who live and work in this wonderful but demanding environment. These were working trips, but it was no ordinary work to be stepping off the north coast of the continent at the world's most northerly settlement, Alert, on Ellesmere Island. At various times I met Inuit leaders and their people in Resolute, Coral Harbour, Cape Dorset, and Nanisivik at Arctic Bay. I spoke with First Nations' leaders in Tuktoyaktuk, Inuvik, and Old Crow in the Yukon. These experiences also included visits with citizens, officials, and resident RCMP officers in these places as well as in Radisson, Yellowknife, Dawson City, and Whitehorse.

My oddest encounter with a native Canadian, however, occurred one autumn morning a few years ago at the Ottawa Airport. I was checking in for a flight to Winnipeg.

Hunting season?

BLAND: You can't take the fall waterfowl migration out of a Prairie boy's blood! Anyway, next to me stood a very handsome, young native man whom I identified to myself as being Cree. The flight attendant looked at our tickets and said, "Are you gentlemen travelling together?"

Puzzled by the question, we looked at each other. We could not have been more different in appearances. I am short, blue-eyed, and grey. He was tall and brown, had deep-black eyes, and his high-cheek-boned face was surrounded by long, thick, black hair. My unknown travelling companion replied, "What makes you think we're together?"

"Well," she remarked holding up the tickets, "you both have the same name, Bland."

After we were checked into our separate flights to Winnipeg, we two Blands—Charlie and Douglas—stood chatting and comparing family histories. He was from the fly-in God's Lake First Nation in northern Manitoba. His great-grandfather immigrated to Canada from Yorkshire, England, in the early 1900s and remained in north Manitoba his whole life, working as a Hudson's Bay carpenter. My grandfather arrived in Kingston, Ontario, in 1911 after he, too, left Yorkshire, England.

As my new friend turned to go to his boarding station we shook hands. He said, "Look, there are lots of us Blands at God's Lake. You should come up sometime and meet the folks."

As Charlie Bland walked away, I called after him, "Maybe I will someday. They might be my folks, too."

The point of this little story is that in Canada if your family has been here long enough and if we embrace the definition of "aboriginal" widely enough, we Canadians are perhaps not as separated a people as some would have us believe.

Authors who sound warnings are sometimes criticized as "alarmists." How would you describe yourself?

BLAND: An alarmist, by most definitions, creates an exaggerated image causing needless panic. I am simply using fiction—some authors call it political fiction—to reach a wide public audience in order to expose what I, and others, see as an apprehended danger.

You mention other authors?

BLAND: Charles Dickens, for example, wrote his ever-popular *A Christmas Carol* which today many read as a heart-warming story about an old man's conversion and reform that led to the rescue of the crippled boy Tiny Tim.

However, Dickens wrote that fiction to describe the ghastly state of the industrial revolution and the misery it caused in the cities of Britain in his day. His three ghosts presented, in turn, images of Britain's happy past, frightful present, and—the apparition he dreaded most of all—the deadly future. Some believe that Dickens' fiction was largely responsible for the development of a social conscience and significant social reforms that followed in Britain.

Other British writers—Oscar Wilde, Bernard Shaw, and George Orwell, for example—used fiction to alert the public to serious social fault lines in an effort to forestall them from becoming reality. Some people may have labelled those authors as alarmists, but in reality they made important literary and social contributions to Great Britain and to many other societies as well.

Uprising was written with the same objectives in mind. It is my hope that there is still time for reasonable people in Canada to ensure that any "exaggerations" in this story can, in the future, be safely remembered as mere "bland fiction."

More great reading from Blue Butterfly Books

If you enjoyed *Uprising*, you might also like the following Blue Butterfly titles on related subjects. Your local bookseller can order any of them for you if they are not in stock, or you can order direct by going to the Blue Butterfly Books website:

www.bluebutterflybooks.ca.

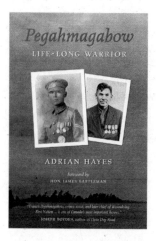

Francis Pegahmagabow was a remarkable Canadian aboriginal leader. He served his nation in time of war and his people in time of peace—fighting all the way. In wartime he volunteered to be a warrior. In peacetime he had no option. His story needed to be told.

Pegahmagabow: Life-long Warrior
by Adrian Hayes
Foreword by Hon. James Bartleman
Soft cover / 6 × 9 in. / 165 pages
ISBN 978-0-9784982-9-0 / $19.95 U.S./Cdn.
Features: photos, maps

Three to a Loaf is the page-turning drama of Rory Ferrall, a young Anglo-German Canadian smuggled into Germany during the First World War to discover the Imperial General Staff's top-secret plan to break the deadlock on the Western Front.

Three to a Loaf: A Novel of the Great War
by Michael J. Goodspeed
Soft cover / 6 × 9 in. / 365 pages
ISBN 978-0-9781600-6-7 / $24.95 U.S./Cdn.
Features: author interview

Following the sudden end to her marriage, Meg Wilkinson, Canada's first woman veterinarian, leaves her practice in Halifax to seek the legendary working wolf-dogs of the Yukon. Arriving in Dawson City in 1897 just as the Klondike gold rush is beginning, she discovers a unique aboriginal connection.

City Wolves: Historical Fiction
by Dorris Heffron
Hard or soft cover / 6 × 9 in. / 449 pages
ISBN (h.c.) 978-0-9781600-7-4 / $36.95
ISBN (s.c.) 978-1-926577-01-2 / $24.95
Features: author interview, maps

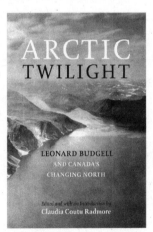

In a series of beautifully crafted letters, former Hudson's Bay Company "servant" Leonard Budgell describes the Canadian north from the 1920s to the 1980s, as could only be done by someone who lived and worked there. He documents an aboriginal way of life that was changing forever.

Arctic Twilight: Leonard Budgell and Canada's Changing North, edited and with an introduction by Claudia Coutu Radmore
Hard cover / 6 × 9 in. / 469 pages
ISBN 978-0-9781600-1-2 / $39.95 U.S./Cdn.
Features: photos, map, interview with editor

Blue Butterfly Books
THINK FREE, BE FREE
bluebutterflybooks.ca

ABOUT THE BOOK

A root cause of terrorism in far-away countries, Canadians are told, is poor, desperate young people who turn their frustrations and anger on their "rich oppressors." Uprising brings this scenario home to Canada.

When impoverished, disheartened, poorly educated, but well-armed aboriginal young people find a modern revolutionary leader in the tradition of 1880s rebellion leader Louis Riel, they rally with a battle cry "Take Back the Land!" Theirs is a fight to right the wrongs inflicted on them by "the white settlers."

They know their minority force cannot take on all Canada. They don't need to. A surprise attack on the nation's most vulnerable assets—its abundant energy resources—sends the Canadian Armed Forces scrambling and politicians reeling. Over a few tension-filled days as the battles rage, the frantic prime minister can only watch as the insurrection paralyzes the country. But when energy-dependent Americans discover the southward flow of Canadian hydroelectricity, oil, and natural gas is halted, they do not remain passive.

Although none of Canada's leaders saw it coming, the shattering consequences unfold with the same plausible harmony by which quiet aboriginal protests decades ago became the eerie premonitions of today's stand-offs and "days of action."